ANDREW SINCLAIR

The author was born in Oxford in 1935, was a Colleger at Eton, and completed his education at Harvard and Cambridge, where he became a don. While still an undergraduate, he wrote his first two novels, THE BREAKING OF BUMBO and MY FRIEND JUDAS. He has written many works of biography and social history, but his major effort over the past twenty years has been the completion of 'The Albion Triptych' of novels, begun by GOG, first published in 1967 and MAGOG, published five years later. His latest novel, KING LUDD completes his vision of the true history of Britain from Druid times to the present day. Andrew Sinclair is married to the writer Sonia Melchett, and they have five children.

'GOG shifts with astonishing facility and learned wit through the history of a people. But the figure of Gog gradually assumes a significance not granted him by history: playing upon the medieval corruption of "God" to "Gog", Mr Sinclair presents us with a modern saviour who does battle against the anti-Christ – against bureaucracy, greed and pretension, against all the corruptive forces which have warred against Albion . . . Gog is a marvellous creation'

The Spectator

'It's a Gothic fairy tale, it's a Norse mythology, full of giants: it's Druidic, Powysian, super-natural, the history of Albion . . . I'm still reeling. I think there's genius in it'

Books and Bookmen

'A bustling, learned, feverish novel . . . undoubtedly a remarkable feat . . . The writing is full of energy, power, lust and humour'

Martin Seymour-Smith in the Oxford Mail

'It's got a tremendous swing to it . . . I enjoyed every surprising paragraph of it'

The Listener

'. . . Fascinating. Its triumphant qualities are surging energy, inexhaustible invention and word-intoxication. It's immensely alive . . . full of unmistakeable comments on the nature of man, on society and on the destructive forces of the nuclear age. Laughter, horror, violence and lust are all facets of Gog's unconcluded quest-journey which may be long remembered'

Wall Street Journal

'Andrew Sinclair is a very talented writer'

San Francisco Examiner-Chronicle

'A dazzling book, and, above all, a very British one . . . it represents an attempt by one of the younger generation of British novelists to grapple with a major theme in place of the private, personal worlds that have so long characterised English fiction.'

John Barkham Reviews

'Andrew Sinclair mounts a time machine and takes a wild ride through history'

Time

SUMMARY OF THE ALBION TRIPTYCH

While the novel GOG deals with 1945 and the history of the struggle of the people against power in England until that year of the victory of the Labour Party, and the novel MAGOG deals with the history of power and its corruption in England from 1945 to 1968, the last novel of 'The Albion Triptych', KING LUDD deals with Gog's version of the history of the Luddites – the machine-breakers between 1800 and 1887 – and the mythology of communications from the age of the Druids to the dominion of the computers.

Andrew Sinclair

GOG

TO MAGOG
MAY HE ROT

First published in Great Britain in 1967 by Weidenfeld and Nicolson

Sceptre edition 1988

A John Curtis Book

Sceptre is an imprint of Hodder and Stoughton Paperbacks, a division of Hodder and Stoughton Ltd.

British Library C.I.P.

Sinclair, Andrew, *1935–*
Gog.
I. Title
823′.914[F]

ISBN 0-340-48608-2

The characters and situations in this book are entirely imaginary and bear no relation to any real person or actual happening

Printed and bound in Great Britain for Hodder and Stoughton Paperbacks, a division of Hodder and Stoughton Ltd., Mill Road, Dunton Green, Sevenoaks, Kent TN13 2YA (Editorial Office: 47 Bedford Square, London WC1B 3DP) by Richard Clay Ltd., Bungay, Suffolk.

Prologue

The naked man lies on the sand spit between the two legs of sea. The waves well up the spit and wash the body of the man, who is nearly seven feet long. He is prone on his stomach, his face turned sideways, his mouth agape with scum running out of his gullet to join the backwash of the water. Long strands of seaweed foul him, dark as drying blood. One string of rubbery bubbled weed winds round his waist and drags back towards the sea. The man does not seem to breathe at all.

On the beach below the cliffs, two soldiers are strolling, their tin hats in their hands. Seeing the body they run forwards. They hoick the man over and pull him by the legs up the beach a little way; they can hardly drag him for his huge weight. Then one soldier squats on the man's chest and pushes down on his ribs, while the other raises and lowers the man's arms. Water and green bile spew out of the man's mouth, he gags horribly. The soldiers release him and prop him forwards, his head between his knees. One of the soldiers thumps his back. The man throws up more water, then, with a retch, he groans, the tears rolling down his cheeks from the salt behind his closed eyelids. The soldier at his back jerks his thumb at the other soldier, who begins stumbling away across the beach towards the cliffs. The soldier who stays by the naked man watches him for a little while. Then he goes over to the edge of the sea and makes a bowl of his tin hat and squats to fill it with sea and carries it back and begins to wipe off the weed from the flesh of the naked man. He works thoroughly, with the man moaning from time to time at the sting of salt on his grazes and cuts.

When the soldier finishes with wiping off the weed, he takes a packet of Woodbine cigarettes out of his pocket, flicks the bottom of the packet with his thumbnail so that the tips of two cigarettes jump upwards, and offers the packet to the naked man. But the man does not see the soldier's gesture. He is hunched forwards, his fingers twined together in one fist which rests on his closed kneecaps, while his forehead in its turn rests upon his locked hands. Above his forehead, a small and bloody hollow pocks his right temple. He breathes heavily and unevenly, occasionally coughing out a mixture of bile and seawater.

"Did you hit a mine on that Yank convoy?" the soldier asks, getting no answer. So he smokes and looks out to sea, as though the reply lies on the stretch of waves which have delivered the naked stranger. From time to time, he studies the bowed figure of the middle-aged man beside him, whose belly is already beginning to drag down the skin on his ribs. Twice more, the soldier opens his mouth to speak, but he closes his lips and says nothing. Eventually, he smokes his cigarette down to its end, until the stub burns the tips of his thumb and forefinger and middle finger, which hold the cigarette in a triangle of flesh pointing inwards at his palm. He throws the stub away towards the sea and squats to examine the naked man closely.

Something on the back of the left hand of the man interests the soldier, who leans forward onto his knees to study the mark. It is a tattoo of blue lines in the form of a fence round three letters that are half-hidden by the man's cheek, so that the soldier cannot read them. But the soldier sees that each side of the fence is pricked out in a sheaf of wheat, while the top of the fence is formed by a sickle.

"What's that you got there?" the soldier says, but the naked man does not give a reply.

The soldier is puzzled. He looks back towards the cliffs; but there is no sign of the second soldier or of other rescuers. So he crawls on all fours round to the right of the naked man to see whether he can find further marks of identification. Nothing shows on the body or legs of the man except a thick covering of hair from the navel down; but, on the back of his right hand, there is another tattoo, this time of five half-hidden letters fenced at each side by a series of wheels joined with a lever and closed at the top by a frieze of crowns linked with a chain.

"You all right?" the soldier asks, anxious to read the hidden letters.

The naked man lifts up his head from his locked hands and turns his face towards the soldier. The soldier sees a long, square chin, cleft in the middle; spreading lips cracked with salt that fall slack to show bleeding gums and teeth jostling for place in a narrow jaw; a nose as pitted and spread as a labourer's thumb; heavy cheeks which sit like two firm pats of butter between eye-sockets and jawbone; eyes bloodshot with exposure and slitted against the light; a jut of bone which pushes out black eyebrows and makes the forehead seem to slope backwards; brown hair plastered back against a knobbled skull with large ears slightly protruding and awry. The soldier has never seen such a strong face, outside films of Chicago thugs. He would avoid it in a bar.

The naked man tries to say something, but he gags and coughs out more water. The soldier looks back to see rescuers in white overalls running with the second soldier across the sand. "They're 'ere," he says, and he sees that the naked man has spread out the single fist of his locked hands on his bent knee-caps. The man is studying the two tattoos, as he gulps in and chokes on the air. His eyelids are blinking continually and tears are running down his cheeks. The soldier leans over the bare right arm of the man to read the three letters tattooed between the square of the sheaves and the sickles; the letters spell GOG on the back of the man's left hand. On the back of the man's right hand, between the square of the levered wheels and chained crowns is spelt the word MAGOG. The soldier sees the intertwined fingers of the naked man arch and pull and wrestle each versus each, so that the blue letters of GOG and MAGOG move in the struggle of the two hands against one another . . .

I

White.

A slab of white with two edges which meet in a corner where a lamp shines.

A white ceiling and three white walls and a green door and a window covered with black-out curtains.

The iron bars of the foot of a bed.

A ridge under grey army blankets that must be a body.

Hands on the white sheet with knuckles and blue veins standing out under black hairs and a blue tattoo on the left hand saying GOG and a blue tattoo on the right hand saying MAGOG.

Each finger can be set to work and move and bend at the joints.

A grey shirt over chest and shoulders and another set of iron bars behind at the head of the bed and a white wall at the back and a brown table at the side with a slop pan and a glass of water.

Silence.

The man places himself in the room. Then he begins to shiver. Perhaps he cannot leave the room. Perhaps the white ceiling will lower itself and the white walls will shrink and he will be crushed within a contracting box of white. Perhaps *they* will come in and tie him to the posts of the bed and ask him questions, day after day of questions, until he cannot even remember how to think for fear that he will never find an answer. Yes, *they* will come into the white room soon. Who?

" Gog," the man says, reading the back of his hands. " Magog." Syllables roll thickly across his tongue like beads of quicksilver. The man feels the sounds slur over fat lips. He must move. He levers himself upright into a sitting position against the iron bars of the bedhead and pulls his legs out from under the sheets and sits on the edge of the bed. He finds that his grey nightshirt reaches to the middle of his thighs. He puts one sole delicately on the floor, then the other, slowly transferring his weight onto his feet. As he does so, he finds himself falling. He puts out his palms to take the shock. His elbows bend. He falls, prone and face down, on the green linoleum.

He draws up his knees. He raises his chest off the floor by pressing down with his knuckles. He begins to crawl slowly in circles round the linoleum. Cold planes his knees, shaves his finger-bones. He reaches a leg of the bed. His hands climb up the bed-post, gripping. They pull his body upright as they climb. Soon the man is standing, leaning on the bed-rail. He is bent, but on two legs. He walks three short paces, leaning on the iron cross-bar. He turns and walks back three short paces. He repeats the action several times, now taking two longer paces, learning to move erect. Then he launches himself on two legs across the linoleum. He reaches the facing wall before falling. He leans, bowing against the wall. When he has breathed deeply a few times, he stumbles to the bed-rail. After ten journeys from rail to wall and back again, he has learned to walk without support. Now he can go over to the door, feeling only the dizziness of hunger in his belly and the salt of thirst in his mouth. His knees bend beneath him as he moves, but they do not buckle. He turns the handle of the door and looks out.

In the long corridor, a single woman in a grey uniform with a white peak of linen on her head, walking away. When she is gone, the man follows her along the corridor, treading delicately on the green linoleum, keeping one hand on the wall to steady himself. When his hand reaches the recess of a doorway, it skips to the far side of the door for fear of making a noise inside the room that may be behind the wooden panel. Eventually, the man reaches a small stone staircase that leads downwards. He slowly descends on his bare feet, smelling cooking. He comes to a closed green swing door and hears voices. He stops. Seeing a cupboard to his right, he clambers inside it, crouching among brooms and brushes, closing the cupboard door nearly shut. He waits. The line of light along the edge of the wood soothes him. If he were enclosed in darkness, he would have to shout.

He hears the voices coming closer, the sound of light-switches being snapped, hinges screeching and leather soles on the stone floor and stairs. The voices and steps pass and fade and vanish. The man emerges out of the cupboard and goes into the kitchen. In all its dark space, there is no person. A thin scattering of light from glazed gratings above is sown over the sinks and tables and bins, so that the man can see well enough to go across to a large box marked BREAD, take out a loaf and begin tearing off lumps with his teeth to swallow. The man eats two loaves of bread and a leg of cold lamb from the meat safe. He drinks two jugs of cold water. In a basket, he finds soiled clothes, including a large pair of stained white trousers and a khaki drill jacket, spotted with grease. He puts on the trousers and the jacket. They fit him tightly, except that his ankles and wrists protrude from the bottoms of the sleeves and the trouser legs.

When the man has dressed, he puts a loaf in each pocket of his jacket and leaves the kitchen, opening the swing door carefully to prevent the hinges from squeaking. He creeps slowly back up the stairway to the corridor. He turns down the corridor, which is still empty, until he finds himself in a large hallway. A porter in a blue uniform, his face shiny and thin under his blue peaked cap, sits behind a desk beside the large glass entrance doors, now covered over with brown paper. The man, seeing that there is no way of avoiding the porter, walks quickly towards the doors.

"Hey, you," the porter says in a nasal voice, "you're new, ain't you?"

The man halts in front of the desk, wanting to walk on, but fearful of raising a cry behind him. "Yes," he says, "I'm new." He looks into the porter's eyes, one of which is clouded white and rolls outwards. So he looks down to the razor-blade in the porter's hand, lying against the pencil it was sharpening.

"I wouldn't have your job," the porter says. "Not for all the tea in China. Cooking. It's bad enough having to eat it these days." He leans forwards across the desk and gives a jerk of the head. "Bet you knock off a few spare rations, don't you?"

"Rations?" the man says, not understanding.

"You're a fly one," the porter says. "Mary's little lamb. You wouldn't know there was a war on, would you?"

"No," the man says.

"We may have beat old Hitler. But, you take my word for it, those Japs'll take ten years to beat. It's horrible what they do to you in the jungles." The porter's cloudy eye rolls with excitement while his good brown eye trembles. "Put splinters up your nails and light 'em. Worse too. Of course, it ain't worse than what they do to you in here. They'll cut off your foot, the surgeons, sooner than cure a blister. As for the doctors, they wouldn't qualify as knackers." He looks darkly to right and left. "I've seen 'em carried in and I've seen 'em carried out. And often you wouldn't know they was the same person. We'll have a lot more bodies here too, the bits the Japs have left of 'em. Ten years more war, I tell you. Ten years more of bloody rations. Ten more years of being posted up here so far North you have to kip with a penguin if you want a bit. Hurry on, VJ Day. Then I can get back to London from the Arctic Circle. It's always better there than what it is elsewhere in Blighty. But I bet I starve before I get back home. I'll even have to turn cook, won't I, chum, to get a square meal?"

"Yes," the man says and turns to go.

"Not very matey, are you?" the porter says, then he sees the loaves in the man's pockets. "Oi, oi, whipping a bit of bread, are you? I should report you."

The man opens the glass doors, and, as he goes outside, he hears the porter saying, "You've forgot your boots. You'll forget your bloody head next. Then where'll you put your hat?"

The man is out of the building and plunges into the pitch of the night city streets. The houses all have shaded windows; the lamp-posts give no light, but serve as bludgeons to those that must grope their way about. The man's eyes soon adjust to the summer-bright dark, with the mackerel sky reflecting the last of the sun's glow off its surface of rusting mirror, so that the man can see alleys skid up and down the cobbled hills off the main street, which is looming and gloomy behind sooted granite fronts, with pillars and porticos snooty above shuttered shops, with pediments high under the slate roofs wondering how they strayed so far and so dingily from Greece. The people that pass in the street are smaller by a head and shoulder than the man; they have closed red faces with the blinds drawn down; they look straight and suspicious in the direction they mean to go. As the man lurches about the pavement, enormous and staggering, the people part to let him by, marking him down and deciding that he is none of their business. Far ahead, he sees two dark blue uniforms walking along under the domes of their dark blue helmets, with pieces of metal shining on their clothes. So the man ducks from some instinct down a side street, where the mock-classical houses give up the pretence and become tall tenements, straggling in black brick and broken papered windows down the hill.

In the cave of a doorway, the man sees a small girl sitting on a step. She wears a ripped tartan dress. Her pudgy face has a bright red spot on either cheek, which might be from fever or from rouge. The man feels compassion well up within him and the need to show it. So he bends down towards her and says, "Shouldn't you be home in bed? Can I take you there?" And the eyelids and snub nose of the girl pucker in contempt; she laughs shrilly and says, "Git awa' wi' ye, King Kong. Or tek me 'ome f'r a dollar. I'm a wee hoar." And the man jerks upright in horror and stumbles away down the flint cobbles, slipping and recovering himself as the stones stud his bare feet.

Soldiers run past the man, soldiers getting out of it, soldiers hiding their cap-badges with upflung hand or else stuffing their berets in their pockets, soldiers forgetting their obligatory off-duty dawdle in the fear of punishment for a crime just committed. And the man sees the bulk of another man in the gutter; a shiny red helmet with a broken strap lies several paces away from him. The fallen man is huge in size. His skull is shaven and his scalp is split open, so that blood is running over his cheeks and ears and crown. A brass whistle on a lanyard, attached to a button on the tunic of his uniform, lies near one of his sprawling hands. By his other hand, a truncheon, tied by a leather thong to his wrist.

The man with the bare feet kneels down to look at the face of the fallen man. At that moment, the lamps in the street glow weakly, then brighter and brighter until they light up the walls and the pavements. A great cheer swells ragged and hoarse over the city so that the very bricks and stones hear the sound of peace switched on with the lamplights, the very houses listen to the cry of war no more over the posters saying, *WALLS HAVE EARS*. And the kneeling man looks down to see an armband round the right bicep of the fallen man, on which is stamped *M.P.*

"Magog," the kneeling man whispers to himself. "Police."

He studies the bloodied features of the military policeman, the sharp nose swelling into an overripe bruise, the flared cheekbones with the sunken flesh beneath them tight on the gums, the ears growing into points as if they had been clipped like a dog's, the jawbone too narrow for the lower row of teeth, the whole effect of the face that of a skull popping out of its wrapper of skin in order to burst its bone into the air. The kneeling man realizes that the military policeman is as tall as he is himself, nearly seven feet long; they are twins in their freakish height.

Then the kneeling man notices the shine of the black uppers of the boots of the policeman. So he crawls down and undoes the elegant spats which cover the lying man's ankles and begins to unlace the closed eyelets. The knots are tight on the laces and the man breaks two finger-nails; but in the end, he pulls a boot from each foot with a great two-handed heave at either heel and toe. Then he strips the grey knitted socks off the policeman's feet, so that these flop back like two gutted white fish on the black slab of the pavement. Then the man puts on the socks and pulls on the boots, without bothering to tie the laces. He is about to go, when he notices the red helmet lying in the roadway. He walks across, picks it up and takes it back to the fallen man. He stoops and props up the head of the policeman with the helmet. The blood has stopped flowing from the wound in the fallen man's scalp; he should live. So the man in his new boots walks away down the cobbles, leaving the policeman lying with bare feet, brought low under the new lamplight, his head cracked open by the clubs of other men.

Out of the side street, into the main thoroughfare. As the man with the new boots watches, a gaudy red and blue light springs out of the stained glass window of a pub. A great roaring within builds up as the stream of light sprays out from behind the glass, until it spatters its colours across the road and waters the spiked golden flower on its sign, THE THISTLE. The man smiles to see the light and walks in through the wooden door of the pub into the boisterous roister and spree.

Men in caps and dungarees, soldiers and sailors and airmen, women in boiler suits and worn-out dandy dresses, chippies and skivvies and troops in their civvies, all pushing up their hands to rip down the black-out and let out the light. And, on the piano, a man with a head the shape of an ostrich egg is belting out Waltzing Matilda on two fingers, Waltzing Matilda, Waltzing Matilda, you'll come a'waltzing Matilda with me, but there's too much of a scrum to do more than a two-step on somebody's toes, and the stench of beer and the stink of smoke tweaks hairs in the nostrils, and it's a frantic fug of fun, with a bald sailor feeling down between the tits of a big blonde, saying that he's looking for spies, and a skinny redhead with a mole on her nose, sitting on a stool and complaining, " I don't want it to be bloody over, I like the war, it should go on for ever," and her fat signaller lover replying, " There's no bloody justice, is there? Like there's no place like home to get away from." Then it's nothing but a hubbub of rhubarb, rhubarb, rhubarb in the large man's ears, as he stands at the door of the pub.

A pack of people shove into the pub behind the large man. They are wearing red rosettes. Their leader, a squat man in a brown suit, with slithery lips and eyebrows as trim as moustaches, yells, " Two 'undred seats. Two 'undred. Up the people." And the bald sailor yells back, " Bugger the Tories." And the pub explodes into laughter and nudges and squirms and bellows and belches and mucks in together. " Two 'undred seats," the squat man shouts. " The Labour Party's in by a double century. And you can put that in your stately 'ome and stuff it. And what's the first thing Labour does for the people? Turns the ruddy lights on." And the pub roars again and the man at the piano begins thumping out the Internationale and the words come into the large man's mind, unasked, the words come in French and he knows that he speaks French and has seen Paris:

. . . Debout, les damnés de la terre,
Debout, les forçats de la faim.
La raison tonne en son cratère,
C'est l'éruption de la fin.
Du passé, faisons table rase.
Foule esclave, debout, debout.
Le monde va changer de base,
Nous ne sommes rien, soyons tout.

C'est la lutte finale,
Groupons-nous . . .

"Brother," the squat man says, putting the gold ring round his forefinger on the lapel of the large man so that his cribbed, brilliantined hair reaches the level of his listener's diaphragm, "we're on top of 'em. And we'll flush 'em out of their palaces. Back to the workers what they took from us. They'll scarper like rats, except this ship ain't sinkin'. All the vermin off after the Allousy Dollar. But that's nothin' to do with us. We've got it now and we'll keep it." His lips move so fast that his words do not trip off his tongue; they skid.

"Got what?" the large man says.

"Westminster. The 'Ouses of Parliament. We've got 'em. For five years, and another ten after that. You couldn't even bomb us out, and they 'ad a try, they did. And you can't buy us out. Because you can't buy the people, can you, brother? Not when they're rulin' like lords in Westminster, London."

"I don't know," the large man says. "Perhaps."

The squat man peers upwards suspiciously at the large man.

"You're a worker, surely, brother. Of course, you're educated, I can tell by your voice."

"Can you?" the large man says.

"But education don't mean you forget your brothers, do it?"

"No," the large man says. "You mean to say, the people . . . people like me . . . they rule in Westminster now . . . so there's no rule, really, because the people rule themselves. Are you sure?"

"What's your name, brother?" the squat man says fiercely. "Rip Van Winkle? You been asleep for too long? The Labour

Party, and that means the people, mister you and mister I, the Labour Party's got in by two 'undred seats for the first time ever."

"Two hundred seats," the man says. "That doesn't sound like much room for all the people."

"Don't be clever, mate," the squat man says. "You know as well as I do, you've got to 'ave representatives. Of course, there ain't room at Westminster for all of us. But now we've sent Joe Bloggs there just like you or me, you'll see the fur fly. Ruddy ermine in shreds all over the Lords. And I wouldn't wonder if some of them war profiteers aren't in for a stretch, brother. And brother who, may I ask?"

"My name," the large man says, "is Gog."

The squat man laughs.

"And mine's Maurice and a gin and lime. You're a big chap so why don't you bollock over to the bar and get me one? And while you're there, get me a double to make your journey worth it. Ta, mate, and up the workers."

Gog looks down at the glossy hair of the squat man and at the half-moon of his white, unworried forehead.

"I haven't any money," he says.

The squat man looks up at him and snaps, "Why couldn't you say so to begin with?" and he's off eeling his way through the press of people so quickly that Gog sees him at the far end of the bar in forty seconds, crying, "Up the workers and down the hatch," to a laughing sergeant, who is buying a round of drinks and adds him into the circle of booze. The smoke is so thick now that Gog's weakened eyes begin to water, until the massed faces of the people in the pub blur and become confused with each other in a pink cracked plate of flesh, and the voices rise into an incessant humming and grinding like a conveyor belt, and the piano has stopped playing and the radio is turned on full blast so that string melodies are blaring out as if drinking also needed Music While You Work, and the sweat of herded humans has the stench of hard labour, and Gog feels the horror like acid in his mouth and he opens his teeth and howls.

Silence.

All look at Gog.

Gog stares about him, stammering at the waiting faces. " I . . . I . . . I," he says, then stops. After a pause, inspiration strikes him and he cries, " Up the workers," and the people in the pub yell the slogan back at him till the smoke eddies from their breath as if out of the barrels of guns, and Gog turns and bursts out through the door into the night street and cold air under the bright-dark summer sky.

Gog begins walking down the pavement; but he realizes that he has no reason to walk anywhere in particular, except perhaps to London, however far that is, because the porter says it's always better there than elsewhere in Blighty, or perhaps to Westminster, however far that is, to see whether the squat Maurice is right and the people are ruling there. But every time he stops to ask someone the way to London, the stranger hurries past, sidestepping quickly and fearfully, until Gog understands that his size terrifies people in the night. So he sits on a door-step, waiting until an old woman, carrying a string bag full of cut grass, walks by, and he says, " Ma'am, would you tell me the way to London?" And the old woman jumps as if she were getting onto a broomstick to skip from the wrath to come; but she stops, clutching her bag to her chest in case Gog means to steal it from her rabbits, and says, " Lunnon? Tha's foor hun'red mile, straight doon Sooth Bridge Road, ye canna miss it, it's verra big." " Is it that far?" Gog says. " Ye no mean to tramp it?" the old woman says. " I do, indeed," Gog says, " I haven't the money for the fare." " It'll tek ye after Sunday," the old woman says and begins to hurry away. Gog rises and calls to her, " What city's this?" The old woman stops in surprise. " Edinburgh, wheer else?" She turns and looks back to see Gog's great height, then trembles and begins to run away at a tottering trot, screaming back, " Ye kin ha' me life but no me grass."

Gog lets her get away, then he starts himself after her and turns down South Bridge Road, past the cold kirks lingering upwards into the night. As he walks, he leaves the people behind him, except in an occasional bus making for the suburbs. On his right, he passes a black dome topped by the thumb of a real giant, on which an impish angel stands, scraping a drizzle of stars from the night with the tip of a cross and pointing to the full-cheeked moon. Gog leaves behind the drab shops with their elegant top storeys, patrician noses ignoring the gobble of the mouths underneath. He strides on past stone proper houses, running to decay because the servants are away, yet with their black lawns cropped to the nap of the grass. Then out sudden by a little bridge over a mumbling burn, already outflanked by a long arm of suburb. The front lawns shrink in size, the houses drop from three to two storeys, then the city peters out in the occasional stone bungalow with twin gables under a tile roof, or a row of box houses with pebbled fronts and pastel woodwork, too cautious to go all out for any crude colour, even by moonlight.

A sign says Liberton Brae, as Gog comes to a cemetery, locked in behind its rails and announcing, ONLY WEEKDAY VISITING. Even the dead get cold comfort on a Scottish Saturday night, and the same on a Sunday. Yet the birds are loud all around, squalling and tanging; the main road is more decorous, presenting a holy hush of no traffic in preparation for the sabbath. Gog meets his first stranger in half-an-hour, a white-haired young man who smiles at him uncertainly; but when Gog asks whether this is the road to London, the young man just smiles and shrugs and points to his ear, where the cord of a hearing aid dangles down uselessly.

At the close of the Burdiehouse Road, the city decides finally to put a stop to itself, where a double-decker bus is parked at the end of its run on a tarmac roundabout. The pylons beyond the last row of houses are the new gatehouse to the South; the lines they carry shed an invisible wall of power, behind which the city can work and heat itself and see by night, if the walls are not breached by the enemy from ground or sky. As Gog turns towards the bus, to see if he can rest a little on its seats before trudging on through the moon-bright dark, a shape rises from the back seat of the bus and stands on its platform, saying in greeting, " Welcome, brother Israelite."

II

In the powdering of the moonlight, Gog can see a spout of white hair on top of an army overcoat. Between the cataract of hoary locks flowing down beyond the coat collar and the cascade of mustachios and beard that deluge the coat's lapels, a fierce nose parts the hairy torrent, while cheekbones like twin rocks break the surface below the spray of joined eyebrows. The man himself under the coat is thin and stooping, as if the burden of a sack of invisible sins sat on his shoulders. He has one palm extended upwards in a form of blessing or telling Gog to keep his distance. The other hand clasps a rusty iron cross chained to his chest. On the platform of the bus, the bearded man is as tall as Gog.

"I am Gog," Gog announces.

The man shows no surprise nor fear; instead, he displays a kind of resignation, as though he has expected Gog's coming.

"So be it," he says in a low cultured voice. "I myself am called Wayland Merlin Blake Smith, otherwise known as the Bagman. The fuzz term me the Wandering Jew and put me inside for vagabondage, as though the King's Highway were not an Englishman's home and castle. But the fuzz will get their orders in due course, when the errant air waves leap to my command ... Come in, my brother of Israel. Enter my poor abode."

He bows towards Gog and, with a wave of his hand, invites him into the double-decker. "Thank you," Gog says, touched by his graciousness, and enters. "Turn left," the Bagman says, "and the couch to the right is thine." Gog settles himself upon one of the large back seats of the bus and the Bagman reclines opposite him, supporting himself on one elbow like a Roman preparing to feast.

"My friend," the Bagman says, "first, the appalling necessities, to which our bellies make us slaves. You, I see, have loaves;

I, naturally, have fishes. A miraculous swap will satisfy the inner man." So speaking, he hands Gog a kipper wrapped in a piece of newspaper, while Gog returns the compliment by giving him a loaf. They begin to eat, the Bagman fastidiously picking the bones of the kipper one by one from between his beard and his mustachios, Gog eating the kipper bones and skin and all in the intervals of swallowing hunks of bread, washed down by swallows from a bottle of cold tea circulated as correctly as a decanter of port between the Bagman and his guest.

"To remove the last obstacle from our perennial friendship-to-be," the Bagman says, wrapping up the remnants of his kipper carefully in the newspaper and stowing it under the seat by his army pack, "how are you for cash?"

"I have none," Gog says.

The Bagman sighs from disappointment or from relief or from a mixture of both.

"Just as well," he says. "Otherwise I would be obliged to find a means of removing it from you. For the cause of Israel, of course. Israel recognizes no robbery. What is done for her cause is done well. Moreover, cash may be a man's best friend, but it's the worst thing for coming between friends. But if you're sure you have no money . . .?"

"None," Gog answers.

"How prudent a reply . . . or how true?"

"True," Gog answers.

"Three times denied means once perhaps," the Bagman says. "I will allow that you may be in that state of bliss called penury. In that case, and only in that case, my conscience is clear. I cannot be accused of trying to convert you for profit, only for the sake of sweet Israel, whose followers are as numberless as the sands of the sea – if only they could see they're part of the bloody beach." The Bagman pauses. "You said your name was Gog."

"Yes," Gog says.

"By virtue of baptism?"

"By virtue of tattoo."

"Ah, the original woad," the Bagman says in a satisfied way. "I might have known it. Gog. Your reappearance was forecast by the Book of Revelations, before the end of the world and the coming again of Israel. It was fated we should meet, as you well know. Although God, I must say, does move in mysterious ways when it comes to choosing a rendezvous." The Bagman looks up and down the empty rows of bus seats, all turning their square backs to him. "At any rate, Gog is fated to meet the leader of Israel on Albion's Ancient Druid Rocky Shore. I am, incidentally, among other incarnations, the original Archdruid – not to be confused with other impostors of that name. Eisteddfod, my Welsh granny! All those official Druids couldn't tell a mistletoe from a pig's foot. I have as much to do with the official Druids as Christ had to do with the church that bears His holy name."

"You said I was in the Book of Revelations," Gog says. "At this moment, I am . . . interested in my past."

"Indeed, you should be. Revelations, Chapter twenty, Verses seven and eight. They are a cornerstone of my own inspired writings, which reveal my mission here on earth, to broadcast the coming of Israel again to this holy island. Only will they give me the transmitters, which a previous emanation of mine disclosed to them? Will they B.B.C.!" The Bagman spits gloomily, then his voice takes on the quality of incantation. "*As saith Revelations, And when the thousand years are expired, Satan shall be loosed out of his prison.*" The Bagman explains, "Some call Hitler Satan, but we know better, you and I. Satan is right here, and we call him – Whitehall. Whited sepulchre, more likely." The Bagman continues with his incantation. "*And Revelations saith, Satan shall be loosed out of his prison, And shall go out to deceive the nations, which are in the four quarters of the earth, Gog and Magog, to gather them together to battle, the number of whom is as the sands of the sea.*" The Bagman recovers his normal tone. "So *there* you are."

"So where am I?" Gog asks. "Excuse me. I don't remember too well these days."

"How could you?" the Bagman says, "when you have just been born again according to the prophecies, as I have, to do battle with your evil brother, Magog. The end of the world is at hand, and you will bring it about by your final struggle with

Magog. The first coming of Gog and Magog drove the first Israel from Albion and the last battle of Gog and Magog shall bring it back again."

"But who am I?" Gog asks.

"You?" the Bagman says. "As though you didn't know." He looks at Gog craftily. "You wouldn't be Satan, would you? The old 'un paying me a personal visit. If so, I should wrestle with you all night." The Bagman begins rolling up the sleeves of his coat, then, considering Gog's vast size, he begins rolling them down again. "I'll give you the benefit of the doubt. Though you could still be a false sign, sent to tempt me. True prophets are always receiving false signs. And Satan is abroad, as Revelations saith."

At this moment, Gog sits up and stretches himself, raising both his enormous arms above his head. He is surprised to see the Bagman quickly slap himself on the beard three times.

"O, thou of little faith," the Bagman says, cursing himself. "Trust, trust, trust, Wayland Merlin Blake Smith. Be thou guileless as a lamb, and the microphones shall be given unto thee. My dear Gog, I'm sure you're on the up and up, though I'd hate to think you were still growing. Where are you proceeding?"

"To London," Gog says.

"Ah ha," the Bagman says happily. "And may I ask why?"

"To see if the people rule at Westminster there."

The Bagman slaps his thigh with glee, although one of his knee joints cracks.

"Perfect. I didn't prompt you. You spoke the words. I didn't put them in your mouth, though they couldn't have been better if I'd been a ventriloquist. You can pretend not to know who you are, but you know all right, you know. Better not to tell, though." He draws his hand across his beard, where it possibly covers a neck, and sags his head to one side, suddenly and horribly. "You never know who's working for Magog, do you?"

"I don't know," Gog says. "But Magog and his men . . . are they everywhere?"

"Everywhere. But you've got to be smart to pick them out.

And the people are a headless beast. That's why, out of sheer self-sacrifice, I have decided to serve at their head against Magog. They must give me the transmitters, which are mine by right. Then I shall proclaim the coming of the new Israel. And the lion shall lie down with the lamb, and the wolf suckle the babe. And it is written that you, Gog, shall aid me."

"Who wrote it?" Gog says.

"I, naturally," the Bagman says. "In my treatise that explains the beginning and end of all things on Albion's Ancient Druid Rocky Shore. That line people think William Blake wrote, though in fact I wrote it, when I stopped off in his fleshy abode for a while." The Bagman delves about in his old army pack and finds a pamphlet, wrapped in brown paper. "Here you are, here you are. This invaluable treatise is not something I normally lend. In the interests of the future Israel, I usually ask five pounds for reading it, a mere pittance to help me install my own radio station, if need be." He hands the pamphlet to Gog across the gangway of the bus, his fingers stabbing at the title inked on the brown paper. "The True History of Albion, As Revealed to Wayland Merlin Blake Smith," the Bagman insists, digging in the pocket of his overcoat to produce the end of a candle and a box of sulphur matches, which he also passes over to Gog. He then settles on his seat, deposits the back of his ankles on the headrest in front of him, spreads his beard delicately as an ostrich-feather fan on his chest, declares to Gog, "Read, learn and inwardly digest, while I have a kip," and is fast asleep within the minute.

Gog lights the candle and reads the pamphlet, which has been hand-printed on five pages in an old type, so that the letters jiggle up and down as though pulled out of their lines by the wavering candlelight.

THIS IS THE TRUE BOOK OF WAYLAND MERLIN BLAKE SMITH, AS REVEALED TO HIM ON THE ANCIENT ISLE OF MONA

1. *In the beginning, Jerusalem was builded in Albion, the golden pillars of Zion; by Thames sweet river, the temples of marble and cedar.*

2. *In Chelsea, the roof-beams of sandalwood; in Hampstead, the oaken floors inlaid with silver.*
3. *All wrought by the craftsman Wayland, the smith of the Lord; I am he in my first coming.*
4. *Builded in nine days and nine nights, to be the temple of Zion in Albion, the son of God.*
5. *And the Druids turned to abominations, to the flesh of human sacrifice.*
6. *And they pulled down the temples to build a brazen city, a city of brass and copper and iron, London the misbegotten.*
7. *And the people were set to toil there, in the service of Moloch and Mammon and Magog.*
8. *And their weeping and their wailing rose to the Lord, and He vowed to destroy their accursed masters, saying:*
9. *Though the Druids dig into hell, thence shall My hand take them; though the Druids climb up to heaven, thence will I bring them down.*
10. *And the Trojans landed from their ships in Devon, and the giant sons of Albion went forth to meet them;*
11. *Magog from the accursed Druid city, and Gog from the vale of Jerusalem.*
12. *And the Lord God gave the victory to the Trojans; yea, unto the enemy went the battle.*
13. *And the Trojans ruled for a thousand years, and after them the Romans; a Queen burned the accursed city of London, but the Romans builded it higher, girt about with walls and towers, and set a great wall to the North, the Wall of Hadrian.*
14. *And after the Romans ruled, there came the Northmen, and after the Northmen, the Normans; and the brazen city grew, yea, walked over the waters upon a stone bridge.*
15. *And Albion groaned under the brass posts of New Babylon; by the waters of Thames, the maidens of Zion wept.*
16. *And Jerusalem fled to stony ground, the rocks near the Dead Sea.*
17. *And my second coming was as Merlin, prophesying woe;*

as the voice of the raven, I sang of blood and sword.

18. *And Magog ruled in London, and his machines ate men; and their wives were harlots in the city, and their sons and daughters stricken.*
19. *And when Gog and the people rose up as wheat in the fields, Magog scattered them as chaff beneath the flail.*
20. *And the Lord called a great plague upon London, as the plagues of Egypt; He called a great fire as the fire upon Sodom and Gomorrah.*
21. *But London rose from the ashes, saying ha-ha to the heavens; and Magog still ruled from the city, with Moloch and Mammon.*
22. *And I rose again in Soho, William Blake the prophet; but I preached to the vain wind and I spoke as the rain upon the sand.*
23. *And Magog sent his minions to the ends of the world, yea, to the uttermost places of the earth.*
24. *And the forests of India and the vales of Africa ran with blood; and the minions of Magog roused up the wrath of the Lord and the nations.*
25. *And the Lord afflicted Albion with warriors from the Northland, two plagues of warriors that ate her young men as grass before locusts.*
26. *And the Lord sent down fire from heaven to consume London utterly; yea, the fires of hell rose up to purge the accursed city.*
27. *And I am come again in my fourth coming; Smith, the leader of the Israelites, come to build again Zion.*
28. *And Magog is burned down in the accursed city, and Gog, his brother; the wrath of the Lord passeth, as the winter into the summer.*
29. *And the Lord saith, how shall I give thee up, Albion? How shall I deliver thee, Israel?*
30. *I am come to restore Zion and the temples of Jerusalem; this is my servant Smith, in him I place my trust.*
31. *I shall be as the dew unto Israel, if she will hearken unto him;*
32. *If she will deliver to him the waves of the air I have given*

her; if she will deliver to him the transmitters, or be cast into utter darkness.

33. *If my fourth servant be not heard, the fire shall come for the fourth time, and there shall be no more London.*
34. *Her towers shall be molten beneath her, the Thames shall dry up as the desert; as wax before the fire, as stubble before the torches.*
35. *But if ye hearken to my servant Smith and deliver to him the waves of the air; ye shall build again Jerusalem, in Israel by Thames side.*

ALL THOSE WHO BELIEVE THAT THE ABOVE IS THE REVEALED TRUTH WHICH IT SURELY IS ARE REQUESTED TO SEND DONATIONS TO WAYLAND MERLIN BLAKE SMITH, c/o CENTRAL POST OFFICE, LEEDS, ALBION (ENGLAND). OFFERINGS HOWEVER SMALL GRATEFULLY RECEIVED; CASH OR STAMPS OR POSTAL ORDERS, NO CHEQUES PLEASE. GIVE AND IT SHALL BE GIVEN UNTO YOU. DON'T *YOU* WANT TO SEE JERUSALEM BUILT IN ALBION'S SACRED LAND? DON'T WAIT–SEND YOUR MITE OR MINT *NOW*!

When Gog has finished reading the pamphlet, he looks across to the sleeping Bagman, who is slumbering the deep drowse of the righteous and the right, of the just and the justified, the iron cross on his chest weighing down his repose. Gog puts out the candle and himself falls asleep. A face nags at his mind, the full face of a thin woman, with black hair cropped close to the skull. She plays with a hoop, passing it over and over her long naked body, until she suddenly breaks the hoop apart in a rage, and Gog starts awake in the first faint grey of morning to find the other back seat empty.

The Bagman is gone, as though he had never been there. No trace remains of him, nor of *The True History Of Albion, As Revealed To Wayland Merlin Blake Smith*. Gog presses his knuckles into his eyes, then pulls them away to see if the pain will make him see differently. But the Bagman is still gone, as if he were a vision in the night. A parable floats into Gog's mind, Is he a Gog dreaming of a Bagman or a Bagman dreaming of a Gog? He searches again for a clue that the Bagman has been bodily in the bus, not only in his own unfurnished mind, hunting desperately for scraps of past fantasy to fill its untenanted places. But all he can find, under the opposite seat, is a twist of newspaper, containing the bones and skin of a kipper.

III

As Gog passes the pylons beyond Burdiehouse, a sharp smell of wet green grain-stalks scrapes his nostrils; the rankness of the moist luxuriance of the weeds and grasses growing on the banks of the road is almost offensive in its reek. In the first light, Gog already sees a tractor driving into a field, to harrow the crops on the boundaries of the city and furrow the limits of the furthest houses. A white sow munches, chinless and inexorable, in a muddy yard outside a farm; its hanging dugs promise litters of piglets innumerable. The fields are rolling and opulent, pushing up sprouts of clover or corn or cabbage with the recklessness of the spendthrift. In all the fertile land, Gog can see no restraint and little control. This riot of plenty seems incapable of being reduced to the coloured squares of ration books.

Sitting on a wall in front of a moulting monkey-puzzle tree in the garden of a sad stone house, Gog sees the knapsack of a soldier. He looks about himself warily; but there are no humans near, only a spying magpie on the tree, cocking its head from its sharp black and white finery. Gog lifts the pack with one hand and is away; out of the corner of his eye, he sees the boots of the sleeping owner stretched out the other side of the wall. The magpie gives a whistle of approval on two notes, "Smart work, smart work," then ceases as though unwilling to sound the alarm. Once round the bend of the road, Gog ducks into a lane to examine his treasure trove; mess tins, a ground sheet, two packs of rations – mainly biscuits and chocolate – a knife and fork and spoon set, a water-bottle, ordnance survey maps of the Borders and the North Country as far as York, a compass, and a printed sheet of instructions headed ENTERPRISE TEST: LIVING OFF THE LAND – THE MARK OF THE TRUE SOLDIER.

With biscuits and chocolate inside him, and the maps and the compass to guide him, Gog branches off down the valley of the North Esk River past foxgloves poking up their ruddy snouts. He sees an old horse in a field actually eating the foxgloves, doctoring himself with digitalis for a cardiac condition. On the hills by the road, the large stone houses squat near the brown bouncing burns that skitter downwards to join the river, which is dammed every few hundred yards in a mill pool that once drove the looms and now carries away the waste. The river is converted from power to sewer, the tall brick chimneys line its banks, the pylons leapfrog across it. The current itself hardly flows, just creeps along carrying the white detergent bubbles from the mills that have stained it mahogany with sweat and grease. The workers' cottages are so streaked with brown damp that they too seem to be dissolving into the brown water. Even on this Sunday morning, the banked fires burn in the mills and the chimneys lay a slow black trail of smoke on a bed of air to make a second crawling dark river above the bed of the North Esk.

Up from the river valley onto the plateau of the fields, and along the tarmac road between hedgerows, from which dog-roses poke out splay-fingered blossoms with pink and yellow palms. Stone walls cut off the castles along the river from the wanderers on the highway; but Gog sees marked on the map in a nearby thicket: *Wallace's Cave*. A memory stirs at the back of Gog's skull, the memory of an outlaw hiding in the greenwood, fighting for Scotland against the English enemy, a patriot of his own time with all men's hands legally against him –

except those of the Scots people and those were many. So Gog turns in off the road into a graveyard, where there are two small old ladies, eighty and after, the three Fates minus one, putting flowers in jam-jars on the gravelled grave plots.

" I'm looking for Wallace's cave," Gog says.

" I don't heer ye," says the first old lady. And she does not, because she is stone deaf as a tomb itself.

The other old lady comes stumbling over between the graves, dodging in and out of monuments and memorials as if through stalled traffic.

" I'm asking for the cave of Wallace," Gog says.

" Theer's no grave o' no Wallace roond heer. Try further East. We doon't ha' truck wi' no Wallaces."

" Cave, I want," Gog says. " Not grave."

The old lady shakes her head at his simplicity. " Ye kin see f'r yesel'. We doon't ha' caves heer. We ha' graves."

" It says on the map," Gog says, " the cave of Wallace, the great Scots champion of the people."

" O, Willy Wallace," the old lady says. " He weer ne'er roond heer. The map's wrong."

There is no appeal, and Gog goes on his way. And so folk memory dies even among the old and the great departed are greatly departed and heroes hide themselves so well that they stay hidden for ever and William Wallace, you are sleeping and your cave is filled in and Esk is brown and bordered by moiling mills.

The road to the South ends with another road cutting across it, so Gog decides to plunge straight onwards past a lodge and along the drive of the estate in front of him, keeping to the left of the stately home or institution marked on the map. The path ahead leads into a wood of oak and ash. The sun at last struggles out of the clouds like a bumble bee thrashing about in grey curds, which suddenly clambers free and breaks away alone and yellow in the bright air. The leaves of the trees change from olive to mustard under the rush of light, the meadows before the wood are a fuzz of green joy. Gog smiles at nothing in particular, and, sensing himself smile, his mouth opens in a wide grin to answer the smile. Then he hears sounds in the wood ahead, mewing and shrieking and humming, shrilling and clucking and gurgling, and round a bend in the path through the wood, monsters proceed two by two in a crazy crocodile towards him.

They come forwards holding hands on limbs gingle-gangle, splaying their feet or dragging them, their outer arms windmill or bent or feeling at the impalpable air. Some parody boys and some parody youths, some possess pin-heads and some possess pumpkin-heads, some have skulls that rise to a peak and some have foreheads that swell outwards, some have squashed noses in moon faces and some have the starting cheekbones of emaciation, some have blubbery open mouths and some have thin lips drooling, some have heads that sit on the shoulders without interval of neck and some have long stalks of windpipe with Adam's apples jigging, some have humps on their shoulders and others humps on their bellies, most have lumpish swollen bodies and a few scraggled trunks and bones, but all, all, all are white, fishbelly white with internment, stumbling in the universal gait of the confined. A few wear kilts, the rest wear tubular trousers with the only creases horizontal across the knees; all carry hand-knitted sweaters of grey or green. Beside them, two young nurses, dressed in field-grey with white bibs held up with bright safety-pins, all plump and pink and professional, are driving them as expertly as a pair of collie bitches drive the sheep on the moors, circling about to head off the strays, making little barks of warning and encouragement, herding the flock in the direction of the meadow beyond the wood.

When the freaks see Gog, they begin to gibber and moan in welcome, agitating their heads and arms in lunatic greeting. The lolling faces holler and the slobbery mouths split open so that the lips seem to peel back and the hands grope and paw at nothing. And Gog sees only the warped flesh of the innocent, who never asked to be born or to be kept alive, and he sees their two trim tidy tucked-in keepers all limber in their uniforms. And he bellows murder and he runs at the nurses. And the freaks huddle together in fright, and one of the nurses begins to scamper back through the wood, screeching, and the other grasps to her stomach a stick-like nodding wraith who clutches her and buries his face in her belly; but Gog picks her up by the waist so that the wraith falls down wailing and he carries her struggling body to a ditch by the side of the path and he throws her in among the nettles and the docks, where nature has been kinder and has grouped pain and antidote side by side. The nurse lies where she is fallen, the wind knocked out of the starched bib between her breasts. And Gog turns back to the freaks, who cluster in a pitiful huddle of despair, clinging to one another and miaowling to the indifferent heaven that has only ignored them all their lives. And Gog shouts, " You're free, free. Go wander, holy ones, simple ones. Go into the sun, sing, do what you will. I give you liberty. Go."

A doughy boy with an old man's paunch falls and jerks on the ground, convulsive in a fit, his tongue between his teeth and his face turning blue. And one shrunken young man comes flailing towards Gog, beating him on his ribs with no more force to his blows than if they were twigs blown by the wind. " Go," Gog shouts, " go free. You're free." And the freaks cling together, wailing and moaning, refusing to move. And the nurse climbs out of the ditch and staggers past Gog to her charges, her hands already red and puffy with nettle rash. The freaks ring her round in their joy, patting her and stroking her and beseeching her for comfort, and she turns on Gog with the arms of the defective about her like withered ivy about a stone, and she cries out, " Monster. You Monster." Then she caresses the freaks, saying, " Poor souls, you poor souls."

So Gog runs away, weeping through the wood, until the gibbering and the moaning is hushed far behind him. And he stops, his breaths making shards of pain in his panting lungs. And he sees in front of him a sapling twenty feet tall. And he hurls himself upon it in a rage, he pulls its bending trunk this way and that, he wrenches at the bark, digging down his heels and throwing his weight first to the right and then to the left and then backwards and then forwards. And he heaves the young tree out of the sucking ground, jerks it free in a snapping of roots and throws it down upon the earth, as though he were wringing the neck of all creation.

IV

On the road bridge over the South Esk river, Gog first realizes that he is being followed. A large black car, driven by a chauffeur, loiters by after passing Gog, who is standing looking down into the brown nibbling water, which bites at the rocks beneath a glossy gleam of rhododendrons in a sunken garden under the bridge. The car turns at the intersection of the road ahead and drives back past Gog. He sees the white face of a woman staring out of the back window. He does not notice the car again until he has walked past the two stone lions crouching on pillars that guard the drive to the great tall-windowed house of Arniston, no longer segregated in privacy and pride now that the war effort has cut away its iron gates for scrap metal and has turned its grilles into guns and its servants into soldiers. But as Gog takes the road to his right and trudges up the hill, with a puzzled bearded bullock eyeing him like a hairy Lucifer over the hedge, he sees the car pass the pillars and stop and reverse, dawdling in pursuit of him.

To shake off the car, Gog decides on a short cut across the fields and moors. He is tiring now, and once over the fence into the meadow grass, he slumps onto his back, resting his head on his army pack. He finds that the only pleasure in walking is ceasing to walk; he feels the exquisite unlatching of his lying flesh. The wan sun eases the lines on his face; a pheasant starts up in a hiccup of feathers. Ahead are coppices on small hills and the scraped hide of the moors.

When he has rested, Gog eats a little and finishes the water in his bottle, which he fills again in a dark burn with the cattle casting suspicious looks from the brown patches over their eyes at this spy mucking about with their water supply. Gog then follows his compass southward along the edge of a long barbed wire fence, set up to keep off animals more than Germans. A sudden stench of carrion offends his nose. He looks for the corpse of a rabbit or a fox; but he only sees some hundred small trailing pieces of black fur, each one carefully placed on a prong of the barbed wire. As thriftily as the butcher bird impales each of its victims among the small birds on a spine growing on its chosen thornbush and larder, so some farmer has killed and stuck each dead mole on a nail of wire. The government is probably paying a bounty for mole corpses, perhaps a penny a pelt; the life of a mole is not expensive, considering how much the skin of a dead human costs to drape on barbed wire.

Beyond the last stone wall of the farm, with its barns lurching about its small grey sides and its trim slate roof like hulking sons about a dapper dad, Gog reaches the first stretch of moor, peat bog, coarse grass, white stalks of rushes among the brown-green turf, blackface sheep used to rough fare and wet hooves. These beasts stop tearing off the grass with the sound of vacuum cleaners to stare at the trudging Gog, the orange tufts in their ears glaring, the jet irises of their yellow eyes thin and horizontal, their dark legs too spindled under their thick grey mat of wool, only their udders and sudden kicking flight belying the ferocity of the horns curving about their black cheeks. Gog makes for an abandoned quarry, where sides of gravel delve a scoop of ochre into the flank of the hill, over which a distant lorry crawls slow as a beetle on the south road. Gog rests again briefly among the iron wheels and levers that flank the abandoned shack of corrugated iron and sacking, which once housed the diggers of the gravel. The machinery is desolate in its uselessness and has taken on the colour of the bleaker patches of the moor, the rusty brown with which the wind and the rain cloak all abandoned things in bare places.

Once back on the straight road over the green Moorfoot hills, wallowing like stranded whales, encrusted by the barnacled lines of the stone walls and by occasional patches of weedy spruce, Gog notices the black car again behind him. This time, it does not pretend to skulk at his heels; but it drives past him to the crest of the hill a few hundred yards ahead. There the chauffeur stops the car on the grass verge of the road and descends and waits for the approaching man. When Gog is a few feet away, he sees that the chauffeur is a slim youth with soft features and full red lips beneath the peak of his green cap, with a round chest and large hips beneath the green jacket and trousers of his uniform. " Madam would like a word with you," the youth says, opening the door of the car, which is large and box-like at the back; a glass partition walls off the rear seat in case contamination may come from the driver's seat; there is a general impression of soft leather and shining metal and polished wood and clear glass that makes the interior of the car seem like the cabin in a yacht.

Against the far window, a woman sits. She is dressed like the magpie on the monkey-puzzle tree, in piebald black and white, black boots and wide black striped trousers, a chessboard jerkin and a white bowler hat on top of her black hair, which is cut in a helmet about her head, so that its long raven sides fall down past each cheek to her shoulders, while its fringe across her forehead is shaped downwards to a point level with her eyes. The woman's face is sallow and bland, her lips ripe and swelling under a sharp thin nose, her eyes pale blue under sooted lashes and eyebrows plucked into immaculate arcs that act as flying buttresses to her pointed fringe. " Get in," the woman says, patting the seat beside her, while the leather gives soft poufs of disgust under her palm. And so Gog clambers inside the black box and settles himself on the soft subsidence of the upholstery and waits, watching the tended face of the woman speak against the background of the rough roundness of the hills, cut off from any contact with the interior of the car by the metal frame and glass of closed windows.

" You don't know me," the woman says in a curiously reflective voice. Gog does not know whether her words are a statement, a question or a wish.

" I don't think so," Gog says. As he looks into her eyes of bleached blue, the colour washed away by that light which seems never to have touched her pale skin, he feels as if the cloud in his mind parts to show a rift of sky and then closes again.

" You don't *think* so," the woman says. " Then you don't. Just plain don't. No one can say he thinks he doesn't know a woman and get away with it – unless he is a stranger." The woman laughs. "I certainly don't know you. In those filthy trousers and that ghastly jacket. You look like a tramp. But . . ." she pauses and smiles again the smile that parts her lips without spreading sideways so that no lines of laughter show from nose to chin, "you *are* a tramp, aren't you?"

"Yes," Gog says. "That is what I am called, I suppose." He finds, to his surprise, a certain subtlety of expression coming back to him, a wariness of phrase that the smooth mockery of the woman conjures up defensively in his mind.

"How's pickings?" the woman says. "I don't suppose the black market extends as far as charity. But in this case, though I don't pretend that these ham sandwiches came out of my monthly pittance of official food, they are all yours. If you can't gobble them down now, take them away with you. Your need is greater than mine and all that. Have you been tramping long?"

Gog picks up the packet of ham sandwiches, wrapped in greaseproof paper, which the woman produces from a wicker basket at her feet. "Always," Gog says, then adds more truthfully, "at least, as long as I can remember." He begins to cram the sandwiches in his mouth, hardly bothering to chew them before swallowing.

The woman crosses her legs so that her right ankle swings towards Gog; it is almost as thin as a stick in contrast to the wide turn-up of her black striped trousers. "I wouldn't care for all that trudging," she says. "I tried it once in the *Landes* . . ." She stares at Gog, her blackened eyelids hooding her eyes.

"The land?" Gog says, his mouth full of bread and ham. "What land?"

The woman laughs shortly, almost without moving her mouth. "I was with someone, a big chap, about your size . . ." Again she looks quizzically at Gog, then continues, "He hadn't anything else in common with you. He was one of those intellectuals playing at hikers that you'd meet in every luxurious ditch in the thirties. He used his feet as if the only way to genius lay in getting bigger blisters on his heels. He had to prove he was a proletarian at heart by wearing a hole in his sole and his sock – and his foot, if he had some iodine handy. He just couldn't get past a peasant without asking him how the grapes were getting along, when he couldn't tell a vineyard from a cabbage patch. He had to prove that he, too, was a man of the people. And he wasn't. Oh, I won't deny his origins were obscure – I call them obscure because people aren't to blame for their origins, however filthy they are, so I prefer to leave them uncertain. He didn't *choose* to come from a Welsh nowhere and he'd got out – not by his bootstraps, he liked people to think *that*, but by his brains. And once you've left the herd because of your intelligence, no perversion of that intelligence can make it accept you back. You may lick a workman's boot, but he'll only kick you in the teeth for being a toff. He was highly educated, my big chap, in a strange sort of way. A bit potty, really, he knew all sorts of strange things about times so far back they were better forgotten. There wasn't a stick or a stone he couldn't tell you a story about – with footnotes. In fact, after some of his more rarefied flights of fancy, I got so fed up with breathing that pure intellectual air I used to send for an oxygen mask." The woman paused and shrugged and put on an appealing mouth, slightly pouting her lower lip. "I'm sure I'm boring you. I do ramble on."

"Please," Gog says, happy to have been able to finish his sandwiches in peace. A pleasant stupor of fatigue makes him slump in his soft seat, so that his slight paunch of middle age presses against his waistband. Yet his tiredness does not extend to his mind, where his brain does not cease hunting the coverts of memory to flush the coveys of the past.

"Well, this other big chap . . . you wouldn't know him, he was before your time . . . this other big chap, he tried to do an Isherwood and a Spender, you know, up the mountain tops to see if you can find a *raison d'être* on high. Personally, all I ever get out of the top of a hill, and I couldn't possibly get higher than a hill, is an overwhelming desire to stay in the valleys for ever. But my big chap made me promise to tramp with him in the Landes in France for a day or two. Of course, he had meant to make it a month or two, sucking in those pine smells with deep yogi breaths, staggering around thigh-deep in sand and ozone, pretending he could scamper over the Pyrenees any time he felt it was his turn to go and win the Spanish Civil War for Stalin, and in the intervals, making love to me under a waxing moon. Well, the first night I gave in. The result? The few square inches that the mosquitoes left for tomorrow were skewered by pine-needles. Where I wasn't a sore, I was a scab. So I struck and took a taxi straight back to Biarritz to recover. The poor lamb, I must say, he didn't understand about a strike so close to home. He used to spend so much time telling people they ought to join the unions and wave the red flag that he hadn't a clue about what to do when he got an individual striker on his hands protesting against all his back to nature nonsense. For four days, I didn't see him. He went off in a huff in the wilds. I took all his money, naturally, he didn't *need* it if he wanted to play at getting away from it all. I wasn't out of the bath for three and a half days, and on the fourth, just as I'd picked up a poor waif and stray, fleeing from a life of idle luxury because it really was too gruelling, the big chap wanders in, all covered with burrs and complexes and stinking like a goat. Well, I forgave him, what could you do, and he really was rather sweet when he was jealous. And after that, I never heard a whisper from him about the great outdoors or best foot forward, we're all toilers beneath the furs. I only had to say, *Gog* . . ."

Gog has been looking out of the car window at the hills, noting the aimless sheep pick at the grass and amble jerkily over the occasional rocks. At the mention of his name, he jerks round.

"Yes," he says, "you were saying?"

"Gog is your name, isn't it?" the woman says. "It's tattooed on your hand. I thought you weren't listening. It's not very polite, when you've broken my bread . . . as my big chap used to say so crisply and Christily . . . it's not very polite not to listen. But, of course, *tramps* can hardly be expected to have manners."

"I've stayed long enough," Gog says. "I thank you for your food. But giving food to somebody doesn't give you the right to give advice."

"That's a shrewd answer," the woman says. "You haven't lost all your wits. You might even have had an education, mightn't you, *big* chap?"

Gog looks at the woman beside him, wondering why she is

taunting him. He presumes that he must remind her of her past lover. She has a crush on big men and can afford to track them down.

"Thank you," Gog says, rising abruptly. He opens the car door and turns away. He feels a vicious pinch on the back of his arm and swings back to face the woman. "Why did you do that?"

The woman is lounging back in her seat, giving no sign that she has made the least movement.

"What?" she says with casual innocence.

"You pinched me."

The woman laughs. "You should pinch yourself to stop dreaming, big chap."

Gog stares hard at the woman, then turns to leave the car again. This time he feels a sharp kick on his left buttock that sends his face lunging into the metal jamb of the door, so that he loses his balance and falls back on the seat of the car. He swivels round furiously, to find the woman sitting in her previous position, her legs crossed and relaxed.

"Clumsy, aren't you?" she says. "But then you aren't used to getting in and out of cars."

"Do you deny you kicked me?"

"Please," the woman says. "I'm really not quite that vulgar. I did once kick a dog for a bet, but the poor pooch turned up such a piteous face at me that I swore to use my toes thereafter for nothing but painting nails on."

"You kicked me," Gog says.

"I did not," the woman says in a bored voice. "I had no motive. And *I*'m not mad. I don't do things without a motive."

Gog looks into the bland pale face of the woman. He sees that the crowsfeet about her eyes have been smoothed away by some sort of grease disguised by powder; every wrinkle that can give interest or age to her face is hidden under a mask of matte paste. Even when she speaks, she is careful to push out her lips as though kissing the air; this pout prevents lines from forming at the corners of her mouth.

"You may have a motive," Gog says, "which I don't know."

"If you're so smart," the woman says, "why are you tramping the roads?"

"I want to," Gog says.

"No one wants to tramp," the woman says. "They tramp because they haven't got a decent alternative – like a sensible life with a wife at home, for instance." Again she looks at Gog with a hint of interrogation.

"I don't agree," Gog says. "I may have an alternative. But I don't want one. I'm tramping to London, because that's what I want to do right now."

"London," the woman says. "You're going back to London?"

"Have I been there?" Gog says. "But why should you know? Perhaps I have."

"You'll take a long time to arrive," the woman says, "at the rate you're going. I presume you'll walk the whole way. Too proud to accept lifts and all that."

"I'll walk," Gog says. "I need to find out various things. Each day I tramp, I'll find out a little more."

"Oh, nature's a *great* teacher," the woman sneers. "Pity I never went to that school. More what?"

"More about myself."

"Tell me what you know about yourself."

"There isn't much to tell," Gog says, "and besides, why should I tell you? I don't confide in strangers. I never have."

"No," the woman says, "you never have." She looks at Gog. "Tell me a little. Just to flatter my curiosity."

"I don't know much," Gog says. "My ship hit a mine and I woke up in hospital in Edinburgh. I'm slowly remembering. Now, if you don't mind, I should be getting on."

"You really don't remember," the woman says. "You've never been to a place called .... Maire?"

"Why do you ask?" Gog says. "Do you know me?"

"I feel I do," the woman says. "It's because you look a little like the big chap I used to know. But he's dead in the war. Everything ended in the war. Perhaps old things will begin again now, perhaps not. More likely not. I'd quite forgotten about the big chap till I saw you on the road."

"Good-bye," Gog says and clambers out through the car

door, leaving his hand on the frame. The woman leans sideways and deliberately slams the tin trap on his fingers. Gog howls and puts his hand in his mouth. The woman raps on the glass partition between her and her chauffeur, who starts up the engine of the car. The woman finally closes the car door and leans her head out of its window. " One thing," she says, " my dear tramp, you should know after a war. Cruelty is gratuitous. Pain is purposeless." The car begins to move off down the road. " And I am particularly a woman of my time." The head of the woman, framed by the two straight sides of black hair and the fringe cut downwards to a tongue between her eyebrows, disappears back into the interior of the car, which accelerates away, leaving the highway and the surrounding hills to Gog and the sheep and the silence of incomprehension.

V

As Gog stumbles on over the hills with swollen and burning feet in the evening, his pack drags on his shoulders like a hump. Gog has never had a hump before. He feels that even the hunchback is luckier, with a hump built on securely and packed well against his shoulderblades. But Gog's hump is a detachable one of twenty pounds weight, with straps that cut the skin over his collarbone so that he has to hook his thumbs beneath them and lean forwards against the dragging load. And the hump has a will of its own. When there's a head wind, it threatens to upend Gog tip over arse; when there's a cross wind, it pushes him round clockwise or widdershins. When he is going uphill, the hump hangs like a Sisyphus stone, more ready to plunge back down to the bottom with each step nearer the summit; downhill, the hump hurries Gog breakneck into the valley. And what a hump! It's no smooth boss of flesh sitting snug upon his spine. It's a khaki canvas tumour sprouting strips of hide to tie down its flaps of skin. Gog would like to hurl it away every few minutes; but he packs stolen food and dry sleep upon his back. So he must malarky on, his monstrous shoulders gradually diminishing with each meal, eating his way through the contents of his hump, the only cannibal whose gorging diminishes his own weight. He envies the luck of the real hunchback, so compact and trim. If people were to rub Gog's hump for good luck, they would get warts.

When Gog's shoulders and soles can stand no more aches and blisters, he stops his stepping on the tarmac as delicately as Agag and he turns aside onto a strip of moorland beside a lulling burn and he takes off his boots and he ransacks his pack and he nibbles at a few more biscuits and he drinks half the brackish water in the bottle and he wraps the groundsheet round himself and he sticks his feet in the top of his pack for warmth and he finds a tuft of soft grass for a pillow and he fits his hipbone into a hollow so that he may lie on his side in comfort and he sleeps as tired as a fox after a chase, stirring each hour to change the position of his pains so that they do not set into cramps. Once he wakes to see the streaky stars overhead, blurred by his filmy eyes. And he feels that the heavens are his personal tent, until the clouds blow up and the drizzle falls and he knows, as he huddles in a ball under the ground sheet, that the tent can leak at any time.

Yet the drizzle passes and Gog falls into a nightmare trance. And the white-bearded Bagman is changed into a black-feathered bird, which sits on a sky-high oak tree and croaks: "*And my second coming was as Merlin, prophesying woe; as the voice of the raven, I sang of blood and sword.*" And on the right of the oak is an aspen tree with each leaf a naked human trembling for the guilt of being the tree and the makers of the tree on which Christ was crucified on the Cross. And lo, a red dragon rises from the roots of the aspen and consumes it utterly in its jaws of fire, with each human leaf shrieking before being swallowed up. And on the right of the oak tree stands the elder, on which Judas hanged himself; and its leaves are of beaten gold and silver and precious stones. And lo, a great pit opens, boiling with sulphur and shit, and it engulfs the elder, so that the gold runs away in pus and the silver melts in piss and the precious stones burst in the boils of the plague. And then the bird that is Merlin opens his black wings as wands. And lo, on the first branch of the oak tree, lambs graze in green meadows and girls sing at the butter churns and men lie in the shade of haycocks and children chatter round their mothers' knees. And lo, on the second branch of the oak tree, a cobbler smiles as he works a shoe and a smith whistles as he hammers iron on the anvil and a weaver laughs as he moves the shuttle of the loom and a baker guffaws as he pulls a pan of hot bread out of the oven. And lo, on the third branch of the oak tree, a sailor opens his sea-chest and pours out spices and silks and green parrots, and a merchant pulls sweets and red ribbons out of his pockets to give to small girls in white dresses, and a banker puts on the red robe and white whiskers of St. Nicholas to shower small boys with bright pennies and oranges. And lo, on the fourth branch of the oak tree, a bishop in a purple cope smiles as he intones a blessing, and a general in shining armour salutes with his drawn sword to his lips, and a minister in a frock coat grins as he throws green banknotes out of the glossy tophat in his hand. And lo, on the fifth branch of the oak tree which curves upwards on either side of the top of the trunk to make a trident of wood, there is placed a golden throne, and the right side of the throne is a lion rampant and the left side of the throne is a unicorn couchant and the seat of the throne is a bulldog dormant, and upon that throne sits Britannia in a dress of red satin and white silk and blue organdie, ruling the waves that lap about the golden basin at her feet and holding in her left hand a blood-red orb the shape of the world and in her right hand a sceptre, the head of which is formed as a ship. And lo, on the top of the trunk of the tree sits the raven which is Merlin, and he croaks no more of woe, but he begins to chant a doggerel, and all the labourers and the craftsmen and the moneymen and the people of power and Britannia herself stand stock still and face the front of their branch and take off their wigs and their hats and their helmets, each in his proper place on his proper limb on the oak rooted for ever deeply in the soil of Albion. And they all sing the song of Merlin the raven, ruling by his magic vision of order:

Merrie England, it has been;
Happy days by fathers seen.
Merrie England, it will be;
Happy days will children see.
Merrie England never is;
But the people all know this –
Merrie England cannot be
If they chop down the old oak tree . . .

At that moment, a light glares down into Gog's eyes, so that he starts awake, his hand shielding himself from this visitation in the darkness, his ears assaulted by the bleating and baabaaing of terror all around. He feels a heavy weight, warm and soft, across his legs, and he hears a voice that he knows say, " Christ, that big sod from the pub, but he's got no pull." And hands jerk him to his feet and other torches send out their masked beams and Gog can see a dozen men pulling the bodies of dead sheep towards the tailboards of three lorries parked by the road. A dead ram, the one which was dropped on Gog's legs, has a wide bloody mouth where its wind-pipe used to be. All about him, Gog can see a massacre of sheep, with men stunning them with hammers or twisting their necks by holding onto one horn to slit their throats with a bayonet.

" Less noise," the leader shouts, and Gog sees that he is the friend of the workers from the pub, Maurice with the glib lips. " Give 'em the cold steel, you bastards," Maurice shouts, " and shut their gobs. If each of 'em were a Jap sentry, you'd all be up the Irrawaddy." He turns on Gog. " Now you wrap up too." He slices his finger across his throat. " It's so bleedin' dark I can't always tell the difference between 'uman and mutton."

While the slaughter of the flock goes on, as the sheep are herded towards the lorries by four collies which rush continually about on the errands ordered by their masters as faithful as camp guards, Maurice grins broadly. " Forty-two, forty-three, forty-four," he says, counting in the corpses past the tailboards.

"We'll prang more than on Battle of Britain day. Forty-five, forty-six. 'Oo's for chops and chitterlin's? Forty-seven. Keep up the bashin', men. It's the people we're feedin'. Forty-eight, forty-nine. And where's the 'alf-century? 'Obbs couldn't 'ave got there quicker. There she goes, fifty. Up the scoreboard. And as for you, mate, you ain't seen nothin' and you don't know no one, do you?"

Gog looks down at the slithering face of Maurice in the torch-light and says, "It's an odd time to run a slaughterhouse." And Maurice laughs and says, "This is war, mate. You can get yours any time of day or night." And Gog says, "Are these your sheep?" And Maurice laughs, and so does his withered tall lieutenant, who has taken up the counting of the corpses.

"They're mine now all right," Maurice says. "But I'm good 'earted. I'm leavin' the baas be'ind for the owner. That's the one bit I can't flog."

At last, Gog sees the point. "Black market?" he says. The words produce a look of injured innocence on the face of Maurice.

"There ain't no black market, brother," Maurice says. "It's a white market, as pure as the driven snow caper, a whiter than white deal. Look, I feel like a ruddy saint gettin' the meat to the people. All that red tape. People'd starve before they could get out of all that red tape. A few ounces of meat a week, are you kiddin'? You should see the eyes of the old-age pensioners light up when I come in with a baron of beef . . ."

"Ye dinna gi' it t' old 'uns, Morrie," the lieutenant says, "if they dinna gi' ye back their pension."

"What's the difference?" Maurice says grandly. "I'm after gettin' meat into mouths, that's what. My best customer's an old girl of eighty and if she's got enough put aside not to need a pension, more chops in 'er chops, I say. It's thrift what brings 'ome the bacon. As long as the meat still gets to them as appreciates it, I'm doin' a public service. They're goin' to decorate me at the end of the war, straight they are. The M.B.E." Maurice laughs. "Meat Bloody Extra."

"Hoo aboot t' C.B.E.?" the lieutenant says. "Costs Bluidy Extra."

" If a bloke's doin' a bit extra, stands to reason 'e's got a right to pick up a bit extra, don't it, brother? Now I'm for fair shares for all, that's why I'm out 'ere, missin' me beauty sleep. Those farmers, they've been cleanin' up a packet, subsidies and all. Ruddy profiteers. Should be 'ung, that's what. If I knock off a few sheep now and then, it sort of shares out the government's money a bit fairer. And if I flog it off 'andsome, you should see me wage bill. Something cruel. And the lorry tax, that's straight stealin' for the government. And the price I've got to fork up for black market petrol. It's sheer 'ighway robbery."

" Bluidy murder," the lieutenant says and adds, " Se'enty-se'en," as another moribund sheep joins the woolly pyramids in the lorries.

" I don't do it for the money," Maurice says. " I could clear more legit. I do it for the people. I do everythin' for the people."

" Which people?" Gog says.

" All the people. Why I'm a Robin 'Ood, sort of. Take from the rich and give to the . . .

" Rich," the lieutenant says. " Eighty-foor."

" Them what deserves it," Maurice observes coldly. " From each accordin' to 'is capacity, to each accordin' to 'is need. I know what's right. Well, I'm good at knockin' off meat, and I give it to 'im what needs it."

" But aren't these people's rations you're stealing?" Gog asks.

" Nah. Anythin' I can knock off can't add anythin' to what you can get in the shops for all them coloured bits of bumph. This is extra meat. The farmers'd only flog it off on the side, if I didn't. I'm cuttin' down their filthy profits, givin' a job to me fellow workers, puttin' away a bit to be used for the cause of the people, which I 'ave up'eld and always will up'old. Get a move on, you bleeders, or I'll 'ave your tripes to tot up the century."

" Ninety-fi'," the lieutenant says. " Tha's tha'."

" You get the 'undred," Maurice says. " I'm runnin' a business, not a rest 'ome for crippled dogs." He whistles and the collies are sent off on a final errand to bring in the last of the straggling sheep from the other side of the burn.

" It's a bit against the law, isn't it?" Gog says. " I know the law's an ass, and I break it often, but you can't go too far, or we'd all be cutting each other's throats."

" But we are, but we are, brother," Maurice says. " We're all cuttin' each other's throats quite legal out in them Jap jungles. And what's worse, makin' a mutton chop or carvin' up your neighbour with a yellow face? If one's illegal and t'other's legal, somethin's wrong with the law, ain't there? And, moreover, the law's agin the people. The law's a club to bash in the people, till the people rule."

" But you told me the people do rule now, since recently," Gog says.

" Ah yes," Maurice says, " but they ain't 'ad time to change the judges. And they can't, 'cause it's agin the law to change the judges in this country. Pretty, ain't it? I want to change the law, but I can't, because it's agin the law. So till they change the judges, I'm a one-man outfit against oppression and for the people. I'm agin property, too, property what's been stolen from the people. And I'm agin all them filthy farmer profiteers, what stayed at 'ome and turned a pretty penny from the blood of the British tommy."

" And you," Gog says, " you fought yourself?"

" Medically unfit," Maurice says. " There I was, all ready to do and die for the people, and what? Flat feet and 'ernia. I've got a certificate to prove it. And I'd like to point out, they also serve what only slaughter sheep."

The collies bring in five stray sheep into the hands of the waiting gang, who leap on them and slice open their throats and heave them into the lorries in a matter of minutes. Maurice consults his watch. " Luminous," he says proudly. " Swapped it with a Commando. What did 'e want to know the time for? Didn't get back from Dieppe." Then he shouts, " All right, men. All aboard the Skylark. Twenty-five mins flat for a century. Bradman couldn't 'ave done it, if 'e'd knocked it all in sixes."

The men pile aboard the lorries, and the engines turn over and catch and roar steadily in the night. And Maurice pokes his thumb up into Gog's navel and warns, " You don't know nothin', brother. Oo's side are you on? The workers, I knew it." And he slips a white bank-note into Gog's pocket and he turns to go, muttering, "You ain't easy to 'ide, a big bloke like you, so if the cops come after me, I won't 'ave far to go to carve up the nark, will I? 'Nuff said, and cheery pip." With that, Maurice reaches the cabin of the lorry, from which an arm descends and hoicks him upwards into the interior. The lorries move off down the road in a sedate convoy. Gog sees for the first time that they have large white circles painted on their sides, and each circle contains a red cross. And so the ambulances disappear from their mission of mercy.

Gog spends only a couple of minutes in getting together his things and making away from the scene of the massacre. Already, light is beginning to trim the wrap of the night and Gog does not want to be found near the bloody pools on the peat. Although all is silence again, he seems to hear the bleating of the murdered animals about him; the blood of the dead ram has stained one of his trouser-legs so that it sticks to his ankle. In the end, he leans down and tears off the bottoms of his trousers and throws them away. Rather bare shins than a bloody flag.

VI

Beyond Innerleithen, the first attempt is made to kill Gog. He has walked through the bruised border town with its hopeful crest of a tame bear and bridled horse, supporting a shield, which shows St. Ronan calming the troubled waters that rear up a full inch high above the mottos *Live And Let Live* and *Watch And Pray*, as though these words had ever been the least defence against the boiling Border barons, who made the local ballads bloodier than anything since the Old Testament. And Gog has passed the old graveyard in the town where a weathered anchor is carved on a sailor's tomb with the pious expectation, SOON LOST BUT NOT TOO SOON FOR GLORY. And Gog has passed Traquair House, standing among its trees in tall granite and freestone rubble, with its windows slit against arrows and crows. And he has sweated up the steep slope of his first real hill, the track towards Minch Moor on the short cut to Yarrow, with flies teeming about his burning face to drive him mad.

As Gog passes a stone wall by a thicket of undergrowth and ash trees, a hare hops mightily just in front of Gog's feet and lands and soars again and slews sideways in mid-jump at a sudden blast from the thicket and falls and jerks on the ground with scrabbling legs that try to dig a grave in air; and is still. As Gog bends forwards to pick up the hare, he hears the second barrel of the shotgun huff out its pellets over his back and send one or two of the balls of lead into his upper arm. He grasps the dead hare by the ears and runs over to the thicket, before the hunter has time to reload. He sees a shape through a thick screen of brush and he throws the hare at the hunter, hitting him with the soft bleeding thud of his victim, as the hunter turns to run, his shotgun in the crook of his arm. But Gog trips in a bramble bush as he tries to pursue; by the time he is on his feet again, all torn and cursing, the hunter is waiting in the coverts or he is lying up as scared as if he were the hunted, he is in ambush or he is in hiding; and all Gog can remember is a thin figure with sloping shoulders and rounded hips under a green jacket, similar to the chauffeur of the black car.

When Gog is walking again on the track up the hill, with the sweat stinging his eyes and his heart rackety in his ribs, he cannot believe the attempt at murder; but lead pellets or imagination smart in his arm, and he begins to consider every wall on his flank as the hiding places of his enemies, Magog or Maurice or the woman in the motor-car. Who knows if the busbies of the redcoats won't pop up over the piled stones in the thin red line of the Peninsular War with levelled muskets and the officer at the far end, all tricked up in gold braid and cockade, won't he lift his sword and shout, "Fire," with the volley crackling out to pit Gog with bloody holes and break his bones with balls of lead and tumble him forwards before the firing squad in a final obeisance? And that blob of scrub, suppose that a thin black executioner rises and points a sten-gun and drills Gog lengthways and sideways for good measure so that twenty little spurts spout from his veins? Or suppose, Gog is struggling head downwards against his pack's weight, counting each pace higher as halfway to peace and utterly oblivious of the threat behind him, when a hand comes hot from heaven to stove in his skull with an iron pipe, a hand belonging to a killer who has crept up behind him unheard on the soft grass in his rubber soles? Gog looks about and each fold in the ground wraps the body of a villain and each rock shields the weapon of a murderer and each trunk shades a highwayman and the very ground may be mined and the very clouds may rain bombs and there is no shelter under earth or in fields or below heaven, only the knowledge that every tick of time is imminent with quick death or slow death, but death certain as the heart has a beat or the pulse a rate.

So Gog hurries on with nature rising in a conspiracy all about him on his way over the next three ranges of hills. He leaves the threat of the stunted firs, each poking up a hairy snout inquisitively from its plantation, and he reaches the windy peaty nothing of the high moors, with the purple ling heather brushing at his bare ankles like dry tentacles and the bracken crackling under his heels to give him away and the dwarf furze pricking his calves to leave a trail of blood droplets for hounds to follow and the tormentil flowers peeping at him with yellow eyes and common speedwell asking him questions with pale-blue petals as taunting as the inquisitive woman's stare in the car and the scattered sheep, deeply suspicious, bleating out his precise whereabouts and the saddle of fell between Glengaber Hill and Peatshank Head making him visible clear down to Yarrow for anyone with binoculars and the soggy stepping down by Deuchar Burn full of boobytraps of bottomless bog.

And once out on the road again, there's no mercy to be expected from passing cars, when any driver can flip his wheel one inch aside and catapult walkers to perdition. And the bonnie banks of Yarrow aren't bonnie any more, but full of smooth white stones handy for chucking at strangers. And it's no better going up over the second range of hills, they're scraped so bare that anyone on the road's as good a mark as a fly on a marrow. And the traveller down the hill is a sitting duck for the squad concealed behind the peering peepholes of that old border tower fifty feet high. And the road along Ettrick Water is so crashing from the cataracts that no one can hear if Magog's not creeping up behind, so glance back, glance back, and if there's nobody, perhaps he's ducked into a gateway, he's a sharp one, he won't get seen however quick a look back, so don't fall into the stupor of the march then, staring at those black boots, slog, slog, slogging it through the Borders, don't let the rhythm of the road unhinge the sense, the hearing what's following, but up now, over the last hills before Hawick, limp-loping in the low sun, hardly daring to fill the water-bottle because the burns are poisoned by foul factory or foul play, and down the last slopes in the twilight, where the dark coppices hide werewolves and botgasties, and the evening wings up like a raven, and back on the main road, it's worse really, with the lorries bashing up to flatten whomsoever, and even at the houses of Hawick at last, they're pill-boxes and waiting dungeons, and fatigue's a double pack on the back and feet drag scuffling and sack-heavy, but then there's the lights of a cinema showing THE BATTLE OF HASTINGS, and Maurice's bribe will easily cover a place to paradise, only one and threepence for a chance of rest and oblivion, with coloured celluloid to chase away the spooks and hobgoblins, and musty plush to recline on, while eyes feast on houris and heroes and happenings incredible.

The script of the end of the film, which Gog sees in the cinema at Hawick, is written as follows:

SHOT 287 *KING HAROLD*, DRESSED IN SKIN-TIGHT CHAIN MAIL WHICH SHOWS OFF HIS ATHLETIC FIGURE TO ADVANTAGE, LEANS WEARILY ON HIS BROADSWORD. AT HIS RIGHT HAND STANDS THE ENGLISH CHAMPION, *GOGFRITH*, WHO IS SUPPORTING *KING HAROLD*'S FAINT-

ING DAUGHTER, THE BEAUTEOUS *HILDA* (Wigs by Arden, Clothes by Lanvin). IN THE BACKGROUND, DRAWN UP IN A CIRCLE FOR A LAST STAND, SHAGGY ENGLISH WARRIORS IN SHAGGIER CHAIN MAIL.

KING HAROLD

So let them come. Here will we stand. On Hastings hill, let all men say, the Britons knew how to die!

HILDA

(WITH PASSION) So young!

GOGFRITH

(WITH MORE PASSION) It shall not be!

SHOT 288 *KING WILLIAM OF NORMANDY*, DRESSED IN SKIN-TIGHT ARMOUR WHICH ALSO SHOWS OFF HIS ATHLETIC FIGURE TO ADVANTAGE, WEARS A SURCOAT OF WHITE SATIN EMBROIDERED WITH SILVER LILIES TO SIGNIFY FRENCH LUXURY. HE LISTENS TO THE EVIL COUNSEL OF *MORTUS*, BASTARD AND ENGLISH RENEGADE, JEALOUS OF *GOGFRITH'S* LANDS AND DESIROUS OF THE BEAUTEOUS *HILDA*. *MORTUS* HOLDS IN EACH HAND THE END OF A CURVED BOW, BENT IN THE MIDDLE.

MORTUS

(WITH EVIL, SUBTLE SMILE) And with a string, break the iron wall. (PRODUCES AN ARROW MAGICALLY WITH A WAVE OF HIS HAND) And with a point, pierce a cunning hole.

KING WILLIAM

Only a brother knows how to beat a brother. HE LIFTS HIS HAND IN A SIGN OF COMMAND.

SHOT 289 LINES OF NORMAN *ARCHERS* SLIP THEIR BOW-STRINGS ONTO THE NOTCHES OF THEIR CURVED BOWS.

SHOT 290 THE CIRCLE OF ANGLO-SAXON *WARRIORS* LOCK THEIR SHIELDS AND PEER ANXIOUSLY INTO THE SETTING SUN.

SHOT 291 A LINE OF NORMAN *ARCHERS* FITS ITS ARROWS ON ITS BOWSTRINGS.

SHOT 292 A SECTION OF THE CIRCLE OF ANGLO-SAXON *WARRIORS* PUTS UP ITS HANDS TO SHADE ITS EYES.

SHOT 293 A DOZEN NORMAN *ARCHERS* POINT THEIR BOWS UP IN THE AIR, READY TO FIRE.

SHOT 294 SIX ANGLO-SAXON *WARRIORS* LOOK AT EACH OTHER, SHAKING THEIR HELMETS IN DOUBT.

SHOT 295 *KING WILLIAM* DROPS HIS HAND AND RUBS IT, TIRED OF HOLDING IT IN THE AIR FOR SO LONG. *MORTUS* SMILES EVILLY.

SHOT 296 LINES OF NORMAN *ARCHERS* FIRE THEIR ARROWS INTO THE AIR.

SHOT 297 *KING HAROLD* RUBS HIS CHINGUARD.

KING HAROLD

To fight is easy. To wait impossible.

GOGFRITH

We shall not wait long.

AN ARROW STICKS IN THE GROUND BETWEEN THEM.

SHOT 298 *WARRIORS* FROM THE ANGLO-SAXON CIRCLE FALL OUT WITH ARROWS STICKING FROM EVERY NOOK AND CRANNY AND CREVICE AND CRACK, UNTIL THE UNBROKEN CIRCLE LOOKS MORE LIKE BATTLEMENTS.

SHOT 299 *MORTUS* GRINS MORE EVILLY.

MORTUS

England is thine, mine liege!

KING WILLIAM

(TROUBLED) A knavish trick to take a kingdom.
(SHOUTS) Charge!
HE JUMPS WITH ONE BOUND IN HIS ARMOUR ONTO A HORSE, WHICH GALLOPS ON SHOT.

SHOT 300 *GOGFRITH* HOLDS HIS SHIELD, AS FULL OF ARROWS AS A HALF-PLUCKED GOOSE, OVER THE COWERING *HILDA*. *KING HAROLD* STANDS UPRIGHT AND PROUD.

KING HAROLD

How shall we fight the air? England must fall when death from the sky . . .
AN ARROW STICKS IN *KING HAROLD*'S HELMET. HE STAGGERS AND FALLS.

SHOT 301 *GOGFRITH* LEANS OVER ONE SIDE OF THE STRICKEN *KING HAROLD*.
THE WEEPING *HILDA*, STILL BEAUTEOUS DESPITE HER TEARS, LEANS OVER THE OTHER SIDE OF HER FATHER. HER BLONDE LOCKS TOUCH HIS HELMET. BELOW THEM, *KING HAROLD* KEEPS A HAND OVER HIS EYE POLITELY.

SHOT 302 (CLOSE UP) GORE COMING THROUGH *KING HAROLD*'S FINGERS OVER HIS EYE.

RESUME SHOT 301 KING HAROLD

(GASPING) I die (GASP) for England! (GASP, GASP) Gogfrith! (GASP) I give to thee (GASP) all I treasure! (GASP, GROAN) The throne is lost (GASP) but Hilda (GHASTLY GASP) was mine (GASP) and (PREGNANT GASP AND PAUSE) ... *KING HAROLD* JOINS THE HANDS OF *GOGFRITH* AND *HILDA* ON THE BLACK CROSS THAT WE NOTICE FOR THE FIRST TIME IS PAINTED ON HIS MAIL CHEST.

SHOT 303 (CLOSE UP) THE THREE HANDS, ONE BLOODY, JOINING ABOVE THE BLACK CROSS.

RESUME SHOT 301 KING HAROLD

Hilda is (GASP) now *thine!* (LAST GASP.)

SHOT 304 *KING WILLIAM* LEADS THE NORMAN *CAVALRY* CHARGING UP HASTINGS HILL, WITH *MORTUS* FAR IN THE REAR.

SHOT 305 *GOGFRITH* PULLS THE KNEELING *HILDA* UPRIGHT FROM HER FATHER'S BODY.

GOGFRITH

The King is dead, but ... his people still live, and shall for ever!

SHOT 306 THE NORMAN *CAVALRY* CHARGES UP THE HILL.

SHOT 307 *GOGFRITH* WAVES HIS SWORD IN THE AIR.

GOGFRITH

Round me, Britons!

SHOT 308 THE NORMAN *CAVALRY* CHARGES UP THE HILL.

SHOT 309 THE LAST OF THE *BRITONS* FORM ROUND *GOGFRITH*.

SHOT 310 THE NORMAN *CAVALRY* CHARGES UP THE HILL.

SHOT 311 THE LAST OF THE *BRITONS* WAVE THEIR SWORDS.

SHOT 312 THE NORMAN *CAVALRY* CHARGES UP THE HILL.

SHOT 313 THE LAST OF THE *BRITONS* WAVE THEIR SWORDS.

SHOT 314 THE NORMAN *CAVALRY* CHARGES UP THE HILL. IT IS A LONG HILL.

SHOT 315 THE LAST OF THE *BRITONS* WAVE THEIR SWORDS. THE SWORDS ARE LONG TOO.

SHOTS 316 to 387 HACKING AND HEWING AND

STABBING AND STICKING AND BELTING AND BASHING AND CLOCKING AND CLOBBERING AND TRIPPING AND TUMBLING AND DASHING AND DRUBBING AND GASHING AND GROANING AND MOANING AND MAULING AND KICKING AND KNOCKING AND WRENCHING AND WRECKING IN A MOUNTED MONTAGE OF QUICK CUTS. *UNKINDEST CUT OF ALL TO*:

SHOT 388 *GOGFRITH* CHOPPING OFF THE HEAD OF *MORTUS*. ALTHOUGH RINGED WITH ENEMIES, NEVERTHELESS WITH ONE SWEEP OF HIS SWORD HE CLEARS A WAY THROUGH THEIR RANKS TO THE NEAREST HORSE, ACROSS THE WITHERS OF WHICH THE BEAUTEOUS *HILDA* IS LUCKILY LYING. WITH ONE MIGHTY BOUND, *GOGFRITH* LEAPS INTO THE SADDLE AND GALLOPS OFF OVER ENGLAND'S MAGNIFICENT DOWNS INTO THE SUNSET (WHICH IS DUE NORTH IN 1066).

NARRATOR'S VOICE:

And so, the lovers rode off into the greenwood, where the beauteous Hilda would bear a son, named . . . (SUSPENSE) Robin Hood! And King William, now called the Conqueror, rode to London Town to build a Mighty England for Robin's Merrie Men!

SOUND OF SEVENTY PIECE STRING ORCHESTRA PLAYING "HAPPY DAYS ARE HERE AGAIN."

THE END.

The critics have called the next feature of the double bill, a sleeper. It is. When the usher wakes Gog after the final curtain in an empty cinema, Gog cannot remember a better ninety minutes of riveting, fun-packed, thrilling, magical, side-splitting, mammoth doze.

VII

By Borthwick Water under the road bridge, Gog sleeps. Occasional noises of army lorries passing overhead on the devious errands of war disturb Gog's restless rest. Morning seeps greyly over the river; on the wilting waters, the reflections of the mill chimneys stretch out their creased fingers. Already, there is the clipping of feet overhead on the bridge and the soft brushing of the tyres of bicycles. When Gog climbs up the embankment to the wall by the river, he sees the first mill shift of men and women going to their work, their fingers already busy at rolling cigarettes or striking matches or stuffing pipes, their faces stitched with threads of wrinkles from lack of sleep, their direction towards their toil as purposeful as the movement of a shuttle. The mill gate is open and it swallows them up, young and old, and the hooter sounds and the gate closes. These are not the mills of God but of men; but they also grind people slow and grind them exceeding small without any intervention from the Almighty.

Gog leaves the dark town of Hawick behind him, a black rage in his heart against the machines of Moloch devouring their sacrifices. And as he takes the road out of the edges of the town into the fields, he sees that a vast and gobbling contraption has broken loose and is eating up the corn harvest, sown early here for midsummer reaping. Instead of a line of men with scythes, swinging at the stalks that bow low before their masters loitering forwards, a red tractor supporting the whirling skeleton of a water-wheel sweeps up the corn stalks, digests them in a clanking maw of wheels and iron plate, and farts them out in neat small oblong turds of hay. These smoking droppings fall regularly in the track of the machine that is eating up men's food, and Gog runs forward along the spoor towards the monster. As he pursues it, it turns at the end of the field and begins crawling and whirling towards him, the reaper-wheel spinning round its cross-bars of death and the goggled devil in the tractor gnashing gears like the teeth of Furies.

Gog reaches up with both hands at the rotten branch of an old oak tree in the middle of the field, standing bare and alone in a patch of grass, in front of which the corn parts as the waves of the sea part in front of the bow-wave of a ship before the prow reaches them. Gog breaks the branch off with the hanging weight of his body and he projects it out before him, priapic and terrible, and he tucks its centre of gravity under the crook of his right elbow and he uses his left hand to raise its point erect off the ground. And he shouts, " Machines shall not eat men," and he lumbers off towards the approaching and gobbling wheel, his oaken lance at the ready, his legs clumping down in a carthorse's trot, his pack jouncing on his spine, with so much sweat trickling down his forehead into his eyes that a vizor seems to be interfering with his sight. Over the sound of the pounding of his blood, Gog hears the yell of the enemy, a roar of dismay. And then, there is a shock that wrenches his lance from his hand. He is flung from the ground forwards into the air. The monstrous machine groans and rumbles and halts. Rods of whirling weight flog into the falling Gog, who plunges from bruising into blackness as he is stretched on the wheel and dragged down and broken against the ground.

Gog opens his eyes to find himself looking through the spokes of the wheel, which has stopped and crushed him. Peering between the spokes are two heads on different levels. The higher head is that of an apple-cheeked country lad, his iron-rimmed goggles pushed up on his forehead to make two black sockets there. The lower head is that of an ageing pippin, yellow and baggy and seamed, as though it has been left on a shelf in the attic to ripen for a winter and has been forgotten for fifty years. The pippin, which wears a red tam o'shanter with a brass cap-badge above an army greatcoat, speaks:

" Back oop," it says. " He's ter great a git t' pull oot. An' if he's croakit, he's not worth t'haulin'."

The lad with the goggles disappears from Gog's view and the pippin withdraws a little later, so that Gog now looks up at a rift of blue in the cloud overhead, a cleft of bright sky barred over by the spokes of the machine. An engine thuds and catches and races, gears clatter and hold, and the spokes move backwards, pressing Gog briefly deeper into the crushed stalks and dry ground, then disappearing out of his sight to leave the sky naked to his eyes. Gog smiles and fills his chest with air and stretches his arms and legs and twists his neck from side to side. Incredibly, he feels no pain, and he levers himself into a sitting position, using his elbows. Before him, he sees that the face like a pippin is attached to a pixie's body, not much more than four feet tall. The pixie, however, does not wear a green doublet and hose below his greatcoat, but corduroy trousers and a leather jacket little bigger than a rabbitskin.

"Thoo's alive," the pixie says. Then he considers his statement and finds it wanting and adds doubtfully, "in a manner o' speakin'."

"Yes," Gog says. Then, feeling a twinge in his back, he too adds, "I mean, quite."

He looks down to where the tractor has stopped a few yards away. The driver climbs down off his seat and walks over and demands:

"Wha' the hell wear ye drivin' at?"

"Thoo wert drivin'," the pixie states. "He were chargin'."

"Why were you destroying the corn?" Gog says. "It's for men like you, isn't it?"

"I wear reapin' it," the lad says. "When wear ye born, mon? The dark ages? The corn's all inside the reaper. It's no hurt."

"And all the men who used to reap the corn?" Gog says. "What do they live on now?"

"They're all in t' army," the pixie says, laughing. "If it weren't fer lads on tractors, t' corn'd rot on t' stalk."

"There's e'en lassies on the land now," the lad says darkly. "Female she-males." He spits into the stubble moodily. "It's nasty wha' goes on under a skirt e'en if a lass is wearin' pants, an' I dinna like it. The land's a mon's job, an' tha' tha'."

"So it'll be agen, when t' men git back," the pixie says soothingly. Then he looks slyly at Gog. "Hoo coom thoo's not in t' army? Or did they let thee oot, 'cos Jerry sent a shell off an' took a leaf oot o' thee?" He taps his head significantly. "Ah can see thoo's got a hole in tha temple. T' war put thee in wi' t' bread an' took thee oot wi' t' cakes, didn't it, like? Left thee ninepence for a shillin'?"

"Dinna ask *him*," the country lad says. "If he's one o' God's oddlin's, he'll no tell ye. I ne'er met a mon sort o' comical in the head who didna ken he was stronger up thear 'n me." He puts a hand in the hip pocket of his dungarees, keeping his fingers moving inside the cloth, as though rolling a piece of dough between them and his thumb. "But as for ye," he says to Gog, "ye're a bluidy menace. Tryin' to booger up me reaper."

"He didn't mean it," the pixie says softly. "He's had a touch ter much o' t' war. Thoo's walkin' woondit, aren't thee, Lofty?"

"Yes," Gog says. "I'm that all right."

"Well, booger off," the country lad says. "Lucky ye didna mash up the reaper." He smiles fleetingly as he feels in his pocket, wincing between smiles as though suffering an exquisite mixture of pain and pleasure.

"Ah'll tek him off," the pixie says. "He may not be oop ter Monday. But even talkin' to a half-rockit man's better 'n talkin' ter thesel' on t' road. 'Cos talkin' ter thesel's three-quarters o' t' way ter bein' half-rockit."

"Half-rocked?" the country lad says with contempt. "He's all crazy." He takes his hand from his pocket. His fingers are bleeding from a hundred little punctures and they grasp the small struggling body of an albino shrew. "Vicious little booger," the apple-cheeked lad says, "eatin' me fingers for yer tay." He tightens his fist round the wriggling shrew, which screams piercingly as its bones crush, and a line of blood comes out from its snout and between its needle teeth. The lad squeezes the shrew finally lifeless, then puts its small face against his ruby nose. "Bite me nose off, yer little booger," he says, smiling. Then he draws back his arm and lobs the body of the shrew into the standing corn. "I've got twenny in the hoose," he explains. "They dinna get lonely while they're waitin', that'd be crooel. They get a rabbit a day, no rations, wish I'd be them." Seeing the look on the face of the pixie, he adds defensively, "Well, a mon's got to hae company in the fields, it's bluidy lonesome." He puts his goggles down from his forehead over his eyes, so that he now stares at Gog out of two opaque circles fringed with black metal. " Ye dinna bring in the harvest be standin' on yer flat feet. Skip, yer crazy booger, or I'll reap an' bind ye for sure." His cheeks shine out red and inviting as he turns to walk back to the tractor, where he climbs onto the seat and starts up the engine, while the pixie pulls Gog away by the hand towards the road.

Gog follows the pixie, too drained in the skull to resist. " It teks a Scot," the pixie says, " ter be reelly gone hissel'. Ah'm from Northumberlan' mesel', but Ah knoo one thin' for certain. Over t' Border is in ter Bedlam. Oonce pas' Carlisle an' thoo'rt in t'crazy hoose. But, o' coorse, tha' wooldn't bother *thee*."

" I'm not mad," Gog says. " Just a bit forgetful these days. But I'm remembering. Slowly. I'm remembering."

" Happen, thoo shooldn't," the pixie says. " Rememberin's all reet, excep' when thoo's got sommat thoo'd do better ter forget. An' they say, they who do t' worsest forget t' most. If thoo've forgot everythin', what hastn't thoo done!" Here, the pixie stops as if scared at the thought. " Still," he goes on, " Ah've done enough bad ter want ter start agen wi' a clean slate. But then, meetin' a stranger's like havin' a clean slate. Thoo dostn't knoo me from Adam. So Ah meet be better'n Adam before he et t'apple!" The pixie chuckles. " But Ah'm not, t' devil be praisit. T' name's Cluckitt."

The pixie stretches out his hand towards Gog, as they proceed slowly down the road towards the South. Gog stoops to shake the pixie by the hand and reply, " My name's Gog."

" Owld Goggie hissel'," the pixie laughs. " Thoo'rt big enough ter be a boggart."

" Who's old Goggie? And what's a boggart?"

" Thoo doesn't knoo? Owld Goggie hides in t' orchards, watchin' over t'apples till they ripen. Chases away t' lads. He's a boggart and bogeyman. Looks like thee, big, braw, fit ter skeer a bairn from his mum's womb."

" Well," Gog says, " *I* thought you were a pixie."

" An' who's ter say Ah'm not?" Cluckitt says. " Ah may be Puck's mate, for all tha'. Ah took thee fer a boggart, t' moment Ah clappit eyes on thee."

" What sort of a boggart?"

" Mumpoker, Tod-lowrie, Clap-cans, Church-grim, Tom Dockin, Knocky-bo, Rawhead, Bloodybones, t' Bodach, or Owld Goggie, all boggarts are t' same, oonce thoo gets ter know them. They're all spookie an' no speerit, all ghostie an' no gutsie. A boggart may be ten feet tall, wi' saucer eyes an' clankin' chains an' shaggy hair an' teeth thoo coold spike a rail-track on. An' he may lurk on t'moor or in t'boles o' trees ter skeer us. But there's no stooff ter him. Thoo can walk reet throo him. He's no match fer t' pixies. Ah tell thee, when t' little people meet t' big folk, it's t'tinies who get on top."

" Nonsense," Gog says. " The strong always sit on the weak. That's what all history's about. Anyway, I'm not superstitious. I'm no more of a boggart than you're a pixie."

" An' no less," Cluckitt says, lagging well behind Gog as they go forward, Gog slowly strolling and Cluckitt nearly running. " Oonce Ah didn't knoo wha' it meant ter *stretch* me legs. Noo Ah do, an' Ah've ploomb stretchit them so far they've snappit. Thoo cooldn't gi' me a lift, Lofty?"

Gog laughs and stoops and makes a ladle of his hand and scoops up the withered body and pippin head of Cluckitt and sits him on his shoulders above his pack, so that Cluckitt rides like an aged parody of the Child on the back of St. Christopher, his legs dangling on Gog's chest and his hands clasped across Gog's forehead. From time to time, as Gog strides away from where the last field breaks against a stone wall and the moors begin, Cluckitt taps out a little rhythm of joy on Gog's skull.

" What's that you're playing?" Gog says. " It bothers me. It sounds like a drum playing reveille, and that's a sound nobody likes to hear." Gog wonders how he knows what reveille sounds like. Yes, there were once many mornings, in a hut, on an iron bed, hearing the brass cheery rooster of the trumpet sound out the rhythm for another bloody day of drill.

" It's revelly, all reet," Cluckitt says. " Wake oop, thickhead. Ah've proovit thoo'rt a boggart an' Ah'm a pixie. An' fer why? 'Cos little people are smarter 'n big uns. They got ter be ter live at all, doon't they? Who else but a boggart woold be tha' soft he'd gi' a pixie a lift on his back?"

And Cluckitt suddenly tightens his legs round Gog's throat so that Gog chokes, then releases them suddenly and laughs to see the moors open free about them.

VIII

The road over the moors is a haphazard failure of tarmac. The sheep graze on its surface in a puzzled way, expecting to find grass in more than the cracks. As Gog approaches bearing Cluckitt, they bleat and stare until the men are almost upon them, then jerk away in a gawky run. The moors themselves are so green, yet so barren and so endless – with each shepherd's cottage no more than a blob against the vast indifference of nature – that Gog feels free from the persecution of yesterday. The black car is no longer following him along the road; indeed, there are no cars at all for mile after mile. This lush emptiness would give minutes of warning before a threat. And there is Cluckitt to chuckle and chatter above Gog's head, spitting out his saws and gleanings of Northumbrian wisdom from his puckered mouth under his red tam o'shanter with its brass cap-badge sporting a cannon and the letters *R.A*.

They rest from time to time on the peaty grass and finish the rations between them. When they have been a dozen miles and have reached Hermitage Water, it is Cluckitt who insists that they turn west along the road by the stream. "Theer's a cassle oop theer, t' biggest on t' Border, an' t' worsest. It's worth a peek. Sooch wickitness theer! T' stones soonk three feet inter t' groond, just for t' weight o' wickitness done theer. All a pixie's fault, o' coorse. A boggart cooldn't ha' done half tha' bad. Red-cap t' pixie's name, an' Ah trust thee marks me own red cap. He was t' fameeliar speerit o' t' Master o' Hermitage cassle, Lord

Soolis, t' wickitest lord theer ever was roond heer. Redcap usit ter live in a chest, an' he helpit Lord Soolis build t' cassle an' do every sin agen t' poor theer was, an' some theer wasn't befor Lord Soolis thought them oop. But Redcap wooldn't let Soolis look at his face – he had an oogly moog like me. But one day Soolis tek a peek, an' then he has his lot. Boilit like a bloater, he was. Boilit like a bloody bloater."

Cluckitt stops gabbling as Hermitage Castle comes into sight between the trees. A great cube of stone sits on the far bank of the water, with round towers cocking up at its corners. It is nearly windowless; only a few slits slice the cliffs of stone blocks. It seems the essence of all castles, bare and accommodating only war – except for one fussy frill of stonework running under the battlements. "If they build a monument as big as tha' on top o' me body," Cluckitt says admiringly, "Ah'll tell Gabriel ter shoot oop when he blows his troompet on Joodgement Day, an' leave me be."

They pass the castle to the right of them. Two hundred yards ahead, a bridge crosses the stream and leads to the green lawns before the castle. Once over this bridge, Cluckitt yells, "Whoa, neddy," and brings Gog to a stop by pulling at his forehead until his chin points up at the sky. Then the little man scrambles down from Gog's shoulders with no more concern for Gog's flanks than if he were clambering off a carthorse. "Not ter t'cassle," he says to Gog. "Not yet. T'other way, theer's a great-great-great-great-great-granny o' a grandad o' thesen burit be t'chapel. We'll see his grave. Nine foot long, it is. Big enough for thee ter kip in."

They turn left and walk along the river bank towards a ruined chapel, marked out by the first few layers of its stone walls and three leaning arches. Ahead, they see half a dozen boys playing between the chapel and the stream. One boy is riding piggy-back on his tall friend. Two others hack away at each other with branches as swords. One flaps his arms like wings and jumps, pretending to fly, while the last one cracks a piece of string tied onto the end of a twig, and yells, "Wurrk, ye dogs, wurrk."

When the boys see Gog and Cluckitt approaching, they stop

frozen in their positions, as if they have been seen playing Grandmother's Footsteps. Then they shriek in terror and run away, scattering and ducking; the devil himself might be at their heels. "Stop," Cluckitt shouts, "or Ah'll blast yoo wi' fire. Yoo'll rot dead in yoor beds this neet if yoo doon't *stop*." The boys freeze again and look back, hypnotized with horror as chickens in front of a viper. "Aye, it's Redcap, Redcap," Cluckitt shouts, "an' he says ter coom back heer. At t' dooble!" The boys scuttle back to where Cluckitt and Gog are and they halt a few feet away, goggle-eyed and trembling.

Cluckitt relishes his role as an evil spirit. A menacing tremolo hints the unspeakable in every sentence, as he points up at the huge Gog beside him. "Ah bring t' Coot back from t' mole coontry wi' me, just ter keep me coompany like. But do yoo knoo wha', boys? He's been moolderin' doon theer so long ..." Here Cluckitt points down at a raised hump of sod nearby, which is nine foot long between its two endstones. "He's ploomb forgot just hoo he coom ter die. It's lucky, then, we've foond yoo lads ter teach him agen, isn't it?" The boys nod dumbly, terrified out of a reply.

"Remember Lord Soolis," Cluckitt goes on in his high and ghostly voice. "T' Master o' Hermitage who lookit on Redcap as yoo are lookin' now. Remember what happenit ter *him*, when he didn't do wha' Redcap tellit him. Will yoo do all I tell?" Again the boys nod in silence. "Thoo, t' tall un, thoo'rt Soolis, lad, Master o' Hermitage, t' wickit magician in person." The tall boy shivers and bows his head. "An' t' rest o' yoo, why, yoo're Soolis's men. Unnerstan'?" The boys shuffle their feet and look at the ground.

"What do I do?" Gog says, dropping his pack onto the ground. "Is this a game or history?"

"Theer's no difference at all between t' two. History plays wi' us half t' time, 'cos we must do just wha' she tells us. An' we play wi' history t'other half, 'cos we never learn from t' mistakes o' others, so we go on doin' just as bad an' just t' same as ever. Thoo'rt history, owld Goggie, an' thoort playin' t' game o' t' Coot o' Keeldar, who was a big braw heero from Englan' like thesel'. An' if terday isn't six hunnerd yeer ago, well, t' weather hasn't changit a bittie. It was hunch-weather then an' it's hunch-weather noo." Cluckitt puts his cupped hands to his lips and blows an imaginary horn. "Tarra, tarra." Then he crouches down, hiding his head under his hands. "Ah'm t' Keeldar Stone, t' same as t' big Coot rode roond widdershins long ago befor he went ter hunt across t' Border in Lord Soolis's land. Theer weer lines wrote o' t' Keeldar Stone.

"Green vervain roond its base did creep,
A pooerful seed tha' bore;
An' oft, o' yore, its channels deep
Were stainit wi' human gore."

The boys shudder, as Cluckitt commands Gog, "Ride roond t' Keeldar Stone, Coot, ride roond. It's an owld Druid stone. So ride."

Gog obeys, jumping a little up and down as though in a cantering saddle and circling the crouching Cluckitt, who cries, "Now Ah'm Redcap an' Ah'm unner t' stone an' Ah'm sayin' . . ." His voice sinks to a sepulchral groan. "Ah coom fer death, Ah coom ter work thee woe." At this line, one of the boys passes out from fright and collapses on the ground, an action which deters the other boys from trying to slink away. "Aye," Cluckitt says, "doon't yoo try ter hoppit, lads, or Ah'll do yoo all in. Now, Soolis lad, t' Coot's heer. Thoo knoost wha' ter do. Nowt's happenit on t' Border for so long tha' even t'lads are all mindful o' wha' happenit hunnerds o' yeers ago."

The tall boy mumbles to Gog, "Cout o' Keeldar, come into me ha', an' hae yoor tay wi' me." And he leads Gog under the shade of a hanging birch by the top of the slope down to the river; there he pretends to pour Gog out a drink into an invisible goblet. Then Cluckitt pirouettes three times widdershins, holds up both hands above his head, and looses an unearthly shriek, followed by a harangue of gibberish impossible to understand, except that the last word sounds suspiciously like, "Abracar-hubarbdabra."

When Cluckitt pauses to draw breath, he puts on his normal tone. "Tha's me spell," he explains. "Ah've witchit all t' Coot's men. They'll linger in Hermitage cassle fer ever an' aye, fixit teeter 'n mortar in t' stones." Cluckitt pauses, then yells, "Now at him, lads. Hack him ter bloody bits."

At this command, the five standing boys leap on Gog and begin beating him with switches and branches and fists; even the fainting boy revives at this promise of a fight and pitches into the bewildered Gog, who is driven backwards down the river bank to where a large pool spreads out a table of brown water.

"Lay off," Gog shouts. "Stoppit, you little devils."

"Go on, beat him," Cluckitt shrills. "Or Redcap'll do yoo."

So the boys bash and strike and slap with a will, and Gog dare not reply in kind because they are too small. He stumbles back down the slope to the water's edge.

"Call 'em off, Cluckitt, you fool," he shouts. "A game's a game, but this is bloody murder."

"Kill t' Coot, kill t' Coot, kill t' Coot," Cluckitt chants, and the boys take up the chant, "Kill the Cout, kill the Cout, kill the Cout," until Gog is forced back by the smarts and stings given him by the six imps, forced back onto a large flat rock that projects out into the pool. Glancing behind him, he sees that the upstream side of the rock has a sheer edge, downdropping twelve foot deep through water the colour of lime juice. On the downstream side, the rock shelves into a brown pool, which is only ankle-deep in shallows rippling over small pebbles. Gog backs across the rock into the middle of the pool, flailing his arms in front of him to knock down the prodding branches of the boys, who edge onto the rock after him. As Gog reaches the end of the rock, where he has to step across a channel to a boulder beyond, he sees the frenzied Cluckitt throw a small stone at him from the bank. He cannot duck in time. The stone catches him on his wounded temple and he slips to his left and goes greening downdrown into the deep pool.

As the cold waters envelop him, a flash explodes in front of Gog's eyes. Clear in the underwater, he sees himself sitting in a khaki officer's uniform reading a book fifty fathoms deep. It was so, it was so, he was reading in his cabin when the mine struck without warning, the war in Europe was over, no one was expecting it, and the mighty disintegration left him reading his book in the dark belly of the ocean, fifty fathoms down and trying to turn over the next page. And the ocean bore him again to the surface and threw him up on the sand. Gog, the new man, now remembers the old Gog, the man who was there before he was spewed out from the sea.

When Gog rises in the pool, choking and spluttering, he meets the points of the branches in the boys' hands pricking him down to bubbledeath, with Cluckitt jumping up and down on the rock, shrieking his incantation, "Kill t' Coot, kill t' Coot, kill t' Coot." Gog is jabbed down again and held under by wooden prongs; but he manages to struggle up for the second time, only to be shoved back under by Cluckitt himself, who seizes a branch from a boy and opens a wound in Gog's cheek, using both hands to rake him under. Gog only just manages to come up for a third and last time, so many branches are pegging him down in his watery grave. And he would certainly drown, except that he swings out a desperate hand and grabs Cluckitt by the ankle and drags him also into the pool.

Seeing Redcap proved mortal and take a ducking, the boys drop their branches and come to the rescue. They stretch out their thin hands to catch at Gog's hair and clothing and pull him out, while Cluckitt clings for dear life onto Gog's neck, whining, "Save me! Ah can't swim! Save poor owld Cluckitt! He never hurt a fly."

So Gog heaves himself out of the pool onto the rock, with Cluckitt stuck onto him like a harpoon onto a whale. And the boys flee away from the dripping pair, away off the rock and up the bank and out of sight beyond the hanging birches, all the way to home, not daring to look back in case the angry Cout and Redcap, all drowned and dead and dripping, will want to munch boys' giblets for their lunch. And Gog picks up Cluckitt and carries him to the bank and holds him a good yard off the ground and shakes him up and down and from side to side, this way and that way and all the way to Biscay Bay, while the spray flies off Cluckitt and he gibbers for mercy, until his false teeth fly out of his mouth and snap against Gog's nose, which gives the big man such a start that he drops Cluckitt quicker than a squirting toad.

"What do you mean, trying to drown me with those little devils?" Gog roars. "You're working for Magog, too, are you? Is everybody? I thought you were a peasant on my side. What do you want to kill me for?"

And Cluckitt cowers, raising up his arms above his head in a pathetic attempt to ward off a crushing fist, and mumbling, "Doon't hit me, doon't hit me. Ah'm a pint ter tha gallon. Thoo'll be in jug for murder."

"*I* was the one being murdered," Gog howls.

"It was only a game," Cluckitt jabbers. "We meet ha' been carrit away a bittie, but it was good clean foon. Can't thoo be a sport?" He picks up his false teeth and clamps them back in his mouth, so that his words separate from their running jumble.

"A sport? For worms?"

"We weer just bein' historic, like. Ah swear it, Gog. T' Coot . . ."

"Enough of the bloody Coot. I was a coot myself ever to listen to you."

"He woor magic armoor an' not a sword coold hurt him. So they droonit him in tha' theer pool, pushin' him doon wi' lances. An' so Master Soolis an' his fameeliar Redcap droonit t'greet Coot o' Keeldar. An' tha' was all we weer doin'."

"I agree," Gog says, beginning to laugh, reassured by the worried earnestness of Cluckitt. "You were making a good job of drowning me. Very historical. Only you'd have had to dig another grave for me. There wouldn't be room for me alongside the proper Cout. I'm sure he'd hog all the graveclothes and push me out of the coffin into the mould."

"We wooldn't ha' reely droonit thee," Cluckitt says. "Thoo mustn't think so."

"I'd rather that," Gog says, "than what you said happened to Soulis in the end. Boiled, did you say? I hope Redcap got boiled too."

"Not Redcap," Cluckitt says. "Thoo can't boil a pixie. He'd just turn hissel' inter steam an' float away. I do it often mesel'." When Gog laughs, Cluckitt laughs too, glad to be forgiven. "But t' Master o' Hermitage, t' wickit Lord Soolis, he did get boilit alive. T' King o' Scotlan' got so fed oop wi' hearin' Lord Soolis did this an' Lord Soolis did tha' an' hoo wickit Lord Soolis was, he said, 'Burn him if yoo please, but let me heer no more o' him.' So they catchit Soolis an' they boond him in steel. But he was a magician an' he bust t' steel. Then they boond him in ropes o' siftit san'. But he bust t' ropes, tho' they still lay theer, t' ropes o' san', by the Nine Stone Burn beyon' t' cassle, wheer t' Druids usit ter sacrifice theer victims."

"And how did they kill Soulis in the end?" Gog says.

Cluckitt begins to intone:

"On a circle o' stones they placit t' pot,
On a circle o' stones but barely nine;
They heatit it red an' fiery hot,
Till t' burnish't brass did glimmer an' shine.

"They rollit him oop in a sheet o' lead,
A sheet o' lead fer a funeral pall;
They plungit him in t' cauldron red,
An' meltit him, lead, an' bones an' all.

An' tha' was t' end o' t' wickit Lord Soolis, which shows ..." Here Cluckitt looks ingratiatingly up at Gog. "Thoo can kill a Coot o' Keeldar, thoo can kill a Gog, thoo can mek poor folk groan an' murder theer heeroes, but t' Big Un on top he'll set them ter catch thee in t'end an' mek pot luck oot o' thee."

"A lot of bad rulers," Gog says, "die in their beds happily of a surfeit of evil. But, I must say, I'd rather be Soulis than the Cout right now. My clothes would be drier."

"Aye," Cluckitt says, "we're like ter shiver t'death."

"Unless we walk ourselves warm," Gog says. "Come on." He grabs Cluckitt by one hand and his pack by the other and sets off across the bridge and down the road at such a pace that Cluckitt is either running or skipping or flying to keep up with him. "Nature's own airing cupboard," Gog says. "Keep the pace up."

"Ah'll bust a gut," Cluckitt whines. "Ah'll die o' breathlessness. Thoo can't dry thesel' *walkin'*. Thoo'rt knowin' as Kate Mullet, an' she was hangit for a fool. Stop, or Ah'll burst."

"Good riddance," Gog says. "A taste of your own murdering habits."

And so they clip lickety-spit along the roads that separate them from Liddel Water, with the Larriston Fells rising up beyond to mark the boundary into England.

They've passed the river and they are going up beyond the last cottage on the track that heads up into the fells, when Cluckitt dunks himself down and says, "Thoo crazy booger, stop. We ha' nowt ter sup an' nowt ter drink an' we're ploomb toockert oot. We got ter stop an' get dry an' rest a bittie. We got ter." So Cluckitt crawls over to the gate of the cottage garden and hauls himself upright and goes through to the kitchen door and knocks. Gog hears him mumbling and whining ingratiatingly for a time, then a woman comes over to the garden wall, all red and rosy and dumpling and dimpled, and she says, "You're to coom reet in, I willna hear no." So Gog follows her into the kitchen of the cottage, where she makes them sit by the side of a glowing iron range; and she takes their clothes away as they strip off down to their trousers, Gog's old jacket and grey shirt and socks, Cluckitt's red tam o'shanter and army greatcoat and raggety sweaters and tartan shirt and string vest. She lays the clothes out to dry on a clothes horse and a line; then she makes them mugs of tea and serves them endless slices of bread and margarine and apple jelly, while they tell her of the drowning of Gog the Cout in Hermitage Water, and she scolds them for being no better than little boys themselves.

At last, it is six o'clock by the large tin clock over the hearth, the sacred hour of national communion over the news that no one has missed for six years of war. The woman switches on the wireless, and the firm soupy comforting baritone begins, "This is Alvar Liddell . . ." The Japanese are being pushed back with heavy casualties and Tokyo's burning and most of our planes are returning home safely and the Nazi war criminals are going to be hanged and the Occupation Zones drawn and Germany quartered between the Allies and all is fine and victorious, until there is a sudden fuzzing of the airwaves, followed by a familiar voice cutting in to say:

"This is Wayland Merlin Blake Smith speaking from somewhere in the North, and I say unto you, give me Broadcasting House, or ye shall be sorry. Already the wrath of the Lord prepareth a cloud in the heavens; with a mighty fist He shall strike down a far city as an awful warning. And if ye heed not that first sign and give me not the transmitters, woe unto you; for the Lord hath revealed unto me that He will strike down a second far city with the great cloud of His wrath, like unto the destruction of Sodom and Gomorrah with a pillar of fire from heaven. And after that second warning, He shall stay His hand at my asking, for that ye should consider the anger of the Almighty and yield me the transmitters, so that I may lead my flock in building Zion again by Thames' sweet side in Albion. Beware, beware, God is nigh and I am His servant, Smith, in my fourth and last coming. Repent ye, repent ye, for Gog is wandering loose in the land, I have encountered him. And Magog ruleth in the high places of London, where we shall meet him. And at that final meeting, shall I beg the Lord to stay His anger, if Magog shall deny me? Give me the airwaves, Magog, or . . ."

At this moment, the voice of the Bagman is suddenly cut off and a smooth announcer's voice says, "We apologize for this break in transmission to our Northern listeners from an unknown radio transmitter. And now we join the Palm Court Orchestra in the Palm Court of the Grand Hotel."

As the sound of violin strings cascades over the listeners, Cluckitt looks quizzically at Gog and laughs and says, "Gog's indeed wanderin' loose in t' lan'."

"Tha' weren't the Bible, were it?" the woman says. "Yet it sounded like."

"No, it wasn't the Bible," Gog says. "It's a man I . . . met once, who writes his own Bibles."

"Thoo *met*?" Cluckitt says incredulously. "Was tha' wheer thoo pickit oop tha' crazy nonsense aboot Magog wantin' ter croak thee? Thoo must ha' dreamt it."

"Perhaps I did," Gog says, and he looks down at the tattoo on the back of his hand which says MAGOG, to check that it is still there. The dark fears begin to rise in the back of his mind again, so that the round face of the woman suddenly becomes a fat mask hiding Magog in the pouches of its cheeks, and the withered dewlaps of Cluckitt conceal Magog in their folds, and the spurt of splitting coal in the range is Magog's boot scraping against the side of his iron box, where he crouches ready to spring out like a ravening golliwog. Then Gog laughs at the folly of his imaginings and says, "Ridiculous. You know, sometimes I think I really am the Gog of the Book of Revelations, and everyone I see is really Magog, and he's after me everywhere. We're all a bit crazy some of the time."

The woman nods and says, "Days coom when I ken tha' e'en the chicks is tryin' to peck oot the eyes o' the bairns. *Fear days*. They coom to us a'."

"Stooff," Cluckitt says. "Tha's mooch cry fer little wool, like shearin' a pig. Better be merry an' bright." And his little eyes shine with glee between the wrinkles that spread out from their corners as thick as hairs on a brush.

"Well, mum, we'd better be oop an' goin', over t' moor from Scotlan' ter Englan'. Theer can't be a better sight ahead nor a worse un behin'."

"Tha's wha' we say," the woman replies, "when we see a Sassenach leavin'."

All three laugh, and Gog and Cluckitt put on their dried clothes. As Cluckitt buttons his shirt, Gog notices that the little man has a large pouch, sewn inside the cloth and stuffed with various objects; but Gog is too busy to inquire what is in the pouch. For he turns to give the woman a pound and ask her for what food she has to spare. She would like to refuse the money, but she needs it. So she loads their pockets with loaves and shortcake and scones and cold sausages and apples, and she fills Gog's waterbottle with cold tea, and she takes her leave with a "God bless ye."

So Gog and Cluckitt leave for England, pretty dry and well-stocked, as the twilight begins to drop its slow summer canopy over them. The track winds gentle over the soft moorland, the peat turf is springy to their tired soles. They meet only the worried sheep, with each ewe followed by a nearly-grown lamb, still trying to suckle whenever its mother stops to chew the grass and practically upending her in its push after her udder, since it is nearly her size and too large to scramble beneath her belly. The ewes, indeed, have such fierce horns curling about their black cheeks that they could throw Cluckitt with one flick; but they always turn tail and run, rather than toss the little man over their backs for good luck. From the ridge of the Larriston Fells, Gog and Cluckitt see the long valley of Liddesdale saunter beneath in soft greens and browns; only a hidden train disturbs the smooth contours of the flattened hills beyond with its poplar of smoke. The track winds on over the saddle of the fells between bile-green moss on quaking bogs. Fern crawls over the brown marsh on curling feet, sundew stretches up its sticky spades covered with hair to trap insects in its lime, and a single butterwort here and there holds up one purple flower on a long frail stalk in disdain at the soft mess beneath.

Where the peat is cut by the deep channel of a burn, Gog and Cluckitt find a decaying stone bridge overgrown by moss and cotton grass. They cannot understand the use of so much labour on an empty track, until they reach a stone pedestal slap by the barbed wire strand that marks the boundary between Scotland and England at Bloody Bush. Ahead, the track wanders sandily down into Northumberland. Cluckitt explains that this is an old raiders' route, which the Border thieves knew was good for rieving cattle and sheep. Then the Union came and the enclosures; and the new owners seized the route over common land and built bridges and put up their sign, telling all men that this improved road was the property of a Bart and an Esquire, who charged:

1st For horses employed in leading coals: 2d each
2nd All other horses: 3 do
3rd Cattle: 1 do
4th Sheep Calves Swine: 1/4d
N.B. Persons evading or refusing to pay at the abovementioned toll gate will be prosecuted for trespass.

Gog spits to see the sign, and says, " I'd like to tear that down. There's no damn right to charge a toll on a road and there never was. A road's open to everyone to wander on. Who cares what it cost to build? Once it's there, it's for us all."

" T'road's open now," Cluckitt says, " wha's left o' it. No coals pass heer, nor sheep nor cattle, other 'n aboot theer own business, not man's. Just a few stray men pass an' precious few o' them. Thoo payit a toll long ago ter pass along t'road an' another toll ter pass back; but that owld toll-keeper, he's payit his toll ter death but oonce an' he's not passin' back. Wha' matter *private* stooff now, when death's always pooblic, for all? Why bother thesel'? Time'll turn t'road back inter a track an' t' track inter moor agen. Only time. It doon't need no help from thee. It'll swallow thee oop, but it'll never let thee doon, 'cos it'll swallow oop tha enemies too."

" I'd still like to tear that toll-marker down," Gog says. " If I had a pick-axe . . ."

" Dreem thoo hast," Cluckitt says. " Let's find a spot ter kip an' thoo can dreem thoo tore doon t' marker. An' if thoo dreem well, thoo'll ha' done it – if thoo doon't pass this way agen ter see thoo hasn't. 'Cos a good dreem after a while's better 'n a bad fact, like luv's better 'n a missus."

So they proceed on down the sandy road towards Keildar. Soon they come to little spruce trees planted in midget groves on either side of the track. The road seems downhill all the way, as though to tempt travellers on to insidious England. When blackness begins to fall and the moon rises with a halo about its shaved circle, they find an empty woodsman's hut by the Akenshaw burn. It is used to store birch brooms for beating out forest fires. Memories of past floggings in some dark schoolroom of some flagellant public school switch at the bare places in Gog's mind, but he cannot remember names or places, only the spread hot pain of the birch twigs against his rump and the choking flush of his face bent down to the floor to stretch his trousers tight against his buttocks and the crackle of snapping twigs spurting across the floor and the switch of the birch ascending and the dreadful pause while he waits for it to slash down again to the count, " One, two, three, four, five, *six*! That's it. Don't do it again."

But these present birches made a good bed, when padded by heather plucked from outside the door. And the burn all night singeth her quiet tune as she mumbleth sweetly along and lulleth them with the sleep of angels, until the frogs croak in the moon and disturb the sleepers with the harsh notes of mortality.

IX

In the morning, Gog and Cluckitt are woken by the sound of foresters whistling on their way to work. They skulk in the hut until the foresters are gone, then they creep out onto the track. And once they are out, their lungs feel the nibble of the milk teeth of the morning, still soft and white with a slight mist near the burn, but the sky overhead already clear and sharp and sporting cheeks of clouds. They cut up over a hill away from the burn which loops towards the west. All is damp and soft in the spruce-pierced hills. There is no noise as they move, until Gog could almost scream from expecting a roar to shatter the yawning absence of sound.

When they reach the crest of the hill, the trees stop short at a stone wall; beyond is a plateau of grass, where black bullocks graze. Gog and Cluckitt walk across the plateau, with Cluckitt dropping his old head towards his left shoulder and looking cockeye at the cruddled clouds, cheeky and fleecy against the blue of the morning. " Henscrattins," he says and spits. Then he wags his finger at a sea-gull, which has the nerve to alight near him and give him a beaky stare from a similarly cocked head.

" Sea-moo, sea-moo, bide on t' san',
Theer's never good weather when thoo's on t' lan'."

Gog stops and drops his pack on the dewy grass and sits on it, looking down towards the Tyne lying silver and winding beneath. Beyond the moorland rushes, spruce hills as shallow as billows roll down past meadows and copses to the gravelled banks of the river. Then up again past Tyne, the frozen sea of the fells stretches, broken only by the finny ridges of firs planted as windbreaks. In the bright and cool and quiet of the morning, Gog hears the racket of the blood pulsing in his ears. The vacuum of sound on the moor makes the intolerable din of the workings of his body audible for the first time. The pump of his bloodstream thumps on each nerve, needles prick at the wound on his temple, until Gog opens his mouth to scream. Then a curlew complains to find the air so thin and the slight noise turns Gog's ears outward to hear the interminable protest of all living things rather than the complaint of his inner flesh. And a small wind begins to bend and rustle the coarse grasses of the moor, making enough of a soughing to encourage Gog to add the sound of his own breath and speech.

"Tell me, Cluckitt," Gog says, "why do the British always talk about the weather?"

"They live unner it," Cluckitt replies, grinning. "We're not in t'mole coontry yet." He wets his finger and holds it up against the wind. "A sly day. Theer's bone in it."

"I think I read once, I can't quite remember ..."

"Read?" Cluckitt sniffs. "Theer's muckle burrit in bad books ter deep ter get at."

"I think I read once," Gog repeats, "someone writing that only a man in a mine or a dungeon could be ignorant of the weather. So it's not worth talking about."

Cluckitt tugs up a handful of grass with his right hand and puts it on the palm of his left hand and blows the blades gently away.

"Tha's toon talk," he says contemptuously. "Thoo doon't groo corn in t'cellar. Thoo's got ter ha' sun."

"But what's the use of talking about the weather?" Gog says. "We all do. Yet all our bad breath can't blow away one drop of rain."

"Happen thoo'd want ter knoo wha'll happen," Cluckitt says, consulting the remaining blades of grass on his palm as carefully as a soothsayer studies the entrails of a sacrifice. "Happen thoo'd need ter knoo when ter soo an' when ter reap in t' fields. It doon't matter what's t'weather in *t'street*, if thoo's got boots on."

"Then why do city people blather on about the weather as

much as anyone else? Do you think all us British have to pretend we're farmers and worry about the weather, just so we can think we've still got clay on our carpet slippers?"

"Aye, tha' city weather talk's all rare overs fer meddlers. Thoo doon't preten' ter be doon on t'farm be pratin', it's a donkey day. But coontry folks need ter know. Look." Cluckitt points to the round hump of a far fell, where a cloud makes a soft black hat over the moor. "Wheer Ah coom from unner Criffel, they say:

"When dingy packs on Criffel lo'er,
Then hoose yoor kine an' stack yoor door,
But if Criffel be far an' cleer,
Fer win' or wet yoo needn't feer.

An' when theer's t'wheel roon' t'moon as theer weer last neet, t'bigger t'wheel, t'neerer t'wet.

"If t'wheel in t'moon be far away,
Mek haste an' hoose yoor corn an' hay."

Gog laughs for the first time that day and feels in the opening and closing of his ribs a great yawn of peace.

"That's all very well, Cluckitt, but you forecast wrong half the time. Anyway, the moon's got nothing to do with the rain."

"T'moon pulls t'sea, doon't she? An' t'sea pulls t'rain doon ter fill it. So it's moon pull sea, sea pull rain, an' rain pull moon onter her back ter fill her lap wi' water.

"T'horny moon is on her back,
Men' yoor shoe an' sort yoor thatch."

Gog laughs again.

"Tell me, with all your superstitions, do you leave your red cap behind, every time it's a red sky at night, shepherd's delight. Are you so sure you can read the weather that you'll risk getting your head wet if you're wrong?"

Cluckitt smiles up at Gog, then rises to his feet so that his eyes are nearly on a level with those of the sitting Gog.

"Happen Ah always weer a cap ter keep me brains snoog, even if it's a sunny glosy mornin' an' Ah sweat good tidily. Thoo can't trust t'weather in Englan', it sets thee oop ter let thee doon. But theer's no harm in tellin' it what it ought ter do."

"So if the weather behaves as you say, it proves you're right.

And if it doesn't, it also proves you're right, because you say the weather always lets you down."

Cluckitt doesn't answer. Then he grins his most crooked smile, showing his yellow teeth at the corner of his mouth.

"Best be on t'road. Last neet, didst thoo hear t'paddocks croak by t'Akenshaw burn?"

"The frogs? Yes, I did."

"When paddocks croak in t'pond at neet,
Thoo may expect both win' an' wet."

Gog laughs again.

"You're incorrigible, Cluckitt."

"But Ah'm reet." He points to a chaffinch, which has begun a monotonous plaint on two melancholy notes. "Heer t'bird. Weet, weet. Dreep, dreep."

"How long then, before the storm?"

Cluckitt smiles again.

"T'weather doon't pay no heed ter clocks, Gog. So Ah can't say fer exactly. But it'd be a wee bit o' a toby-trot if theer weern't no win' an' wet befor Candlemas. T'weather in general may be skeowy an' skittery, but thoo can be sure it's never long wet nor yet long dry. So Ah'm always reet in time. Always reet in t'end."

And Gog laughs and rises and puts his pack on his back and scoops up Cluckitt and hoicks him high and athwart his shoulders and strides off over the yielding grass down towards the silver windings of the Tyne. And the clouds are sucked into the blue and the sun shines all day.

The Tyne makes a brown boundary of shallows beside their morning's walk; even the sun can do little with such a sluggard muddy river, except where an occasional ripple glints as it rises and breaks by the rare pebble which is not yet rounded enough to let the water slur past. By noontide, the travellers reach the moulting sign of a game-bird, bearing the legend *The Blackcock*; so they turn across the bridge to Falstone, and drink beer and eat sandwiches in a pub lined with painted dark wood and low plaster ceilings. Four aged men sit at a table wearing old suits of Sunday blue. They are playing at dominoes; the sharp click of the pieces has all the violence of snapping teeth. One old man has eaten his lips, another has snuffled his nose away into a snub one, another is so hard of hearing that he has grown a tin trumpet ear, and the last has led with his chin so often that it meets his hook nose, enclosing his lips sunk onto his gums.

That afternoon, Gog and Cluckitt cut across the forests towards the Chirdon burn. The spruce trees are tall and seem to breed a particular torment of flies that surround the men's faces in a whizzing and settling hood of insects. Cluckitt is useful here, for he can shoo the flies away from his position on Gog's shoulders. But Gog gets too hot to support the little man's weight and sinks to the ground at a cross-roads, where two meeting tracks have been hacked out of the forest. They lie side by side on the sandy earth, slapping at the flies until their sweat dries and the flies vanish to irritate other victims. The spruce trees are closely planted in careful rows. Between their slim aisles, nothing grows, and their needles lay a hushful floor.

Far in the gloom of an aisle between the firs, Gog sees a movement of black and white. Yet as he sees it, it vanishes.

"Dost thoo see owt?" Cluckitt says, rising to his feet and looking about, as though expecting something or somebody.

"Something black and white in the firs. It must have been a magpie."

"Hoo many o' them?" Cluckitt says, beginning to open up the layers of his clothing to get at his shirt.

"Just one. It couldn't have been more."

"Wheer Ah coom from," Cluckitt says, "theer's a rhyme fer seein' magpies, an' it's never wrong.

"Wun's sorry,
Two's merry,
Three's a weddin',
Foor's death,
Five's heaven,
Six is hell,
An' Seven's t' devil's own sel'."

"I'll be sorry, then," Gog says.

"Aye, but Ah've got a magic hat Ah've made ter ward away

t' evil. An' it'll keep off t' sun too, it's not particular."

Cluckitt produces out of the pouch under his shirt an old brown felt hat. It has obviously been salvaged from a dustbin and would be as full of holes as a net, except that Cluckitt has made it into a downy helmet by covering it all over with brown grouse feathers, plucked from the game-bird and held down by a fine mesh of yellow brass wire. As a form of thwarted artistry, he has even made the hat resemble the shape of the flying grouse itself; two false wings curve down the sides of the hat to its rim, the top of the hat is sewn with black feathers and ends in a spray of tail, and the front of the hat cunningly supports a brass-ringed neck and a black head.

"That's very magical," Gog says. "I hope my head doesn't fly off." He puts on the hat and finds, to his surprise, that it fits his large skull perfectly. "Thank you," he says to Cluckitt. "How did you know my size? I'd love to wear it, as long as a gamekeeper doesn't mistake it for the real thing and blast off."

"Theer's no chance o' tha'," Cluckitt says, smiling. "Thoo looks like a man in a feathery bonnet from t' *side,* Ah can tell thee."

The two men start off down the track again between the spruce trees, enclosed in a hot trench of air, with the smell of pine needles a drowsy and acrid intoxication. Gog offers Cluckitt a lift on his shoulders two or three times; but Cluckitt refuses fiercely, saying that he has tired out the big man enough. So they plod along in silence. Gog looks down at his boots, monotonously following the line of the deep rut on the side of the track. He wipes the sweat away from his forehead, then glances up into the intolerable blue of the sky.

Above and ahead, a black M hangs in the heaven, sometimes sliding down the slipstream before checking to lie on another invisible shelf of air, sometimes catching the current by an inclination of its wings so that it is wafted upwards and sideways by the merest flick of feathers. The hawk hovers so lazily that it hardly appears to be hunting. Yet in its heavenly sauntering, it watches the whole area below from its high patrol.

"I wish I got along as easily as a hawk," Gog says, as he stares upwards in jealousy. Then he feels a pluck at his sleeve, and he looks down to see Cluckitt pointing ahead. "Theer, theer." And Gog looks along the track, but he can see nothing in the corridor between the trees. "Badger wi' yoong uns. Tha's wha' thoo sawst." Yet hard as Gog looks, he can see nothing but the lines of firs standing on each side of the track, as regular as the troops lined up with staves in their hands to flog to death a guilty comrade as he runs the gauntlet between them.

At that moment, a bolt from the blue stabs Gog's skull. His head is spiked and riven. As he sinks to his knees, he claps both hands to his crown. His fingers are cut by hacking wings. He grasps a bunch of quills. His wrist is savaged by a claw. He pulls a wingtip down towards his shoulder. The wound on his cheek from Cluckitt's branch is laid open as if by a razor. Briefly, he sees the curved beak of a hawk, its eye bright as a slick speck of coal. Then his hand slips and the hawk flails free, ripping from Gog's head the hat which is shaped like a grouse. Gog puts his palms on his scalp and feels the blood trickling through his hairs down his forehead.

When the scissors of fire stop snapping in front of his closed eyes, he blinks his lids open to see Cluckitt far away along the track, running towards a thin woman's figure in black trousers and a white shirt. It is the woman from the car. On her hands, she wears large gloves; on her right wrist, a leather guard. She halloos to the heavens, "Icarus, Icarus, my sweet Icarus." And the hawk comes slipping out of the sun all the way down a long slope of air to the wrist of its mistress, who wrenches the grouse cap free from its claws and laughs shrilly and ruffles the bird's head and slips a scarlet hood over its beak down to its neck.

Gog tries to rise and pursue after her and Cluckitt, who has joined her and is gesticulating. But his skull seems split in two and he falls again onto his knees, and he has to pause, his hands pressing against the pain in his head lest it should explode like a grenade and spatter his shrapnel brains all over the sand. After a while, the pieces of his head come together and he can ease the pressure of his hands and look up again. There is no woman along the track and no hawk and no Cluckitt in his red tam o'shanter. Perhaps the little man really was Redcap and has vanished away. Perhaps he only existed in Gog's mind, as the woman in the car, and even the hawk. Granted, blood trickles down from Gog's scalp and cheek. But there is a sharp stone at Gog's feet and it is dark with gore. Gog knows that he is a little out of his mind and that he imagines conspiracy everywhere. He has walked too far in the sun, he has got dizzy, he has fainted and opened up his head on a stone. The second explanation is far more reasonable than the first. Yet . . .

After a quarter of an hour, Gog collects enough of his wits together to stumble along the track out of the forest as far as the Chirdon burn, where he climbs over a split-rail fence and reaches the river bank and a pool beneath the hollow of an elder tree. There Gog strips off his clothes and stands in the water, which comes up to his waist. He scoops up the cold stream in his hands and pours it again and again over his scalp, until he can bear to lie down in the pool. But he is scared of somebody coming, and desperately as he would like to duck his whole head beneath the water, he will not risk being attacked when blinded and defenceless. So he rises from the pool and wipes himself dry with tufts of grass wrenched from the river bank and dresses and goes slowly on his way towards the south-east.

Gog walks by the burn back to the Tyne past the few stone blocks on the hill called Dally's Castle. Then he turns towards Bellingham, with the thunder clapping its hands towards the sea and a few drops of rain falling on him out of a bright sky. But the good weather lasts and the thunder huffs and puffs away over the coast, as Gog reaches the stone coolie's hat high on the Georgian house of Hesleyside. And luck stays with him. For as he feels the pains begin to shiver in his head again and his legs buckle with fatigue, he reaches the edge of Bellingham and sees a green bus panting up the hill towards him. He thankfully waves it down to a stop and climbs aboard, glad to sit on a jouncing seat and grudging springs, among women in mackintoshes carrying home a whole family's rations for a week in one small shopping bag, yet overweight from the eating of starchy foods over the war years.

When the bus has groaned a dozen miles to Simonburn, Gog gets off. For his map says that a short walk will take him to Hadrian's Wall, and he remembers the Bagman's verse about the Romans, that they set a great wall to the North, the Wall of Hadrian. So Gog decides to approach the wall as the Northmen did out of Scotland. He turns on the small road through the village past a field of stubble, where he sees an old hare lying. The hare is too decrepit to run away; it flattens itself against the ground, its giveaway ears laid upon its back, thinking itself invisible although there is no cover at all. Only the hare's head moves slowly round as it watches Gog passing. When Gog has gone by, he kindly looks away from the hare to allow it to hobble off on its last legs, proud at taking in stupid humanity once more.

As Gog reaches the angle of the road, where it turns sharply to the left, he sees the square back of the black car ahead of him. It has pulled onto the grass verge by a hedge; the two heads of the woman and Cluckitt are shown through the rear window. Gog moves onto the verge of the road and gets onto his hands and knees and slowly makes his way under the lee of the car. He crouches between the running-board and the hedge. He listens to the conversation inside the car, which comes to him clearly through the half-open window. Yet, although he hears every word in the present, a quirk of his mind makes him feel that he is hearing words said long ago, as though the steel and glass between him and the speakers carried all three back to a forgotten age of the thirties, where luxury was taken for granted; there were poor people then, but they weren't us, and there were wars, but they didn't affect us, and if the deluge were to come after us, at least it would be after us. Gog closes his eyes and sees himself where he is in place, sitting between the running-board of a black car and a hedge, eavesdropping on a conversation; but to his inward eye, his face is the face of a younger Gog, clean-shaven and wearing a tweed suit instead of torn cook's trousers and a khaki jacket; and, to his outward ear, the conversation about him is too apt to be more than the memory of words once overheard from a much longer dialogue.

"Took *you* for a peasant," the woman was saying. "Impossible."

"Absolutely, my dear," Cluckitt says in an accent that bypasses cut-glass and approaches crystal. "My make-up was rather professional. I wore the gardener's clothes and a ridiculous red tam o'shanter I use to yacht in, with a R.A. capbadge on it, meaning Royal Academic rather than Royal Artilleryman. But my accent, that was my pride and joy. The worst pseudo-Northumbrian you could find, all padded out with pithy saws and wise sayings from every folk-lore book I've wasted my long university life over. I can't tell you what a success I was, after I'd pretended to bump into Gog on his hike. He almost took out his notebook to record all my genuine folk memories. I tell you, I was more of the earth than the earth ever is. Sheer sub-soil. In fact, I was so much so, I wouldn't have taken in a *child*."

"But we're dealing with an infant," the woman says.

"Precisely. Dear Gog, you know I'm really rather fond of him and his delusions. He's got a touch of egomania and paranoia, but rather lovably so. Of course, he's always a bit too much, too big, too bold, too generous, too naïve, too plodding, too banausic, just too too. But I don't have to tell *you*!"

"No. The man isn't merely excessive, he's gargantuan. Of course, some of his appetites *do* rather please a woman ..."

Here Cluckitt laughs a light leering laugh that is knowing without being impolite.

"And he has the infinite advantage," the woman continues, "of always being at one's mercy. I could search the whole world over and never find a man so exquisitely torturable. He doesn't have that helpless passivity which is no fun to jab at. He has a sort of bewildered capacity for suffering, a flustered lunging back that never connects. He's the perfect victim."

"I must say, I agree," Cluckitt says in his cultured voice. "He's the Saint Sebastian of our time. All those lovely Italian primitives where seraphic Sebastian looks nobly surprised to find every cranny of his punctured with arrows ... But, Maire ..."

"Yes, Miniver."

So these are their real names. Maire the woman, Miniver the man. Of course, Cluckitt was a pseudonym, a made-up name for a made-up man, pretending to be the peasant that he never was nor could be. And Gog, O Gog, he's a real fool.

"Do explain to me a little about his delusion over Magog. Who *is* Magog? I've asked him, Maire, but he simply can't make any sense of it. He burbled something about a bit of Old Norse he'd discovered and translated. He gave it to me to read as an expert. He says it's a fragment of a lost prose Edda, called the Gogwulf Edda. Of course, it may just be that his translation is so poor . . . but I think he's trying to plant a forgery, rather like Ossian. He won't produce the original Norse. He can't, because it's only in his own mind, like all his obsessions are. Especially Magog."

"I'd like to read it some time," Maire says.

"In a moment," Miniver says. "I've got it in my pocket, rather the worse for wear. But he does take all this nonsense so seriously. He's even had Magog *tattooed* on his hand. I mean, I know it's all very patriotic in these hard times to support the Navy, I'm sure it'll save us all, but you needn't go as far as a sailor and get pricked blue like a baboon's bottom."

"I know," Maire says. "But he's always had to do everything the *people* did. I used to ask, *what* people? There's a limit. One man can't tread grapes and mend roads and hew coal and catch fish and hold down a university job all at the same time. It's either one thing or the other. Nothing's worse than *playing* at being part of the people – they loathe it, and quite right too. I sometimes think the proletariat even prefers being patronized to being enthused over. I mean, I know I resent being *joined* by those I dislike even more than I resent being loathed by them."

"But Magog!" Miniver says. "I know all that folklore stuff, about Gog fighting Magog, the old giants of England, and their images being set up in the City. But Gog still thinks he's fighting Magog. He thinks we're all agents of Magog, trying to kill him. I don't mind a good healthy delusion of persecution, as long as I'm not included in it. Soon he'll begin persecuting us because he thinks we're persecuting him."

"But we *are* persecuting him," Maire says. "And if he wants to call us all Magog, it's as good as calling us *They*. He doesn't mean anything specific by Magog. Something rather amorphous, like the spirit of ruling, of power, of persecution. Gog, naturally, stands for the people, the enduring ones, those who suffer, *him*. Trust him to want the *beau role*! Anyway, he thinks in rather black and white terms that the rulers and ruled, the torturers and victims, they and we, Magog and Gog, are all bound to fight forever and forever, world with end, and I hope that comes bloody soon to stop the boredom, amen."

"It's probably just a new fad of his," Miniver says. "Nothing serious. He gets galloping fads, and they may last a whole day. Do you remember the time he got all dreamy about chopping wood and he had to go and spend the whole day thwacking that oak with an axe? And when it fell down on his left foot, as of course it did, all he could say was, *Theoretically* it should have fallen the other way."

The woman laughs. "What's the next step, Miniver?"

"The mixture as before."

"So *Magog's* still keeping after him?"

"The more the merrier."

"What a born victim he is, Miniver. I really do adore him. I couldn't live without him to screw."

"I'm glad you don't adore *me*. Think how you'd make *me* suffer. I'd much rather adore you, my dear, and be kept at arm's length."

"Except when Gog's away," Maire says, laughing.

"When Gog's away, I must admit you do occasionally agree to rub skins with me. But you couldn't keep me further away, emotionally."

Gog outside the car feels a knot in his belly. His loins contract. His blood hammers. Jealousy? Why? He knows nothing of this woman now. But once?

"I couldn't make you suffer, Miniver," Maire says, "however hard I tried. Every ounce of feeling's been squeezed out of you years ago."

"Except my feeling for you, my dear. If Gog's really *certifiable* . . ."

"He's no more mad than you or I. And if I ever left him for you, Miniver, you'd know I'd accepted death."

"You'd better," Miniver says. "Because death's already accepted you."

"Don't talk like that," Maire says. "I don't like it. At least, *he* always likes life. Always makes things exciting. I mean, you can't have two people sneering together, or it just makes one nasty noise. Gog always shoots things up and I shoot them down. A happy arrangement, don't you think?"

"Like the friend of the family," Miniver murmurs. Gog hears the sound of him kissing Maire. "When the Gog's away, the mice do play. I think you two are made for each other – to stay away from."

Here, Gog decides to rise and jam his head and two elbows through the window.

"Exactly," he says.

He sees an unrecognizable Cluckitt-Miniver gaping at him. The skin on the man's face is still wrinkled, but pasty pale. He is shaven and smoothed off, his black hair is singed back flat on his skull in the style of the male leads of the thirties. He wears a dapper, striped suit and a carnation in his buttonhole; his wide trouser legs sport creases fit to slice butter. While Maire's face is blander and slightly fuller, it needs no cream to give it the oil of youth. Her hair is cropped to the nape of her neck, her dandy suit is of black and white checks, with black velvet lapels on her jacket and wide trousers like Miniver's. She looks out at Gog quizzically through the clear glass of the copper monocle set in her left eye, and says, "Surprise, surprise." Miniver jerks nervously on his seat, then tries to settle back casually, but he has to pull, pull away at the lobe of his left ear.

Gog hears himself say, as if from a distance, "What would you say if I wrung your neck, Miniver?"

"Quack," Maire says, and laughs.

"What for, my dear Gog?" Miniver says, uneasily.

"Deceit," Gog says.

"Miniver wouldn't deceive you, Gog," Maire says with great conviction. "Unless he were *pretending* to deceive you because he knew you were eavesdropping. Just for a giggle, Miniver, wasn't it? Pretending to be my *lover*." Maire goes into a particularly nasty laugh and pushes the edgy Miniver in the ribs with the point of the scalpel fingernail on her middle finger, which causes him to leap as if stabbed. Maire leans confidentially towards Gog in the window. "As if I could make love to that excuse for masculinity after *you*. It doesn't make sense, does it?"

Looking down at that face of immediate innocence and infinite lies, at that guileless and knowing expression, at the woman who is a stranger and yet who is the only woman who declares herself bound to him, Gog feels simultaneously the urge to strangle and the urge to embrace. His hands open in a curious groping clutch through the window into the interior of the car. Maire seizes his right hand and bites the thumb hard; then she sucks the thumb, kisses it, licks it, nibbles it, and turns yearning eyes up to Gog. And Gog feels his wrath melting; but he looks up to see Miniver smiling at Maire's expert turning away of anger. A bubble of bile bursts in his gut and he wrenches at the handle of the car door with his left hand and he opens it and he pulls his right hand from Maire's lips and he grabs at Miniver. Yet all he seizes is a few pieces of paper from Miniver's pocket. For Miniver wriggles and squirms away, slips the far door open, and is off down the road, running at a spritely clip for all his air of decay. And as Gog turns to pursue, he sees the thin-shouldered chauffeur behind him with a wrench raised in his slight and long-fingered hand. And Maire nods and the wrench is brought down and the iron stuns where the hawk has bitten and Gog falls into unconsciousness.

When Gog comes to his senses, it is nearly night. There is no car. He is alone. His head is a hive of pain, where bees feast on his honey brains. He looks for the tracks of the car on the grass verge; but there is only one deep rut made by a heavy ribbed wheel, probably a tractor's. Gog knows that he has fainted again, that is all he knows for sure. The hawk or the stone was certainly enough to give him a delayed concussion. And the conversation in the car was surely a returning memory of an incident long ago before the war. Yet there are a few sheets of paper lying near Gog, fallen from someone's pocket. So he picks them up, and, when his head stops buzzing enough to allow his eyes to focus, Gog reads slowly through the pieces of typed paper by the bright light of the moon. The paper is headed:

THE GOGWULF EDDA

Author Anonymous: Undated

Translated from the Norse by George Griffin

And we come to the battlefield of the giants and the dwarfs. Great bones are white on the side of the hill; the grass is sown with the bones of the giants, and the bones of the dwarfs, smaller than the bones of Northmen. In the ground, ribs; through the ribs, great swords. We grasp the swords and they are brown rust in our hands; we take up the shields and they vanish away. Six thousand six hundred and sixty and six skulls are there; above, the great skull of Ymir that holds up heaven. Two ravens sit on the thighbone of a great giant: Huginn and Muninn watch for their master Odinn; they shall bring him the news, that many shall join him in Valhalla. The sacred trees are burned on the hill by the fire-God Surt; King Aesir bids us hew and haul a mighty tree to the place; King Aesir, who has brought us over the dark sea in our winged ships along the dark river we call Tweed in answer to the command of the Wyrd. We set up the altar to Odinn; Magog, younger son of Aesir, son of the Gods, puts on his sacred cap of the raven for the sacrifice. The omens are good and the Wyrd abides; the dwarf natives call this place in their tongue, Camlann.

Beyond is the country of the giants; they have built a mighty ditch and a wall as a boundary. The ditch is as wide as six men and as deep as a giant; the wall is the height of three tall men and topped by square teeth of stone and every two thousand paces a tower. The blocks for the building are large and square; six men cannot carry a fallen one, nor can they shape one without magic axes. We dare not cross the wall into the country of giants; did not Hrungnir the stone-giant break the skull of Thor himself with his whetstone? But Magog, younger son of Aesir, sacrifices a horned ram from the hills; and I Gog, elder son of Aesir, tall as an ash and leader of the warband, am ordained to pass the wall of giants.

In fear and dread, I approach the mighty wall; shame on me, I wet myself, jelly is my marrow. My hands will not grasp the great stones, they are weak as a new-born babe; I am faint in my bowels and I cannot move. Behind me, I hear the jeering of the warband; Gog of the faint heart, shall you grind corn with the women? So I clamber over the wall that stretches from sunrise to sunset; the wall is deserted, the giants all perished or gone away. And I call to the warband, saying, "The giants are fled before me;" Magog waxes wroth, saying, "Gog, the ugly ogre, the giants are fled in fear to see your goggling ogle." But Aesir, the King my father, says, "Gog, the brave one, he is my chosen son and he shall follow me."

Behind the wall, the giants have trodden a way with their feet; we follow it eastward, back to the sea about the Northland. We journey along the road, the wall to the left side; we meet many halls, camps and empty cities. There is grain in the storerooms, iron weapons in stone chambers; towers and turrets with no one to people them. Mint grows in the halls of the giants, mort and vervain; by great copper cauldrons, docks and nettles. And we meet no one, save only dwarf natives, they live in square broken houses about a courtyard, fit only to be slaves; they speak a strange tongue and we must slay them. For my brother Magog has made us swear the great oath; to Odinn is given all men and all booty. Gold and silver to be drowned in the river; war-coats and horses deep drowned under. Men to be hanged, and women and children; naught to be left to us, all to Odinn. So the oath taken by the great oak tree of the Northland, the true root of the world-bearing Yggdrasill; naught to be kept, if Odinn aids us in battle, naught to be kept save the empty land of the giants, all to be broken there and burned and buried.

Then one morning, on the way eastward, by the bank of the river, we meet a way to the northward through a turreted city. Upon that way, ten armed horsemen; between them, a bier; round that bier burning one hundred torches. The leader wears a purple cloak of fine wool; his armour is silver and his helmet is gold; his horse bears a white cloth with red crosses on its side. And his nine horsemen wear red cloaks of thick wool; their armour is bronze and their helmets are silver; each horse bears a black cloth with white crosses on its side. And I say, "Let them pass, they go for a hero's burial." And Magog says, " Slay them for the oath to Odinn." So we come upon the horsemen, and the battle is bloody. They are not men, but sons of giants, fighting furiously. They kill Snorri Baldhead and Gurmi Gaptooth; half a hundred heroes they send to Valhalla. I hack at their horses, hamstrings hewing; blood bursts forth bright and bloodily boiling. Nine horsemen we pull down and ring with our axemen; weary and woeful, they slay us with their short swords; like wolves we set about them and drag them down to death.

Only the leader in the purple cloak of fine wool stands his back to the bier, slaying and slaughtering. Then Aesir my father says, " Odinn gives me this warrior." And he walks forwards, his long sword held high as a fir tree; he brings it downwards and cleaves the warrior's left arm from his shoulder. Yet the warrior lunges forward with right arm and short sword; between shield and war-coat the blade enters my father's neck, it slips in sweetly as into its own scabbard. And my father is stricken and bows forward on his long sword; the warrior falls against him terribly bleeding; they hold onto each other, groaning, the blood spouting as a river; they look at each other as if they were brothers; they fall together and the Valkyries call them, to fight daily and daily die with the Chosen Warriors, and be reborn nightly to feast in Valhalla, that waits to perish on the day of the Ragnarok.

And sorrow bursts forth in my belly; I fall down on my father's body, bitterly lamenting. And I rise, waxing wroth, and I seize the bier boldly; without the dead hero, there would be no dying. The lid of the coffin is wondrously wrought, worked in amber and bluestone and jewels beyond telling, set in golden crosses over a sheet of silver, worth the ransom of a king and nine kings beside him. And I wrench off the lid, gold bolts bending and bursting; I look down at the carrion that once was a hero. Tall is he and clad in iron armour, hewed and rusty; against his neck, a shirt of hair, his palms streaked with blood, marks of the scourge on his neck and bare feet, cheeks sunken inwards till they cleave to his skull, starved unto death as a dog forgotten on his chain. And I lift him from the coffin and I break off his armour, cracking it from his bones as the shell off a nut, until only his helmet sits upon his shrunken head, his helmet with two iron wings straight down his cheeks, his helmet with an iron beak down over his nosebone. And I bear him in my arms to the brown river, that flows under the stone bridge of giants by the temples, where stands a stone lion slaying a stone deer lying. And I cast him in the river and his weighted head sinks downwards, yet the summer river is shallow and his legs float upwards. So scraping on the pebbles, swollen as white weed, the dead hero is sucked out to sea, an offering to Odinn.

I go back to the warband, to cast away the horses and the armour, the gold and the silver, the purple cloaks and the red cloaks, to cast out all the spoils as an offering into the river, for Odinn has given us the victory and asks for his sacrifice. But Magog has stripped the corpses and has them piled on faggots; yet the arms and the armour, the gold and the silver, are put on one side in a pile of glittering. Magog sets fire to the wood beneath the nine dead horsemen; the savour of their flesh rises sweetly to Odinn. "Tomorrow," Magog says, "when we have raised up our new King, raised him up on our shields as the chosen of the warband, we shall carry the armour and the gold and the silver, worth the ransom of a king and nine kings beside him, we shall carry them with the body of Aesir down to the North sea, and build him a ship with the spoils set about him, and send him off burning to the gods in Valhalla." The warband is silent, mourning its dead king Aesir; then the warriors shout, swarming about me, tall as an ash and the leader of the warband; they raise me up, their new King, high on their long shields – all but Magog the priest, my younger brother, his eyes are as hot bronze under his helmet.

There is mead and corn in plenty in the stores of the dead horsemen; I ordain a feast for the weary after battle. I drink deep from the King's cup, the ox-horn wrought with silver. Straightway I fall into sleep, for Magog has put mandrake, cun-

ningly mixed in a powder, in the sweetness of the mead. And I awake bound by the hands and the ankles, bound to a great cross of two timbers of oak, its form taken from the bier of the hero. And the warband lifts me, bound on the oak trees, lifts me high among the winds and leaves me hanging. And Magog takes his spear and casts it upwards; it strikes me on the left side and the hot blood drips downwards.

So it passes that I myself am an offering to Odinn, as Odinn offered himself to himself in the Lay of the High One, praying:

> I vow that I hung
> On the windy tree
>   Swung there every night of nine;
> Gashed with a blade
> Blooded for Odinn
>   Myself a sacrifice to myself
> Knotted to that tree
> No man knows
>   Where the root of it goes.

And below me the warband, feasting and chanting; they wear the spoils of the horsemen, the oath of Odinn broken. Magog has won them, sharing out the gold and the silver, risking the wrath of the gods, turning to new ways. He wears the purple cloak and the white cloth with red crosses; yet on his head still, the priestly cap of the raven, its wings folded down and its beak on his nostrils. And the warband rejoices they have put aside the law of their fathers; for their share of the spoils, they have put Magog over them.

As I hang dying, the winds are my winding-sheet; and a bard comes up the South road, honoured among travellers, and speaking our tongue and the tongues of many warbands. His name is Taliesin, from the West and far country; he sings of a great battle, the battle of Camlann. It is not the place of the last battle of the giants and the dwarfs; but the place of the last battle of

King Arthur, lord of the natives called Britons; he went down to the nether world to steal a magic cauldron, kindled by the breath of nine maidens; a cauldron that would not boil the food of a coward. And King Arthur brought it back from the nether world, where the noon is as midnight, and he made himself the hero of the people against the Northmen and warbands. He won twelve great battles and, on the thirteenth at Camlann, he slew his son the usurper Mordred, begotten in incest, and he was taken wounded on a black ship to an island named Avalon. And his sinning Queen Guenevere, she perished long afterwards; also her lover, the voyaging Lancelot. I follow his body, sings the bard Taliesin, I follow his body with the nine knights and bishop attending, on the bier of Guenevere with one hundred candles burning, I follow it northwards to Joyous Gard, his castle glorious.

As I hang dying, the winds are my winding-sheet; and I see Taliesin fall silent in front of Magog, who brings forth the coffin of jewels and gold and silver. And Taliesin weeps and turns back to the West and far country; Magog would kill him, but dares not break the oath of greeting, not for fear of Odinn, but for fear of the warband.

As I hang dying, the winds are my winding-sheet; my eyes swim as fishes and I see the weighted body of Lancelot, scraping head downwards on the shallows along the river to the North Sea. And Magog will rule the Britons now by cross and by raven.

As I hang dying, the winds are my winding-sheet; and the ravens of Odinn sit on the oak tree above me . . .

When he reaches this point in the Edda, Gog feels a black cap being pulled down over his inner mind and falls into unconsciousness again. In his stupor, he hears the ravens croaking closer and closer. The noise provokes a waking dream, in which he turns his head to see that the sound comes from the idling engine of the black car. Maire gets out followed by Miniver. She is scolding him. "You fool. It's got his *name* on. You don't want him to know who he is, do you? All those years, breaking down his sense of identity. You might as well not have had a war, if you couldn't at least do *that*." And Gog sees Miniver scuttle forwards like a crab and pinch the Gogwulf Edda and sidle back into the car again with Maire, the car that makes off down the road, its engine croaking like a flock of ravens.

When Gog comes properly to his senses, again there is no trace of what he has read or done or dreamed. So he staggers on towards Hadrian's Wall. And the Wall is not there. A great shelf of earth is the only barricade that survives below Simonburn. On the top of the barricade, following the straight line of the Roman fortifications, a tarmac road has been set, down which the convoys of lorries pass all night, rolling towards the North Sea. A ditch on either side of the road shows that the Romans feared a stab in the back from England as well as the frontal attack of the Picts and Scots. The wall was not so much a wall as a strip of fortress a hundred miles long, dividing the South from the North, defending each from the other, preventing their coalition; but now it is gone and the people are uneasily one.

Gog crosses the road and climbs to the top of a small hill, where his map marks the site of an old Roman camp. Under the moon, he looks back over twenty miles of the hills that hump slowly down from the quiet Border into England. He unrolls his groundsheet from his pack and curls up in the roots of an old hawthorn tree, twisted into ridged curlicues by the blast. The set whorl of its roots has been hollowed out by sheep into a dry, bare resting-place, which provides a break of root and earth against the prevailing wind from the south-west, a wind that wails through the hawthorn all night, while Gog sleeps fitfully, waking occasionally to see boles and branches like great black jellyfish supporting trailing black weeds in the sea-howling sky.

X

When the rain sifts through the first grey crack of morning, Gog wraps his groundsheet tighter about him, trying to conserve the warmth that seeps away from his skin, which seems to be cut into patches of cold and warmth that have no connection with each other except for an invisible seam of epidermis. Gog feels the rain gather on his neck and form a puddle above his collar-bone; it beads his hair and fills the drum of his exposed ear. Eventually, he is forced to sit up and thank the dawn for being a wet flannel to his face. He rises and pulls his sodden pack onto his shoulders over the groundsheet, which hangs as a gluey cloak about him. So Gog stumbles off, Learlike into foul weather. "Fool," he says to himself, "fool." He does not know why he is where he is, only that there is nowhere else he can think of being.

Gog has not gone ten paces over the slopping hummocks and slimy tufts of grass towards the shelter of a distant stone wall, when the ground gives way beneath him. He finds himself sliding down a ventilating shaft and dropping into a vast underground hangar, roofed with corrugated iron and lit with electric lights. Racks stretch into the distance supporting every form of military equipment; it is as if the genie had let Aladdin into the quarter-master's store which supplied the whole world war. There are wirelesses and webbing, bayonets and barbed wire, bazookas and belts, light tanks and hobnails, mess tins and iron rations, socks and spats, camouflage netting and flares, picks and rifles, sten guns and spoons, spittoons and polish, and all the etceteras of survival and destruction needed by the compleat soldier in his combined role as navvie, skivvy, tramp, dummy, gunner and ripper.

At a table in the cleared middle of this cornucopia of war materials sits the Bagman, fiddling away at a massy pyramid of valves and tubes and wires and lights, and holding a black microphone in his hand. His white beard is a tuft of filaments, sparks seem to fly off his mustachios, as he berates the deaf world.

" Give me the airwaves, or I shall destroy a great city in the Far East. You shall see a cloud rise higher than the Rising Sun, the awful wrist of God raising Itself from the cursed city and opening into the spread hand of His wrath. And this warning shall be as nothing to you in the hardness of your hearts. And again the Lord shall open His hand and smite a great city utterly, yea, the dust that bloweth in the wind shall be of more substance than the foundations thereof. This second warning shall bring you peace on earth, but that peace shall be as the poppy in the fields of corn, a peace that passeth and is taken away. For how shall ye pacify the heavens when ye deny the Lord's servant in your midst? The time of the final solution . . ."

Now the Bagman deigns to look up at the bewildered Gog, who has collected his limbs together in their due order and has advanced towards the Bagman.

" It is the time of Gog and Magog," the Bagman intones, " the time of the last act of the world. To prove this, who should *drop in* at the studio but Gog himself, who was here at the beginning of Albion and shall be at her end. Well, Gog, tell the people, your people, what you shall do to Magog when you find him in London."

Gog looks at the microphone which the Bagman holds towards him and then he looks round the visible audience, the gape of haversacks, the eyes of binoculars, the snouts of rifles, the ears of buckles. The invisible audience at the end of the airwaves, the men and women yawning and stretching as they rise to go to work in the shiver of the dawn, he can imagine them. Out of sight, in mind.

" Magog?" Gog says. " In London? He is here. Everywhere. He wants to kill me. To kill us. Daily. In the farm. In the factory. He's there, Magog is. In the plough that crushes your foot. In the lathe that takes off your thumb. In the loom that threads your guts into the weave. In the potter's dust that poxes your lungs. In the dum-dum that makes a stew of your chest, the incendiary that lights your hair like a wick. Magog's there.

His machines can kill you as you tend them. What comes from his machines can kill you if your brothers use them on you. Magog! We are Magog's men set to murder our own, till we can turn on Magog and kill him."

The Bagman nods his hoary head, approving. "And when you get to London, the great wen?" he prompts. "When you find Magog sitting in his cesspool of pride and corruption, what then?"

"He is as the hydra," Gog says. "So many heads. Every hair a stinking chimney stack, every pore a sewer. Magog covers the earth and the millions live under his brick rags like lice. What shall I do when I meet Magog in London? Magog is London and he has swallowed up Albion. How shall we wring the neck of a whole city?"

"Call down the fire," the Bagman says, "unless they deliver unto me Broadcasting House."

"Even if they do," Gog says, "will you not destroy London? How can you build Jerusalem on the Thames in the smut of Mammon and the belching of Moloch and the maw of Magog who consumes all? When Jerusalem was first in London town, before she fled to the Holy Land, what was she like?"

"I am Wayland Merlin *Blake* Smith," the Bagman chants. "And in my third coming as William Blake after the second destruction of London by the Great Fire, I set down my memory of the first sacred Jerusalem in London, which I built in my original incarnation as Wayland, the smith of the old gods of England.

"The fields from Islington to Marybone,
To Primrose Hill and Saint John's Wood,
  Were builded over with pillars of gold,
And there Jerusalem's pillars stood.

"Her Little-ones ran on the fields,
The Lamb of God among them seen,
  And fair Jerusalem his bride,
Among the little meadows green.

"Pancrass and Kentish-town repose
Among her golden pillars high,
Among her golden arches which
Shine upon the starry sky . . ."

"Yes, London was Jerusalem," Gog says. "Before memory, before history . . . Jerusalem here . . . the golden age . . . What went wrong?"

The Bagman continues his chant, sad and low:

"What are those golden Builders doing
Near mournful ever-weeping Paddington,
Standing above that mighty Ruin
Where Satan the first victory won?"

"And what's my bloody watchman doin', muckin' about with me wireless sets," a voice says from down the hangar. Gog looks up to see a dumpy field marshal slithering towards him, with medals clinking against each other all the way from his gold epaulettes to the shine of his Sam Browne belt. Then the marshal takes off his cap of red and gold to reveal the sleek scalp of Maurice. He rips the microphone out of the Bagman's grasp and pulls its wire from its socket. "I'll 'ave your whiskers one by one with tweezers, if you give 'em a wireless bearin' on me whereabouts."

Maurice turns on Gog. "Lofty again, bugger me. Turn up, 'ere there and everywhere, don't you? Like a bad dream. Can't close me peepers without you poppin' up your ugly mug. What brought you down 'ere to me depot?"

"I fell through a hole in the ground."

"Got to 'ave ventilation. We ain't worms, you know," Maurice turns and waves expansively round the vast dump of war goods. "'Ow do you like my little 'ome from 'ome?"

"You could start a war yourself from here," Gog says.

"I will, I will," Maurice says, grinning. "You know what these big wars are for, Lofty? To give cash back to the people what gave it originally to the White'all bandits. Look at this lot. I pick it up dirt cheap, the government practically gives it away. Now the war's over against the jerries, it's surplus. You can't pull an 'aycart with a tank, can you now? Shoot a rook with a six-pounder? Now the army's bein' demobbed, they've got piles of this junk just layin' around disfigurin' our 'eritage, England's beautiful countryside. I'm a preservationist, I am – I preserve what I can flog. I cart away the eyesores. Just to 'elp tidy up the place for peace and all. I don't charge 'em 'ardly nothin' for carriage. I must admit, I do cart away the junk by night sometimes, without askin' a by-your-leave, when the sentry's 'avin a kip on the side. But it's just to get rid of the eyesores. Then I tuck the junk away 'ere, leavin' England's green and pleasant land green and pleasant, sort of."

"What's the use," Gog says, "of storing up all this war surplus, if it's surplus?"

"Use your loaf, Lofty," Maurice replies, his glib chops sliding about like two lumps of lard in a hot pan. "Of course, it's so 'igh up where your loaf is, the bats may 'ave nested there. What's surplus 'ere may be needed express over there. No sooner 'ave big blokes stopped a big war in one place than little blokes start a 'ole lot of little wars somewheres else. Then they need all this junk again. Stands to reason. War's based on surplus. You get too many blokes, so you've got to put 'em down. So you make too much stuff to put 'em down with. So you 'ave to get rid of the stuff. But then the blokes begin breedin' up again and the 'ole ball rolls on, keeps on rollin'.

"Me, I'm all for surplus. Buy cheap, sell dear, that's the gravy. Like I told you, I'm a sort of Robin 'Ood. White'all screws you to pay for this lot, then I screw White'all and get it for a whistle. Then I flog it to foreign bleeders, what don't know better than carvin' each other up like Christmas turkeys all the year round. So the wogs knock each other off with the 'elp of me surplus, and we don't 'ave the bother of knockin' the wogs off to keep the White Cliffs of Dover white and all. They can 'ave a good punch-up on their own, they don't need us, thank you kindly. What's usin' a gunboat compared to floggin' two gunboats to two blokes what 'ate each other? So the wogs take care of their own and we don't 'ave to spend nothin' on defence, which 'elps the economy and 'elps the British people like you and me. Buy British, I say. You Croak Better That Way."

"Render to Caesar that which is Caesar's," the Bagman warns sombrely, "and to Gog that which is Gog's."

"But I am," Maurice says. "I bleedin' well am doin' just that. The stuff I can't flog to the wogs to keep 'em 'appy murderin' one another, I change over to peaceful purposes for people like old Gog. Swords into ploughshares, that's old 'at. But bayonets into brassière 'ooks, cartridges into cosmetic cases, parachutes into knickers, you name a necessity and I've got it 'andy. There's nothin' I can't turn into somethin'. If I can't flog a gun, I'll use it as a fishin' rod. Every bullet's got its billet, and if you can't fire it and blow a bloke's breakfast apart, you can 'ave it flat in a fancy pattern and use it to keep your cuffs together. Don't matter 'ow the bullet ends, war or peace, do it? So long as you get paid proper."

"It's all the same," Gog agrees, "all the same. War or peace. The people get killed fast or they get killed slow. But they die all the same, without doing what they want to do. And someone's always making a packet out of it. Fast or slow, a profit."

"We all would if we could," Maurice says. "That's why I get along all right. 'Cos I'm doin' what comes naturally to all of us."

"Naturally?" Gog says in despair. "This?" His eyes rove round the stacks of mortars and the racks of bombs, round the myriads of burnished buttons, the flashes piled on badges piled on stars piled on piping piled on pips piled on ribbons piled on redcoats piled on flags piled on every fol-de-rol and geegaw of glory invented by the peacock military. "Are we naturally *this*?"

"Tooth and claw behind fine feather," the Bagman says. "Nature's fang behind the fur. By their bite shall ye know them. *Men.* The beasts are better."

"This?" Gog says. "Naturally?" He moves over to a hump of tin hats and gives it a kick that sends fifty metal crania rolling over the floor of the underground hangar.

"Hey, keep your feet to yourself, Lofty," Maurice says, dodging the hats. Gog ignores him and scoops up grenades with both hands and lobs them at Maurice, who leaps aside from the iron pineapples. "Their pins'll drop out, you crazy bugger."

But Gog has just begun. Volleys of munitions and material begin to fusillade Maurice, broadsides of revolvers, shoelaces, great-coats, valves, tyres, berets. The Bagman joins in the assault, firing off anything near at hand. Maurice backs screaming until he reaches the central prop of the hangar, where he falls to the ground and rolls himself in a ball to protect his vitals, his chest on his thighs, his hands under the soles of his shoes. The munitions cover him up, make a junk heap above him of canvas and steel and cloth and brass. The surface of the growing heap is always skidding or slipping, as Gog and the Bagman keep hurling stuff onto the pile and as the buried Maurice kicks and struggles in the interior. But after a quarter of an hour of bombardment, the heap reaches thirty feet high to the ceiling of the hangar round the main roof prop, a vast mound fit for the tumulus of an ancient hero instead of the detritus over a modern profiteer.

Gog and the Bagman stand watching the burial mound. There is no movement from its inner recesses. Maurice lies still under the garbage of destruction. As a *coup de grâce*, Gog swings round a six-pounder to point at the pile, opens the breech as if he had been an artilleryman all his life, slides in a shell, closes the breech, and fires. The effect of the explosion in the subterranean space is volcanic. The corrugated iron reverberates and eardrums thunder. The racks fall inwards and the mound flies outwards. The main roof collapses, bringing down the middle of the ceiling and layers of falling sod.

A great rift is opened up to the cleft of blue above, which makes a tear in the bright cloth of the morning haze. Gog and the Bagman clamber up over gun muzzles and canvas straps and cloth tunics, all now covered with the soft khaki uniform of the soil that insidiously infiltrates and eliminates everything with the slow guerrilla stealth of time. They climb out of the hole in the ground onto the meadow and walk down the hill that looks back twenty miles over the Border. The meadows lollop up and down lazily under their grasses. The trees saunter upright, their branches backed by such clarity of milk cloud that they seem pinned on opaque glass. A white-walled farm-house exhales a puff of white smoke, which teeters in the still air, unwilling to disperse. A rook croaks and a cow answers it, as if a moo could reply to a caw.

Dew beads Gog's boots, crushed grass jets its sharp smell onto the hairs of his nose, so that he sneezes. He smiles and opens his palms towards the Bagman, as if the view were his own creation. "Naturally," he says, "*this*."

XI

Down the road is Chester's Fort, and Gog and the Bagman hop over the wall to view the remains. A groundplan of stones divides the tufts of grass, the huge grid of a compass with the foundations of gateways to North and South and East and West, with barracks and bath-houses and quartermaster's stores and officers' mess and H.Q. Soldiers' camps come and go, but their ingredients remain the same. Most camps are transient; but the Romans tried to deny their impermanence and build for ever. Canvas and pegs were derisible to them; even bricks and lime were not enough. Only stone would do for the legionaries, even if the quarries were distant. Yet, after all, the Romans also left and the stones fell or were carted away to make the walls of nearby manor houses. Only the ruins of what the Romans built remain, although they were right in one of their convictions. The state of war is permanent and camps of soldiers, although they are always struck even when pitched in granite, are always pitched again.

Gog and the Bagman cross over Tyne and climb the ridge, which Hadrian's Wall follows. On the top of the hill above the river they find a timber cross twelve feet high. At its base, a plaque:

Heavenfield

Where King Oswald, being about to engage in battle, erected

the sign of the Holy Cross and on his knees prayed to God and obtained his victory as his faith deserved. A.D. 635
LAUS DEO

Under the shadow of the symbol of the God of self-sacrifice and of the sacrifice of others, Gog and the Bagman rest to eat their food. The Bagman has filled his haversack with army rations from Maurice's stores; he is clever at opening tin cans of spam with a bayonet. Gog still has the remnants of the food given to him and Cluckitt before they crossed the Border. The two men eat in silence, too drowsy and hungry to speak.

An army convoy grinds up the hill, nose to tail, gears gnashing and exhausts farting. Somewhere ahead there is a breakdown or a halt. The middle of the convoy has to brake on the hill, engaging every cog to avoid slipping backwards. Gog sees the Bagman, till then sagging weakly with his back against the cross, suddenly lean forward, his sharp nose above his beard twitching with attention. Then he is on his feet, his haversack in his hand, running towards the road before Gog can even open his mouth.

A solitary jeep sandwiched between lorries has stopped level with the cross. Its engine is idling, the lone soldier inside is yawning at the wheel. Without even a stumble, the Bagman clambers through the open space at the side of the jeep, clouts the driver with the haversack, and knocks him onto the roadway through the other side of the vehicle. Then the Bagman, spry as a youth, springs into the driver's seat, reverses the jeep with a crash into the lorry at its back, and locks the wheel to swing the jeep in a tight semi-circle, narrowly missing the assaulted soldier who is sprawling on the tarmac. Gog watches agape as the Bagman accelerates downhill back towards the Tyne. He cannot understand this sudden mania, until he sees in the rear of the jeep the cause of the attack – an immense army radio set covered with knobs and dials and sporting an aerial as tall as a shivering aspen.

Gog quickly gets to his feet and walks away from the cross. A knot of drivers in khaki has gathered round the fallen soldier. They pick him up and dust him off, carefully picking every piece of grit off his uniform, while he adjusts the hang of the creases of his trousers. One of the rescuers takes a cigarette from behind his ear, lights it, draws on it once, then passes it on to the victim of the Bagman's assault. He in turn sucks at the cigarette, before passing it round to the next soldier, and so on, until the cigarette has done the ritual round of the pipe of peace and poverty and has been returned to its owner, who pinches out the glow carefully between finger and thumb and replaces the butt behind his ear.

As Gog tries to creep away, the soldiers move forward to surround him.

"Oi," the sharp-faced driver of the jeep says, "what about your mate? What about 'im?"

"My mate?" Gog says. "I've never seen him before."

"He were with you," another driver says, his face as crumpled and cherry as his beret. "Muckin' about under that cross there."

"Five minutes before you came, he did," Gog says. "He cadged a bit of bread off me."

"'E's lyin'," the driver of the jeep says. "An' even if 'e ain't, someone ought to suffer."

The soldiers bring up their fists to batter Gog, but the convoy begins to move in front of them, so they have to drop their hands and run to the cabins of their lorries. The driver of the jeep, now finding himself alone before the hugeness of Gog, opens his fist in mid-air as it sails towards his foe, catches Gog's palm and pumps it up and down. "Ta, mate. An 'elpin' 'and is always grand." He runs for a passing lorry and hops in over the tailboard. Once safe inside and on his way, he yells back, "An you an' your muckin' mate are goin' to swing for it. Bloody 'ighwaymen."

The lorries grind and cough and racket by without intermission until Gog, walking on the far side of the road, finds that the metallic caterwaul trepans his skull and fills his lungs with the bad breath of exhaust. So he turns down the side-roads away from the military wreckage of Hadrian's Wall, still conveying the endless errands of war. Around him is the anarchy of the summer greenery, where the loudest engine is the buzz of the bee or the susurrus of the breeze in the leaves of the hedgerows. Gradually, the peace of the lanes which passeth all understanding flows into Gog's ears, then seeps down his mind and damps his hot nerves, so that a languor wells through him and his stride becomes a saunter, then a stroll, then a lagging. In this drowsy meandering of the day, the memory of the underground hangar and the stealing of the jeep are as mere nightmares, spooks and waking dreams provoked by the shadow of combat that lingers wherever the Romans once passed.

When Gog can hardly move any more for fatigue and the heat of the swelling sun, he chances on a large hay-tip to the right of the lane. Its reek of moist steamy rotting grass shrouds him with wet cloths of smell. He feels like the Duke of Clarence circling the vast butt of malmsey, trying not to reel under the influence of the rising fumes, trying and failing, then falling into the sweet wet stickiness of his final intoxication.

Groggy and swooning, Gog stumbles across the lane and falls into the hay. The tip stretches twenty yards square and its depth is almost as much. It rests on a sunken field; wooden rails confine the hay and pack it into a dense cube below the level of the lane. Into this solid bath of stalk and softness, of prickle and give, of snap and sag, Gog plunges. His pack falls from his back, he slips off his coat and his sweater and his long shirt. He tumbles backwards, kicking his legs in the air. He pulls his wide cook's trousers off over his boots, unlaces these, lets them sink off his feet, strips off his socks, and rolls sideways through the waves of summer stink that drown his senses, the spume of rotting sap, crushed blades, carrion greenery. Naked, Gog swims on the surface of the hay, his limbs threshing, throwing up the moist stalks about him until they wash over him. Then Gog dunks his head beneath the hay. The acrid reek of steaming and dying grass lines his nose and makes him cough and hold his breath. Each pore of his skin is pierced by a stalk, as stinging as salt spray. He wallows. The hay buoys him up, yet yields beneath him as the brine of the sea. Gog raises his face for air, gulps deeply, and plunges his face back beneath the surface. He is wrapped, swaddled, lulled, as the prickles of the stalks are crushed by his weight into soft waters. Vapours rise from the hay all about. The sun burns down on Gog's back through the lapping blades. Then Gog sleeps, floating on the heady rankness of summer, his body supported as inevitably as upon a Dead Sea.

Behind closed lids, Gog sees himself as a young man lying on the body of a woman, ammoniac from making love. He feels the hardness grow between his legs, the muscles of his thews and stomach tense and contract. On the blinds of his eyelids, nipples hard as bosses on shields of soft white flesh. A black-fringed red cleft splitting arched legs. A head thrown back in an agony of penetration, its helmet of black hair a jagged jet frame for ecstatic pain.

"Maire," Gog whispers, his lips mucous on the hay. "Maire, Maire, Maire, Maire, Maire, Maire." And his desire seems to flow into his repeated incantation of the name of the object of his desire, until the sounds are a charm to his sleep.

When Gog wakes, he feels his eyes gummed together and his body laid out immobile. He cannot stir for two or three minutes from his drugged doze, then he manages to turn his head aside and rest his right cheek on the grass. He blinks through an arch of hay-stalks to see an angel kneeling at the edge of the road, watching him. The angel is surrounded by a red-gold net of light. Gog puts up a hand to his eyes and rubs the film of sleep away on the inner side of his lids. Then he looks again towards the angel and discovers that he is a man, bare to the waist and covered with a fuzz of golden hair all over his red-brown skin. The hair grows on his flat belly and his spreading chest; it flares out over his nipples so that they look like two buds in a burning bush; it wraps his arms in an orange down; it thickens at his beard and moustache, becoming spiky and ochre; it softens again to yellow at his cheeks; but then it coils in thick curls over his scalp, so that he seems to be wearing a helmet of gleaming bronze springs.

From the waist down, the man is wearing stained brown leather trousers, tight as the hide of a beast, so that there is a large bulge at his crotch which suggests the capacity of a bull. He stands up, and Gog sees that he is lean and strong, broad at the shoulder and nipped in at the hip so that his loins are scarcely wider than his waist. He bends one leg at the knee and raises his foot to scratch the calf of the other leg with his toes. He wears no shoes. Golden hairs also cling to his ankles and cluster on the bridge of his foot. In all his body, only his sole is hairless, and it is as black and rough as a hoof.

The man stands watching in silence, as Gog bellies up to his clothes to hide his stiff cock in an envelope of trousers. Gog dresses, burning with sun and shame. He does not blush for his nakedness so much as for being found playing the fool. When he is ready, he lunges forwards over the hay, springing and sinking until he reaches the tarred surface of the lane. The hairy man continues to stare at Gog steadily, surrounded by his yellow fur of sun. As Gog approaches, he sees that the man's eyes are yellow, too, and strange. Gog cannot understand why they disturb him so much, until he notices that one of the pupils of his watcher's eyes has spilt over into the iris, making a blob of black that does not alter with the light.

"I was just having a sun-bathe," Gog apologizes. "You caught me at it."

The man nods. A slight sneer lifts the corner of his mouth. "I don't say for why," he says. "Never."

"Yes, better not to explain," Gog agrees. "Just do what you want and need to. Like a beast."

The man jerks his thumb towards the South. "Trampin' that way?" he says.

Gog nods. "I'd be glad of company."

The man nods, too. "They call me Crook."

"Gog," says Gog, happy at last to give a full explanation to the silent stranger in a single syllable.

The two men set off side by side towards the South.

XII

The two curses of walking are feet and flies. The flies raid in squadrons as soon as sweat indicates their target; only a barrage of wind will keep them away. Round Gog in the sun, the flies are as thick as a funeral veil. Every time that Gog waves his palm in the air in front of his face, he scores a hit on one or two flies. If he drops his hand for a moment, the flies dive in on his cheeks, neck, wrists. They do not even move when Gog stuns himself with slaps and murders his attackers as they suck the beads off his face. If Gog stops for a moment, the attack becomes a blitz. Gog can make a fly cemetery round his feet in a matter of a minute, but thousands more of the black insects will still whine about him and land on the runway of his skin. Only when his sweat dries will the flies take off for some Pandora's Box with its lid open, where they breed in their myriads waiting for the radar of perspiration to scramble them into flight.

Crook, however, does not slap at the flies. He seems hardly to sweat at all. So few flies approach him. Those that do are caught by a quick snatch with a cupped hand; they are squashed between finger-tip and palm and then are flicked away. Crook never misses a fly. His reflexes would outdo a cat. He moves stealthily, making no noise. His eyes dart from side to side, always on the alert. His thin mouth is usually a little open, showing the flickering point of a tongue between the hairs of his golden muzzle.

Gog and Crook pass the tall old grey houses of Corbridge. They buy apples and bread and cheese and beer in the town, leaving Gog with some fifty shillings still to spare. Then they climb up a hill on the way to Durham with the Tyne still beside them. On their left, a high stone wall borders the road. Behind it, a park in which a dark wood grows.

"Time for grub," Crook says. He runs at the wall, as if to dash his body against it. But his momentum is such that he walks up its surface, catches the top with his hands, and is up and over.

"It's meant to keep us out," Gog says. There is no answer from the other side of the wall. So Gog shouts, "Hey, I can't climb that."

Crook's head reappears on top of the wall like a bronze cat. "I'd leave yer," he says, "if yer didn't 'ave the beer. Keep up. Or yer on yer own."

Crook hangs down a thick wrist. Gog runs at the wall, leaps, catches the wrist with both hands, and is drawn up by a jerk that brings him chin-high to the top. Another hand grabs his waist and plucks him onto the wall. Crook's snatch and heave is perfectly timed, that of a champion weight-lifter.

"Yer can 'op *down*, I suppose," Crook sneers. Then he jumps onto the fringe of meadow that borders the dark wood beyond and lands lightly on all fours, immediately springing up onto his feet. Gog jumps after him, landing heavily and falling on his knees before the jeering Crook.

They eat and drink. Then Gog lies back on the grass in the sun, his paunch full, his eyes closed. A shadow comes between him and the red light on his closed lids. He looks up, expecting to see Crook's head. Indeed, it is Crook's head, but he has grown curving horns and his muzzle is black. The eyes are the same, yellow, and the beard; the same orange tufts of hair grow out of his ears. Then Gog hears Crook's laughter behind him and Crook leaps over his body and seizes the blackface ram by its horns and twists its head sideways, until the ram falls on its knees, then kicking on the grass. Gog rises and claps at this throwing of the male beast; but Crook does not stop. He kneels behind the ram's neck, lets go one horn and transfers his grip to its foreleg, then gives a sudden jerk and wrench. The ram's spine snaps like a stick.

"Christ, you've killed it," Gog says.

"Who dares ter meddle wi' me?" Crook says, rising and laughing. He takes a knife out of the pocket of his leather breeches, bends, slices three times, strips back a layer of fleece from the ram, severs sinew and thew and joint, then carves off three strips of bloody flesh which he stuffs into his mouth one after the other. As Gog pales, he carves off another strip of flesh and offers it to Gog on the point of his knife.

"Eat it," he says in a hard voice. "Fer *me*."

Gog takes the raw meat off the knife and looks at it. He is about to throw it away, when he sees Crook's eyes narrow and the point of the knife come forwards at his throat. So Gog smiles, throws back his head, and drops the strip of meat into his open mouth. He expects to vomit; but instead, he tastes a curious pleasure, flesh still warm with blood. He chews, then swallows quickly. His tongue licks the dark salt from his lips.

"More," Crook says, a statement rather than a question.

Gog nods, and eats another slice.

"Yer can git a taste fer it," Crook says, smiling.

Gog wipes his lips on the back of his hand, leaving a streak of blood on the blue veins between his finger bones. "Shouldn't we get back on the road?" he says.

Crook does not answer. He turns towards the cluster of ewes and lambs that huddle and tremble at his approach. He crouches on all fours and crawls up to the ewes, who bleat pitifully, yet seem mesmerized by the glare of his yellow eyes. When he is upon them, they each and all turn their rumps towards him, kneeling on their front legs, so that Gog has to laugh at the sight of the row of woolly backsides turned towards the human ram, their tails like downy G-strings waiting to flick out of the way.

"You've got a way with sheep," Gog says.

"I were brung up on the moors," Crook says. "'Swhy I'm called Crook. I were suckled on a sheep's tit. Baa means Ma ter me, don't it? An' girl, when there's nowt else." Crook laughs and smacks the puckering rumps of the ewes one by one, sending them jerkily fleeing and bleating, their lambs skipping after. "But I like cunt when I can git 'er. An' that's when I want 'er."

"Really?" Gog says. "Even now? Here, for instance." He waves his hand at the meadow, empty except for the sheep, and at the dark wood, where the trees wait.

"I call for 'er," Crook says, "an' 'er come." He begins to trill, piercingly and sweetly, then deepens his sound to a succession of throaty notes, somewhere between a gurgle and a chuckle. Then he opens his mouth wide and shouts high and clear, a noise of triumph and exultation, the call of the wild male beyond all challenge of rival. Crook pauses to draw breath, then calls again in rampage. And through the trees, a girl shows herself, wearing a maid's overall, perhaps a servant from the hall lost in the dark wood. She is curious and diffident, peeking out her plump red face from behind a bush, cocking her round chin with wonder, shaking her curled brown hair at such a carry-on. "*'Er,*" Crook says.

Then he is gone after his prey in a crouching run that skims the grass, barely leaving the servant girl time to turn and flee, screaming, through the pitchy alleys of the wood. Gog stands, watching Crook's golden body and brown leather legs twist, dark-dappled, among the trees, until Crook vanishes into a black cleft, where a dead branch has fallen against the trunk of an oak to make an entrance. There is a silence, as Gog watches the wood. Then he hears a girl scream twice. Cloth tears, muffled and far. The girl calls, " No." Then she stops crying on a choke. Gog lumbers forwards into the wood.

Between the first trees, fern grows, green and hairy. But Gog has not gone ten strides, when brier begins to prick and bloody his ankles, and brown bracken to scrape his calves. Gog cannot see, for the darkness of the wood puts two wet black leaves on his eyes after the sun. He blunders on, scratching his forehead on a low branch, so that he has to put up an arm to shield his face. His sight adjusts to the twilight of the trees, and he can hear ahead of him a rustling, a grunting, the rooting of a pig. He passes between the cleft through which Crook has disappeared, and he comes into a tunnel between two rows of oaks. Under the shade of their branches, which intertwine like veins, the ground is mushy with decaying leaf mould.

Gog walks down the tunnel between the oaks towards the humps of red at its end, where it narrows into a cranny of dark boughs above dead stumps of elm trees, the colour of gore. Over one of these stumps, the girl is bent, naked and still. Her arms and head flop over the far edge of the timber. Her chest and belly is laid on top of the rotting stump. Her right breast is squeezed into a split in the wood, its nipple askew and pointing towards Gog. Her ribs crush small toadstools that sprout from the decay. Her near buttock swells upwards like a vast white fungus from the back of the stump. Below it, her thigh and leg trail down the bark near Gog, so that her toes just touch the dank earth.

Behind her, Crook stands, his two hands on her hip bones, working and pulling his screwing belly deeper between the tops of her thighs. As Gog watches, he shudders, clawing at the haunches of the girl, scoring blood from her flanks. Then he bends, his chest against her back, and bites her in the nape of the neck. Her head twists, then lolls again. And Crook draws back, his cock still erect and dripping, and he turns towards Gog.

Gog strikes at Crook's face with his fists, but Crook ducks and lunges at Gog's gut, hitting him in the lower belly, so that Gog grunts and jerks downwards. By chance, his plunging elbow chops with force on the back of Crook's neck, sending him sprawling. Gog drops his great weight on Crook's body. He hears his foe grunt beneath him, then draw in a rattle of breath through his downturned mouth. As Gog puts his hand round Crook's neck, Crook goes limp. Gog tightens his grip on Crook's windpipe, but his foe stays motionless. Still straddling Crook's shoulderblades, Gog continues to throttle, suspecting a ruse. Still, no movement. So Gog rises, one leg on each side of Crook's back and looks down at his fallen enemy.

Behind him, he hears a moaning. As he raises his left foot to turn towards the girl bent over the stump, Crook twists over onto his back, rears upwards, and butts Gog in the balls with his skull. Gog yells and falls, rolling over, his hands between his legs. He hears the snap of wood as his temple explodes from a heavy blow. Then darkness.

Cold.

Gog wakes to the cold. Cold belly, cold face, cold left arm. Only his right side is warm. He feels a ticklish pain at his crotch. He puts down his left hand to find his cock erect and swollen and hurting. A piece of bracken is flicking at it, stroking it. Gog hears Crook laugh and opens his eyes to see his enemy hunched between his legs. At his right side, the naked girl lies on her back, her eyes turned towards him, looking at him with terror. And yet, she lies there, as if staked down by invisible thongs. Gog sees that her plump breasts are gridded with welts and scratches; bruises make patches of indigo on her white flesh.

"'Er's yers," Crook says. "I've 'ad 'er every way there is. An' some there isn't. So 'ave 'er 'ow yer fancy." He looks down at the girl and flicks the bracken between her thighs, so that she trembles. Then he fixes her with his hard yellow stare, still bright in the twilight under the trees. "Yer's willin', if I say?"

The girl nods dumbly. She shivers, but draws her knees up, opening her thighs.

"Git up on 'er," Crook says to Gog. "Try it out. Or did I geld yer fer good?"

Gog sits upright, meaning to defy Crook. But as he sits, he sees the white belly of the girl, the hairy triangle arrowing the red sore between her legs, the spread and fallen pillars of her thighs. The sick agony of his cock swells and thrusts outwards. Gog looks at the girl's puffed red face, as if beseeching forgiveness. But she has closed her eyes, her top teeth tight on her fat lower lip.

"Go on," Crook says. "Or I'll crush yer balls proper. What's them fer?" And he grabs Gog by the waist, lifts him half-way onto his feet, turns him in mid-air and drops him between the girl's knees onto her body. "I hope yer know what ter do *now*," he says. "I don't 'ave ter teach yer *that*."

Gog closes his eyes, all thought, all feeling, all himself concentrated on the erect pain between his legs. He fumbles with his hands to guide his prod of lust into its sheath. The soft point of his being scratches on hair rough as bracken, then suddenly plunges deep into a warm stickiness, slippery, gripping. And Gog can feel the body under him shudder and the girl gasps under his chest and Gog shifts his weight forward to dig deeper into her. But he is so tall that he crushes her face beneath him, so that he must squirm sideways a little, allowing her mouth and nose to get air under his armpit, while he lies with his face downwards on the dampness of the earth, one eye buried, the other looking at the red and rotting stumps of elm.

Gog hears the girl sob again and squints back to see Crook standing, one of her ankles in each hand, forcing her legs apart, for her pain or Gog's pleasure. As Gog watches, he sees Crook bend the girl's legs back again at the knee, so that each of her soles rests on Gog's pumping buttocks, making a white M of thighs and shins above Gog's rump. Then Gog buries his face in the soil, projecting images of naked breast and belly and buttock on the screen of his closed lids to hurry on his desire. To perform rape, he has to act out rape in his mind; not the real rape of a red cold bruised plump girl, but the mock rape of the remote tall sneering Maire, stripped of her black coat, her body of cream spilt before him, screaming halt. So Gog has a quick coming, so that he may have a quick going away from his fall and degradation.

When the spurt of Gog's release is over, he rises and buttons himself up and turns to the watching Crook, without daring to look down at the lying girl.

"We'd better get away," he says. "Fast."

Crook shrugs. "Slow, if we want ter. 'Er won't tell." He bends over the girl, his knife in his hand. "Will yer say owt?"

The girl shakes her head against the ground, her eyes trembling wide.

"I were good ter yer," Crook goes on saying. "I didn't carve yer. So yer can 'ave more. I should 'ave left yer so other men would be sick ter see yer. So forgit us, see. If yer don't, an' a copper come after me, I'll be back ter carve yer."

He stoops, plucks at one of the girl's nipples, and swings down the knife he holds in his other hand to slash off the nipple. But he swings the arc of the blade short, so that the point of the knife merely scratches the skin of the girl's breast.

"Next time, I won't miss," Crook says.

He stands up and turns towards the recesses of the wood. As Gog looks back at the girl and opens his mouth to ask if they can help her, somehow help, Crook catches Gog by the elbows and pushes him beyond the stumps of elm into the thickets ahead. Twigs and branches jab at Gog's eyes, so that he has to push his hands in front of him to make his way. Lunging forwards, he bursts through the thickets and he turns to find Crook on his heels and the girl cut off from sight.

"On," Crook says, and pushes him stumbling forward between the trees.

The forest begins to change its nature. A blight has struck the trees. Their boughs are covered with a white webbing, a cocoon over whole branches that swathes them in moist gauze. Bulbous growths, the colour of curds, split the bark of trees. Mistletoe festoons the oaks, its sticky pearls of berries sweating on its green and mucous leaves. A curious albino lichen spatters the surface of the detritus of wood, which makes a verminous barricade feet high between many of the trunks. A kick clears a way through; but the kick also raises up a stink of maggoty wood, an odour of wet rot, a scurrying of lice and spiders and earwigs that briefly scatters the forest floor with a confetti of orange and yellow and grey movement.

"Let's turn back," Gog says. "This is foul. I'm not going on."

But Crook clouts Gog against the earhole, forcing him onto one knee. He picks up a splintered branch and prods Gog in the thigh, compelling him onwards through the litter of decay.

The trees begin to thin at a clearing. The twilight brightens to a grey clouded day. Through the trees, Gog can see a white summerhouse, curiously carved. As he reaches the edge of the clearing, he discovers that a Gothic fretwork encloses the summerhouse in whorls and curlicues and gargoyles of fantasy. The snake-haired heads and vast breasts of four Medusas support the roof at each corner of the building; the wings that sprout from their shoulders hold up the gutters; their waists are as scaly as mermaids; but a horn projects from where their legs divide into haunches of wooden fur, ending in wooden hooves. The walls of the house are a saturnalia of still coils and immobile writhing. Satyrs enwrap whales, goats leap upon the backs of serpents, eagles alight on sleeping nymphs, bees pollinate sea-anemones, sailors impregnate giant worms. There is no permutation of copulation between fish, fur, flesh and fowl, between insect and plant and mammal, that is not carved grotesquely upon the walls of the summerhouse in a carnival of coupling, peeling all over with scabs of flaking paint.

Between the orgies of the fretwork are windows, opaque with grime. Crook shoves past Gog and sidles up to a pane and draws back his fist to smash it. At that moment, there is a murmur of voices from within the summerhouse. Crook pauses, then moves on cat's feet past the twisting length of a naiad embracing a buffalo, to where a broken pane rises above the nipple of a griffon rearing upon the rump of an elephant. Crook begins to smile at what he sees, and he motions Gog to join him at his peephole.

The broken pane makes a sooty frame for Gog the *voyeur*.

Through the hole in the glass, he can see a brass four-poster bed set in the middle of the boards of a bare enormous room. On the black coverlet of the four-poster, her right arm holding the yellow metal bars of the bed head, Maire is lying naked, facing them. One leg rests on the bed, the other is bent at the knee so that its sole is upon the floor. The chauffeur with the narrow shoulders kneels at Maire's feet, wearing his green uniform but without his cap, so that Gog can see the back of his bobbed, slicked, black hair. As the chauffeur licks the lying Maire, he runs his fingers up her thighs and over her belly to scratch at her nipples, then down again. From the glint on his fingernails, Gog can see that they are varnished.

Maire arches her back against the coverlet, her breasts swelling and her nipples opening like spread lips. She moans four times, luxuriously, pulling at the short hair of the chauffeur until a tuft comes away in her fingers. He remains, kneeling on the boards in the dust, until she relaxes again. Then she commands sharply, " Get up, Jules. And take off your clothes." He obediently rises and begins to undress, facing her with his back towards Gog the *voyeur*.

Gog is sick with a compound of jealousy and curiosity. He wants to crash through the window, yet he has not seen enough. And Crook, for once, shows no sign of violence nor aggression. His pointed tongue runs rapidly along his lips, sucked in round his teeth.

The chauffeur takes off his shirt and drops his trousers to show himself bare-backed, but wearing a black garter belt above his rounded white buttocks and black stockings held up by the shiny metal grips of the belt. He walks forward towards Maire, and she pulls down the garter belt and unrolls the stockings off his hairless legs delicately and slowly. Then she kisses him on the belly and pulls him onto the four-poster beside her. And Gog sees that the chauffeur is another woman. " Julia," Maire says, " my only one." The two women entwine their bodies until they join in a mesh of limb.

Rage wells up in Gog's windpipe, so that he chokes. He raises his fist and crashes it through the pane. " You Sapphic bitch," he shouts, while Maire and Jules start up.

" Gog," Maire cries, " you dare?"

Jules leaps off the four-poster, her small breasts swaying, and rummages in her clothes. She comes up with a small automatic pistol in her hand. She squats, crouching, resting her elbow on her thigh to steady her aim, and fires at Gog. The pane near him smashes.

" Scarper," Crook says.

He and Gog run as another two bullets are gnats by their ears. They are as fearful as beasts at the noise of any gun. They do not pause until they are safely within the coverts of the wood on the far side of the clearing.

Again the wood changes its nature. It becomes spare and barren, with pine trees standing upright in kempt rows like soldiers in the ranks. There are also firs, stretching out their straight branches with horizontal precision. The ground is dry and crisp underfoot with brown pins, while the olive needles on the trees sting and prick and stimulate Gog's skin as he passes by. The air is sharp now, so that he breathes deeply to fill his lungs with piercing oxygen, and he straightens his back to approximate to the stiff spines of the trees.

The sun comes out from between the clouds and catches Gog in a grid of blaze and shade. The horizontal bars of the straight branches, the vertical trunks of the trees, make a cage of shadow about Gog. He stops and turns back to see Crook stop behind him, covered with black lines as if he were scored with pokerwork. In this definition of dark and light, Crook takes on even more the look of the beast, on whose head and ribs and haunches nature has laid the stripes of camouflage.

And Crook comes forward, his yellow eyes staring at Gog, his broken iris compelling fascinated stillness, and he puts his forearm behind Gog's neck, and he kisses Gog full on the mouth.

Gog does not recoil at the hair rasping on his three days' beard, nor at the tongue that thrusts between his slack lips and open teeth. He stands as if playing statues, while Crook rubs up against him, belly to belly, a little shorter than Gog, but equal in height on tiptoe. Only when Gog feels Crook's free hand fondling his buttock does he step back, breaking from the forearm round his neck.

"What?" Crook says. "Don't yer fancy me? Ingratitude."

Gog shakes his head, dropping his eyes to avoid the hypnosis of the black blob of broken iris. "I'm not that way," he mumbles.

"What d'yer mean?" Crook jeers. "We're all all ways. Bent sometime, straight sometime. As long as we git it."

He sidles forward through the grid of light and dark, the many stripes of shadow making him tyger, tyger, burning bright in the forests of the night. But no mortal hand nor eye could frame his fearful symmetry. That comes from the force of the inner cock-screws of desire, of the nervescrews of instinct, of the gutscrews of perversity that knows it must succeed. Crook's left hand plunges for Gog's crotch, grasps, loosens and strokes, while his right hand is raised, ready to chop or claw or strike.

Gog stands, looking willy-nilly into the yolk-bright eyes in the striped hairy face. A great weariness comes over him, a resignation in the face of power. He feels his muscles drain into syrup and lust begin to rise in his belly. But when he sees Crook begin his thin grin, he suddenly jerks forward with his shoulder, catching Crook on the side of the head.

This time Crook is not caught unawares. He chops terribly with the side of his hand into Gog's neck, and as Gog sags, he brings up his knee onto Gog's chin, knocking him unconscious. Again Gog slides into the black recesses of his hidden mind, the winding crannies among the roots of his brain cells. There he sees myriads of red maggots twisting desperately to get into a mesh of tiny slits and holes, their red tails squirming and thrusting as their heads burrow and search and enter. His inward eye cuts to an image of himself standing by the rollers at the back of a police launch on Thames river. The naked drowned corpse of a girl suicide is bent over the rollers, her head and arms flopping forwards, her belly flat on the wooden spokes, one breast squeezed through them, her buttocks high, her legs trailing down until her toes just touch the water. In every orifice, the tails of eels jerk and heave, blue-black as the vomiting policeman by the rollers. And then, Gog is the corpse, and the eels writhe within him, and he screams dumbly in his dream.

Gog wakes in a wash of relief, to find himself safe in his own skin, alive, dry pine needles under his face, belly down flat on the earth, relaxed and still, his bare legs apart. He feels a pain between his buttocks, but his body responds when he moves its parts slowly, fingers first, followed by arms and legs. He turns himself over to lie chest up in a shaft of sun. His aching head gradually feels only an occasional throb rather than a continual hammering and the sun puts its warm balm on the knots in his muscles. After a while, Gog sits up, wipes himself below the waist with abrasive handfuls of pine needles to cauterize his flesh, finds his trousers and puts them on. Then he begins limping on slowly through the wood, hoping that the animal Crook will finally leave him alone.

Again the light and the forest change. Black clouds sweep angrily over the grey. The trees are low and gnarled; the soggy soil cannot support the weight of height. Gog's boots begin to sink into the swamp at his feet. Onyx pools exuding vapours make hollows of polished jet among the roots, which creep into them as entrails into the stomach. Twining buckbean bares the pink lumps of its fruit from the white beard of its corolla. The hairy stems of hemp agrimony matt the reddish flowers into lung linings. The fleshy leaves of brooklime curl from stems crawling intestinal. There is a brackish sweet smell as if syrup were mixed with slime. Gog squelches on, sometimes sinking in mud or stagnant water up to his knee.

Plump drops of rain begin to fall one by one. Gog hears thunder clap its hands many miles away. He hurries forwards to where the dark curve of a hillside shows above the swamp. As the rain turns from a spatter into a torrent, he reaches a driveway of sodden timber sleepers, raised above the surface of the marsh. A ruined oaken gateway is set on each side of the drive. Its uprights are two rounded poles fifteen feet tall; at each of their tips, the wood has been carved into the shape of a swollen cloche hat. The crossbar between the uprights is cracked in the middle so that it is half-fallen in the centre. Gog can just walk straight under the splinters in the middle of the collapsing bar.

In the side of the hill ahead, the façade of a pagan temple has been built, a northern Baalbek, some aristocrat's folly. Massive fluted square pillars supporting a broken pediment stand in front of the hill like the bars in front of a cage in a natural zoo. As Gog approaches, he sees that black doors three times his height make an entrance into the granite hillside within the pillars. One door is a little open. Gog walks through it out of the thunderstorm, past the black bolts that stud its surface. As he enters the hill, the door closes behind him.

He is inside a cavern lit by ten thousand candles, sending out black smoke and yellow light equally. In crevices along the rocky walls, naked boys and girls are chained and stretched into every contortion that the body can bear and ingenuity devise. On the cavern floor, the harlots of the temple, painted in vermilion shellac from head to toe, embrace beggars, dogs, monks, apes, bluejackets, stallions. Dancing transvestites strip off their breasts with their seventh veil, then couple with hyenas. The dugs of fat brothel madams shake in their frenzy, as they whip and rack girl children for the golden coins that drop one by one from the lacquered nails of old men, feeling themselves below their paunches. Androgynes play with hermaphrodites under the benevolent kisses of eunuchs.

Dozens of impish bare children, not more than six or seven years old, clamber over Gog, tearing off his drenched clothes, sitting on his shoulders or clinging onto his thighs, scratching and caressing. Youths with mouths of honey suck at each finger and thumb, girls with small breasts of silk brush his belly, the orange hair of whores switches at his shoulders. But Gog bursts through the teasings of the flesh, while his ears are full of the moaning of sexuality and his nostrils are stuffed with the cloying acridity of sexuality and his fingers touch the velvet nap of sexuality and his tongue tastes the moist gelatine of sexuality and his eyes see the sag and tautness of the sexual flesh.

The floor of the cavern rises sharply towards three thrones, set above the orgy. On one of the lower thrones sits a fat elderly man; on the other throne, a slight and younger man; both are breeched and powdered; the first flogs a naked woman with a whip and fingers at the same time between her thighs, the second fingers himself while a dwarf girl wearing only red boots dances with her heels on his thighs and thrashes his cheeks with the knotted pigtail of her long hair.

Above Sade and Sacher-Masoch sits Magog, whom Gog sees for the first time. And Magog is as the toadstool rearing on his long stalk through the knot in the wood, as the worm moving slyly into his burrow, as the sulphurous mud boiling in the hole, as the wedge splitting the log, as the lightning cleaving the forked oak, as the frog plopping into the rain barrel, as the heron picking in the pool, as the grab of the crane dropping into the hold, as the piston thrusting into the cylinder, as the smoke-stack penetrating the swell of the cloud, as the barge parting the bow-wave, as the spire between folds of air, as the bit in the horse's mouth, the syringe in the bottle, the pipe in the rack, the brush in the pan. As all these things, the changing shape of Magog is, so that he bewilders Gog with his continual presence and metamorphosis. He is everywhere in everything, an obsession to the sight, a ceaseless skirmish to the imagination, a sniping at the senses.

Gog feels his rage hone him, pare him to a cold skeleton of bone, inviolate from these pluckings of the senses. He kicks to right and left, sending Sade and Sacher-Masoch and their thrones sprawling. And as they rise, he seizes each round the neck with a great hand and cracks their skulls together as if these were gongs. Sade reels screaming back, his wig awry, his hands clasped to his shaven scalp, while Masoch rolls on the ground, his mouth fixed half-way between a leer and a grimace. Sade kicks with his stacked heel into Gog's ribs; but while Sade laughs, Gog clouts him breech over buckle, so that he stumbles over the body of Masoch and treads on the fallen man's guts. Masoch now whinnies with trampled pleasure, while Sade boots him contemptuously in the rump, merely to hear the whinny change to a cackle of ecstasy. Then Sade leaps upwards, twining his fingers in Gog's hair and bringing up his knee into Gog's kidney. As Gog bows forward under this punishing weight on his back, Sade slowly twists at his hair, not wishing to conquer Gog so much as to make him feel his locks extracted slowly, root by root by root. The sloth of Sade gives Gog his chance. He reaches back, grabs Sade by his powdered neck, and dashes his foe over his shoulders onto the body of Masoch, whose last act before falling unconscious with the stunned Sade on top of him is to give a great grin as his ribs cave in like a broken basket.

Then Gog moves forward to grapple with the stupefying, enfolding, mutable Magog.

And Magog is a coat of wild honey, but Gog sheds him onto the cavern floor and covers him with stones.

And Magog is a bath of warm slime, but Gog dams him up with the fallen thrones of wood and lights them to burn him away.

And Magog is tongues of fire, but Gog pinches them with horny hands and stamps them out.

And Magog is black fog, but Gog cups his hands to catch and pocket him.

And Magog is a green serpent, but Gog knots him and squeezes the venom from the sac behind his forked tongue.

And Magog is a springing web of vines, but Gog crushes the grapes and tears up the vines by the roots.

And Magog is a swarm of dragon-flies, but Gog swipes at their bright bodies and snaps them between finger and thumb.

And Magog is a tawny eagle, but Gog breaks his beak and crushes the bones of his wings.

And Magog is a ladle of boiling pitch, but Gog pours him through a fissure into the burning core of the earth.

And after his nine forms, Magog appears as himself, a vast rearing sceptre of ridged silver, from which golden spears protrude as hairs. At its tip, a ruby orb that swells out over the circumference of the sceptre and rises to a split point, from which black oil spurts. A crown of white gold rings the ruby orb and holds a circular spilling pool of the black oil; from the crown, manes of coarse hair curl forth, matted and sticky.

At the sight of the rearing sceptre crowned with the ring of white gold and hair, a frenzy overtakes the multitude in the temple sanctuary. They tear, bite, wrench, twist each other's bodies. The cavern floor heaves as a leggy sea with interlacing strands of limb and hair. There is a din, a slavering, a baiting of lust.

The knees of Gog tremble, his bowels loosen, he begins to bow and fall beneath the mighty emblem of Magog into the fleshy swell rolling at his feet. But as he bows and falls, his hand meets the splintered timber of the leg of Magog's throne. Oaken thorns drive into his palm, so that he screams in agony. And he seizes the stump of the throne with his free hand, and he plucks its wounding end from his pierced palm, and he smites the rearing sceptre once, twice, thrice, yea, even nine times. And the sceptre cracks in its silver sheath and its golden spears rattle upon the earth and its ruby orb splits in twain and its hairy crown of white gold topples. And Magog tumbles and lies at Gog's feet. And Gog puts the splintered stump of oak upon the sceptre's corpse and leans upon it.

And the people of the temple break apart and look at one another and are ashamed. They cover themselves with their hands and huddle each in his own private modesty. And the black doors are blown open by the storm and the chill rain enters.

Through the doors, the hairy fallen angel walks into the sanctuary, his yellow mat of hair sodden against his skin, so that he seems to be of flesh rather than fur. He passes by the bowed bodies of the multitude, and he lays himself on the earth at Gog's feet, saying, "I'm Crook no more."

And Magog speaks with his voice of brass from the fallen rod of silver and gold, saying, "Gog, spare my life, and I will be a servant to you. For when the mind shall flag, I shall be the spur. And when the prayer shall fall short, I will give it wings. And when the arm shall drop, I will nerve the sinew. And when the voice shall be dumb, I will be a trumpet in the throat. And when the foot shall be weary on the road, I will be as the spring of turf. And when the land shall be empty, I will fill it with children. And when the house shall be dark, I will light it with the content of wives. Harness me, yoke me, chain me, bind me, keep me within the cage of your lawful desire. But spare me, for you cannot live without me."

And so Gog bends to make of the silver of Magog plates for his table and of the gold of Magog bracelets for Maire and of the split ruby of Magog twin hollowed cradles. But Crook rises from the earth and speaks, his knife in his hand:

"Kill 'im. Yer saw me. A beast, I was. A cock, an' cock all else. 'E did it, Magog. Yer can't trust 'im. Turn yer back an' 'e's up yer arse. 'E made me an animal. A screwin' beast. Kill 'im."

But Gog says, " Let Magog be. He is my servant. And he will be a good servant. Only as master is he evil . . ."

" Kill 'im," Crook says. " 'E's the devil." And Crook runs forward with his knife and lets it in between the ridges of silver and turns the blade in the rent, until the black oil pours out and Magog groans. And Gog pulls at Crook's arm and wrenches it backwards. But the knife in the wound is sunk home as deep as to the womb.

" Fool," Gog says. " You cannot kill Magog. You must govern him. If you try to destroy him, he will devour you even more."

As he speaks, the black oil flowing from the wound becomes a horde of drops, which grow legs, and lo, they are ants which scurry forth. And they grow wings and take to the air and cover the people in their swarming, so that the masses in the sanctuary forget their shame and modesty in order to scratch, then to slap, then to dance, then to laugh, then to shriek. And the winged ants of Magog drive the people into a frenzy that passes the fury of the maenads, the screeching jig of the Bacchantes, until the naked men and women and boys and girls and androgynes and hermaphrodites and eunuchs are clutching and pawing and coupling over the cavern floor, with the ants driving them on to every experiment of pain and torture of lechery.

Squadrons of the winged ants of Magog attack and sting Gog and Crook, who are driven howling from the temple under the pillars out through the cracking gateway into the swamp and the wood. Weeping and flailing, Gog plunges blindly on through marsh and bush, losing Crook. He tries to lie in a swamp pool to drown the ants upon his naked flesh; but as he ducks himself, Magog sends hundreds of leeches to hang onto his flesh, until Gog rises bellowing with black tails sprouting from chin to toe. So Gog lumbers on. The thorns of the thickets tear away the leeches, which leave bloody kisses where their black lips have been. The stinging ants eventually drink their fill of Gog's veins and drop off. And twigs scrape off the remnants of Gog's skin, until he is one pulp of raw meat.

He can run no more. So he starts to crawl on all fours

towards the sunlight which begins to sift through the branches of the trees and show its yellow doors between their trunks. Sobbing and torn, Gog comes out of the dark wood into a meadow. And there, set above him, is a giant cube of hay, kept in by wooden rails from falling. With the last of his forces Gog clambers up the rails and reaches the surface of the structure and collapses, naked and belly down on the steaming hay. Thus Gog sleeps with the hot stink of erotic decay rising into his mouth and nose.

A shower in the evening makes Gog waken on the hay-tip. He is suffering from sunburn, which has made his skin raw. His whole body is a rash of red discomfort from head to foot. He gropes for his clothes, then remembers that they were stripped off him in the temple of Magog in the dark wood—if he has ever stirred bodily from his original sleep in the hay-tip and has not merely wandered through the forests of the night within the windings of his own skull. His clothes, indeed, are gone; but there is a small bundle beside him, and a note, which reads:

I leve you the suit of my dead husband wot was big like you and wont need his no mor. Good luck.

So Gog soon finds himself dressed in a clean grey flannel shirt and a red tie and a green pullover and a brown suit, shiny at seat and elbow. He has knitted socks and brown boots for his feet. The cloth burns his raw skin, but Gog is happy to wear clothes that are half-way respectable, even if the kindly widow has taken away the rest of his money from Maurice in the pocket of his old trousers.

So Gog shoulders his pack and walks on towards Durham in the evening. When he passes the old grey houses of Corbridge, he could swear that he has already passed the houses with Crook at noon. But the grocer's shop is closed, where they bought their lunch, and Gog cannot check whether he went inside the shop that midday. He walks on fast over the Tyne, taking the way South that does not allow him to pass again the wall in front of the dark wood. He keeps going, until his legs and the light begin to tucker out on Whittonstall Rise, where the big-rumped farmers stand at the pub door talking fat stock prices.

Once over the hill, Gog overlooks the medieval town of Consett on its hump above the Derwent. The town seems to be on fire, its turrets and keeps blazing. Then Gog looks again and sees that there are no turrets nor keeps, only chimneys and kilns, blazing on an artificial hill with sides of slag above the black and red roofs of a workers' town. The white smoke drifts out of the kilns, as the golden sunset goes grey and the usurious day banks the sovereigns of its light in the night vault, the gold of the light that makes men work all day in the cannibal kilns.

Gog eats his last loaf of stale bread and sacks down in the lee of a haystack. The rain begins to fall after an hour or two. So he struggles over to a nearby haycart and spreads his ground-sheet over its cracked planks and crawls underneath, curling head on knees like a hedgehog despite the cramps in his legs, dozing in fits and starts as the rain drums and drips down. In the night, Consett is a dark fleet getting up steam to move from its berth; in the first dawn, its grey stacks stick up into a grey sky.

During his last nap in the dawn, Gog sleeps waking, as if one eye were perpetually half-open. He seems to be watching an old film, grainy and scratched and silent. In it, Maire, dressed only in a black skin-suit with a silver dagger at her belt, stalks noiseless through the Paris of the Belle Epoque and Feuillade, past *art-nouveau* interiors and horse-drawn trams and kiosks plastered with posters of Jane Avril at the *Divan Japonais* and Rosa-Josepha, entwined Siamese girl twins for ever. Maire carries in her arms a hairy porcupine of a cat, its slant eyes blazing through its soft quills of fur. She creeps up behind men in top hats and cloaks, then she slips her dagger in their backs and they fall without a whimper. Their only warning of death is the running of the porcupine cat past them. Then Maire stalks away, her body suggesting white where the black skin-suit is tauter at swell of breast and buttock.

As Gog dreams waking, he wakes dreaming to find his mouth and nostrils stopped up with fur and his eyelids closed with claws. He chokes, then tries to brush away the animal from his face; but his palm meets the wrists of someone trying to suffocate him with the warm body of a beast. He writhes and sweeps with his arms, striking into the soft give of a breast. And then, the animal is gone in a scrabble and a scamper. And Gog rolls over to see Maire in the skin-suit and the hairy porcupine cat running over the stubble towards the open gate of the field, where the black car waits. As Gog gets onto his hands and knees, ready to jump up and pursue her, he squashes with his palms two fat black slugs, the glossy ones which crawl out with the rain and undulate as enticingly as the Queen of Sheba's little finger. But revulsion at this sudden cold squish sets Gog back on his heels, and by the time that he has wiped his hands on the hay, Maire and the cat are in the car and away.

Gog ponders over the attempts of Maire to kill him, that seem more threats of death than attempts at murder. They are surely warnings, not failed assassinations. And Gog dozes again, squatting on his haunches, until another drizzle disturbs him and sends him drowsily on his way, as heavy-headed as if he had just woken from sleep.

The green fields end suddenly below Consett in the fluid sludge of the Derwent, which is no more than an open sewer, while above rises the first bastion of the industrial revolution which Gog has seen since Hawick. It is the Grey Country as yet, the outpost of the Black. Gog climbs slowly, until he reaches the great mine which tops the hill above Consett on the way to Leadgate. Men don't build earthworks to defend themselves against other men any more, but they build slagheaps to rid themselves of refuse. Yet it is all the same to the weeds and grass that are already climbing over these new banks of black grit. Men dig out coal, use it, tip out its remains, which goes back under grass and slowly becomes coal again.

Gog passes the bungalows of Leadgate with their shining wet slate roofs, which jettison themselves down the hills and straggle up the slopes in cocked rows. Everywhere, monotonous repetitions of plaster and stone and slate and grime. All the way beyond Leadgate to Durham, there is nothing but the slick road and the soft hills, turning more and more grey and less and less green, petering out in allotments and red villas. And so Gog comes down the hill into Durham, drawn into its hub by the towers of the Cathedral on its mound. And Magog waits there, holding his second rod of power.

XIII

Gog lurches down North Street under the vast viaduct of the stone railway bridge, marvelling at the mighty Victorians, who erected arches to hail the triumph of steam and iron, arches greater than the Romans built for the baths of a conquering emperor. A train rumbles overhead and black grit falls on Gog out of a white puff of cloud, as he hears the stutter of the wheels punctuate his reveries. The noise gathers and departs along the rails over the arches, keeping to the lines of its coming and going, the iron lines that divide England even more decisively than the stone lines of the Roman roads, separating the people from their land by a skein of metal and machines that shuttle from station to station the factory goods and the labour force (no longer counted one by one as men are counted), until the roots of the villagers in earth are pulped by pistons and the desire of humans for the fruits of the soil is baled in crates for carriage and the river water hisses in boilers and the fields gape open in pits to produce coal for the fiery maws of the rolling behemoths and the patrols of the iron monsters along their beats make the people expect their regular passing so that they are missed when they do not come, as though the engines were now the guardians of prosperity rather than the seasons, as though the engines were not the sentinels on the perimeter of the concentration camp that condemns England to toil in the sweat of smoke and grime and din and slum, to sell what she does not need to make in order that she may consume what she does not need to have.

On the facing hill at the end of North Street, Durham Cathedral sends up its square central spire, pointed in position by the pediment of Bethel Chapel; the Methodists have gone classical now and they proclaim their respectability from pillared doorways; the fire of Wesley and Whitefield is snuffed out under pseudo-porticos. Gog sees a canopy of glass and wrought-iron project from the line of the shop-fronts; its solid delicacy makes it worthy to be the roof of the stable of the horses of the sun, but underneath its shadow, double-decker buses now squat in heavy oblongs, waiting to box the people together for their necessary journeys. For the signs are everywhere, insisting – IS YOUR JOURNEY REALLY NECESSARY? until Gog feels like shouting, No, no, no. I walk because my feet move, I wander because I wish to, I voyage towards uncertainty, I tramp in service to myself, I am of necessity a man and of necessity I travel because all men must on their slow trudge from light to dark. IS YOUR JOURNEY REALLY NECESSARY? Yes, but I don't use your transport, I go on my own way.

The old stone terraces plunge down the side-streets until checked by the corner houses in mid-topple before they crush Gog, descending past the Durham Miners' Hall, proudly stamped 1875, when the men-moles had decided that digging and delving was not enough and had organized to build their temple under the props of heaven; but the depression had made them poorer and the coal seams had grown narrower, and now their temple has golden letters tacked onto its tower that spell out ESSOLDO and the wooden chairs of the protesting pit-workers have become the cushioned seats of the liquorice-suckers, who stop their gobs on sweet glue while they watch the jerry bombers in flaring explosions on the newsreels and cosily dream of daring-do from their dark cockpits only two feet off the ground.

Gog keeps to the left side of the street, under the dangling floors of old window-seats on the second storey of the shops, until he reaches the bottle-necked bridge over the River Wear, where the convoys pant endlessly on the slow trail down to Catterick. On his left, Gog sees the weir over the river making a scimitar of sunken stone under the shallows and carding the slow green water into white threads falling transverse down. Green weed lines the edges of the river, houses and factories hem the banks with red brick and square windows, all powdery with the rot of time. Dark trees screen the far view at the bend of the Wear, as though a forest stretches up two fingers to nip off the stream between them. Above the end of the bridge ahead of Gog, Durham castle is jetty-long, with great windows in the shape of perpendicular arches cut into its yellow stone sides in a vain effort to disguise the fortress as a university.

Gog now crosses the road between the lorries of stalled convoys, past soldiers staring glumly down over green tailboards. The men seem dazed at still being ferried about, although the fighting in Europe is over; they are waiting for the demobilization that does not begin, but is always promised for this year, next year, sometime, never, as the army authorities count heads mysteriously and pick the lucky few for civvy street by some arcane principle that is no more just than the eeny-meeny-miny-mo of children. On the right side of the bridge, the trees continue to clothe the small hills on either bank of the Wear; the branches near the river make drab-olive shadows on the wan waters in a zig-zag of camouflage more perfect than on the hoods of the trucks. Half a mile upstream lies another low weir and a bridge between so much sloping greenery that Gog might have imagined himself in a glen, fringed with a few stray roofs. Yet the convoy starting behind in a grind of gears recalls Gog to the world of the incessant machine and his eyes rise upwards over the trees on the left bank towards the great crown of the west end of the cathedral, which raises its two flanking spires sheer into the sky for the armrests of the throne of Magog, whose giant and invisible spirit squats between the pinnacles and broods over Durham on the roof of the west nave.

Gog takes the narrow path through the trees up the hill toward the cathedral; the gravel is dappled in sudden sun all the way to the peaked roof of the old prebend's house that hats the top of the path. When Gog reaches the garden wall of the building, he turns left down a shadowed narrow street. Someone is playing a piano within the prebendary; he plays two shrill notes over and over again, with the shriller voices of choirboys imitating the notes a little flat, a little late, a little false, until the piano notes stop and are succeeded by a shrill shriek, "No, no, no."

Then Gog emerges out of the street and, as he wheels, the full glory of the cathedral close bursts upon his eyes, so he senses that he has been kicking upwards out of a trough of dark water and he has broken the surface into bright air and he is gulping down life again into his lungs and his blood is pulsing and his mouth gasping with joy. The sun strikes out the gravestones in white squares and rounds and barrows and slabs of light against the cropped green luxury of the grass. Occasional trees spawn other dark trees on the turf; the shadow leaves in the wind become shaking black garlands over the graves. Three of the tombs are lying men, weathered by the centuries until their smooth stone flesh is pale as a girl's body. The choirboys sing again on two high notes to the nagging piano and Gog's eyes swim in the glare of sudden light and the standing gravestones shake and shimmy like bleached robes, they whirl about the maypole trees as if in magic circles to woo the summer sun, and the lying stones are white couples writhing in the smooth interweavings of love, and the very grass quakes in an ecstasy of earth, yes, the skin of green and stone and flesh is all aquiver on the film of Gog's eyes so that his whole body shakes in the shifting spurt of delight that sometimes pierces and fuses all creation in one shudder of sudden joy.

Then the shrill voice shrieks crescendo, "No, no, no, no, *no*," and Gog blinks his eyes clear and he sees the great holy place of Magog threatening the close from above. The whole shape of the cathedral is the one distorted initial of Magog, with the square central spire jumped up in authority between the end spires, which are themselves built as smaller M's, as is the cathedral doorway over the main entrance, where wooden slabs hide away the interior of power.

And Gog walks down the gravel path to the cathedral door, on which is fixed a brass lion's head with a ring in its nose, a sanctuary knocker where the fugitives from the king's justice could once cling and beg the bishop for refuge inside the cathedral safe from the king's men. But the lion's head is bodiless and without strength; the ring in its nose is to lead the beast, not to proclaim its might. The knocker only saves the outlaw from the king's men at the price of making him a slave to God's priest; the ring is the gyve about his neck. Magog in his holy place grants sanctuary for the condemned to prove his power over kings and to enslave those men weak enough to try and evade the justice of other men. The mercy of the most high is no mercy; it is the mere proof of power over the less high. The arch-priest of God absolves in order to bind men to himself and to spite their laws; he never forgives a man still proud enough to stand on his own. Magog rules because he denies both men's justice and their injustice, in the name of the Almighty; and in the name of the Almighty, men bow down before him to receive the heavenly hope of the opposite to their fate on earth.

Gog passes the sanctuary knocker into the black hole of the cathedral doorway. A velvet pad is laid over his eyes and ears as he reaches the massy aisle of Magog's house.

The organ sounds in the darkness; it is being tuned and one pipe is blown and held and stopped, a small pipe that does not shrill as the choirboys, but hums high and intermittent, until Gog's very brain becomes untuned. Gog rams his fingers in his ears, but the hum skewers through his plugs of flesh and unhinges his thoughts, so that he can feel his eyelids pucker back and his eyeballs begin to roll and his fears start out in cold sweat on his skin. He sidles against one of the great ridged pillars that fence off the north aisle from the nave and he supports himself with his spine pressed to the stone and his arms braced backwards against his feeling of falling to the rear.

Sweet Jesu, the cracks over the paving stones . . .

Wisps of cloth . . . shreds of dresses rising . . .

Women in kirtles and hoods grovelling . . . beating their shaven foreheads on the stone . . . clawing the nails off their fingers on the pillars . . . tufts of hair pulled free, blood at the roots . . .

Women stretching at the raised font . . . making a pyramid of praying, of writhing hands . . . beggar women, poor women, cook women, peasant women, market women . . . screeching like roasting cats . . . gaping up, teeth bare . . .

The fanged round arches thirty feet overhead yawn back in silent howl . . .

Above these under the second tier of arches . . . more women weeping, scratching the satin off their breasts . . . scourging their bare backs, screaming for mercy . . . Mary, mother of God, have mercy . . . Magog, master over man, have mercy . . . milky ladies and gentlewomen, shrieking repentance . . . squalling their submission in their soiled finery . . .

Above these, gargoyles sneering, stone-lipped in frozen spite . . .

Higher, higher, half-way to heaven . . . under the top arches, by the small far windows . . . abbesses in ripped purple, stained with their own blood more purple . . . scoring their cheeks to let out their sins . . . peeresses in sackcloth, flogging each other with gold chains . . .

All women, all keening, all begging mercy . . . all women, all this side of the black boundary cross . . . black stone cross set in the paving . . . Cross that grants no crossing, no ford for Jezebel . . . no bridge into the main body of the church for Lilith . . . yes, no way past, not even for Ruth nor Judith . . . back, at the back, you too, Queen of Sheba . . . Women may not cross my black stone, boundary marker at the rear of Magog's holy house . . . Women are evil, are sinful, are slow death to men . . . Back with you, skulk lucky to be let into the byways of grace at all.

On the forward arches towards the altar . . . the arches high as towers, keeping up the roof of plaited cloud . . . gouged deep round the arches, the dread initial of Magog . . . hidden in mouldings or patterned squares, squeezed out in waves . . . Magog's initial, to terrify the faithful . . .

And in the nave proper, a great bellowing . . . a sobbing and moaning and sighing . . . varlets and tumblers, quacks and glee-men, minstrels and chapmen, palmers and gypsies, bakers and butchers, smiths and shoemakers, farmers and labourers, all of low estate lowly and weeping . . . trampling one another down, prostrate three deep . . . a heaving brush, a moving bush of flesh . . . fingers shaking as twigs in a mighty wind of beseeching . . . the packed, stinking, common people, herded to seek mercy . . .

In the second row of arches overhead, level with the ladies . . . fat burghers and merchants, gentlemen of quality, traders and lenders . . . meaty and milch lush, yet scrabbling loose their purses . . . spilling out coins for charity, any price for absolution . . . stripping off their doublets and hose, their rich slashed stuffs and silken linings . . . standing bare-legged and round-thighed in shirts with ropes round their puffy necks . . . muling and puking . . . Magog, Master Magog, mercy, mercy . . .

Above these, on the top tier, lords lying prone . . . naked and despairing, their jewels heaped before them . . . gashing their ribs with swords, lacerating their shaven polls . . . not daring to ask absolution, so great their sinfulness . . .

And high, high, high, all praise to the highest . . . in the great square hollow of the central spire, a red swing . . . redder than whale's gore, finer than damask, rich as the morning . . . backward and forward swinging, a crimson-clad boy at each corner . . . a boy to north, south, east and west . . . on their wrists are bolted burning censers . . . the censers burn wormwood, acrid and stinging . . . between them, two naked stooped men, manacled to act as armrests to the throne . . . on their heads, crowns; round their ribs and limbs, chains . . . as the seat of the throne, two naked queens . . . their flesh as an eight-legged stool, the backs of queens bearing the burden . . . the burden of seated Magog, dressed in flame and crimson . . . on his head an eagle's mask of burnished copper . . . from its beak, a trumpet flares open its brazen mouth . . .

Magog raises high both bronze gloves . . . the right one clutches an iron cross . . . an iron cross that is a three-pronged trident, with a barb at tip and two sides . . . the left bronze glove holds a steel orb, burning with light, so that the people are blinded by the orb and grovel, weeping . . . begging Magog on high for mercy, have mercy, Magog, Master Magog, set over men . . .

And Magog sounds his trumpet from the red swing and makes a single unceasing note of brazen breath that topples reason and sends all sense reeling to worship the majesty of Magog . . .

Before the cataracts . . . of the stone-falling fountain of the screen behind the High Altar, monks and priests lie on their faces . . . their heels towards Christ's mystery . . . each tonsure turning its bald eye upwards at the blinding orb of Magog . . .

Bishops in the choir stalls rend their mitres and chasubles . . . tears are slimy on their soft jowls, as they intone their *peccavis* to Magog . . .

Lofty in the embrasures of the upper windows . . . cardinals vomit into their scarlet hats . . . throwing up their pomp and pride in fear of Magog . . .

Even the Archbishop of Canterbury on the wooden throne of red and gold over the choir stalls . . . even the Archbishop cries out . . . Mea culpa, mighty Magog . . . even the Archbishop hems and haws for mercy . . . even the Archbishop havers his old noddle forwards to rub his nose on the wooden floor in abasement . . . Mea culpa, mighty Magog, mea culpa . . .

And Magog still sounds the brazen note of his horn.

Then the note stops.

And all is still.

And there is peace, dropping slow.

And Gog looks about himself and finds that he is at the east end of the cathedral in front of a placard on a wall, which tells him that he is standing in the transept of the nine altars, the altar to Saint Michael, the altar to Saint Aidan and Saint Helen, the altar to Saint Peter and Saint Paul, the altar to Saint Martin, the altar to Saint Cuthbert and Saint Bede, the altar to Saint Oswald and Saint Lawrence, the altar to Saint Thomas of Canterbury and Saint Katherine, the altar to Saint John the Baptist and Saint Margaret, the altar to Saint Andrew and Saint Mary Magdalene, the nine altars of the favourite saints of the North, a medley of missionaries and warriors, of men and women, of Hebrews and British, a fit stew for any Northerner with faith in his heart. And Gog knows that the truly meek can find an altar there to venerate, showing their backs to Magog while all the rest of the people scrape beneath him. And Magog will let them turn away to the true God. For the strong shall inherit the earth and the meek shall work it. The humble at heart shall have their peace, if they sweat for it. The mild in mouth shall find their quiet, if they do not protest. The charitable shall lay up their treasure in heaven, if they are taxed on earth. The gentle shall bind up the wounds that others inflict upon them. The compassionate shall be given more than they can sorrow for, yea, even their own plight. The forgiving shall be judged for what they have not done. The generous shall be deprived of that which they do not wish to give. And the good, ah the good, it were better that they are not born. And if they are born, it were better that they die at birth. And if they live to the natural end of their days, they shall live to curse their life and they shall go into the grave gladly, as no one else goes among men.

"Can I help you, sir?"

Gog looks down to see a small verger, staring at him with sharp green eyes under the white fuzz of his brows. Gog is about to tell him that helping is the short way to hell on earth, when he realizes that the verger only wants an excuse to show the giant madman out of the cathedral, before telephoning the police to take care of such a suspicious character. "I help myself," Gog mutters and strides down the nave out of Magog's holy house, leaving the verger nervously checking the locks on the offertories, just in case Gog has helped himself too much.

XIV

As Gog walks down the hill from the cathedral on its loop of land overlooking the Wear, he meets a familiar, wizened, waxy goblin of a man, Miniver alias Cluckitt, looking even more aged than before. Miniver now wears a black academic gown that billows about him and wraps him in blackout, if not in learning. He smiles to see Gog, his face withering with his grin like a balloon losing air.

"My dear Doctor Griffin," Miniver says. "We have not had the pleasure of your company for an age. Have they let you out of His Majesty's Forces, now you've won the war for us? I see from your clothes, you must have been issued with a demobilization suit."

"You haven't seen me recently?" Gog demands in a threatening voice.

"Not since the war, my dear fellow. You know *that*."

"*Cluckitt*."

"Who?" Miniver says.

"You don't remember being dressed up in a red bonnet and answering to the name of Cluckitt? Just two days ago?"

"Two days ago?" Miniver says in astonishment. "I was here, of course. A red cap, did you say? Cluckitt?" Miniver scratches the few remaining hairs that are slicked down against his pate, then suddenly laughs. "Why, yes! That was seven years ago. Or more. Before the war. When I dressed up like a peasant from Lady Chatterley. I had a bet with Maire I could take you in. And I did. Except she wouldn't pay. Maire never pays if she loses a bet. She just refuses to admit she's lost it. How is she, by the way? *Darling* Maire."

"You haven't seen me for *years*?" Gog says. "Do you *swear*?"

"My dear Gog Griffin," Miniver says, "I never swear on principle. But you know perfectly well you haven't set eyes on me since '39." Miniver's own eyes narrow to black pips between his cheeks of withered appleskin. "You're all right, old chap, aren't you? Nothing the matter? Shell-shock? Anything like that?"

"I'm fine," Gog says.

He looks round helplessly at the stone walls of the university, which give him no answer. Then his eyes stray down a plunging alley to the slow river. Flow, flow, flow, all the day, tomorrow, yesterday, what matter? This year, last year, since the beginning until the end, for ever and aye, till all the seas gang dry, my dear. Time past, time present, time future, the same sluggish current, careless of the marking of the hours. The Wear of memory.

"Did you have the time in the service to go on with that odd research of yours?" Miniver is saying. "What was it? I've still got a piece of it tucked away in my files. Gog and Magog. That was it. All that curious prehistoric British mythology, mixed up with some wild theory about populism. Nothing much to do with *history*. Or archaeology, I'd say. But suitable for somebody with an imaginative temperament."

"I have that all right," Gog says ruefully, still looking down towards the river.

"Miscast in academics, my dear fellow," Miniver chatters on. "I always thought so. I know your pupils liked you. They found you very stimulating. But when all's said and done, it's research that counts. My few modest works on phonetics and dialect may not be very much, but, do you know?" Here Miniver does not so much ask a question as give an answer. "*The Times Lit*. called them seminal only last week."

"Seminal," Gog says. "Yes. I'd like to get at the germ . . . the sap . . . of *this*." He shrugs his arms vaguely at the river, the cathedral, the university, the city, the factory worker who passes in her turban and dungarees. "This . . . Why? Tell me why? What's it all for, Cluckitt?"

"Miniver," Miniver says coldly. "A joke's a joke. Professor Miniver, if you please, my dear Doctor Griffin." He takes out a silver cigarette case, opens its golden interior, selects a cigarette for his mouth, and closes the case without offering Gog a smoke.

"I'm sorry," Gog says, menacing once more. "I'm not good at remembering *names*. And *time*. Only *faces*."

He examines again the lined, glossy face of Miniver, the eyes mere slits in the paunches under their dark brows, as Miniver lights his cigarette from a golden lighter. But Gog can find no evidence that Miniver is telling a lie. Miniver seems so certain that he has not seen Gog in years. And surely, Gog himself knows well enough that he is amnesiac and sick and dizzy. All truth is a question of evidence. And there is no evidence, except the evidence of Gog's own memory since his waking in the hospital. And that evidence must be a mixture of the dream and the fact; it must be his recollection of the gone melting into his experience of the immediate; it must be his own remembered history confused with his research into pre-history.

"A dish of tea?" Miniver says. "You won't refuse that?"

"I'm starving," Gog says. "I'll eat you out of house and home."

"I'm out of rations," Miniver says quickly. "I have to hand them all over to the university. They don't leave me a coupon for myself. But some bread, perhaps."

"Anything," Gog says.

He follows Miniver's sweeping gown through the gate into the university, across a lawn, up a stone stairway into a panelled room that again seems familiar. As if compelled, Gog's eyes search out a chip in the panelling surrounded by a darker stain.

"A bottle of wine smashed there," Gog hears himself say. "I threw it at your head."

Miniver seems startled at Gog's remark, then recovers quickly.

"There's nothing wrong with your memory, then," Miniver says. "Though you do bring up the past in a most disconcerting way. Some things, I'd say, are better left dead and buried." He rings a bell set into the panelling. "Yet I suppose it's a historian's bad habit. Thinking what's happened is more important than what's happening. But I must say, I'd have thought the war would have cured you of that. It would have kept your mind on everyday things. What sort of a war did you have, by the way?"

Gog cannot remember, so he says, "I lived."

"I'm glad you don't want to talk of it, actually," Miniver says. "I'm so bored of heroics. Or of heroes who got bored in some camp and never managed to do the heroics at all, so complain of it to me."

An old woman limps in, her face cobbled with warts, arthritic lumps on the knuckles of her hands.

"Tea, please," Miniver says. "And my friend here is hungry."

"I'll see what I can do," the crone says. "I don't promise."

"Who can, these days?" Miniver says.

The old woman leaves. Gog has gone over to the chip in the panelling and is fingering it. "You know," he muses aloud, "I remember even the wine. Pommard '31. But I can't remember why I should have lost my temper so much that I tried to stove in your skull with a bottle."

Miniver seems relieved at Gog's forgetfulness. " You always did have uncontrollable moments, old chap. Still, I forgive you."

" Why did I?" Gog says.

Miniver pauses, then seems to test Gog's powers of recollection. " You . . . were annoyed at something I said in committee about mythology being so hypothetical it didn't need *real* people to study it. You took it personally. You thought I wanted you out of your job."

Gog hears Miniver's earnest tone and knows that he is lying.

" It was about Maire," he says. " You know it was." He remembers the conversation which he overheard in the car. " You were lovers."

Miniver scuttles over to the door, opens it, looks out, closes it again, and turns agitatedly to Gog. " I say, not so loud, if you don't mind, old fellow. Walls have ears, and all that. You'll compromise me dreadfully. This isn't one of your southern universities, they've got the morals of rabbits down there. This is the north. A wee bit puritan, you know, but I like it. We don't sleep with our colleagues' wives up here. You can't have it thought that Professors . . . I mean, I have a Chair . . ."

" A throne," Gog says. " A seat of power, Miniver?"

" Someone has to run education. See the young don't forget all the decency and wisdom of their fathers. And, candidly, I can't think of anyone more suitable than myself to instruct them. They say, as soon as the Vice-Chancellor retires, and he's past it, dear old boy . . . no disloyalty meant, of course, I'm merely stating the fact . . . *when* he retires, they say that I . . ."

" Why does Maire want to kill me?" Gog says.

" You do ask the most extraordinary things, my dear Gog. Kill you?"

" Oh yes. Frequently."

" When I used to know your wife . . ."

" We're married, then?" Gog asks.

" Of course you are," Miniver says, surprised. " You seem to have great holes in your memory like a gorgonzola . . . oh, why must I torture myself with thoughts of those pre-war goodies? You forget all the important things. And you remember the unimportant, especially if they're embarrassing to other people."

"Tell me about my past," Gog says. "I don't remember too well, I must admit."

"What is it?" Miniver asks. "A sort of amnesia?"

"Yes," Gog says. "Chunks of the past suddenly come to me. Rather vividly, as though they were happening to me now. But I've lost all sense of time. And there are great gaps."

"Amnesia's like that, so a doctor friend once told me. You never forget everything. For instance, you'd still know a policeman was a policeman ..."

"True," Gog says. "I knew that straightaway."

"And then you remember more and more daily. But it's rather disconnected."

"Tell me about my past, then," Gog says. "Let's see what I can fit in." Gog's voice becomes hard. "And don't you lie to me, Cluckitt ... Miniver, I mean. Or ..."

"Please don't threaten me, Gog. I know you were an amateur boxer in your youth, and you have just been trained to be a professional murderer for six years. But I'm not a Nazi with your bayonet at my throat. Doubtless, your mind's been spilling over with blood and slaughter and outrage for years. But it's peacetime here. And it always has been. Ah, the tea!"

The crone enters with a pot of tea and a plate full of sandwiches, spread thinly with margarine and plum jam. She sets down the tray and leaves. Gog wolfs the food, while Miniver speaks.

"I first met you, my dear Gog, when I knew you as a graduate student at Cambridge in the thirties. Ancient and Roman and Dark Ages. British history up to the Normans. You were rather fervent, then. One of those lapsed Catholics flirting with communism, who were arguing in every corridor after the General Strike and the Depression. Except your communism was rather agrarian and backward – anarchism, really. You should have called it communalism, but you've never defined your terms very carefully. And you were a great man for tramping. All over the moors, you were. All the way to Edinburgh you went once. Then another time, from Tolpuddle to Avebury. You didn't have what I would call an academic mind. Too unsystematic. Not scholarly, really. You'd always be enthusing over the last weird trifle you'd picked up. So your mind was a ragbag of the strangest sort, full of oddities which were doubtless asserted by ancient chroniclers and not invented by you. But they'd hardly be verifiable by modern standards of documentation. You grubbed around with the passion of those old antiquarians like John Aubrey. You really liked the gossip of history, its lust and its scatology, its funny stories and curious remnants, its byways and its teases. None of the hard slog after *truth* for you. Everything was grist to your mill, sagas, flints, hymns, tomb inscriptions, assertions by proven liars centuries after the event. You never had a discriminating mind, God. You were no scholar, though you tarted up your thesis enough with footnotes to get your doctorate. Just a fascinating magpie, you were. Your mind full of bright bits."

Gog nods, his mouth full of sandwiches. He believes Miniver's explanation. "Maire," he mumbles.

"Maire?" Miniver says. "I didn't meet her till you resigned your post to marry her just before the war. You'd met her in Paris. She was half-English, half-French, and every ounce a devil. The eternal artists' mistress, you know the type, Kiki without the blubber. Trust you to try to make a decent woman out of her, you always did have an appetite for the impossible. I remember her telling me about a disastrous time you tried to take her tramping in the Landes. Still, she liked you all right . . . a liking that soon ripened into love, when you inherited that wallop of money from your great-aunt. For all your love of the red flag, you didn't turn down that legacy. It bought you Maire as a wife. She wasn't your type, of course. But then you seem fated to create difficulties for yourself, even when none exist. There was a joke round here, that you were the only man who could walk under a clear sky and have a brick fall on his head."

"More about Maire, please," Gog says. "It's not every day I discover I have a wife."

"She's a bitch," Miniver says blithely, "but everything in a bitch one could desire. She has to torture, to see just how far she can go and then go further. Of course, you were the perfect victim for her. Long-suffering, blundering, lunging, strong, always interesting, but basically as sloppy as a bull-calf. She ran rings round you, Maire did. She lacerated you, used you. And you loved it. And her. I don't have to tell you *that*. You remember."

"A little," Gog says. "She comes back to me just as you say. Memories of her behaviour, mixed up with memories of my war experiences, I suppose. I see her or her chauffeur ... she does have one, doesn't she?"

"Jules," Miniver laughs. "A real rum do."

"That's him. Or her, should I say?"

"*It*," Miniver says bitterly, "would be the most accurate term for Jules."

"Well, she or Jules is always sniping at me, or trying to do me in. I must put their faces on real snipers, who had a go at me in the war. But tell me, *you* and Maire?"

"Let's skip that," Miniver says sharply. He drinks his tea and goes over to the tall windows to look out at the quadrangle. "I haven't forgotten her, Gog. One doesn't. There's only one Maire. If there were two, the world would disintegrate. One's as much as the human race can stand. Once she's got her claws in you, you stay scratched. Though I can't expect sympathy from *you*, of all people. Why should I?"

"She has a weakness for intellectuals?"

"Oh yes," Miniver says ruefully, his back turned to Gog. "She won't let anyone touch her, who can't think or paint or something. She sees herself as a sort of creative goad. A scorpion to the lazy writer. She'll sting him till he dies – or till he tries to work her out of his system by scribbling a masterpiece in his despair."

"And you? What have you done because of her?"

Miniver shrugs. "She failed with me. I know dialects, but I'm no dialectician. She thought all my riddles funny like ..." here Miniver slips into Cluckitt's voice, while Gog watches him suspiciously:

> "Clink clank doon t' bank,
> Ten against foor.
> Splish splash in t' dish
> Till it run oor.

"Answer: the milking of a cow. Or . . .

> T' bat, t' bee, t' butterflee,
>   T' cuckoo, an' t' gowk,
> T' heather-bleet, t' mirensnipe,
>   Hoo many birds is tha'?"

"Seven," Gog says.

"No, two," Miniver says. "The rest of them are insects or something, not birds. You may like peasants, Gog. But you totally lack all peasant knowledge. And cunning. How about this, then? If an' herrin' an' an half coom ter three ha'pence, wha' will an hundred o' coal coom ter?"

"I wasn't ever any good at arithmetic," Gog says.

"Ashes," Miniver says, "is the proper answer."

"They're too smart for me in the country," Gog says. "I admit it. That's why I admire them."

"They don't work out the riddles there. They learn them from childhood. We think they're smart, because we hear them for the first time. Like Maire did. But I was merely parroting the smartness of some rustic Sphinx centuries back. And Maire soon found out and got bored with me. As I wasn't original anyway, she didn't stimulate me to anything. Except sloth."

"Thanks," Gog says. "I appreciate your frankness."

Miniver turns and raises one brow slightly, so that Gog can see a gleam in the ball of his left eye. "Since frankness is at a premium today," he says, "why are you here?"

"I found myself in hospital recently," Gog says. "Hit a mine off Edinburgh after the last day of the war, I suppose. I don't know how long I lay there. It may have been months. I didn't remember anything. Some instinct made me begin to walk. Towards London. I gather that the Labour Party has got in by a large majority. The people at last rule in Westminster."

"The *people rule* in Westminster?" Miniver begins his jeering laugh that sets his whole tiny frame shaking. "You really are incurable, Gog. Your myth about the people. Who are the people? They're not what you've always thought they were, a lusty, brawling, anarchic, kindly, bawdy bunch of red-blooded peasants, somehow cooped up by a ghastly mistake in tenements and terraces and semi-detacheds by the foul fiend of industrialism. In fact, your friends the Communists would have put you straight in front of the firing squad for thinking heresies like that. You wanted the worker to go back to being the Merrie England peasant, while the Communists wanted just the opposite, the worker to march on as the factory proletarian. And they were certainly righter than you were, with your nostalgia for the non-existent. The English labourers were always a cowed, beaten, lick-spittle race of serfs, who'd much rather tug their forelock at the squire than raise a club against him. Look at all the English peasant revolts. They never came to anything. Every time the King said, "Go home," like in the Pilgrimage of Grace, they downed their billyhooks and went and were hanged at the King's leisure. They hardly ever killed a gentleman. In fact, gentlemen usually led them when they revolted. Leaders are born, you know. It's in the blood. This isn't a countryside of rioting revolutionary labourers. It's died-in-the-wool conservative. And quite right, too."

"The people," Gog says. "They fight the government. They always have and they always will."

"Nonsense," Miniver says. "They can't govern themselves. If you didn't have laws and police, the people would all murder one another. I'm sorry, old man, but a few people are born to rule and the rest to obey. And it's as well to recognize that fact, because fact it is. My family, for instance, the Minivers, we were sturdy yeoman stock, never serfs. And when they dissolved the monasteries, we got our chance, got some land, and became gentry. I will say one thing for the Papists, your old people, they were useful in getting together the land which we took over. The people round our place know us and like us. They trust us. If you say Miniver in our village, it means generations of kindness, firmness, order, *trust*."

"Generations of exploitation, abuse, hate," Gog says. "It's your version of the people which is unreal, Miniver. They have to hide their true natures from the likes of you. It's so much more convenient for you to believe the play-acting version of the grateful rustic. Oh, we've got our Uncle Tom Cobley and all!"

" I agree *that's* all over, and the more's the pity," Miniver says. " I'm a realist. In fact, now people of my sort are considered as lower than vermin by the government, it'll have a shot at putting us down. Except, of course, it'll fail. You mark my words, the Labour government won't put us down. Who else will act as unpaid Justices of the Peace? Who else will run the shires for next to nothing? They'll have to keep us on, because the country's too bankrupt to pay a salary to our inferiors to take our place. You can't afford not to use *noblesse oblige*, Gog. Who else will do something for nothing?"

" The people's government will get rid of you."

" Even if they did, it'd be like the end of the monasteries all over again. A new class would rise and take our place. Yeomen into gentry, profiteers into lords, politicians into patricians. The people govern at last, Gog? You know in your heart of hearts they don't. It's merely a new government and it'll be like all governments. It'll carry on much as before. Because governments can't govern themselves."

" It may be different," Gog says. " This time."

" Take your fascinating Mr. Bevan, the white hope of the social revolution. Your Nye, I bet you, will end with a pig farm and a Rolls Royce. Ebbw Vale, he'll shake the coal-dust off his feet all right. Even though the present government wasn't born to rule and can't rule properly, it'll pick up a few of the tricks quick enough. Governments are like monkeys, they all look alike and they do just what the others have always done."

" Perhaps you're right," Gog admits. " Perhaps Magog has always ruled and always in the same old way. Till now. But he's been toppled for the first time. There's never been a Labour majority like that. At least, give them a chance."

" They don't intend to give me one," Miniver says, " so why shouldn't I return the compliment? One thing, though, even if they shift me out of my country house, they won't shift me out of here. Here I'll stick, teaching their children that the old ways are best. Which they obviously are. So perhaps the new generation, my dear Gog, will not follow you. After every revolution there's a reaction. And, anyway, you're pretty inconsistent yourself. You've always wanted to preserve every stick and stone from the past. You hate change in old things. You loathe new buildings. You're the true reactionary, far more than me. The revolution you want is to turn the whole clock back to the golden age when all men were free and equal. Which was never. And never will be."

"If it never was," Gog says, "you can't say it never will be."

"Visionary," Miniver says. "Incurable." He goes over to a filing cabinet, opens a drawer, looks through the files, and comes out with four sheets of typed paper clipped together. "You asked me to comment on this just before you left your job. I forgot to return it. I've kept it for you over the years, though it's pretty average trash and I've smothered it with red ink. Still, if you haven't changed, perhaps you'll like all that sheer propaganda and romance you used to come out with, pretending it was history." He hands the sheets over to Gog and goes over to the door. "If you'll excuse me, I have to visit the bursar briefly. All these damned forms. You'll have time to peruse your past productions. Then you'll see that your present folly has deep roots."

Miniver goes out of the door, closing it gently behind him, while Gog reads the papers in his hand.

THE CONCENTRATION OF POWERS IN THE MIDDLE AGES
by Dr. G. Griffin

Perhaps the concentration of powers in one hand has never been better illustrated than by the case of Henry Despenser, Bishop of Norwich, during the Peasants' Revolt. The rising was, naturally, justified, even if its success was unlikely. The feudal system pressed intolerably on the rights of Englishmen and their liberty; the position of the serfs after the Black Death was an insult to humanity.

(Here Miniver has added in red ink: NONSENSE – LIBERTY IS FREEDOM TO STAY IN ONE'S PROPER PLACE, WHERE MOST OF HUMANITY SHOULD STAY.) *The English rural labourer – and that was the mass of the English people – lived in poverty, insecurity and degradation. In the late fourteenth century, rebellion was his only way out.*

(Miniver here added – WHAT ABOUT PRAYER? SUICIDE?)

Near Norwich, Geoffrey Lidster was the leader of the peasants. When John Ball rang the bell of the revolt, Lidster raised forces in East Anglia. Among them was his lieutenant, a peasant named Griffin, who may be some ancestor of mine.

(LIKE ADAM IS OF MINE! WHAT'S YOUR SOURCE ON GRIFFIN? HE'S NOT MENTIONED IN THE USUAL DOCUMENTS ON THE PERIOD.)

Lidster took Norwich and had the Mayor killed, the local symbol of authority, since the Bishop, Henry Despenser, had fled to raise forces for the King. Despenser gathered together eight horsemen and a company of archers. These were sufficient to rout a group of rebels near Newmarket and to set up their leaders' heads on spears. The country gentry now plucked up courage and rallied round Despenser, who marched on Lidster and his men. Lidster retired with his rebels to North Walsham. There, Despenser charged and routed the rebels, who could hardly stand up to armoured knights with mere scythes. Lidster and Griffin were captured.

The first strange role of Despenser, Bishop of Norwich, was as a military officer. Actually, he had been given the bishopric as a cheap method of paying him off for armed services rendered to the Papacy in the Italian Wars of the time. This is not to say that Despenser was ungodly. Between slaughtering peasants, he performed daily the religious rites in the cathedral. The gauntlet was, and is, the pillar of the Church.

(Miniver's comment: AND REBELLION WAS, AND IS, THE DRY ROT IN THE ALTAR.)

The second role of Despenser was as a judge in the King's Court. Despenser took off his armour, put on a wig, and condemned Lidster and Griffin to death for taking arms against the King's Peace. As traitors, they were ordered to be drawn, hanged, and quartered. I should point out here that a skilful executioner could draw out a man's guts and show the man his own tripes while he was still alive, could cut him down choking from the noose in the middle of his dance on air, and could thus sever the limbs from a man who was still breathing.

(SHEER EMOTIVE PROPAGANDA! SO, PUNISHMENT WAS BARBARIC AT THE TIME. BUT WHO WERE THE GREATER BARBARIANS GENERALLY, THE PEASANTS OR THE KING'S MEN?)

The third role of Despenser was as the Bishop of Norwich. He took Lidster and Griffin in chains to the church, confessed them, and gave them absolution. One record here states that, while Lidster accepted absolution, Griffin spat into the Bishop's face, thus incurring the punishment reserved for heretics, to be burned alive. The same record states that Griffin was quoted as saying, " Whatever happens to my soul, even if it may rot in Hell, it will surely meet thine there, Master Despenser, yet thou canst but kill my body once."

(SOURCE!! WHO IS THIS GRIFFIN? YOUR INVENTION?)

Thus Despenser had played the role of military officer, of judge, and of priest. Now he had a fourth role to play in the affair, that of a humble Christian man. Mercy is, of course, the prerogative of Majesty. Only power can afford to forgive. The people, normally powerless, cannot in their brief moments of power afford to spare, which is why they are often cruel during rebellions.

(SPECIOUS AND FALSE REASONING. THE BETTER MAN ALWAYS SHOWS MORE COMPASSION THAN THE WORSE, BY NATURE AND TRAINING.)

When Lidster and Griffin were being dragged behind the cart's tail to the place of execution, Despenser walked the whole way over the rough road at the back of the cart, holding up the head of Lidster to prevent it from being bruised and broken against the tailboard as it jolted up and down on the potholes. Griffin, it is said, refused Despenser's helping hand. " Master Despenser," he declared, "when thou livest with both thine hands in the wallets of the poor, how shall I accept one finger of thy charity?"

Despenser probably would have liked to have filled the role of executioner as well:

(UNFOUNDED ASSERTION – PROFOUNDLY UNHISTORICAL!)

but as the calling was shameful, he contented himself with watching the executions, until Lidster's quarters were stuck on the spikes of the gates of Norwich, and Griffin's ashes had been collected and scattered on the dungheap. Griffin's last words seem to have been a rhyming addition to the famous lines of the Peasants' Revolt:

When Adam delved and Eve span,
Who was then the gentleman?

Griffin's reputed gloss ran as follows:

When Gog and Magog brothers were,
They lived in peace and not at war.
Now Gog doth toil and Magog rule,
Who is the knave and who the fool?

(SHEER INVENTION ON YOUR PART. GIVE SOURCE, FOR GOD'S SAKE!!!)

The Middle Ages saw the great peasant revolts, not only because the life of the peasant was hard, but also because the various powers of government were all concentrated in the person of one local magnate. I have shown how Henry Despenser represented military might, the King's Justice, priestly pardon direct from the Pope, and the human mercy of the great; but he also had the local money power through feudal inheritance and church dues; and he even had sexual authority, through sitting in judgement on cases of adultery, not to mention his feudal right of the jus primae noctis.

(REALLY! DO YOU HONESTLY THINK THAT A *BISHOP* INSISTED ON PERSONALLY DEFLOWERING

LOCAL VIRGINS ON THEIR MARRIAGE NIGHT? A GROSS OBSESSION, GOG! OR MORE LIKELY, AN OBSESSION WITH GROSSNESS!!!)

Each power that is now scattered in the many branches of government, the Houses of Parliament, the Courts, the police, the army, the Church, the local councils, the income tax authorities, etcetera, ad nauseam, bureaucracy without end, all these powers Despenser exercised spasmodically in his own person.

Thus Despenser incarnated for the people of Norwich that mythical figure of supreme authority, whom I will refer to as Magog in my projected work, after the original giant of Albion described by Geoffrey of Monmouth. The serfs could certainly be called one " class " in the strict Marxist sense at this period, bound as they were to the land by a similar social system of oppression; therefore, they also can be referred to generically as Gog, Magog's original brother and final foe.

(A POET MIGHT REFER TO THE SERFS AS GOG: BUT A HISTORIAN CERTAINLY SHOULD NOT!)

Thus, to me, the struggle of Lidster and Griffin and the peasants against Henry Despenser, the Bishop of Norwich, is once again the reworking of the old struggle of Gog against Magog within the framework of the Peasants' Revolt. And with this struggle of the people against the powerful, of the countryside against the city, the history of England began and is ending with the total triumph of London.

(Miniver's final comment reads: I DISAGREE PROFOUNDLY. ALL PEOPLE HAVE ALWAYS HAD A GOVERNMENT AND ALWAYS WILL. GOVERNMENTS ARE MADE *FOR* PEOPLE. IT IS IMPOSSIBLE TO THINK OF A PEOPLE WITHOUT A GOVERNMENT. THE GOVERNMENT IS NOT YOUR ENEMY, BUT YOUR NECESSARY FATHER, AND YOU OUGHT NOT TO BE TRYING TO WRITE HISTORY, BUT POETRY OR FICTION, AND I WOULD HARDLY RECOMMEND *THAT*! MINIVER.)

When Gog has finished reading the piece he wrote before the

war, he understands many of the obsessions and visions which have been plaguing him on the road from Edinburgh. A breeze blows through the open window of the room, as if to promise coolness in future for his hot head. A cupboard door, left half ajar, begins to bang intermittently. Gog rises to close the door. As he opens it before slamming it shut, he notices something red hanging on a hook inside the cupboard. He takes it out into the light. He finds that he is holding Cluckitt's red tam o'shanter, still moist from the ducking in Hermitage Water, with the brass capbadge green from decay.

Miniver comes into the room again and immediately begins to back out, as he sees Gog advancing towards him with the red tam o'shanter held out in a great fist.

"Liar," Gog shouts. "Here's evidence. Cluckitt's red cap. So you say you didn't try to have me drowned at Hermitage under orders from Maire? Liar!"

"It's my gardening hat," Miniver alias Cluckitt protests.

"Liar," Gog shouts and rushes at Miniver, who runs into the corridor, slamming the door in Gog's face. By the time that Gog has wrenched the door open, Miniver is safely in the shadows of a pair of large beadles, dressed in faded uniforms of red and gold. He is pointing to Gog in the doorway of his room, then pointing at his own head and shaking it sadly. As the beadles begin to advance on Gog, he turns and lumbers off down the stairs into the quadrangle and out through the stone gateway of the university, which was once a fortress. He slows down to catch his breath, glancing over his shoulder all the while. But there is no one pursuing him.

So Gog walks on the bridge over the Wear and turns south through the streets of Durham, to leave the hard smack of tarmac on the soles of his boots and to feel again the suck and spring of the moors. He still holds in his hand the red tam o'shanter and he puzzles over it as he leaves the suburbs of Durham behind him. The bonnet is evidence, all right. But evidence of what? A lying Miniver? Or merely that Miniver had impersonated Cluckitt before the war and has kept a gardening hat for several years?

XV

Gog would have had a long walk to reach the Yorkshire moors; but he does not have to trudge. To his surprise, the large black car draws up beside him on the outskirts of Durham without trying to run him down. The back door opens and Maire coos in her deepest voice, " Gog darling, as we're both heading south, do let me give you a lift, at least part of the way."

Gog suspects a trap, but he is intrigued by the change of approach. So he answers, " As far as the moors, I'd be delighted." And he climbs into the car, which indeed starts towards the south.

Maire is wearing a black turban over her hair with a large white pearl pin stuck through its folds. The effect of the turban is to make her face from the front seem like that of an oriental despot of some beauty and indeterminate sex. The darkness of her shadowed blue eyes above the pallor of her full cheeks makes her seem somewhat Balkan, Slavic with a dash of Mongol from the time of Genghis the great Khan; her hawk nose is foreshortened to a snub one. Her suit is square-cut at the shoulder. Pearl buttons gleam on a check as bold as a chessboard. The suit actually has a skirt, a concession to femininity which surprises Gog; but below the skirt, he sees that Maire is wearing black stockings and high white lace-up boots, more suitable for skating than walking.

" I owe you an apology, Gog," Maire says. " I've been a bit cruel to you. So has Jules." She looks forward through the glass partition between her and the cropped nape of the chauffeur. " I should have told you who I was right at the beginning. Your wife, Gog. Your own Maire."

She leans towards Gog, puts a palm on each of his cheeks as if to pat butter into place, and gives him a full kiss, passionless and expert, on the mouth. Then she drops her hands and lolls back in her seat.

" But it was such fun, such a marvellous game, to see how

much I could *hint* at without actually telling you. It really was remarkable. You didn't even recognize your own wife. I couldn't believe it, but there it was. They'd told me it might be like that at the hospital. So I decided to give you some home shock treatment, to see if I could jolt you back to your senses. But it didn't work. I'm so glad you're remembering things now."

"How many times have you seen me since Edinburgh?" Gog says, looking at Maire's bland face intently.

"Once," Maire says. "You know that. In those hills just after Edinburgh. We had a talk and I slammed the door on your hand. I admit you had irritated me. But also I thought it might make you better. Jules and I have been looking for you ever since. We've been up and down every track in the North of England. We've spent the past two days in Durham, waiting for you to turn up. We thought you might be coming through here, back to where you were working when we met. The murderer returning to the scene of the crime."

"Talking of that," Gog says, "you haven't been trying to kill me lately, I suppose?"

"I?" Maire says, with genuine astonishment in her voice. "Are you crazy?"

"Yes," Gog says, "I am a little crazy. Have you got a cat?"

"Not with me. I left Mishkin at home. I'm glad you remember him. He'll purr for pleasure."

"Is he black and hairy like a soft porcupine?"

"There, you *do* remember. That's what Miniver told me, when we visited him in desperation and he told us we'd just missed you at the university. So we followed you out of Durham, Jules and I. And here we are. Alone at last, if you don't count Jules. And chauffeurs aren't really human, are they?"

The car passes on like a great otter in the stream that is the road, cleaving its way forward without a jolt, seemingly buoyed up by water rather than springs and tyres.

"I've been dreaming you were trying to kill me, Maire. You and Jules. I suppose my memories of you are all mixed up with the war and old films."

"I've seen so many films on the war," Maire says, "I can never remember what I actually did or what Greer Garson pretended she did. Poor Gog! There, I'll get your head better soon. You'll see."

Maire pulls Gog's head down onto her lap, so that Gog is lying sideways on the seat of the car. He feels Maire's fingers stroking his forehead. They are cool and fluttering like the wings of a live plucked bird. His wariness of Maire grows numb and dissolves away.

He is half-asleep, when he feels Maire lay him out on his back on the seat. She kneels beside him on the floor of the car and begins to unlace his boots. When she has removed the boots, she puts his feet on the seat and pulls down the black blinds that are rolled up above each window of the car. When the interior is in partial darkness and hidden from outside watchers, she begins to undo Gog's trousers and to bare his belly. She strokes him softly, so that he can feel the lust rising in his groin. Then Maire hitches up her skirt and lies on top of Gog and begins kissing his face a hundred times over.

"Gog, Gog, Gog, Gog . . . I love you, you know. No, you don't know. But I do. I love you. Enormous you. Vulnerable you. Forgetful husband of mine."

Gog begins kissing the white face of the woman above him and pulling her body closer to his own. She licks his cheeks all over as though she were a cat showing affection, yet her tongue is not rough, but as smooth as a hot twist of wet silk. Then she begins to finger his belly and thighs. Soon she rises astride of Gog on her knees, slowly working her body onto his with each sway of the car, so that he can feel himself penetrate her deeply, deeply, oh warm and plucking, to the very knuckle of her womb, and he can see her face riding above him, wincing with lips apart, breathing quickly, nostrils flaring, below the black curve of the turban with its pearl navel.

With her palms, Maire presses on Gog's belly and chest, moving her body in little circles round its fixed hub. Then as the car lurches, she pulls at Gog's haunches with both her hands, digging in with her nails and crying out aloud. And Gog feels himself come with a jerking that makes him clutch at Maire's shoulders and draw her down on top of him.

Maire is lying on Gog, when he looks to his right and notices that the blind over the glass partition has rolled up. In the driving mirror, he sees the thin smile of Jules, who has adjusted the mirror to see the interior of the back compartment rather than the road. "The bastard," Gog says and rolls half-over, depositing Maire suddenly on the floor, while he yanks down the blind. "I hate being spied on. You and your bloody chauffeur. You sack him. I insist."

"You needn't be such a brute to me. Men always are, *after*. What was poor Jules doing?" Maire rises, aggrieved, off the floor.

"Playing Peeping Tom. Or is it Peeping Tomasina?"

"Well, the poor dear, it's so boring up front, all alone. I can't sack Jules. There's still a war on, don't you know? She's a treasure. I'll never find another like her, even if I ransack the whole of the A.T.S."

"Why does she have to dress like a man?"

"It makes her look more like a chauffeur, doesn't it?" Maire wipes herself with a handkerchief and begins pulling down her chessboard skirt. "We've got to pretend there are more men around than there really are, to forget the war which took you all away. That's what we call doing our little bit."

"I suppose so," Gog grumbles. He dresses himself and draws Maire beside him on the seat and kisses her. "That was very sudden, darling," he says. "You could have waited till we were in an hotel."

"Again, how like a man!" Maire says, smiling. "You only complain you've been seduced *after* it's all over. Anyway, I had to seduce you, to remind you how nice it was with me, so you'd stay with me. Instead of wanting to go back to the moors and leave me again. And I should think it ought to have been sudden. I haven't seen you in a year, with you dashing all the way to Berlin with the army."

"You've been virtuous for a whole year while I've been saving the country?" Gog asks. And then he looks into the ripe pout of his wife. And they both burst out laughing simultaneously at the absurdity of the question.

"Of course I haven't, darling," Maire says. "But I only love you."

She lets up the blinds of the car one by one, to show Gog more and more of the grimy brick terraces of a northern industrial town, with nothing but honest toil to make an excuse for itself. "You do get me to go to outlandish places," Maire says. "When the hospital finally tracked me down, I raced up with Jules, only to find you'd left the night before without permission. I've used up half my petrol coupons, and I simply can't flirt with yet another M.T.O. to fiddle more; every time they make a pass, you feel they're changing gears. I've more than half a mind, you know, not to let go of you again. It's the very devil finding you. You don't even stick to the roads. In fact, I may have said I'd loose you on the moors again. But don't you think, Gog angel, we should make it straight back to London? You do like sleeping with me, don't you?"

So Gog remembers one of Maire's tricks, tacking two questions together which have nothing to do with each other, yet demanding one answer. "Of course I love sleeping with you," Gog says. "But I really would like to get out at the Yorkshire moors, when we reach them." He yawns. "But perhaps not. We've got so much to talk about. If you talked for days, I'd still hardly know you. There are so many gaps in my mind. So perhaps I'll stay. Or you could tramp the moors with me."

"None of that, Gog Griffin," Maire says. "I've tried tramping with you. And frankly, I'd rather be raped by the Red Army than keep up with you on a hike." She plants firm kisses on each of Gog's eyes. "You're not to open them. You're dropping. Sleep, my giant friend. And when you've woken up, I'll chatter so much the holes in your mind will overflow."

"The moors," Gog insists. "Wake me at the moors. I want . . ." Yet he is so tired, the words become a mumble in his mouth and his head leans on the back of the seat and he falls into a dreamless sleep in the back of the black car.

He wakes to find Maire shaking him by the shoulder. It is night. Outside the car windows, Gog can dimly see the frozen breakers of the moors.

"Borrowby," Maire says. "The moors, as promised. The Hambleton Hills are to your left. Just what Dr. Griffin ordered. Now, do you seriously expect me to leave the car with you and spend a night in that howling patch of nothing?"

Gog rubs his eyes with his fist. "We could sleep here," he says, "and start tramping the moors in the morning."

"Not bloody likely," Maire says. "Whatever folly I may be prepared to commit, Jules likes her creature comforts. She'd give in her notice, if she didn't have a swansdown mattress and lavender sheets every night."

"Yours, I suppose," Gog insinuates.

"Are you trying to insult me?" Maire says. "I don't happen to sleep with my chauffeur."

"I've seen you," Gog states.

"How too Proustian! Are you sure you didn't call up some literary lesbian memories? Your mind is, after all, choc-a-bloc with fantasy."

"Which allows you to start again with a clean sheet, Maire. If only I knew what you'd really done."

"Nothing," Maire says. "I'm as innocent as a new-born lamb. I wasn't born yesterday, I was born today. And since you can't remember for *sure*, who's to judge me? I'm totally absolved."

"You could judge yourself."

"Then I'm bound to get off, aren't I, Gog? I've never felt guilty in all my life. I've always done just what I wanted to do. So I couldn't feel guilty, could I? We only feel *real* guilt – not that false religious kind – if we think we've missed a chance."

Gog laughs. "Perhaps ... Let's discuss it in the morning on the moors."

"I'm not coming," Maire says coldly. "Don't be a fool. Drive back to London with me now and start up your normal life."

"I'd rather tramp right now," Gog says.

"Why? It's pure self-indulgence."

"Hardly. It's a form of personal treatment. I do remember I always used to go off and hike, when I got into a bit of a brainstorm. And it cured me. This time, I reckon I need a good long hike."

"In London, my psychiatrist ..."

"Nature's the best one."

“Don’t be a fool, Gog.”

“Come with me, Maire. But I have to tramp.”

“I certainly won’t. I’m not going to catch my death, even if you are. Be reasonable. Come to London. Do you really love the Brontës more than me?”

“No. I must cure myself.”

“I’m trying to be patient. I know you’re ill, Gog. But you really would try the patience of a saint, and I’ve never pretended to be anything but a devil. Will you or will you not come with me?”

“I must walk,” Gog says.

“You’re forcing me to persecute you, Gog.” Maire’s eyes close and her white face hardens to wax. “God, martyrs bring it on themselves. Who wouldn’t crucify Paul upside down, after what he said about women? I’ve tried kindness on you and I’ve tried cruelty. And, dammit, you force me to be cruel. When I’m kind, you’re stubborn and intolerable and plain stupid. It’s only when you make me vicious that I can get any sense into your thick skull.”

“Thanks for the ride,” Gog says coldly. He puts his hand on the nearside door of the car. “I’ll see you in London.”

“If I’m waiting patiently, which I doubt,” Maire says. She takes the pearl pin from her turban and jabs its steel point into the leather seat.

Gog half-opens the car door. He shivers at the cold wind blowing in off the moors.

“If you take that step out of the car,” Maire says, “I’m not responsible for what I do in the future. I *won’t* be left flat. Not by *anyone*. You just think you can screw me and get out. You’ll see.”

“I must be by myself,” Gog says. “To cure myself. Or I’d stay.”

“Just step out,” Maire says, “and you’ll regret it.” She almost smiles. “Why not stay? It’s warm here. And there’s me.”

“I can take care of myself,” Gog says. “You can’t always sit above me in judgement, Maire. Even making love, you have to dominate, don’t you?”

Maire laughs. “Better be ruled by a clever woman than by

a stubborn fool, even if the fool happens to be yourself."

"Good-bye for the moment," Gog says and steps out. Just as he loses his balance, he hears a miaow of triumph and catches a glimpse of the face of the porcupine cat rising in the front compartment beside the grinning chauffeur. And then Gog's feet slip and he is slithering down a cliff of shale and stone, on the edge of which the car has been deliberately parked. A minor avalanche hammers about Gog's ears. And then, above the miaow and the lying Maire's harsh laughter, the bitter chuckle of water. And Gog is plunged into a shallow pool, his ankles cut open by the rocks at its bottom. He slips, falling full length into the icy pitch of the water and he hears Maire's voice calling, "Pride. Fall." Then the noise of the car moving away.

The wind slices through Gog's sodden clothes, seeming to cut between his ribs into his innards. He shivers uncontrollably, then stops shivering, too frozen even to shudder. He knows that he will freeze to death if he does not find some warmth. So he begins to stumble and climb back up the shale towards the road, to signal a passing car.

Gog stands for ten minutes beside the road, yet no vehicle comes. He feels himself chilling and losing feeling in his limbs. He must move. Dimly he can see the walls of a farmhouse set back some hundreds of yards from the road. So he begins to trudge towards the black blocks of human habitation, shuttered up against the night. Two stone walls block his way; but he clambers over their scraping edges.

When Gog reaches the farmhouse, he bangs on shutters and door, shouting, "Let me in, I'm freezing." He hears movement within, voices, a mutter of argument. But however loudly he shouts, no one will unbolt the door.

Cursing and sodden cold, he makes for a large barn, where he hopes to find some hay as a covering. The barn door is shut, but only with a spike. He removes the spike and enters the dark interior. It is warm within, meaty warm with the stench of dung and animal heat and hay. He walks a few paces forward, then meets with his knee the lying flank of a beast. He puts out his hand and feels the hot hide of a cow, which does not stir at his touch. Thankfully, Gog lies by the rump of the sleeping cow and gathers in warmth from the body of the animal. And eventually he sleeps on the trodden hay, his body curved round the beast that is drying him back to life.

At crow of rooster dawn, Gog wakes. The grey light dusts the rafters, the hanging leather harness, the cubes of baled hay, the pitchforks, the teeth of the rusting machinery for ploughing and reaping. Gog sees the dark flank couched above his body, and he lies grateful in the shadow of its warmth. Then he rises, stiffly, as the cow begins to shift and turn its face towards him. Only it is not a cow, but a heavy dew-lapped bull, looking at him with eyes blurry with rheumy lashes over the iron ring through its nose.

The bull that has spared Gog regards the man, whom it has not crushed nor gored in the night. Creases of puzzlement at its action ridge the white patch on its forehead, while slobbers of gratification at its own generosity run from its nose and the soggy corners of its mouth. It stares at Gog, then yawns cavernously, while Gog slowly backs away in fear. At the door of the barn, Gog has the grace to bow. "Thank you, good bull," he says, "for your patience." And so Gog quits the farmyard, leaving the barn door open in revenge, so that the bull may get out and perhaps gore the farmer, whose light in his bedroom now mocks Gog with its ray of comradeship denied.

Once out onto the moors, Gog takes a course towards the south-east, where the Hambleton Hills rise, their limestone and grit scarps as spume on the top of the choppy swell of the foothills, which run their breakers up the slopes, the wind making ripples in the bracken and heather, a little movement that cannot affect the still waves of the earthy sea. Above the moors, a buzzard is soaring; but, as Gog watches, it becomes a meteorite and plummets down, only breaking out its wings a thousand foot below to sweep again upwards. The buzzard plays its freefalling game thrice, and then, in an upsweep, it is attacked by a horde of ravens, angry at its presence above their nests in the limestone peaks. The ravens pierce in at the buzzard as if to skewer their large enemy on their beaks. The buzzard flaps its wide wings lazily ahead of its black pursuers. But when one of its foes dares to come too close, it turns on its back in mid-air, holding its talons towards the presumptuous raven, which sheers away in alarm.

Gog keeps his body moving up the hills, the hot blood in his veins drying out his moist clothes, until the sweat pricking through his skin makes his shirt moist again. He feels hunger nag at his belly, until the nagging becomes a gnawing obsession. Thoughts of tinned peaches fill his mind all the way to a saddle between the hills where the limestone crags give way to a swell of bracken and furze and gorse. So Gog crosses Boltby Moor and looks down past Old Byland to Ryedale, a green and unlikely trough in the high moor before Brontëland, with far copses of oak and ash breaking in occasional permanent spray.

Gog does not take the road to the village, preferring the hard slog through tuft and thorn, breaking bracken and edging past gorse. His eyes scan the sheep-tracks for manna from heaven to allay his hunger. Heaven remains indifferent, but man comes to his aid. There is a rustling and whimpering. Gog comes upon a rabbit, choking and plunging in the wire noose of a snare. His hunger makes the saliva of a beast of prey spurt in his mouth at the carnivorous desire for raw flesh, which Crook made him taste. But as he feels the warm life pulse beneath the brown fur of the rabbit and sees its small head twist up with rolling white eyeballs and its legs scrabble against his thighs, Gog pauses. He remembers the past night and the clemency of the bull. If an animal can show mercy, why not a human? So he changes his grip, slipping the wire noose off the rabbit's neck and letting it free, so that it can hop and burrow into a clump of gorse. A life for a life, but still no breakfast.

It is Gog's fortunate morning. As he reaches the road just beyond Old Byland, he finds the litter of a day-old picnic, crusts of bread thoughtfully wrapped in greaseproof paper for tidiness' sake, chicken bones not properly gnawed, even salt in a twist of blue paper. Gog scavenges for the starving belly that has become all of him. He bolts down everything, even to the last scrap of sinew adhering to a drumstick. His hunger is not satisfied, but allayed. He now crosses the little Rye river and walks through the cornfields on its far bank, breaking off the stalks and rubbing the ears between his rough palms and blowing the chaff away with his breath and chewing the raw corn grains into a mash between his teeth. So, filled with a surfeit of litter and fresh grain, Gog comes with a swollen belly to the ruins of the great abbey of Rievaulx.

The broken stones of the abbey skirt the valley's edge as it plunges into the Rye. Through the fallen arches of the cloister, Gog sees a throng of boys in straw boaters sitting on the grass, while rows of bright-coated ladies and cassocked priests sit in folding chairs behind them. They face a narrow stage, set up beneath a brown tent on the site of the old chapter house. The gutted west transept of the abbey church flanks the left side of the stage; three tall perpendicular windows without glass stare blankly down from the bald flat face of wrecked religion. The right side of the stage is bordered by the ruins of the monks' lavatory; the scrubbed stones crumble and totter above the rounded arch into the old washplace as they try to keep their square stance on the rain-scoured walls. Beyond the tent, the woody hills to the south roll upwards to the grey fells of cloud in the sky, indifferent to the roofless abbey, fallen, fallen, fallen, fallen from its high estate and sombre in its stone.

As Gog approaches, a pimply youth in grey flannels and a black blazer, his boater more of a soiled straw rim than a hat, presses a leaflet into Gog's hand. It announces that the Downforth Public School Players are presenting the medieval miracle play, *Everyman in Albion*, to the greater glory of God; the profits from the sale of the five shilling tickets will go to buy the rear turret of a bomber. Gog reaches his hand into his pocket to find a coin; but his pocket is naturally empty. So he withdraws his hand and shrugs, waving his arms. The boy cowers back, bowing Gog into the cloisters. Gog cannot understand the boy's reaction until he squints down and sees that he has forgotten to unclench his fist. He walks over to the back of the folding seats, and he looks past the flowered hats firmly pinned onto the permanent waves of the guardian mothers and past the greased strands of hair failing to cover the bald patches on the crania of the priests, too old or too holy to go to war, until he sees the boaters of the sitting boys above the fluffy down fluttering on their necks with all the soft promise of catkins in the breeze.

On the stage a youth appears, dressed in pieces of sacking that fail to suggest a doublet and hose. He stoops as if overcome by the woes of the world, or perhaps he has merely outgrown his strength. In the high-pitched boom that passes for clear enunciation, he declaims:

> "*A wretched wight, I, Everyman,*
> *Am here to tell ye all I can.*
> *All harken to me now . . .*"

With a stage effect worthy of the Book of Genesis, the sides of the tent shake mightily and a golden sun and a silver moon fall from the roof of the tent on strings, bouncing like yoyos, while a turreted canvas wall is wheeled onstage from the left with a screeching of wheels, its painted bricks infinitely more cheerful and credible than the rotting ruins of Rievaulx. Everyman shouts valiantly above the din:

> "*A strife I shall tell to you*
> *Of Magus and of Grim –*
> *Scratch, dog at cat and cat at him!*
> *Satan's dam she was their mother,*
> *And horrid hate between both brothers.*
> *Bloody born in woeful sin,*
> *Crouchit and scratchit twin at twin.*
> *They sorrows suffered many on,*
> *Each beating each through Albion.*"

A cross now shoots upwards between the floorboards of the stage, unfortunately in the spot where Everyman is standing, so that he is hoisted into the air astride the timber. He continues to declaim his lines, hanging onto the top of the cross with both hands to keep his balance.

> "*Ah! Lord Jesu, where may we go?*
> *Must we be in such wicked woe?*"

At this moment, a Jesuit priest in a black cassock rushes from behind the scenes and pulls Everyman down off his high seat, audibly whispering, "Get off that cross!" The shaken Everyman is then propelled forwards out of harm's way by the priest, who disappears as suddenly as he has come. The boy continues in a trembling tone:

"*Certes, Lord, we must make moan*
At Magus' rule so sorely borne.
Yet barns do burn and widows weep,
If Grim do rouse us from our sleep.
Thou art wise, Christ, who sayest this:
Peace is but in paradise."

No sooner does Everyman shut his mouth, when a fat boy, draped in a cassock far too long for him and wearing a gold crown of paper, comes galloping in, pretending to ride on a hobbyhorse. As he mimics the pawing of hooves, he treads on his cassock and takes a toss. Quickly recovering himself, he strikes a proud pose and tries a tentative strut or two, carefully hitching up his cassock about his bare calves as he does so. So Magus declares:

"*A prince I prance, prickit in pride,*
My sovereign Satan, at thy side!
Full faint and feeble creatures are,
Yet kith on kin he wageth war.
When Magus ruleth, none shall harm
The naked babe on mother's arm.
None shall murder, none shall steal,
Nor rust corrupt the commonweal.
Would ye be rich? Bow down to me,
Else all is grisly misery."

Everyman duly bows down before Magus, who puts his foot on Everyman's back and drops his cassock over Everyman's head. There is the thumping of a drum off-stage, and a tall boy dressed in a false brown beard and a red tablecloth clumps in on three-foot stilts. He tries to balance on the stilts without using both hands to steady their tops; but he immediately goes into such a desperate wobble that he has to catch a turret to stay upright. The turret bends alarmingly so that he staggers forwards and saves himself by grasping the cross. With one hand hooked round the beam, he beats his chest with the other, declaiming each word in a slow monotone:

" *Alarum! Alarum! tro ro ro ro!*
'Tis Grim, thump thump, come come, go go!
False Magus, while thy rule shall last,
Cometh the flood fleeting in full fast.
Drown dead crops and drown dead men,
On fowl and beast a great murrain.
Magus, avaunt!"

With Grim's final word, he makes a mighty gesture with both hands and topples forward off his stilts, crashing down on Magus and the bowed Everyman, who yells, " Bugger it." The Jesuit rushes on with a cane and whips Everyman off-stage, saying, " And ten thousand Hail Marys and a mouthwash." Magus and Grim pick themselves off the boards and square up to each other, trading insults as sweetly as if they were exchanging cricket scores, and grappling with each other as though they were loving each other up. The dialogue runs:

MAGUS

" *Fly, else I trow*
The blood shall flow bright on thy brow!

GRIM

" *Lose thy hands from off my ears!*
Take thy fingers from my hairs!

MAGUS

" *What, curst knave, art not down yet?*
I trow to lie thee at my feet.

GRIM

" Rascal, wouldst thou scratch and bite?

MAGUS

" Yea, marry, will I, if thou dost smite."

Grim now swings at Magus with a straight arm and catches him a clip on the ear, for the poor Magus is so tangled in his cassock that he cannot duck in time. The result is that Magus bursts into sudden tears and runs off-stage, finally tripping over the hem of his robe so that he literally falls into the wings. Grim struts about the stage and a pasteboard trumpet descends from the sky on another string, knocking the sun awry in its path. Grim seizes upon the trumpet and pretends to blow it. Off-stage, the scratching of a gramophone is heard, followed by the music of a wild ukelele. Grim, annoyed by the accompaniment, makes a valiant attempt at realism by pursing his lips and producing a rasping noise, followed by a halloo of " Tarrah, tarrah." Then one of those exquisite thirteen-year-old boys, who make English public schools a heterosexual's hell by the enticement of their pink lankness and blue-eyed blondness and segregated innocence, wriggles onto the scene in a sequined shimmy dress from the twenties. The Jesuits have allowed Lechery no breasts for decency's sake; but they cannot stop the dress from being too tight on his rump, which waggles delicately behind him like two blancmanges in a satin bag. Batting his eyelids in the style of a vamp and chucking Grim under the chin, the moppet declaims in a cracked treble:

" Come to me,
Lechery,
Je vous prie,
  Sir, I say.
In licking and lust,
He shall rust –
Till death's dust
  Do him to clay."

Grim blushes at such a straight proposition and seems ready to go along; but another boy, supporting a cushion with both his hands under the front of his purple shirt, rushes on late for his cue, then remembers the part that he is meant to play and waddles exaggeratedly, sticking out the cushion on his stomach like the bow-wave of a vast belly. And Gluttony speaks in a deep voice that would be bass if it did not sound like a tenor drowning in the depths:

> "*Ya, ya, man,*
> *Drink red wine,*
> *Eat fat swine,*
> *Swell belly.*
> *In hell shall sweat*
> *He who doth eat*
> *Too much at meat*
> *His soul to slay.*"

When he has finished his lines, Gluttony fiddles with his hands to unstring a goblet, tied round his neck; his belly, now unsupported, falls on the floor. Gluttony hands Grim the goblet and begins stuffing his belly back inside his shirt; Grim quaffs great draughts of air from the goblet, making jolly enjoying noises, as Lechery paws him timidly well above the belt to avoid Jesuit anger. Magus enters again, his cassock now securely hitched up by a cord about his waist. He carries a noose of rope in his hand, and, creeping up behind Grim, he slips the noose over his head and neck and pulls tight. Grim immediately begins choking to death, while Lechery says, " Round his arms, you fool." The noose is unloosened and put round Grim's arms, while Magus declaims:

> "*Mickle the worse, wail and woo,*
> *Thou shalt thy rebellion rue!*
> *With folly full from Envy's school,*
> *Must peasant madmen make to rule?*
> *I'll whip thee sore!*"

As Magus raises his arm to beat Grim, Grim backs away, pulling Magus after him, since Magus has forgotten that he has used the other end of the cord which binds Grim to hold up his own cassock. Both boys begin tugging at the rope which ties them together, declaiming in turn:

GRIM

"*Mercy, pardee!*

MAGUS

"*I'll break thy bones till thou shalt die!*"

While the tug o' war of life and death continues between Magus and Grim, there is a creaking from the top of the tent and a pair of sandals appears, dangling beneath the brown canvas that cuts off the view some twenty foot above the stage. Magus and Grim and the two Sins look upwards in horror and wait without speaking. After some thirty seconds, the sandals descend another two feet, until the waist and legs of a boy are visible; his knees are covered by a white robe and are locked about a knotted rope. He remains stuck and lopped off half-way down; but his voice sounds heroically from beyond the canvas top of the proscenium:

"*Ye peevish pests, patience I pray!*
Hark to the horn of Judgement Day!"

As there is no sound from the wings, Grim improvises his "Prrrrp, tarrah, tarrah," several times to prove that Gabriel blows no mean trumpet. Above him, the bottom half of the white-robed boy continues:

"*Christ cometh . . .*"

With a screech of pulley, the boy suddenly drops ten foot into sight, oscillating fearsomely on the end of the rope, twirling this-away, thataway and hanging on for dear life. Lechery hitches up his dress above his pubescent thighs, scrambles up Magus and leaps onto Grim's shoulders. Sitting astride the tall boy, Lechery can just reach the feet of the swinging Christ, and catching them, he steadies their owner by this superb display of team spirit and pulling together. Thus Christ, standing on the hands of Lechery, at last faces the audience in a state approaching equilibrium, and declaims:

> "*Christ cometh to save all this isle*
> *From grisly Grim and Magus vile . . .*"

Gog looks at the white-robed boy on the rope and suddenly sees himself twenty-five years before, his long square chin beardless and soft, his spreading lips blooming with ignorance, his broad nose not yet rough with age, his cheeks rounded rather than fleshy, his hair long and loose instead of short and stuck down, his body lean and disjointed, not set by the fat and the purposes of the years. And the boy on the rope sees the great Gog standing at the back of the rows of folding chairs, and his eyes widen and he shouts, "Father," and he falls off the rope, knocking down Lechery and Grim and landing with a soft crash on his head on the boards.

The whole audience swings to stare at Gog, some hundred faces looking at the author of this final catastrophe, which has overtaken the miracle play of *Everyman in Albion*. And Gog, the father, turns and runs away out of the green and fallen cloisters of Rievaulx, as two Jesuits pull the curtains of the tent closed on the drama of chaos. And Gog flees up the way towards the south, leaving the road for the high bareness of Scawton Moor, overlooking Ryedale. And he turns to look back at the ruins of the abbey. And behold, the audience on the green square of the cloisters is vanished away, and the brown tent between the west transept and the lavatory is struck and gone utterly, and only the grey ruins sit in their squares and lines, a regular labyrinth that gives no clue to the puzzle of half an hour ago.

And Gog wonders if he has seen his own son, forgotten until now in the crannies of his brain, his own son playing Christ in a miracle play for his public school. Or he wonders whether he has seen a vision of his own past in the ruins of Rievaulx, when he himself once came down from the heavens on a pulley and had a vision of parental authority and fell down and concussed himself. And as he looks down at Rievaulx, the squares and oblongs of stone walls yawn at him with their roofless mouths. And he knows that the past is the past and cannot be checked. What is remembered is. Whether it were fact or fantasy, doing or dream, memory makes it history. And if there is evidence remaining from time gone, letters or documents or other witnesses, letters may be forged and documents may be untrustworthy and other witnesses may suffer from mass hallucination. Each man carries his own past within his own skull. That is the truth for him and there is no outside appeal nor confirmation. Gog as a boy or Gog as a father, what does it matter who he was or is, what does it matter to the great chain of the living and the dead, which begets Gog after Gog after Gog, world without end, amen.

XVI

Fire has purged the slopes of the moor, spreading its black absolution over turf and root and thicket. Low tufts of dead grass raise their bristles like old paint-brushes embedded in an abandoned builder's yard. Briers are reduced to twists of wire, gorse bushes to burned splinters. Powder fine as dirty concrete rises at each tread of Gog's boots. Beyond the dark blodge of the limits of the fire, runs of ochre pebbles make channels among the heather and felled trunks, weathered into silver pipelines by the wind. Gog makes his way towards a ruined tower near the crest of the moor, where ivy has spread its green-gloved hands up the stone walls and over the trunk of the nearby oak.

Gog rests with his back against the tower wall, lolling in the staccato peace of the day, where only birdsong and the rustling creatures of the undergrowth punctuate the silence. Then, in front of the drowsy blinking of his eyes, he seems to see a troop of cavalry dressed in iron breastplates and round iron helmets as it wheels over the crest of the hill and disappears. Gog stares after the horsemen; but they are gone. "Roundheads?" Gog says to himself, thick lips mumbling. "Roundhead cavalry. In sixteen hundred and forty-four, Cromwell went to Marston Moor." And Gog laughs to recollect this doggerel of childhood that tells of King Charles and Prince Rupert and the Cavaliers routed by Cromwell's troopers in most uncivil war.

When he has rested, Gog strolls up the gentle swell of the ground to the height of the moor. But as he crosses the ridge, he finds that the Roundhead horsemen are really charging the massed peasants, ranked round their peacock Dukes as dun and earthy as furrows. To Gog's left, the Cavaliers gallop behind Prince Rupert, black curls and white feathers flying, gilt spurs and bright blue doublets a garish assault on the discretion of the moor. By Rupert's horse, a small black-and-white dog snaps and yaps, Boy, Boy, not yet sliced in two by a Roundhead sabre, but gambolling along in the best chase of all, the hunt of men.

"Cut!" the voice of distant rage sounds faintly through the wind. And Gog turns to see a round bald figure in black britches and a brown hacking jacket jumping up and down with fury, while the minions grouped about him all begin running towards Gog and the operators leeched to their great cameras fall back like ack-ack gunners at the wail of the all clear.

The minions in their uniforms of grey trousers and canvas jackets and caps hustle Gog off towards the bald man, who has stopped jumping up and down and is tearing the tin of a megaphone into strips as though he were shredding silver paper.

"You schmuck!" the bald man says in an accent that seems to be a mixed cocktail of Viennese and Brooklynese with a dash of grated British. "You have cost me two thousand pounds. That wasted take cost two thousand pounds. Is any man worth two thousand pounds? No. Except me, who am worth millions, many millions. You know, of course, who I am. Hon Sternheim. You have heard, *perhaps*, of Hon Sternheim, the greatest director in the history of motion pictures."

The minions' heads nod like poppies in the breeze, while memory stirs lazily in Gog's mind as he watches the bald and oblong skull, the eyes that are mere gashes at right angles to the straight nose, the mouth as fat as cruelty, the chin blunted at its tip, the obese body strutting as only a small man's body can strut who seeks to dominate. Gog can now close his eyes to see the figure striding in jackboots, monocled and leering, across the screen of his projected memories.

"Von Sternheim," Gog says, opening his eyes again. "The man you letch to loathe. Von Sternheim."

The greatest director puffs like a turkeygobbler and saliva sprays out his mouth. "*Hon* Sternheim, you Frankenstein! I am Mr. *Hon* Sternheim. Ever since the war. Do you think, fool, that I could remain *Von* after Hitler had raped my beloved Vienna? I am Mr. *Hon* Sternheim. And you will pay me the respect my honourable title deserves. Ach, Vienna!" Like bath-water from a loofah, tears suddenly begin to roll down the seamy cheeks of the greatest director. "The cafés, the coffees, the Imperial Guard! The cream cakes, the Habsburgs, the corsets! The frauleins, the steins, the wines! How should you know? When I was Prince von Sternheim . . . but you will have seen *Deaf Husbands, Dumb Wives, Crippled Children, Twisted Princesses, Queen Paralysis*. My classic movies of dear Vienna, where the strong and the straight and noble once ruled and loved the Austrian Empire . . . Ah, King Charles!"

Gog turns with the greatest director to see a withered vine of a man hobbling towards them on crutches. His right foot is encased in a floppy black boot with an elegant pointed toe; his left foot is a club one. His left hand wears a dashing elbow-length suède glove, his right hand wears a hook. Below the broad crown of his plumed velvet hat and below his long ringlets, his chin rests on the curious hump that protrudes from the middle of his chest.

"How well you look today, King Charles!" the greatest director rasps. "Too well! *Make-up!*" At his shout, a swarm of girls in overalls cluster about the twisted king, powderpuffs and combs at the ready. "I want bags under his eyes. Make them *portmanteaux*! And a scar at the end of his moustache.

Age him! I want him to gain twenty years in five minutes." In a moment, the King is beset by the horde of cosmeticians, he is hidden behind a waving bush of etching and plucking and stencilling and applying arms. "My dear Charles," the greatest director purrs, "remember, you are *suffering* for the woes of your people. That villain Cromwell, with all the gold of London in his saddle-bags, makes war on the King and his country folk. And you *suffer!* My God, how you *suffer!* I want that suffering to show."

Here Gog dares to interrupt. "But King Charles the First was surely a healthy upstanding man . . ."

The greatest director whirls round on one heel, his hands on his hips. "If this was Vienna, I would *whip* you. Insolence! Do you think a painter can capture the reality that I, Hon Sternheim, can show in a movie? What can you show on flat canvas? A tinted photograph! While I, I capture the essence of the man, the *suffering* King, Charles the Martyr, crucified for the people and the good old days. *Ach*, in cinema, we must show the inside on the outside, portray the warpings of the soul." His hand sweeps out to include the armies on the barren moor. "You might say, why Scawton Moor? Why not the real Marston Moor? But have you been there? No. It is all cows now, meadows and pretty hedges. It looks like a postcard, not a moor. But this, this is a wild moor, as Marston was once a wild moor. This is more like the original than the original. And that is film, my friend, that is the truth of the movie. We make people, we make places more like the original than the original. For the moving picture convinces more than any place, any person, any event there ever was. And if we convince more, we are then more true. We deny time, we resurrect the lost, we recreate what never has been. Do you know, there were *no* steps in Odessa? But now, because of that little Eisenstein, the guidebooks of Odessa, they have to put a cross on the map saying, 'The steps were once *there*!'" The greatest director pauses for a moment, overcome with philosophy, then he commands Gog, "So put on your peasant coat, my giant schmuck. Pick up your pike. And go and stand over there, in the front rank of Good King Charles's foot soldiers. You're a big man and this is a big picture. And when you die, you can be proud of one thing. Once, the greatest director of them all, Hon Sternheim, talked to you, a mere extra, of the art which he invented and which shall die with him."

So the greatest director rears up on tiptoe and strikes a pose, his chin cleaving the breeze. And the minions say ah and yes with the soft assent of moving grasses. And Gog is taken away by the wardrobe lady and fitted out in a smock (made of brown paper) and a pair of cloth britches (made of nylon parachutes) and an iron helmet (made of cardboard) and a wooden pike (made of wood by some error). This war material, when filmed, apparently resembles the real objects more than the real objects do. With time and reality so well suspended, Gog finds himself drawn up in the front ranks of the King's Men waiting for the clapper-boy to rap his boards together and start the Ironsides charging over the crest of the moor again.

By Gog's side, three extras stand, leaning on their pikes. They are the dregs of war, the rejects from national conscription, the epitome of the unfit, a long man and a short man and a tall man. Yet, like soldiers before a battle, they talk of war and wages.

"John Bates mate," the long one says to the short one, "it must be time for a tea-break."

"I think it be," the short one says. "But we won't get a cuppa before the take's over."

"The next take won't be the last take," the tall one says. "We shall never see the end of it." He turns to Gog. "Hullo, mate."

"Hullo," Gog says.

"Are you in the union?" the tall one says.

"Mr. Hon Sternheim engaged me," Gog answers.

"That Nazi? We'll see what the shop steward says about that, if you haven't got your cards. He'll call a strike, he will. We'll down tools."

"Down pikes in face of the enemy?" Gog says, smiling. "I don't know what Sternheim will make of that."

"He didn't want to hire us," the short man says. "But the union made him. Trash, he called us. Refuse. Just 'cause we couldn't get in the real army. Give him a whole bleeding Panzer Division, and he still wouldn't be happy. Worse than Hitler, he is, though he calls himself a Yank."

"He seems pretty much like you and me," Gog says. "He may get a bigger wage, but then he's got more to worry about. After all, he's got to act like the master, or you won't fight the way he wants. And if it's all a flop, he suffers. You don't. He's probably more scared than you are about the outcome."

"I don't care how shit scared he is," the long man says. "I bet he's not as insecure as us. We don't know where the next battle's coming from. The good shooting weather's nearly over. They don't want camera fodder in winters. So how do we eat, then?"

"You don't have to be here," Gog says. "You're not conscripted. Perhaps you enjoy making films like he does. I think he would not wish himself anywhere but where he is."

"Well, why doesn't he shoot a solo film?" the short man sneers. "Starring Sternheim, directed by Sternheim, written by Sternheim, produced by Sternheim, one long continual passionate close-up of Sternheim kissing Sternheim. It's all his fault. If blokes like him didn't offer us occasional jobs, we'd have to settle for regular ones, wouldn't we?"

"Perhaps the Battle of Marston Moor will be a bloody good film," Gog says, "and you'll have helped to make it."

"Marston Moor?" the long man says. "I thought we were waiting here for Agincourt. Day-for-night shooting. And whoever wrote the script, give Shakespeare a credit, he's box-office. I was just going to shout, For God, King Harry and St. George, and all that."

"No," the short man says, "it's the Wars of the Roses. Get you confused, all these battles do. Here today, gone tomorrow, as they say. You never know what side you're on. One day I was a Saracen, next day a Crusader. You don't even know who's winning or losing. It doesn't matter, really. You just go on slugging and nobody tells you what for. One week it's the Vikings you're clobbering, then the Normans. Then the Frenchies, then the Micks. Of course, it's mainly Jerries and Japs we clobber now; but me, I prefer this costume stuff. Except it's always the same old costume. They've only got two peasant dresses in the wardrobe from the Dark Ages to Waterloo. If it's not a smock, it's bare toes and a sack. Still, the action's always the same. Waggle your cudgel when His Royal Mightiness yells at you, step out of the horses' way, and don't count your pay-packet, it'll give you the screaming dib-dabs. Whoever wins these battles, it ain't us. We just do what we're told. Smear on the ketchup, count our bruises, lay around for the final corpse shot, then pack up and go home to starve, till the next epic rolls round. And don't ask why."

Through a megaphone, a minion yells, "Action!" And the pikemen lift their weapons in a rattle and hold them forwards. And the Ironsides come charging over the hill and canter towards the King's Foot. And Gog finds his hands trembling as the armoured men on their heavy horses loom up like bobbing tanks, their progress as inevitable as if they were on tracks rather than hooves. "Run, you fools, run," the greatest director shouts, and the pikemen drop their pikes and turn tail and begin jog-trotting backwards. Gog stands alone and facing the enemy for a moment, hero and afraid, as the flanks of the horses of the godly Ironsides part on either side of him like the Red Sea waves at the command of de Mille. Then a Puritan captain leans down from his saddle, cursing blue murder. "Bugger off, you big nit! Who do you think you are, Douglas Fairbanks?" And a clout on the side of his head sends Gog reeling and staggering along with the horses, pursuing the fleeing King's Men in the ranks of the New Model Cavalry, backed by the gold of the City to shatter Court and people, to confirm the rule of London.

This charge should end the battle of Marston Moor. But on the flank of the Ironsides, a fox whisks past in a rusty puff of hairy wind. By its tail it drags along a yelping string of hounds, speckled in brown and white and black. A horn sounds (not in the script) for the counter-attack of the Cavaliers. And though the official King's horsemen are streaming away in their gay doublets over the hill, a shock troop of mounted redcoats out of the wrong century and the wrong battle come charging in on the Roundheads' flank, for King, for County and for St. Reynard. With a yoicks and a tally-ho, the Yorkshire Hunt rams the

Roundhead charge and sends it into chaos and milling, rearing and rout, stalling and stampeding. In the maelstrom of hooves and boots, with whinnies and curses clapping like thunder and lightning in his ears, Gog lumbers out of the ruckus, climbs over a hedge and through a ditch, to lie hidden and safe beyond the fray where the bloodlust of the shires is once again wrecking all the best-laid plans of cameras and money and reasonable men.

There is a rustle in the patch of nettles behind Gog, and he looks round to see the muzzle of the fox staring at him out of the stinging weeds. The fox looks at the man and the man looks at the fox and each decides to leave the other be. But at that moment, through a hole in the hedge, the hounds begin to scramble before they fall yelping into the ditch, Butcher and Bellman and Bugler and True, Slasher and Snitcher and Scurvy and Toast, Trumpet and Trusty and Jorrocks and Blight, the twelve pooches of the apocalypse scratch and scrabble their way from the depths to bark havoc behind the fox and to flush their quarry out of the nettles on his travels again. Gog only has time to glance at the sky above the hedge before it is filled with four-legged bellies big as convex parachutes sailing over the twigs or merely clearing their path straight through the obstacle. Clods of mud fly like a cluster of soft grenades, hooves rip open the sod like booby-traps. With his position totally overrun by the hunt, Gog only wishes he had a foxhole to cower within. But all he can do is to curl up like a bristle-less hedgehog, his knees to his chin and his elbows tucked in and his hands clasped about his bowed head. Gog would even pray for safety, if he were not afraid that opening his mouth would lead to him gargling a spurt of mud.

The assault seems miraculously to pass over Gog's body without doing more hurt to him than soiling his smock from neck to hem. He is about to uncurl, when he hears a last and tardy horse galumph into position the other side of the hedge. The harsh voice of a Valkyrie shouts the winged command of the gods, "Hup, you bastard!" and the horse blunders straight through the thickest part of the hedge and collapses in the ditch. A great scarlet cuckoo in black bowler and jodhpurs is jounced from her saddle-nest and lands with the force of the yolk of a roc's egg on the crouching Gog, timorous as any Sinbad. The wind is smacked from his lungs, the senses scattered from his skull, and the neighing of the foundered horse bids him a sweet good-afternoon.

Gog wakes to see the scarlet cuckoo squatting beside him, smacking his cheek systematically with her black-gloved hands. Then she bends down her ripe, heavy face with the squeezed-grape veins of good living standing out in her full aged cheeks, and she nips the lobe of Gog's ear with teeth which seem more suitable for the bit than the toothbrush. Gog squawks and sits up, gasping for air.

"Keep your teeth to your own mouth," he says.

The woman lifts her large nose high and hoity-toity as a true lady, who can do as she pleases because even if she were found stark naked pissing in a Bible, the people would only close the holy pages reverently to preserve the mark of the true lady.

"How dare you speak like that, Gog," the scarlet bird-of-passage declares, "to your own *mother*!"

The harsh and hensure tone of the woman's voice stirs a reflex in Gog's left arm, so that he crooks his elbow over his head as if expecting a rap from her knuckles on his skull for some childish crime.

"Mother," Gog says softly, not daring to question, yet equally afraid of binding himself to the stranger by such a lifeline.

"Your mother Merry," the ripe lady says. "And don't you be so insolent as to pretend not to know me! Everyone says I don't look a day older than when we last met. When was that? About ten years, wasn't it? Well before the war."

Gog looks for a sign of himself in the heavy and creased features of the woman beside him. She is still handsome in her sixties in the glossy, spongy way of a pumpkin left to ripen a little too long, a pumpkin which some near hallowe'en will deliver into the hands of small boys to disfigure with penknives into the mask of monster old age. Yet in the jut of bone over brow, in the spread mouth and puffy nose, Gog can catch a glimpse of himself bloated and unsexed by food and years.

So Gog bends forwards in duty and obedience and kisses the hunting lady on the veins in her left cheek. "Mother," he declares.

"What are you doing," Gog's mother Merry says, "dressed in that ridiculous smock? I never thought any son of mine would dress up as a girl, and a filthy girl, too. You look just like a pregnant peasant."

"I've been playing a part in that film you interrupted, Mother," Gog says. "I was one of the King's men."

"Well," Merry says, "it's a change to hear of you on the right side for once. Has the war knocked all those silly pinkish notions out of you? I suppose fighting alongside our ally *Ivan* showed you just what a terrible fellow a Red is."

"The Russians," Gog says, "did win the war for us, you know. They bore the brunt of the fighting. I'm just the same, Mother. On my way to London back to Maire, I suppose. And to see how the Labour government's doing. The people ruling at last."

"Sometimes I wonder who was the bastard," Merry says, "you or that brother of yours. You talk such utter rot I can't have given birth to you. You're somebody else's child." Then Merry's face suddenly breaks up into a hundred wrinkles that run rapidly as ripples over her cheeks, so that an irresistible twitch of imitation breaks up Gog's own set face into a smile. "Cat and dog, aren't we, Gog my son? Always were. You're your mother's boy all right. Just as stubborn, always going your own way like her. But how you *can* talk of the people ruling when a member of the present misgovernment calls people like your mother *lower than vermin*, I simply can't imagine. Unless you're going up to Westminster to give them a good black eye from me."

"I'll give them a pat on the back from you," Gog says laughing. "What was that about my *brother*? Our ship hit a mine on the way back home and I was fished out of the water and my memory's still drying out. So you'll have to forgive me and remind me. My brother? He's not called . . . Magog, is he?"

Merry laughs. "You haven't wholly forgotten, have you? Though I must say, it was a bit of a shock, finding you didn't even recognize your own mother. My little slip-up and your love-a-duck of a stuck-up half-brother, he's called Magnus. Though you always call him Magog. You told me all about him last time we met. You'd seen him for the first time and he was already a pompous little ass on the make. Not like you and me, my dear. I'm afraid we're a bit too much of the earth, earthy. Or of the county, county. But Magnus, he's on his way up. Of course, he wouldn't see *me*, his real mother. He pretends he belongs to those stuck-up Ponsonbys who adopted him. Though, my dear, what I don't know about the Leicestershire Ponsonbys! It makes my little peccadilloes look like the vicar's sermon to the young ladies' finishing school. But Magnus, he would rather die than admit he was born the wrong side of the blanket. Though I can't see that it matters what side of the blanket you're born on so long as you *are* born. I mean, it can be very distinguished to be a bastard, depending on whose bastard you are. And Magnus's dad owned half Shropshire, or was it Worcestershire, I can never get those western counties straight. I read in a book that mathematics prove we're all descended from William the Conqueror, which makes us all bastards. I really can't see what Magnus is fussing about."

"I'll see him when I get to London," Gog says, "and tell him not to fuss. I always thought I'd find Magog there."

"He's in the Civil Service now. Doing terribly well, or so my spies tell me. Not that you do so badly yourself, since you inherited all that lolly from your great-aunt. I must say, Gog, thanks for that allowance which comes in every month, though I bet that mean wife of yours doesn't know about it. You're a good son. It's nice not being a charity case any more. After all, though I'm pretty spry for my years, I can't go on and on shaking rich boy-friends like conkers down from the trees. It's nice to depend on my son, for a change, instead of on some old beast who doesn't know the difference between his stable and my bed. Ever since that allowance began coming in, I've been able to pick and choose a bit. And didn't some of those old Oliver Hardys get a thumb in their eye! They used to say there was a test to join the Inner Circle of the Hunt. You had to be able to ride three miles, drink three bottles of champers, and ride me three times in three hours. So they said. Now my reputation's better than Queen Victoria's. And why? Because I can *afford* to be discreet, my dear. We're all sinners, Gog, but a steady income draws a blind over the bedroom windows."

Gog looks at his mother's rueful, sensual, sagging face and feels a swell of love go out to this last redoubt of frank reaction and open lust. "You know, Merry," he says, "you're a marvellous lady to have for a mother."

"The very worst mother a child could have," Merry laughs. "That's what I've always been told. And that's why you love me, isn't it?"

Gog is about to fling his arms round the rosy rogue who gave birth to him, when he feels his right palm driven excruciatingly into the sod. "Will you kindly ask your horse to move?" he says politely to Merry. "It's treading on my hand."

"Satiricon!" Merry says sharply to her fat gelding. "Stop shaking my son by the hoof." She rises and pulls her horse to one side, while Gog delicately massages the back of his hand and feels his finger-bones one by one to see if they are still whole under the imprint of the iron horse-shoe.

"My father's dead, of course," Gog says. "Was it the First War?"

"A dirty murdering bog Papist shot him in the back of the head in Dublin," Merry says, "God rot his soul. I'd have been a respectable woman, but for that. You and your wars. They're not a matter of men against men, you know. Wars are really fought when men are fed up with being run by their respectable wives in peace. So they up and murder each other, till there're too few men to go around and the respectable women have to become whores to get a chance at what's left. There were times I'd rather have been dead like your dad than what I had to be to get a bit of *paté* on my melba toast."

Here Merry puts one foot in the stirrup and tries to swing herself onto the back of her gelding. "Give me a hand, boy," she calls, and Gog shoves her astride by hoicking her free instep up on his shoulder, so that she can throw her other leg across the saddle, clipping his ear on the way. "Call in at Cropley Hall down the road," Merry says, "and you can have a bath and a change and a good long natter with your old mother. And I'll tell you how Arthur's doing. It's been a long time, too long . . ."

Merry's words break off in mid-flow as a hare gets up a few yards away and jinks off crazily through the brambles and feathery tall grass. A glaze drops over Merry's eyes as if they were two balls of sudden porcelain, the toes of her riding-boots both kick out sideways like a jumping-jack's before falling back with full spurpoint into the gelding's flanks, and the horse bolts off breakneck down Scawton Moor after the hare. In less than a minute, flippety bobtail and bowler hat and flying mane have all disappeared into a fir grove so that Gog can follow after them slowly southwards, wondering if the saucers of torn turf at his feet were thrown up by hooves vanished a moment or a memory ago.

XVII

"Pegs, kind gentleman. Or shall I tell your fortune, sir?"

So the gypsy girl speaks to Gog as he stands outside the ruins of Byland Abbey, with its arches broken into giant keyholes and the twin stone stumps above its entrance propping up the grey and closed sky. The toppling of time has turned one of the two taller remains of the Christian church into an Egyptian obelisk, the other into a minaret, so that the centuries seem to have confused the religions in their decline and fall. Gog turns away from the abbey to the speaker plucking at the sleeve of his paper smock. He sees a tall and thin girl, her black hair agley down to her hips, her skin swarthy as a toad, her soiled red silk blouse ripped carefully as a stripper's to hint at bare breast and belly, her legs naked under a white draggled petticoat, and her eyes bold and black and slightly askew, so that she seems simultaneously to be staring at Gog and signalling to an enemy just behind his back.

"I can't cross your palm with silver," Gog says. "I haven't got a penny and I've lost my clothes."

"You're from the film, sir, on the moor. Take me with you, sir, and I'll ask no silver to tell your dukkeripen." She seizes Gog's hand and begins reading his palm as if a litany were written there for her to chant. "God bless you, pretty gentleman, much trouble will you have to suffer and much water to cross. But never you fear, pretty gentleman, you shall be fortunate at the end, and those who hate you shall take off their hats to you, if you take a Romany chi with you as your mort to the land of the gorgeous gorgios by the Western Sea." The gypsy girl gives up her chant and turns her shrewd left eye upon Gog's staring two eyes. Her voice suddenly acquires a transatlantic twang. "That means, brother, take me with you to Hollywood, and I'll add the noughts onto your contract. That's what the stars say."

Gog begins to protest. "I'm hardly anything to do with films. I'm an extra. I was only taken on today. Really I'm on my way to London ..." But before his explanations can explain anything, the gypsy girl claws open the rip in her blouse until both her brown breasts are bare to the breeze, then hurls herself scratching and writhing closer into Gog's arms, so that Gog does not know whether she is assaulting his virtue or defending her own. He is not puzzled for long. She lays back her head, opens her gullet, and looses a howl for help.

As if waiting for the signal, a sleek horse pulling a yellow caravan brighter than the sun appears out of a hidden lane. The mumping mugger on the driver's seat of the caravan appears in no hurry. He lets the horse amble along until it reaches the scene of the supposed attempt at rape; then he stares down at the bare-breasted Gog and girl, for she has now clawed off Gog's paper smock and is trying to remove the skin off his ribs in strips with one set of nails, while the other set digs into his back so that he cannot fend her off.

"Would you mind," Gog says, "getting your lady off my chest?"

The mumping mugger hitches the reins of the horse round a post on the driver's seat, rises slowly, spits in one hand, rubs it on his leg, spits in the other hand, rubs it on his buttock, lowers himself off the caravan, walks slowly towards Gog, raises his right hand, and swings it across with the force of a thrown discus. Only the blow does not strike Gog; it smashes the girl's cheek, so that she spins ten yards sideways and lands in a heap by the horse.

"Thank you," Gog says, "for that helping hand." But his gratitude is a little chastened by the appearance of his saviour. The mumping mugger is nearly Gog's own size, burly and black with wind and sun, his face lumpy with permanent bruises, his snub nose cleft at the tip like a split plum. He wears a brown oily cap rammed over his frizz of curls, a red kerchief knotted tightly over his Adam's apple, yellow braces over his checked shirt, and gumboots over his corduroy trousers that seem more mud than cloth and are held up for double safety by a brass-buckled belt. He takes off his cap and dashes it violently on the ground. Gog, conciliatory, bends and picks up the cap and restores it to its owner, who wrenches it violently from his hand and dashes it on the ground yet again.

"Do I bash yer," the mumping mugger mutters, pausing with menace between each word, "or does yer marry her?"

It is a good question. Gog cannot decide which is the more painful alternative. So he decides to temporize. "I'm married," he says, grateful for once to Maire.

The mumping mugger becomes even more violent at this remark. He jerks off the handkerchief from round his neck, crumples it into a squashed tomato, and throws that on the ground. "Don't chaffer," he says. "I says, do I bash yer or does yer marry her? I ain't asking yer if yer's got a mort. Does yer marry *her*?"

"Perhaps she's married too?" Gog suggests.

Indigo with rage, the mumping mugger pulls loose his yellow braces, rips off his checked shirt and throws that on top of the cap and handkerchief. His chest looks like a coal-face after blasting. "I'm married to her meself. I says, do I bash yer . . ."

"Bash him," the girl says, one hand to her bruised cheek and the other holding her torn blouse together and her rolling, evil eye fixed for the moment on Gog.

" But if she's married to you," Gog says, " how can she marry me?"

One by one, the mugger unbuttons his hanging braces. He is about to dash them also to the ground, when Gog takes them from his hand and lays them tidily on top of the pile of his clothes.

" If yer marry under an hedge," the mugger says, " yer can marry all yer please. Now will yer marry her or . . ."

" Before I say anything," Gog says, " are you going to take your trousers off next, or your gumboots? There is a lady present."

On hearing this, the cheeks of the mugger turn darker than pitch, froth flecks his lips, and he goes into a clomping war-dance as he tugs off first one gumboot and then the other, before hurling them onto the road. Stripped down now to his trousers, he looks as tall and dangerous as a pit-shaft. And Gog, for fear that one more word will peel his opponent down to the naked Caliban, dabs his enemy with a left fist on his split nose.

So it's round one of Gog versus the Mumping Mugger. And it would do you good, young Tom Sayers long gone to worms, O Peerless Little Wonder, to see how Gog taps the ground with his left foot, his arms held down and his head thrown back, ready to smash out with either fist, as the Mumping Mugger, bigger than even the Benicia Boy, hurtles in for the kill. And see, Gog now raises his fist out in front of his shoulders – just so, Bill Neate, you once set out your arms, so that none of the Fancy could plant a punch on you and tap the claret, not even the spry braggart Gasman who went in and out of a boxer's guard quicker than a viper's tongue. You too, Tom Cribb, Champion of All England, never fought so mountainous a blackamoor, no, not even when you milled twice with Molineaux and fibbed him so mercilessly the final time that you cracked his jaw like plaster and stove in his ribs like laths.

Yet the onrush of the Mumping Mugger against the raised fists of Gog is so fierce that, though Gog smacks him with another left on the chin, the force of his assailant knocks him clean off his feet. Then he's down with the Mugger's knees in his belly and the Mugger's hands round his windpipe, choking him senseless. And Gog's a gone goose, but a sudden thump of soft flesh sends the Mugger sprawling. And Gog is buoyed onto the lap of a billowy shape so full of swell and fury that the whole sea seems to be contained in a sack under him.

"Fair's fair," Gog's rescuer says. "I woant have no bloody murder. War's over. It's rules now, an' doant yer forget it, yer gyppo mardarse. Or Rosie'll bust yer." Gog looks up at the speaker of these coaly and loamy vowels to see the fattest and pinkest girl in all the world, dressed in a white circus tent that seems hardly to cover the amphitheatre of her robust charms. "Crippen," the Fat Girl says, "if it ain't ole Goggie. 'Ow's yer keepin'? We'll 'ave a reight chinwag after yer've smashed 'im." Then she says, "I'll 'ave five pound on Goggie, 'e's a reight 'un in clinch."

"Done," the gypsy girl says. "I'll hold the stakes."

"We'll 'old our own," the Fat Girl says. "An' if yer doant pay oop, yer'll 'ave ter settle with me."

So the second round begins with Gog rising from the Fat Girl's lap as Champion of Albion, to fight the Mumping Mugger, over the sea from Egypt or Barbary or even God doesn't know where. Each has his second, the thin gypsy girl crouching like a stoat on the caravan steps in the Mugger's corner, the Fat Girl spread out opposite her as cushioned as an arm-chair fit for a Gargantua or a mere Gog. The ring has one side in the yellow slats of the caravan and another in the fence before Bylands Abbey, but on the other two sides the open road points north to Edinburgh and south to London. The gypsy girl bangs a whip on the iron rim of the caravan wheel, and the champions set to in earnest. Eternity deep on the roadway, the ghosts of the old Fancy and the Flash and the Swells collect, in silent hubbub to lay the odds, as the Champion of Albion fights for purse and country against the black invader in the noble art of self-offence.

Second Round: The Mugger leads with a left-hand blow which does not tell; when Gog plants a most tremendous blow over his adversary's right eyebrow; this does not have the effect of knocking him down, he only staggers a few paces, followed up by the Champion of Albion. Desperation is now the order of the round, and the rally recommences with uncommon severity, in which Gog shows the most science, although he receives a dreadful blow on the mouth that makes his teeth chatter again, and exhibits the first signs of claret. Evens on Gog, as the heroes fight again in the valiant style of the sporting annals of the past, hot with the dukes and red with the blood of Black Richmond, Dutch Sam, Mendoza and Maddox, The Pride of Westminster, Tom Belcher, Paddington Jones, Tough Tom Blake, and matchless Tom Cribb, who also defended the honour of England against the dark foe in the pages of Gog's youth, and now nods among the battered faces of the Fancy to see his boy crib him to feint and strike at the Mumping Mugger by the ruined abbey and the caravan.

Third Round: After a short space occupied in sparring, the Mumping Mugger attempts a good blow on Gog's nob, but the Champion of Albion parries it, and returns a right-handed hit under the Mugger's lower rib, when he falls rapidly in the extreme. Two to one on Gog.

Fourth Round: On setting to the Mumping Mugger rallies, when the Champion of Albion stops his career by a severe hit in the face, that levels him, the tarmac being set and slippery.

Fifth Round: The amateurs are uncommonly interested in this round, it is a display of such united skill and bottom, that both the combatants claim peculiar notice from their extraordinary efforts. The Mumping Mugger rallies with uncommon fortitude, but his blows are short. Gog returns with spirit, but the Mugger knocks them off, and puts in a tremendous hit on the left eye of the Champion of Albion. A rally, at half-arm's length, now follows, which excites the utmost astonishment from the resoluteness of both the heroes, who hit each other away three times, and continue this desperate milling for half a minute; when the Mumping Mugger falls from a feeble blow. The Knowing Ones are lost for a moment, and no bets are offered.

Sixth Round: The Mugger plants a blow upon the nob of the Champion of Albion, who falls from the bad state of the ground.

Seventh Round: Gog in a rally gives the Mumping Mugger a hit on the side of the head, when he goes down.

Eighth Round: Gog shows himself off in good style, and deals out his blows with considerable success and effect; but he has experienced from the determined resolution of the Mugger that he is somewhat mistaken in his ideas of the Black Man's capabilities, who rallies in prime-twig, and notwithstanding the severe left-handed hits which were planted on his nob, and the terrible punishment he has received on his body, directed by the fine skill and power of the Champion of Albion, still he stands up undismayed, and proves that his courage is of no ordinary nature in exchanging several of the blows, till he falls almost in a state of stupor, from the milling his head has undergone. This round is equal to any that precede it, and only different in point of duration.

Ninth to Eighteenth Round: The battle is fought with superlative milling and fibbing, with the odds now on the Champion of Albion, now on the Mumping Mugger, so awesome is the skill and bottom of both opponents.

Nineteenth Round: To distinguish the combatants by their features would be utterly impossible, so dreadfully are both their faces beaten – but their difference of colour supplies this sort of defect. It is really astonishing to view the determined manner in which these heroes meet – Gog, acting upon the defensive, and retreating from the blows of his antagonist, though endeavouring to put in a hit, is got by the Mumping Mugger against the fence, which is in height about five feet, and in three rows. The Mumping Mugger with both his hands catches hold of the wires, and holds Gog in such a singular way, that he can neither make a hit nor fall down; and while the seconds are discussing the propriety of separating the combatants, about two hundred goats rush from the middle of the abbey field to the exterior fence; and the gypsy girl asserts, if one of the Mugger's fingers is not broken, it is much injured by some of the goats attempting to bite off his hand; all this time the Mumping Mugger is gaining his wind by laying his head on Gog's breast, and refusing to release his victim; when the Champion of Albion by a desperate effort to extricate himself from the rude grasp of the Mugger, is at length run down to one corner of the open ring; and the Mumping Mugger having got his head under his arm, fibs away most unmercifully, but his strength not being able to the intent, it otherwise must prove fatal to Gog, who falls from exhaustion and the severe punishment he has received. Half an hour has expired during this round.

Twentieth to Twenty-eighth Round: Gog recruits his strength by keeping back from the Mumping Mugger, who rushes in boring and hitting. Gog manages to darken his left peeper in a scientific manner, his opponent's desperate onslaughts notwithstanding.

Twenty-ninth Round: The Mugger is running in with spirit, but the Champion of Albion stops his career, by planting a hit upon his right eye, and from the severe effects of which he goes down, his peeper materially damaged. The fate of the battle may be said to be decided by this round.

Thirtieth Round: If anything can reflect credit upon the skill and bottom of Gog, it is never more manifested than in this contest, in viewing what a resolute and determined hero he has to vanquish. The Mumping Mugger, in spite of every disadvantage, with a courage and ferocity unequalled, rising superior to exhaustion and fatigue rallies his adversary with as much resolution as at the commencement of the fight, his nob defying all the milling it has received, the punishment appearing to have no decisive effect upon it; so he contends nobly with Gog right and left, knocking him away by his hits, and gallantly concludes the round by closing and throwing the Champion of Albion. The Mugger is now convinced that if he does win, he must do it off by hand, as his sight is much impaired.

Thirty-first Round: This is the last round that may be termed fighting, in which the Mumping Mugger has materially the worst of it; but the battle is continued to the thirty-ninth, when Gog evidently appears the best man, and at its conclusion, the Mugger for the first time complains, that "He can fight no more!" but his second, who views the nicety of the point, persuades him to try the chance of another round, to which request he acquiesces, when he falls from weakness, reflecting additional credit on the manhood of his brave conqueror, Gog Griffin, who, in falling back on the lap of the Fat Girl, is in the very position that he was upon the commencing of the second round.

If anything has been wanting to establish the fame of Gog, the above conquest has completely decided his just pretensions to the Championship of Albion. With a coolness and confidence, almost his own, and with skill and judgement truly rare, he has beaten his man with more certainty than any of the professors of the gymnastic art. He was called upon to protect the honour of his country, and the reputation of English Boxing – a parade of words, or the pomposity of high-flown diction are not necessary to record the circumstances; however, let it not be forgotten, that Gog Griffin HAS DONE THIS . . .

Gog wakes from a brief moment of insensibility to find himself again on the Fat Girl's lap, his face and chest hardly bruised and the ghosts of the dead Fancy gone for ever down the open road. She is whispering fiercely in his ear, " Now, will yer use Low Crooked?" And Gog feels her put something heavy in the palm of his left hand and close his fingers round the object into a fist. " Doant loose that, luv, till yer've fetched it be'ind the Mugger's lug'ole. It's loocky charm an' all." Then with a heave, the Fat Girl ups the groggy Gog onto his feet as the whip handle sounding against the caravan wheel singles the opening of yet another round. And Gog sees the Mumping Mugger come rushing at him, but his foe is so miraculously unmarked that Gog fears he has dreamed the thirty-nine rounds from the lap of the Fat Girl, his mind has cribbed word by word the progress of a great victory once won by a Champion of Albion in the past. But if Gog finds that he has imagined a victory by the high straight left and right, now he has only Low Crooked to save his skin. And as the Mumping Mugger strikes and strikes so that the wind of his blows whistles unpleasantly in Gog's ears, Gog collects all his strength to give the Mugger a left hook on the ear, which fells him to the ground like a pit disaster. The gypsy girl runs forwards with a loud cry and throws herself on her fallen champion, while the Fat Girl raises Gog's right hand in triumph, slipping a half-horseshoe from his left palm into the bosom of the marquee that hides her breast.

" Gog's woon fair an' square an' above board," she declares, " an' that'll cost yer five pound, yer Romany chi."

The gypsy girl rises from the body of the Mugger and throws

herself, all scratches like a brierbush in a gust, upon the Fat Girl, who merely envelops her in two broad arms and squeezes the breath and the sass out of her. When the gypsy girl is nearly pressed flat, the Fat Girl removes the gold sovereign that hangs from one ear of her rival and the gold napoleon that hangs from the other. " I'll 'ave 'em, doocks," she says, " till I get me five pound. I like matters 'onest like. I'm joost simple coontry maid goin' oop ter big city. An' yer'll 'elp me fare."

The gypsy girl protests her poverty, she weeps at the Fat Girl's feet, she swears by every oath of heaven and hell and by many a curse heard in neither place, that she has no money, not even a tanner. But the Fat Girl is hard as a churn for all her appearance of being a mountain of butter. " If yer'll not pay," she says, " we'll wait in caravan with yer mardy Mugger. Yer might as well lift us on way ter York. Happen yer'll find soom quids theer, happen not."

So the Fat Girl bends and lifts the fallen Mugger in her voluminous arms and carries him up the caravan steps into the yellow interior of the wagon. And Gog follows her inside, while the gypsy girl gets onto the driver's seat and starts the horse on a slow walk towards York, pulling the six humans on their way if the Fat Girl is counted as three.

Once Gog enters the caravan, he feels that he has stepped into a miniature theatre. Along the wooden sides of the single moving room painted in red and yellow, two leather-topped benches are fixed, one of them ending in a wrought-iron stove with a chimney that projects through the roof. The bed at the end of the caravan is a small stage, inbuilt between a proscenium arch of plumed wood with two red curtains gathered at head and foot, ready to drop across the profiles of mattress and ochre coverlet that rest on the long cupboard beneath. Every cranny has been converted into a space for sitting or eating or sleeping or stowing the petty baggage of existence.

Ahead of Gog, the Fat Girl is laying out the Mugger, a huge black length that scarcely fits the bed which can be no greater than the width of the caravan. As Gog turns to rest on one of the leather benches by the slatted side of the vehicle, he sees a little window cut into the wood and framed with polka-dot curtains and a pelmet no bigger than a frilly ribbon – the only superfluous thing in the whole small room that clops and sways by the tall hedgerows. A caw makes Gog look back towards the entrance door, which is constructed in two flaps like a stable's. There he sees a pair of wooden cages hanging from the roof. From one, a raven with clipped wings regards him with tilted head and bold-bright eye. And in the second cage, a fox desperately circles, chasing its own tail as if it could escape by entering its own rump and burrowing to safety down its intestines. Gog thinks he recognizes the fox as the one chased by the hunt; perhaps, in seeking refuge from hound and horse and horn, it has found only the slower death of bar and gate and peg.

Gog leans over towards the fox's cage and slips the twine loop that secures its latch. The fox bursts out, falls scrabbling on the floor, and scurries out of the doorway, red brush whisking into the nettles of a ditch. The raven, however, does not take kindly to release. It considers the open door of its cage, then uses its beak to pull the door shut and put the twine loop back into place, cocking a knowing eye at Gog as if telling him that he will not get rid of this black-feathered spy so easily by the offer of mere liberty to limp about defenceless with docked plumes.

"War's bashed yer oop a bit," the Fat Girl declares. "I doant think I'd fancy yer like I did oonce, if it weren't fer ole times. 'Ow's Arthur?"

"Arthur?" Gog says, while words such as Lancelot and Bors and Gawain pound into his skull with each clip of a hoof outside.

"Our boy," the Fat Girl says. "Doant play mardy. Yer remember 'im. I know yer does. 'E's in school oop way yer've coom from. Yer've been visitin'. Yer sly 'un! Yer doant need be with Rosie. I'm joost simple coontry maid what all world takes in."

While she speaks, the Fat Girl is padding about the room, tapping and listening at each slat on the walls and twisting the small rosettes that hide the joins in the wood.

"Yes," Gog says, "I did see a boy who could have been my son. Arthur, you say? When was he born?"

Gog sees the boiling plum duff of the Fat Girl's face break open in joy as if a great hot bubble has burst in her mouth. Her fingers have found a rosette which turns. She pushes the nearest slat, a section of which revolves outwards. Then she stuffs in a pudgy hand and pulls out the plum, a small leather bag tied with a thong. When she peers inside the bag, her whole face pops and explodes with glee. She tucks the bag away in some recess under the awning of her skirt, then she closes the slat. "That'll learn 'er," she mutters. "'Er'll wish 'er give me five pound, all reight."

"You can't steal whatever's in there," Gog says. "It may be all they've got. You're always saying, Honest and fair's fair."

"Hoosh," the Fat Girl says, rummaging in a cupboard and throwing some corduroy trousers and a red shirt and a tatty jersey across to Gog. "Put on soom Christian clothes. Fair's fair all reight, so long as it's them treatin' yer fair. But fair's unfair, if yer's but a poor coontry maid in wicked world. Do unto others what they woold do, Good Book says, but if yer do what they woold do yer'll be done proper. Me, I do unto others what they woold do, but I do it first."

Gog puts on the Mugger's spare clothes, which fit him tolerably well, then he begins to put on a pair of the Mugger's socks and boots, which are tucked under the stove. "You're not quite such a simple country maid as you make out, are you, Rosie? I should think when you get to the city, you'll teach them a thing or two. Incidentally could you spare me a couple of quid? I'm out. And I did win the fight, after all."

The Fat Girl looks in her bosom, finds a single half-crown, and passes it to Gog. "Look at simple mardy me. Ruinin' mesel' fer a great git what ruined me. Yer didn't win feight, Low Crooked did. An' 'oo put Low Crooked in yer 'and? I shooldn't give yer a lead farthin', but me 'eart's pure gold."

"If your heart's pure gold," Gog says, feeling the bruises on his neck with one hand and pocketing the solitary coin with the other, "I understand why you're giving none of it away. Some people have milk in their breast, you've got a bank vault."

"Yer say that," the Fat Girl says threateningly, "after all yer've doon ter me? Theer yer weer, wicked squire an' all – it doant fool me yer callin' yersel' a stoodent – an' yer coom up ter me perlite as a daisy an' say, Wheer's way ter Derby, miss? An' next mo I'm rollin in 'ay, doant know 'ow fer life of me I ever did get theer. Ain't all bootter an' cream bringin' oop brat on yer own, with father away gettin' married ter French tart. Yer paid brass regular, I'll say, but it wasn't same. No dad aboot t' 'ouse. Yer made me what I am, Gog, so 'elp me. An' if I 'ave ter look after mesel' in wicked world, yer learned me all reight."

The caravan passes through the grey stone walls and red roofs of Coxwald, the name of the town mounted on an old millstone that grinds flour no more, its use almost a forgotten memory. And hard as Gog tries to recollect something about the Fat Girl, his mind jibs at the thought of himself coupling in any hay with such a jellied Everest, even in the sharpest lust of his forgotten days of whisky and wild oats.

"You like conning city folk, Rosie," Gog says. "You're not conning me, are you? I was mined, you know, I don't remember very well. I don't even know for sure if I have a son, and certainly not whether he's yours or not."

"'E's yers, all reight," the Fat Girl says fiercely. "An' mine. 'Appen mind's like pocket, ain't it? If it's got 'ole in it, yer can say all yer brass slipped oot, an' yer doant 'ave ter pay fer what yer've 'ad. 'Ow coold I con yer, Gog? If yer've seen Arthur, yer've seen 'e's yers. 'Appen 'e coold 'ave 'ad other dads, an' 'appen I took fer 'is dad a gentleman like yersel'. But nature's foony, like. An' it looks like 'e's yers after all. Ain't no con, Gog. It's t' loock of t' kip."

"I'm sorry, Rosie," Gog says, "I simply didn't remember. You must have changed a bit in a dozen years. Arthur's about that, isn't he?"

Rosie sits on the leather bench opposite Gog. She seems to spread over the entire length of the caravan which takes a dangerous tilt to the left, so that the rim of one of the wheels scrapes the outer slats. "Sit central, you gorgio cow," the gypsy girl shouts from above and Rosie settles herself on the bending floorboards of the caravan to restore a semblance of equilibrium. Her bulk totally fills the space between the benches, so that

Gog's calves are enveloped in a deluge of thigh. Rosie sighs. " I moost 'ave put on a pound or two," she admits.

" I didn't promise you anything, did I, Rosie?" Gog says. " I mean, I didn't let you down particularly."

" Arthur weer more'n I bargained fer," the Fat Girl says, " but I always knew yer wooldn't make no 'onest girl oot of me. Yer gob weer always open. I didn't lissen. I liked way yer gob moved an' yer cooldn't be kissin' all t' time, coold yer? Yer used ter go on, 'ow yer 'ad ter get back ter t' people. But it weer only way of sayin' yer wanted ter 'ave me. Yer talked of roonin' away ter Australia, t'last frontier yer used ter say. We coold 'ave seventeen brats theer, yer said, an' we coold people t'empty earth. But I'd still cough after every time, 'opin' I'd 'ave none. Then one day, yer oop an' gone back ter books an' stoodyin'. Fact is, yer weer off ter Gay Paree an' tarts. I doant blame yer, Gog. Yer helped pay fer Arthur. But curds an' whey doant mix, do they, tho' both's milk."

" I'm sorry, Rosie," Gog says. " Still, Arthur's off your hands now at school. Who looks after him in the holidays?"

" Yer ma Merry," the Fat Girl says. " I like 'er. 'Er's real lady. Yer know what 'er said when 'er first saw Arthur? Gog's little bastard, 'er said. Boys're better that way."

A jealousy of his unknown bastard brother Magnus clots Gog's belly on the sudden. Does his new-found mother Merry really love the smart-alec civil servant more than him, her legitimate child? Gog stares out of the open flap of the door as the caravan passes a small lake, sporting royal swans and muscovy ducks in the convenient alliance of the Second World War. Even the hedges of the great priory with its entrance hidden by gabled stables are clipped into a menagerie. Foxes and dogs and geese and deer stand in a line of green privet on the hedge-top; the careful clippers of the monk gardeners have made the lion lie down with the lamb in a vegetarian Utopia. " You're not doing too badly for yourself now," Gog continues. " At least, my mother's taken the little mistake off your hands. She adores bastards. Why, it looks like I'm rather worse off than you are."

" Yer'll be set oop cooshy when yer're back in Lonnon all

reight," the Fat Girl says. "Yer're not playin' fer real now, no more'n yer weer playin' fer real when yer first met me. Yer've got yer ritzy French tart an' big 'ouse in Lonnon. An' yer moost be rollin' ter send me what yer do regular fer Arthur. I'm joost simple coontry maid but I 'ope I do 'alf as well as yer in Lonnon, when I get theer."

"If you play the simple country maiden like you do up here," Gog says, "you'll whip the tiara off Her Majesty in two minutes."

"'Oo's talkin'?" the Fat Girl says. "'Oo's boots ye're wearin'?" And as Gog takes a guilty look down at the clodhoppers on his feet, the Fat Girl says, "Takin' fer yersel', that's property, ain't it? Losin', that's larceny."

Gog lies down on the long bench of the caravan and the Fat Girl also lies back on the floor, her head supported on the side of the inbuilt bed. Both snooze, with the Fat Girl snoring from time to time in counterpoint to the hooves. Once Gog, overcome by a ravening hunger, rummages in the cupboard over the stove and finds a half-filled saucepan of cold stew containing some indescribable savoury cold meat, which he devours. At other times, between dozes, he watches the countryside slowly retire in a shimmy behind the tail of the caravan. He sees the tall skittles of churns set out on roadside tables waiting for trucks to knock them down and take them away. He sees the farmhouses built now in grey stone and red brick with red-tiled roofs. He sees a pub pass by at Crayke, "The Durham Ox", black bull hanging at the top of the final hill, down which the rosy houses of the village tumble onto the flatlands that stretch towards York. Once a white Yorkshire terrier follows the caravan for a few yards, parting its wide moustaches for long enough to loose a volley of black yaps after its disturber. But generally, the landscape is little more than an invitation to another doze, as level meadow beyond tall hedge succeeds level meadow beyond tall hedge, and the moors are gone away to the north like a fright in the night goes away in the day.

A splintering, a cracking, a tearing, and a yelling wake up Gog from a deep drowse. He looks down to see the Fat Girl's monstrous head and shoulders wedged between her ankles and jumbo feet. The middle of her body has vanished through a hole in the snapped floorboards so that her barrage balloon of bountiful buttocks is scraping and skidding along the tarmac. The Mugger is still out to the world on his bed; but the cart comes to a halt and the gypsy girl soon appears at the caravan door. When she sees her rival at her mercy, she dashes in to fetch the Fat Girl a clout on the left cheek, and then begins on the right cheek, gouging with her nails a tribal mark of four bloody parallel lines. Gog catches her hand before she can deepen the scratches into troughs, and he is bitten in the wrist for his pains. Then the gypsy girl is out of the caravan quicker than the fox. Gog hears her jump onto the driver's seat and begin lashing at the horse, yelling, "Dearginni! Grondinni! Ta villaminni! Hup and go! Scrape off the lubbeny's arse till she's rawer than a rasher!"

The caravan begins lurching off down the road at a furious pace. "Stop," Gog howls, "stop!" But he is hurled from bench to bench and wall to wall, unable to keep to his feet in such a pitch and toss. "Pull me out!" the Fat Girl shrieks. "Pull! Me arse, me brass! O me brass in me arse!" Gog seizes her by thick wrist and thicker ankle, though his hands can scarcely get a good grip because they have such a vast circumference to span. He heaves mightily, while the caravan jolts half-way to the sun and three-quarters to the pit, and the shrill shrieking of the Fat Girl and the gypsy girl keen louder than a northern gale through a crack in a tunnel. A sudden plunge of the offside wheels into a hole in the road unbalances Gog, who slips his grip and lurches, flailing helplessly, through the open flaps of the caravan door. He falls in a heap onto the roadway, the hay knocked out of his bale. And the gypsy girl whips up the horse, singing above the wails of the Fat Girl a shrill Romany lilt:

> "Here the gorgio lubbeny see,
> With her jellicle arse on the tarmaci,
> She'll rue the day with Romany rye
> She dared to meddle with a Romany chi.
> Romany chi . . ."

So the last sight that Gog has of the Fat Girl is of a pendulous sack of flesh protruding beneath the wheels of the yellow caravan, as it disappears round the corner of the road. The bottom of the sack of flesh jounces and scrapes along the roadway as the Fat Girl is painfully and inevitably reduced in size and to shreds.

The rest of the way to York is well-marked. Gog merely follows a trail of scraps of canvas and blobs of flesh and blood. Every so often, he finds a piece of leather and a gory gold guinea from the gypsies' hoard which the Fat Girl stowed unwisely below her skirt. Gog picks up the gold and cleans it on his trousers and collects a fair handful of loot by the time that he reaches the watchtower on the outskirts of York, a large Rowntrees' Cocoa factory. "The wages of sin," he murmurs, counting the gold in his palm, "may be the death of poor Rosie."

Past the high red jetty of the factory, which breathes out a dark rich belly-washing smell fit to make Gog disgorge all into the scuppers of a ditch, he sees ahead the twin-funnelled stone ferry of York Minster moored on the horizon above the choppy red and black tiles of the city's houses that break beneath it as ineffectively as wavelets beneath the ribs of a steamer. Now Gog has found his mark, the last three miles between him and the Minster seem as short as a walk down a pier. At one point in the suburbs just before the city walls, the trail of blood and canvas suddenly comes to a stop. In the gutter, Gog finds the spokes and the rim of one of the wheels of the caravan, now broken into twenty pieces. He imagines that the forcible slimming of the Fat Girl and the gallop ended with a spill, needing a smithy and a hospital. At any rate, there is no sign of Gog's recent companions on his way to the Minster, and the line of white dashes in the middle of the street is a more certain and reassuring guide than the gory blazes of revenge and loot.

Just before Gog turns towards the evening towers of the great church, he decides to slake the dryness in his throat that feels as if it were lined with flour. He turns into a pub over which hangs the sign of a large anchor, for some odd reason labelled *The Pick and Mattock*. Curiously enough, the flukes of the anchor seem to have been used to dig the foundations of a tombstone that is painted in the background. Gog is puzzled by the sign, and when he has ordered his pint of bitter from the pubkeeper, a keg of a man with tattooed arms and the stern civility of ex-petty officers, he asks the reason why.

" It's me own pub," the keeper says, " and a Free House too. Named it meself. I was twenty year at sea, and I allus swore that when I docked for good, I'd walk inland till I met a bloke who said, What's that pick on your shoulder? And I'd lay me anchor down there in the middle of the land, where they'd never heard of the bleeding sea. And I'd drink meself to death. What's this? A guinea? A golden guinea? I haven't seen one of them for many a year, since we was docked off Aden. The Ayrabs won't have nothing else but sovereigns and guinea gold. And it's to drink me good health with? Well, I thank you, sir. That's noble. For it's a bad health I can drink meself with a whole gold guinea. And if you're drinking yourself to death, it might as well be quick as slow, the beer's all the same ...

" I've already carved me cross for me grave, sir. In whalebone it is, harpooned it meself, you don't see that these days, either. And you know what it says, sir?

Here Rests Nelson Smith
Mariner
Docked At Last
NOT LIVETH BUT DEAD."

XVIII

Greyly through the grisaille glass in the grey north transept of the grey Minster, the evening smears its wan oil of holiness on Gog's eyes. The perpendicular windows called the Five Sisters stand side by side in their obscure transparence, wearing the slender habits of nuns so purged by prayer that all cloth and flesh is translated into luminous pointed shafts patterned with infinite panes of cloud. As rags of silver light sometimes patch the tears in layers of dark mist, so tatters of brilliance here and there break up the grisaille's innumerable subtleties of shade between near-black and olive-green. Each of the Sisters wears a different pattern on her habit, as abstract as the symbols and keys that may unlock one of the ways through the skiey labyrinth towards the Almighty. Some Crusader in the thirteenth century must have returned with the idea of Islam, that the way to God does not lie through the reproduction of the human face, but through the ascending pattern; and the Crusader made Christian these patterns of the worshipping infidel by enmeshing them in the colours and web of chain mail. Thus the Five Sisters stand in front of Gog in all their glory of grey, chaste in their mysterious clarity, alike in their extraordinary differences, harmonious as a whole but contradictory in every part, the most unearthly hint of heaven ever set up in Albion.

And as Gog prays standing and void in front of the Five Sisters, the First Sister on the left comes before him in the shining fleece of meekness. And she speaks:

"I am Meekness. I was born of a winter lamb. I grew among the bulrushes bending to the East Wind. My school was the grain beneath the flail that maketh the bread of men, the berries beneath the press that flow as the wine of men, the children whom the rod doth not spare, the daisy that boweth to the split hoof, the wattle pen that yieldeth to the flock but doth not allow it to pass. He who taketh me by the hand shall fall and yet he shall not fail. He shall follow his enemies while he leadeth them, he shall kneel before the proud who shall be humbled in front of him. Without me, the people shall be as the thunder and the lightning that come before the flood of their weeping and the rain of their tears on the day of retribution. With me, men shall wax fat in times of joy and preserve their bodies in times of sorrow. I am the sister of all and the stepmother of none. Shall I be thy coat, Gog?"

Before Gog may answer, the Second Sister steps out of her narrow place on the wall on the left hand of the First Sister and comes before him in the bright bark of an ash tree. And she speaks:

"I am Endurance. My father was an oaken bridge and his wife the Severn River that floweth and floweth without ceasing. Where the millstone grindeth and doth not complain, where the bollard maketh fast the merchant ship in hail and storm, where the stone paving supporteth the carriage and the slate roof covereth the hall, there I am. When the fury of the tempest lasheth the people, I shall put my cloak about them so that they may shelter until the morrow. When the wheel turneth and doth not stay for an answer, I shall give strength to all that they may serve the wheel for their bread and yet not stay for a rest. He who stands at my back shall not want, nor shall he falter. I am the staff of all men and without me there can be no men. Shall I be thy crutch, Gog?"

And lo, as Gog is about to embrace either Sister with either arm, a black breath, stinking of burned coal and oil, fumes forth and melts with its searing blast the lead strips that hem together the innumerable panes of the robes of the First Sister and the Second Sister. And from their like height of fifty feet and more that is fourteen times their breadth, the Sisters are reduced to two little pyramids of broken grey glass, from which silver trails of lead run away like the tracks of snails. And as Gog looks forwards toward the north wall, he sees that the twin stone embrasures on the left, from which the two Sisters have stepped, are now the narrow black nostrils of Magog, whose dread initial appears as the raised stone skin about his pitchy nostrils, once plugged and made holy by the two Sisters in their set places at the side of the other three Sisters. And Magog speaks:

"What is Meekness to me but the clove that I insert in my left nostril to perfume my foul breath as it issues out? And what is Endurance but the quill through the cork that I insert in my right nostril so that I may take in air through the clogged passages of my diseased nose? Through the quill of Endurance I take in the draught that my iron lungs need to ignite the fuel that drives my piston ribs. Past the clove of Meekness I expel the filthy odours of the crippled servants of my machines, their sweat and piss and pus, and these rank scents are turned into the wafting breezes of sweet bowers and orchards despite the moiling midden of their sources. Without you twin grey Sisters, Meekness and Endurance arm in arm, how should I make the mob perform its daily and necessary labour? Bring me the virtue of Lasting, and I will pin a testimonial of parchment for forty years' service on the dewlap of withered skin about her neck. Bring me the virtue of Humble Duty and I will trick her out with a linen sheet to shroud her bony frame. In your absence, the people kick against the pricks and rear up to their ruin and my own. In your company, they walk to the grave in labour and are content. Am I not your true master, Gog?"

And as Gog groans in bitter wisdom, the sight of the fuming slits of Magog's nostrils is hidden by the edge of the robe of the Third Sister from the far right of the group as she stands before Gog in the lowly glow of the pilgrim's shift. And she speaks:

"I am Faith. My cradle was the green weathervane on Salisbury spire built on a swamp. Where I go, the orphan Hope also goeth. For she hath no cover but the edge of my shawl, she must die in the tempest but that my hood shieldeth her nakedness. Yet without this orphan on my arm, would not every man and every woman put a penknife into their vein? I am stronger than Hope, and yet she is prettier and vainer and littler than I, and she needeth her lessons. For the few who favour me shall be the arks of the people, while the many smile upon the dimples and babble and dreams of the child. A multitude of places are built to give me shelter, yet none shall find me there but those who know how to seek me. In the dark night when the white Word of Truth walketh about the room, then I alone can drug the hour-long minutes until the footfall of first light. Call on me boldly and I shall answer boldly. Call on the orphan child Hope and she shall answer as a child. Shall we be your glove and your pretty ring, Gog?"

Before Gog may answer, the Fourth Sister steps out of her narrow place on the wall on the right hand of the Third Sister and comes before him in the clarity of a pillar of grey matter. And she speaks:

"I am Understanding. Begotten on a sun's shaft by an old owl at break of day. Where the pool encompasseth the frog and doth not let him sink, where the swallow laceth her nest more careful than the thatcher of cottage roofs, where the spider threadeth his warp and shuttleth upon his web, where the bat turneth away from the horsehair and doth not touch, there I pass, gone before I am seen to come. In my pouch I carry a legless girl, who knoweth affliction. And wherever I wander, she scattereth the dry soil with her tears and the melancholy puddle with her smile. To the fallen, she giveth a twig with which they may begin to raise themselves. To the lost, she giveth a little key which may open one of the many iron gates closed against them. She is too pleased with her own merits, my little legless Charity. And yet, without her, who would remember the unrecorded, who would discover the wants of the forgotten? Shall we be thy cap and thy wallet, Gog?"

And lo, as Gog is about to embrace either Sister with either arm, a blinding beam, bright as the fiery furnace, strikes forth and shrivels with its searing blast the lead stitches that bind together the myriad pieces of the robes of the Third Sister and the Fourth Sister. And from their like height of fifty feet and more that is fourteen times their breadth, the Sisters are charred to two small mounds of glittering ash, from which silver dribbles of lead run away like the droolings of idiots. And as Gog looks forwards toward the north wall, he sees that the twin stone embrasures on the right, from which the two Sisters have stepped, are now the narrow black eyeholes of Magog, whose dread initial appears as the raised stone lids about his pit-deep sockets, once blinkered and made holy by the two Sisters in their ordained positions at the side of the other three Sisters. And Magog speaks:

"What is Faith but the patch that shields the maggoty socket from which my blind and sinister eye was removed? And what is Understanding but the smoked lens of the monocle set before my seeing and dexterous eye? Strip off the patch and the smoked glass, and I would cringe in the light of Truth. If I can turn my blind eye to all believers, the fools who always trust and are always disappointed, then I may ordain according to my whims and they will have faith that my fancies are revealed wisdom. When I yawn, 'Country . . .' they will crowd the cemeteries in certitude of the righteousness of their cause and of the orders of their betters. When I snigger 'God . . .' they will bruise their knees and beggar themselves to build me a stone barn for my ease. And as for the smoked glass called Understanding, how it prettifies my bloodshot eye! If that eye were bared so that men could see the surface of red veins streaking the yellow ball and the flecked iris spotted with flies like a hot turd, then they would jeer and tear it out and leave me in darkness. But as it is, they elect to have a Cyclops above them to call their natural deeds misdoings and to spy on them for the benefit of judges and courts and jails and hangmen's knots. But Understanding, my downy Understanding, how you are my guise and badge of respectability! I speak to you only words of honied reason, and you nod and say, 'So shall it be, for so it has always been. I understand thee, Magog, thou couldst be worse. Better the devil thou knowst . . .' So blessed be Faith and blessed be Understanding, for they shall veil the loathsome look of Magog. Am I not your true master, Gog?"

And as Gog groans in the terrible smart of perception, the sight of the filthy holes of Magog's sockets is hidden by the edge of the robe of the Fifth Sister from the centre of the group as she stands before Gog in glory without seam or edge, the glory of love. And she speaks:

"I am Love. At the cry of the newborn and at the blood of the afterbirth, on the splint by the broken bone and on the lint that wipes clean the wound, in the choir of the morning and in the coupling of the evening, where the worms embrace in silver slime and the woman scrubbeth a table for the family meal, there I am. If I am not present, living things are but things that move and are not alive. The beasts of the field and the forest, the birds of the air and the fish of the sea, these know me in a small measure. But men may know me in a great measure, or they may deny me. My name is called often, and often in vain. I come without asking, I go before I am known. Shall I be thy shirt, Gog?"

And lo, as Gog is about to embrace the final Sister with both arms, a putrid puff, ripe with dung and waste, belches forth and withers with its pestilence the lead ribbons that wave between the countless lights on the robes of the Fifth Sister. And from her height of heaven that is as broad as the world and all that therein is, the Sister is powdered to one small heap of grey dust, from which silver trickles of lead run away like the tears of angels. And as Gog looks forwards toward the north wall, he sees that all the five embrasures are empty and that the pillars of stone between them have become the four fangs of the black mouth of Magog, surrounded by the puckering of raised stone lips, once stoppered and made holy by the Five Sisters in their serene hierarchy. And Magog speaks:

" I adore Love, the perfect hypocrite. That word is the blanket for all the vices through which I rule the race of men. He who speaks the name of Love, lies. He who practises the art of Love, is debauched. He who gives up all for Love, gives up his precarious way through the world, and then he has no other way but mine. To die for Love is to live for ever and die no more, they say. But it is, in fact, no more than to die. Death asks no reason when he comes. Yes, Love is my favourite word, the most debased. Even God is Love, they say, and God does rule, they say. Then say Magog is Love, for Magog surely rules. Am I not your true master, Gog?"

A hand touches Gog's shoulder like a thief in the night, and Gog wakes with a start to the fact of a darkened Minster, with all the light of evening gone from the backs of the Five Sisters so that they are indeed mere black slits between the four stone fangs of Magog's black mouth. The verger of the Minster is pulling at Gog's coat. " Sorry, sir. We have to lock up now. Sorry to disturb your meditation. Powerful holy, this place is." And he ducks in deference to the far High Altar, as he conducts Gog back across the transept to the outer door and the night city of York.

As soon as he leaves the Minster, Gog finds himself in a Tudor Street that some butcher wag has called the Shambles. And shambles it is, but the shambles of straight lines that can be the lilt of architecture. The heavy black beams that support the projecting upper storeys of the old shops are aslant and agley with warping and subsidence. The cross-timbers on the house fronts, which contain the white plaster, curve and bend in answer to the grain of the wood rather than of the structure. Occasionally rose-red bricks fill the heavy wooden frame of the houses, which wear their pointed caps of tile as rakishly as jesters once sported their headpieces.

In a doorway, Gog sees a wandering minstrel, a troubadour of old in a profession gone to seed. Once royalty was his open purse; the courts are less kind now. He is lean and shaggy and dressed in soiled army fatigues. His lute looks like a half-strung tennis-racket backed by an orange box. His sandals are old gym-shoes with holes cut in them to let his corns breathe. Yet a smile on his face springs up from his dejection, and he chirps cocky as a sparrow undaunted by a thousand attempts to get near a large crumb just out of beak.

"Tanner for a song, sir. Tanner for my supper." He strums a few chords on his home-made guitar. "I've got songs on love and war, sir. Very popular, war now. Though I've got a lovely number on peace, there's no demand. Or highwaymen. This is Dick Turpin's home base, they hanged him here. Or Robin Hood, he was a bandit too."

"Robin Hood," Gog says. "I'd like to hear a song on him. The first of the Resistance heroes. Fought from the forest. The Normans never got him either, did they? The church bled his life away and ..." In the distance, a klaxon sounds on a lorry, its far gears crack like branches and its moving tyres sigh like wind in the leaves. "You can still hear his horn."

The minstrel smiles and begins to pluck his chords. Then he sings as a bird sings, unforced and a little shrill, yet the notes cosseted in the throat.

> "*I sing a song of both now and then*
> *The song of two Lincoln highwaymen ...*
>
> *Little John and Robin Hood*
> *Stand by the road through the greenwood.*
> *They meet a Giant in doublet grey:*
> *'I shall not let you pass this way.'*

'Oho!' quoth Robin and bends his bow:
But with a clout he is laid low.
The same befalls poor Little John
By the fist of the mighty champion.

'Your merry men, my Robin Hood,
Might do better if better led.
The people groan 'neath the Norman yoke,
While ye lurk in the forest brake . . .' "

"There's substance in that song," Gog says. "There always was in the old ballads. And just to show you there's still some substance left, I'll give you a golden guinea when the song's over."

"I'll have to take three quid in notes for it at the jeweller's in the morning," the minstrel says. "But it'll be nice having the coin a wee bit. It'll keep me warm all night and keep me for a fortnight after. Have you been robbing the gypsies, or something?" He then begins to sing again.

" *'If leading be such an easy thing,*
Goodly Giant, then be our king,
My merry men shall thee follow,
By thy word, I'll bend my bow.'

'I will not,' quoth Little John,
'I will now hunt the deer alone.'
'Little John, that shall not be.
As Robin's man, thou art to me.'

Bound are the arms of Little John;
The Giant is chief of the merry men.
He leads them forth to Lincoln town,
There the Normans to throw down . . ."

"It's very difficult of course," Gog interrupts, "the whole

question of what you do about discipline in a Resistance group fighting for freedom. I really don't . . ."

" I really don't like interruption," the minstrel says, " even for a guinea. And I don't like talking about songs much. They're for singing." So he begins to chant again.

" *The Norman lord, Magus the Black,*
With mace of jet leads the attack.
Knights on horses are now seen
Trampling down the Lincoln green.

Back to the brake flee the merry men,
Back flee the Giant and Robin,
They come upon a darkling pool:
' *Look in here who seeks to rule.*'

The Giant looks and sees his face
Blacker than Magus' jet-black mace.
He cuts the rope from Little John;
He leaves Robin and his merry men."

The minstrel's voice rises as he sings the moral flooded by a cascade of low chords.

" *Robin sat under the greenwood tree:*
' *He who would rule cannot be*
Better than he who ruleth now.
For your own self, bend ye your bow.' "

At the end of the song, Gog is plunged into silence, while the minstrel gets to his feet and waits for his pay.

" Where did you find that song?" Gog asks eventually.

" When I was a student at Durham," the minstrel says. " There was a crazy old teacher there during my time. Doctor Griffin. He soon left, but he'd grubbed up this ballad from somewhere and one of the blokes I knew put a tune to it. I've never heard it elsewhere. Original, maybe. You can't tell with these ballads. They may have been made up any time."

"Any time," Gog says. "Do you know what happened to Doctor Griffin? George Griffin, wasn't he?"

"Got killed in the war, I think," the minstrel says. "Did you know him?"

"A little," Gog says. "Yes, Doctor Griffin got killed in the war." He fishes in his pocket and catches two of the small golden coins. "Here's two guineas. It was a very good ballad."

"Ta," the minstrel says. "That's handsome. I can have a really good blow-out. And I don't get it often. Nobody much wants to hear the old folk-songs any more. Sometimes I wonder if I'm not the last of the minstrels."

"In twenty years," Gog says, "who knows? Perhaps every doorway in Britain will be full of a folk-singer with a guitar. You can't ignore the past for ever, you know. It has a way of coming back and tripping you up."

So Gog parts from the minstrel of the ballad of the Two Highwaymen. And he wanders on through the night city towards the south. On his way, he finds a fish-and-chip shop open, where he spends his two-and-sixpence on a vast cornet of fried cod and fat-brown potatoes, wrapped in the messy newsprint of *The People*. The grease stains through the items on crime and gambling and sex and war that tidily smudge the pages for the sabbath entertainment of all true Britons. But Gog is only concerned with stuffing into his belly the traditional night snack of beery Englishmen. And so, full and warmed, he comes to Micklegate Bar and the southern arches that run beneath the city walls.

Under the long-faced gateways with two round towers like protruding ears beneath a frizz of battlements, Gog sees the black car of Maire progress and stop by the kerb. He ducks into a doorway, for he thinks he is unseen. Over the car's bonnet, he watches the head of Jules appear in her peaked cap, as disembodied as the head of a traitor from the Pilgrimage of Grace or the Jacobite rebellion, a traitor's head once made gargoyle by the elements on its spike upon Micklegate. Then Maire appears in a long black trailing cloak as queenly as any royalty coming up to the capital of the North in procession from London, to pardon the city for its sins. Leaning on the arm of her chauffeur, Maire walks into a lighted doorway just by the gate, as Gog sidles forwards to cut off her pursuit of his journey towards Magog.

When Gog reaches the driver's door of the black car, he sees that lady luck has left the pea under the thimble for once. Jules has forgotten the car keys in the ignition switch. So Gog can climb into the seat and turn the key and look along the dashboard in front of him for the starter. The various buttons and levers and dials of the dashboard seem strange, yet familiar, as a boyhood crystal set discovered after a lifetime can seem to an ageing man. But by trial and error, Gog discovers the right button, presses the engine into life, and allows his reflexes to put the car into first gear, to take off the hand-brake, and to drive out of town under Micklegate at a trotting pace of ten miles an hour. A scrabbling of fingernails on the boot of the car makes Gog switch into second gear and a cantering twenty miles an hour, so that the screaming face of Jules in the driving mirror falls back to a mere white point in the night and then to nothing.

So Highwayman Gog rides out of York on his good steed, Black Bess, the paint on her flanks groomed into a glossy coat fit for Old Nick to wear. The engine snorts and the tyres paw the road, as Gog misses gear or reins in the brake too sharply. A constable blows his whistle as Gog gallops by without lights; but Gog presumes that the law will be after him and has forgotten under the streetlamps that cars need to carry their own lanterns. Horses never did.

So ride again, Turpin, ride again from York, outlaw and highwayman, pistols cocked at the gentlemen and cock pistolled at the wenches, ready to lift a fob or crack a nob at any time in the line of trade. O sit there, steady as china in your three-horned hat, your black curls a-falling round your rosy cheeks and fringe of beard, your red frock-coat as bright as blood over your pink weskit, your high boots black as your mare and the saddlecloth green as the fields of your getaways. So you also sit in the Staffordshire piece that stands on the high shelf in Merry's kitchen (where? where?) in the boyhood days gone by except in mind, the days when Gogling child is a-riding on the broom-handle down the streets, a wooden gun in his hand and in his mouth, " Bang, bang, you're dead, don't get up again!"

Yes, hang, hang, you're dead, Turpin, but do get up again, Gog the man is still riding the King's highway on the leather saddle of his horsepower, riding to London town with stolen guineas in his pocket, riding to fight all the King's horses and all the King's men, all the machines of Magog and all the might of Mammon, living as only a lone outlaw can live, by his wits, on his own, fearing daily betrayal by the people, the people who'll sing him as hero only when they've shopped him and laid him in lime in his prison grave.

Outskirts of streetlights.
Can't see the road.
Christ, headlamps! Which switch?
Wipers moving, scraping on pane. Switch off.
Own face staring in black mirror-back.
Slow down.
Approaching dazzle on windshield.
Switch. Nothing.
Press. Nothing.
Dazzle growing, growing, burning comet all over glass.
Slow, slow.
Roaring dazzle shrivel eye.
Swing wheel.
Screech.
Tilt fall.
Black glass slam face.
Wheel crash chest.
Death?

As Gog pushes his chest off the wheel with groggy arms, he finds himself beginning to smile with the surprise of being alive. The near door of the black car rammed deep into the ditch has sprung open so that Gog can fall out of the vehicle easily into softish mud. He picks himself up and finds glee welling up like a haemorrhage inside his bruised ribs, while his fingers explore to confirm that his cage of bending bones is still intact. Swaying and buoyed by joy as if smashed only on brandy, Gog climbs onto the tarmac to find the Bagman denouncing him out of his torrential white beard, with the radio jeep from the convoy parked unharmed down the road.

"You, is it?" the Bagman thunders. "Anti-Christ and wrecker, minion of Satan. Coming like the Worm in the night to destroy the wheeled Word that wingeth its way over the airwaves to the ears of the multitude. For the time is nearly at hand, when the twin Far Cities of the East shall perish. The awful engines of destruction are already in the silver bellies of the avenging archangels of the Lord. And Gog rageth with Lucifer across the land, already half-way to London before his mighty battle with the supreme fiend, Magog, which shall herald the end of the world. But thou shalt not try to wreck the wheeled ark of the covenant, which the Almighty hath put in the care of his servant Wayland Merlin Blake Smith. Weak though I may be, Pilgrim, in the face of Apollyon, God shall nerve my right arm to destroy thee!"

With these words, the Bagman lunges with a concealed metal aerial held in his hand and gives Gog a deadly thrust, which makes him give back as one that has received his mortal wound. As the Bagman makes at him again, Gog luckily falls backwards into the ditch on top of the ruined bonnet of the black car and faints clean away.

When Gog wakes, he is being laid on a stretcher by a uniformed nurse, driver and orderly. They raise him past a large red cross painted on a white circle on the canvas side of a curious ambulance, which has been converted from a troop-carrier. Gog is slotted into place inside the vehicle and looks up past a lighted spirit-lamp and a medicine cupboard at the camouflage colours of brown and green that make blotches of false nature above the iron struts of the frame of the hood. "The Bagman," Gog mutters. And the nurse bends over him, red and disinfected and reassuring, "There's no one here but us," she says. "No one at all."

"I am no one at all," a low voice says behind the nurse.

"Raise your hands for no one at all." Gog turns his head with the nurse to see a figure completely shrouded in a black cloak, wearing a white silk hood over its face. "I don't exist more than a nightmare does," the figure adds, lifting forwards the silver blue gaze of the twin barrels of a shotgun. "I am a bad dream but *this* can fire."

"Maire," Gog mumbles. "Yes, you're a nightmare. Do you know the old English word for a woman was a mare? And you're a nightmare. Always springing on me as I sleep."

"Hush yourself, man," the figure says. "Deluded." She motions the nurse out of the ambulance with a flick of her gun-barrel, and the nurse climbs down to join the orderly and the driver on the roadway, where they are being forced to drop their coats and trousers by Jules, still wearing her green uniform and cap, but now sporting another white hood over her face and another shotgun in her hand. When the nurse reaches the two men, she is made to take off her own uniform and pick up all the clothes and throw them in the back of the ambulance. Then she is lined up with the men and Jules walks towards her and slowly rips open the front of her slip, so that she is forced to clutch her arms about her to cover her breasts. Jules now walks round to the driver's seat of the ambulance, while Maire covers with her shotgun the three shamed messengers of mercy. The engine of the ambulance starts, the vehicle moves off towards the south. Maire goes to sit on the bunk opposite Gog and turns the shotgun on him.

"Quite a day for highwaymen," Gog says. "You're the fifth I've met, including myself."

"Kidnapping the kidnapper," Maire says, removing her hood. "It's poetic justice. Wrecking Boanerges, my favourite car! I should fill *you* full of holes. Still, the insurance will pay. They always do, don't they, it's their job."

"The police will catch you," Gog says.

"If they do, Jules and I will be wearing hospital uniform. We'll bluff our way. And since when did you ever say one good word for the *police*?"

"Why do you follow me, Maire?" Gog says. "Why can't you leave me alone?"

" We're linked, my dear," Maire says, " by our four bare legs. You drag me around with you, wherever you go. And *you* were following *me*. You stole my car. I was only trying to get it back. And as you wrecked it, I took the first available transport. You may leave whenever you wish. Though if you do, the gun may go off accidentally."

Gog smiles. " You wouldn't really kill me, Maire."

" Who talked of killing?" Maire says. " I never did. I'm not a professional murderer, miscalled soldier. I'd just pepper you, my dear. Fill you full of shot so that you could suffer a little more exquisitely than usual. Then I could certainly get you to the place where I'm taking you."

" And that is?"

" What they call a rest home, Gog. No one is called a lunatic there, because all pay to be called merely resting. You need a rest and a psychiatrist. In fact, you need a *team* of psychiatrists – the English do so love to take their sports in company. I know an excellent secluded spot in Cornwall near Land's End. You can go for walks on the cliffs and feel quite at home in the lucid intervals between the electric shock treatment. Just to show you how much I care for your fantasies, very close to the rest home there are a couple of large rocks in the sea. Gog and Magog, the locals call them. So you will be happy there, won't you? Your fantasies will reach bedrock at last."

Gog moves to sit up and take the gun from Maire; but he sees her face stiffen into hard paste and her finger whiten on the trigger. A sudden sharp headache makes him lie back again on his bunk. " Please, can't you leave me alone?" he begs.

" Never," Maire says. " Not till you're back to normal. They'll get you back to normal down there in a few months with the shocks."

" And what is normal?"

" Normal," Maire says smiling, " is when you can't leave me alone."

XIX

Jolt, bump and sway, looking up at the canvas roof, dark and ribbed as a mackerel evening sky. Drop, jar and shake, a yielding hardness under the back, a smell of iodine rank and erotic as rotting grass, its stain yellow as corn-stalks. Lids drowsing, flicking open, drowsing back on the willy-nilly journey, arrival out of control. Long, long since, the sprawling Gogling lies thus dreaming of tall and impossible women on the top of a haycart in the short summer journey, rumble-mumble from rut to rut down the track to the farm, while the twilight drives the labourers and the small boys home, small boys creeping out from their slums by the docks of Holyhead, small boys winter-white as mortar before haying time, brick-red by the autumn before they go back for bad to their coal-black terraces running in seams down to the salt shore, where the ferries to Dublin sound their mourning horns night and day after the deadly crossing over the Irish Sea.

Each morning, the wrapped bacon-sandwich and bottle of cold tea waits on the table, the dawn light so dim that the soot in the air seems to have layered the ledges and the china Turpin in dark dust, and Gog is out and away in jacket and buttoned boots before his parents have stopped moving and muttering in their chapel-holy bedroom, he's out and away running through the shivering streets with the air sharp as a mincer, running towards the ball of the sun bobbing red-bright on the seal's nose of the promontory above the rim of the flat black sea. Turn up off the tarmac down the twin titchy trenches of the cart-tracks, and hop from one to the other across the no man's land booby-trapped with thistles and coarse grass with edges rough as rusty bayonets and beaded with the gory dew. Into the hay-field as the men and women yawn and stretch and lean on their pitchforks, gabbing in thick voices and drowned vowels, growling in Celtic gibberish and mockery of English. Soon the squat men pull at their fingers and begin to pitch and toss the hay bales high onto the slatted cart, resting on its wheels big as millstones, with the heavy horses slavering at the harness and making earth pancakes among the stubble with their iron-bound hooves. Dodge the prongs of the forks swinging alternately to the rhythms of the men and pick up the stray scraps of hay and pass them on to the women, squatting and chattering in their wide plump skirts as they bind the bales. And so until the noon is a white splash of glare and the sweat trickles down into smarting eyes. Then it's the break and the sun-warm tea washes down the gritty bread folded over the cold salt fat meat and the boys' voices wheel as swallows while the men and women rest as crows. Then to work again through the long afternoons that never end, no never end, and the boys slip away fading with the falling sun, wilting by the cart until it's piled high and they can clamber up the scratchy slipping sides with the men prodding up the pitchforks in play at their scrabbling breeches. Then the final jog home with body flopped back on the cart, arms and legs asprawl, sleeping-waking under the dark fingering sky.

It is not always this. No, later the time of the troubles, the Irish troubles. What cares Holyhead for Flanders and poppies and mud, when it's the bog Papists across the water that are shooting down the King's men and helping the Hun and making the khaki boys tramp away from France where King George is needing them, tramp away sullen onto the gangplank of the old paddlewheel steamer. See them file into her, men hangdog and silent, never a song among them, with rifles shaped like crutches and puttees wound round their ankles careful as brown bandages. Watch them go sullen and slouching into the iron bowels of the ship, as you stand with your mother Merry, and she is blubbing and crossing herself, and you pull at her sleeve, Mother, Mother, not here, Mother, as the crowd about you shrinks back from her sobbing Hail Marys, as the black-garbed Wesleyans recoil until the only clear space on all the cobbled quay is a ring about Gog and his mother. And the Welsh are all mumbling and whispering and pointing to the two Papist spies among them, Gog all of ten years old and his praying mother, with his father suddenly stepping up the gangplank among the line of soldiers, his father with bare neck under brown cap and Kitchener moustaches desperately drooping, his father looking backward in fear and weariness, looking until he sees Gog and his mother, who runs forward screaming, Griffin, George Griffin, you can't kill them, you can't kill them, my own people, you can't kill them, Blessed Virgin, he can't kill them, his brothers. And the two policemen seize her and pull her back and Gog runs forward and bites the policeman's hand on his mother's wrist, sinks his teeth into the knucklebones and hangs on, until a swipe on his ear sends him cowering onto the cobbles, hands over his head. And he peers upwards again through parted elbows to see his father turn away in denial as he is prodded forward by the khaki men advancing behind him, his father's back turn away bowed under big pack and kitbag and rifle, his father turn away on the treadmill of uniform that falls into the belly of the paddleboat. And he sees no more of his father, except the sepia photographs yellowing at the edges, except the telegram that Father is dead for his country in Dublin, except the letter from the adjutant that the dirty Irish Papists have shot Father in the back off duty for the wearing of the khaki.

It's short commons now in the shuttered house with the pinched fingers of charity bringing bowls of dripping for the bread, and the plump priest offering consolation when there's none to be had, and the relatives always at their requiem. Well, what did you expect, Merry, if you would marry beneath you? And one day, Mother puts aside her drab weeds and rises in scarlet and feathers and she's off to the town for the pickings from the processions of soldiers. And the uncles begin to stop by on their way to the ferry, hanging their braided caps on the deer's horns in the hall, their Sam Brownes smelling of polish and linseed, the metal tips of their tan shoes digging dents in the Persian patterns on the carpet. And the uncles give way to a steady comer, the garrison Major ready for an Irish counter-sortie, the English squireen who treats Wales as a tribal reservation and Holyhead as a feudal village and Merry as a temporary wife, for any woman he is with must be a lady too respectable to be a whore. And the boys call out at Gog in the streets,

"Blimey, blimey,
Your ma's got a limey . . ."

till he's so bruised with blind bashing at his tormentors, his mother forbids him to go out. O, the fights are bloodier and not so classy as the Fights of the Fancy and peerless Tom Cribb in *Boxiana*, conned page by loved page. But the Major keeps on coming, bold, bluff and booming with small spiky mustachios, brown and rough as an oak, used to striding across a whole shire and calling it, My Estate. And when Merry swells at the belly and talk changes to marriage, How would you like another Father, Gog? How would you like to go to boarding school? Don't make a face now, say thank you to Major Meredith, don't you want to make me happy? Then the Major's off to the Somme for ever, transferred by request, and the relatives descend like cormorants and gulp down Gog like a codling, ready to disgorge him to the Jesuit fishers in the cold Northern moorland, where Catholic schoolboys learn to avoid perdition by Rod, Rigour and Restraint, the trinity of three R's so good for the soul.

But on the last day in Holyhead on Holy Island before the train will take him to the cassocks of Downforth, Gog runs across the narrow neck of land to Trearddwr Bay pointing towards Anglesey. And from the straits the sea creeps in crook-fingered along the low-lying mud-scratches that separate the hillocks of heather and granite and gorse. And the rabbit-tracks wind and scurry through the furze and the bracken, marked by brown pills of droppings. And Gog follows an inlet as it limps towards the straits, he follows it clambering over the stone walls and squeezing along the bushy ways until he reaches the brackish shore shelving in front of him, half-marsh and half-sand crying with curlew and gull. Crouch in the old familiar tree, the blackened bole of the old oak, charred and improbable, stricken and twisted and burned by some great heather fire or bolt from heaven. And watch, watch over the ridged table of the brown waves, watch the far shore where the trees mass like an army, watch like the Druids that Evans the Latin shouts over in school, Evans the Latin as thin as a ruler but snapped at the shoulder from a cradle-fall, his comma of black hair plastered down in a lick on his forehead, his teacher's voice fierce and nasal, the holy horror of small boys. " Construe, construe, you, Griffin bach . . .

You don't sit at the top of the form to warm your bum . . . Construe your Tacitus . . . It took the Romans to beat us." Halting and stumbling, tongue like a finger in treacle, dragging English words out of an alien language that has no relation to normal talk, Gog says, "*Hostes* . . . The enemy . . . many with many arms all together . . . stand on the shore. Women with black robes . . . with hair, I don't know, sir." "All out of place, like your construe," says Evans the Latin, then he's all wild and private and onto the old story, the dark story of old Holy Island or Mona which the fools confuse with Anglesey. And Evans raises his arms like the Druids from their white robes to call down fire from heaven and the Welsh women are howling and brandishing torches that flare among the sacred oaks and the Roman legions are massed on the far shore of the straits in a wall of bronze and iron, struck still by the force of magic called down by the Druids making their last stand by their last sacred grove. And the Druids cast mistletoe onto the waters to make the sea boil and bubble as pitch, but the old gods are deaf and Suetonius sounds the trumpets, ha ha, and the men of bronze and iron move into the water with their brass eagles held high, the cavalry swimming by their horses, the legionaries pushing off in captured coracles and timber rafts. And they swim across the straits as steady as the tide and the Druids pray to the gods to swallow them up in the great mouth of the sea. Will ye not listen to the Druids, the oldest and holiest of men of all time, the Druids who sent wisdom to Greece and Persia, the Druids who are the fathers of all religion and the teachers of the Brahmins and the Magi, the authors of all faiths after chaos and before Christ – or so says Dio Crysostom and St. Clement of Alexandria and Evans the Latin? But the gods of the Druids are still deaf, for the Druids have long sinned by following the heresies preached by Magus, son of Samothes and king of all the Britons according to Holinshed. So the sea does not boil nor swallow up the legions as a great mouth, and the Romans ride up the shelving shore on their horses or march in bronze and iron, and the Welshmen cast their clubs and spears and rush at the Romans in the breakers, but the lines of metal drive on and crush the Britons and the Druids, stamp them under and smite down the true faith and wrap the high priests in the flame of their own brands. And blood runs on the sand, the blood of Druid and seeress, of warrior and woman, until the last place of the ancient faith of all the world is razed and red and the sacred groves are hewn down and burned with fire and only one charred bole stands still by the shelving shore looking towards Anglesey and England, from where all evil comes, the men in boots and uniforms bearing swords or bayonets to cut up the true Britons of Wales and Ireland, to put out the light of the old faith called Celtic, to harry and occupy the land that was from the beginning the land of the Celts and their fathers' fathers till time before memory.

So speaks Evans the Latin in the ears of the small boys sitting at the benches and chalking pictures of hunchbacks on their slates called TEACHER, while they look at the broken body of Evans, who speaks fierce as ever in the mind's ear of the lying grown Gog jolting along under the canvas roof of the ambulance. And he thinks back to that day, the last day in Holy Island before he's packed off to Downforth to waste his youth among cassocks and corridors and skirted harsh holy men, black-robed where the Druids were white, their home a cell not an oak-grove. Never, never, never does he see Holy Island again, only the bleaker ruined rival holy isle across the sands from Northumberland, the wreckage of Lindisfarne where nature has taken back its own from the barren hands of the Benedictines. But on that last day in the true Holy Island, the young Gog sits in the charred oak, surely the last tree of the sacred grove, and looks over the straits to Anglesey like the last of the Druids. And he sees a curlew on the sand walking deliberate as a councilman, his neck stretched out and his long down-dipping beak held high. And the Devil puts a flint close to Gog's hand and he picks up the stone and chucks it at the bird, as he's done a thousand times as a boy and a thousand times missed. But today is the last day on Holy Island and the flint flies true and catches the bird on the shoulder as it begins to open its wings and run, so that it falls back onto the sand in a thrash of speckled feather. And Gog runs forwards, the blood hot in his ears, and he reaches the curlew as it staggers upright and begins to drag away, one wing crooked, and the sight of the escaping victim is thunder in his skull, and he jumps forwards and stamps and strikes with metal hobnails at the spread feathers until the bird is a still sandy lump on the corrugated sand. Then the cold wind chills the heat on Gog's cheeks and he bends down, his fingers touching the gritty down of the bird's white belly, then recoiling at the slime of blood, then creeping back again round the upstretched legs of the bird to pull it off the ground level with his own triumphant and terrified eyes. And Gog sees long scaly legs thin as a grass-snake, he sees a white underside, streaky with blood and sand and flecked with black arrowheads that also spot the grey-brown swell of the bird's breast and its head loose-dangling and its wings flopping downwards from dead joints and unstrung sinews.

Now bury the body. Bury the evidence. For this is murder, murder. Find a cranny, there's one, in the hollow at the side of the rock, where the wind's scooped the sand away. Drop the body down, then crush it flat with both fists, feeling the thin bones breaking under knuckles, until the curlew's sunk in sand and squashed on rock into a dish of feathers. Then up and scuffle the sand with boots until it covers the body, before bending to make a sandpie like a baby over the top of the curlew. Wipe, wipe bloody hands on the white sand, lick, lick at the last streaks of dried darkness on palms and knuckles, rub away the bloody mingling of boy and bird, of Gog and curlew, scrape till there's no evidence of murder, until the black guilt of the stuck salt streaks is merely red raw skin to take home, where mother will never know before she packs Gog away for ever, for ever and a night from Holy Island where the Druids lived by oak and blood and live raven and died by iron and blood and brass eagle.

So Gog remembers in the ambulance, jolting and dozing, while Maire sits on the bunk at his side, watching him with eyes hard and blue on either edge of her beaky nose. And she says, "Remembering? Remembering, Gog?" And he says, "Not a thing. I don't remember." And he lies back, his eyes closed, his arms crossed over his stomach. And he sleeps. And he wakes to Maire's grip on his elbow and a piercing pain in his bare underarm and the sight of Maire rising from the bunk beside him and stepping back in the still lorry. She has a syringe in her hand and she says, " Remember. You'll remember now. You'll have to remember all I ask you. You can't lie to me now. You'll tell me everything, and you'll remember it for good." And drugged with sleep, Gog hears himself mutter thickly, " Maire, Maire, what is it? Maire. Poison?" And she says, smiling, " Pentathol. The new truth drug. For making spies tell all. I found a bottle in the drug cupboard. I've given you an abreaction, I had a doctor chap tell me how the intelligence does it in the war. Now you'll remember. You haven't got an option. You'll answer all my questions and remember all you answer. Yes, you will, Gog. Then you'll be mine, as you always were, before this blasted war. Mine."

And Gog feels the drug rising in his veins, exploring, thrilling, quivering until his tongue begins to tremble in his mouth, loosening ready to jabber in answer to the interrogator with the full lips who knows his past and who lies for her own interest.

And Maire says, " Where were you born?"

" From the sea, the sea, the bloody sea. Like Albion, born from the bloody sea."

And Maire says, " Who was your mother?"

" A woman called Merry, who married beneath her and left her Catholic country house for a poor Celtic radical teacher. She could as well have been called Mary or Magog or Maire. All mothers are matriarchs. They rule the world through their sons, who cannot escape what they learned at the breast."

" And your father?"

" I hardly knew him. I was ten when he was killed in the Great War that killed all the best and the least. I never even knew what sort of a man he was, because everybody lied about how noble and good and true he was meant to be, and nobody in the twenties ever believed a word they were told about the virtues of the Great War, not to mention the Irish Rebellion. What price glory? My father had Kitchener moustaches like two black sickles. But he didn't have a chin, even before his jaw and the back of his head were shot off and he died of the khaki plague in Dublin."

" So you were brought up by women?"

" Yes. Women in skirts and women in cassocks. Jezebels and Jesuits. Rapped on the knuckles with thimbles or rulers. Made to put on swollen gloves and bash in other boys' noses, in case they bashed in mine in the name of sport. Always cold in parlours or schoolrooms. Sundays, strange scents and a chanting of Latin."

" An only child?"

" There was a half-brother, but we didn't mention him. He was born more than a year after my father died and sent away to London. Must hush up the scandal. I only found out years later. We had to think of the family. Griffins stay good or shut up."

And Maire says, " Why did they call you Gog?"

" I didn't like my name George and I used to like gooseberries. We called them goosegogs. And Merry used to say, ' Don't be a silly goose, George.' Then one day, ' Don't be a silly goosegog.' So I came to be called Gog."

" And Magog?"

" That was my half-brother, after I'd found out about him. I called him that secretly, after Gog and Magog. I never knew his real name till much later. It was Magnus. He went into the Civil Service before the war, the Ministry of Defence. He had been adopted into a family with connections. And he connected all right."

" Did you ever meet him?"

" Yes. Several times on leave in the war. He was thin and slick and suited. My looks skidded off his sharp surface. He used to call me Dr. Griffin, though we were brothers. He didn't want to acknowledge he was really a bastard. So we had to meet in secret, because he was curious. But in public, he'd have cut me dead, if I'd said Brother Magog. I was his skeleton in the closet, so he couldn't call me his own flesh. He wouldn't admit we had a blood tie."

" You envied him, didn't you?"

" Well, he's very successful. He never makes a mistake, which isn't a permissible error. Always moving up the ladder of success wrong by wrong. Always ahead on the promotion table. Everything calculated in advance, for his own advancement. You have to admire him. Though I don't want to be in his shoes. I don't like power. It corrupts."

And Maire says, "But you do really like power, don't you?"

"Not if it means being like Magog. He makes me squirm. I couldn't lie like him, if necessary. Too much the politician. He does a good job, perhaps. But if it makes a man into a Magog, we shouldn't have jobs like that. Or we should rotate them."

"You envy him?"

"Sometimes. He's so sure of himself. He likes ruling and knows he can. You have to envy him."

"And your marriage?"

"It was in the Coupole I saw Maire. She was like a Modigliani. I could see her naked through her silk dress. It was September, flies too lazy to crawl off you. Sweat stuck her dress to her breasts. She smiled at me, made me pay for her beer, went back with me to my hotel, was bored with me making love. She took my money, blued it on her painters and her girls, sucked me dry. Then, when I was packing to go, she came in with a handbag. That was all she had. 'Take me with you, Goliath,' she said. 'Enough of this *merde* of a morgue.' She always said Goliath without the h. 'Golly-at,' she used to say. She looked like a Renaissance David, a rounded beautiful boy with her back turned in her trousers, her bag like a sling-shot in her hand. She just wanted me to pay for her summer holiday. Then I got rich from my aunt. And I wanted her. So she married me. Maire."

And Maire says, "Liar. It wasn't like that. Did you love her?"

"Yes. I itched for her. I couldn't keep my hands off. She had such a skin, soft surface, muscle beneath. She could make love any way, as if Jesuits and sin didn't mean anything. I loved her. Even when I hated her. She deceived me. I knew it. But it was best to seem not to know. If I accused her, she always had an answer. Then tortured me for doubting her. And wouldn't let me have her. And I had to have her. Maire. I cared for people till I met Maire. Then I damned them and cared for Maire."

"Then the war came?"

"Then the war came. I joined the Intelligence. I was seconded to Africa. Then Italy. Then France and Germany. They can always use historians in Intelligence. It's what we're trained to do. Piece together bits of information to make a pattern. Sift the true from the false. Oh, that's possible in war. The job's easy. Merely to kill one another. But in peace, the job's impossible. You can't sift the false from the true. What's killing one another compared to living with one another? That's impossible. And what's the truth, when it's a question of loving one another?"

"Did the war change you?"

"It freed me from Maire. I learned to love the tommy, the soldier, the human. The people I said I'd loved before, oh they were an abstraction. Merely the folk. I wasn't more rational than a Nazi. But I saw men crawling out to die, just to try and save a wounded stranger in the same uniform. I saw them laughing when they were croaking. And even at the worst times, a sense of decency. Imagine, we were shooting a spy in Caen. And we made him dig his own grave. Then he asked to crap before he died. So the sergeant pointed to his grave and said, 'Crap in there.' So he did and we shot him. And after he was dead in the grave he'd crapped in, a man in the firing squad said to the sergeant, 'You didn't need do that. A bloke shouldn't have to crap in his own grave'."

"How did the war free you from Maire?"

"I didn't see her. I couldn't. At first, she'd crawl on me in my dreams. I'd wake crying. Then I got more scared of bullets than of her. Not so much of the bullets, but of not dying bravely. I didn't know whether I could stand up under torture, if they caught me spying. I didn't know I wouldn't scream like a baby from a flesh wound. But they didn't wound me or catch me. I got through scot-free, except for a scratch on the side of the head that makes it ache a bit. I may still be a coward, I don't know. But I lost my fear of Maire because I feared my own cowardice much more."

And Maire says, "But you're going back to Maire in London?"

"Oh yes. But peace won't be the same. The people rule in London."

"You know Magog still rules. The Civil Service doesn't

change. It's permanent. It rules the ministers, doesn't it?"

"Then I must fight Magog."

"And Maire? She'll still rule you, Gog."

"I'll fight her too. She doesn't know what war does. You learn to depend on yourself. There's no one else sometimes. You can do without women. They become irrelevant. Except to buy when you pass through a city. Two cigarettes, they cost in Germany now. They tell us to give no more, in case we spoil the price. I once gave a girl a whole packet of Player's and she wept with joy. Her breasts were better than Maire's."

And Maire says, "You bastard. You still love Maire?"

"I don't know. I haven't thought of it. For whole weeks, I didn't even think of her. I don't know. She's so remote."

"What did you do in the war you were ashamed of?"

"Nearly everything I did I was ashamed of. Taking a week-end's leave off a man because he had dirty boots. Telling raped girls we couldn't find the men. We could have, but we didn't have the time and they were only Eyeties or Krauts, you know. There was one girl who just put a child on my desk and said, 'Il vostro. Fatto in Inghilterra.' And spat and ran out. We caught her, made her keep him. She hated him."

"What were you really ashamed of?"

"Once they told me my good friend from Cambridge, Putney Bowles, was a spy. We knew he had been a Communist and pro-Hitler before the war – you could be both in those crazy days. They couldn't prove it officially, they had no tabs on him. He was working for the Germans, they said – or the Russians, except they were our allies, only there was top secret stuff that shouldn't go to Moscow. They told me to make it look like an accident. We went out duck-shooting near Cairo. He stopped to have a pee, turned his back. I blew off his head at five paces. An accident, naturally. I mistook his head for a duck in broad daylight. I didn't even know he was a traitor. But orders, you know. I went through his pockets. Found nothing. We never did find anything, not even in his effects. There was just a tip that he was a traitor, which H.Q. believed. So I shot a friend in the back of the head while he was having a pee. And I don't know. Perhaps all he did was only to believe in Stalin and Hitler for a time, some quite good chaps did before the war, I suppose."

And Maire says, "You did nothing shameful to women?"

"Nothing. I paid for what I bought, above the market price. Yes, I was ashamed. They wouldn't have, but for the war."

"Rape?"

"Never."

"You imagined it?"

"Yes. I always do. I lived with Maire."

And Maire says, "You swine. When you lose in life, you imagine your triumph within your skull. Then you blame women for hurting men, when women know perfectly well that men do nothing but humiliate women in their lusts. But I'm going to master your mind, Gog. Tell me now, what do you fear most?"

"Blindness. I'd rather lose all my legs and arms than my eyes."

And Maire lights a cigarette and puts it in a metal holder and says, "If someone tried to burn out your eyes, would you obey her? In everything?"

"Yes. I fear so."

And Maire puts the cigarette in its holder towards Gog's right eye, "Obey me."

And his instinct makes Gog snatch against the bonds of the drug, his nature makes him jerk from under the narcotic net, and he grabs the lighted ash near the skin of his eyeball and crushes the cigarette out in his palm, before his hand falls back limp on the bunk, and he says, "You'd have to have me held. You couldn't do it alone."

And Maire says, "I could, if you were asleep beside me. Why are you going back to Maire, if you don't still itch for her?"

"Habit. It's my home. I know the way. War's a state of mind. It's over. I have to find another state of mind. Perhaps it'll include Maire. At least, she's familiar. We can't start again without something from the past."

"Why not a clean break? Like . . . amnesia?"

"The past haunts me. The past all the way back to the beginning, the very beginning of men and women on this island, the past that from the very beginning made us all. I'm a historian. I can't forget."

And Maire says, " Surely the more you recollect, the more you belong to Maire?"

" An army psychiatrist told me, the more I recollected the past, the more I'd be able to free myself from it."

" Nonsense, Gog. The more you're bound by it." And Maire rises and goes over to Gog's bunk and sits beside him and takes his left hand and puts it to her left breast. " Remember the Coupole. My breasts stuck to my dress. You had to take me to your room. You had to. And I was bored. Yet you still had to have me again."

And Gog strokes Maire's breasts until the nipples are hard against his palm, then he moves his head and lays it on her lap, his crown against the small swell of her belly, his mouth buried in the hollow between her thighs. And he says, " I had to have her."

And Maire says, " The past. You remember. You're mine."

And Gog says, his voice muffled by the body of Maire, " We love what we've lived with. Because ..."

" Because?"

" Because we can share the past with them. We have to hang onto people we've known well, for we can check with no one else what we have done. They were our only witnesses most of the time. They were there with us, they still are."

And Maire says, " Mine, Gog. Mine?"

And Gog says wearily, " Yours."

And Maire says, " Is that the truth?"

And Gog mumbles, " Yours," slithering on the lips of the womb of sleep, then falling back into forgetfulness, as Maire cradles his head in triumph, whispering, " Mine. Men abreacted with pentathol can't lie. And you said you were mine. You can't lie, Gog. You're mine. You said so. Mine." And her eyes look up, blue and thin with glee, at the clear bottle of liquid, from which she has filled her syringe. And the bottle is marked ALCOHOL, not PENTATHOL. And as Gog sleeps, Maire feels the laughter shake her belly and rock Gog's head. For she has put mere spirits into Gog's veins to trick him into revealing how much he really remembers, how little he has recovered from his obsession for his wife.

XX

If weariness has brought about Gog's downfall, wakefulness brings about his escape. He opens his eyes to find Maire asleep in the other bunk, the shotgun lying on the floor between them like the drawn sword which lies between the chaste lovers of legend. Jules is, presumably, also asleep in the driver's compartment, for the lorry has pulled up off the road. Gog puts out one hand cautiously towards the shotgun and diddles it into his grasp. He then rises softly in his socks, his boots in one hand and his gun in the other, pausing only to scoop up a cache of maps of the Southern roads. He reaches the tailboard of the lorry and steps cautiously down the iron rungs to the highway. Maire stirs behind him, but only to clutch the pillow on her bunk and say, moaning, "Gog . . . uh, Gog," as if she would lull him back to her. Is she asleep or mocking? Gog does not want to know, especially when he opens the breech of the shotgun to find that it is empty of shells and threats to kill, so that Gog throws away the useless weapon into a nearby hedge.

The dawn glances in silver slivers off the wet slate roofs of the straggling town, which Gog sees ahead of him. He puts on his boots and hurries away from the lorry, fearing yet another trap and surprise, determined to avoid being outwitted again. From a sign on a bakery, he sees that he is in Totnes in Devonshire, the grey town falling down from its tumulus through narrow streets of tall houses to the bends of the River Dart. No wars seem to have disturbed Totnes for centuries. The round keep of the castle on the mound overlooking the town seems more like a bull-pen than a serious effort at defence. The granite houses sometimes have old leaded glass in their windows, spared by bomb-blast. As Gog walks down the High Street towards the river, he sees the pillars and tile-fronts of colonnaded Butterwalk and Poultrywalk, untroubled through the centuries in their steady sale of chickens and churned goods. There may be a war on and rationing, but Totnes is always Totnes and who knows what's under the counter? So down past the tall spire of the red sandstone church, holding up its stone splint through the ages in a call for peace and mercy, which God seems to have granted locally. Then on through the East Gate which spans the street with its pretty toy battlements and ornamental clock, and into Fore Street, where the carved gargoyle gables project the Elizabethan merchant's house over the pavement. There is a milkman delivering bottles outside shut doors from his pony and cart, otherwise nobody is about so early except for a bent figure standing by a granite stone set into the pavement.

As Gog approaches him, a sense of the familiar teases his mind. The greying cowlick—so loathely if it's Hitler's and so lovely if it's Chaplin's playing Hitler—the shoulder badly set into the back, the thin broken body and the seamed face that seems to have had an ice-cream scoop taken out of each cheek, where from, where? But Gog does not need to jog his own memory, for the tall hunchback turns in greeting. "Griffin bach," he says fiercely, "you're six years late for the Latin."

Gog cringes momentarily as if he'd had a sharp rap with a ruler across the knuckles, then he blinks his eyes and sees in the blink a chalk-dusty schoolmaster declaiming Druid curses against the English and dragging Gog's slow wits to construe, construe, use your gammon, Griffin, as Gog tries to tug meaning out of alien verbs and declensions. "Mr. Evans," Gog says in surprise. "I was thinking about you only last night, thinking about being in Holy Island when I was a lad."

"*Eheu, fugaces, Postume, anni,*" Evans declares, shaking Gog by the hand. "I know there's been a war on, man, but that's no reason to be late for the Latin. There's things more important."

"But here?" Gog says. "How can you be here, in this foreign country? You don't look a day older."

"Foreign, be damned," Evans says. "Merely occupied, it is. Like Wales is occupied, and France was. I'm not a day older, I'm years older. I spend all my summers here, as you well know. Doing the researches, indeed." Here Evans winks in complicity at the uncomprehending Gog. "When was it we last met?

Thirty-nine, the same month, August. There was our *job*, remember you. To faze the limeys."

Gog hasn't an earthly about what Evans means by their mutual job, but Evans looks so eager and plotting that Gog answers diplomatically, "Yes, the job. I've often thought of it. Did it turn out well?"

"The vellum, that was the trouble," Evans says. "When you find a good piece, it's been written on. Rare stuff, mind you, the scribes couldn't waste it. If you had to have a piece of hide every time you wrote a letter, you wouldn't waste words, would you? The day they invented paper and printing, there was an end to tight thought. Though William Caxton, I suppose, is partly why I'm here, mind you. Just like a bloody limey, he took it all from a Welshman."

"But the Welsh didn't invent printing first," Gog says, then, seeing Evans's face darken, he adds quickly, "though they invented everything else that matters, like magic and prophecy and mining and . . ."

"Not printing, Griffin bach. Don't mock me. Totnes! Tysilio the Welshman found this place first, and well you know it. You remember the lines he wrote seven hundred years before Caxton came and stole it with his . . ." Evans's voice suddenly rises to a derisive falsetto, "*Brute come to Totnesse*," before returning to its normal pitch of dark disclosure. "Tysilio called this place Talnus, that foxed us, till I began reading a scrap of Phoenician. And look you." He swings out a long arm from his hump as if to include the whole round hill of the town in the crook of his elbow. "What's the Phoenician for tumulus? Telneshua. That proves it, indeed. Brutus got Phoenician sailors to take him here after Troy fell and they called it Telneshua or Talnus, corrupted to Totnes hill, mark you. And indeed, what does Tothill mean, but a sacred place of worship for the Celts, who are the true Trojans?"

"Clear as crystal," Gog says quickly. "A most *convincing* case." A titbit of history comes back to his mind, so he adds ironically, "The Phoenician sailors, naturally, sailed on and discovered America a few thousand years before Columbus."

"Oh no," Evans says. "There's a pestilential error. And I

thought you were the next best thing to being a Celt, a half-Celt. Everyone with an ounce of gammon in his noddle knows who discovered America." Here Evans makes a pregnant pause, as if his next sentence could be a surprise. "The Welsh did. Hu Gadarn went there and back in a day in his coracle. Every Celt knows *that*. It stands to reason."

Gog wants to laugh at this fantastic statement, but Evans looks so penetratingly at him that Gog cringes again, still in the skin of the small boy, quite unable to contradict his teacher.

"The job," Gog says, "we were doing . . . you said you had trouble with the vellum."

"In the end," Evans says, "I had to forge it. Sometimes you can't show the truth any other way, can you?" Gog nods in agreement. "Look at that stone I was by, the one you came all that way to see in thirty-nine when we met again." And Gog looks down dutifully at the small granite block by him; above it, the legend is inscribed, *BRUTUS STONE*, 1185 *B.C.* "Of course, it's not the original. I mean, it could be, but it isn't. If you ask me, when the limeys occupied here, they broke up the original stone just for spite and put down an English one. Brutus Stone, in Roman lettering, it fair makes you vomit." Evans looks far too happy to throw up more than antiquarian bile. "But there's no matter if it's not the original stone. The original stone was just a stone, mark you. It's the *spot* that matters, the spot which Tysilio named when he wrote that King Brutus founded Britain."

"There's some virtue in having an original thing, isn't there?" Gog says. "It convinces more people if it's historically true."

"Who cares for history? We want the truth, not facts," Evans says. "That's what the Celts know, it is. And true, it is. It's the spirit, man, the spirit. The truth's in the spirit, not the facts. They're always telling us, those bloody limeys, you *say* that's Druid, you *say* that's ages old, but it's all spurious, all made up far later, all resurrected in the eighteenth century when you'd forgot your ancient wisdom and lost all your sources. But nothing's spurious in Wales, man. Nothing's dead, there. It's all living, it is. In the spirit of the people. That's a Druid truth, and the Druids know it well. The spirit comes round again and again and again, ever renewing, never dying with the body, always coming again, bearing the truth. So the truth can't die. It speaks through different mouths in different centuries, but it's always the same truth. It can't be spurious. As long as the mouth's the mouth of a Celt, as long as he's from the Celtic folk, who keep the ancient wisdom in their spirits, ever renewing it from the spirits of the past. Though most of the Welsh don't know the ancient wisdom to speak of, would you believe it, man?"

"I wish I was a true Celt," Gog says. "All of me, not half of me. Then I wouldn't have to worry whether I was looking for true things or false things. I'd know that the folk memory was driving me on and nothing else would matter."

"Half Celt's better than none, man," Evans says. "You can't be a bard, mark you, but we'll let you *listen* to us. We aren't exclusive like the limeys." Here Evans almost swells with his own generosity. "Especially when there's a Gog Griffin tracing back his ancestors to the ancient Britons, the very first giants here to meet King Brutus and the Trojans. Gogmagog, the *original*, you!" Suddenly realizing that he has given Gog an even more ancient lineage than himself, Evans quickly adds, "There's certain an *older* giant Evans was with Gogmagog to meet the Trojans, only Geoffrey of Monmouth didn't think it worth the mentioning, Evans is the very oldest name in all Wales, there's never a happening without an Evans there. Even the Crucifixion. An Evans held the vinegar."

"I'm sure you're much more ancient a Celt than I am," Gog says, pacifying. "But this research I came to do about Gogmagog?"

"It was a fine piece of work, a fine piece . . . for a *half*-Celt, which is no worse and no better than being a half-wit. Lucky it was, the meeting with me, your old teacher Evans. I put it to rights, the Druid wisdom that you could hint at, never hold and put down. When I had the vellum off a modern sheep, there's pity, I aged it in tallow and tannin and sunlight. Then I lettered it in old Latin with a goose-quill pen, no lying metal nib for me. No scribe was more careful, not St. Asaph himself." Evans looks round carefully to see if spies are eavesdropping, but there is only one sparrow cocking its head, hoping for crumbs rather than secrets. "I've got it hidden in my lodging, five years I've had it, mark you, waiting for you to come and get it, when the fighting was over, the limey troubles that take good Welshmen all the way to Singapore, God help them. And there's pity, they should never leave Montgomery, and I don't mean that damned limey-serving general."

"I gave you something in old Latin to put on vellum?" Gog says, bewildered.

"Ah, I see they've taught you well, pretend not to know then, there's best for all of us, who knows what limey's listening? Come." And Evans sets off at great pace down Fore Street, pulling Gog after him and muttering all the while so loudly that the West Country postman the other side of the street can easily hear them and pass it on by telegram to the cabinet, if he wants. "You couldn't do the Latin, the old Latin, there's too difficult, you can't learn *that* in a ninniversity. You must have the ancient wisdom. No, remember you, you brought me that thing in *English* translation, the fight of Gogmagog and how they broke apart into Gog and Magog. You said it wasn't spurious, you'd found the Gaelic original and done the translation, then you'd lost the original. And no one would believe you. They said your translation was a forgery, out of your own mind. And so it was, so it was. But the *truth* comes out of our own mind, the Celtic part, that is. The limey part's all falsehood, the limeys have no folk memory, they're a jumped-up bastard people. But I could use the Celtic half of your translation that was the true half and I put it into the old Latin on old vellum in my scribe's hand, no one will know it's not the original. Show it at the gate of heaven as your passport and St. Peter'll let you through with one hand, while he's using the other to throw out the Papists with all their damned forgeries." Here Evans reaches an old green wooden door directly on the street and begins to fumble through his pockets to find a key. "Of course, *I* haven't done a forgery, there's impossible. No Celt can do a forgery if his spirit's speaking the truth of his people, the original Britons." Evans produces a key the size of a monkey-wrench and pushes it into the keyhole so large a rat could saunter through it on its hind legs. "There's fools up at that ninniversity of yours, demanding the original, when they've destroyed all the originals with their own hands, to try and stamp out the ancient Celtic wisdom, the true Druid religion of Albion." Evans turns the key in the lock, which groans mightily, and he leads the way into a dark corridor that opens up on a little courtyard, containing an oak tree growing out of some paving-stones and an iron bench beneath its shade. "But they can't stamp out the Druid wisdom, because it's not written, it's in the folk memory. And if they're fool enough not to believe without a little piece of vellum, why, they'll get their *vellum*, the original vellum as true as the original Brutus Stone!" Evans laughs for the first time with a low cackle and takes Gog through a small door off the courtyard which leads into a room that is literally so lined with books that the walls are invisible. Pillars of volumes soar and sag on every side of Gog, so that any moment he expects to be buried under a toppling of tomes. Even the window is shaded by a pile of old manuscript on the window-seat. Every indrawn breath brings a stink of bookworm and mould, every breath exhaled threatens a deluge of paper. Evans sweeps a leather-bound set of rustic sayings off the only cane chair and declares, "Sit you down and make yourself at home. Pretty, isn't it?"

And Gog, looking round the palatial igloo of reading matter about him, can only nod and say, "Pretty, that's just the word for it."

Evans goes over to the window, peers out to make sure that the courtyard is empty, then bends and pulls at a panel below the window-seat. The panel slides back to show a small recess. "They don't think of looking here, indeed, the limey spies. They're after me, they are. Ever since cursed King Magus perverted the secret of Druid power and sold it to our enemies."

"King Magus?" Gog says. "Any relation to Magog?"

"What else? The bastard son, the ruin of the Druids, the apostate, the heretic Magus, who with his wicked ways made the gods turn away from the Druids for the stink of his abominations. Tyranny, may it rot! Magus sat in his shame and oppression in London and worshipped the golden calf, and now the Druids are no more, except in our spirits, that is. We shall return."

Evans straightens up, holding a brown roll of parchment in his hand. He scuttles over to the door, opens it, checks that the corridor is empty, closes the door, turns the key in the lock, and returns to Gog to give him the parchment as regally as if he were handing over the secret of the universe.

"There you are, there you are. The true story of Gog and Magog, from the very beginning. The original version, set down by some old Welsh monk twelve hundred years ago, and he was drawing on a tradition of thousands on thousands of years. We had nothing to do with it, indeed. The monk, he did. And if his spirit speaks through our voices and his pen writes through our hands, it is the spirit of the bards come again, come again, to speak the truth to the Celts and remind them of the ancient wisdom."

Gog unrolls the parchment, brittle and stained and transparent with seeming age and looks at the crabbed script that covers it on both sides. His eyes can hardly decipher the sentences and the words make no sense, for Gog cannot remember any Latin, let alone old Latin. He sees certain repeated words, *Goggus-Magoggus . . . Talnus . . . Brutus Rex*. But he cannot understand this document which at last may give him the secret of his origins in the giant, from whom Gog sprang, son of Gog, son of Gog, son of Gog, son of Gog, etcetera, etcetera, since the first rising of Albion from the waves of the North Sea.

All the while, Evans chatters on triumphantly. "There's proof, it is. Oh, they'll raise their eyebrows in the ninniversities, they won't want to believe, mark you, but there's the original fragment, they can't deny that. It's not the same as your translation, the one you brought me in thirty-nine, I told you, I could only use the half that was the true Celtic spirit speaking. Because half *was* spurious, the false pen of the lying limey, no offence meant, a man can't choose his own mother. And there were omissions, indeed. There's shame on you, not mentioning the old giant Evans who stood at Gogmagog's right hand against the Trojans and never fled at all, the only one, but lay left for dead on the field, before returning wounded to Wales undefeated. I set him in the Latin text, for there's the truth, the Druids told me when I was working on the vellum."

Gog pretends to study the parchment and allows his eyes to travel along the lines of Latin, as though he understands what he is reading. Then he says, "You've done a marvellous job. It doesn't only look like the original, it *is* the original account of the fight of Gog and Magog. The truth of the Druids revealed to you. But, one thing, you wouldn't still have the English translation I first brought you? I'd like to compare it with what you've done on the vellum, if I could."

Evans looks at Gog with suspicious eyes, his shoulder hunched under his brown tweed coat like the shoulder of a long-legged bird with a broken wing. "For why do you want your translation, that is half-false and half-limey, when you've got the Celtic truth between your hands?" He seems ready to snatch back the vellum from Gog, as though Gog were a sudden enemy.

Gog cannot confess that he has forgotten how to read Latin, so he says, "I must learn, Mr. Evans. I must learn to tell when the limey in me speaks falsely, so that I can guard against the devil's inspiration of my bad heredity. If I can compare my old translation with your Latin script, I'll be able to see what part of the truth I saw and what I didn't. And, in the future, I'll be able to do much more, much more for the Celtic cause because I'll be able to guard against the limey spy born inside me, who is always intercepting my true thoughts and putting down lies through my pen."

Evans is reassured by Gog's explanation, and he returns to the recess and produces several typed sheets, yellowed and brittle with time. "This is what you gave me," he says, handing the sheets to Gog. "But there are bad errors, mark you, which I had to correct in the Latin. Learn to avoid them, Griffin bach."

Outside, a bird calls, *zit zit*, *zit zit*, *zit zit*, three times. Evans hears the call, pulls a turnip watch out of his top pocket and consults it with satisfaction. "The martin's call, that is. There's the signal it's safe." He cups his hand about his mouth and whispers to Gog. "There's a secret meeting this morning along the street. The Celtic Council. Now the war's over, we're going to send representatives to the United Nations they're talking of setting up. We're going to secede, we are. Form the Celtic Union, the true Albion, the old land. We're going to petition for a new federated country, Britanny, Cornwall and Devon, Wales, Eire, the Isle of Man and the Western Isles. The countries where the last of the Celts are and where the Druids will rise again in power and glory, indeed. And if Magog and Magus try to stop us in London, why, we'll burn it down like Boudicca, the fiery Queen. Oh yes, the Romans may have killed off the Druids in Mona, but at their backs, London was burning. And if they don't let us rule ourselves now, home rule for the Celts, London will burn again, though I have to do it myself."

Gog is almost ready to laugh at the thought of Evans the Latin with a Druid brand setting fire to all of London, but he checks his laughter when he sees the fierce light in Evans's eyes, as he pulls an old cap low on his forehead and moves towards the door.

"One fire in Pudding Lane and the whole of London burned in 1666. They'll see it flame again, mark you, if they don't let the Celts have their Union." Evans takes an old bottle-green scarf from behind the door and winds it round the lower part of his face. "I have to disguise myself, I do. They follow me everywhere. Everywhere. All limeys are spies, by their crooked nature. They're always spying on me, the immigrants in Celtic country, and sending back word what I do to Whitehall, indeed. But they won't know me now." Evans swings back towards Gog, his face swathed in his scarf and his head swallowed up in his cap, but his hump making him the most obvious man in all of Totnes, if not in all the West Country. "Read you, mark you, learn you, and inwardly digest you the original Druid lore of Gog and Magog, as revealed to you in part and to me in whole six years ago in the original spot where King Brutus landed in Albion. And if *they* knock on the door to take you, Magog and his men, swallow it whole."

Gog looks with horror at the decayed inky hide in his hand and suddenly realizes he hasn't had any breakfast. "You haven't got anything to eat, have you?"

"What need you food, when you have the words of the spirit?" Evans thunders. "Swallow it whole, mind you, if *they* come. You won't have time to chew it. Swallow it whole, lest the truth fall into their cursed hands once more. Cymru ambeath, Gog Griffin." And Evans turns and goes out to the clandestine meeting of the Celtic Union, slamming the door shut behind him and turning the key in the lock to keep Gog inside with the precious manuscript. At the slam of the door, however, the columns of books ripple and shake and begin to slide downwards in an assault of dust, so that Gog has to leap up and be a constructive Sampson and shore up the pillars of the temple of Evans from bringing down the roof on top of him. Choking and spluttering, Gog manages to push back the skidding volumes into a precarious equilibrium, before settling down on the cane chair to read the version of the discovery of Albion by the Trojans, ascribed to him by Evans the Latin. And as he turns the cracking pages, he does not know whether he is reading a true transcript of an old document or a forgery suggested by his own imagination, half-Celt and half-limey and all myth, mysticism and muddle.

The typescript is headed, *A Translation from the Gaelic of a fragment about the early history of England, author unknown, probably a Welsh monk at Jarrow, circa* 600 *A.D.*

... In that dark awakening, when the green belly of the fell of Albion heaves nine times and the earth of the valley of Albion cracks long and the sinews of the hidden creeks of the sea beneath Albion press the sides of white chalk deep underground and nooses of closing stone squash me forth in green slime out of the cave into the gorge flooding with the torrent of the weed from the buried waters and I bawl in the hollow of the hands of the hills and the heaven opens its black pouch to empty down the washing rain and the great raven of the darkness cuts with his beak the cord of earth that plaits me to the cave and the wild goats slough their skins as a blanket for me and the dawn pours its yellow sand into my eyes so that I can first see, in that dark awakening is all I know of Eden. For I wake to find a monster lying at my side, his ankle touching my ankle. He lies twelve cubits sprawl, dressed in a tunic taken from the skin of wolves

with leggings taken from the belly of otters. His legs lie white on the ground in two ridges and the white bridge of his lower belly points down because a wolf's tail from his tunic falls between his loins. And the face of the monster is lean and pitted, his nose the iron blade of a scythe so sharp that his eyes lie far back in their sockets out of fear. And he smiles towards me and he says, Brother Gog. And I howl again and I rise to my own height of twelve cubits so that I may flee and there is a trap on my left leg and I look down and behold, where my ankle meets the ankle of the monster, we are joined by the flesh under one skin and one blood flows through our veins.

And the monster rises and smiles and says, Brother Magog, Brother Gog. And he steps forward towards the South, swinging his right foot that is joined to mine at the ankle and I must stumble willy-nilly with him or fall, although the surface of his skin is cold and scaled as an adder and he has no more smell to him than a dry stone. Where he goes, I must go, and as I shrink back from him, I am tugged forwards by the pain of my ankle that is joined to his. As I cry out, he only smiles and says, Gog-magog. And he puts his arm about my shoulder so that our bodies touch at ankle and hip and rib, and we stride together with our three feet taking one hundred paces to each league.

Behind us is the gorge which is called Cheddar and we go past the Hole called Wookey which is the navel of Albion until we cross eleven rivers, Axe and Brue and Cary and Parrett and Otter and Clyst and Culm and Exe and Yeo and Teign and Bovey, so that we may come to Totnes on the Dart river. And the soft knees of Albion hump about us as hills and the streams run brown with the peat of the moors and the badger scuttles away at our passing, only Magog stoops with his hanging hand and scoops the beast as a morsel into his mouth, breaking its back with a gnash of the iron points of his teeth as its head jerks from one corner of his lips and its hind legs scrabble from the other corner of his lips. Then Magog pushes the beast into his mouth with the flat of his palm and chews three times and swallows, while I root out the red-berried elder and strip off the clusters and squash them into my mouth. And Magog licks clean his lips and the iron points of his teeth so that he may sneer at me with the red juice running down my chin. And he will not rest, even to drink from the rivers, for King Brutus and the Trojans have set up their camp at Totnes and the giant sons of Albion must fight.

Round the holy ankle-bone of Albion, the mound of Totnes, the Trojans have dug a ditch and set up a rampart of earth. The brush of the roofs of their tents rises as a thicket within their walls and a great hum of many men walks the air with the neighing of horses and the screech of iron against stone and the bleating of sacrificial sheep and the chant of priests. For Albion, wounded in his skin by the digging of strangers, has called together a score and four of his giant sons, my half-brothers from the Southland and the Midland. Although Magog and I are spawned from the mother sea herself that girdles Albion and supports him as an ark, the mothers of my half-brothers are from the three and thirty daughters of the King of Syria, Diocletian, who banished his daughters to the ends of the earth when they slit the throats of their three and thirty husbands. When these furies came to Albion, he sweated up devils in the likeness of walking oaks and they came to the three and thirty daughters of Diocletian at Ogbury, on Avon, where Albion threw up a great camp for their spawning with walls three and thirty feet high and one mile round. And there our half-brothers were begotten on the daughters of Syria by walking oaks, that went away and were rooted by Albion on Hampstead Hill in a sacred grove outside the marsh of London. And the three and thirty daughters of Diocletian died behind the great walls of Ogbury, each giving birth to a giant, my half-brother and only six cubits tall.

The leader of the score and four giants met outside Totnes is Caugherigan of the single eye and the middle hand which grows from his chest that he may strike his enemies without loosing the ash tree that is his club and the millstone that is his shield. And on his right hand stands the giant Tregeagle from Dozmare Pool, who is condemned for rebellion by Albion to empty the pool for all eternity with a limpet shell and is now released to fight the Trojans, bearing a barnacled rock of three cubits' girth to crack the helmets of the Trojan warriors. And Little Grim is come from Lincoln, bearing a pouch of stones as large as a man's head and smoothed by the waves to cast at the foe. And Bolster of Portreath with the stretching legs, so long that he can put one foot on the Beacon and the other on Carn Brae, stands by Trecrobben of the ten fingers and the two thumbs and the twelve toes and no joints, and at their back is Termagol of the trident arms. And the giants of the Welsh country are there, Palug riding on his mighty cat with the jaws of fire and Annwfn's Chief of the tusk teeth sharp as stakes and Tyrnoc of the hair of vipers and Pen Palach of the oaken skull and Manawydan of the dark net that holds in the darkness and Pryderi that leaves no shadow, so black is he. And they draw themselves up about me, making a rampart of stone and wood and night to the right and the front and the back of me, and to the left I am joined by the ankle to Magog.

[Here Evans the Latin has made his only written comment on the translation – *LIMEY LIAR, WHERE'S MY ANCESTOR, EVANS THE GIANT, THE OLDEST AND BEST OF THEM ALL?*]

And there are the twelve giants of brass and copper and iron come from the marsh of London, Hand of the two brass faces upon his cheeks and Hyle of the clubfoot bound with iron and Coban of the copper arm studded with bolts and Guantok with sickles growing upon his wrists and Peachey of the clashing maw and Brereton of the burning cauldron and brass gloves and iron-girt Slayd with the headless Hutton on his back with spiked flails for limbs and Scofeld of the axe-pointed tongue one cubit long and Kock of the hammer head and Kotope of the crushing ears of copper and Bowen of the rolling brass barrel set about with glass. And they draw themselves up about Magog, making a tower of brass and copper and iron to the left and the front and the back of him, and to the right Magog is joined by the ankle to me.

And the Trojans come against us out of their rampart, leaving their ceremonies of blessing the new land half-done. And they draw up the spearmen in the middle squatting behind a row of shields, as close set together as the scales on a red dragon. And the Trojan horsemen stand on each flank, with manes of horse-hair on their curved helmets steady above the waving manes on the necks of their mounts. And they await the charge of the giants with the wall at their backs and the gates of the camp closed. For King Brutus with his champion Corineus of the red beard, the hero of the Trojans, does not wish to flee back over the seas from Albion, the White Island, but to build a New Troy here or to die with all the Trojans, whom he has led out of captivity under the Greeks.

And Little Grim casts his smooth stones so that many a rider finds himself astride a headless horse and the row of shields is broken as if a tooth has been pulled from a mouth. And Treg-eagle runs forward with his great rock and slays seventy horse-men, crushing them down on the broken backs of their mounts. And Caugherigan smites with his ash tree many men and breaks in the ribs of others with his millstone and strangles yet others with his middle hand, so that the number of the slain is one hundred and seventy and three. And Bolster squeezes to death seven spearmen at a time between his stretching legs and Tre-crobben writhes about a dozen horsemen and flings them in the air by a sudden straightening and Termagol sticks six times six men through at once with his trident arms. And Palug's Cat grasps forty spearmen in his jaws of fire, melting the bronze heads of their spears in his gorge. And Annwfn's Chief impales nine warriors on each of his tusk teeth sharp as stakes. And twenty-three horses and their riders turn blue and swell mon-strously as Tyrnoc passes by with his head of vipers and Pen Palach of the oaken skull slays seven men at a blow by ramming them with his head against the wall of the rampart. And Manawydan casts his net of darkness about whole lines of warriors and strangles them in its black cords, while Pryderi makes him invisible in darkness, so that no man can wound him.

So would I follow my champions, but Magog stands still behind his champions of brass and copper and iron, and I am bound by my ankle to his side. And the Trojans beset the giants as yellow flies beset heaps of dung, hacking and hewing at their ankles and calves, until Tyrnoc flees on bloody stumps and Palug's Cat runs away with mighty mewling for its pierced paws and Annwfn's Chief breaks his tusk teeth between clashing shields and engulfs himself in the underearth which is his house and Pen Palach charges the rampart so hard that his oaken skull becomes caught in a crevice in the wall and he is cut into twenty pieces and Manawydan's net of darkness is severed in seven places and Pryderi, pierced by a barbed arrow, flees, leaving Manawydan without cover and pricked on the points of a hundred spears. Little Grim, seeing the fortunes of the battle go against him, scuttles back to Lincoln, saying that he must search for more smooth stones, which only are found by the East Sea. Tregeagle is cut so much that he limps back to Dozmare Pool, finding his penance easy after such tribulation. And Bolster's legs are knotted by the many legs of the milling horses so that he goes off groaning on his knees and the backs of his hands. And the ten fingers and twelve toes of Trecrobben are lopped one by one until he rushes away howling and holding up his two thumbs for mercy. And Termagol of the trident arms flees with his prongs splintered inwards so that every time he strikes at a shield, the blow glances back and wounds him grievously in the ribs with his own wooden barbs. Only Caugherigan still slaughters the Trojans, until he finds himself before Corineus of the red beard, who lops off the middle hand of Caugherigan with a magic axe of sand-blessed iron and breaks the millstone of Caugherigan about his head and splits the ash tree of Caugherigan in twain with the point of his shield and slices Caugherigan into two parts from crown to thigh so that each half of Caugherigan falls away from the other on one leg. And still Magog and his champions of brass and copper and iron do not stir, even though I howl and plead to join in the battle.

When the champions of stone and wood and night are dead or fled, the Trojans blow the trumpet for the advance against the metal giants standing before them. And the horsemen charge against the giants and brass breaks them and copper scalds them and iron severs them and they fall about us until we are walled nine cubits high by a rampart of heaving horses and twisting men. And Hand of the two brass faces upon his cheeks shatters many a jawbone with a swing of his head and Hyle of the clubfoot bound with iron breaks fetlocks as faggots for the furnace and Coban of the copper arm studded with bolts cracks necks as nuts for the oven and Guantok with sickles growing upon his wrists lays spearmen low as weeds before a scythe and Peachey of the clashing maw grinds down men whole in his bronze mouth and Brereton of the burning cauldron sears horses and riders into screaming steam and iron-girt Slayd with the headless Hutton on his back with spiked flails for limbs winnows the Trojans and beats them bloody with iron points and Scofeld of the axe-pointed tongue one cubit long hacks furrows in the faces of warriors so that there are bloody mouths where there were once noses and Kock cracks rib against spine with the blows of his hammer head and Kotope of the crushing ears pulps arms between copper lobe and copper flap of each ear as in a vice and Bowen rolls back and forth upon the fallen in his brass barrel set about with glass.

Then the rampart of the slain and the wounded and the neighing and the wailing is wrenched apart and Corineus of the red beard and King Brutus rush upon us as a mighty wind. And King Brutus picks up Bowen by either rim of his brass barrel and hurls him a league high and three leagues South so that he falls in the watery mouth of the Dart and plunges to the depths. And King Brutus puts out either hand round the copper ears of Kotope and twists them out and widdershins until they loosen in his grasp, and he kicks Kotope earless clean from off the field with one blow of his boot. And King Brutus meets the hammer head of Kock with the knuckles of his right mailed fist and shivers it into a hundred pieces, and he winds the axe-pointed tongue of Scofeld about his wrist and swings him round and round as a flail to knock the headless Hutton off the back of the iron-girt Slayd, so that he may beat the two fallen giants to death with the body of the third.

And Corineus of the red beard spits into the cauldron of Brereton so that a dense fog arises, and he seizes Brereton by the throat and burns off his head in his own scalding weapon. And Corineus of the red beard reaches deep into the clashing maw of Peachey with his mailed hand and drags out the brass-bound gizzard of the giant, who chokes on his own tripes. And Corineus of the red beard bends back the wrists of Guantok so that his two sickles pierce the red points of his two nipples and his life's blood flows in two streams down his chest. And Corineus of the red beard wrenches off the copper arm studded with bolts from the shoulder socket of Coban and drives it as a stake through the iron-bound clubfoot of Hyle. And Corineus of the red beard spreads his mailed palms wide as a roof beam and boxes the cheeks of Hand of the two brass faces, so that they shatter in splinters of metal.

And so King Brutus and his champion, Corineus of the red beard, stand before Magog and me, and the Trojan host stands in a great circle about us so that we cannot flee.

And Magog my brother in his voice of iron struck on the anvil says, O Strangers, by what right do ye dare to slay the sons of my father Albion, on whose skin ye tread and in whose holy name I speak?

And King Brutus gives answer, My right is by the oracle of Diana, in whose temple I set up three altars to Jupiter and Mercury and the goddess and spoke nine prayers and walked four times about the altar of Diana and poured out the sacred wine and lay down before the altar on the skin of a hind until the third hour of the night. Then the goddess Diana appeared to me and spoke thus:

> *Brutus, past land of Gaul and the bed of sun,*
> *There is an island, an ark upon the ocean,*
> *Its moat is ocean – there few giants live*
> *And it is solitary for thee and thine.*
> *Find it! And thereafter stay for ever.*
> *And for thy sons, another Troy shall rise,*
> *And from thy blood will stem the island's Kings,*
> *To rule in blood the quarter of the world.*

For this reason, I now call this island Britain and my companions Britons, after my own name, for this island was Albion and thine and is now Britain and mine.

At this speech of the usurper, Magog throws himself upon King Brutus and I grapple with Corineus of the red beard.

I grasp Corineus of the red beard by the neck with both hands to pull his head from his shoulders, but he drives his knee into my vitals so that I bow forwards in pain, bringing him down over my back and shifting my grasp. And now I catch him by haunch and shoulder with my arms behind him and crush him against my back ribs and straighten upwards until he screams and clasps my hair with one hand and puts a thumb in my eye so that I have to fall upon him to drive the breath from his body. But as I fall, our joined ankle brings Magog topsy-turvy upon me, just as he has King Brutus in a lock and is about to slice open his throat with the scythe in his nose. King Brutus steps back and leaves the field to his champion and Gogmagog, for the prophecy is that he shall live to found Troynovant or New Troy, not be carried into the site of the city on a bier.

And Corineus of the red beard, rising from the ground, catches Magog about the ribs with his left hand and catches me about the ribs with his right hand and presses out the breath from our bodies until our ribs crack like the skin of roasting pigs. And

Magog and I link our four hands in one mighty fist behind the back of Corineus of the red beard and we press against his ribs. And we each hug the others tight in the shackles of our arms, making the air quake with our breathless gaspings. And we hear the ribs of Corineus of the red beard split, one, two, three, two on the right side and one on the left. But the splitting of his bones rouse him to wrath and with a mighty heave he throws us up over his shoulders so that we slip down the further side of his back and our heads dangle on the ground and our joined ankles are a halter round his neck. Now he rushes forward with both hands pushing at the fork of flesh about his neck and the speed of his going knocks our faces against one another so that the scythe on the nose of Magog slashes my cheeks and I strike out at my brother and we fight, tearing at one another, as we are dragged swiftly over gorse and rock and heather to the top of the high cliff above Plymouth, where Corineus of the red beard swings us about until our two heads dangle over the edge of the granite and he slips the halter of flesh from about his neck and pushes us down and we fall joined through the bright air, howling and the sky moaning blue tears above us.

And a great darkness comes upon me falling and a great pain and I am again in that cave where I was begun, but now my own red blood is washing me for my death. But in the void that is the starting and stopping of all things, I hear the voices of the Trojans and I am raised up and I wake to find cloths bound about my wounds and chains bound about my feet. And behold, the teeth of the rocks have severed me from Magog at the ankle and we are two. Gogmagog is dead and we are Gog and Magog. Once I had been bound by links of flesh to my brother; now I am bound to him by links of iron with a chain about our legs.

And we are made to march the full circuit of the island, while the site of New Troy is chosen by King Brutus, who now wears the white fur leggings of Magog as a border to his long robe of royal red, so that two strips of white fur run up the front edges of the robe from ground to shoulder and then run down at a slant to meet in the middle of the chest of King Brutus where he wears a clasp of gold wrought in the shape of a bull. And Magog always strides ahead of me, reproaching me for his fallen state and dragging me by the chain on my ankle behind him. And the brass shields of the Trojans are all about me pressing me onward. And over the tops of the armoured ranks I can see the dew as tears on the rotting brown grass of Albion.

And we come to the marsh of London. And a league towards the river Thames from the hill of sacred oaks at Hampstead, King Brutus makes the Trojans build the first gateway of New Troy towards the North. And they chain Magog and me to either tower of the gate and call the gate Aldermanbury, for King Brutus dies and his son Locrine comes after him and is an evil ruler and breaks his pledged word to marry the daughter of Corineus of the red beard, so that the father rises up against Locrine and is put to death by a stratagem and his body is hanged upon a gibbet of alder outside the North gate, above the chains from which Magog and I rail and spit and throw filth at each other, for we cannot grapple unto death since we are separated by the twenty cubits of the full width of the gate.

And so the new Britons build the New Troy on the site of London marsh and the sons of Albion are chained as porters to the gate of Aldermanbury below the gibbet where Corineus of the red worms is hanging. But Magog begins to give counsel to Locrine how he shall put down the followers of the hanging champion, called after him Cornishmen. And Magog is released from his shackles and is taken to the palace of New Troy and sits at the right hand of the King and he knows the Queen and she begets a son, the apostate Magus. And I stay chained by iron at the gate under the shadow of the body of the dead hero of the Trojans, and I stand upon another body, the body of my dead father Albion . . .

At this point in his reading, Gog moves an elbow which catches the edge of a heap of books and dislodges them. As they topple, dust rises as sharp as lime to the throat and nostrils, so that Gog hacks and sneezes and splutters. This movement of air trembles the pillars of leather and paper and print and glue; they quake and shimmy and slide and finally crash on one side of Gog, on the other side, over him and under him, behind and before in a great tumbling of volumes that entombs him in a rubble of learning. He feels the Gogmagog translation in his hands and the vellum in his lap tear and crack into fragments. He kicks and struggles as the books crush him with their masonry of covers and pages, he is interred as fully as a blitz victim beneath a wall. He coughs again and again to clear his lungs of the grime of ages; but each time that he draws breath, he gathers a throatful and two lungfuls of ancient dust that make him hawk once more in desperation. With each heave of arm or leg, another cornice of books thuds down onto the pile, adding to the weight of archaeology and mysticism on Gog. After three or four gigantic jerks and splutterings, Gog has only succeeded in bringing most of the library upon his head or his limbs, while his final kick merely causes a smashing of glass in the window-seat and a blast of wind from the courtyard which blows the dust even more cloakingly into Gog's windpipe, so that he is buried alive and gassed simultaneously, as if he were an Old Contemptible in a Flanders trench assaulted simultaneously by poison clouds and mortars.

Gog lies prone for nearly a minute, feeling the dead weight of the research materials of the past crush the blood in his veins, until his fingers and feet begin to go numb. Carefully he tries to breathe through the hairs of his nostrils without moving ribs or diaphragm, yet he cannot suppress a choking belch of dust that makes him gasp for the air which will not reach his lungs for the puffing powder of the pages. And Gog knows that he will be slowly pulped and choked under the documents of Evans the Latin, if he cannot move. So slowly, slowly, he begins to draw his limbs close to his body. His left arm, its wrist scraped bloody on the metal hasp of an old tome, is pulled through the crevices of piled paper until Gog feels his elbow against his belly and his fist against his chin. Then his right arm is inched in, although bent backwards by the collected works of some forgotten historian; Gog has to move that arm sideways and upwards by an agony of force, until he can bend the sinews and draw it in, dislodging another layer of dust into his mouth, which explodes in a further detonation of exhalation. But Gog's two fists and elbows are now touching beneath his chin and can force the weight of the burying books a little way off his chest.

Now for his legs. Gog swivels both feet in the sockets of his ankles to make two crannies, then suddenly heaves sideways with the trunk of his body into the little space cleared by his forearms above him, the space no higher than the coffin lid above a corpse. This successful heave allows Gog to get his legs together, one on top of the other, and it is only a matter of time before he forces his knees upwards until they touch his elbows and eventually his chin.

So Gog lies in a ball of flesh below the pyramid of books, Gog lies under the dust of learning, gathering his forces to erupt out of his living tomb. And then, with a violent splaying of limbs and jerking upwards, Gog explodes out of the paper blocks of wisdom, sending books flying about him as though they were shaken by a trembling of the earth's crust, his coughing sounding as loud as huffs from a volcano. Fearful of a quick reburial, Gog continues to scrabble and flounder among the tearing of paper and the ripping of bindings and the haze as thick as ash. Like a sea-monster thrashing on a beach in a sandstorm, Gog makes for the window as for water. Kicking and lunging through the flotsam of the library, he reaches the remaining panes of the window and hurls himself through the glass onto the paving-stones of the courtyard and into air and life. He leans back, clearing his throat and spitting against the wall of the house under the window, sensing the indrawn breaths line his lungs as sweetly as spring water lines the casks of thirsty sailors, feeling the hot blood throb in his forehead from the wound in his temple.

Yet the dust of the books still eddies from the broken panes and Gog begins to cough incessantly again. So he rises and lumbers out of the courtyard past the oak tree down the dark corridor, where he fumbles at the latch of the street-door until the door opens and looses him into Fore Street in the white clear morning. And Gog must drink or cough up his lungs in shrivelled scraps of paper. So he runs up the street until he sees an old tap leaking on the outside of a grey-walled house down an alley. And Gog clambers over the garden wall and turns the handle of the tap and scrubs his hands under the falling jet and cups his palms and begins to scoop and splash water into his mouth and face as if he were used to the Sahara rather than the rainy island of the world.

When Gog has laid the dust in his lungs and has slaked his thirst, he returns to Fore Street. He is guilty at the mayhem which he has left in the den of Evans the Latin and he is determined to go back and put the worst of the mess to rights. But look as he will in Fore Street, he cannot find the door leading through the corridor into the courtyard. No door seems exactly the door he once entered, yet all doors look vaguely like the door. He tries knocking on several doors, only to be met with silence or angry stares or curses. So Gog goes back down the street to the Brutus Stone. But there is no one about, only the spurious inscription. *BRUTUS STONE, 1185 B.C.*, placed there somewhat after the event.

Hunger gnaws like a rat in Gog's belly, so that he walks eastward into the rising sun over the bridge that crouches upon a green sliver of island and crawls on diamond piles to the far side of the river, where an hotel promises good scavenging in the dustbins. There is stale bread enough to be found even under rationing; for the West Country does not go short of food, and the hotels always justify their prices by what they waste. And there is fresh milk on nearly every doorstep, for the hand moving quick enough to tuck the bottle out of sight under a coat. Thus Gog feeds and turns left onto the road towards Exeter. At least, he hopes it is the road towards Exeter. The signpost says so, but who can trust signposts in Britain any more, ever since the Home Guard twiddled all the signposts around so that the way to Plymouth is marked Paignton and the way to Ashburton is marked Kingsbridge, all to confuse German spies who may be trying to find their way around – as if a spy wouldn't have a map and a compass and find his way around perfectly well despite the heroic Home Guard. In fact, the only people confused by the signposts pointing the wrong way are the various foreign troops trying to get to the South Coast on the way to Europe, and these poor souls are always finding themselves in Bristol rather than Plymouth Hoe, with the natives chuckling over the stupidity of all aliens and saying, " Everyone knows the way to Devon's tother way." Yet an instinct for the past makes Gog cross the silver Dart and swing left, trusting to the signpost saying *EXETER via NEWTON ABBOT*. Magog and his men may have turned the directions round to confuse; but as Gog walks up to the rise and sees the serpent river flash its scales in the sun while it slithers along the vale below and beside him, he feels sure that he has walked this way before in 'thirty-nine, in 'thirty-nine, when just such a morning peace fell in brightness from the air and war was a threat rather than a presence and nature made a like Munich of light and green and road and stone to appease the most troubled spirit.

Past the nostalgia of Roman lettering on the milestones to Newton Abbot, past the fat porker tooting on a fife and hind legs at the inn sign of the Pig and Whistle, past the slate roofs of the cottages glistening like slicked tents, past the giant's stilts of the telegraph poles mired behind tall hedgerows, and over the rise to see the curdled ridges of fields in pats of olive and emerald butter all the way to the burning side of the churn of the sky. The peace of the road is only broken by one convoy of army lorries, which grumbles by on its ordained and mysterious errand, forcing Gog into the nettle and brier patches on the side of the road. These sting and scratch him into a brief awareness that rural quiet is bought sometimes at the price of world war.

The very permanence of the landscape that ignores the passing of all men on their petty businesses would seem to Gog to involve the same perceptions in all men. As peace steals like an earwig into the sleeping shell of his soul, so he expects it to steal into the souls of the army drivers, looking from their high windows at the green conspiracy of truce about Gog. But perhaps their eyes are boxed in by their artificial cabins, their ears are deaf except to the right running of their motors. Or else there would be an immediate mutiny and all the drivers would flock out and loll on the grass and take time off to watch the Devon hills and tors hump towards the North.

Yet Gog supposes, although men cannot see the same things

in nature because each man reads into a scene his own hopes and despairs, yet some things are common to all men. The common fear of bolts of lightning and hammers of thunder. The common joy at sun on water or buttercups in meadows. And the naming of places by common consent. On Gog's map taken from the ambulance, he can see marked Mamhead for a mountain peak, Ipplepen for a shepherd's village, Ugbrooke for a nasty stream, Shillingford for the way over it, Hope's Nose for a promontory into the sea towards the sunrise, Coffinswell to remind him of the human sunset. Names by Celt, by Anglo-Saxon, by Norman; Dunchideock, Bovey Tracey, Cheriton Fitzpaine giving way to the neighbouring Stockleigh English. Names by races, by spot, by tree, by animal; Jew's Bridge, Exmouth, Ashcombe, Otterton. All place names agreed mutually by past villagers from the evidence of their eyes and now hallowed by time. Once perhaps, when all men were close to the soil, there was a common sight, now going, going, gone to blindness behind the many layers of brick and metal and glass that men have erected between their eyes and nature.

Gog reaches Newton Abbot past a cider factory and a cemetery, and he enters the somnolent suburban town, all cooped and cosy. Only the crazy-paving fronts of the Grace of God Mack-rell's Almshouses, only the yellow gothic pinnacles of the Victorian Science and Arts Library, are insane enough to jolt the town from its mild monotony. Gog finds a jeweller's shop open where he hopes to trade in his guineas for pound notes to buy food and appease his bubbling belly. But the quick, ducking jeweller snatches the golden coins and scurries into the back of his shop, making Gog crane over the counter to hear him hissing into the telephone, "Police? Come quick, come quick. A tramp selling me guineas, stolen no doubt." So Gog runs out of the shop, penniless past the cattle market with its straw stinking of scared beasts, ammoniac with the same terror of hunger and confinement that sends Gog panting towards Exeter.

The town ends in an old pipe factory of white brick with tall octagonal chimneys that bisect the low mounds of the hills beyond. And as Gog staggers north dizzy with emptiness and fatigue, he sees the insidious yellows of the southland disease the summer greenery like a fever. The leaves are flushed with ochres; streaks of yolk run along the ferns; whitish lichen poxes the bark of trees. The haunches of the hills are tattooed by the harvested fields so that red earth and mustard stubble make patches of contagion on their flanks. Then, on the sudden, the green horns of a hawthorn are moved by two brown spiky branches, and Gog sees a stag gazing shocked at his approach, until it kicks away and thrashes through the thickets.

As always, the suburbs holding up the joined palms of their high tiled roofs pray at the approach of the city of Exeter. Among them, a few cottages are stranded, yokels with hairy thatches out of place in such a kempt congregation. Ahead lies a goal for Gog's stumbling steps, the oblong bleached length of a cathedral rising up above surrounding rubble. And this sight is enough to carry Gog forward up the hill over the last two weary miles into the bomb-blasted centre of the city. The cathedral itself seems to have made an unholy pact with Satan for its preservation; no miracle would have been powerful enough to save it among such a surrounding shattering of brick.

There are few people in the street in this late July afternoon in that lost half hour between the closing of the shops and the opening of the pubs. But in front of the red sandstone ruins of an old Tudor almshouse, Gog comes on a horde of women, shoving and pushing at each other to get closer to some Pied Piper of housewives, whose siren music can make them forget their tired feet and heavy shopping-bags and waiting children, and charm them into scrumming about in front of a ruin. And sure enough, above the pre-war felt hats turned inside-out for that new look, above the frizzed hair done up with wooden pegs and tongs at home, above the knotted cloth scarves bright with blurry flowers, Gog hears the luring notes of the greatest salesmen of them all, Maurice the Supreme Wrangler.

XXI

" The very latest," the voice of Maurice chants. " Supersheer nylons. Stockin's so thin you can't find 'em 'cos they're invisible. The latest fashion in the U.S. And 'ow do I know they're the latest fashion? I nicked 'em off the legs of Laureen Bacall last night, and that was a sight, I can tell you. Transparent 'ose for ladies. They make your ankles so thin witches'll nick 'em for broomsticks. You ain't seen such nice bits of nothin' even pre-war, 'cos they weren't dreamed up then. No coupons, no rationin', just a quid a pair, don't tear me 'ands off, ladies. Yes, I know they cost a bit, but the best always does. And if you knew what I 'ad to pay for 'em, you'd know I was givin' 'em away. Five pair, that's a fiver, lady. Put 'em on and the 'ole navy'll be queuin' at your door. You can't get stockin's like these 'olesale, retail or blackmail, just cash on the nail to yours truly."

The dowdy women on the outskirts of the female mob round the stall turn ugly in their frenzy to get near the purveyor of all delight. They kick with their blunt-toed shoes, hack with stacked heels, prod with elbows and the points of umbrellas, swing tatty leather handbags, claw at shoulders, and whine threateningly, " If you don't mind . . . you've had your turn . . . If you were a *lady* . . . Don't shove, I was here first." The discipline of years of waiting in queues is forgotten in a moment at the siren's song of thin stockings, the last pairs worn out years ago into joined ladders. And Maurice keeps on the pressure, turning up the pitch.

" Don't kill me, ladies, I'm doin' me best. Ta, dear, 'ere's your change in frillies. I ain't got nylon only for the legs. Ho no! I got nylon knickers edged with lace, prewar stocks from gay Paree, what our brave boys liberated just to trim your panties. Don't 'oick my eyes out, ducks, you blind that madam next to you. Fifty bob a pair, the panties, four a tenner. No reductions for quantity, I 'ad to give me 'eart's blood for each of 'em. Course there may be some of you ladies what don't care 'ow you look underneath it all. But 'oo knows when '*E* won't be comin' 'ome just to 'ave a look at you underneath it all? An' if '*E* won't ever come 'ome again, why, there's plenty of others comin' 'ome these days. Or passin' through, if you don't fancy '*Im* permanent, like. You've ripped me sleeve, lady. That pair'll cost you a fiver. Look, I ain't a polished nigger, and this ain't a lynchin'. Easy does it. Don't pull them knickers out of 'er 'and, dear, they'll bust. There, I told you. That'll be twenty-five bob each, as you've each got one leg. Don't tear 'er 'air out, dear, she may be wearin' a wig. That's all in knickers, ladies, but I ain't through yet. There's slips to come."

The mob of women begins to heave and swell as a few triumphant ladies, their hats pulled over their eyes and the buttons ripped off their jackets, come burrowing out of the mass and run away with their purchases cradled in their arms more carefully than a day-old infant. The gaps they make in the crowd are filled quicker than a hole in junket, with tempers rising and arms starting to flail and voices screeching. But the voice of Maurice shouts even higher than the combined din of the bacchantes about him, all clawing at this true Englishman, the Orpheus of all the hucksters in the world.

"Now, ladies, these 'ere are slips what even 'Er Royal 'Ighnesses wouldn't mind slippin' in. Look at 'em, all the colours of the rainbow. Peach, tangerine, plum, you'll bloom like an orchard. Put 'em on, and you'll feel like you came out of a can from California, yellow-cling peach 'alves, that's the ticket. Slip into these, and '*E*'ll be apple-pickin' all night long. Five nicker a slip, and I'll tell you what I'll do. For every two slips, I'll throw in a pair of nylons. Big-'earted Morrie they call me, I'm givin' 'em away. Ta, lady, you're into a good thin'. As me favourite readin' matter, Mister William Shakespeare, says, There's many a slip 'Twixt the 'ip and the 'ip. And I wouldn't mind slippin' in there with you, dearie, why not see me after?"

Gog watches two tall policemen turn the corner and quicken their pace as they see the frenzy of women bobbing and fighting about the stall. They try to part the women at the back of the crowd politely; but they only get shoved and dug in shins and ribs for their pains. So they draw back and bullock their way in among the women, using shoulder and knee and boot to reach the cause of the riot. Gog sees first the useless scuttle of one blue-black helmet, then of the other, sail over the hats of the crowd. The policemen's heads just keep above the wrack of ladies' bonnets askew and clawing fingers; but one copper's bleeding from a bloody nose and the other's got a prune swelling up on his right eye. Gog hears Maurice shout, " That's all, ladies, God bless you," and then a convulsion shakes the mass of women, a shrill keening rends the heaven as if the body of the dearest of dear departed had departed. And the policemen's heads go down, as the ladies begin ripping off their uniforms and battering them with brollies and bags in a mayhem of lust disappointed and longing frustrated. And there is a small eddy on the skirts of the maelstrom and Gog sees Maurice's head emerging between the legs of the women. As Maurice crawls into the clear street between the calves of a large blonde, engaged in slamming her shopping-bag onto the glass cherries of another woman's bonnet, he looks upwards into the hidden thighs of the blonde and sighs, " Woollen drawers, it fair drives you to chastity." Then he's out of the rumpus and scuttling down the street, as fast as his fat legs will carry him, his hands plunged deep into his pockets to hold down the loot. But as he scampers past Gog, Gog reaches out a long arm and brings him up, short and snuffling.

" You," Maurice says in horror. And he tries to eel off, but Gog holds him by the arm and whispers, " You better walk with me, friend, or I'll tell the coppers who you are."

" 'Ow much?" Maurice says, resigned, and pulls out a fiver, which Gog takes with his free hand and puts away in his pocket, thinking of all the meals he can buy now to fill up his hollow belly. " 'Olesale, retail, and *blackmail*. I was really talkin'."

" I don't want money," Gog says.

" Then give it back."

" I want food," Gog says. " Here." He pulls Maurice sideways into a convenient Kardomah and plunks him down at a brown table in front of the mirrors and drapes of gentility, where the padded shoulders and thick stripes on Maurice's blue suit make him look like a thief in a parlour.

" Something of everything," Gog says to the waitress, " and

pots of tea." "That means something of nothing," the waitress replies, going off, "and pots to pay." Gog turns back to Maurice. "Back to street-selling," he says. "Last time I saw you, you were dressed like a general and you could have supplied ten armies."

"And 'oo ruined me?" Maurice asks furiously. "As if 'e didn't bleedin' well know. Left me for dead, you did. Blew a bloody 'ole in me underground 'angar and piled up the works on top of me corpse. I couldn't get out, could I? I couldn't 'ardly breathe. So course they find me, the coppers and the lot. Ask me where I got me stuff. And you know me, lofty, I don't 'ave no bills for nothin'. Anythin' wrote down can always be used in evidence against you. So they said I'd nicked the stuff, *me*, 'onest Morrie, the lad you can trust. They even said they found serial numbers on stuff what I'd bought fair and square on the black market. If you ask me, the coppers planted it. Jealous, they were. And they would 'ave sent me down, too, only I did 'ave *one* paper what me old right 'and man 'ad signed, that Scotch lunk 'ead you met on the moors. And the paper said '*e* was the legal owner of some of the stuff, but I 'adn't signed nothin'." Maurice chuckles. "So they 'ad to send 'im down and I lost the best friend I ever 'ad. I'd rather they'd 'ave cut me arm off. 'E were a good lad and 'e kept 'is gob shut."

"Didn't he object?" Gog says, snatching a plate of bread and margarine off the waitress's tray and stuffing the food hand over fist into his mouth, while she sets down the tea-things with a disapproving clatter of china.

"Object? 'Im? 'E were glad to pay me back after all I'd done for 'im. 'Is last words to me were, When I get out, I'll do you. What do you think of that? 'E were too overcome with emotion to finish what 'e was saying. What 'e meant was, when 'e gets out, 'e'll do me another favour."

Gog pours out cups of tea for himself and Maurice and goes on wolfing the strawberry jam that tastes of sweet splinters and the mock cream that tastes of shaving soap and the sponge cake that tastes of the absorbent absence of all taste. Maurice watches the ravening Gog with interest.

"You ain't 'ungry, are you, lofty?" Maurice says. "You

wouldn't catch me ever goin' 'ungry. You may 'ave reduced me back to the gutter, you stupid yob, but the gutter's not a bad place for a pitch. You saw me out there, coinin' it in faster than the mint. You can't keep a good man down. Nah. Bet you I'll be in the 'Ouses of P. by the time you get there. In the Lords, too. Sent there by a grateful people for signal services rendered to 'is country in the line of 'osiery and 'aberdashery." Maurice laughs and looks at his watch. "Go on, take the last cake in your pocket, lofty, I've got a meetin' with me suppliers. An' there's another fiver in it for you, you big lump of brisket, if you 'elp me cart away the gear. I could do with a strong man what keeps 'is mouth shut. And though you're as thick as a door-knob, you ain't never blabbed, which is more than I can say for most. So, let's scarper."

Maurice rises and makes for the door. And Gog, swallowing his last cup of tea, makes after him, only to be stopped short by the waitress shoving out her open hand in front of him. Gog gives her his new five pound note, large and white and scripted, and she puts it up against the light, suspicious of forgery. But she sees the metal line embedded in the paper and she has to give Gog back his change, four pounds and fourteen shillings, the seven florins so heavy that they pull down Gog's hand like small weights. Then Gog's out of the café after Maurice, who is waiting for him, signalling impatience with slithering eyebrows as black and thin as twin brackets. Maurice leads Gog off at a trot down alleys and byways through the old streets of Exeter. The British natives in their civilian drab and macintoshes grow thin on the streets and the new Trojans dominate with their pink and brown and black faces, always hairless even on the backs of their skulls below their caps. Strange accents sever the hazy air with the twang of bow-strings. The invaders do not walk with either of the gaits of the English, they do not shamble nor clip along straight-backed and heel-digging. They move loosely without slouching, as if floating in a state of alienation from the foreign soil under their boots and from the contamination of the Old World. They are spick and span in mustard or olive uniforms, where the English soldiers lurking on the corners are dowdy and slouching and creased in khaki and green webbing. The foreign sailors from the ships of the New Troy of the New World are likewise scrubbed and shining in white bell-bottomed trousers and tunics purer than the spray, while the limey sailors are crammed into coarse blue uniforms, rough and rolling as the swell. The forces of the two nations do not fraternize; they walk on opposite sides of the street as though it were as wide as an Atlantic; when a brave convoy of men makes the crossing, it plunges into the harbour of a safe pub to berth as quick as possible. So Gog sees the invaders come again to England in their ships to the West Country. They may call themselves allies, but so did Hengist and Horsa and the Saxons, when they had really landed to plunder the wealth and women of Albion, before taking it over.

Past the hurrying Gog and Maurice, an old man walks, purposeful and unexplained. He bears a large placard on his chest, which proclaims in red letters the message:

LONDON IS DOOMED,
Unless
The Bishops open JOANNA'S BOX!

He is handing out leaflets to the uninterested and Gog would dearly like one, but Maurice at that moment pulls him sideways into a pub. Over its door of frosted glass, there swings the sign of a hook-nosed man in a cocked hat with all severity on his face and the legend beneath him, *The Duke of Wellington.* And under the sign of this fearsome patriot, the Yanks pour in and out past Gog and Maurice, who find themselves in a public bar boiling with beer and roaring with whores, with the invaders packed in ranks round the horseshoe bar of polished oak. And the strange soldiers and sailors pull temptation glossier than apples out of their pockets, nylons and chocolate and cigarettes in shiny packets, perfume and chewing gum and lipsticks in gilt cases, so that the eyes of the women of the town glisten like peeled grapes and they dart forwards their hooked fingers to snatch and they let the troops suck at their lips and feel at their breasts. And Maurice eels into the hubbub and racket, pulling bank notes from his pocket and trading them for the treasures of America, what price Araby? And from every foray, Maurice returns to Gog, loading him with plunder until Gog's arms seem to be supporting the merchandise of a small department store.

Then the door of the pub is kicked open and a battalion of native soldiers sweep in, crushing the invaders back against the far end of the room. It's the Gorblimeys, their flashes green on their shoulders, their berets black as their hearts. Behind them come a covey of camp followers, the loyal tarts of the district, true to home and regiment. And as the Gorblimeys ram in ready for a punch-up to take back *The Duke of Wellington*, Maurice sees his supply arrangements about to blow up in blood and slaughter. So he leaps onto the bar and begins spieling to keep fists down and hearts up, Maurice the trucemaker and troubadour of commerce. And such is the flow and honey of his tongue that the noise dies down and the soldiers drop their knuckles and their bottles and everyone turns to the tattler on the bar.

" Steady, boys, steady," Maurice shouts. " You can 'ave a punch-up all right, nothin' I like better, only I've seen it all before, nothin' else for six bleedin' years. Why bother to go to Alamein when we've got Iwojima right 'ere in our own back garden? Go on, 'ave a scrap then." And Maurice yawns elaborately.

" We don't need to ask you, buddy," a Yankee says, and there is an ugly eddy in the mass, which Maurice quickly counters.

" I've done me bit, too . . . and it was a nice bit . . . of tit. While you was away fightin' to keep the 'Un out of British mothers and daughters, I was stayin' at 'ome 'avin the fun of makin' British mothers out of daughters." There is a little chuckle. " Like the Grand Old Duke of Wellington said to me personal, Morrie me old, 'e said, Don't fire till you see the whites of their thighs." The chuckle swells into a roar of laughter and Maurice is away. " Look at all the lovely ladies in the room, only don't call 'em ladies or they'll slap you for sauce. And while you've been away a-fightin' and a-dyin', what's they been doin'? Just sittin' on their arses keepin' the tea and the beds warm. So what I say is, you've all done your little bit for 'em, why don't you let 'em do their little tit for you? You'd like to see a bit of boobs, wouldn't you, lads? A free strip? Let's see oo's got the tarts with what nature distended. Don't tell me the Yankees 'ave got a better lot of United Dairies than the Gorblimeys."

"They probably have," a tired Gorblimey voice drawls. "While we win the wars, they win the whores."

"Ho no," Maurice says. "You ain't lost before you're off. Where's that old British never say die?"

"Dead," the same voice says, "at Monte Cassino."

"Nah, it's up and doin'," Maurice insists. "And I bet, underneath it all, the Gorblimey girls 'ave got a lot more to show for 'emselves than meets the eye. 'Aven't you, girls?" A chorus of cheers greets him, with jeers coming from the Yankee ranks. "But the proof of the puddin's what's dished up on the plate, ain't it? So I propose, lads, not a punch-up what'll only bring in the M.P.s and put you all inside. I propose somethin' to tickle your fancy, somethin' for the sportin' spirit of old England. A great Breast Match, the Yankees versus the Gorblimeys. And may the best span win."

There is a shout for the rules and Maurice willingly obliges.

"Each mob to put up four 'ores, picked by a democratic vote, up the people. When you've fielded your top team by common consent, the ladies show what they've got above the navel." There are a few female shrieks, but these are quickly suppressed by a great roar of male approval. "The referee's that great big lug over there in the corner of the room . . . give 'im a big 'and, boys. 'E's so neutral, 'e's a bloody pacifist." Gog finds himself picked up with all his goods and passed over the heads of the mob and hoisted onto the bar by the side of Maurice. "This 'ere is Gog, and 'e'll treat you fair and square." A great booing and catcalling shakes the room, while Maurice grabs all the goods from Gog's arms and whispers fiercely in his ear, "That'll teach you, lofty, to bury me in me own 'angar. If you get out of this in one piece, it's no thanks to Morrie." The yelling dies down and Maurice pipes up, "The ref, me old sport Gog, 'e'll judge the titties of the lovely ladies, and 'e'll score 'em. Ten points the pair for what providence put there." A cheer rocks the rafters. "And ten points for what each lovely lady can do with what she's got. So if you ain't well stacked, me lovelies, you can always do a little shimmy and a shake and if the lads give you a big 'and, why, the ref'll give you up to ten points for performance. So it's ten for what you can do and ten for what you've got from nature and I bet she gave you 'andfuls. So it's eighty points possible, four a side strip, best breast forward, and the winners take The Iron Duke. 'Ow's that?"

The soldiers and sailors whistle and halloo and pull their tarts into a circle and nominate their favourites by a show of hands. And in the general ruckus, Maurice is off the bar and away with his loot clutched to his belly, he's out of the frosted glass door and into the street. Gog also tries to scarper, but the press is too thick and the moment he tries to get down from his oaken throne, the military turns nasty and shoves him up again. "You stay there, ref. You'd better. Till close of play."

So the teams are nominated for the great Breast Match in *The Duke of Wellington*, and Gog feels he's wandered into the pages of the favourite reading of the wartime troops, *Lilliput*, where the girlies bare their all and the jokes are spicy and sporting enough to keep a tommy warm o' nights in his foxhole.

And for the Gorblimeys it's Gloria with the frigid face and lank blonde hair, Gertie the stick all willowy and willing, plump Gilda fresh from the churn, and Glenys the Magnificent, all curds and copper curls. For the Yankees, it's Mildred the hairless gorilla girl, Mirabelle the mincing and oh-my-dear-really, trim Maisie tight as a trivet in her twin-set, and black Mayhem from Martinique who came for the Free French and found the Yankees much freer with their lolly.

"Seconds out of the ring," Gog calls. "Strike one. Bails on. Gorblimeys to drive, and she's off." Behind him, he hears the pub-keeper desperately shout, "Time, please," but there's the thud of a bottle on flesh and no more sound from the voice of law and order.

So the great Breast Match begins. And Gloria opens for the Gorblimeys and she comes out of the pavilion and takes her stance at the crease and examines the placing of the Yankee fielders, who are ready to swoop on her every stroke. She fiddles around in front of the crease and, as the eyes come up to bowl out of everybody's sockets, she lifts her blouse and plays forward with a nice neat pair of low-slung breasts, shaped like white cricket boots tipped with red pompoms. The Yanks try to barrack her, shouting, "Keep it closed," but the Gorblimeys cheer her all the way back to the pavilion, because she stonewalls and keeps a straight face and puts the shutters up until Gog the umpire closes play and she can drop her blouse. Gog scores her five for a decent show and none for her stiff upper tit.

And second into the ring is Mildred for the Yankees. She peels off her scarlet shirt to show a pair of desperate pink reinforced silk cups trying to hold back the deluge. When she looses the support at the back, the deluge plunges down to her navel, making two short slack extra arms sprouting from her chest which end in soft fists sporting red gloves on their knuckles. While the Yanks howl, "Ten, ten count it again," the Gorblimeys groan, "Nowt, nowt, she's knocked out," and Gog yells, "Two for the milk round." But Mildred is equal to the insult. She walks over to the bar where Gog is sitting, hops onto it, puts a hand under each breast, and slugs him with the old one-two, hitting his left eye with her right pap and slamming him as he bounces with an uppercut from her left pap. "Nine, ten, out," the Yankees shriek, and Gog has to score her so, while she struts up and down the bar, her left forearm pushing up her breasts in triumph, her right hand clenched above her head in a fist of victory, and her voice screaming, "Tit for bloody tat."

And next into the arena, facing up to a deficit of five points to twelve, is Gertie for the Gorblimeys. She does several knee-bends, then a somersault out of her mauve sheath, which falls onto the floor, leaving her only in her orange track pants. She shows nearly all, only the Olympics would close if that was all there was to show. The two slight bumps beneath her nipples might pass for promise on a ten-year-old boy. The Yanks howl, "We was robbed," while even the Gorblimeys can't defend the theft. And though Gertie gallantly beats her bare chest and hallooes, "Me Tarzan, you Jane," pointing at a blue-bearded, red-blooded, black-souled and lilywhite Marine sergeant, Gog can only score her two for audacity.

And next Mirabelle is off the Yankee bench and ready to swing on the plate. When her white shirt peels open, and two firm mounds palpitate above the lucky black catching mitts of her brassière, the Yanks yell, "Strike two," and she looks as if she's going to hit twin homers. But come the unhooking, when the mounds dissolve into two tiny baseballs with all the stuffing knocked out, the sass all turned to sag, the Gorblimeys shout, "A pair of ducks." In a breast as in the rest, nothing is further from achievement than potential. Gog scores her three for not being offensive, then adds on another seven for sauce, when she puts on a great goofy toothy grin over her inadequacies and pats them from palm to palm, saying solemnly, "Ping ... pong ... ping ... pong!"

And she's off for Milord Gorblimey, Gilda in the chocolate and cerise ... and my, o my, she's whipping off her racing colours, because the stewards want to weigh her in ... and it's a two horse race all the way ... on the right on the rails, Titillation, a lovely filly, one hand tall and what a shape, a bit soft in the withers but bred for staying, by Pectoral out of Sensuosity, made for soft going ... and on the left on the outside, Corsage, another lovely mare, one hand tall and who would want more, curved for the saddle and bred for stud, by Cleft out of Easy Come, doesn't mind a fast pace ... and with three furlongs to go, it's Titillation, by half a length from Corsage ... and with two furlongs to go, it's Titillation, Titillation and Corsage ... there's not a gap between them ... and it's Titillation and Corsage, Corsage and Titillation ... and at the post, it's Titillation and Corsage, nipple to nipple, a dead heat, and the prize is shared between them, eight thousand guineas if it's eight points ... but the race is too much for them and they're stabled at once and Gilda just stands there, proud of nature's bounties and doing nothing with them, when their natural gyrations have settled to rest. So the Gorblimeys win nothing for performance.

Next onto the golf course is Maisie for the Yankees, with the score standing at twenty-two points to fifteen. She swings a useful niblick with her left palm into the right-hand bunker of her twin-set and the ball is blasted out into sight, a lovely orb though a little on the small side. And again Maisie swings a mashie shot with her right palm into the rough and another little ball pops out onto the fairway in full view. Each of the balls is dotted with a large red spot for instant recognition; what there is of them is nice and the make is good. So Gog scores her two holes in a par five, giving her ten in all, when she gives a terrific swing with her hips and follows through by a jerk of her shoulders so that the two breastikins pop back into their bunkers without using a blaster.

So it's a desperate situation on the Centre Court, as Glenys goes into the final for the Gorblimeys, with seventeen match points to save in the last two sets. But there's guts in the fighting lassie, and with her first serve, she throws up a beauty out of her blouse, as firm as rubber and as round as perfection, and the second serve's the same, so that even the Yankees whistle, and it's game and set for the magnificent missie, who never says die and knows there'll always be an English rose, or a pair of them. And in a tight corner, still seven match points down in the last set, inspiration strikes our Glenys and she takes out her lipstick and quickly strings her breasts with a web of crossed red lines so that they look like rackets. Then she shimmies her titties so fast that the rackets seem to be batting the nipples from one to the other, while her head tocks from side to side watching the play, until with a mighty final effort, she lobs one breast upright while doing a savage overhand smash with the other. The spectators break forward onto the Court and carry her off on their shoulders, shouting that she's won every point going and handing her up the twin cups of victory that house her remarkable genius for tennis.

So it's thirty-six points to the Gorblimeys and thirty-three to the Yankees. And Mayhem from Martinique comes in to wind up the affair by a bull's eye from thirty paces. And she strings the cupid's bow of her lips and she notches the first black arrow of flesh between the buttons of her dress and aims and lets fly. And the right breast scores an outer, a bit ridgy and odd and hard as a shield. She doesn't seem eager to try a second shot and she says, "Score me on that. We only need four to win." And Gog scores her two and a half. And she still won't try a second shot, though all the Yankees are yelling, "Shoot, sister, shoot." And, in the end, very carefully, she takes aim and fires a second breast of such ebony beauty that the very spheres would fall silent in worship. But there is one thing wrong; the second breast doesn't match the first and also seems a little rough at the edges, so that, while the Yankees are yowling, "Ray, ray, the

USA," a lank Lancashire Gorblimey creeps up behind Mayhem and snatches off her second breast and throws the falsie in the eye of the blue-bearded Marine sergeant, while amazon Mayhem pleads, "Give it back. Anyway, I won't need it. I've saved up enough to have the other one paraffinned." But no one listens. For the blue-bearded Marine sergeant is about to lay out the lank Gorblimey and start the biggest free-for-all ever seen by the Iron Duke since Waterloo.

But Gog tries to pour oil on troubled soldiers. "I score her half," he shouts, "for artifice. That makes a tie. Thirty-six each. You *share* the Duke of Wellington."

There is a mutter and a moan. Then Maurice's voice croons again from the rear of the crowd, where he has slipped back to collect more loot. "When it's a tie, lads, I say, knot it round the ref's throat and string 'im up." There is a roar of approval. "But we're a sportin' lot, so why not give 'im a small chance? Let *'im* be the target, and let the 'ores (God bless their darlin' 'ides) 'ave another game, the Tarts' Darts Match. Strap a dart-board on each 'and of that dirty old ref, and one over 'is cock, in case any of you ladies wants to make 'im sing soprano for the rest of 'is life. Then the 'ores will 'url their darts at Goggie, an' 'e will try not to get 'it by puttin' a dart-board in the way. The 'ores score what the dart-board says if they 'it one. But if they 'it Goggie, why, they score thirty for a limb, forty for a body, fifty for an 'ead, an' an 'undred if it's a man's eye." A great hurrah shakes the room at this prospect of slaughter without tears by the slow puncture of a helpless man.

Gog tries to leap down and run for it, but he's caught by a score of willing hands, and a dart-board is tied onto each palm and a round cork codpiece over his crutch, and he is left exposed and alone on the range of the bar counter.

"Elevation thirty," Gog hears a voice call. "Armour piercing. One round, prepare to fire."

So the great Tarts' Darts Match begins, with Gloria stepping up to the mark and pushing off a slow feathered shaft on a high arc. Gog finds it easy to intercept with his left platter, and he can feel the dart thump home into the cork. "Thirteen," a voice calls, "unlucky for some." But Gloria's quicker off the mark with the second dart, which whizzes straight for Gog's front teeth. More by instinct than thought, Gog ducks and puts up his right platter horizontally, so that the dart sticks without scoring in its side. "Zero," the voice shouts, and the furious Gloria hurls her last dart low, driving its point home into Gog's calf. He howls and tries to pluck it out, forgetting the platters on his hands. But all he can do is to increase the pain by pressing the end of the dart sideways with the edge of the board, so he has to give up trying to remove the missile, which stays stuck in his leg.

Gog concentrates on the enemy in front just in time, for Mildred has already launched her dart and Gog has to duck and let it whistle by his left ear to smash a bottle on the bar shelf behind him. Mildred is so enraged by his evading action that she throws her other two darts simultaneously, so that both home in on Gog at once. He fends one off with his right platter, and by the grace of feather, the other dart plunks home in the circle round his vitals. "Eight plus seventeen," the voice calls, "making twenty-five to forty-three for the Gorblimeys."

Next on the throwing mark, Gertie the stick favours an underarm lob which sets Gog highstepping along the mahogany bar like a bucking cart-horse. One dart he stops with his left platter, one impales his trouser-leg and the third nicks the skin on his jawbone as it flies by, its feathers whisking Gog's bristles. "Three," the voice calls. "Nowt for near misses."

Then it's Mirabelle with a high roundarm swing that brings the darts out of the blind spot level with the lights so that she notches one in Gog's thigh and one on his rib that is turned back by the bone, yet sticks long enough in his clothes to score. Her third dart homes in on his cork crutch, making a score of thirty plus forty plus eighteen. "Yankees one hundred and thirteen. Gorblimeys forty-six," the voice calls amid a barrage of boos and cheers, while Gog hops up and down, swearing at the iron points pricking his flesh.

So it's Gilda, the plucky wee lassie with loads of British guts, throwing the javelins from the mark. And with her first she's pierced Gog through the skin of his left arm and with her second she's skewered him in the nape of his neck, and her third would open a hole straight between his eyes, only he gets up his right shield just in time to swipe the dart away, so that all true Britons cry, "Foul," and the referee scores sixty for the Gorblimeys.

Maisie, alas, has not had a sporting education, so she releases her first dart on the backswing, piercing a lanky Gorblimey sergeant through the earlobe. With a howl, he wrenches out the dart and slings it straight into the bicep of the blue-stubbled Marine sergeant. And then the darts begin to fly in all directions. The two surviving players empty their quivers at the opposing uniforms, Glenys and Mayhem both scoring three flesh-wounds on the enemy. And the whole air is suddenly full of flying bottles and mugs and fists and heads, so that Gog is battering down a fusillade of objects that would have kept a German division penned in its trenches on the Marne. He is horribly cut and bruised, the real Aunt Sally of the pub, with the slings and arrows of outrageous fortune making him the martyr that Maurice intended.

And as he stands on the bar, dodging and blocking and suffering the bombardment, Gog feels a curious kind of pleasure at the danger and the pain. The voice of Maire seems to whisper in his ear, "I could search the whole world over and never find a man so exquisitely torturable ... He's the perfect victim." But Gog does not duck behind the counter. He stays up above the mêlée, as though he seeks his own perfection in being the victim, as though he chooses himself to endure all the pain that the free-for-all of humankind can inflict upon him. If Maurice hadn't put him on the bar, perhaps he would have put himself there. Perhaps he'd have chosen to be standing above everyone, St. Sebastian Gog pierced by darts and glass, the martyr in the frail armour of his skin and the steel mesh of his righteousness. Or if he hadn't chosen to set himself up as a holy coconut shy, his imagination would put him there.

A flying beer-mug in silver plate, however, catches Gog a glancing blow on the temple and knocks him off his perch on high. He collapses beyond the bar, landing softly on the lying body of the bar-keeper. Once down, he finds his strength drained and his many small wounds hurting like measles, so that he is on fire to pick away at each of his fifty irritations. By knocking the dart-boards on his wrists against the back edge of the bar, he manages first to free his hands and then to unstrap the circular codpiece from his midriff. Exhausted, he sits back, slowly picking out the darts from their home in his flesh and allowing the trickles of blood flowing from his wounds to harden into scabs. The blows and the thuds and the screaming of the women and the curses of the men sound like a loud lullaby to him, as he squats peacefully within the recess under the bar. A Gorblimey leaps behind the counter and begins tossing bottles like grenades into the fracas; but he never looks down to see the hiding sacrificial victim at his feet; and soon he is felled by a flying table-leg and tumbles beside the bar-keeper. A new note joins the soporific roaring, the shrilling of whistles, and Gog hears distantly through the oaken panels the clubbing of truncheons and the shouting of orders. But he sits, hugging his knees, content to be forgotten in the battle, until the noise beyond the bar dies to a murmur and then to silence. And Gog congratulates himself for keeping out of trouble for once. But he is complacent too soon, for a large pair of shiny boots suddenly plunks itself back of the bar and stands by Gog, who looks slowly up glistening spats and up creases sharp as bayonets, on past bright belt-buckle and brass tunic buttons to the square red jaw and flaring nostrils and brows of a Military Policeman, looking down at him from under the bald dome of his helmet.

"Up, you mother-fuggin' bastid," the M.P. says, in a broad voice that seems to drawl and menace simultaneously.

Gog rises in front of the M.P. and finds that, for once, his eyes are on a level with another man's eyes. What Gog has not realized is that the huge policeman is a true dandy. The truncheon in his hand has a gold-plated grip, as does the revolver-butt sticking out of the patent leather holster at his waist. Round his wrist, the policeman wears a silver watch-band, studded with rubies; even the whistle at his breast-pocket is silver and set with a large turquoise. The red scarf round the man's neck is knotted with an attention to casual detail worthy of a Brummel. Only the face of the policeman is coarse, the flesh on the cheeks hanging puffy down to the jawbone and the eyes tucked away in pouches of lids.

"Git'n the paddy-wagon," the M.P. says. "Off'n the guard room."

"You have no authority over me," Gog says. "I'm a civilian. And, as you see, I wasn't fighting. I just got out of harm's way until it was all over."

"No authority?" the policeman mocks, swinging his club round and round on its thong so fast that it looks like a propeller. "One thang Ah know. This riot stick kin bust the skull of any cott'n-pick'n bum talk'n crap. Now, git'n the waggon, or Ah take you."

The policeman puts his hand on Gog's bicep and shoves him up against the bar. Gog wrenches himself free.

"I said you have no authority . . ."

Gog sees the truncheon descending through the air and he moves his head sideways and the wood lands shatteringly on his left shoulder. He swings with his right fist into the face of the M.P., sending him crashing back into the shelves behind the bar, so that empty pre-war liqueur bottles topple and shatter everywhere. As the policeman begins to slide down, Gog catches him by the neck with both hands to pull his head from his shoulders. And while he squeezes the windpipe of the M.P., Gog has a flash of hallucination that he is standing behind his own body, as if watching a film of himself or of his twin brother, a film in which he plays a British giant strangling an alien invader. Then the M.P. brings up his knee into Gog's vitals, and Gog rejoins his own agonized body as he bows forwards in pain, bringing the policeman down over his back and shifting his grasp. Now Gog catches his dandy enemy by haunch and shoulder with his arms and crushes the policeman against his own back ribs and straightens upwards until the M.P. screams and clasps Gog's hair with one hand and puts a thumb in his eye so that Gog has to fall backwards upon him to drive the breath from his body. But the falling Gog catches his foot under the body of the bar-keeper so that his ankle is wrenched and he cannot use his weight to crush the policeman. And the policeman rises and catches Gog about the ribs with his right hand and presses the breath from Gog's body until Gog's ribs crack like the skin of a roasting pig. And Gog links his hands in one mighty fist behind the back of the M.P. and presses against the other's ribs. Both men hug each other tight in the shackles of their arms, making the air quake with their breathless gaspings. And Gog hears the ribs of the policeman split, one, two, three, two on the right side and one on the left. But the splitting of his bones rouses the policeman to wrath and with a mighty heave he throws Gog up over his shoulders so that Gog slips down the further side of his back and Gog's head dangles on the bar floor and Gog's ankles are joined in his enemy's grasp like a halter round the other's neck. Now the policeman rushes forwards with both hands pushing at Gog's ankles about his neck and the speed of his going through the bar-flap and across the pub and out into the street knocks Gog's face cruelly against the face of the lying bar-keeper and scrubs his nose along the floor-boards and bangs the back of his skull on the pavement as he glances up to see the sign of the sneering Duke of Wellington above, the Iron Duke who certainly wouldn't have let a foreigner do such a thing to *him*. Then other hands lift up Gog and swing him so that he lands on top of a pile of bodies, his head dangling over the edge of the lorry. And Gog howls as his head falls backwards and he sees the bright air and the sky again moaning blue tears above him.

Then Gog's head is shoved inside the truck and the policemen clamber in on top of the heap of bodies and the truck's under way and Gog remains lying where he is, for every time one of the piled soldiers raises his skull, it earns a crack of a truncheon and sudden relapse. Gog feels like a living corpse in a plague cart of the dead; but he does not stir until the lorry stops and the tailboard is let down and military policemen begin hauling out the clubbed soldiers and sailors like haunches of beef. Then Gog walks giddily into the Nissen hut ahead of him, going quietly, his hands held up over his scalp and face for fear of another welt on the skull. And he is led straightaway into a cell and locked up there with a dozen assorted groaning men in various uniforms. Luckily, he is near a wooden plank with a wooden pillow that looks like the chosen bed of an embalmed mummy, and he sprawls on the hard board and falls at once into a deep sleep from the effects of his long walk and delayed concussion.

Gog wakes to the sound of whistles, but these are whistles of lust and appreciation. " Git," the threatening voice of the military policeman drawls, " or Ah'll bust you bums." Then a hand shakes Gog by his bruised shoulder, so that he groans. He sits up to see the huge M.P. standing with Maire at the end of the wooden bunk. Maire is wearing white kid boots and white bell-bottomed trousers tight as a sailor's round her hips. Her white pseudo-naval tunic is slashed low between her breasts and laced loosely together for indecency's sake by a lanyard running between gold eyes. On her hands, black gloves; on her black hair, a black peaked hat with a ridiculous white daisy stitched in the place of a cap-badge. She ignores totally the men slouching about her and leering up. She has eyes only for the vast policeman, who swells with pride and says, " He's all yourn, ma'am. Know he was yourn, Ah'd bruised him gentle."

Maire plucks at the silver whistle set with turquoise on the M.P.'s chest and says clearly, " I don't want him bruised gentle. I want him black and blue for being such a bloody fool as to get into a bar brawl. I hope he didn't hurt such a fine man as yourself. May I compliment you on your manners? I haven't felt so well treated since before the war. Whoever wins a war, courtesy loses."

" Ah'm from the South, ma'am. And we know how to treat ladies ther."

" And niggers," Gog says. " I see where you learned to treat us."

" Shut up," Maire says furiously, then turns honeyed to the M.P. " What did I tell you? He deserves all he gets. He won't ever learn. He provokes punishment. Oh, *officer*," she pleads, tapping delicately on the non-ranking policeman's chest, " if only I had a large and sensible man like you to protect me, I wouldn't ever feel frightened and alone. But it's *I* who have to get this born fool out of all the scrapes he gets in. You wouldn't believe the awful situations he drags me into. When he should be defending me, protecting me, keeping me from the sordid side of life. Oh, officer, give him back and I'll take him home and you won't be bothered again, I promise you, the word of a lady."

" You don't need swear nothang to me," the M.P. says graciously. " Ah know a lady when Ah see a lady. Ah don't need no word from you more'n Ah need a word from my mother." He turns and hoicks Gog onto his feet and pushes him stumbling towards the open cell door. "You, git. You ain't worth a hog's bladder. Lady, take him home and scoot him down with a hose and reckon you ain't no luck hav'n a cott'n-pick'n bum round the house and no man."

"I thank you kindly," Maire says, and she takes the policeman's hand and squeezes it and says in a low voice, "If only we'd met in different circumstances. But that's life, isn't it, officer? A matter of Too Late."

"It's never too soon, ma'am," the policeman says, "for you to visit my home town, Troy, Georgia." "I will," Maire says, as she follows Gog out of the cell door and down the passageway and past the group of policemen standing by the entrance to the hut, who greet her deferentially, "Good-bye, ma'am. Call again soon." And Maire says, "I certainly will call again soon, when I can call alone. Thank you for all your kindness." And she's out of the Nissen hut into the night, pushing Gog before her. And he sees a white square car ahead of him, with Jules standing by the rear door, supercilious and thin-shouldered and capped as usual.

"Where does *that* come from?" Gog says, jerking his thumb towards the car.

"Never you mind," Maire says, "I happen to have *friends*, good friends, who'll lend me anything I need. They know they'll be repaid, in *kind*. Or if not, they hope they'll be repaid, and that's even better than actual repayment sometimes, especially when they're getting on a bit and are worried about putting up a poor show."

Gog jibs at the door of the car, which Jules holds open for him. "I'm not getting in, I don't have to."

"But you do," Maire says. And she produces a signed Army Form in her hand, a pass out of the camp which Gog sees all about him, dark box after dark box after dark box to the limits of the barbed-wire fence enclosing them all. "You can't get out of here, Gog, unless you drive out with me. I had to work for this bit of bumph, sucking up to those revolting morons. But I've got it. You can't get out without it, Gog. It's always like that, isn't it? I'm your passport to sanity and the outer world. Left to yourself, you're always in a bloody mess."

So Gog climbs into the back seat of the white car where the porcupine cat is lying and Maire climbs in beside him and Jules gets into the driver's seat, no longer partitioned off from the rest of the car. And they drive to the entrance of the camp and present the pass to the sentry on duty and the red-and-white bar across the roadway is raised and they move on, heading without compass bearing into the night. Maire sits triumphant and straight in the corner of the back seat and she stares at Gog with her pale eyes and the porcupine cat on her lap stares at Gog with its eyes of amber-green, until he is forced to look down, and Maire says, "I told you so. When will you learn? You can't get away from me. You can't live without me. All roads lead to Maire. Wherever you go, all roads lead to Maire." She pulls at the quills of fur on the back of the cat's neck until it miaows. "And to Mishkin."

XXII

The road from Exeter is lit by an overfed moon with bulging cheeks, which leers down at the stubble on the silvered fields as if it had gobbled all the grain of the harvest. The complexion of the moon is flushed and pink from its feast and it hangs in a charcoal sky as sober as the suit of an expensive businessman.

For a long time, Gog sits dumbly in the back seat, while Maire remains silent beside him. She seems thoughtful, as though she were considering a change of tactics. Thus Gog is not surprised, when he asks where she is taking him, to get the answer, "I'm taking you back to the West Country by the route I drove you down to Totnes. It's on your way."

"On *my* way," Gog says. "You're helping me on my way. I thought I was only allowed to go on yours."

"I've been thinking," Maire says, "that perhaps I've been trying to influence you too much. If you say walking will cure you, perhaps you should give it a try. You can't escape me, Gog, anyway. So perhaps you should have the illusion of brief freedom. After all, even when you think you're alone, you carry me around inside your skull, ready to leap out on you at any time. I'm always there, deep inside you, however far away you think I am. And you are walking back to me in London, aren't you?"

"I'm walking back to London," Gog agrees, "and you will be there, won't you?"

"Yes," Maire says. "I'll be in London." She takes a piece of paper out of her bag and writes on the paper and puts it in Gog's pocket. "That's your home address, in case you've forgotten it."

"So you're not taking me to the psychiatrists any more? Why, have you lost faith in them?"

"No," Maire says. "Only I sometimes have more faith in other things. Like in faith, for instance. It's got a longer history of successful healing, particularly of people possessed by demons like you. You'd have been burnt for being possessed by Magog in the Middle Ages. Or you'd have been sent on a pilgrimage till you were cured. Well, I thought of burning you, but we've had a little too much of burned people, what with the blitz and the V-2's. So I decided that perhaps you should try a pilgrimage to the holy places, a long pilgrimage. That's what you want, isn't it?"

"Does it count as a pilgrimage," Gog asks, "when you're in search of yourself, not of God?"

"God may help you to find Himself through your quest into yourself," Maire answers piously. "Or so a charming Dominican told me before the war. They're so sexy, wearing those long priestly skirts, yet you always know there's a *man* below – even if there may not be a God above."

"You don't sound very much of a believer yourself," Gog says.

"Nonsense. I'm very much a believer. I shall certainly repent on my deathbed, but I must have something worth repenting about during my life, mustn't I? What's the use of all God's infinite compassion and forgiveness, if He doesn't have a chance to use it on a real sinner? So you go off on your pilgrimage, Gog. I'll set you off at the holiest place in England, Glastonbury, and you can put a few prickles from the Holy Thorn round your deluded brow, if you really want to feel religious. Then you can walk off to the second holiest place in England, Canterbury. Via Stonehenge, if you want to go back to all your old Druidic nonsense. If that isn't a proper pilgrimage, what is?"

"It's as good a way of getting to London as any," Gog says. "An almost sacred way."

"And you," Maire says, lighting a cigarette so that her pale eyes wink sardonically in the flame of the match and two smaller flames spurt in the eyes of the watching Mishkin, "you will be a saint *en route*, naturally."

"No," Gog says, "just a man walking to London."

"A saint," Maire says. "That's how you like to think of yourself. As a suffering saint who can endure all the torments the world and his wife can inflict on him. Your mock humility doesn't take me in. But let me tell you a story about a true Saint. A very *moral* story. It'll pass the time to Glastonbury and it might make you think a bit on your sacred way."

And so Maire tells the story of the Saint's Wife to Gog, as Jules drives them towards Glastonbury through the summer night. And Maire's round pale face is a second moon within the car, smiling as the full moon sometimes smiles, the point of her cigarette a comet in the darkness.

"Once there was a Saint," Maire relates, "who was the holiest man in all the world. He flagellated himself with whips and scorpions, he fasted for months on end until he was mere skin and bone, he sprained his wrist from laying his hand on the multitudes of the kneeling faithful. He couldn't meet a beggar without giving him his whole coat and his trousers, too. In fact, the Saint (whom we'll call Gog just so that we can *identify* with him) was so holy that people flocked to England on their coracles from all over the world just to gawp at him and touch the hem of his robe – if he hadn't also given that away to some poor naked cannibal, who didn't want it. After Stonehenge, Saint Gog was England's greatest tourist attraction, and his fame spread to the length and the breadth of the whole earth.

"Of course, Saint Gog would have been England's greatest *dead* tourist attraction, if he hadn't had someone to look after him. And that person was his ignored wife (whom we'll call Maire just for fun). Saint Gog had, unfortunately, married early in life before he had become holy and wise. And though he tried to flee from his wife into the wilderness, somehow she had enough devotion to follow after him – difficult though that was – and to keep him alive when he was nearly in the grave. After all, when he'd given away his trousers, who had to scrounge him another pair? Maire. When he was on the point of starving to death, who had to force oysters and brown bread down his unwilling gullet? Maire. Who swept out his lonely cave, who prevented the tourists from tearing out his finger-nails and hair for holy relics, who chased away the would-be Salomes after his bed or head, who charged an entrance fee to his lair so that the rabble could be kept away and enough ground be bought to allow him a little solitude? Why, Maire, of course. In return for her services to the Saint, the world called her a dragon, a shrew, a monster of avarice, a harpy, and worse. And they pitied the Saint who, in the folly of his youth, had misallied himself to such a creature.

"In the fullness of time, Saint Gog died in the odour of worms and sanctity and he immediately rose to heaven on a golden push-chair. Or so the faithful reported. His gorgon of a wife shook down the believers for a vast marble tomb to be set up on his favourite meditative hill-top on Glastonbury Tor, visible for twenty miles all around. This hill-top immediately became the most crowded and sacred doss-house for all the pilgrims of the world. Maire also channelled some of the funds aside to bring up Saint Gog's son, whom she had never mentioned because the Saint preferred to ignore the child as a youthful peccadillo beneath the attention of a holy man. (I know we have no children, Gog, but it improves the story.) And so, Maire lived out the rest of her days, fading into obscurity more and more each year, as the queue at Saint Gog's shrine grew and grew until it stretched seven times seven round the Tor. And then Maire died in her due time and was buried underneath a little wooden cross in a neglected spot at the foot of the Tor, on which stood the marble tomb of Saint Gog.

"And so it seemed that, in life on earth as well as in heaven, the Saint and his wife had found their rightful resting-places. But one day, many years later, Joseph of Arimathea passed by the foot of the Tor on his way to plant the Holy Thorn at Glastonbury (where you and I are now proceeding, O beloved). And Joseph stopped at the wooden cross at the foot of the Tor and he picked it up from the place where it had fallen on the ground and he set it up again above the grave of the Saint's Wife and he cleared the plot of weeds and he knelt there to pray. And when he had started again on his way towards Glastonbury without ever looking upwards at the vast tomb of Saint Gog on the high ground above him, one of his twelve disciples asked, 'Master, why did you not pray at the grave of the true Saint?' And Joseph answered, 'I did'."

The dawn wrinkles the puffy skin of cloud, as the car stops at Glastonbury outside the ruins of the Abbey. Maire ushers Gog out of the door and kisses him almost coldly on the brow. "Be a good pilgrim," she says, "and remember who set you on your way."

XXIII

Gog does not feel holy, once he has lumbered over the wall onto the sacred soil of Glastonbury Abbey. He merely feels sleepy. The dawn light may lend the abbey ruins that mysterious clarity which provokes awe in the religious soul, but it also exhales a mist of fatigue as if the whole earth were breathing out a silent yawn. Gog yawns, too, in sympathy with the tired break of day, then suppresses the heretic yawn guiltily, only to yawn twice as loud and long from the effort of trying to suppress it.

Gog walks on the turf between the fallen walls of the abbey that seem no more than an ornament now to the perfection of the cropped lawn. He is searching for a starting point which may bless him on his journey and take away the dullness of his spirits. He finds a healing well in the crypt of a ruined chapel; but the well is set behind plate glass. No wanderer can wash himself free from his diseases or from his sins there; Gog can scarcely see the round lip of the well for the reflection of his own self in the dark glass. The sites of the High Altar or of King Arthur's Grave might, indeed, be the marks for the beginning of Gog's quest after the grail of self-wisdom; but their oblongs of turf are surrounded by low spiked black chains that seem more mantraps for the ankles than spurs for the inspiration. Arthur, Arthur, were you really buried here in this island of would-have-been Avalon, once set about with marshes and now set about with mainland? Or is the king's grave, which they looted to find your bones, the resting-place of mere royal calcium that was never the white lie of a legendary hero? From such a questionable beginning, no pilgrim ever should start forth. And even when Gog follows the sign that reads TO THE THORN, thinking that such a holy tree must prick him into a spurt of leaving, he finds the sign leads only to another sign, saying that the original thorn was never in the abbey grounds at all, but elsewhere. The thorn tree which is there claims to be a graft from the original holy thorn planted by Joseph of Arimathea; but it hardly seems to justify its name. It is spikeless and spineless and without flower, however much legend makes it bloom forever and Christmas day.

So Gog would wearily leave the sacred soil of the holiest place in Albion, the home of pagan temples before the coming of Christ, did not the first shaft of sun strike him blind as he clambers back over the girdling wall round the ruins. He turns away from the light to see a gout of blood spattering up from the broken stone top of the abbey church. It is a miracle. And Gog feels his own flesh spout out a spray of wonder and curiosity that engages him on his way to the East. If a blink of heavy eyes reveals the miracle to be red valerian blooming on the wall, nothing can take away the first jolt of worship and surprise. So Gog starts out towards Shepton Mallet, bearing a little hope to balance his dragging steps.

The road follows the crests of the chain of hillocks that used to be the only stepping stones above the marshes from the hills to the Island and Tor of Glastonbury. On Gog's left, the Tor rises in a series of giant steps of grass and gravel to a square tall tower which might indeed be the tomb of Saint Gog, looking down in the arrogance of holiness at mere mortals far below. Yet Gog, as he trudges step after step, can hardly see the point of Maire's story. A holy man may make a woman evil by leaving his dirty work to her; but a walking man is no more than a walking man, alone on a road, affecting no one and nothing, merely moving from place to place, with all the useless private purpose of the truly irresponsible and the truly free. If mankind chooses to think hermits and wanderers holy, it is because mankind must explain away the person who wishes to have nothing to do with his own species, for good or bad.

Two miles out of Glastonbury, Gog reaches a ditch and rampart cut athwart the road, which ignores the old earthwork on its level-running way. The map calls the rampart Ponter's Ball, and nature has strengthened its defences over the thousands of years by fringing it with nettle and bramble and thorn. Ponter's Ball, Ponter's Ball, the name nags at Gog's mind. Built of earth by the men of the Iron Age, surely? Built to enclose a great Celtic cemetery on the Tor, built to keep out the impious from the sanctuaries of the Druids, which the later Christians came to desecrate and consecrate as their own? Ponter's Ball, surely that was it? A massive bank and ditch running from marsh edge to marsh edge, barring the only landward approach to the " Island " of Glastonbury, later claimed to be Avalon. As a military obstacle the earthwork does not make sense; it could be too easily turned at either end. So it must be the temenos of a great pagan sanctuary. Ergo, q.e.d., proven, the right answer by archaeological reasoning. So Gog would write, if he were once again sweating at his desk with the hundreds of other students in the dark hall that swims up in his mind, the hand of the clock on the wall twitching at the nerves in his stomach as he strives to set down all he knows against time, against time, against time. But time won then as time wins now. The examiner might give full marks for Gog's answer on Ponter's Ball; but time has made even the question pointless and has swallowed up the truth in weed and tree and forgetfulness. Ponter's Ball is merely the overgrown ditch and bank before Gog's eyes. Whether this sudden trick of memory tells him truly or falsely about what he once read, Ponter's Ball will remain indifferent, a name and a scene to the wanderer on the road, whom time will move on as surely as a policeman.

The wayfaring tree ahead first betrays the stealthy advance of the chalk under the soil by revealing the white bed of its roots in the white powdering of its flowers. After his long dip down between the breakwater hedges keeping back the flooding buttercups of the marshland meadows, Gog now begins to climb the first slopes of the grassy hills past the dark-stone cottages that have lost the yellow tints of the fallen blocks of Glastonbury. Shepton Mallet itself wears grey dungarees on its walls to show its workaday spirit. At least, a village shop is open for early risers and its owner will sell Gog some stale biscuits and lemonade. But Gog is glad to move quickly through the sprawling town towards the chalk ridges. He thinks nothing will stay him, but the tail of memory gives its second flick of the morning, as he reaches a discreet blue-and-red sign pointing down an alley and bearing the initials, *M.P. & D.B.*

Suddenly and hey presto, he's Captain Griffin of Army Intelligence striding down the alley, wearing shoes waxed with oxblood and a dark-gory Sam Browne, his khaki uniform trim on his body like a hide, the swagger stick in his hand ready to bruise and maim. Ho, ho, ahead lie the cringing prisoners, the suspect spies, the traitors waiting for the grill. See the Military Prison and Detention Barracks hidden in the hollow, with its dungeons contained in a block of crazy paving. See the prisoner peer down through the bars set across the mocking fan-top windows. Wonder at the high iron chimney that smokes away by the slate roof of the prison, belching out oily fumes that may be the charring of flesh. There's no help from outside for the prisoners here, not with the warning boards in gold letters on baby-blue background, stating under the crown and royal initials, G VI R, that it's two years inside for helping the escape of an army man gone wrong, six months for smuggling in liquor or fags, and an excessive postage of ten quid for taking out a letter.

When did you first come here, Captain Gog, commissioned as the ferret on the trail of enemy intelligence, chosen to save the English people from the Fifth Column rotting their resistance from within? And what evil did you do in the name of good, how did you wrack the flesh of the friend suspected to be foe in the name of the rights of man and democracy? The opium of oblivion has scattered its merciful poppy powder over Gog's recollections of war, and he no longer knows as he stands under the high walls of the Detention Barracks when he came here or whether his precious errand ended in an inquisition or a joke, in a trauma or a farce.

At his feet, Gog sees the torn pages of a horror comic. He picks them up and smooths them out against his knee. He is not surprised to see that the garish reds and purples and yellows of the comic strip bear the title:

SPECIAL CHRISTMAS ISSUE

SWEENY GOG

The Demon Barber of Secret Street

Gog reads on fascinated, his eyes skipping from lurid picture to the white balloons of the text that fly before the characters and whoosh them into action.

At His Underground Hideaway, Sweeny Gog Manicures (ha, ha!) Enemy Agents Into Revealing Their All (Especially Mata Haris ! !). Read Yet Again How Sweeny Gog Saves The White Cliffs Of Dover And Makes Mincemeat (ho, ho !) Of England's Enemies To Put A Bit Of Body (hee, hee!) In The Bangers Of Her Soldier Sons.

PICTURE ONE : SURROUNDED BY HIS MIGHTY MEANS FOR EXTORTING THE TRUTH FROM THE DREADED FIFTH COLUMN, SWEENY GOG DUCKS BEHIND HIS DEMONIAC ELECTRIC (BARBER'S) CHAIR, AS THE

CHOLERA-TIPPED DART FLUNG BY THE DEADLY ARM OF THE RAVISHING EYETIE BRUNETTE SPY, MISS MAMBA, WHISTLES THROUGH HIS BRISTLES.

SWEENY GOG: Close shave!

MISS MAMBA: Spaghetti! Mussolini!

PICTURE TWO: IN ONE MIGHTY BOUND, SWEENY GOG STRAPS MISS MAMBA IN HIS DEMONIAC BARBER'S CHAIR, RIPPING OPEN THE BLACK SHIRT ON HER CREAMY AMPLE BOSOM WITH HIS RED-HOT HANDY-PACK CURLING TONGS.

SWEENY GOG: Ha, would you like-a da friction massage, no, in my demoniac death-dealing barber's chair that connects by a hidden trap door to my Win-the-War Sausage Factory in the cellars? Or will you spill all, Miss Mamba?

MISS MAMBA: Caramba, no! Arrivaderchi, ravioli! I justa simple country-a maiden!

PICTURE THREE: SWEENY GOG READS THE MESSAGE TATTOOED ON THE CREAMY AMPLE BOSOM OF MISS MAMBA, AS SHE STRUGGLES IN THE DEADLY GRIP OF THE BARBER'S CHAIR.

SWEENY GOG: (WITH DEVILISH CUNNING) Then what's justa simple country-a maiden doing with Heil Hitler palpitating on her creamy ample bosom? You are unmasked, Miss Mamba!

MISS MAMBA: Sapristi! Risotto!

PICTURE FOUR: SWEENY GOG PULLS THE LEVER THAT SENDS MISS MAMBA DOWN THE CHUTE INTO THE SAUSAGE MACHINE.

SWEENY GOG: You fry with the chippolatas tonight!

MISS MAMBA: Uuuuughi! Eeeeechi! Tuttefrutti!

PICTURE FIVE: SWEENY GOG IS DISCOVERED IN HIS CONFIDENTIAL THINK-ROOM SOMEWHERE BENEATH THE SEWERS OF LONDON WITH HIS BLONDE SECRETARY, MISS VENUS FLYTRAP. HER BOSOMS, BEING BEST BRITISH, WEAR A LOW-CUT ARMY SHIRT AND ARE EVEN MORE CREAMY AND AMPLE.

SWEENY GOG: (THINKS) Was that a menu? Or a code? We'll crack it. (TALKS) The English people must be saved again in this soul-hanging, breath-shattering, cliff-taking instalment! Or how shall we find readers for our next stupendous number? I hate war, Miss Flytrap. But we must do terrible things – especially to girls with creamy ample bosoms, to save all us honest blokes. I don't like what I'm doing, but England expects! It hurts them more than it hurts me.

MISS FLYTRAP: You're marvellous, Captain Gog. (THINKS) Shall I call him Sweeny?

PICTURE SIX : SWEENY GOG'S INDISPENSABLE RIGHT HAND, SHERLOCK BONES, GIVES A SALUTE WITH HIS INDISPENSABLE RIGHT HAND AT THE THINK-ROOM DOOR. BEYOND IN THE SEWERS, THE BLOODY BODY OF FRITZ VON PIPZ BLEEDS BLOODILY ALL OVER THE PAGE AND INTO THE MARGIN.

SHERLOCK BONES: (WITH FRANK OPEN BRITISH SMILE) A confession from Fritz Von Pipz alias John Smith, extorted by your razor-dealing, battery-sharp, death-operated scissors. He will tell all, as he lies outside on a stretcher as per Geneva Convention! And we have reached our target! Miss Mamba's bountiful left bosom gave us our millionth sausage, enough to bring a sparkle to the eye of many a bangerless old-age pensioner on this frigid Xmas night!

SWEENY GOG: Take a week's leave till the next instalment and this bag of gold-wrapped jellybabies, off ration!

FRITZ VON PIPZ: Aaaaach! Heeeeeil! Sauerkraut!

PICTURE SEVEN : WITH SEWER RATS CRAWLING ALL OVER HIM, A BLACK-CLOAKED FIGURE DRINKS FROM THE THROAT OF THE READY-TO-TALK KRAUT AGENT. IT IS COUNT MAGNUS, THE VAMPIRE FROM OUTER SPACE, WESTPHALIA, JUST LANDED FROM HIS FLYING COFFIN! HIS LEECH-TOOTHED, SABRE-SUCKING, GAP-SHARP MOLARS DRAIN THE VITAL JUICES OF HE WHO MUST CONFESS!

FRITZ VON PIPZ: Gluuuuuuuuuuuuuuuuuuug . . . . . .

PICTURE EIGHT : WITH HAWK-JAWED, JUT-EYED, STEELY-NOSED STARE, SWEENY GOG CONFRONTS HIS ARCH-ENEMY.

SWEENY GOG: Count Magnus! This isn't the Crimean War! Fly back out of date! My Fritz, my precious Pipz!

COUNT MAGNUS: Where the bee sucks, there suck I! (This is a Kulture Komic – ED.) The Vampire always walks where there is war! Too late! I've drunk a toast of vintage von Pipz, chateau-born when his pop was bottled, 1919!

PICTURE NINE: ROCK-HEELED, SPRING-SNORTING, RIP-FISTED SWEENY GOG BLATS THE VILLAINOUS VAMPIRE ACROSS THE BOKO IN AN ABYSMAL BATTLE.

ZAM! BLIM! BLUNK!

PICTURE TEN: SWEENY GOG HOLDS HIS DREAD ADVERSARY UPSIDE DOWN AND SQUEEZES THE BLOOD OF FRITZ VON PIPZ OUT OF HIS SLAVERING FANGS. THE GORE RUNS INTO THE CRACKS IN THE COBBLED SEWERS AND WRITES A MESSAGE IN RED!

SS PANZER STUKA TIGERS LAND WHITE CLIFFS TONIGHT BLITZ NELSONS COLUMN TO TOPPLE MORALE IF BETRAYED PERISH WITH SECRET LOVE ADOLPH

PICTURE ELEVEN: SWEENY GOG SPEAKS EXCITEDLY INTO HIS ELECTRO-BLUE, SKY-WAY, TWO-MAGNETIC TELEPHONE CONNECTED DIRECT TO SOMEWHERE IN ENGLAND, WHILE COUNT MAGNUS SLINKS OFF INTO THE THINK-ROOM. BEWARE!

SWEENY GOG: Demon Barber to Whitehall 121* (War Secret – ED.) Deploy British fleet off white cliffs soonest! Ring Nelson's Column with the Guard! I have saved England again, until next week's rib-racking, suspense-tickling, nerveful instalment!

COUNT MAGNUS: Revenge!!

PICTURE TWELVE: OVER THE EXECUTION DESK OF THE THINK-ROOM, COUNT MAGNUS LAYS THE NUDE BODY OF THE ALL-BRITISH, DOUBLE-CREAMY, MORE-THAN-AMPLE MISS VENUS FLYTRAP, SINKING HIS FANGS IN HER THROAT WHILE HIS CLOAK HIDES WHAT HE IS DOING ELSEWHERE TO HER DAIRY CHARMS.

COUNT MAGNUS: Tea-break!

MISS FLYTRAP: Ouuuuuch! Leeeeeeeeeeggo! You cad!

PICTURE THIRTEEN: SWEENY GOG IS PULLING A MODEST MAP OF BERLIN STUDDED WITH PINS AND MARKED *FINAL VICTORY* OVER THE RECUMBENT FLESH OF MISS VENUS FLYTRAP. AT THE SAME TIME, CONSCIOUS OF THE YULETIDE SPIRIT, HE HOLDS A SPRIG OF MISTLETOE OVER HER APPLE-TOOTHED, PEARL-RED LIPS. THROUGH THE WINDOW, COUNT MAGNUS IS SEEN SAILING OFF THROUGH AN ACK-ACK BARRAGE ON HIS FLYING COFFIN.

SWEENY GOG: Happy Christmas! In the nick of time!

MISS FLYTRAP: Too late, you fool. I'm soiled again! (Dear Readers, she will be soiled again next week, *twice*! ED.)

COUNT MAGNUS: Auf widdershins, Herr Gog! Till next week's spine-defying, hair-chilling, death-raising instalment!

PICTURE FOURTEEN: THE BRITISH FLEET BLOW UP THE SS PANZER STUKA TIGERS UNDER THE WHITE CLIFFS OF DOVER, NOW RED WITH GORE.

SUPERZAM! JUMBOBLIM! UTTERBLUNK!

PICTURE FIFTEEN: THE YEOMEN OF THE GUARD CARVE UP THE FILTHY FIFTH COLUMN UNDER NELSON'S DITTO.

SUPERJUMBOZAM! JUMBOUTTERBLIM!
UTTERSUPERBLUNK!

PICTURE SIXTEEN: THE KING DECORATES SWEENY GOG THE DEMON BARBER OF SECRET STREET IN FRONT OF THE CHANGING OF THE PALACE AND BUCKINGHAM GUARD.

KING: We've run out of medals for you, Sweeny Gog, but we haven't run out of instalments! I'll have to invent a new one by next week. The Georgia Garter and Bar!

SWEENY GOG: Thanks, your majesty. (THINKS) What a spiffing new attachment to my demoniac electric barber's chair!

AND SO . . .

DON'T MISS THE NEXT NUMBER OF SWEENY GOG VERSUS COUNT MAGNUS! SEE THE GASPING GAR-

ROTE OF THE GEORGIA GARTER ON PETAL VON PIPPIN, THE NUBILE ARYAN MAIDEN WEARING WHAT NATURE DISTENDED! PALPITATE WITH FEAR AS SWEENY GOG SEEKS YET AGAIN TO SAVE DEAR OLD ENGLAND FROM THE WICKED WILES OF ADOLPH'S APPARITIONS! TREMBLE WITH TERROR AS COUNT MAGNUS FLIES IN AGAIN WITH THE V-I's ON HIS CADAVEROUS COFFIN! YOU CAN'T AFFORD TO MISS OUR NEXT SURE-DUPER, WHIZZ-FIRE, SUPER-BANG ISSUE!

A shadow falls across the comic in Gog's hand and he lets the sheets of paper blow away in the wind as he blinks up at the shape of a Military Policeman standing between him and the sun. First the unconscious one in Edinburgh at the start of the journey, then the American one in the bar at Exeter, now a third M.P. They seem to be after Gog as remorselessly as Maire.

"Sleeping?" the M.P. asks.

"I was reading," Gog says.

"What?"

As Gog looks round for the comic pages that blew away in the gust of wind, he finds them vanished out of sight, so that their lurid pictures remain only in his memory.

"It's blown away," Gog says.

"Your *book*?"

"My comic."

"A grown man reading a comic?" the M.P. says. "Rather childish."

"You've no right to question me," Gog says.

"You're sitting on army property," the M.P. says. "Where's your I.D. card?"

Gog rises and stands at the level of the tall M.P. whose face remains shadowed by the peak of his cap. "I.D.? What's that?"

"Identity card. It's wartime regulations. You have to carry one, as you know."

"I haven't got much of an identity these days," Gog says. "Not much more than you could write down in a card. Or a horror comic."

"Could I see your I.D. card?" the M.P. insists.

"No," Gog answers. "You've no authority."

"While you as civilian personnel are on Army property . . ."

Gog takes two steps onto the tarmac of the roadway and smiles at the Military Policeman.

"This is the public highway," he says. "You can't make me now."

"Don't be difficult," the M.P. says. "When were you demobbed? You could be A.W.O.L. Where's your discharge papers?"

Gog looks at the high prison walls in front of him that no longer seem a comic strip but a vicious circle closed about all life within them. And he turns away and begins to walk back up the road.

"Better come quietly with me," the M.P. says at Gog's back, grasping him by the arm. But Gog shakes off the other's grip and finds himself taking the evading action once taught him by the class war of Old England.

"Take your paws off me, my man," Gog says in his most clipped and gentlemanly tone. "If you don't, you'll be in trouble. My wife's the local Justice of the Peace." Who knows if Maire is not a J.P. in one of her many guises?

The assurance in the M.P.'s behaviour and voice cracks a little. "I'm sorry, sir," he begins. Then he rallies. "But it's my duty. If you wouldn't mind coming along to be identified by the civilian police."

"I would mind."

"Not having seen you before, sir, I wonder if you wouldn't mind staying five minutes in the police mess while I go round to the station . . ."

"If you arrest me, my dear fellow," Gog says with the light menace of those sure of their place in the county, "you'll have to charge me. What is the charge?"

"Acting suspiciously in the vicinity of His Majesty's Detention Barracks . . ."

"Reading a comic is acting suspiciously?"

"There wasn't a comic, sir. And what would a *gentleman* like you . . ."

" I can do as I please," Gog says curtly. " According to you, I was asleep. Is that a crime?"

" There's no harm in sleeping," the M.P. says. " But if you do it in the wrong place or the wrong bed, there can be trouble."

The M.P. takes courage from his insinuation and walks in front of Gog to bar his way. The light shines on his face and for the first time Gog can see his small head, set like a pumpkin on a pole, incongruous with saffron cheeks above his height.

" If you arrest me," Gog says, " I'll sue you in the civil courts. That mightn't affect you much. But I'll also see your commanding officer, my man. He's Colonel . . .?"

The M.P. is too wily to be caught by such a simple trick. " He's Colonel who?" he replies. " *You* answer."

" My wife will know him," Gog says. " She likes army cops. Then you'll bounce, my man. A head will surely roll, and I think it will be yours."

The M.P. is no longer sure of himself. He stares at Gog with large, baby-blue eyes, then takes a half-step to one side.

" Who are you, sir?" he asks. " It would make my job easier . . ."

" I?" Gog says. " I'm an eccentric local squire. Can't you tell by my accent?"

" Your clothes, sir, don't seem quite . . . and you haven't shaved . . ."

" I said I was eccentric," Gog says. " I've taken a vow not to change or shave till the end of the war in Japan."

He feels the long stubble on his cheeks and chin and strokes the forgotten bristles as if he was indeed fingering his beard of wisdom, which has taught him how to use the rotten caste system of England to extricate himself from the still more rotten intrusions of wartime.

" I'd still feel happier, sir," the M.P. insists softly, " if you'd come with me . . ."

" And I'd feel happier finishing my stroll on my own," Gog says. " Will you let me pass?"

He takes a step forwards and is relieved that the M.P. steps aside. He does not feel like fighting yet again the strong arm of the law, since his shoulder is still badly bruised from the truncheon of the Military Policeman of Exeter.

"I'll let you go on your way," the M.P. says. "I'll take you at your word."

"The word of a gentleman," Gog says firmly, "has to be taken, doesn't it? And gentlemen can be eccentric, can't they? It's the polite way of saying they're lunatic. And it means they don't have to be locked up for their follies like ordinary people. Good-day, my man."

He strides away up the road with the soft voice of the M.P. speeding him on his way. "All the same, sir, I would advise you not to hang around the Detention Barracks again. Or we might make a mistake, even though you're a local gentleman, and put you inside."

Gog increases his pace to something approaching a trot, thankful to make so easy an escape. If he had not retained something of the arrogance of the gentleman so that he could play the part with ease, what then? He glances back to see the Military Policeman running towards a jeep, obviously hell-bent on sending the civilian police after him. So, once he is round the bend and onto the main road, Gog begins a lumbering clop away from Shepton Mallet past a redbrick hog factory with green windowsills, the inbuilt career of the pig from grass into blood, with a railway right by to bring home the bacon.

Go right by the tracks down a side-street towards the south. Walk until the sign of the hanged man outside the pub at Cannard's Grave. Look up at the corpse of the innkeeper turned sheepstealer, as he hangs from the black gibbet above his open grave, with ten of his white woolly victims making a frieze of pallbearers above and below. And run, run out of town from the gruesome pub sign, run Gog without identity, run from the policemen just as Gog Turpin once ran from the law in York.

At the outskirts of Shepton Mallet, veering south-east into the Mendip hills, Gog reaches the last refuge of the old ways, a thatched cottage with a thatcher on its roof. The thatcher whistles *The Foggy Foggy Dew* as he packs in osiers under a wire hairnet pegged over the eaves and shears away unnecessary ends. He has curly black hair and a crimson nose, and he warbles as merrily as the sparrows that try to make more holes in the thatch for their nests the moment he has filled in all the old holes. "Hey, thatcher," Gog calls up, "the cops want to put me back in the army. Tell them I went the other way." The thatcher grins. "Right you are," he shouts. "Good luck on the road." And he continues to plait and clip and trill on his perch, as ready to misguide inquirers as any swallow's flight misguides diviners seeking signs of rain.

The tower on the top of Glastonbury Tor, which Maire called the tomb of Saint Gog, mocks the fleeing Gog as he takes the ancient lead route towards the old ridgeways across the high chalk downs ahead. Gog can almost see the small dark men with their ponies carrying baskets full of ore, as they trudge along the way over Maes Down towards the rivers that can float the metal down to the sea and onto Gaul. Yet to them, the far Tor swelling like a green breast from the flatlands must have been a marker on their way rather than an echo of Maire's derisive voice reminding her husband that the price of his wanderings is the willingness of society to feed and clothe him on his solitary way. From hilltop after hilltop, the tomb remains as distinct as the sight of a rifle pointing due west down the vale from Gog's position.

Gog walks slowly all the afternoon under the alternating dark and bright patches of day. The separate clouds that spot the blue sky are lopped off underneath by some dark blade of wind that leaves their topsides white as washed lambswool and shears their bases greasy-dark and even as a stretched fleece. His strolling progress gives Gog time to look at the little things by the wayside, the flowers that pullulate at the foot of the hedgerows. There is hogweed or fool's parsley tall as Gog's shoulder and powdered with white on its skeletal rayed stalks; there are the violet shaved tongues of meadow.cranesbill, the green spiky froth of ragless mayweed, cuckoo-spit hanging in gobs from thistles; there is bittersweet with its fool's petals round its pointed cap, poison warning in the yellow peak darting from the nightshade's purple hood; there are ox-eyed daisies with yolks big as hens' eggs between beaten white splashes, and the red filaments of sorrel that taste acrid in the mouth. One by one, Gog picks the hedgeflowers, while their names and properties spring unbidden to his mind, as if mere sight and feel of each conjures up old botany lessons and wildflower rambles in the distant past. Yes, once there had been another quest, the never-ending search after British flora, so boy Gog could paint in the white spaces between the outlines of each specimen in the holy writ of Bentham and Hooker. Gog is happy to find little details creep back into his skull as well as the immense obsessions of his past. "Eggs and Bacon," he finds himself murmuring as he cups the bright yellow flowers of birdsfoot trefoil, and the homely name on his tongue makes him smile at the hope of recovering an ordinary way of thought and the interest in small things that is so much of the love of life.

Another tower set among woods on a rise ahead greets Gog as he pants up to the crest of Seat Hill. He pauses to consult his map and finds that the new marker is called Alfred's Tower. Its appearance seems almost too apposite. For, as Gog turns towards the West, he realizes that the crest of Seat Hill will finally cut him off from the sight of the tower that crowns Glastonbury and Arthur's Isle of Avalon. Yet, as Gog looks back, the miracle that sent him from Glastonbury seems repeated in his last view of the holy place. The clouds have interwoven to spread their dirty cloth over the whole sky, turning the meadows into drab olive and the stubble into dirty mustard. Yet over the Tor, the sun is sending down a few dark spokes of light through the rents in the cumulus. Rungs of rays connecting earth and heaven climb from the distant tomb of Saint Gog to the base of the clouds, like that Jacob's Ladder held by the stone angels flying in squadron over the entrance of the Jacobean Church which Gog has just passed in the village of Batscombe.

The far Tor is too distant for Gog to see whether men are climbing the ladder of light to God above. Only faith would name this effect of afternoon sun through cloud a miracle, and Gog wishes to have no faith despite a miracle. Yet there it is. And something stirs in Gog's soul, a reverence for nature and for whatever stages its seasons and its tricks. Gog chokes on a gulp of awe and closes his eyes to clear his throat. Behind his lids, he sees his son's face or his own kneeling at a red altarcloth. Saliva flows back into his mouth as sweet as communion wine.

He opens his eyes again to find the dark spokes of light moved on from Glastonbury Tor into the flatlands. He feels a grimness drag down the muscles on the corner of his mouth. He begins to curse at the priests, who taught him long ago and who can still make him see their Catholic visions, however far he journeys from them down his own road. " Christ!" he shouts, " Christ, Christ, Christ! Can't you leave a man *alone*?" And there is no answer from the indifferent grey of the sky, only the nagging voice of Maire inside his ear, " You will think yourself a saint *en route*, naturally."

XXIV

" Roughing it," Merry says. " We're just roughing it."

Gog sits under the high pinnacle of Alfred's Tower, taller than a tall story, longer than the long arm of coincidence which makes Gog fall upon his mother again. The brick triangle of the building climbs perpendicular between its three corner columns, crowned with skiey and absurd battlements. In the shadow of this Victorian delirium which outdoes in madness any rich man's folly and builds a memorial to look like an ornamental chimney, Merry is sprawling on a chaise-longue that squats insanely on its four wooden beasts' paws scratching at the grass. The couch has four gilt griffons' heads which snarl from each corner of its up-curving ends, and its cover is of damson silk threaded with gold. Merry reclines in a limp lump, dressed in a gown of claret velvet. At the far end of the chaise-longue, a toad of a man sits, squat and low-lidded, his cheeks pocked with scars, his skin rough with tweed.

" Otto, this is my son, George," Merry says. " He's dropped in by chance to take pot-luck with us. He's on safari across England. Gog, this is Otto. For a man with a kraut mother, he's almost a Britisher. Or else he'd be in detention camp under 14B."

"I *am* a Britisher," Otto says in an exquisite Oxford accent, more English than the English. "How's hunting, Gog? I can see you're very sophisticated. You don't even carry a gun. You like to give the game a sporting chance. And it's more fun, I admit, to kill with one's bare hands – if you can catch things."

"I'm a bit slow," Gog says. "So I'm starving."

Otto claps his palms together. From behind the tower, two aged footmen appear, wearing dun liveries, threadbare and patched, but with silver buttons shining. Between them they carry a hamper. A third old footman follows behind, bearing a Chippendale table, while a creaking butler brings up the tail of the procession, solemn in tail-coat and white-wing collar, too frail to support the weight of a damask tablecloth. "I'm sorry the servants look like an old folks' home," Otto says. "But the army's left us with only the ancient monuments, third class."

The table is spread with the cloth and a feast is set out in front of Otto and Merry and Gog. There are the luxuries that are beyond price and out of the range of coupons. Partridge and grouse, hare and venison; quail's eggs and asparagus, *pâté de foie gras* from a pre-war tin; burgundy from the year of the Armistice, hock from the vintage of the General Strike, port only as old as Guernica. Gog eats and drinks himself sick and silly, while his mother apologizes, "I'm so sorry. You shouldn't have dropped in to see us on the one evening we decided to camp out and picnic."

"*Déjeuner sur l'herbe*," Otto yawns over his brandy, which dates from the Kaiser if not Napoleon. "Take all your clothes off, Merry my dear, and the illusion would be complete."

"I would with pleasure," Merry says, "on such a clement evening. But really, a son can see too much of his own mother. At least, Gog thinks so. He hardly ever comes to see me."

"I'm right here," Gog says, "by some sort of accident. It's like a dream. To be gorged when I thought I was starving. I'm sure I'll wake in a moment and find only a mouthful of straw."

"To return to the most serious of subjects," Otto says, "your hunting. I can see you're covered with burrs and dried grass. I presume you disguise yourself as a heap of manure, until a rabbit tries to dig a burrow in you. Then you strangle it. Very original."

Gog finds the offensive banter of Otto revive in him the role of the gentleman so effective against the Military Policeman.

"No," he replies, "I disguise myself as a ditch. And when a hunter comes by, I break his ankle."

"Can a son of yours be against blood sports, Merry?" Otto says. "It's like Nero turning Christian and feeding himself to the lions."

"Gog's against everything," Merry says, patting her son fondly on the head. "Everything except his mother."

"You eat grass then," Otto says, "when you aren't being polite and wolfing down our poor meaty fare?"

"I agree," Gog says, "I'm not consistent. I'm not even consistent enough to be against everything. I like eating meat and I hate killing it. It's a natural end-of-the-war reaction. I mean, murder may soon become a crime again, and mass murder be considered rather bad form."

"The size of the bag," Otto says, "shows the talent of the shot . . ."

"I should warn you, Gog," Merry interrupts, "there's hardly a country on earth that Otto hasn't hunted in. He's declared a sort of permanent world war against animals, and he's winning it. Hippo in Rio, wildebeeste in Vancouver, penguin in Sierra Leone, I simply can't count the corpses."

"Your geography, my dear," Otto says, "does credit to your sense of romance. It's true, my friend, that I have pursued the rarest of beasts over the more lonely parts of the globe. Panda, oryx, white rhinoceros, I've shot them all. It has been most informative, as well as damn good fun. Do you know, the Himalayan bear, when potted, makes the noise of a weeping child? Unbearable – excuse the pun – if you didn't know what the noise came from."

"You must find England very boring after all that refined slaughter," Gog says.

" Not at all, not at all. Even hunters grow old. And the shoots are so well-organized here. The English alone have the true sense of the kill. Anyone can organize the killing of humans, even my ghastly Nazi mother's family, because humans co-operate so readily in their own massacre. But only the English know the most difficult of arts, the organization of the killing of the unhelpful birds. It's a sort of national genius, the bringing up of the chicks on eggs and grain, the killing off of the foxes that might disturb the hen pheasants about their maternal duty, the sending out of armies of beaters to make sure that every bird has its chance to share in the glorious Twelfth of August and add its contribution to the grand total of the bag. Six hundred brace in a day, I've done it."

" I've known Otto bring home a mountain of grouse," Merry says. " You'd think nothing ran or flew on the surface of the earth when he'd walked over it. I must say, Otto, you're God's gift to the twelve-bore."

The vision of hunters with shotguns stalking the crust of the globe confuses in Gog's mind with the vision of the red area of the British Empire spreading its stain over the same crust.

" It's just occurred to me," Gog says, " that Otto's the real reason for our Empire. The gentry got bored of shooting pheasants and hares here. They wanted bigger game. So they set out on a safari that turned into a permanent colonization, just to find larger beasts and huger reserves of wild meat. In their quest after the okapi, they discovered Africa. The tiger was the reason for the conquest of India. Allow wogs to kill so noble a beast? Impossible. The British explorers were hunters first, last, and all the time. They planted the Union Jack to make sure of their sport. We must preserve our game preserves, they said. And where the sportsmen led, the merchants naturally came after. Trade follows the bag."

Otto looks up to heaven at the end of Gog's speech as if the dull sky were less boring than the speaker. But he suddenly becomes alive, reaches quickly behind the chaise-longue, brings up a shotgun hidden behind the silk, aims aloft and fires. A pigeon falls slipping sideways down the air and comes to rest a yard from Otto. He has to rise to pick it up. "Damn," he says. "Another tenth of a second and I'd have dropped it in my lap."

"Dinner with Otto," Merry says, "can be a dangerous affair. You never know when he won't produce a revolver from his buttonhole and take a pot shot at something. Champagne corks pop all right when Otto's near, but only because he's shot them off the bottle. I've seen him convert a chandelier into a brass meat-hook by picking off the glass droplets one by one till there was only the metal left. He never misses, Otto . . ."

"He misses me," Gog interrupts, "completely."

"Would you mind," Otto says, "putting this *petit four* between your front teeth and opening your lips a little? I will then miss you completely, but remove the cake with a bullet. William Tell, I've always thought, was a yokel, despite his popular appeal. Only knocking an apple off his son's head, and the child probably budged and knocked the fruit off himself! I'd rather fling my answer back in someone's teeth – sportingly, of course."

Without a word, Gog takes a *petit four*, wedges it between his front teeth, curls his lips back over his gums and turns his profile to Otto. He waits, while Merry says, "For God's sake, no." Then there is a snap and the hard cake disintegrates, driving dry crumbs into Gog's mouth so that he chokes and his teeth clack together.

When Gog has finished coughing, he turns towards the smiling and triumphant Otto, who has the right arm of ownership round Merry's shoulders while his left hand holds a long-barrelled revolver.

"It's my turn now," Gog says. "Would you please lend me your pistol and put a grape on the parting of your hair, so that I can shoot it off?"

Gog watches Otto's sure smile dissolve into a frown and then become a flickering rictus. "Don't be absurd, my young friend," Otto says. "How do I know you can shoot well?"

"I know enough to pull a trigger," Gog says easily. "Doubtless the gun will do the rest. And why should you worry about my aim? You're a sportsman, aren't you? What I let you do to me, you have to let me do to you. Fair's fair, isn't it? A game's a game. Each side has to have the same chance. Weapons are equal. You can put a grape-pip on your head if you like, if you want to make it even more difficult and sporting for me."

"Merry," Otto says, "will you please explain to your son that there's a world of difference between a *trained* sportsman and an amateur playing at sport? I know that I will hit what I aim at. But your son George . . ."

"I know I'll hit what I aim at, too," Gog says. "It rather depends what I aim at, doesn't it?"

Otto begins to tremble a little, while a look of concern that may even be a grin crosses Merry's face. "I must say, Otto," she says, "that much as I adore you, Gog has got his point. It's only sporting to let him have a pot shot at you. You can't always do the shooting, you know. It's only fair that you should get in the line of fire from time to time."

"But he may kill me," Otto shouts. "He may even mean to kill me. I'm a sitting duck. I haven't got a chance."

"I'll let you fly off, if you like," Gog says. "Let nobody say I didn't give another Anglo-Saxon a sporting chance, even if his Saxon half on his mother's side was a bit too recent." He makes a sudden grab and snatches the pistol out of Otto's left hand. "Put the grape up," he says, levelling the gun at Otto. "I won't fire till I see the green of its skin. Or else you'd better run for it."

"I protest," Otto yells.

"So does everybody who's a target."

"It's not cricket."

"No, it's not."

"It's . . . murder."

"Very probably."

With trembling hand, Otto reaches forward towards the bunch of grapes on the table. Then his nerves give way with a shriek, and he's off at a shuffling hop towards the dark entrance into Alfred's Tower, followed by the laughter of Gog and Merry.

"I'll give you a minute's start," Gog calls. "Then I'm hunting." He turns to Merry. "I hope I'm not about to wing your nearest and dearest."

" Oh, there's plenty more where he came from," Merry says. "It's time for me to move on, anyway. I've spent a day over a long week-end with Otto and that's too long. Country houses are only built for week-ends, and one week-end at that. By Monday, it's limbo in one of those stately mausoleums, and by Tuesday, it's doomsday, and by Wednesday, it's inferno. Luckily, there are so many of them, all filled with exactly the same type of conquering zero, lecherous as a rabbit and just about as brave if the rabbit had the shotgun. But I shouldn't complain. I've lived off the county all my life. There's always a squire ready to take me in, as long as I can be bothered to take him in. I've never yet had to stay in an hotel, or hire a man or a horse. Alas, my dear Gog, I'd have been a respectable woman, if only I'd had my own stable. But the wrong men own the right nags. You can't get a good horse between your legs without getting an indifferent chap ditto."

"If you can't join 'em," Gog says, laughing, "leave 'em." And he helps his mother to her feet and walks with her towards Alfred's Tower in search of Otto, who has disappeared into the black hole of the decayed entrance. A large sign warns: WAR DAMAGE – DO NOT ENTER THE TOWER. Royally impervious to the risk, King Alfred still stands in his stone oyster-shell over the doorway, his right hand clutched to his heart and his left hand on the cross that makes up the hilt of his long sword. Beneath him, a legend is cut into the stone.

ALFRED THE GREAT
A.D. 879 on this Summit
Erected his Standard
Against Danish Invaders
To him We owe the Origin of Juries
The Establishment of a Militia
The Creation of a Naval Force
ALFRED The Light of a Benign Age
Was a Philosopher and a Christian
The Father of his People
The Founder of the English
MONARCHY and LIBERTY

As Gog reads of the achievements of King Alfred, who was the originator of so many of Magog's devices of power and law in the name of defending the people, he does not want to walk under the heel of such a genius of ruling into the tower named after him. But Otto has gone that way, so Gog follows with his mother into the darkness of King Alfred's neo-gothic chimney-stack, miscalled monument.

"Monarchy and liberty," Gog grumbles, "they're enemies, not allies."

"Nonsense," his mother answers. "The first ensures the second. You wouldn't be free to sing the National Anthem if God didn't save the King."

As Gog enters the tower, he is blinded. There is a sudden wind by his face and thump at his feet. He stoops to find a brick embedded in the soil, fallen by chance or thrown by choice from above. He looks up to see that the roof of the tower has tumbled down and a triangle of grey sky is his only cover from the wrath of God. A faint light trickles half-way down the two hundred feet of crumbling brickwork which make up the walls of the tower. Weather has blackened the bricks so that Gog seems to be looking up the immense length of a flue.

Another brick crashes against the wall at the left edge of the doorway, just missing Gog. He quickly moves his body to one side out of the dangerous silhouette of the entrance. And he studies the darkness of the lower reaches of the walls, looking for Otto.

"You'll ruin your tweeds, Otto," Merry calls up, "if you will insist on pretending you're a chamois. And Gog'll see you soon and make a bit of leather out of you for wiping windows. Why don't you surrender and say you're sorry?"

"I surrender," Otto calls out of the darkness.

Gog peers in the direction of the voice and can just make out a dark crouching blob in the darkness that looks like a crow, huddled into itself against the cold.

"Then stick up your hands," Gog calls back.

"I can't. Or I'll fall down."

"Then fall down."

"I can't. Or I'll break my legs."

Another brick whistles by Gog's ear, scattering rubble over his head.

"What are you chucking bricks with, Otto? Your teeth?"

"No. I'm hanging on with them."

"Then what are you talking with?"

"My tongue. No one talks with their teeth, you fool."

"Then where are the bricks coming from?"

"The whole tower's falling down."

"Then you'd better fall down."

"I can't. I'm stuck. You'll have to come and get me. Help! You can't leave a fellow Anglo-Saxon stuck in a crevasse. Was this the spirit that braved the Matterhorn? Help!"

So Gog tucks his pistol in his belt and starts up the sheer north face of crumbling Alfred's Tower. Without crampons, without pompoms, without icepick or toothpick, without hope or rope, Gog starts a traverse over the dread brick cliff that no human foot has ever trod before. It would make the stoutest heart quail to see the human fly nearly seven feet tall inch his way upwards, fingers dug into the toeholds made by mortar crumbling between bricks, and toes dug into the fingerholds although his fingers are still there. "Ouch!"

"I can't hold on much longer," Otto calls. "Will yet another life be sacrificed to the fearful north face? This is no sport, to pit one's wits and nails against the brick. It's murder."

Up, up, Gog scrabbles, scrambles, ambles, shambles, rambles, rumbles, grumbles, fumbles, tumbles, tangles, angles, wangles, tingles, jingles on this Alp of an Eiger of an Everest of a Popacatapetl, until Otto artfully dislodges seven lucky bricks onto his skull, making him see seven lucky stars. As Gog throws up a despairing hand, it clutches onto the left boot of the odious Otto, which is safely planted on a ledge. And down comes Gog and Otto and most of the north wall of the tower in an avalanche of rubble. As Gog skids into the ground, the pistol in his belt goes off and proves the last bullet which breaks the tower's ribs. With a thunder louder than Thor dropping his worst clanger, with a topple worse than Babel's curtsy, with a crack more absolute than the shattering of Humpty Dumpty's shell, the whole tower of King Alfred's Monument comes falling down,

falling,
        falling,
                falling,
                        falling,
                                brick
                                    after
                                        brick
                                             DO
                                                  W
                                                      N.
                                                          .
                                                             .

When Gog has coughed the dust out of his lungs and has pulled his limbs out from under the few fragments that miraculously are the only ones which have tumbled on him, he begins squirming, worming, storming, stalking, walking, baulking, bucking, mucking his way up the great pothole of red rubble above him. So the speleologist Gog comes out of the bloody womb of the earth to the peak of the high mountain of the fallen tower of might and majesty. And the breeze is blowing the red dust like a rusty mist. And an apparition clothed in powdered scarlet rises from the peak of the mountain, as the climber approaches the summit of F666 and says in an awful voice, "My son, you always used to bash in other boys' sand-castles on the beach, but this is a bit too much."

XXV

Gog leaves his mother sailing off stately home behind Methusaleh, who is the chauffeur of Otto's Silver Cloud Rolls Royce. Merry wants a bath and what Merry wants, Merry gets. "After that, I'm staying with my steady in these parts, Sir Clifford

Chastity – only he isn't. Do you know, I've sometimes spent a whole *week* there. We're almost married." So Gog's mother, really the scarlet woman under the layers of brick-dust, bids her son farewell and rides off, leaving Otto's aged retainers to pick among the bricks in search of their master. But their task is like finding a powdered toad in an apothecary's shop. It will take them light years to locate Otto among the débris.

So Gog walks off, whistling *Lili Marlene*. He takes the old Saxon Hardway or Harrow Way along the ridge, past the smooth bark of beech groves hanging down the pointed fingers of their leaves. A sudden vale takes his eyes to the right; it ends in a herd of cows grazing in the jaws of the beech wood; the cattle also ruminate beneath a ruined stone pavilion set in the centre of the grass for no reason except to bear a little cross and to remind wayfarers that Christ, perhaps, cared for them. Gog looks back soon afterwards and seems to see the top of Alfred's Tower still rising above the beeches. How can that be, when he has just seen it topple? Yet the quirky light of evening has already obscured Gog's vision, so that the three turrets of Alfred's Tower may well be three treetops, and Gog is certainly not returning a mile to check on whether his latest encounter is merely another dream. He hurries on to where the beech woods end on the high meadows and the chalky linen of White Sheet Hill ahead lures him towards London, as it flies its flag of truce from the earthworks of the ancient fort miles away, promising Gog repose.

Gog plunges down the longest lane in all the world, walking on the tongue of grass between the two tractor ruts, with the high banks of brier and nettle and foxglove and cowparsley and buttercup putting blinkers on the willing horse following his nose straight towards the east. From the occasional thicket, pigeons get up in a mocking rattle of musketry, disturbed by Gog's approach. But even the longest lane has its ending, and Gog arrives eventually on the hard chalk track across the downs proper. He is tiring now as if his strength were ebbing with the light and fatigue were cloaking him in the folds of the night. But the way is milky beneath his feet and it leads him under an arch of oak branches up White Sheet Hill past the ramparts of the old earthwork, until he finds an entrance into the fortress cut through the sloping walls. He climbs up the causeway across the ditch and double wall, his boots pushing through feathers of grass as tall as arrows, through plantains as heavy-headed as darts, and past pyramid orchids flaming purple in points of fire. He sinks back onto the slanting inner bank of the earthwork and turns the two balls of his eyes down the entrance slope across the dark-olive fields, sliced sideways by the hedgerows, to the crow-winged hills, above which the last curve of the single ball of the sun is shut between the lower lid of the earth and the upper lid of the night. And sodden with good food and tiredness, Gog tumbles into sleep as deeply as down a shaft dug by an archaeologist on an interesting site.

" This intriguing specimen of Neolithic man," Miniver's voice says in Gog's ears, " has just been excavated, as you all see, *in situ* beneath this old causewayed enclosure on White Sheet Hill." As Gog tries to move, he finds to his horror that his limbs have turned to bone or stone, and that he is bound down in place as if by the grasses that bind down decayed shells and fossils which the years in their millions have translated into the chalk subsoil of the downs. " The skull of this Neolithic man, as you see, has the prognathous jaw and protruding ridgebone which we would expect on a primitive of his type." And indeed, as Gog tries to open his eyes to see Miniver discoursing over his body to a group of students, he finds that he has only sockets in his skull which can discern nothing at all.

The lesson continues. " Although the earthwork we are inside is a Round Barrow of the Bronze Age, the skeleton before us is one of the earlier Neolithic or Windmill Hill people. Of course, he was uncommonly large for his time; he may even have been superstitiously thought to be a *giant*. We may reasonably suppose that he died defending his tribe from the superior weapons of the Bronze Age warriors, attacking from their mines in the Mendips and elsewhere.

"You may well ask, what sort of a life did our Neolithic skeleton friend lead? He was semi-nomadic, cultivating grain here and there on virgin soil and moving his cattle and pigs and sheep to the increasing areas of cleared grassland on the chalk downs. As he did not yet know how to weave, he wore cow-hides, prepared by antler combs and flint scrapers. Now that flint, indeed, which exists in large veins beneath the chalk, was mined by our Neolithic friend and gave him the advantage in war over his predecessors. You might well say that the men of flint conquered the men of softer stone and of wood, while they in their turn were conquered by the men of bronze, before these gave way to the men of iron.

"So the Ages passed from Stone to Bronze to Iron to Roman to Dark to Middle and to Modern. Our friend here has returned to the chalk from which his weapons and his life came. Look at the hole in his skull just by his right temple! It would just fit the edge of the small bronze axe, which you will recall we saw in the British Museum recently. Thus we may reasonably suppose that our skeleton friend is a Neolithic warrior, entombed by the conquering Bronze Age attackers as a sacrifice to their king in his Round Barrow. He was doomed, despite his huge size – as the dinosaur and all brute strength is doomed – by the advance of superior technology in the hands of brainier people. So study, my students, study, and you can safely bury the mass."

The voice stops and Gog struggles to move beneath the mesh of grass-roots that ties him down, Gog Gulliver the victim of the Lilliputian archaeologists. But he cannot move or see, and he must lie in dumb stillness, bearing all that Albion must bear. Albion, lying beneath the green skein of nature, Chalk on Upper Greensand on Gault on Lower Greensand on Oolite on Shale on Carboniferous Limestone on Calcite on the most ancient rock of all, Old Red Sandstone. Albion, sunk layer after layer into the crust of the globe and washed about by the cold vein of the sea, while tiddly folk dare to sink shafts and scoops into his pores, while minimal men comment on his innards and past as ignorantly as Miniver comments on the fossil of Gog.

At last, a whisking irritation unbearably repeated a dozen times rescues Gog from his stonebound nightmare. A volcano of a sneeze looses his rocklike trance, and he wakes with a jerk to find a cow dusting his face with her tail. He shoos her away through the dawn and the grass, ripe with slugs and dew, while he gets to his feet to jog up and down and to warm his blood against the coldness and stiffness that reaches down into his marrow-fat. The old wound in his temple throbs as if the point of a weapon were tapping it in rhythm to his jumping blood.

Then Gog's through the grassy plateau of the earthwork, over its southern walls nearly levelled by centuries of ploughing, past tumuli raising their vast bosses of soil above buried heroes, and down a tongue of hill, where the cows have trudged and worked the clayey chalk into floes and troughs fit to break both ankles. At the bottom of the hill lies the town of Mere, and Gog turns into the Old Ship Inn, with the cleaning woman and the manager shrinking back in terror from his gigantic, loamy, smeared and burry shape. Gog takes the talisman against their fear out of his pocket, a green pound note, and he is immediately ushered into a hidden corner of the huge dining-room under the vaulting beams that curve to a central apex. Gog looks upwards from his seat and seems to be beneath a Viking ship, set upside down as a hall for its rowers and plastered between the ribbing of its sides. And Gog wolfs down two breakfasts in a row, one for the inner man beginning to kick infantile within his ribs, and one for the terrifying outer man, whose bulk and bristles scare the other guests as they seep in and hide away from the sight of Gog behind the pages of newspapers, screaming of military victories against Japan and of election victories for Labour and the people.

On through Mere towards the South-West and the old way to Salisbury across the high downs. At present, the road lies through flat and farm lands. A curious sense begins to come over Gog that Maire has been on the way before him, leaving her signs scattered throughout nature. It is as though she thinks herself a treasure trove, and she has left her true colours behind her as clues to tantalize Gog and tease him forwards in the chase. A black-and-white cat stalks along the hedge with the fearful boldness of half-wild pets; she complains to see Gog, but she will not let him touch her. A herd of Friesian cows chews the cud in a field, blobs of ink spattering the paper of their flanks. A wallow of coaly saddleback pigs seem to have their skin deliberately scraped over their forelegs and front shoulders to show Maire's cruel white traces. Interminable magpies in ones and twos flick their tails derisively in flight. Within the mysterious intestines of barns, great dark metal guts of abandoned machinery rust away in front of bleached wood walls. Even through a cottage window, Gog can see a loaf and a white bowl of apples set out on a chessboard of oilcloth, while a crow perches on the corner of the black bedroom sill in front of whitewashed bricks. Gog is certainly walking towards London and Maire is there. If she is his treasure trove, then perhaps, like fairy gold in the stories, she will turn to dried leaves and ashes in his hand, blowing away in the wind, leaving him alone at last.

The old tree-trunks of the telephone poles hobble along the road, their wires keening in the wind and telling runes, mysterious messages only intelligible to the high priests speaking and listening on either end of the cable. And the rain soon adds its counterpoint, driving Gog into a miraculous sentry-box of old red brick, built for wayfarers by some charitable gardener. There Gog rests until the squall is over. Were such providential shelters everywhere beside the road, the whole population would be on the tramp, always progressing towards the joy of never arriving at disappointment. Gog dozes, propped up against the bricks, glad that even Maire seems to have lost her terrors for him now, so he can almost smile at his thought that the haphazard palette of nature might be painted by his wife. As though Maire had invented the contrast between black and white rather than stolen it, as usual, from the creation of God etcetera!

When the rain has stopped, Gog moves past Huggler's Hole into Semley. He turns off by the railway tracks tying the village by twin metal bands to London, and he goes into the Kingsettle Inn under the pub sign of a monarch reclining at his ease on a plush throne, his feet resting on a footstool under the roof of a golden palace. Gog himself lounges royally inside the pub on the leather seat of an old oak bench, a pint of bitter and a plate of rabbit sandwiches in front of him. There are a few farm labourers also at the bar, talking weather and plonking dominoes together fiercely, while the pubkeeper has a snub bullseye of a nose and a round-cheeked face fitter than Gog or a board to be the target for darts. Half-way through his midday rest, Gog sees the oldest inhabitant make his entry on two sticks amid triumphal cries of "Joe!" Only two teeth remain in Joe's right gum, even the skin on his bald head is wrinkled, the hairs sprouting from his ears and nose are white, while his middle is a flannel pumpkin beneath wide grey trousers braced up as high as his nipples. His striped tie and the crested badge on his blue blazer proclaim him a veteran of the Boer or the Crimean War, while his slow shuffle and settling at his favourite chair are hailed loudly as if his entry proved that old soldiers never die and men can live for ever. Seeing Joe's living denial of death, Gog wonders if death is worth denying at the price of living like Joe. Yet the old man's belly, now balanced on his haunches as he sits, looks the same as the belly of a woman about to give birth. And Gog feels a little compassion scrub at his heart to watch the very old carrying within themselves the signal of the very new.

Beer and fatigue make Gog move blindly on, lost in muzzy thinking, through the sunny afternoon. The tick-tock of his pace induces a walking doze, so that hundreds of yards pass by without him taking in their passing. A fork in the narrow lane always jolts Gog back to consciousness because of the need to choose one path rather than the other. Otherwise he would sleepwalk unseeing on past the bracken and trees of the wooded hills, with foxgloves dumbly clapping their bells and bees hung silent in the air with black legs dangling ready for landing and nettles massed in their stinging ranks reserving their green darts against any intruder. But the beer and the sleepiness wear off with the wind on the crest of Semley Hill and with the view of the flat hills ahead across the Nadder Valley, chalk scours and scars and squiggles marking the green flanks of the downs with cabbalistic signs. The sun is suddenly swaddled in dark cloud on this unpredictable day, which reveals the alchemy of the weather only to the initiate, while the rest of mankind must suffer the fair and foul weather as it comes.

While lying on the parapet of the small stone bridge over the Nadder by Donhead St. Mary, Gog discovers that he is becoming a new man. Without his noticing, his walk has hardened his body and is healing the dark wounds of his mind as stealthily as the flesh heals itself unnoticed under the armour of a scab. The stupor induced by his tramping has been a balm to his obsessions. He can feel the outward signs of his inward cure. His stomach has become a series of parallel ridges of muscle between which he can fit the fingers of his exploring hand. His thighs are knotted hard as a tangle of wet hawsers, his calves are two balls almost as tough as skulls, his feet are so inured to walking that they feel only the heat within his boots and not the fiery furnace of trodden tarmac.

Within such a firm frame almost equal to the condition of a workhorse, there is room to cradle a fresh spirit. The superfluous has been melted away with the fat, the necessary may begin to enter. Proud at the strength of his renewed body, fearful at the first stirrings of something like a soul, Gog looks down at the trickle of the Nadder beneath him to see an external image of spreading peace. Within the banks of the little river where the water runs as steadily as through a vein, a peacock's tail of green weed spreads itself out in a feathery fan from a point in the middle of the current. The grey light reflected on the ripples glances in a hundred eyes of brightness, so that fire and water and feather and plant combine in a trembling arc of beauty. If Gog seeks a picture of his inner mood, it lies there.

Yet as he watches, a cloud of midges rises about the spreading weed to make a furious head-in-air. And rain begins to pat his cheeks and crown, reminding him that peace is only a momentary state. Cures do not come at their first sensing; to feel well can be to begin a relapse. So Gog flees on up the steep chalk path that leads to Old Salisbury Way, with the rain like the tongues of the Furies at his heels. He is cheered to pass a wrecked and rusted lorry with its bonnet split open and its engine become a bush spearing out sprays in green silence. But it is Gog's last cheer before the rain and the high downs plunge him back into his passion for persecution.

For he's out exposed on the ridge of the downs now and the rain's falling in a slant on his front like the Norman arrows at Hastings and drops are pricking their barbs into his whole forward body and wetness spreads over his skin like a seeping of blood and he's running between the two strands of barbed wire that flank the straight track for mile after mile on the treeless grass and a stone sign mocks at him, XCVII TO HYDE PARK

CORNER, XIV TO SALISBURY, 1756, such a flood of a way to go still, and a shard of flint embedded in the chalk cuts into his foot through a hole in his boot to remind him that this is Maire's country after all, with black slicing edges of stone hidden in the milky clay. Yes, this is Maire's favourite southland, where the thick-woolled sheep aren't smut-dark like the northern ones on the moorland. No, the southern sheep are fluffy as whipped cream, their silly ears sticking out sideways like twin handles on a sugarpot. Beware, Gog, beware, the southland manner, the bland beguiling, then the hidden weapon, the smiler with the knife. O yes, the southland is like that, and the weather and the soil made the southerners like that and gave them the victory over the midlands and the northland; a weather of rare storm and much shower and breeze and sun; a soil of high ridges easily fortified, of full living from herds on the plain and vegetables in the valley, of flint weapons springing like dragon's teeth ready to hand. O yes, by the time the midlands had discovered that their fields had the power of food and the northland had discovered that its mines and factories had the power of iron and coal, the southland had learned all the wily ways of chalk and flint and it coaxed the rest of Albion to curtsy to London, to holiday in the south and spend its brass there, before the provincials went back to the north to labour and wonder how they had been conned and cozened and plucked and packed off penniless home by the soft southland, which now whips Gog along on the barbs of the rain, his sole bloody from the cut of the flint, the victim of the sudden brutality that the southland only shows to prove its easy mastery.

It's a long ridgeway that has no shelter, even the Old Salisbury Way, and Gog eventually reaches a large beech grove where the high props of the branches and the irregular layers of the leaves catch the rain before it touches the ground. Gog sinks back, panting in the lee of a tree-trunk, while the heat of his running gradually becomes a soggy warmth and ends as a clamminess. He has to rise and flay the wet clothes off his skin. Once naked, he wrings out his corduroy trousers and red shirt and socks and jersey, jumping up and down like some parody of an almost-human mechanical mangle. He puts on his clothes again and huddles into the roots of the tree, torn between the need to rest and the need to pump his blood into motion and heat. In the end, the rain stops and the wind soughs on, so that Gog decides to plod through the evening and let his shoulders serve as a drying-rack for his clothing.

It is nearly dark when Gog reaches another ringed earthwork, Chiselbury Camp overlooking Compton Chamberlayne and the Nadder Valley from the high ridge. The corn is browning, sodden and bowed within the low circles of the ancient fortress; the rationing of modern war has set the ploughshare to till the old place of the sword and feed the many-mouthed warrior island. Gog sits briefly on an iron water-tank, fairly dry and very hungry, but cocky at being tough enough to endure such weather without even a sneeze. The new Gog is a strong Gog, even if he is still forgetful.

Yet Maire does not forget to leave behind her last and most horrible clue of the day. On top of the green scum in the tank, a bird floats on its back, with long wings and fanning tail spread out in a flat trident's head of feathered blackness. Yet the centre spoke of the trident, the belly of the bird above the tail, is swollen and split. Within the gash is a crawling curd of maggots, a thousand thousand white worms that make up a tongue of decay among the jet feathers. Gog runs off to shelter in a thicket for the night, his stomach heaving from hunger or horror or fear.

XXVI

The morrow is a southland day, with the air as warm and steamy as a laundry and the birds rising at Gog's approach from thorn and chestnut with the noise of wet flapping towels. It is a day to knead the stiffness from muscles and meander through the cool rinse of the atmosphere, with just enough breeze up to spread the smell of drying leaves and plants everywhere in sharp sweetness. Of course, as the chalk track is in the southlands, it is soggy and treacherous underfoot with deep brown puddles enough to drown a foot in, with lumps of clay and gravel that could break an axle, let alone an ankle. The raindrops stored on the bending blades of the tall grasses soon make a smaller puddle in each of Gog's boots by way of the swamp on his trouser-legs, so that he walks on water, at first cold and squelching, but soon tepid and moulding his sock and leather uppers to his feet. Perhaps the greatest pleasure of the early morning is to take leave of the ridgeway at last by pissing against a tree, the yellow arch curving onto the lichened bark and the urine running down black onto the black whorls of the roots. It does for a man to make a little water when the sky has made so much.

It's the Hoop Side track that Gog goes skating and ski-ing and bob-sleighing down. For Wiltshire summer sports, visitors are recommended to wear on the slopes a filthy jersey crocheted in purled twin-stitch with irregular holes big enough to put your five heads through, a pair of corduroy trousers so mud-caked that the ribbing of the cloth has long since disappeared under a sheen of slime, a red shirt smelling as meaty as a month-old steak, and all-purpose army boots, fitted with ready-slip hobnails which serve as skis and skates and runners without the need to strap on anything else. For cocktail lounge wear, there aren't any cocktail lounges. For dining and dancing, try picking hips and haws and berries from the briers and hopping up and down to the eighty-piece brass band of the north wind howling through your soaked smalls. No need to reserve places. There'll be few other fools summer sporting in the Wiltshire rain.

Down the Cresta lane at sixty inches per minute, a hard turn on the bank of the old tumulus, straighten out of the swerve on the dropping track towards Barford St. Martin (the St. Moritz of the Wiltshire Alps), skid vertical down between the fifteen-foot banks of nettle and thorn, slide between the twin ruts cut deep into the ice-smooth chalk by tractor-sleighs, check and christie by the bend, lean into the jump over the five-barred gate, and tumble arse over tip, ski over shoulder, boot over ear, knuckle over nipple, sleigh over foreskin, onto the main road at the foot of the sporting Salisbury slopes of Hoop Side and Burcombe Without.

Tuck-time at the village shop fills Gog with all the various forms of saccharine-sweet dough that he can find. Not much is off-ration except the artificial and the heavy and the tastelittle; but hunger does not discriminate, and Gog wolfs down fruit pies and wool-filled doughnuts as if they were pomegranates and manna. He even swills down lemonade that is impossible, being both gluey and fizzy at the same time. And Oliver Gog asks for more. His body cannot drink in enough sweetness. With his belly full, he sets off towards Grovely Wood, his heart light and soaring because he has again seen the sign of the previous afternoon's peace, the peacock's tail of weed feathering in a large pool of the Nadder, with every plume of green now bearing white flowers. The whole river is solid with petal and weed so that a moorhen jerking on its swim across the pool seems to be walking on a carpet just below the surface.

Again the feeling of peace does not last. This time, an inner aggression takes Gog back to the wars from which he has just returned. As the pigeons and the crows rise from the hedges at his coming, Gog finds his hands also rising, willy-nilly, and pointing at the birds with fingers outstretched like pistol-barrels, thumbs cocked in a hammer, while his lips explode, " Pow, pow," left and right, never miss in the mind, though the birds fly away before the eye. Even a blackbird or a thrush scirring upwards from a bush makes Gog's reflex thrust his fingers upwards, his breath puffing, " Pow," until he grows ashamed of his automatic habits of slaughter, left over from animal rough shoots before the war and civilized human shoots during it, mow down anything that moves, fire before you see the whites of their feathers or fur or faces. Only by a great effort of the will can Gog stop himself from pretending to aim and fire, so that he may look at the winged and furry things to enjoy their flight or run. Yet even so, the reflex twitches at his hands from time to time, so that he has to drop his half-raised arm and swallow a " Pow " like a belch in his throat. Trained killer that he is, no better than an Otto, Gog tries to learn the ways of truce.

He fails. Across the green-dark fringe of Grovely Wood, two hundred yards ahead at the hedge's end, four hen pheasants run across the path through the field, jerky and camouflaged in dun spots like soldiers on patrol. On the sudden, Gog finds his body stooped and crouched, his fingers hooked as if round invisible handles in front of him, his shoulders pulling round a heavy barrel of thin air along the moving line, his teeth chattering like a machine-gun. The pheasants run out of sight into the flanking cornfield. The spasm passes from Gog, leaving him collapsed and quivering on the ground. Across the screens on the back of his closed eyelids, lines of brown men start their jumpy run and the stutter of his nerves brings them kicking down, hands to their belly like himself. The pictures cut behind his lids to another scene, where he stands in a bivouac by a hurricane lamp, swigging a whisky and soda, bragging with the quietness that is the supreme insolence, " Bagged a whole Eyetie patrol in between forty winks . . ."

A passing shaft of sun makes Gog blink and return to his feet and trudge heavily onwards into the wood. Midges like little worries buzz in his lashes and his ears, as he treads the soggy trail between birch and beech and ash. The two muddy ruts through the wood lead him onto a cross-road of tarmac, where the old Roman way used to bisect the forest regardless of ups and downs and trees and meadows, as straight as a parting through shaggy hair. Gog continues on the ancient Saxon way through the woods that follows the contours; for the flat-footed Saxons would rather march five miles round than one mile straight up and down, preferring the ridgeway to the rule, the level to the line. Just beyond the Roman way, Gog crosses the northern part of the ancient Grim's Ditch, now clogged with leaf mould and bracken and brier. Did Giant Grim really stop here on his way from Lincoln to gouge out this ditch against the Trojan invaders soon to defeat him and Gogmagog at Totnes?

On the far side of the wood, in the last clearing before the slow drop down to the Wylye Valley, Gog comes on a shepherd's caravan of corrugated iron on metal wheels. As he approaches the iron steps leading up to the open door of the caravan, he can see that it is boxed with planks inside. He has only time to notice with surprise a great brass bedstead filling up most of the floor-space of the caravan, when an extraordinary figure stops him short in his stride. A dropsical naked female Bacchus comes spinning and weaving down the steps and slowly twirls across the clearing. Flowers are plaited into all her available nooks and crannies. Between her toes, helleborine opens its white flowers with lascivious yellow tongues; knotted in her pubic hair is a posy of sneezewort and black horehound and bastard balm; from her hairy armpits grow the parasite broomrape and ramping fumitory and tufted vetch; her fingers are pink-red with dumpy centaury and dodder and bindweed; her lips smoke the stems of policeman's helmet and bouncing bett; in her eyelashes, scarlet pimpernels, in her eyebrows, forget-me-nots; dog's mercury entwined with cuckoo-pint make a green garland full of poison-seed round her crown; from each ear sprouts a hoary plantain, from each nostril curls a rough hawkbit, and from her navel springs one perfect sowthistle. It is Merry, getting back to nature.

Following her from the caravan comes a gamekeeper, wearing gumboots and scarlet shirt and close red moleskin trousers. He sits down on the iron steps, stuffs his brier pipe with shag tobacco, looks at Merry expressing herself all over the woody glade, and spits.

"Look at 'er," the keeper says bitterly to Gog. "Lady Chastity 'erself from the 'All! Visitin'! Canna keep 'er clothes on, neither! This is Lady Jane, 'er says, pointin' to where 'er shouldna. Here I shits, 'er says, bendin' down an' showin' me where. An' here I pisses, 'er says, bendin' up an' showin' me where. As if I didna know! I'd ha' bust by now if I didna know. Lay tha hand on 'em both, 'er says, an' like me for it. Well, I keeps me hands in me pockets, an' I dunna like 'er for it. We all ha' what 'er has, but we keep it private. Then 'er tells me to take me trousers off. All right, Your Ladyship, I says, but if thee wasna Your Ladyship, I'd keep 'em on. Then when I've got me trousers off, 'er takes me balls in her hand an' says, 'Ullo, Sir John Thomas, 'ow about gettin' up for Lady Jane? Has thee ever heard such bloody cock? So I says, Keep tha hands to tha own parts, I mun do me job. Then 'er makes me wear these close red trousers, so tight I'll split me arse if I bend in 'em. Once the men walk with legs close bright scarlet, 'er says, an' buttocks nice an' showin' scarlet under a little white jacket; then the women 'ud begin to be women. I'm not wearin' no white jacket, I says, not even for Your Ladyship. Go an' dance the tango in the nude if tha pleases, but I willna wear no honeysuckle on me balls nor no white bumfreezer to do me work. An' if women 'ud begin to be women an' dance round naked with daisies in their cunts once men wear red trousers an' white bumfreezers, I'm bloody well goin' to bed in a macintosh, just to keep 'em off. But 'Er Ladyship willna listen. Off with 'er jodhpurs, stick enough flowers in 'er mount of Venus for a village fête, then 'er's ready to step on top of me poor little game chicks. O dear, O dear, it were very simple bein' Sir Clifford Chastity's keeper before Lady Chastity began readin' books on 'ow she should take an interest below stairs."

Gog prefers to leave Merry to the pursuit of her nature by the rules of liberty prescribed for the intellectual savages of the thirties. So he pats the gamekeeper on the back. "I'd take over from you, my friend," he says. "But she's my mother. Don't worry, she'll be after another Sir John next week-end." And he wanders out of the wood on the way the map marks as leading to Stonehenge.

In the field beyond the trees, Gog sees how the gamekeeper does his job of rearing the chicks for the slaughter. Through the wooden bars of little cages, anxious white hens poke out their red combs, looking for their bastard offspring, changeling pheasant chicks, all speckled and strutting as they run in and out between the bars into the grass. An iron pot stands over some blackened stones; from it comes a strong smell of mixed meat and grain. So these are the fowl raised for the ceremonial massacre of the twelfth of August, the yearly Verdun and Dresden of the game birds, when Otto and his friends come out with their shotguns to train themselves and younger men like Gog for the killing of anything that moves. Yet nature is as cruel, if not as deliberate. As Gog watches, there is a bolt from heaven, a scrabble on the grass, and the sparrow-hawk is away with a chick between its claws, while the gamekeeper is sidetracked from his sentry-duty as Merry leads him a dance in Grovely Wood.

Gog strolls down the hill to the red-tiled roofs of Great Wishford and crosses the river Wylye at the stone bridge. Beneath him, the trout lie facing upstream, no more substantial than shadows. Their tails move lazily just enough to keep themselves still against the current, waiting for the river to drift its food into their open mouths. And in the large meadows beyond the village, all other living things seem as lazy. The swallows merely lounge on the breeze with an occasional flip of their wings to adjust their position to a more comfortable one on their mats of air. A rabbit does not even bother to move off at Gog's approach, but crouches down, obvious and oblivious, until he has gone. And as for the chase that should add some vigour to this summer's drowse at doze of day, why, the hare and the pursuing hound are set immovably in iron over one farmhouse on the peak where the weathercock should be, and they turn only with the breeze, never closer to each other, never further away on their still hunt.

For mile after mile, Gog meets not a soul. The country tracks of England are empty, the people are forgetting how to walk, the rights-of-way are disappearing under the plough. He is a man alone in a deserted countryside. Yet he knows that sometimes he does not see a passer-by, because he is lost in a reverie or in the monotony of the trudge. And he knows that the people of the southland shrink back from the stranger, who may well carry the plague or a knife. Why should the traveller be welcome now, when he can bring no news as quickly or as well as the radio and the newspapers? The wires and the metal type that have made the countryfolk the eavesdroppers of the gossip of the city, have pushed the traveller from the hearth. For he can tell nothing so novel and curious now, that it will outweigh the natural fear of his unknown coming.

A hall called Druid's Lodge marks the way from the south towards Stonehenge. Yet Gog can hardly believe that the great remembered stones really exist over the rise; for all he can see ahead are the chimneys of incinerators sticking like black needles from the cloth of the earth and trailing threads of smoke, while the familiar oblongs of Nissen huts squat smaller than dung-beetles on the slopes of Salisbury Plain. Gog looks at the map and finds that the name of the army camp beyond Stonehenge is Larkhill. Larkhill? when the artillery is singing a staccato barrage of broken caws and the mortar bombs are booming like distant bitterns and the familiar noises of war make Gog tremble so that he longs to confuse them with the unfamiliar noises of nature, and he cannot. Yet it is evening now, and the actual birds begin to shrill in the stubble and the copses, and the soldiers manning the far guns cease fire and pack up in time for dinner, and the mad hares begin bounding about everywhere, rarely stopping to listen while poised on their hind legs, their ears pricked high and their short forepaws hanging down like another set of ears. And the evening is buttery on the golden bowls of the fields, as the southland beguiles with its soft bright ways. So it is in peace that Gog walks up the little slope in the track and finds himself looking two miles ahead to the grey giants of Stonehenge.

XXVII

A grove has put up its ragged palisades to shut off the huts of Larkhill Camp, as the stone giants walk down from the north to meet Gog walking up from the south, the stone giants alongside the wooden giants from the tall copses at their flanks and alongside the giants of the night that walk in the long shadows of the sunny evening. "Caugherigan," Gog finds himself murmuring, "and Tregeagle from Dozmare Pool, Little Grim from Lincoln, Bolster of Portreath, Trecrobben of the ten fingers, Termagol, Palug on his mighty cat, Annwfn's Chief, Tyrnoc and Pen Palach, Manawydan of the dark net and Pryderi that leaves no shadow, so black is he." So Gog calls the roll of honour of his twelve giant companions of stone and wood and night that come marching on to meet him from the woods about Stonehenge in the summer's close of day. They have come to help Gog fight the new Trojans of the new metal, steel and aluminium and tungsten, who tear up the old places of Wessex on their manoeuvres and testing-grounds beyond the fringing woods round Salisbury Plain.

The old trail from the south dips again as Gog walks forwards. and he loses sight of the stone giants. All he can hear is the gathering noise of a convoy of lorries passing along the main road before him, a din that grows from a rumble to a roaring. Up another rise and the stone giants have walked nearer in their broken circle. They face outwards, ready to meet attack from all directions, especially from the back, for this is the wily southland. As Gog crosses the main road and approaches Stonehenge, he sees that the new Trojans have hemmed in the giants by roll on roll of barbed wire. The great stones are making their last stand, back to back in their doomed ring, fronting the thousand thousand wire points of their enemies. They can no longer advance nor retreat. They wait over the many centuries for the final attack from the war camps on the plain, the ultimate assault of the metal things from Larkhill, propelled by the mechanics who have ringed them with iron barbs.

The low evening light chips out mill-stone faces from the standing monoliths, flat-cheeked, snub-nosed, mongoloid. Where the lintel stones still bridge the gap between two of the standing stones, they seem to be the pelvis joining the stubby thighs of some Ozymandias. From outside the besieging rolls of barbed wire, the stone giants appear broken into limbs and torsos, some leaning in rest and some dead from their fight over the millenia with the encroaching forces of metal that ring them closer and closer in fanged manacles.

As Gog stands outside Stonehenge, wishing for a pair of clippers to cut his way through the outer wire, he sees that his wish has spawned the deed. A burrow has already been opened, the iron barbs bent backwards so that a man can easily crawl within the sacred enclosure on hands and knees over the grass. And so Gog crawls into the henge. As he rises to his feet, he sees a priest clad in a white robe standing within the inmost circle of the stones, invoking the aid of the red sun that is blinking on the rim of the west. Gog approaches softly to see that the priest is tall and hunchbacked and speaks in the fierce voice of Evans the Latin.

"Ogmios, god of the mouths of the Celts, come down in your lion-skin and touch Evans your servant, indeed. Touch him with your club, that he may speak with tongues of fire. Teach him to drag the limeys behind him in chains, as you drag all men. Give him strength to put the accursed city of Cockaigne to the torch, that the sweet stink of English flesh can roast in your nostrils. Look you, Ogmios, I go against London. There's no time now for forgetting the champion of the druids. I go against the false Cockaigne, the city of Gog and Magog. And burn it, I will, down to the twin hills on either side of Walbrook, where Gog and Magog sit, ruling Cockaigne and all the lands of the Celts. Ogmios, *bach*, be you a coal on my tongue, a spear in my breath. I go to tell the wicked parliament of London to let the Celtic peoples free. If they say nay, then burn, burn, burn! Ogmios, aid me. Who else calls to you? Ogmios, hear me. The last of the true Celts, the last of the true druids, calls your holy name. Ogmios! And, look you, it'd be a bloody shame to let down another taffy."

As Evans swings round towards the approaching Gog, he reveals that he is carrying an inverted broadsword; round the hilt are twined a twig of oak and a sprig of mistletoe. The front of his white robes is covered with golden signs for the sun and the moon, the scales of justice and the pyramids. When he sees the intruder, he looses a fiendish Celtic yell and runs at Gog, holding the broadsword above his head ready to slice Gog in two. Luckily he trips over a sunken bluestone just before he can amputate Gog's split self into twins, and he comes clattering down at Gog's feet. Gog picks Evans up and dusts off his embroidered sheet, but he keeps the broadsword warily in his own hand.

"It's no good trying to split me asunder," he says to Evans. "However expert you are, I doubt whether you could separate the true Celt in me from the lying limey. Not with a broadsword, at least. Maybe with a pair of tweezers."

"Oh, it's you, Griffin *bach*," Evans says. "I get that feared in this accursed land, I think everybody is an enemy. And enemy they are, if they won't let the Celtic peoples go."

"I used to think everyone was an enemy in England," Gog says, "but I'm not so sure now. Don't you think the limeys may be merely misguided?"

"The limeys are so steeped in error," Evans says, "that the only way you'll get their heads straight is by cutting them off their necks. A bloody folk and they must be dealt with bloodily. But, mark you, I'm a man of peace like all true druids. I'll give them a last chance, indeed. If the new parliament of the Labour Party sticks to what it says – though what else does a limey eat but his own words? – if the socialists do what they pledge, then they'll give freedom to all the British Empire. And that means Wales and Cornwall and Scotland, too. Conquered peoples, we are. And if the free Celts choose to form together and make me their archdruid and ruler, why then, it's only right, look you. So Ogmios, let me change the wicked ways of the limeys at their Westminster, accursed in history. Or I'll burn the whole bloody lot."

"I didn't know you were a druid priest," Gog says. "There's an awful lot I don't know."

"Hush," Evans whispers, looking fearfully among the stone giants at his back. "Don't shout. Limey spies are everywhere, mark you. Stones have ears." He pulls Gog's own left ear close to his mouth and fills it full of words and the fierce froth of his passion. "There are always druids and I am one of their leaders. We don't declare ourselves, mark you. Why should we, in the land of our enemies? We've been the fifth column of the truth in two thousand years of occupation, since the bloody Romans came. We are always there when we are needed, indeed, though you may not find us even when you ask. We may seem to have disappeared over many centuries, but we were always there. For the truth is always there. From the druids, all religions come. Pity it is, they wither. But the druids are always there, waiting until another religion is needed, in its own due time. Christ was a druid, for what is the old druid name for the saviour to come but Yesu or All Heal? And Buddha, and Mahomet. Wherever a new religion arises, know you that the druids were there first. That legend that Joseph of Arimathea came to Glastonbury, of course, it's true. Why wouldn't he, when the source of holy things is here?"

The ring of giant stones backs Evans's words like some loyal guard, the ranks of the faithful stones that endure as long as the words of truth and long after the flesh has turned to dust.

"We have records, Griffin *bach*, that hold all wisdom, but we only reveal them in due time. We have always known of the powers of the centre of the body, look you, and now the scientific fools talk to us of endocrine glands. Nothing is new, indeed. All is rediscovered, because all is known before – by the druids.

"And if we know all knowledge, why do we conceal it? It is because wisdom is like the seasons, it shows itself in its own due time. For instance, we know how the people of Atlantis destroyed themselves. I would tell you, indeed. But then you would ask, What weapon did they use? Horror it is, that you should all ask the wrong questions and make us hide the truth and the wisdom from you. You do not want to know what happened to Atlantis, you want to know what was the machine that destroyed it, so that you can make it again to destroy us all."

Here Evans pauses, and a shadow crosses his face, as if a raven has passed over him in flight.

"Ah, but the infernal machine that destroyed Atlantis is already discovered again. We pray to stop its use, but it will be used. In a few days. Pity it is, and terrible it is, but they will not listen, they will use it."

"It will destroy two cities in the Far East soon, won't it?" Gog says.

Evans the Latin looks at Gog with surprise and suspicion. "How know you?" he says. "You're no druid."

"I'm half-druid, perhaps," Gog laughs. "Actually, someone called the Bagman told me."

Evans's face grows dark and the froth on his mouth becomes spume. "That apostate! That false druid! That traitor! Broadcasting our secrets to alien ears. Judas Iscariot was a saint compared to Wayland Merlin Blake Smith. Why talk you to such lying fools?"

" He talked to me," Gog says. " I didn't know you knew him."

" He was a maggot in the oak-apple, a blight in the grove. He wormed his way in, deceived us by fair words. Then he tried to set himself up as our false priest, and we expelled him. Since then that mad villain has paraded about, blabbing all the sacred secrets to limey ears. Lucky it is the limeys are so mad themselves they do not like to know the truth when they hear it, the holy wisdom of the druids. But if I ever see that traitor again, I'll quarter him in four parts and stick his bloody names on each bit of him, Wayland on his arms, and Merlin on his black heart, and Smith on his legs, and Blake on his rotten head. Ah, Griffin *bach*, that he should claim those marvellous old names. William Blake, he was the archdruid and some of our teachings are revealed in his writings . . ."

" I know," Gog says, " that poem of his about Jerusalem being once where London now is. The Bagman quoted it in the underground hangar. It begins, doesn't it?

" The fields from Islington to Marybone,
To Primrose Hill and Saint John's Wood,
Were builded over with pillars of gold,
And there Jerusalem's pillars stood."

" Right you are, *bach*," Evans the Latin says. " Haven't you heard that lying tongue tell you Blake's magnificent truth, All Things Begin and End in Albion's Ancient Druid Rocky Shore?"

" I have," Gog answers. " The Bagman always says *he* said it, when he was William Blake in a previous incarnation."

" The lying sod," Evans yells. " Of course, we druids believe that there is no death, we all come again and again in the form of all living things. But that apostate never was Wayland, never Merlin, and never never William Blake. He may be Smith, that's a dirty filthy limey name. You can't just *choose* who you were in the past. You were who you were. It's all in the archives, and I have the key to all the archives. All is in the archives, who everyone was and is and will be. And that filthy Smith, he wasn't William Blake. And when he comes again, he's going to be a toad, and I'm going to tread on him, I am."

"If everything's in your archives, all the past and the present and the future," Gog says, "they must be pretty big."

"They grow," Evans says. "They always grow. We don't write down *all* the truth, mark you. Only what's necessary to be written."

"And what's necessary?"

"What men should know at this time."

"But you said you knew what men were going to be."

"We do. And we will write it when they are. Always in our minds, the archives are, as well as in our pens. But we can't spend our whole lives writing, can we now? So we only write down what's necessary for today, though the archives know it all."

"If you know it all," Gog says, "and you even know my future, who do the archives say I am and was and will be? I've been looking for that on my tramp, you know."

"I can't tell a non-druid what the archives say, not even a bastard druid."

"Then can I become a druid?"

"No. Not like that. You're a druid only when you know and we know you're a druid."

"And if I did know I was a druid, and you did . . ."

"Unlikely it is."

"But if I *did* become a druid, then could I consult the archives and find out just who I am? Everything about myself?"

"I told you," Evans says, "you don't ask the right question. So how shall you receive the right answer? You want to know about your selfish self. But the druids, learn you, they ask only the holy questions, and these the archives answer. Our records aren't available for personal peeking and prying."

"So your archives, in fact, don't tell you anything interesting about yourself?"

"They tell us all things interesting to druids, which are all things interesting, excluding mere selfish curiosity."

"So if I want to see the archives to find out about myself," Gog says, "I must become a druid. But if I become a druid, I can't ask the archives about myself."

Evans the Latin nods. "You take the first step towards the true wisdom, indeed. And more than that. Though we know all wisdom, and though everything is rediscovered by others because we have discovered it first, yet we only write down a discovery in our archives when others have rediscovered it. Else those filthy limey spies might steal our written archives and destroy us all with our wisdom wrongly used."

Gog gives a wry smile. "I see why the druids are the source of all wisdom," he says. "No people have ever been wiser after the event."

"Oh, Griffin *bach*," Evans the Latin chides his old pupil, "that's the limey unbeliever speaking in you. We are wise before the event, wiser when the event is happening, and wisest when it is over."

A series of shrill pips pierces the still evening air, then a familiar voice begins to deliver his message from somewhere within the ring of ancient stones.

"This is the voice of Wayland Merlin Blake Smith, broadcasting briefly from fabled Stonehenge, where the wisdom of the druids is revealed to me, the voice of the Almighty. And the Lord saith, Give my servant the airwaves, or else I will smite the ungodly . . ."

"I will smite the ungodly," howls Evans the Latin, rushing back into the circle of sacred stones, his broadsword cleaving the air as if he would cut the very atmosphere into a thousand pieces.

"Owing to unforeseen circumstances, your warning voice from the hereafter must break . . . Aaah." The voice of the Bagman yelps with terror, as there is a mighty clang of sword on stone, and the dark interior of Stonehenge is lit by a comet's tail of sparks.

Gog walks forwards into the most famous sanctuary of the druid faith to a noise that would not disgrace the Ragnarok, the final battle of the gods of the north against the giants. And Gog sees the Bagman capering around on top of the lintel of a mighty trilithon. The Bagman skips and hops, while Evans the Latin thunders his long sword overhead into the stone, trying to slice off a foot or a knee of the prancing Bagman. Never would Gog believe that such a venerable prophet with hoary locks could dance such a jig, never would he credit that the frail Evans could swing his broadsword twenty times over like the avenging Arthur and twenty times strike a cataract of flame from the sarsen stone. But fear is pepper to the Bagman's toes and fury is salt on Evans's wounds.

Yet, as Gog watches, the wily Bagman decides on a counter-attack. He whips off the long aerial of the jeep radio, which he has mounted on the trilithon, and he pokes it down at his enemy's face, as Evans is on the long backswing of the broad-sword. And he draws blood at once, twitching a patch of skin off Evans's forehead. But his shrill cry of glee is nearly his last. The broadsword arches up like a jag of lightning and lops off his beard close to the chin, so that his white locks are thistle-down on the holy soil, and the rusty iron cross on its chain round his neck is cut off to bed itself in earth. With a shriek of fear, the Bagman tumbles backwards off the lintel stone onto the ground.

That would be the chopping-block for the Bagman, if Evans the Latin did not forget to lower his broadsword as he gallops between the two upright stones to finish his enemy. As it is, his death-dealing weapon is raised so high for the final execution that it catches on the lintel and jerks the heels of the charging Evans from beneath him. So he lands on his sheeted arse, while the Bagman rises and jabs at him again with the aerial, opening his eyebrow so that his blood obscures his vengeful right eye. But then Evans is up again and slashing, while the Bagman's scarpering round the ring of stone giants as fast as his old hams and pins will take him. So Gog sees the two enemies vanish into the night, the iron force of ancient wisdom trying to ampu-tate the whippy rapier of the perennial rogue, while the stone giants watch the chase round and round their perimeter with all the indifference that the great feel for the little, the enduring feel for the passing, and the stone feels for the metal which can only sharpen itself on stone.

Gog walks away through the gathering night towards the south again, fearing to involve himself in the battle. It is not his quarrel, for neither prophet can tell him about himself. He does not stop to rest in the woods that occasionally flank his path. It is as though he has a rendezvous somewhere in the night. As though he knows someone is waiting for him in this stumbling darkness. As though there is a pit a few yards ahead, just at the limit of his eyes, and into this pit he must fall to discover his fate. As though he is walking down the unlighted gangway of a cinema while the screen is black and the film of the next episode of a serial about to begin.

The meeting Gog expects does not come for many miles. The moon is high and Gog has crossed the Avon, when he comes upon the two fates waiting for him in the castle of Old Sarum. He has climbed down and up the huge ditch and rampart of the outer work, over the sprawling cross of Bishop Roger's fallen cathedral, down again into the inner moat and up again over the jabbing flints of the walls of the Norman keep. Maire and Jules are sitting on a pile of their stones, the flints of war; they are equally dangerous in black cloaks and white faces; each of their hands holds a nickel-plated revolver sharper with threat than any stone. They lead Gog down and back to the River Avon, where a black barge sits on the black water, that is both mirror-bright and opaque under the moon.

And Gog says, " I thought you were going to leave me alone until London."

And Maire replies, " I was. But I got bored with no one to play with. We have a game to play, the most interesting game of all, the only true game, and the only wise game. If you win it, you will be free for ever. And if you lose it, you will solve everything. Will you step into my cabin, said the black widow to her mate?"

" Black widow?" Gog says. " You're not that yet."

" Not yet," Maire agrees.

XXVIII

The cabin of the black barge is plated with silver paint and furnished by couches with gilt legs and off-purple upholstery, by lamps each made from a single false baroque pearl, by carved pine tables touched up to resemble Carrara marble, and by twin Corinthian pillars supporting a frieze of nymphs and satyrs which swings open to reveal a stainless steel cocktail cabinet. Choice viands such as salt beef and native luxuries such as pease-pudding add a gourmet's touch to the queenly surroundings.

Gog says nothing and begins to swallow the beef and pudding as fast as the muscles of his throat will operate. Maire watches him, smoking a black sobranie marked *Red Army*. She takes off her cloak to show herself wearing a skin-tight pyjama-suit of white satin, which fits tight as the skin on a melon at breast and belly and buttock, but which flares out in wide bell-bottoms below the thigh.

" I specially stocked peasant fare to suit your taste," she says. " It does."

Gog pauses for long enough between mouthfuls to ask, " Where did you get the barge?"

" From a bargee. Where else? You should have heard the language – mine. I paid him half what he wanted, so I had to swear twice as much. Then I added the woman's touch to the cabin. How do you like it?"

" Very tasty, Cleopatra," Gog says. " Duly honouring the bard on his home river. The barge she sat in like a burnished throne, etcetera. I hope you've got an asp in aspic ready for your creamy ample bosom when I die."

" You do remember a lot these days," Maire says, " remembering Shakespeare. And don't fret, my pet. You'll die all right. What do you think you're here for? Now you've finished the condemned yokel's dinner, we might as well start the dice."

" Dice?" Gog says. " I didn't know dice was your vice."

"The truly vicious," Maire says, "have all the vices. And all the virtues as well to make their sins even more shocking." She takes six dice out of her pockets. Three are white with black spots, three are black with white spots. "Choose your set. Most people play with two dice, I prefer three. It's luckier. All the dice are loaded – with nothing but hazard."

"What are we playing for?"

"A literary man like you?" Maire laughs. "Don't you know what you're on? A black barge. For carrying a body."

"Like the barge that carried King Arthur's body away from his last battle to Avalon? I've just come from there. That's Glastonbury. You can't carry me back there. The Avon flows the wrong way."

"Look out of the porthole," Maire says. And as Gog looks out through the circular silver filigree that surrounds the purple glass of the portholes, he can see the dark banks of the Avon rushing past.

"I can't hear an engine," Gog says. "And we haven't any sails. Why are we moving so fast?"

"The air is cut away before us," Maire says innocently, "and closes from behind. Now do you know who you are, you fool, and what boat you're on?"

"No," Gog says. "It must have an engine."

"Ten little nigger boys are running round and round a treadmill in the keel turning a rubber paddle-wheel. You really do say the obvious, Gog. Of course, there's a silent engine. And you're the Ancient Mariner, idle upon the painted ship upon the painted Avon. And I'm Lady Death-in-Life and I'm playing dice for your life. And you'd better play with me and you'd better not lose. Or, brother, this barge is going to become a hearse."

"You're mad, Maire. What do I get if I win?"

"My life," Maire says. "You're always wanting to get rid of me so that you can be on your own. You're always complaining that I won't ever let you go. So I was reading old Samuel Taylor Coleridge and I thought, Why not the Death-in-Life Game? At least, it'll rid one of us of the other. I don't see how else we can."

"You're being very extreme as usual, Maire. What are the rules? They're sure to suit you."

" Not this time. The first to throw seven or eleven with three dice wins. Eleven's better than seven. Three sixes mean a free turn."

" And if you win?"

" Then the other person's got to do what you order him. And you must give him something dangerous to do. I mean, he doesn't have to *die* doing it, because that's murder, but it's likely he'll die. That's life, isn't it? And war, especially. No one ever survives in the end. We have to die, sooner or later. I just want to accelerate the whole process so we can be free of each other before we suffocate each other. So the dice is chance and the dangerous order's our will and the carrying out of the order's our skill at survival. That's existence, don't you think?"

" No," Gog says. " I don't. But I'll play the game. If you promise to leave me alone till London."

" For ever," Maire says sweetly, " if you lose."

Gog tosses both the sets of dice to check that both fall at haphazard, and both seem to do so. He selects the set of white dice with black spots, and he hands the black dice with white spots across to Maire on the other side of the false marble table.

" Let her roll," Maire says. " You can start. You can't beat me at games of chance, because I never give anyone any."

Gog rattles the dice against each other between his cupped palms, then rolls them across the painted wood. Three black spots up, three black spots up, the last dice spins and hangs and falls, one black spot up. " Seven," Gog says. " You won't beat that. I wonder how I can best get you to risk your neck?"

Without even bothering to reply, Maire rolls her black dice out of the side of her right hand. They fall smoothly into place one behind the other, four white spots, four white spots, three white spots. " Eleven," Maire whispers, passing her fingers in a blessing across the cubes of bone. " Who would believe such *luck*? The game is done! I've won! I've won!" She whistles three times and laughs, as Gog grabs the dice and throws them again to see if they are weighted. But no. However often he throws, he never makes up eleven.

" I've got a keel-haul ready on deck," Maire says. " Jules and I are going to strap you on and winch you slowly under the keel of the barge. We may take up to five minutes to do so. So you'll have to hold your breath for that long. One or two of Nelson's sailors did it and survived, so they say. And one murderer in an American gas chamber is meant to have held his breath for six and a half minutes, while the prison governor and the reporters watched him through the plate glass window growing purple in the face as he tried to prolong his agony for yet another few seconds. But, in the end, he had to breathe in, like you will."

"If you really want to go through with this," Gog says, "I won't survive. I don't like living enough to fight so much to live."

"You may change your mind," Maire says, "down under the keel."

So it is that Gog is stripped and strapped to a leather harness attached to a rope on a winch. Jules and Maire slowly turn the spokes of the winch so that Gog is dragged headfirst over the edge of the deck, his back to the wooden sides of the barge. His last view of the world is topsy-turvy, with the night sky as earth and the tree-tops their own black roots into heaven. But as the waters of the Avon touch his hair, Gog takes a deep gulp of air and manages to close his mouth just as his lips go under the surface.

First, Gog feels the splinters and nail-heads on the side of the barge tear at his back. He opens his mouth to scream, but the water enters, so he has to lose a little air puffing out spray.

Then the blood begins to hammer at Gog's right temple, then in his cheeks, then his heart.

His shins are still above water, dry. Winch, faster, damn you, Maire. Do you want to kill me?

Spine begins arching backwards on the keel. Body sticks on iron patch, halts, jerks on.

Air in mouth stales.

Lungs pump and pump faster and faster.

Less and less air.

Hurry, hurry.

Head hits keel, bends forward, bumps over iron, floats a little up.

Heart thumps chest, angry fist knock, knock, knock.
Shoulders scrape over keel.
Ribs squeeze out, in, out, in.
No air.
Cheeks blown out, bursting.
Rump jibs at keel, jerks over.
Bellows torso.
Huff out.
Brief relief.
Less suck in.
Huff more.
All body shudder shake.
Force lips close.
Retch belly.
Hold in.
Can't can't can't.
Hold.
Can't.

As Gog's lips explode open to suck in water and death, his scalp breaks the surface so that his first swallow is a mixture of river scum and air, and he chokes and gags and pukes all the rest of his slow dragged way up the other side of the black barge onto the deck, where he is laid out and unstrapped and turned over onto his face and massaged until the water runs from his lungs and the splinters are pulled from his back and the raw flesh covered with soft cream and dressed with lint held down by plaster. And he is sat upright and clothed in a clean white shirt and clean white trousers and canvas shoes. And brandy is forced down his throat and becomes fire and strength in his guts and he is walked up and down the deck between Maire and Jules until he is unsteady on his feet and breathing easily. Then Maire says, "Four and a half minutes under. We took pity on you and winched quicker at the end. You want to live pretty much, Gog my friend. Ready for the next roll?"

And Gog nods and he goes back to the cabin with Maire and he picks up the black set of dice with the white spots and she picks up the white set of dice with the black spots. And Gog throws again, this time each dice in turn. Five spots. Six spots.

Six spots. Then Maire throws her three dice together, one, one, two. Then Gog throws again, two dice and then one dice. Three spots and three spots, then two spots. And Maire throws again her dice all together, six, six, and six. Her turn again. Again she throws, six, six, and six. She smiles mockingly at Gog and throws again, this time each dice singly. Six. Six. Six. " I shouldn't prolong the agony, should I? I mean, *mental* agony, *anticipation* of pain is worse even than a keel-haul, isn't it?" And Maire blesses the dice, rubbing them on her sleeve, and throws them once more, four and four and three, making eleven.

" It's very traditional and sporty, Gog, my second order. It's the greasy pole with the pig on top. There's a special collapsible mast on deck, covered with oil. It would be impossible to climb if it weren't covered with nails as well. You'll slip on the oil, but then you'll stick on the nails. There's a small penalty if you fall, but you'll see what that is. If you return with the greasy pig safely onto deck, then there's no penalty, of course. Shall we begin?"

Once Gog is on deck, he sees that Jules has stepped up a mast some thirty feet high above the barge, so that the wood bisects the face of the moon. At the top of the mast is a small yard-arm, from which a screaming piglet is dangling by a noose round its neck. " I forgot to add," Maire says, " you'd better shin up that mast quick before the pig hangs itself, because if you come down with a dead pig, you're bacon too."

So it is that Gog starts up the greasy pole. And the surface of the mast is just as Maire says. If Gog can find a place for his palm among the nails, then his hand slips down until it is driven onto the point of the nail below. Gog can only make progress upwards to the squealing and choking piglet by clasping the pole to his chest with locked arms and thighs and by heaving himself upwards on the nail points. Each foot in gained height starts up twenty trickles of blood from twenty rips in Gog's skin, so that blood is seeping from his chest and biceps and legs in a hundred places before he has reached five foot up the pole. He is ready to drop back here and risk slaughter at Maire's hands rather than endure this slow death by the thousand pricks, when he sees that he cannot fall. Jules and Maire have dragged up two steel semicircular mats under the mast, through which fifty sabres glint their tips upwards in the light of the deck-lanterns.

So Gog is forced to climb, tearing the front of his body to shreds, while the plaster on his keel-hauled back breaks loose and his previous wounds start to bleed again. He is a gory twenty feet high, mounting slowly, slowly, when the piglet stops squealing above him and he sees that the brute is at its last kick. With three great jack-knives of his lacerated body, Gog makes up the last ten feet and swings one arm loose to grab at the piglet. He cannot hold its larded hide, but at least he pushes the piglet up enough for the noose round its throat to open a little and allow it to snuffle in a small breath. Gog dares all at his next attempt, flinging both arms round the piglet and holding onto the pole only with his legs. The piglet kicks its hooves into Gog's face as he drags its body choking down on the noose, while the nails in the mast drive deeper than ever into Gog's thighs, now supporting his full weight as well as the piglet's pounds. Suddenly, Gog's flesh can stand it no longer. His legs splay apart and he swings out from the pole, spattering a bloody rain on the deck from his myriad wounds, his arms squelching the slippery pig, unable even to hold on to an ear or a tail. By some grace, as Gog swings outwards, the yard-arm breaks, and down come Gog and noose and piglet and all in a parabola that lands him stunned just outside the sabre-toothed mats.

Gog wakes to find himself propped in a chair at the false marble table, the two sets of dice ready at hand and Maire smiling at him from the opposite seat. Bandages have been wound tightly round his body so that he is swaddled like a baby or a Lazarus. He cannot decide whether he is reborn or resurrected, until the pain over the whole surface of his body makes him opt for the second choice. "You really do struggle to live," Maire observes. "That's twice you've survived. All that tramping's made quite a Bulldog Drummond out of you. A tough customer. Still, as they say, third time lucky. You're sure to expire on the next instalment. Your throw, as usual."

Gog moistens his thick, numb lips. "You throw first," he says. "It's your turn."

"Chivalry won't get you anywhere with me," Maire says.

" Except to the grave, quicker."

She picks up the white set of dice with black spots and rolls them quickly out of the side of her hand, as she always does. Two black spots and two black spots and three black spots make seven. " You've got a sporting chance," Maire grins. " A last sporting chance. Don't say that Maire would deny you that, though the odds are pretty much against you."

As Maire fans out her fingers in her usual way to bless her lucky dice, Gog makes a sudden effort and jerks out his hand to catch Maire by the right wrist. Underneath his torn fingers he can feel six hard growths beneath Maire's cuff. He squeezes her wrist tighter and tighter until she screams and six hidden dice, three white and three black, come popping out of her sleeve and fall like cubes of false mosaic on the false marble tabletop. Gog picks up the black set of dice with white spots and rolls them one by one. Four white spots. Three spots. Four. " Eleven," Gog says. " You lose."

Maire jerks her cuff into place and massages the blood back into her wrist. " So you had to palm dice into my cuff to win," she says. " Pretending I was cheating to disguise the fact that you were planting loaded dice on me. Still, I don't care. If you have to cheat to win, so be it. I'll do anything you say, even if you win unfairly."

Gog pauses a moment. " I could ask you to stop the propeller screw with your bare hands," he says.

Maire rises. " Of course," she says, her face pale even beneath its usual whiteness. " I hope you won't mind being clawed in future by your wife's twin hooks."

" I won't make you do that, really," Gog says, also rising. " I'll tell you my actual terms. We stop playing out this murderous fantasy right now. And you leave me alone till I get to London. That's all."

Maire storms in front of Gog, her face suddenly raw with fury. " I won't have your charity, Gog. I won't. You're not better than I am. You just haven't the courage to work out your fantasies in fact. I do. I act what I think, you repress it, till it's a hundred times more foul and beastly than anything I've ever done. And all the time, that pie-face, that martyr's look, that *beau role*! I won't stand for it, I won't. I won't have your bloody nobility. You can go and stuff that saintly bit up your navel. I'll risk something far worse than I've made you do. Come on. Come. The engine-room. I'll show you, you holy turd."

So it is that Gog follows Maire down to the engine-room of the black barge. It is a low narrow space with immense pistons driving their way into brass cylinders and cogs grinding round their circular teeth to spin the propeller shaft and steam hissing out of boiling valves and grease making a dark scum on metal and wood. Just above the pistons and the cogs and the steam-heat is the wooden ceiling of the engine-room. Each six inches along the beams, iron rungs have been screwed in, as if they were a ladder for a gigantic fly. Without a word, Maire picks up a spanner and puts it under the tight satin between her breasts and begins climbing horizontally along the iron rungs by hands and feet, squeezing her body up against the beams to keep her shoulder-blades and rump out of the gnashing of the machine beneath her.

"I'll stop your bloody propeller," Maire yells above the clanking of the metal. "I'll put a spanner in the works. That's what I know how to do."

As she shouts, the rung supporting her left hand gives way and part of her body drops like a gobbet into the teeth of the machine. Her arm vanishes between piston and shaft, while the giant cog rips the satin from her breast, making the spanner fall and a nipple show in a rose of blood. She screams, as if she is being drawn inexorably into the maw of the machine, first the cheating fingers, then the hiding wrist, then the quick arm, then the soft shoulder, till the thin skull will be pulped and all that trickery and joy in life be mashed into a mud of blood and bone and brain.

As Gog gawps at the imminent end of Maire, he is whirled round by Jules and pushed out of the engine-room. She stays inside the room, slamming the door in his face, and bolting it tight. So the munching machine is shut off from Gog's sight at the moment it devours the Pearl White, Jet Black Maire. And Gog knows that he'll have to wait for the next thrilling instalment of the weekly serial, when Maire will somehow be plucked out of the jaws of disaster and appear larger than life in black-and-white on the screen of life or cinema before his eyes.

As Gog walks away from the engine-room onto the deck, he hears a scream, then a shearing whine of machinery. Has Maire's body or her spanner stopped the works? Perhaps this is really the end of his serial fight with Maire. Perhaps the game of death-in-life has really finished in her dying. But who can talk of dying while the memory of the living still conjures up once-known ghosts to walk with film stars through its nightmares in the Alhambras and Rialtos and Ritzes of the unconscious mind?

Then Gog looks over the stern of the black barge and sees that the propeller has, indeed, stopped. The barge drifts towards the bank and grounds on a shallows three feet from the land. Gog leaps onto the earth and stumbles away across stubble from the hearse upon Avon. And the night presses upon him as heavily as the swaddling bands press upon his body, so that he does not know where or when he falls into a fainting sleep.

XXIX

Gog wakes with the light of day tweaking at his short hairs. He blinks and feels the bandages round his wounds still wrapping his ribs in a strait-jacket. But as he stretches, the bandages crack and split. And when he opens his eyes, he finds that the weight on his back and front is the weight of a haycock, in which he has wedged himself. He pulls himself out of his press of a bed to find that he is smeared all over with thick-caked mud, so that elementary tiles of straw and dried earth hang onto his clothing and case him about as if he were a small tower. He spends half an hour picking off the mud and finding out that his skin is unmarked. He has no wounds except the old one on his right temple and the bruised left shoulder given him by the policeman at Totnes. The game of death-in-life with Maire has been a nightmare unrolled by the projector of his mind. Or has he been healed miraculously, after all? For he has no recollection of how he passed from Old Sarum to where he finds himself, several miles beyond Salisbury and east of the Avon by the village of Whiteparish, except his memory of the voyage in the black barge. He must have truly walked in his sleep for many miles along river bank and over marsh and clay field, to wake up so far away and so mud-armoured in the morning.

Again Gog manages to buy the stodgy things available in the village store for those without the coloured magic squares of coupons. And he wanders on towards Winchester, leaving behind him the curious local church with its small slate spire strayed in from dissenting Wales, but with a fine gold clock to display a bit of Anglican mummery and earn the catholic name of All Saints. On past the White Hart, too, closed as most English pubs are closed when a traveller needs a beer; the albino deer of its sign is also confined by a golden chain attached to the golden crown and manacle round her neck. Closed, too, the garage, where a sign says NO PETROL; but a grey-haired girl canters in on her gelding and fills him up with water.

It is a dull day, with the clouds in a low and threatening stance, but not striking with the rain in their fists. Gog feels the same sense of blunted menace in the things about him; the scarecrow in the cabbage field with a cap pulled over its blank sack of a face and a wooden dummy of a shotgun under its arm; the placard in the main square of the town of Romsey, where the abbey squats like a grey fat hen above the red-chick houses, the placard below an elaborate projection of iron – *It is recorded that in the year 1642 Two Soldiers of Cromwell's Army were hanged from the wrought iron sign bracketed on this wall – This Bracket is a good example of Old Hampshire wrought iron work.* Yet, it was good iron-work all right. It bore the necessary weight of guilt. But Gog cannot bear the weight of guilt that hangs on his spirit as heavily as the clouds on the air or the bodies on the gibbet. His is the worst of guilts, the guilt without name that makes the body feel a sodden skin of bogwater, the guilt that has no cause and therefore no limit, the guilt that makes men invent a God and His priests so that their sin can be tagged and filed, the guilt that is the lead in the blood of all men for ever and ever because they are men in a world without end, amen.

So Gog hopes for a cleansing rain beyond Romsey. But the rain will not fall and wash away his sins. The sky is indifferent to his needs. In the wooden-pillared temple of Ampfield Wood, however, a man stops his pony and trap by Gog and cries the one word that can free Gog from his heaviness of spirit. "Pardon," the man says from the height of his driver's seat above the huge spoked suns of the wheels of the trap. "Pardon me, sir, would you care for a lift?"

So Gog is elevated onto the seat of the jaunting-car above him by a heave-ho from the hand of the driver. He settles himself in the narrow seat of the vehicle, while his new acquaintance begins lashing the pony into a trot with stroke after stroke of a long yellow whip. "Lazy beggars, ponies," the man says. "They don't understand the whip, unless they get it all the time. Like men, really. Anything they get regular gets to be a pleasure. Even intimacy with their own wives, if you'll pardon me mentioning it, sir."

"I'll pardon anyone," Gog says, "who gives me a lift on a day like this."

He looks at the driver beside him and sees a face that is all bone and no skin, with white protrusions marking nose and brow and chin and top of cheek. The man wears a black riding-coat and a black round hat, with small cockle-shells sewn around its broad brim.

"Ah," the man says, "I see you're looking at my hat, sir. And curious it is, very curious. It's the badge of my trade. I'm an educated man, sir, I've read a lot of books." And Gog does notice, indeed, the vowels of learning which polish the coarse consonants of the man. "And I learned from 'em just what I was fit to do. I'm a pardoner, sir, the only one travelling in the length and breadth of this fair island. And what you see is a pardoner's hat. If you've got a worry on your mind, something you've done, why, I'll set your mind to rest for a small fee, just to put some hay in the feed-bag of my friend Jonathan. That's the pony, sir. The labourer's worthy of his hire, don't you think, sir, pardon me?"

"You or the pony?" Gog asks. "We're well-met. I was looking for a pardoner."

"I can tell, sir," the Pardoner says, lashing the pony again. "I can tell. It's a certain light in the eyes. You can see it, if you're looking, even in a blind man. Of course, every man needs a pardoner, yet I'm the only genuine one left in the trade. Non-union, that is. I believe in free enterprise. I won't get my cards and join one of those churches. There's no incentive there, sir, they take the joy out of the job, the craftsman's pride in the personal touch. And talking of the personal touch, you do have a few shillings, don't you, sir?"

"Yes," Gog says, "I do. It's been funny, this long walk of mine, you know. Just as I'm thinking of people, just as I think I need them, they always seem to turn up."

"It's God's good grace," the Pardoner says. "It's often like that. Ask and it shall be given unto you. I'm glad you've got a few shillings for my dear beloved pony, who's like a brother to me." The Pardoner now begins to flick his whip up between the pony's hind legs, to excite a little more speed from the beast. "Of course, I'll pardon your sins for free, sir. I wouldn't accept a fee for my holy work. I hope they're spicy sins, sir, pardon me for saying so. Pity the poor pardoner! Sins used to be much more interesting before the war, no end to the perversions and all. But the war's made most of the countryfolk very normal. No *bestiality*, like there used to be." A curious light flickers in the goatish amber eyes of the Pardoner, as he flicks with his whip the quivering rump of his friend Jonathan. "Even the shepherds have got so little time on leave together, they only do the quickest and most boring things. And only with *women*! But when I caught sight of you, sir, I said, There's a hardened old goat if I ever saw one, pardon me for the liberty of thinking so."

"I probably am," Gog agrees. "But I can't remember quite what I've done. I'm feeling guilty all right, but I don't know quite what for."

"Then it's an all-purpose pardon you need," the Pardoner suggests. "It's like an all-risks insurance, sir. It covers almost anything except rape, sodomy and beggary. They need special pardons."

"Why beggary?"

"I don't like it, sir. How can a beggar pay for hay for my horse to get a pardon? And if he can pay, then he's no beggar. He's a liar, and that's worse."

"It sounds as if your pardons come out of the pony, smoking hot," Gog says. "The sinners feed in hay at one end and the pony brings out the pardon in turds at the other. I don't think I'll have an all-purpose pardon. He might piss on it as well."

"You're mocking me, pardon me, sir," the Pardoner says. "If you don't take me serious, then I'll be thanking you to step off my trap. That'll be a shilling for Jonathan for the ride, sir, and nothing for me. I'm always glad to give a fellow Christian a helping hand."

Gog lays a hand on the whipping arm of the Pardoner, which is as thin and hard as a flail. This action has the merit of both soothing the Pardoner and stopping the lathering of the pony, who immediately settles down to a moribund amble.

"Don't take *me* so seriously," Gog says. "I was only having a little joke. I'd be glad to buy your pony a whole mangerful of hay and offer you a drink, if you'll find a pardon for my vague sense of sin. The trouble is, I don't really know what the actual sin is. I've done many bad things, even on the road, but I don't feel guilty about them. I'm feeling guilty about everything, I suppose. About being a man."

"That's a very guilty thing to be," the Pardoner agrees, biting the bony knuckle of his thumb. "But you're a rare and honest man, pardon me saying so, sir. There's not many as admit how guilty they are, these days of war. There's too much to be guilty for, I suppose. There's so much sin been done, murder and all, that people have to pretend they're innocent, when they're not. Or they'd go mad. But, of course, that's why a pardoner doesn't hardly make a living now . . . for his horse, I mean."

"Really," Gog says, "I suppose all our sins come out of our obsessions. It's just easier to do one's worst in war. I probably got used to doing all the horrible things I wanted to do, fighting. Then I came home, and I don't know how to behave here. I'm looking for my true self so hard these days, I seem ready to do anything which my inner nature tells me to do, without question. So there you are, Pardoner. Anarchy's my sin. Too much liberty. I couldn't care a damn what other people and society say. I might be revenging myself in an occupied country, rather than coming home to peace. Why, I often want to tear down every shred of law and order, the whole of London and everything that comes from it. I'm a fool for freedom."

The Pardoner shakes his head so that the cockle-shells on his hat tinkle like a little knell.

"That's what the war does, even to good honest gentlemen like yourself, sir. I haven't heard a worse case for many a year. Free enterprise is a good thing, but only in the way of business, for my dear pony's sake. But free enterprise in the way of pleasuring yourself, why, sir, there's no ready-made pardon for that! It includes everything, Babylon as well as Sodom and Gomorrah! Oh, sir, you warm the cockles of my heart as well as shake the cockles on my hat, to hear such a marvellous sin. Jonathan'll need a whole barnful of fodder for me to absolve a crime like that. But never you mind, I'll forgive you anything you've done and will do from a full heart, freely and for nothing. I'm only a poor Christian man doing my poor Christian duty. Pardon me for having to mention it, sir, but my beloved friend and source of locomotion, my brother Jonathan, is partial to a pint of stout. And as it's just opening-time, kind sir, don't you think you might pop in to the ale-house right here where Jonathan has happened to halt and bring out the wherewithal?"

And indeed, the pony has stopped exactly outside a convenient pub, whether by his own will or by his driver's. So Gog descends and buys two pints of stout and brings them out to the trap. He takes the Pardoner at his word and holds one of the pints to the pony's mouth, while quaffing the other himself. Yet you may take a horse to the stout, but you cannot make him drink. Jonathan seems to prefer to hang his tongue out at a dripping tap, which Gog turns on fully for his benefit.

"What my friend Jonathan spurns, four-footed brute though he may be, yet I shall humbly accept it. Bring that pint over here!" So the Pardoner commands and Gog obeys. In three long swallows, his Adam's apple wobbling up and down his scrawny windpipe, the Pardoner empties the mug. "Jonathan's usually very partial to the stuff," he explains, wiping his mouth. "But I don't like the taste, not at all. That's why I drink it quick, so as not to have to taste it, and not to disappoint a kind sinner who's been spurned by my ungrateful Jonathan. Oh, I'll beat him for it, I'll teach him to turn down the gifts of friends with a full purse and fuller heart." The Pardoner here seems almost to wink at Gog, but it may only be a temporary drooping of one yellow eye. "But if you want to be a true Christian and wet the whistle of a true Christian who occasionally likes a glass, why, mine's a black velvet."

So Gog finds himself buying another drink for the Pardoner, before they can set out again on their slow ride towards Winchester. But the Pardoner now seems to be in a merry mood and he even forgets to thrash the pony again, so full is he of the malt and hops of human kindness. And he tells Gog of the tale of the three youths of Winchester, to try to ease Gog's soul of the crime of his unpardonable sense of liberty.

"Once long ago, there are three youths of Winchester," the Pardoner relates, "wily William and proud Henry and rotten Richard. And they are riotous and gambling and wenching young men, ready to dare anything and defy anyone – like you, sir, pardon me. One day, they are playing dice, a wicked and accursed game, sir, never you try it, you may lose your life that way. Then as they are rolling the barren bones, they hear a funeral bell. And in the coffin lies a friend of theirs, sir, who has gone to London to demand something of the King. He has sworn he would get an answer, he would not return home without it. So he returns home with it.

"'Odd's blood,' cry the three youths, wily William and proud Henry and rotten Richard, 'we will make an end to this monstrous monarch.' So they set out to London there and then, the wine boasting in their tongues and their swords hot at their hands.

"They have not gone half a mile, when they come on an old mother, who says, 'Pardon me, kind sirs, good day.' And proud Henry gives her a cuff on the side of the head for daring to say anything at all – manners are bad then, but they're worse now. 'And the same to you, mother,' proud Henry says. 'We're off to London to kill the King.'

"'The King's not in London, young sirs,' the old mother says. 'Why, I saw him sitting under an oak tree just in that wood over there by the road.'

"So the three youths run off to the oak tree to find the King and kill him and free all England. But all they find beneath the oak tree is a cope and a mitre, a chasuble and a crook, covered with gold and jewels. Likewise a scarlet hat, sir, and a vestment embroidered by the hands of queens. They each try on a piece of the treasure. Wily William wears the golden cope and proud Henry holds the jewelled mitre, while Richard has the chasuble and the vestment, until that is torn from him by wily William, who loses it in turn to proud Henry.

"'Pardon me,' wily William says, 'there is only enough here for one of us to wear. So I suggest we cast dice for it.' He is the best gambler.

"'Never,' proud Henry says. 'We will fight for it.' He is the strongest.

"'I say divide,' rotten Richard says. He is the best thief and he hopes to steal away the rest from the other two.

"So the three youths begin to quarrel over the treasure, as people who love licence tend to do, pardon me, sir. And a harsh word leads to a hard fist. And a hard fist leads to a sharp stone. And a sharp stone leads to a pointed dagger. And a pointed dagger leads to a deadly sword. And in no time the three youths are trying to kill each other, not the King.

"And as all three are lying badly wounded round the treasure, gathering their strength to renew the fight and finish each other off, there is the sound of a horn. And the King himself comes into the wood, surrounded by all his huntsmen in coats of green and gold.

"'So you are the three youths of Winchester,' the King says, 'who set out to London to kill the King. The old mother tells me that she sent you here. Now the King is here, at your service. But you seem more ready to kill yourselves.'

"And the three youths kneel before the King to beg his

pardon. And he raises them up and tells his servants to bind their wounds and give them wine mixed with herbs and honey – very good for the digestion, sir, I have a special herbal remedy under the seat, if that should interest your honour, only two bob for the horse."

Here the Pardoner pauses, but as Gog says nothing, he continues his story with bad grace. "Then the King says, 'Fight no more. There shall be not one mitre, but three. There shall be not one chasuble, but three. There shall be not one cope, but three. The King has need of many servants and all shall be rewarded. Your friend did not choose to serve Me, so I sent him home to his mother in his coffin. But you have seen that all your rioting for the sake of liberty is merely rioting for the liberty of serving Me. Your quarrel is not about who should kill Me, but about who should serve Me best. So serve My Majesty first, quarrel in My name, riot against My enemies, and My purse and power are freely yours.' "

By the time that the Pardoner has ended his tale, his friend Jonathan has dragged the trap into the middle of Winchester, where the perennial shop names of every town afflict Gog with the sense that he has been here ever since boyhood, even if he has never been here before. Mac Fisheries, Cadena, Timothy White's, Boots, Marks and Sparks, Woolworths, Lyons, all are there, the places of fug and terror for infants, of treasure and joy for small boys, of scorn and derision for smarmy youths, of necessity and familiarity for adults. Because of them, every high street in England is the same, and the traveller is never lost in a strange town.

And yet Winchester seems a different place, the ancient capital of Wessex and of all England, rose-brick and half as old as Tudor, quiet and seemly in its thank-you-nicely privacy. But the Pardoner does not stop until he has driven the trap down to the cathedral close and has hitched his friend Jonathan to a stone pillar, where the pony can take a free snack from the lush turf among the graves. Gog hardly has time to admire the vast bulk of the cathedral supporting the low cloud, before he is pulled behind the Pardoner into the cathedral entrance.

"I'll show you my tale isn't just a tale," the Pardoner says.

" It's true. How can I ease you of your guilt and tell you the way out of your woe, if my tale isn't true? I'll prove it to you."

And prove it he does. He takes Gog under the high-lacing pillars of the southern aisle and stops him at the tomb of a bishop, who lies in full vestments on top of a high bier, his face smug and complacent in its smooth skin of stone. " Wily William," the Pardoner whispers, and Gog reads by the tomb that this is indeed William of Edington, Bishop of Winchester, Treasurer to good King Edward the Third, satisfied with a life lived in piety and order under his monarch.

Then the Pardoner hurries Gog onwards almost to the end of the aisle. And there is a tomb of fatness and magnificence. A plump cardinal lies in state, puffed out in scarlet and blubber and glory, dressed in painted red robes from head to toe, his fiery hat as broad-brimmed as the Pardoner's above his beaky nose, his black-gloved hands folded in unlikely piety over his chest. He seems to be praying to himself in his overweening pride. It is Cardinal Beaufort, four times Chancellor of England, brother of King Henry the Sixth, arbiter of the War of the Roses, and Bishop of Winchester. " Proud Henry, I told you," the Pardoner announces to Gog, hurrying him backwards a little way.

The tomb of rotten Richard is in a barred enclosure let into the wall. It is the tomb of blind Bishop Fox, Secretary and Keeper of the Privy Seal to Henry the Seventh and Eighth before the Reformation. Gog sees that the insolence of proud Henry Beaufort has destroyed the world nicely balanced between Pope and King, and the Monarch is about to crush the over-free church, and rotten Richard is buried crying out against the death-rattle of himself and his faith, his flesh withered away from his effigy of marble skin and bone, so that he is naked and sunken and starved, his clawing hand holding only a rag over his shrunken balls, the tragic caricature of the body after death. So wily William gives way to proud Henry and ends in rotten Richard, and the mighty Bishops of Winchester pass into the State Church under the rule of the King, and the Pardoner's Tale is proven. And as Gog closes his eyes for a moment to reflect, he sees himself standing in front of the same tomb of rotten Richard; but his suit is narrow-shouldered and striped, and his hair is slicked back, and his face is that of an undergraduate with a dutiful copy of Chaucer under his arm to swot up for a First.

Gog opens his eyes again to find himself shabby and middle-aged, walking away down the aisle with the raffish modern Pardoner. Although all seems proven, yet Gog ventures a question. "I'm sorry to be so stupid," he says, "but the three youths of Winchester couldn't have been friends. Each of them lived a century earlier than the other. They weren't contemporaries."

The Pardoner looks at Gog with a humble sneer on his sucked-in lips. "What's truth got to do with time?" he asks. "As though a true thing that happens at one time isn't true in another! Pardon me, sir, you're too intelligent not to know that you saw the mere effigies of the Bishops of Winchester. What I said was generally true. Who cares about the particulars? I speak in parables of eternal wisdom, my honoured sir. I leave statistics to plumbers."

With this lofty reply, the Pardoner leaves the cathedral entrance in front of Gog. There is a loud neighing from the direction of his friend Jonathan. Gog goes out onto the close to see a verger hitting the pony away from the gravestones. The pony rears and bolts, dragging the trap on its twin spoked suns on a collision course across the cobbled street into the arcade by the close, scattering old ladies with baskets and schoolgirls with books like scraps of mist before the rush of light. And the Pardoner breaks into flight himself after his bolting friend, his limbs splaying out in propeller-blades from his bony fuselage. Gog expects him to take off at any moment and prove to be the first man since Icarus to levitate himself merely by his own frantic motion.

Gog begins to steal away from the close in another direction, when he hears the snorting and splintering crash of the pony and the trap trying to bring down the stone arcade, and failing. He cannot bear to look back, as he slinks away from the cursing cajolery of the Pardoner, who hymns his lament for his dear departed trap, pony and friend.

"O Jonathan, thou wast slain in high places.
I am distressed for thee, my brother Jonathan:

Rise, my beloved, or thy hide goeth to the knackers.
Very pleasant hast thou been unto me:
And very unpleasant shall I be unto thee.
If thou dost play dead, thou art catsmeat.
Thy love to me was wonderful,
Passing the love of women.
How are the mighty fallen!"

XXX

Some are born sour, some are born curdled, some are born vinegary, and some are born postmistresses. The post office and store on the outskirts of Winchester, where Gog stops off to buy something to eat with his last pound, is tenanted by a lady of a certain age and more certain hostility. The moment that Gog begins pointing to any of the few poor fruit pies and rolls visible on the bare shelves of the shop, she snaps, "Already sold ... specimen ... where's your ration card?" All the time that she is speaking, she is cutting the air with a heavy pair of scissors, obviously used for slicing off children's fingers as they try to steal humbugs. Gog is glad to flee the shop with two old sausage rolls, given him grudgingly for sixpence. "They're last week's," the postmistress declares. "Or I wouldn't let you have them." Gog can almost swear that he hears the bolt of the post office door slid home behind him as he walks out, or perhaps it is only the noise of the open scissors being held in the sign of the cross against the postmistress's steel bosom.

With his appetite both whetted and disgusted by the sausage rolls, Gog moves along the main road east that loops under the shoulder of the hill like an armpit, slowly rising in its lazy winding between Longwood Warren and the tall trees on Cheesefoot Head. Although the road is fairly empty as all war roads are, an occasional battering bus or lorry grinding up the hill makes Gog wince and plug his ears with his thumbs. He supposes that when there's no shortage of petrol and cars any more, a new breed of Englishmen will have to be born, like Kotope with deaf ears of copper that reject the noise. Or else all peace will be forgotten, except if the seeker turns off with Gog down the little lanes that vein the face of England.

The small road towards the South Downs and the sea is patched and full of holes from lack of labour in wartime. A fierce brief sun makes the tarmac smoke with drying dampness as if the holes have really been made by exploding shells. Yet fighting cannot have been here. For Hampshire is not the refuse-dump of no man's land. It is ordered and kempt, the fields tidy, even the grasses lying in place under the rakes of the breeze. It is countryside on its best behaviour as it approaches the towns and the cities, it is a vast back garden which hopes to keep the houses away by making itself so pretty and appealing that it will be left to grow crops rather than prefabs.

The afternoon is a time of relapse. The mild heat of the south-land, the puffs of wind, the drugging smells drawn from grass and flower by the drying rain, all induce a feeling of fatigue in Gog that is very different from his guilt of the early morning. In some strange way, the Pardoner does seem to have eased Gog's soul, but less by his words than by his final disaster. Gog is so satisfied at the Pardoner's deserved fate that he is too smug to feel guilty about his own sins. His spirit is not weary now, but his toughened body. For some reason, his feet begin to swell like hot buns within his boots and the many days of bad diet tell on his will. He sits on the verge of the lane, then lies, then is carried away by a sudden tidal suck of oblivion.

He wakes. How long has he slept? He does not know. A minute, a year, a lifetime? He rises and trudges off automatically up the hill, his mind shocked into emptiness by the depth of his slumber, his thoughts wiped free of all memory of past and hope of future, his brain the clean slate handed to the infant in his first class at his first school.

While Gog walks stunned up Old Winchester Hill, sense gradually returns to his skull and he finds himself saying, " Old fortress, ramparts and ditch, defence against the enemy," as he sees the green wrinkles in the earth on the flat top of the hill. Slumber can only return Gog briefly to the mindless state of the beginning of his walk from Edinburgh. He retains now what he has learned and remembered on the road, except in the few minutes after waking. So he can consult his map and see that all the hilltops of Wessex are covered with the earthworks and tumuli and barrows and ditches and hidey-holes of antiquity. He can see the sickness of his mind, which fears an enemy in every tree and fold, translated to actual history on the ground. Does not the chalk soil over there bear the dark yew trees, springing with scores of hidden longbows in their branches? Gog does not have to imagine war and persecution any more. Its traces lie hidden beneath the grass about him in every long barrow and battlefield where the old heroes and giants lie sleeping.

Gog sits on the crest of Old Winchester Hill with the turf a cushion to his rump and thought. He looks about him at all of man's grubbed defences gone to green. And he feels himself smile as if his sickness had lifted off the top of his skull and flown it away like a kite in the soft wind that comes soughing up from the south-west. War, perhaps, shall be no more – at least for Gog – if grass conquers all. The sword may not become a ploughshare, but it shall certainly become buried rust. And time shall pass until generation after generation has succeeded each other in peace, no longer caring nor knowing that in this hollow the Beaker people slew the Neolithic tribes and on that hill the last of the Romans slid to earth before the Saxon rush. For who now can tell which man in the south is Jute or Dane or Saxon or Norman? Where they mingled their blood in battle, their heirs now mingle their blood in children. Miscegenation settles all.

Gog hears a far sound of tally-ho and rises to see what beast the countryfolk are chasing to its death. Only he sees no beast, but a swollen envelope of silver-grey with a blunt point and three fat fins on its tail, floating some fifty yards above the ground and trailing long wires beneath its underside. Midges seem to be clinging to the wires and running in their hundreds after the floating envelope; but Gog soon recognizes that the midges are distant people and the envelope is a barrage balloon. As he watches, he sees two pin-points of smoke and hears the tiny double pop of a shotgun. The balloon drifts nearer and nearer to the ground, eventually disappearing behind the trees to Gog's left. The yelling grows to a howl at the kill. Gog runs between the trees to find a crowd of labourers and country-women and children jabbing the bulging mass of the balloon with pitchforks and kitchen knives. They leap onto its undulating flanks, they roll about its wallowing hide, they slash it and rip it and scream with laughter as if they are intoxicated on its oozing gas. The balloon first becomes a sagging marquee and then a struck big top, a vast area of grey material beneath the boots of the country people. One solitary fin still rears up its monstrous sausage; but that, too, pops and deflates at the slash of a scythe. The cheer that greets the final death of the barrage balloon would raise a cirrus sky of white doves in the air, all bearing sprigs of laurel in their beaks, if white doves and laurel were local, which they are not.

Gog leaves the crowd to stomp the balloon into the soil and walks slowly, slowly, on through the afternoon. He is lucky to find a pub, which will sell him illicit ham sandwiches, in the last valley before the South Downs. So he fuels the fire of his burning feet with a little warmth of good food and beer in his belly. A windmill heralds the coming of these last downs before the sea; it looks into the eye of the south wind from the Channel. Gog's way up to the heights would be as hard as the other tracks of chalk and flint; but nature seems to be relenting and a soft tongue of turf allows him to walk easily up the hill on his aching feet.

Half-way up the hill to Huckswood, a chalk pit waits for Gog. Its bleached scoop, more curdy and solid than a snow crevasse, makes him wander wondering into its hollow. In front of him, one sifted breast of white rises thirty feet from the ground and one black iron finger tracks up the breast to push down its nipple. Up the finger, the tips must climb like hairs to tickle the breast into a slow rising of chalk.

As Gog watches, the surface of the chalk splits open to reveal two thrones of smoothed flint. One throne is empty; on the other

Magog sits in the guise of a frail, petulant, crowned boy, who plays with a cup and ball, the cup painted with waves as the sea, and the ball as white as the cliffs of Albion.

"Why fight me?" Magog says with a pout. "Come. Let's be friends. I haven't anyone to play with. Sit beside me. See, your place is empty. It'll just fit you. We'll play catch." And he reaches under his throne to pull out a blown-up pig's bladder crudely painted as a peasant's face. "It doesn't matter if it pops. I've got hundreds of thousands of these. Just come up and play."

And Gog comes up and smites Magog with his fist so that his skull smashes like rotten pumpkin into a mash. And the mash smokes and becomes a heavy vapour, and the vapour freezes in the shape of a dignified old man with thin lips, who smiles.

"Now, my child, where will all this violence get you? Where would we be, if we all raised our fists against each other? Surely you can see that you've been a little hasty. Sit beside me and watch how I do things. And little by little, you shall take my place. I am an old man and old men do not live for ever. Here." He takes from his pocket a lead skull cap shaped as the dome of St. Paul's. "Wear this and begin your lessons. Whatever you do, you cannot make me your enemy. I merely want to guide you to be my friend."

And Gog opens his fly and pisses on the leg of the dignified old man, who immediately dissolves into a yellow cloud that settles down as an imposing, but cheerful, matriarch.

"Whatever you do, my dear, you can't shock *me*. Nobody who's the breed we need can shock us. I mean, what can you do that I haven't seen a hundred times worse before? It's the boring people who shock us, and that's most people. But if you're interesting, why, we'll be amused at you. Go on, fart in my tiara, and I'll say, It's good for the diamonds." She holds out towards Gog an old English chamberpot with an eye painted on its bottom and the inscription, *Thou Seest Me*. "It's bawdier at the top than the bottom, believe you me. So why not come and join us, and have a really good dirty laugh?"

And Gog wrings her neck like an old rag until all the dirty water runs out and becomes a hearty bloke in a cloth cap.

"That's right, sir. 'Ave your bit of fun wringin' me neck.

Them what's born to it are born to 'ave a bit of a lark with them what ain't born to it." Gog drops his hands from the red neck of the speaker. " Me, I'm a union man. You can get to the top there, too. There's union blokes what've been lords an' ladies an' all, by the time they ended. Know your place, don't envy, work your way up, and who knows that you won't be able to 'ave a lark with the best when you're sixty. There's union men what've shaken 'ands with 'Is Majesty, God save 'Im. Us workin' blokes are just like the rest of you. We just want a chance to join you, get on. Fair's fair. So don't muck things up, Gog. Leave things be, 'cos it's what workin' blokes want."

And Gog kicks the Tory union man to a pulp, which becomes a milk-white mannikin with bright-red hair.

" I love them rough. Do, do it again. Thank God they've never abolished the birch at Eton. What else can the plebs inflict on us, when we've endured far worse at school – and loved it? Come up and punish me some time. Call me any names, and I'll revel in them. The filthier the better. Beat me and I'll kiss your boot. Tell me I'm rotten, bent, corrupt, slim-gilt, pansy, and I'll shriek, Yes, I am, I am, I am, your Algernon. I love insults. So come up and stand by me and tell me how vile you find your equals – that language doesn't do coming from inferiors." He hands Gog a spray of birch twigs. " Be my master and I'll be your fag.

" Birch, birch, is my favourite tree,
The more I'm beaten, the better I'll be."

So Gog is forced to kiss in kindness the mannikin on both cheeks to make him vanish in a faugh and a fie of disgust. But as he vanishes, Gog hears Magog's voice cluck, " I've won, I've won, he kissed me." And lo, Magog squats on Gog as if Gog were but a white egg beneath a vast broody hen, an egg that the warmth of the feathery welcome of Magog will hatch into just such another universal mother and mistress. And fight as Gog will, he cannot break out of the warm walls of his eggshell, let alone the pressing downy underbelly of the maternal Magog.

Yet as Gog is yielding into a yellow yolk of submission beneath the total incubation of the vast hen, he finds that the egg-shell cracks as his eyes suddenly open and the hen rises into the night until her wings are the whole darkness of the sky. He is lying on the chalk, looking upwards by the white breast in the pit, with no more than the heavens above him. And the air does not heat him and soften him and include him, it chills him and hardens him and makes him alone. So Gog huddles within himself in the roots of an old tree and dozes a few uncomfortable hours until first light sends him on his way, sad and solitary in the rain.

XXXI

So Gog survives the last and worst temptation of Magog, the temptation of inclusion. Those that are not for us are against us – true. But how shall we be against those that are for us? Gog knows that England is a country of joiners, of clubs, of old schools, of teams, of matches, of locals, of sides, of unions, of mates, of muckers, of chaps. How can a man, in all common decency, resist the friendly hand or the kind smile or the invitation to share? Magog in Albion is powerful and enduring because Magog in Albion has always known how to win his enemies from the ranks of the mass. O, Magog, Magog, how clever you are, when you make nearly all people believe that freedom is anti-social, solitude is misanthropic, refusal is hating, pride is improper, and passion certifiable. Yet one thing you cannot take from the people, for they take it from the example of the island. You cannot call each man's lonely suffering a mere form of masochism, when the whole body of Albion is only an island suffering alone in the north sea, when a national pride in being each a good loser makes the nation usually win by each man losing so often and indifferently that the winners give up and go down before such a callous virtue of lasting.

It is also Gog's last and worst day of walking. The rain wipes dawn and morning and midday into one. Sometimes it lovingly washes the South Downs, sometimes it scrubs them, sometimes it bathes them, sometimes slaps, sometimes pats, sometimes frets in a fine spray scarcely distinguishable from sea air. Gog walks along, sodden and uncaring, as much a creature of the storm as any sheep in the open. Though his belly is empty, his head is full of the beauty of English names and the singing rhythm of the places he passes. From Hooksway through Phillis Wood past the string of mounds called the Devil's Jumps, on to Didling Hill and beyond and between Linchball and Venus Wood and Cocking Down. The track descends at Hacking Copse and rises past The Butts towards Forest Hangar and Graffham Down, Lamb Lea and Teaglaze and Woolavington and dips again to Bishop's Ring and Dogkennel Cottages. Who would not chuckle to rattle out those names?

As Gog strides over the rainy downs, mile after mile in wet and driving mist down the grass track that leads straight into more wet and mist, he finds himself in court before invisible judges, their woolsacks the wet hems of the clouds, their voices the wind and their words the inescapable rain.

"Guilty or not guilty?" ask the wind and the rain.

"What is my crime?" Gog shouts back into his inner ear.

"You were Gog," say the wind and the rain. "Guilty or not guilty?"

"What else have you got?"

"One or the other," says the wind.

"Neither."

"You must choose," says the rain.

"I choose not to choose."

"Then you plead not guilty?" says the wind.

"I am a man."

"Then you plead guilty?" says the rain.

"I am not God."

"Do you think God is guilty?" says the wind.

And the near copse echoes, branch after branch after branch,

" He thinks God is guilty, guilty, guilty . . ."

" Of making us, God's guilty," Gog says. " But aren't we guilty, too, of making God?"

" Give us a proper answer," says the rain.

" Give me a proper question," Gog says.

" Give yourself a proper question," says the wind.

And the near cornfield echoes, stalk after stalk after stalk, " And we shall judge your answer, answer, answer . . ."

" Am I innocent?" Gog asks his inner soul. " Yes, I am innocent."

" He says he's innocent," mock the wind and the rain.

And the near grasses echo, blade after blade after blade, " Of what is he innocent, innocent, innocent . . .?"

" I am innocent of living," Gog says. " I did not choose it."

" But you did commit the crime," say the wind and the rain. " You were Gog."

" I was alive," Gog says.

And the wind and the rain and the trees and the corn and the grasses all give the judgement. " You must die for it, must die for it, die for it, for it, it . . ."

" Then," Gog says, " I must have lived."

So Gog is judged by the wind and the rain and the downs, and he sits in judgement upon himself. And he wakes from his inner monologue to find the mist lifting and fields of grain and stubble stretching out hundreds of yards to where the clouds have pitched the corners of their tents. And Gog knows he is in the set of a Russian propaganda film of the thirties. At any moment, the Fat Girl will come driving up on her tractor and pull off her huge goggles and give a great grin as broad as the steppe, the grin of the lady Stakhanovite tractor driver who has ploughed a thousand versts before sunset, fulfilling her norm by ten quotas and a half. And she'll say, " Comrade Gog, I'm joost simple Rooshian maiden what all capitalist world takes in."

Only the Fat Girl and the tractor don't turn up and Gog has to plough through the original dinosaurus' wallow outside a farmyard in a cleft between downs before he can rise again onto the high places under the driving clouds that shred more every minute, as the wind freshens from out of the invisible sea. And walking in his clammy clothes, Gog begins to feel the peace that passeth all repose, which comes only when judgement is received and accepted. And then he begins to notice that a grace is touching him. It is a grace towards living things. He finds himself striding a long pace to avoid a chalk-smeared worm or a slug, he steps around beetles, he shoos away flies without swatting them, he replaces ants on the ground with his little finger when he finds them crawling on his trousers. Gog's new-found care extends even to plants and flowers so that he weaves through the long soaking grass trying not crush it despite a further wetting; he jinks about the tall cowparsley to spare its spindly sprays. He cannot avoid treading the short-bladed turf between the ruts to pass by the puddles and flints in the hollows; but he minds his boots enough to pass round the larger living things.

Yet Gog's care about the placing of his feet makes him lose the way ahead. The track over the downs swings low into a forest and then splits and splits and splits again, sometimes offering five different routes at once in wide fire clearings between the trees. Yet, however wide the clearings, Gog knows that a blaze will surely come that will reduce all man's little precautions against fire to cinders. The forest is misleading and mazy, but Gog keeps on taking the way that leads towards higher ground until he breaks out of the trees onto Waltham Down. There he opens a wattle gate before a herd of sheep and lambs, and he is immediately bitten in the thigh by a collie dog. Alas, Gog's thigh is too toughened now for the dog's teeth to penetrate and it falls back with blunted bite and sharpened bark. The shepherd runs up to restrain the collie and tells Gog the way towards the main road. Gog follows the route to a cornfield just below the swell of the down. And, on the sudden, over the dark and rotting ears of grain, over the dun ridges of the hillocks in the middle distance, over the last grey ledge of land, he looks at the sea.

As the Ten Thousand knew, there is only one thing to say when the sea is in sight after a long march. And that is, "The sea! The sea!" with ten thousand voices. So Gog says, "The sea! The sea!" with one voice. The sea lies in a long blue-black lip beneath the sky, tucked between the slope of Burton Down and the promontory of Selsey Bill. It is part of the mouth that encircles all Albion, the mouth that has tightened round Gog and expelled him to wander over the body of Albion from the north sea to the south sea. And now he has found again the slate salt lip that spat him onto his journey, he can hope that his tramping is over and his time of settling near.

On Gog's left a metal viper suddenly rears its head, soon becoming a small tower among the corn. Gog pushes through the wet grain and the indifferent ears on the corn-stalks that do not listen to the excited voice coming from the tower.

"Flee from the wrath to come, pack your bag and baggage, this is my final warning, give me the airwaves and the B.B.C., I cannot hold back the holocaust in the Far East, and it shall come here . . ."

Gog finds himself on the edge of a hidden dip; at its bottom the Bagman sits in his stolen jeep, broadcasting his final message to the British people. Gog expects to see the Bagman's beard shorn just below the chin by the broadsword of Evans the Latin. But no, a hairy cataract falls from the Bagman's chin as frothily as ever. Either he is a true saint and can grow new hair by the effort of prayer, or else his beard is as false as the rest of him.

"Ye shall not hear me again, O ye of deaf ears, ye shall be not warned again by the inspired words of Wayland Merlin Blake Smith. Tremble, Magog, in your high throne beside Moloch and Mammon in the gilded dunghills of murdering London. Give me the transmitters now, now, now! I come to London now! If the servant of the Lord be not heard, he shall call down fire and brimstone, sulphur and treacle from heaven. What shall not be given to God and his minions with full heart shall be plucked away by fire and sword. I, Wayland Merlin Blake Smith, call out for the last time to give the last message of the Lord. Deny me at your peril!"

As Gog watches, he sees khaki men with bayonets on their rifles rise up out of the corn in a ring. "Surrender, Bagman," a fat officer calls. "You're surrounded. You're under arrest for illicit broadcasting from stolen War Department property." Without replying, the Bagman switches on the jeep's engine and ploughs off through the corn, swerving and jinking as the bayonets jab at his tyres. One sharp turn brings him roaring straight for Gog, who leaps for safety, is caught a bad blow on his bruised left shoulder, and is spun by some trick of ballistics into the open seat beside the driver. The Bagman immediately drops the wheel and lets the jeep bucket about at random, while he grabs a spanner in each hand to stove in Gog's skull. But when he sees who his uninvited guest is, he drops the spanners and takes up the wheel just in time to stop running down the fat officer, before he junkets off down the hill, muttering, " It would be *you*. Gog, the sign of the end of the world."

No sooner on the main road to Chichester, then the chase is on. All the transport of the British army seems to be in hot pursuit, tanks, troop carriers, scout cars, lorries, spotter planes, prams. But the Bagman's driving is as inspired as his words. One moment he's in Petworth, the next in Pulborough, then back to Arundel and round the corner to Amberley. In an alley, down the dumps, up the creek, under a truck, over the wall, the Bagman tries them all. Everywhere about him, transport crashes. Tanks go into churches, spotter planes into telephone poles, lorries turn turtle, motor-cycles play ducks and drakes. And still the Bagman hots up the pace, while the vehicles charge him and veer at the last moment before his bonnet, piling up in bow-waves of scrap in the ditches on either side of the road. It's the Keystone cops in rapidest motion, W. C. Fields taking a pregnant elephant to the hospital, must deliver the little jumbo, always faster, faster, faster, till the pictures flicker so quickly behind Gog's terrified closed lids that the images blur and smear even more than the landscape rushing past the rampaging jeep. Gog cannot bear to keep his eyes open to see death missed by a fender twenty times a second, nor can he bear to keep his eyes closed, since the thrills and spills of his cinema memories are just as bad. In the end, Gog screws both fists into his face and holds them there, until he is jolted into vision by being ejected through the air and serenaded by the noise of a gargantuan crash.

He lands groggy, but in one piece, on the grass outside Brighton Pavilion. A hole has been torn in one of its walls. Out of the hole, the traditional tyre on the traditional wheel comes rolling and falls at Gog's feet, bearing what seems to be the Bagman's last awful message, *Goodyear*. Gog hasn't time to check on the survival of the infernal broadcaster, because the pursuers are jammed in the neighbouring streets and soldiers are piling out of their lorries and running in through the hole in the Pavilion and swarming over its minarets and cupolas and domes and turrets and curlicues and whirligigs and filigrees and all the mad baroque follies of the Prince Regent, who never said a wise word until his last ones, which suddenly float into Gog's mind as the Bagman's epitaph, " So this is death. My God, how they have deceived me!"

But certain of the chasers in uniform are turning towards Gog to ask questions, so he's lumbering off himself, pursued down the back streets and alleys of Brighton. He ducks into an angle of a wall and from there into a dark doorway, while the chase pads past. And after a short time he emerges to find no one on his trail. Or so he thinks, until the yelping of tracker dogs approaches him and then suddenly fades as if they are following a false scent.

Gog finds himself facing a fence of tall boards covered in creosote, through which a fresh hole has just been splintered. He crawls through the hole to find himself on cinders in some sort of botched stadium. In front of a crowd of several thousands, six girls in white coats and bowler hats are parading six greyhounds, dressed in muzzles and coloured jackets. As Gog watches, a man in jodhpurs comes forward and shoves each dog brutally in turn into a row of traps with grids over their front. From these half-dozen joined and narrow cages, the hounds yelp piteously.

Gog finds himself shaking with anger at this dog-baiting and he bullocks through the crowd to the barrier round the circular grass track of the stadium. A curious humming begins from a wire in a metal groove at Gog's feet, as he vaults over the barrier. But he ignores it and runs over to the grids in front of the six traps and tries to wrench them off to let the greyhounds run free. The crowd roars and boos, cheers and whistles. A small swaying gobbet of fur mounted on the humming wire flicks past and all the grids simultaneously fly open in Gog's face. And number one greyhound, Magnificent Misfit, is off down the rails, and number two's well away, O'Toole's Wonder, but number three and number four and number five all pile up on Gog's shins, so he's down in a jumble with Lollipop Luscious and Call Me Nightly and Gruesome Gertrude, with number six dog, Watch My Tail, swinging wide at the first bend as he lopes after the electric hare.

Then the punters with their money on the three middle dogs are over the barrier and drubbing Gog unmercifully, but he's up between their hands and away round the track himself, and the bookies are offering seven to four that he's not round once before the greyhounds are round three times, but it's no bet because there's a welcome committee of stewards and judges and policemen and punters fingering lumps of true Brighton rock who are waiting for Gog on the last bend, so he's back over the barrier and scrambling through the hole in the boards and off down the alleys and back lanes onto the evening solitary pebble beach. And Gog has learned his last hard lesson, that it doesn't do to give a dog a chance, if he doesn't want one.

Gog walks down to the last suck of small stones at the fretting edge of the tide. He stands now on his strong legs at the rim of the mothering sea, from which he was retched forth by the pangs of the waves. The salt water is black and shot with twists of white, like a great cloak Maire may have worn to the opera of the deep. The wash of the sea licks Gog's boots humbly, as though he had endured as much as the white land of Albion in resisting all the storms and furies flung at him by the encompassing ocean. And Gog looks down at the tattooes on the backs of his hands. Between the square of the levered wheels and chained crowns on the back of his right hand, MAGOG. Between the square of the sheaves and sickles on the back of his left hand, GOG. It has been a long walk to find out little about the five blue letters of his enemy's name and the three blue letters of his own name.

Gog turns up the dark beach under the struts and amusements of the pier. And he comes upon a strayed sideshow set against the sea-wall under the boardwalk. The weariness of his escape and the dizziness of his drained body and empty stomach make him fall back against the painted canvas of the shut attraction. Dimly in the last light of day, he can see the life-size poster adorning the booth.

ROSA – JOSEPHA

See The Stupendous Siamese Twins!
Joined Since Birth – And Before!!
What God Hath Put Together,
No Man DARES Put Asunder!!!

The blue-and-orange poster shows a brace of thin girls with pouting lips, who are joined at the hip. They wear only a double sequined bodice and a single four-legged pair of brocade pants, from which their four bare legs project as if they were a beautiful stool supporting the immaculate curve of their arms. Gog racks his mind to find out why he seems to recognize the poster. But all he can know for certain is that it is the style of the Belle Epoque, as so many fairground signs are, advertising the attractions of long ago and showing the substitutes of the minute.

But Rosa-Josepha is not dead. As Gog lies against the painted canvas, he hears two little voices whispering and answering in the same voice as if one girl were speaking to a gramophone record made by herself.

"Ah, Rosa."

"Ah, Josepha."

"What times."

"What times."

"In the night."

"On the beach."

"Ah, Rosa."

"Ah, Josepha."

"A man."

"Yes, a man."

"But who shall he choose?"

"But how shall we choose?"

"If I have him ..."

"If I ..."

"You'll be jealous."

"You will."

"If you have him ..."

"If you do ..."

"I'll kill you."

"And you'll die too."

The waves murmur their soft hubbub against the single voices.

"If he has us both ..."

"Ah, both ..."

"Then we'll both kill ..."

"Each other."

"Ah, Rosa."

"Ah, Josepha."

"A man."

"Yes, a man."

"In the night."

"On the beach."

And the single voices sound together as one strong voice.

"For us."

And Gog sees them standing above him, silver and naked and joined at the hip, and they are taking off his clothes and they are caressing him with twenty long nails and they are brushing him with two pairs of lips and their four legs twine round his own legs and his waist. And he is rutting and ready and does not know which one to satisfy. And he kisses one and holds her little breasts in the great splay of his hands and the other climbs onto him and trembles and shivers and moans at his rising within her and his going down.

And afterwards, as he lies with one of them cradled in each arm and their joined hips over his belly, Gog says, "Thank you, Rosa-Josepha."

"Thank Rosa."

"Thank Josepha."

"*Her* lips."

"*Her* belly."

"*Her* breasts."

"*Her* thighs."

"You don't love me."

"Me."

"I'll kill her."

"I'll kill her."

"I love you both," Gog says. "Rosa-Josepha."

"I'm Rosa."

"I'm Josepha."

"I'm one."

"So am I."

"Two hearts, not one."

"Two, not one."

"Choose," demands Rosa-Josepha in a single voice.

"Can't we do it the other way round next time?" Gog asks. "Then you'll both be satisfied in a different way."

The girls begin to weep and claw at Gog and he finds it hard to defend his eyes from the twenty nails at once. But at last, he locks their four arms in a tight embrace and says, "Rosa, I love you. Josepha, I love you. But I love you both in a different way, and I'll have to make love to you both in a different way. I love one of you above the navel and one below . . ."

"Who?" demands Rosa-Josepha in a single voice.

"Rosa above and Josepha below," Gog says at random.

The girls both cry out with rage.

"No, Rosa below."

"And Josepha above."

"I'm Rosa."

"I'm Josepha."

"Except when I'm Josepha . . ."

"And I'm Rosa."

"You won't ever know who is who . . ."

"We're so alike."

"No, no," Gog vows. "I'll know you. I'll treat you always the same. Both differently."

"*Her* lips."

"*Her* belly."

"*Her* breasts."

"*Her* thighs."

And both girls break into passionate weeping and wriggle free from Gog and cling to one another and cry on each other's shoulders and support each other, and Rosa or Josepha wipes away Josepha's or Rosa's tears with her hair, and Josepha or Rosa kisses the salt from Rosa's or Josepha's eyes.

"A man."

"A man."

" Always the same."
" Always."
" Like the other one."
" I had *him*."
" *I* had him."
" Some of him."
" Some of him."
" Never a whole man."
" Never a whole one."
" But I love you, Rosa."
" I love you, Josepha."

And they both say in their strong single voice, " Then we shan't need another man."

And they walk away, silver and naked and joined at the hip, over the pebbles of the beach. And Gog calls after them, " I love you, Rosa-Josepha. Tell me, who was the other man?" And their voices laugh together and answer together in one mocking sound, " Magnus, Magnus, Magnus . . ."

Gog blinks by the painted canvas to find himself cold and alone. He does not know whether he has been awake or dreaming. There is not even the poster of Rosa-Josepha there; only the bare canvas. If the Siamese twins came to Gog, silver and naked and joined at the hip, they must have gone away with the poster rolled up between them, the poster of the Belle Epoque that Gog knows he has, either in the furnished room waiting for him in Maire's house in London, or in the slowly filling room of his once-bare mind.

On the promenade, Gog finds a fish-and-chip shop open, and he spends his last shillings to wad his hunger with grease and ground-tuber and sea-fruit. Then he moves north-east on the road to Canterbury. He passes the Georgian terraces of Brighton with their tall oblong windows and white regularity and good proportions that seem to have stolen the golden mean from the Greeks, as the Greeks once stole the golden fleece from Colchis. When Gog asks himself why the Regency terraces are so perfect, his answer is that everything in them is built in the shape of a man. The height of the houses, of the windows, of the doors, is exactly the height of a large man in ratio to his shoulders.

The houses contain no squares nor circles nor horizontal oblongs to destroy the vertical spaces, into which a giant may fit from shoulder to shoulder, from crown to toe. Perhaps a man sees most beauty in the house which most follows his own ideal shape. Yes, the Regency terraces are like rows of pale soldiers standing in their ranks. They are built for men to inhabit, and, since they are built like men, they seem the best to men to inhabit. Gog is content to find even the buildings representing his new-found harmony with his own kind. And he remembers that the other beautiful buildings he has seen, the great cathedrals of Durham and Winchester, the ruined abbeys of Rievaulx and Glastonbury, why they, too, are beautiful because they are based on the shape of a crucified man.

So Gog leaves the south sea on his last night's tramp, because he has nothing else to do and feels ready to reach London. And, indeed, he never gets to Canterbury on his way there, he never finishes the pilgrimage suggested to him by Maire. After several hours of slogging along the Sussex roads above Brighton, he sees a glow in a wood and turns off his almost sacred way, as though it were enough to feel a living man again and to renounce any spurious holy purpose.

XXXII

Gog follows the lights wavering between the bars of the trunks of the birch trees that stake the torches about like haphazard pickets. He dodges from trunk to trunk, concealing his approach. Soon, he is looking over a bush at the edge of a clearing, where a circle of people dances about a bonfire lit beneath an iron tripod. If this is an orgy of devil-worshippers, it is a godly one; for the dancers wear Sunday clothes of blue and strike up a chant suspiciously like a hymn to the tune of *Rule Britannia*.

"Come, loud hosannas let us sing.
By all the earth let praise be given.
Praise God for giving us a King
To make this earth resemble Heaven.

Rule, King Shiloh! King Shiloh, rule alone,
With glory crowned on David's throne."

The dancers throw themselves on their knees as an old woman leaning on two blackthorn sticks hobbles out of the ring towards the fire. She stops by the flames and raises both sticks up towards the heavens. Trembling and shaking in her long robe of black, she calls to the sky for vengeance.

"O Lord, who still keepest Joanna with Thee in a Trance and hath not yet given her back to us in Reawakening, who caught up her Son and Thy Son Shiloh unto Thee at His birth, grant that the Day of Their coming again may be soon, O Lord, and grant us a Sign, grant that the hearts of the black Bishops may be turned from their Wickedness and that they may open and examine Joanna's Box, in which her True Prophecies have lain sealed for many generations, grant us this, O Lord, that London may not be consumed again in fire and brimstone by the anti-Christ. Amen."

The kneeling people reply, "Amen," and rise. And the old woman leans again on her sticks and hobbles back towards the ring. As she moves forwards, a sudden flare of light from a cracking log illuminates her shadowed face. In her long nose and thin jaw, in the crab-apple lumps on her cheek-bones that gather the lines of cracking skin from eyelid and cheek into polished red knobs, Gog seems to see a woman he once knew. His mouth opens in a cry of recognition; but he stays silent out of policy and fear, when he sees the old woman nod at a man in the ring, a man who bends down to pick up a small squealing box and lopes with it into the firelight so that Gog can recognize the abominable Crook, as tawny and furry as ever, but with his black pads in boots and his chest in a sailor's jersey above his stained leather breeches.

When Crook reaches the edge of the fire, he wrenches off the end of the box and pulls out a small black pig, which wriggles and screams continuously. Crook drops the box and takes a firm grip on the pig by tail and hind legs. Then he walks slowly round the fire, displaying the pig to the ring of people.

"And Joanna wrote," the old woman chants, "that the Devil came unto her in the likeness of a black pig, and lo, He was chastised by the True Believers and cast into the furnace."

The people of the ring bend and pick up stones or branches from the ground. And Crook throws the pig into the air with the cry of, "Hup, Satan." And the pig dashes for safety across the clearing away from the fire; but every time it tries to break through the circle of people in their Sunday blue, it is chopped or bludgeoned or stoned until it is dragging itself about on three legs, still screeching out of its bloody snout. Then the people break the ring and surround the pig and batter it to death. And Crook runs in with a hook and chain, and he pulls out the corpse and he puts it on the hook and he takes it back to the fire, where the chain is put on the tripod and the corpse swung over the flame. And Crook watches the blood drop off the broken porker into the embers with a hiss and a splutter, and he licks his hands clean of gore, and he laughs to see the people begin dancing again in a circle, singing a new hymn.

"Now Satan's gone, shall Shiloh come,
Descending in Millenium.
  Pour Satan's ashes on thy head,
  And God will waken all the dead.

Halleluiah, now no more
Shall evil flourish on our shore.
  Halleluiah, good is nigh,
  Joanna cometh from on high.

Let the faithful's holy praise
Rise to . . ."

A rifle shot. The singing stops as if all the voices had been cut dumb by one bullet. The people of the ring turn. Gog sees khaki uniforms advancing in the moonlight from the far side of the clearing, as the local Home Guard charges with fixed bayonets. "Theer," a yokel's voice shouts, "I told 'ee. Spies. Signalling the Jap bombers." The worshippers turn and run back towards Gog. "Halt," a voice shouts, "or we fire." But the worshippers scuttle off, with Crook in the lead dodging and jinking away into the birches quick as a stoat. One portly figure trips and the Home Guard surrounds him, pushing its bayonets at his throat and belly, while he weakly protests, "I say, we're not spies. Really. Just followers of Joanna Southcott, the prophetess, don't you know?" But the Home Guard pulls him up mercilessly and frog-marches him off and seeks further victims. The village soldiers, however, are too scared to stray out of the clearing into the recesses of the wood, who knows what enemy may not be laying in wait for them with machine-guns, and they already have their single captive to prove their devotion to duty. So even the old lady is allowed to hobble away to safety on her sticks as they shout, "Let the old witch go, or 'er'll put the evil eye on 'ee." She crouches down behind the bush by Gog and waits, panting. The Home Guard fires off a dozen shots into the air to ventilate the rusty barrels of its Lee-Enfields, then it forms up and smartly marches back through the wood along the way it has come, bearing off its prisoner to interrogate at leisure.

When the village soldiers have gone, Gog looks out at the clearing and sees that the corpse of the pig has been reduced to a twisted stick of ash on the end of the hook and chain.

"You've burnt a pig," Gog says bitterly to the old lady. "You haven't burnt Satan, granny."

The old lady peers up at Gog's face, then suddenly cups her scaly palms about his cheeks and drags his face close to her own. "Granny?" She studies Gog's face. "I can't see in the dark. You're not one of us. What are you doing here?"

"I saw the light through the trees," Gog says. "I'm on my way, walking if I can, to London. I turned off to see what it was. Pure chance."

"There's no chance," the old lady says. "It's all intended. Intended. Revealed to Joanna and locked in her box. What's your name?"

Gog looks down at the old lady's withered face, so familiar and yet so distant beyond memory. And he says, "They call me Gog." And the old lady hooks her bent arm round Gog's neck and kisses him on the mouth with her dry gums and snivels, "Ta, Gog. Gog Griffin. Granny indeed. Your own father's mother. Maria, your own granny. There. Nothing's chance. It's all intended. All intended by the mind. The mind of God as revealed through Joanna his Bride."

Gog looks at the dark face of the old woman and he cannot remember, but as she seems to recognize him, he kisses her dutifully on the cheek, saying, "How lovely we should meet again."

"Home, my Gogling. Home. You and your old granny should not be sitting behind a bush in a damp wood at night, when there's a home not far away, your home." The old lady rises and says to Gog simply, as if she has always said the same thing, "Carry me."

So Gog picks up the woman who says she is his grandmother, he picks her up sticks and bones and all, and he carries her through the birch trees. She weighs no more than a large Christmas turkey and she lies in his arms, light and trusting, as though cradled again in contentment. She directs the way by pointing with one knobbled hand. Gog takes paths soft with wet leaves, he follows tracks that wind and double back through the trees. After a quarter of an hour, he comes to a rotting gate in a high wall so overgrown with moss and ivy that he cannot tell in the summer-dark whether it is built of brick or stone. He carries the old woman through the gate and up a paved path to the porch of some Victorian Gothic rectory, abandoned in the wood. He reaches a wooden porch, set askew on its supporting pillars of cast-iron frondage, and he deposits the old woman on her sticks and on the ground before the front door, chequered with lozenges of dark red and dark blue from the moonlight shining through the leaded glass between the pillars, with an occasional silver diamond in the pattern to indicate that a pane is missing.

The old woman looks in the black pouch attached by a thong to her wrist and produces a large iron key, which she gives to Gog. He feels round the face of the door with the fingers of his free hand, reading the braille of entering, the recognition of the keyhole with questing fingertips and the guiding of the key into the lock, so that it can be turned to let the outside inside and gather men from nature to the protection of their own built imaginings. They enter a dark hole redolent with rank dampness, and the old woman strikes a match and lights an oil lamp in the cavernous hallway. In the streaks of wavering light Gog can intermittently see Persian carpets and pre-Raphaelite paintings hung alternately on the high walls. The carpets repeat the forms and the colours of the porch, so that vermilion and marine sprays and ferns run across lozenges and diamonds of deep black and red and blue. The paintings, too, are azure and turquoise and scarlet and crimson, with the white faces of the women bright as bare canvas under their copper hair and the medieval backgrounds as gaudy as fantasy fairs.

" I left it just as it was when he passed away," the old woman says, hobbling off to light another oil lamp. " Not a thing altered. He doesn't like it. I only have to move a chair a foot or two and he tells me to put it back." She sighs. " Ta, he bothers me all night, if I've budged even an antimacassar."

" I thought you said he was dead," Gog says, following the old lady from lamp to lamp, as she continues her round of lighting the wicks.

" You know *that*," the old woman says. " You know George Albert passed away twenty years ago. But he always was a talker. And now I can't stop him talking . . ." The old woman sighs. " Ta, that's the trouble with spirits. It's very comforting hearing them when you live all alone. But it's all one way. They talk and you listen. It's not like a conversation."

Now that four of the lamps are lit, Gog can see that he is in a vast mock-baronial hall. Blue rafters studded with gold stars span the ceiling; where they meet, a red rose of carved wood opens its giant petals; where they join the walls, a dragon's mouth erupts out of the brick and swallows the beam between its jaws. A great stone fireplace, the size of an attic, makes a cave in one wall. Strewn about the floor are tables and carved chairs of dark polished wood and covered with tapestry, so that the uncertain lights seem to make the embroidered griffins and unicorns and maidens dance and retire on the backs of benches or the seats of stools. Yet nothing in the hall is as it pretends to be. The tall windows are leaded and black; but where the moon shines through one perpendicular window, Gog can see that the glass is brown and yellow in a pale imitation of the medieval style. Everything in the room is copied from a heroic feudal age and nothing is correct. On the tapestries, the maidens are too maidenly, the lions are fierce and life-like instead of being sweet-mouthed and imaginary, even the griffins look as if they were copied from a zoo rather than a traveller's tall tale. Gog feels that if a fair lady in a long flowing robe and trailing tresses entered the room, she would surely turn out to be a housemaid in a dressing-gown on her way from the bath.

"It's providential you've come, Gog," the old woman says, lighting more lamps until the hall becomes relatively bright. "We're always having so many disappointments in the Movement that it's time Providence did something for us. Oh, what am I saying? Questioning the working of the Will of the Lord? But He doesn't have to run an organization as *human* as mine. Still, as if He didn't know best! It's all your fault, Gog. Especially with a name like that, so unfortunate. I should call you George like your poor father. But everyone calls you Gog, although the name's not at all well mentioned in Revelations."

"I know," Gog says. "Magog and I are meant to put an end to the Millenium. And the world."

"Well, you'll come in very useful for once," the old lady says, sitting on a form of throne with a carved lion's head at the end of each arm, its body the arm-rest, its tail the side of the chair-back, and a lion's paw on a ball at the end of each leg. "I'll have to explain to my flock why the Almighty allowed those stupid soldiers to break into our Service. And I'll be able to say it was because Gog was at hand. They'll understand *that*."

"What were you doing out there, granny?" Gog finds the word "granny" slips easily out of his mouth for the first time, although he still does not recognize the old woman sitting in front of him. "I thought it was a witches' sabbat at first. And where did you meet the frightful Crook, the man who held the pig?"

"Of course, it wasn't a sabbat," the old woman says, scandalized. " Ta, you naughty boy. You're like the fools who call me a witch round here, just because I live alone and I'm old and I have the power of healing and know the truth, that Joanna was the Bride of God. The man who held the pig? I've never seen him before. He just happened to have a pig under his arm, when I was looking round for one and didn't have the coupons, of course. He stole it, I suppose. Black pig, black market."

" You have the power of healing, granny?"

" You know that, too. Don't tease me, pretending you don't know what you do know. *Come here.*" Although the old woman's voice is thin, her commands lash the ears like a cane. Gog obediently goes to stand beside the throne-chair. " *Kneel.*" Gog kneels and bows his head so that his face is level with the seated woman's. " Now tell me, what's wrong with you, and I'll intercede with the Most High that you shall be cured."

" Well, I've a bruised shoulder. Nothing much else wrong, except being alive."

" Don't be clever. Which shoulder?"

" The left one."

The old woman puts out her right hand onto Gog's left shoulder and lays her left hand crossways upon the back of the other. She presses down on the shoulder, while Gog winces with pain. Then she raises her wrinkled eyes towards the rafters and says, " May the Divine Power flow from Thee, Joanna, Bride of God, through thy Divine Daughter Maria into the shoulder of this miserable sinner, and make him whole. Amen." She lifts off her hands and Gog's shoulder immediately feels a little better, since it has no pressure upon it. " Your cure's not finished," the old lady says. " Go over to that jug of water and dip this in it." She hands Gog a small linen handkerchief, which she takes from her pouch. " It has been blessed by the Breath of Prayer," the old lady says. " Wet it, put it in your mouth, suck, then lay the handkerchief on your afflicted member, and the pain will be taken from you."

Gog crosses the room, wets the handkerchief, sucks the linen, and puts the damp square under his shirt on his bare shoulder. He smiles inwardly as he does so; but the authority of the old lady's voice and vestigial memories of boyhood make him obey with a grave face.

" And while you're over there," Gog's granny orders, " fetch me a bottle of the cordial by the jug."

Gog picks up a black bottle without a label, stoppered with a twist of paper over a plug of wood. He carries it and two glasses back to the throne-chair. " Ta, invite yourself to a nip, too," the old lady says. " You never waited to be asked, ever. But manners makyth man, Gog." Gog pours out two glasses of the cordial, gives one to his granny, and raises his own.

" Here's health to you, granny, and may you live to be eighty."

As Gog tosses back his drink, he feels his palate split in half and his gullet corrode into flakes of rust. Meanwhile, his granny says, " I'm already over eighty, you fool. And I'm past the age when you can flatter me by calling me younger. I'm not a young lady, you know, though I may look it." She puts on a little simper, then says sternly, " You shouldn't have swallowed my cordial in one gulp. You should sip it. Savour it."

Gog has put his hand over his mouth and is blowing breaths of fire that scorch his palm. He rushes over to the water jug and begins draining great gulps to quench the arson inside his belly.

" You don't need more water for your cure," his granny says. " You've had quite enough. And water will dilute the taste of my cordial. I brewed it especially weak this year. I couldn't find the belladonna. Ta, things are still shockingly short, though the war's officially over. Did you like it, Gog? It's a mild stimulant."

While Granny Maria sips down her cordial with little smacks of the lips, Gog finds his heart bouncing like a yo-yo and his eyes swivelling round in their sockets. The hall begins to whirl about topsy-turvy and helter-skelter and roller-coaster and uphill down-dale and askew-agley and clockwise-widdershins, until Gog feels himself spinning and falls into a large settee, manorial-style with escutcheons cut all over the wooden rims and hauberks embroidered all over the seat.

" Would you kindly get up and serve me another glass?" Gog's granny says. " It's so weak I can hardly taste it. Ta, I shall have to give it to the Vicar."

" Do you mind," Gog says, " if you serve yourself? I'm feeling a bit giddy. Not your drink, dear, just tiredness. I've walked a long way towards London. All the way from Edinburgh."

"How ungallant of you, Gog," the old lady says, pouring herself another stiff drink. "And if you've walked from Edinburgh, you're walking backwards. The army has made you uncouth, and I hoped it would make you into an officer and a gentleman. But *you* wouldn't have come running out of the woods with your pig-sticker fixed on the end of your musket to break up a Holy and Sacred Occasion?"

"No, granny," Gog hears himself say, while the cordial in his stomach makes him see the strangest phenomena, tritons leaving their tapestries and floating away up the chimney, auburn-haired beggar girls sprouting lilies until a deluge of blossom covers the whole pre-Raphaelite painting, and Granny Maria levitating on her throne-chair and sticking to a carved rose on the ceiling, so faraway and distant is her voice in Gog's ears.

"I agree, Gog, that to the uninitiated, the ceremony must have appeared a little *outré*. But it was a Commemoration Service, begun by my Celtic father, your great-grandfather George Edward, not George Albert like my husband. I told you about him, how he fathered me when he was a very old man. He even fought Boney. He was a sailor at Trafalgar, only fourteen he was, and he saw Nelson as close as you now see me."

To Gog's skittering eyes, Granny Maria seems to be half a heaven away, riding her wooden lion among the stars and the black beams that hold up the universe, swooping past the dragons' mouths that bellow and belch at her out of the walls of the firmament.

"Well, when the war was over, he sailed back to England to find all the labourers starving and the machines in the factories making paupers out of free Britons. So a terrible rage came over him. He had fought the French all over the seven seas, he had endured hard tack and cannon-balls and years without stepping ashore, all for a handful of profiteers eating up the poor in their slum factories. So he gathered together a group of out-of-work labourers and they went round wrecking all the threshing-machines they could find."

Who was it, then, who was it charged the threshing-machine

on the Border when Cluckitt first sprang up like a pixie? Was it Gog who charged the machine eating men and men's food, or was it great-grandfather George Edward, the first Ned Ludd, charging in the veins of Gog?

"My father, George Edward," the swooping witch calls far and away, "called his band of machine-wreckers, the Luddites, after King Ludd, who built old Celtic London full of palaces and towers and parks, not a chimney in it, all craftsmen plying their own trade with tools they used with their own hands. He wanted to get back to an England like that, fit for a free man to live in and work for himself, not an England where machines ate men. But he and his men didn't wreck many threshing-machines. The moment the magistrates saw his flag, *Bread or Blood*, they called out the soldiers and all the band ran away. Ta, they weren't men of stuff like George Edward. The soldiers put him in Norwich Gaol, where someone gave him William Blake to read, all about how we had the first Israel here, then one of Blessed Joanna Southcott's works. And he read it and he was converted to the true faith. And he heard that the Lord had just taken Her in a Trance to heaven, for, although She was immortal, yet He could no longer do without Her on High. And He also took Shiloh, Her Son born to Her according to Her prophecies at the age of sixty-five years, a miraculous birth. For the Lord in His Infinite Wisdom saw that the time was not yet ripe for the Millenium, when Shiloh would rule with His Mother Joanna at his side for a thousand years, until Satan should rise again with Gog and Magog to destroy the world before the final Judgement Day.

"When George Edward heard the true faith, he prayed to Joanna, and lo, his prayer was answered. A trembling shook the earth and the walls of the jail were parted and George Edward walked away to safety. And he gathered together other followers of Joanna and he performed the ceremony you saw tonight, when the Devil was burned in the shape of a black pig and the ashes were to be scattered over the heads of the faithful in order to hurry the coming of Shiloh back to a cleansed earth. Only, just as tonight, the military appeared and they took away George Edward and they put him in chains and they sent him away to

Bantry Bay. And he did not return from the Antipodes until he was sixty years of age, when he married my Welsh mother and begat me in the true faith of Joanna and passed away."

The words of Granny Maria thunder or pipe in Gog's ears, as she swoops and banks and glides on her wooden lion round the spacious firmament on high, through all the blue ethereal sky under the rafters, now brushing past Gog's nose, now whisking away almost beyond his sight in the eddying smoke of the oil lamps. His senses reel as he tries to follow her whirligigs and gyrations. Gog tries desperately to focus his sight and establish that his granny is a witch on a lion-stick or else a respectable old lady sitting in a chair with a powerful line in home-brew; but his eyes won't align themselves for long enough to clear his own mind, which is scooting way over the moon on its own.

"Of course, I had to marry in due time, and I should have been a boy. Although what's wrong with a woman, ta, she's got two legs and two arms and a head like any man? And the rest of her's private, anyway. George Edward made me swear that any son of mine should take the name of George Griffin, and that I shouldn't marry a Celt who wouldn't take the name of George for love of me. So Albert, my husband, became George Albert and your father was called George Griffin like my father. And both of them were a credit to him, they were. George Albert knew Keir Hardie and Lloyd George. He used to tell them, that's how the people think, bless 'em, that's what you should do. They called him, The Public Pulse. You just had to feel him and you knew what the people wanted. The Public Pulse. But my son George, your father, he broke my heart, as well you know. He left the true faith and married a Papist, your wicked mother Merry. And I never saw him from his wedding-day till his funeral, and then he was in a box. Still, he was his grandfather's son in a way. He was what the Griffins always are, a fighter and a doer for what he thought was right. He read a fellow called Bakunin, and he used to talk of getting rid of His Majesty's Government and letting everyone look after themselves, as though we hadn't always had a King. That's why, of course, he would go and live on nothing near his Celtic roots in Holyhead, where he said he could get the Welsh to demand their rights and break away from England. Decentralize. Ta, decentralize, he always used to say, and it didn't do him a bit of good. They put him in the army all the same. He thought he could make the troops rebel and help the Irish, but the Papists killed him for his trouble. They would."

Granny Maria on her lion-stick begins to hover above Gog and slowly drift down to earth. After a few seconds, she does a perfect four-point landing on the legs of her lion-chair, and, lo and behold, she is sitting on exactly the same spot from which she departed.

"Ta, when you were born, what a time ago! They wouldn't let me come and see you, and it nearly broke my heart. I wrote that you had to be called Shiloh, my Voice told me. But they didn't listen, though you were called George. I suppose a family name's the next best thing to a Divine Name. And George, I'll have you know, is a Kingly Name! But Gog, ta, what a corruption! When I heard you were called that, I knew it was a Sign and a Portent. And I said to myself, How can any Griffin be called Gog? When Gog is Satan's chief lieutenant who'll put an end to Shiloh's Reign after a thousand years and bring about the End of the World. So I hunted through all my Bible, to see if there wasn't another reference to Gog. And, of course, there was. Just one reference, Ezekiel, Chapter Thirty-eight, Verse Two. *And the word of the Lord came unto me saying, Son of Man, Set thy face against Gog, the Land of Magog.* Ta, it was all clear to me. You were to be the greatest Griffin of them all, the true fighter for the people. Though everyone was against you, though all the sons of men set their faces against you, you were going to fight for the right, yes, even in the Land of Magog, the cursed city of London where Magog rules. Yes, my Gog, you will pull the walls of parliament down about the heads of the wicked Bishops, who will not allow the Sealed Box of Joanna to be opened in their presence. For they fear that Her prophecies will foretell their doom. But their doom is already nigh, for my grandson Gog goes to London to force them to open Joanna's Box. Swear to me you will go direct to London from here, not through unholy Canterbury, where the Archdevil himself rules in his red pride."

Gog nods his assent, for he has already decided to take the shortest road to London.

" And when you get to London and tell the foresworn Bishops to open the box, if they refuse, ta, then all the Accursed City will be destroyed with fire and brimstone. For Gog is the forerunner of the End of the World."

Gog's whirling brain comes to rest for long enough to allow him to speak. He hears his words sound as if they came from a foreign tongue.

" Joanna's Box? I saw a placard about that in Exeter. Why won't the Bishops open it?"

" For fear. They fear that their lies will be shown up and their false authority exposed. Ta, poor Blessed Joanna. That She should have believed that the Bishops would ever cause the Box of Her Sealed Prophecies to be opened in their presence to prove that She spake truly the Word of the Lord. For one hundred and fifty years, even while Blessed Joanna was still alive, the Bishops have refused to recognize the Truth, that Joanna is the Inspired Bride of Christ. And now She is long taken up to Heaven in a Trance, we may advertise on boards and in the London newspapers, yet the Bishops turn a deaf ear to us. But you, Gog, you will make them listen."

" Do they have the Box?" Gog asks, his stirred senses beginning to settle like mud at the bottom of his skull.

" No, an old Southcottian family has *The* Box. And it cannot be opened, by Order of the Blessed Joanna, except in the presence of the Bishops Assembled." The old woman leans forwards, her stays or her bones cracking. " But there's another Box." She laughs and beckons Gog towards her. " Come closer. Another Box. Closer. We don't want anyone to hear."

Gog looks round the vast empty hall, in which an army could be concealed, only what army would not run screaming in terror out of such a nightmarish bivouac? And he rises delicately onto his feet and spreads his arms out as if balancing on a tightrope and walks across to Granny Maria's chair. Once there, he squats in front of her, so that she can lean forwards and whisper into his ear.

" In the minstrels' gallery. Up there." Gog looks round to see high over the entrance door a small balustrade of railings carved in the shape of rams with their curving horns supporting the parapet. "We'll go up there and find it. In a leather chest. Triple locked. You can't get in. No one can. I always carry the keys on me. Ta, they're heavier than a ball and chain. But safety first. If unholy eyes ..." The old woman's irises briefly glint under her hooded lids, as a nearby oil-lamp splutters and flares. "Shall we look? Not in five years have I seen it. But you are come. As a Visitation. You, Gog. You shall be armoured with Faith, now you go to London. Help me up."

As Gog aids the old woman to rise from the lion-chair and support herself on her two blackthorn sticks, he feels her claws push some banknotes into his pocket. "For your journey to confound the Bishops," she says. Then she makes Gog stoop as he walks, so that he can buoy her up with his right hand under her left elbow. As they reach the end of the huge hall where the stairs mount up to the minstrels' gallery, Gog sees a gas jet flaming in an alcove. Over the gas jet, a large iron saucepan bubbles and brews, sending out an aroma of herb and gamey meat and unspeakable intestinal odours that seem to signify that the liver and lights of Lucifer are in the pot.

"It's my stew," Granny Maria says. "On the boil for six years, ever since war broke out. I never empty it. Just add to the top. Anything that's handy. Scrag-end and sweetbreads and nettles and mugwort and clubmoss and the pimpernel that grew on Our Lord's grave. And ..."

Gog cuts the recipe short, feeling his hungry stomach heave and turn inside him in horror at such a bill of fare. "It sounds marvellous, granny. But I'd prefer not to know what's in the stew. Let it be one of those mysteries, like witches' broth."

"After we've seen the Box," the old woman says, "we'll tuck in to a nice plate of stew. You'll like that. Granny's cooking's best." Again she drops her sticks and says simply to Gog, "Carry me." And Gog lifts her up in his arms and carries her up the steep stairway to the minstrels' gallery.

The gallery is as small as a sofa and the boards below Gog's feet crack and give alarmingly when Gog treads upon them. Half the area of the gallery is filled with a great leather trunk, upon which Gog deposits Granny Maria. The top of the trunk sags under her weight; but she is so bird-light that the old leather manages to hold her without tearing. "Lift me down, Gog, you fool," she says. "How can I open it from on top?" So Gog lifts her down beside him; but the space in the gallery is so narrow that he is squashed against the railings and the parapet, which wobble outwards, barely containing Gog's sideways thrust. He tries desperately to edge towards the centre of the gallery; but the old lady is squatting on the floor, fumbling with three enormous keys taken from her pouch of ironmongery. So Gog is left to squint over the edge of the hand-rail at the drop of twenty feet beneath him straight onto the flagstones of the hall, as far as he can see. Bats, disturbed from their rest, begin to flit and twitter under the starry rafters, glancing in and out of the black columns of oil-smoke like charred sheets of paper rising in the hot air.

At Gog's feet, Granny Maria mutters as she tries the keys variously in the locks. "Not *all* Joanna's Writings were Sealed. George Edward was given one, in Her Own Hand. He kept it and passed it on to me. He said it was written especially for the Griffins, and indeed, it foretold that Gog would be born in the likeness of a griffin and that he would hasten the coming of Shiloh. There are many other Prophecies about you and about your children and your children's children unto the Millenium. And also in the Box, there is the family tree of the Griffins, George Griffin after George Griffin after George Griffin, how they were champions of the people and heroes of the poor, ever since the lost Ten Tribes came to this holy island and settled here. In the ancient Hebrew language, do not Gog and Magog signify our name George, the patron saint of all England? And did not the Ten Tribes of Israel, fleeing here, bring the name of George with them to these sacred shores? And did not they bring also the name of Griffin, signifying Defender of the Poor? So you shall see, Gog, how the generations of the Griffins have begat you, how you are as they were, how you do what they did, how you live but as a plaything in the hands of the Almighty, the instrument of the Lord."

Granny Maria manages to turn a key in the first of the locks, raising a screech and a cloud of rust. She fits a key into the second lock and twists it, unavailing. Her voice rises until it sounds as the incantation of inspiration.

"I have set down all that the Voice of the Lord hath told me of the generations of Griffin, since the House first landed on these shores with the Tribe of Japheth, son of Noah, and his son Magog. The Griffins were all giant men, and their women were as fierce as tigers. Some of the House turned to the abomination of desolation in their pride and they ruled over the people in tyranny and lust. But always from the same House rose up a George Griffin to topple them from their high places and work the Will of the Lord."

Using both hands, Granny Maria turns the key in the second lock, which screeches even more piercingly than the first. She fits another key into the third and final lock, while her thin old voice chants and prophesies.

"So thou shalt find out at last who thou art, Gog Griffin. Thou shalt discover that the seed in thee maketh thee do all that thou doest. Even if the unworthy vessel through which thou didst pass to this earth was an accursed Papist, yet the seed of the House of Griffin triumpeth over all things, yea, it is the chosen of the Lord. Whatever the errors the teachers shall instruct thee, whatever ways the unholy paths of the world shall lead thee, yet shall the seed of the Griffins and of Noah cause thee to fulfil the purpose of the Lord and to defend the maimed and the halt and the lame and the old and all who cry unto thee for succour. For thou art Gog Griffin, the heir of the Tribe of Japheth, Defender of the Poor and Servant of the Almighty!"

The third lock opens, wailing to the high beams of heaven, and the minstrels' gallery sways and moves as a bough in a wind. And Gog sees his grandmother opening the locks that close the documents of all the generations that begat him, he watches the lid rise on the revelation of the great chain of the living and the dead that ties all men to the dim and distant prehistory from whence they all came, the great chain that shackles the ankles and wrists of every child in his crib so that he does unconsciously what he would not do and seeks for a reason why that he shall never find. For the seed of men blows on the wind as the dandelion puff, it roots itself where it may and it keeps no records. We sow our children blindly, and blindly they spring from the womb, and they reap the harvest in blindness. If they know the generation of their fathers, they are fortunate; if they know the generations of their grandfathers, they are blessed; if they know the generations of their great-grandfathers, they are aristocrats; if they know the origins of their tribe and their people and their race, they are historians, doomed to squabble together with rakes in their hands among the cinders of the past, unable to see for the dust they turn over, the dust which the wind bears away along with the seeds of new men floating in balls of down.

And when the lid of the trunk is open, Granny Maria screeches louder than the turning of the three keys, shriller than the bats twittering about the hall, more menacing than the floorboards splitting beneath them. And Gog peers down to see scraps of yellow paper, screws of documents, shreds of evidence made up into nests for innumerable mice, scurrying and squeaking round the confines of the trunk or running out of a vent in the corner of the trunk to clamber onto Gog's boots and to scatter off to a safe hole behind the panelling on the wall.

"Gone, gone!" Granny Maria wails. "The Prophecies eaten, the generations lost, the House of Griffin fallen!" She turns in fury on the giant Gog, squashed up against her in the trembling narrow gallery, and she begins beating on Gog's chest with her old knobbled fists. "You, you! You are no Griffin. Another bastard, like your brother Magnus your wicked mother bore out of wedlock. Your father did not sow you. The Devil did. You are the true Gog, come to destroy us all. The Gog of Revelations! Fall, deceiver! Fall!"

She pushes Gog and the railings give way at his back with a crack as if the crust of the earth were splitting and he is swallowed up into the bowels of the air. And he would shatter his spine on the flagstones, only the spirit of the late George Albert has prevented his widow from removing a large baronial dais from beneath the balcony, a dais padded with horsehair and sprung with the most enduring and resilient of Victorian springs. So Gog bounces up from the earth and comes to rest again sprawling on his back, looking upwards at Granny Maria perched on the edge of the broken gallery like a raven on a ruin. And she begins screaming unintelligible curses that should blast Gog dead on the spot or wither him to a toad, although he still seems to remain a sprawling seven foot man. But more serious is the smell of the stew, which enters his nostrils and cranks his stomach into turning over like a cold engine on the point of vomiting into life. And most serious of all is the volley of splintered rams' heads and wooden horns that the old witch begins hurling at Gog, so that he is forced to spring to his feet and run to the entrance of the hall. As he passes under the gallery, the leather trunk is pushed down, missing him by inches and shattering apart in a shrapnel of paper and a concerto of mice and a stink of rotten hide. And Gog flings open the outer door and runs out of the red-and-blue glazed porch into the winding ways of the wood, where he blunders about in the night for nearly an hour until he finds his way back to the King's Highway and the protection of sense and reason.

Once Gog has been walking along the road to London and the North, steering under the clear sky by the mariner's star that points the pole, he can hardly believe that he has been visiting relatives. But he realizes with a start that the pain in his bruised shoulder is gone, gone for ever as though it had never been. And when he feels with his hand under his shirt, he takes out a damp linen square from the hollow of his collar-bone.

XXXIII

Gog walks on through the night, approaching London, with an occasional glow-worm making a smear of light in the darkness. At last, rain and fatigue drive him to hunch in the hollow roots of an old oak by the roadside, his back supported on the trunk.

He lies in a half-stupor, beached on the Dogger Bank between dry wakefulness and the deep of sleep. But as the cold and the dawn begin to shiver his limbs, he pushes his fists into the two peeled eggs of his eyes and forces himself upright on cramped and set legs. He is still compelling his sinews to work against the pain of willed movement, when he hears the bray of a donkey, the creak of wheels and the words of a song sung by a familiar voice:

" Duck-legged Dick had a donkey,
  And his lush loved much for to swill,
One day he got rather lumpy,
  And got sent seven days to the mill . . ."

Gog looks down the road to see an old donkey hobbling on splay legs towards him. The white muzzle of the beast nearly touches the ground in its effort to pull at the black harness set about its shoulder-bones that start out of its hide as prominently as two scythes. Behind the donkey is attached a green cart with slatted sides, supporting a placard:

MOKE'S TOURS
We Get You There For Half
Take Time Off To See The Sights Slow

The cart is loaded with bodies, perhaps a dozen lying hunched in a heap for warmth. On a box at the front of the cart sits the Pardoner, a long whip in his hands. The points of his nose, his cheekbones and his chin form a diamond of skeletal points of light under the shadow of his broad black hat. He continues to sing in his prissy and coarse tone, the voice of man who has educated himself to con his own.

" His donkey was taken to the green-yard,
  A fate which he never deserved.
Oh! it was such a regular mean yard,
  That pardon! the poor moke got starved.
Oh! bad luck can't be prevented,

Fortune she smiles or she frowns,
He's best off that's contented,
To mix, sir, the ups and the downs."

The bony Pardoner reins in the donkey by the side of Gog, although the beast still trembles and sways so much that it seems to be progressing at its former slow pace. He points his long whip at the pile of bodies that fill the surface of the undertaker's cart behind him, and says, "Well met, sir. Only a tanner to London, just for the moke's hay. You can spare sixpence, surely, for my friend Absolom. Pardon the crush, but this is a popular tour. Plenty of room there, plenty more room."

Gog looks at the human débris littered on top of each other on the cart and sniffs the smell of stale beer that hangs over the bodies like the mouldy umbrella of the Black Death. "I'd say you were overloaded," he says. "If a sparrow fell on that heap, you'd break an axle."

The donkey sinks onto its two front knees and the Pardoner begins to whip it with relish and accuracy, trying vainly to pick a spot on its concave haunches that is not a sore nor a scar. "Pardon me," he says, flipping the lash, "plenty more places behind dear Absolom." He flicks his whip too far back on accidental purpose and twitches a piece of skin off the cheek of one of the sleepers, who curses and rolls over further onto the human pile and relapses into sodden slumber. The swearer does expose, however, an area as large as one buttock on the edge of the cart. "There, what did I tell you?" the Pardoner says. "You hop on there, sir, among the hop-pickers coming back from their sweet ramble among nature's gift to beer. You lounge back among your fellow creatures and relax. You won't think you're on King George's golden coach, I admit. But you'll be in better company, pardon me, able to take your ease and survey the glories of the universe, while we progress on our merry way to London Town."

All the Pardoner's exquisite flogging of the donkey produces no reaction except shuddering flanks, until the beast collapses in the end on the roadway. The Pardoner bends forward to screw the point of his whip into an abcess on the withers of the donkey; but Gog reaches out and pulls at the lash and gives the whip such a yank that the Pardoner is lifted out of his seat and is tumbled on the ground, his hat flying off and clinking its shells like castanets. " Pardon me," Gog says. And he sets about flogging the Pardoner as hard as he can.

The screams and howls of the Pardoner for mercy do not disturb the sodden mass on the cart. The donkey, however, revives enough to climb on its legs and watch with a large and grateful eye the beating of its master. Eventually, Gog breaks the whip, then leans down and pulls the blubbering Pardoner to his feet and sets his broad hat stitched with cockle-shells again on his skull.

" I don't care about beasts being cruel to each other," Gog says. " That's nature. But when a man's cruel to a beast, he's making a brute of himself, and he's better than that."

The Pardoner smears the tears out of his rheumy eyes and looks at Gog through his crooked claws. " And when a man beats a man," he says, " isn't he a brute too, who ought to be beaten? Pardon me, isn't it just brute force which sets one man above another?"

Gog feels the cold of the dawn lay its wet cloth on the righteous anger of his blood. " Yes," Gog says. " I shouldn't have beaten you. And I'm a brute for doing so."

" And what's the use," says the Pardoner, " if I'll only beat Absolom ten times worse when you've gone? He's got to get us to London and he's got such a thick hide, he only understands the whip. If he sat in the driver's seat and I was in the harness, he'd flog me. Pardon me, I wouldn't beat him, you know, if I didn't have to earn my way through the wicked world. Oh, you're all right, sir, a big bloke like you, you can always get a bit of bread with a heave of your hand. But us thin ones, it's not so easy. I've got to get my investment back. After Jonathan did the dirty and died on his old pal, I only had enough of the ready to buy old Absolom and the cart off a coster down at the hopping, and I'm skinned. If the moke gets a bit skinned getting us to London, he'll get his gilt back quicker than I will. Pass it on, pardon me, sir, pass it on. That's all we can do. People is like that. Pass it on."

Yes, Gog thinks, pass it on. Blows, breath, diseases, lungs, jobs, hare-lips, beds, crookbacks, deeds, cleft palates, photographs, paranoia, last wills, leukemia, pass it on. Never suffer what you suffer, give as bad as you get, pass it on. It's not me, no, not me, sir, it is the past, the family, the country, the city, the weather, the wind, the gods, the government, the memory, the mind, the mistake, never my intention. Pass it on. We are here merely to pass on what we are to more passers-on in the chain of labourers humping the sack of existence, passing it on from Adam to oblivion.

"Here," Gog says, "this will pardon me for everything." He reaches into his pocket and he takes out the twists of green notes that he finds there and he puts them in the Pardoner's palm. And the Pardoner bends, brushing the rim of his hat with a clatter of cockles against Gog's sleeve. And he tries to kiss the back of Gog's hand; but Gog pushes him upright and drags him by the arm over to the donkey. "I'm buying Absolom," Gog says. "Unharness him." "He's worth double," the Pardoner complains. "Double what?" Gog says. "Double any money I can give you?" "He's worth more as dogsmeat," the Pardoner says. "No dog would touch him," Gog says, examining the welts and scabs and rubbed patches of bare hide that make up the surface of the beast. "But being a man, Pardoner, I'll take him."

The Pardoner unharnesses the beast. When he has done so, Gog takes him by the scruff of the neck and ties him up with straps and buckles in the place of the moke. "If you want your profits," Gog says, "*you* haul the hop-pickers to London. They've paid their fare, they won't want to walk. When they wake up, they're not going to like it, stopping for so long." And Gog sets off down the road with the donkey ambling beside him, until the soft whimpers of the Pardoner die away behind them, die because the Pardoner dare not shout from the harness in case his drunken cargo wakes and whips its human moke all the merry way to London Town.

So Gog reaches the outer suburbs of the great wen, London, with the hoary muzzle of an old donkey poking at his shoulder and a stupor of fatigue making a balloon of his head and cannonballs of his feet. The streets are cleared by the daily air raid of the early morning, which keeps the people in the linen shelter of their beds and allows only milkmen and postmen and coppers to patrol the empty avenues and deliver their duties. The war-grimy villas flaunt their unavailing eccentricities that cannot deny the horror of the box after box after box now built over the once-holy way to Canterbury. Here a house has a yellow door, there a green one, there a red. Here is a modern Tudor beam only an inch thick stuck onto pink plaster, there a cathedral spire a full two feet high dominating a porch. In this garden, a bird-bath rests on the crown of a plaster pixie; in that lawn all of two yards square, a goldfish pond big as a sunken bowl sprouts up an iron Cupid no larger than a rusting fungus. Yet all is the same in these family villas, three bedrooms and one attic, living- and dining-room, tool-shed and strip garden, fit for mother and father and only two children, never more and never less or something might change and all change is for the worse. In their hundreds and their thousands, the villas line the King's Highway, only their hopeless nameplates crying out silently against the tyranny of numbers, showing in their dumb oblong mouths the protesting letters, *Strathclyde*, *Mon Repos*, *Shalimar*, *Shangri-La*, *Aviemoor*, *Bonnie*, *The Lilacs*, *The Laurels*, *The Laburnums*, screaming unheard for the utopias and the greenery and the wilderness that cannot be there in this no man's land for respectable everyman between megalopolis and byre. Yet the vain quirks that speak for lost individuals in the ranks of the outer villas give way to the regimentation of desolation of the inner Victorian and Edwardian terraces, three rooms up and three down, where the clerks still breed and butter their thin bread with the oleomargarine of old glory. And there the paint and the bricks and the stucco are shabby as a regiment in retreat, carrying its battle-honours cut in plaster scrolls on the yellow brick flags of its fronts, *Alma*, *Inkerman*, *Sebastopol*, *Balaclava*, *Khartoum*, *Pretoria*, yes, *Roberts* villa and *Kitchener* villa cheek by jowl with *Jubilee* and *Imperial* and the pub at the end, *The Empress of India.*

Gog's courage runs down into his toe-caps at the repetition of this interminable gentility and he begins to stagger and weave all over the pavement as tiredness makes him into a drunken man. Absalom, however, finds the decayed hedges and shrubs of suburbia very much to its taste, and it fills up the drum of its belly with shrewd passing pilfering from the front gardens. It becomes almost skittish, and when Gog reels against it by mistake, it lets fly with a kick that fetches Gog up winded on a garden wall with two iron stumps pile-driving into his buttocks, the remnants of railings cut off to help the war effort.

"Well, moke," Gog says to the donkey, "if you're feeling that sassy, you might as well give me a lift to anchor your feet to the ground." So Gog catches Absolom by the rope halter attached round its head and he throws a leg over its sagging spine and he sits astride the beast with both of his soles still planted firmly on the ground. He finds that, if he bends his legs at the knee, he can lock his ankles under the donkey's belly with his downdropping toes just off the tarmac. As Absolom moves on, Gog tends to fall off right or left, so he slouches forward, embracing the neck of the beast, his nostrils pressed against the rank mane of the moke, which slowly drags its way towards the city. The slight pitching and rolling of the donkey make the choppy swell of Gog's fatigue wash over his consciousness and drown him in a billow of doze.

Jogging into London with the Kentish men ... men of Kent, the Kentish men ... Jack Cade our leader, call him Mortimer ... Jack Cade, old soldier, with twenty thousand Kentish men ... How much longer will we stand for it? Tithes and extortion, stinking breath from Westminster, Lancaster and York, Wars of the Roses, thorns for the people, thorns and oppressors, we've come to rout them out, burn them out of London, Jack Cade and twenty thousand Kentish men ... Cade on his horse, in gilt spurs and gilt helmet, in robe of blue velvet, striking his sword on London Stone, crying, Now is Mortimer Lord of this City ... No taxes for the commons, sting the foreign merchants, take Lord Say from the tower, off with his head and spike it on London Bridge, drag Say's lordly body at the cart-tail till the flesh cleaves to the cobbles from Cheap to Southwark, walk on the meat of the rich that waxed fat from the bones of the poor, slip on the bloody stone greased with the blood of the great ... but the mob riots and plunders and Cade wears a crown and the

Mayor goes to the Tower and the Kentish men plunder and flee back to their forests and furnaces with a pot or two of gold and silver . . . and Cade's off with his loot downriver to Rochester, gulled by a free pardon, a free pardon for the Kentish men . . . but there's no pardon for a rebel, once Magog's sitting pretty in the City again . . . and the soldiers go out and Cade's wounded and carried in a cart back to London, pitching and rolling to Blackheath where his great camp was, wounded unto death, the boards of the cart slippery with his own spewing veins . . . O, the poor bleed as bad as the rich do, what matters your estate when your ribs are stove in and your side is slit and your life ebbs spattering the boards of the cart and your head's chopped off to rot on the same spike as Lord Say's (now buried in hallowed ground), left to rot like a marrow in the sun on a spike on London Bridge, not falling down, not falling down, but standing up to the Kentish men and sending the soldiers South to pierce the people with their pikes and halberds . . . Cade is gone to London once, Cade he wears a crown, Cade is gone to London twice, stinking out the town . . . and the Kentish men, O you men of Kent, black with charcoal and toiling at your forges, never again will London be in the hollow of your hard hands, never, never, never . . . and London will creep out on grimy nails along the King's Highways, creep out brick finger by brick thumb until the forests are gone and the forges are parlours and a Kentish man is a South Londoner, saying I'm all right, Jack Cade, what were you so fussed about?

Gog wakes to find himself sitting in a puddle, embracing the donkey's neck as it squats on its haunches eating the stuffing out of an abandoned chair on one of the many bombsites that pock the kempt rows of the city. By the side of the puddle in the rubble, daisies and marigolds and dandelions grow among the long grass that has already made the ruined houses into a plot of pasture. Gog climbs to his feet, brushing the wet off his buttocks; but as he rises, so Absolom falls onto its side, sticking out its four legs briefly and stiffly before they also collapse to the ground. Gog hopes the beast has expired; but it breathes rhythmically beneath the huffing cage of its ribs. Gog decides to leave it in its arcadian meadow among the broken bricks; but as he turns to abandon it, he notices a crowd of early morning housewives watching him over the wall, ready to denounce him for abandoning such a walloped old moke. So he turns again and tries to pull the donkey to its feet, crying, "Giddup," but Absolom just reclines, occasionally rolling an eye and shrivelling its lips back over its yellow teeth to laugh the better at the idiotic efforts of the man. Gog is exasperated at the immobility of the moke and he is about to kick it in the haunch to force it upright, when he hears the crowd murmur behind him. So he yanks again, "Giddup, will you?" while Absolom lies like so many hundredweight of knacker's prime cut. And the murmur of the crowd rises to a shrill protest and the housewives begin to wave their umbrellas and shopping-bags about and a policeman will come upon the scene any moment, so Gog is forced to turn and address the mob.

"Dear madams," Gog says, hoicking away at the donkey's rope, "this poor brute I saved from a fate worse than death. I am but a poor Samaritan and I am taking him to the vet to be cured of his many wounds. I love our four-footed friends just as much as you. I am not responsible for the moke's sorry condition, he was beaten by his former master." Pass it on, pass it on, Gog, that's the ticket, pass it on. "Could some kind lady direct me towards the nearest vet? And I promise you, if the poor beast is not well enough to walk, why, I'll carry him myself."

So it is that Gog rashly promises and has to cross the River Thames at Westminster Bridge carrying a donkey on his back. It is a heavy scarf. In his left hand, Gog clasps the hind quarters of the beast; in his right hand, he holds the forelegs; on his bowed shoulders, the full weight of the belly of the animal bears down. Happy to be conveyed in its turn, Absolom rests its jawbone on the side of its neck and snuffles in Gog's ear, occasionally licking away the salt sweat and the skin from his lobe with a tongue rougher than a file. As Gog crosses the bridge, a ship blows a derisory horn on the Thames, a paean of mocking, "PRRARP, PRRARP, *proo-proo*, PRRARP, PRRARP." And the sun spills over the white wraps of the cumulus clouds, gilding the blackened towers and spires of the Houses of Parliament ahead, where the gutted windows of the bombed building open their square mouths as unheard as politicians. And the bright light strews palms at Gog's feet on the ripples of the puddles that he sloshes through. And as he staggers over the bridge with the donkey on his back, he stops the passers-by with his question, "The vet. Where's the vet?" And they sing back their hosannas, "I don't know, I don't know, I'm not from round here, I don't know, why not ask a bobby, I don't know, I'm a stranger myself, I don't know," they chant the muttered litanies of the great metropolis of the unknown and the unknowing and the visitors and the aliens and the passers-by and the passers on and the passers through, they mumble the matins and the evensong of the great human wash that flows and ebbs once a day, while the dirty tidal Thames sucks at the piles under the bridges twice as often in a feeble imitation of the great land tide above.

And Boudicca's charging with her spear held high behind horses of neighing bronze, her raped daughters clutching her haunches on the chariot floor, she's charging full tilt across the bridge to put the Houses of Parliament to fire and sword, to burn out the misrule of London over Albion. But her chariot is bogged in immobile stone and the Houses of Parliament are guarded by Richard the Lionheart still standing in Old Palace Yard, iron Richard horsed on his plinth, still holding up his sword in his raised right hand, undamaged by bomb and fire and blast, except that the heat from the blitzed parliament has bent the sword a little way above the hilt, so that his weapon seems cracked by many mighty deeds of war, dented by the helmets of the million German houses he has riven in revenge with the downdropping iron hacking home from the high mailed glove of the bomb doors. And a tarpaulin backs the broken crosses of the windowless great window of St. Stephen's Hall and an immense emptiness seems to sit behind the shutters upon the gutted House of Commons. But the donkey, seeing the vast stable of stone, scents good company, and it kicks free on Gog's shoulders and scrambles onto the ground and gallops past two startled policemen through the entrance of parliament, braying its contribution to the deliberations of the representatives of the people. And Gog, lightened of his load, takes to his heels back towards Trafalgar Square, as the policemen yell and chase the hee-hawing beast through the corridors of parliament, stopping it from eating the brief-cases of undersecretaries and delivering the plans of the future in a series of smoking turds. And Gog runs towards the high column of Nelson, runs until he is winded, then floats, giddy and glad and alone, floats towards the North where a lost instinct drives him wafting and blowing as a pouter pigeon with tail feathers fanned out by a following gale.

One skip and I'm high as you, one-eye cockhat Horatio, kissing the starlings like Hardy, any room on your platform, I bet not, reserved for admirals only ... Why not take up the pavement, old artist squatting by your chalked racehorses and madonnas, take up the paving stones and hang 'em in the National Gallery, next to the Hogarths, genuine folk art, who else would buy it? ... Spin in and out of the double-deckers climbing the Charing Cross Road, burbling and burping on bad petrol and old motors, one step off their roofs onto the second floors ... Sway up Denmark Street where the brass nightingales swing and bebop from their celluloid nests ... Stop by white palladian St. Giles-in-the-Fields, all overgrown with Bloomsbury now, stop by the old leper hospital ever mindful of charity, where the St. Giles's Bowl was always full to give the condemned man a last nip of ale before the gallows at Tottenham Court Road or Tyburn, now turned to Marble Arch ... Run out, you priestly potboy, run out with your silver bowl, put it to the lips of old Gog staggering up towards Hampstead, dry as a lime-pit and tied to the cart's tail of instinct dragging him home to execution for treason to Maire, Maire and the past, Gog traitor to the old faith, lapsed Catholic and heretic of love ... Over huckster alley Oxford Street, up Gower Street with its black terraces, past University College where Jeremy Bentham's bones sit like calcium wicks in wax behind glass, no, all's not the product of pleasure and pain, Jeremy, there's the past too, driving us on unthinking to do what we would not do and cannot help ... Float on, dragging feet like anchors, into North London, with the houses careening by, their brick sails battened down, tiled roofs tight as hatches, the pavement rising and falling like a coaly sea, smack into the arms of a looming bobby, Can I help you, sir? ... Help me, help me, I know where I'm going, yes, I know where I'm going, I'll float there, I'll wash there, you needn't help me, I'll get there, look, there's Maire's paper in my pocket, telling me where I'm berthing, I'll get there, copper, only I'm sinking, that's why I'm sitting down, full fathom five my father lies, I'm diving, but I'll get there . . .

And Gog falls in a faint across the glossy black boots of the policeman, who looks down at him from the height of heaven under his moon of a helmet, his belt buckle flashing as bright as Orion.

XXXIV

White.

A slab of white with two edges which meet in a corner where a lamp shines.

A white ceiling and three white walls and a white door and a window covered with black-out curtains.

Two carved horses' heads at the foot of a bed with a ridge under lilac soft blankets that must be a body.

Hands on the black sheet with knuckles and blue veins standing out under black hairs and a blue tattoo on the left hand saying GOG and a blue tattoo on the right hand saying MAGOG.

Each finger can be set to work and move and bend at the joints.

A red silk Chinese robe embroidered with golden dragons over chest and shoulders and two more carved wooden horse's heads at the top of the bed and a white wall at the back and a mahogany table at the side with a copy of *Salome* by Oscar Wilde and a glass of water.

Silence.

The man places himself in the room. His room. His bedroom. His bedroom at Hampstead. If the curtains are drawn, he will see clear over Hampstead Heath to the city lying beyond the trees. His home. His place. His pictures on the walls. The blue-and-orange poster of Rosa-Josepha, showing the Siamese twins joined at the hip, thin girls with pouting lips and four bare legs that make them look as if they were a beautiful stool supporting the immaculate curve of their arms. The *Divan Japonais* of Toulouse-Lautrec, with Jane Avril sitting pug-nosed and round-breasted in profile and black skin-dress and orange henna hair, with Yvette Guilbert from the neck down clasping her bony hands together in the long gloves that have turned yellow with the yellow background of the poster, and the *monsieur* leaning over the indifferent neck of Jane Avril, tickling her nape with the edge of his pointed beard, propositioning her with offers of lusty sheets and gold. " Our poster," Maire had said, and theirs it was, hanging in Gog's bedroom by the large double-bed borne on the backs of four wooden horses.

The door opens and Maire enters. Her hair is piled high under a false bun of black tresses, piled high under the little bangs that fringe her forehead. She wears a kimono of black, on which jet swans fly above pitchy rushes. The kimono is closed at the neck with a gold brooch, but slit at the sides to the hip-bone, so that Maire's long white legs show and vanish to the height of her round white thighs.

" You're awake, Gog," Maire says, going to the window and drawing the curtains until a dab of bright day slaps Gog in the eyes. " How do you feel after your journey? I'll ring for coffee." She presses the bell by the table and sits on the blankets beside Gog and brushes his forehead with lips cold as slices of melon and takes his hand and kneads it between her own.

" I feel . . . rested," Gog says. " Yes, rested."

" You know where you are now?"

" Oh, yes. In my room, at home."

Maire smiles. " You are better. Back to your senses."

Through the door, a maid comes, dressed in black dress and white apron and white cap, an Edwardian maid dating from the World War before the last. But her hair is cropped beneath her cap and her face is familiar, the face of Jules the chauffeur, now wearing lipstick and rouge. "Julia," Maire says, "coffee and toast for the master." Julia curtsies and leaves, mincing on high heels.

"Haven't I seen her before?" Gog says. "Dressed in a man's clothes as a chauffeur? Green cap, very dikey."

Maire laughs. "Of course not, silly. Julia in drag? She's so proper, she'd give in her notice if I suggested it. You must be dreaming."

"But when you were following me in the big black car, she was your chauffeur. Or has she a twin sister, Jules?"

Maire looks at Gog in astonishment. Her eyes widen above her bland moon cheeks, the pout of her lips becomes a droop of wonder. "Follow you?" she says. "My poor Gog. You're not as well as I thought you were. Follow you? I was with you all the way from Edinburgh. Sitting beside you, in the ambulance, all the way."

Gog looks into the pale eyes of Maire, limpid and untroubled as twin glass eyes on an optician's counter, reflecting exactly as much faith and truth as the beholder can see in them. "You mean to assert," Gog says, "that I came from the hospital in Edinburgh to London, all the way in an ambulance, and you were with me all the way?"

"Exactly," Maire says. "I'm so glad you remember now. I wondered if you would remember anything. You tossed and turned all the time, babbled in your sleep a lot of things I bet you wish I hadn't heard. But I didn't think you were really awake. It was very nice of me to keep such a long vigil by the wounded warrior, wasn't it? Just like Florence Nightingale, except I'm married, of course."

"It's a lie," Gog says. "It's a damned lie. I walked all the way, except for that time you kidnapped me between York and Totnes so I had to walk in from the West. And you know it. You devil. Why do you have to lie? Why? You can't tell the truth. It offends you. You're the only person in the world who feels guilty if she says what's actually happened."

"Stop raving, Gog. I don't mind you malingering when you're perfectly well. But I won't have you playing mad. Of course, you lay in the ambulance the whole way. Walked? On your back, if you insist. You just don't want to admit how nice it was of me to sit up with you the whole way. It's typical not admitting that I do anything for you. You always want to think of me as some sort of monster. Well, I'm not. I can be a perfectly loving wife, if I want to."

In the righteousness of her reply, Maire speaks with such passion that Gog is almost convinced against the evidence of the past weeks in his memory. Then he feels under the bedclothes at the soles of his feet, which are blistered and calloused and horny.

"I walked," Gog says, "and you're lying. Feel my feet. The skin on the soles is like shoe-leather."

"Feel your feet," Maire says. "No thank you. I'm not one of those German tramps you've had lately kissing your boots for a fag-end. Of course, your feet are hard. You've spent five years tramping around in the silly old army. What do you think your feet should be like? Lavender bags?"

"They shouldn't be as hard as they are," Gog says. He looks round the room for his corduroys and his boots, but he can see nothing. "What have you done with my kit? My boots and everything?"

"I burned them on the bonfire," Maire says, "last night while you were sleeping. What awful pyjamas you came in! They weren't fit even to be given to the refugees. You were picked out of the sea naked. Boots? You're dreaming."

The maid Julia comes into the room, carrying a silver tray loaded with thin-buttered toast and marmalade and a silver coffee-pot and a milk jug and two large, blue, French peasant coffee-cups. She sets the tray down on the table and turns to go.

"Jules?" Gog says, "Where's your green cap, Jules?" The maid walks away, apparently deaf.

"Julia," Maire says, "the master's talking to you. Humour him. He thinks you're called Jules and you wear a green cap. It'll pass. It's a form of shell-shock."

The maid turns and looks at Gog with cool green eyes. "I don't have a cap, sir," she says. "Is that all?"

When Gog nods, the maid turns again to leave. As she turns,

the back of her hand brushes Maire's cheek by accident or intention. Maire closes her eyes at this contact of flesh and she grimaces quickly from pleasure or anger at the chance familiarity. Then Julia walks out of the room.

"Really, Gog, I won't have you upsetting the servants with your silly fantasies," Maire says. "It's simply impossible to replace them. So you can rave to me as much as you like, I'm quite used to it. But please be a bit discreet in front of poor Julia."

"If you two are in a conspiracy to persuade me I'm out of my mind," Gog says as Maire pours him his coffee, "you may well succeed. Provided I can't find anything or anyone to check up with. But if there's anyone I met on my walk who'll say I did walk, you'll catch it, lady."

Maire hands Gog his cup of coffee and a plate of toast spread with marmalade. "Just who could tell you where you've been these last twenty-four hours on the ambulance?" Maire says. "Only a psychiatrist. They're very good at telling us just why we took one particular journey through the mind, though there's not a word of truth in what they say."

"I suppose," Gog says ironically, "you'll be able to produce an ambulance driver and a doctor from the hospital in Edinburgh to swear I was put on a stretcher and driven all the way here?"

"Of course," Maire says tranquilly, sipping her own coffee. "I've got your discharge certificate in my bag. And if you want a *sworn affidavit*, I can get that too, Mr. Prosecutor."

Gog looks at the smooth kempt woman in front of him stocked with the assurance of the worldly-wise and the provocative tongue of the ready answerer. And although he knows that his defeat is certain, yet he plods on into the riposte.

"Cluckitt," he says, "I mean, Miniver. And the Pardoner, I met him yesterday morning. And Merry and Granny Maria. And Evans the Latin. And everybody. I met them, just now."

"You've met none of them since before the war. You've lost contact with all of them for six years. You've been having nightmares, Gog, in the ambulance. Tell me, in your *journey*, did you meet all these people in *likely* circumstances?"

"Well, no," Gog admits. "Just like in a dream. They were

suddenly there on the route, without explanation. Popped up again and again. But they *were* there. I could tell you everything about them."

"You always did have a fantastic memory," Maire says. "No one can doubt *that*. I should think even your nightmares are clogged up with telling details. I bet your dreams are full of the right facts, the verifiable facts, the academic facts. You don't ever get a place or a name or a recollection wrong. I bet in your imagination you're the Baedeker of the English byways. You remember every lane you ever strolled through in your old walking tours of the thirties, every bloody ramble you used to take. Why, you once walked the whole length of what you said was a lost sacred way, from Glastonbury nearly to Canterbury, day and night like a pilgrim fleeing from hell fire. I bet you took that route in your dreams."

"Yes," Gog admits, "I did. When did you say I walked that?"

"In 'thirty-eight."

"Then why did I see a barrage-balloon on the way?"

"Because dreams don't discriminate. You mixed up your memories of old walks with what you see roundabout you now. Dreams are a dreadful hodge-podge. They're nothing to do with time. Confess, you thought you were jumping backwards and forwards through time every second."

"Yes," Gog confesses. "I did think so."

"And weren't you always having endless idiotic fights, just because you've been fighting idiotically the last six years? And just because you boxed even more idiotically when you were young?"

"Yes, again," Gog says. He finishes eating and he lies back on his pillow, looking up at the white blank ceiling, trying to find there the clue that will prove he has walked his journey on his feet in nineteen forty-five, the year the war in Europe ended.

"Who'll believe you, anyway," Maire says, "if it's your word against mine? Your doctor's certificate says you're a case of total amnesia with slight paranoia. Did you think I was persecuting you, too, my poor darling?"

Maire bends down and kisses Gog softly on the mouth. She

picks up his hand and puts it against the swell of her breasts, rubbing it up and down on the soft silk yielding of the kimono. "You used to like that." But Gog's hand remains limp, so that she drops it back on the sheets.

"I wish I could believe you, Maire. I wish I could. But you know you're a congenital liar."

"You needn't insult me, Gog," Maire says, annoyed. "Just because the world's so unspeakably dull that anyone with a grain of wit has to embroider things a little to stop themselves dying of boredom." She rings the bell by the bedside again. "I'll get Jules to clear away the things."

"Jules?" Gog says.

"Of course, silly," Maire says. "She was in here a moment ago. You saw her. I couldn't have done without her. Who would have driven the car? You know I don't drive."

There is a knock at the door and Maire calls, "Come in," and Jules enters, wearing her green chauffeur's uniform, her hair slicked close to her skull, just as Gog remembers her from his journey. Without a word, she comes forward, stoops her narrow shoulders and picks up the breakfast-tray. "Will that be all, sir and madam?" she says without expression.

"Get the car ready," Maire says. "I have to go out and cadge a few more extra ration-cards, now my husband's back." Jules turns to go, but Gog restrains her by tugging at the back of her green jacket.

"Were you in here a few minutes ago in a maid's uniform?" Gog says. "Julia, weren't you?"

"I'm sure I don't know what you mean, sir," Jules says, and she twitches her coat free with a swing of the hips and walks out of the room.

"You are trying to drive me mad," Gog says. "You really are. It wasn't a dream. You and your precious Jules. Do you deny she came in here just five minutes ago in a maid's uniform?"

"Jules isn't *that* kinky," Maire says coolly. "Though I must admit, it's an idea. Still, dress Jules up as a woman now, and she'll give in her notice. She's got so used to her chauffeur's kit, I don't think we'll ever get her out of it. Except in the way of pleasure." Here Maire laughs mockingly and puts a soothing hand immediately on Gog's wrist. "I mustn't tease you. I really mustn't. I promise you, I didn't do anything naughty with Jules all war long. It would have been too easy. I'd much rather torture her disappointed desire."

"But the maid's uniform ... Julia ... do you admit?"

"Admit that we've been playing a joke on you?" Maire says, her eyes wide with innocence. "I'd never admit that. You'll have to prove it, dear, won't you?" She looks up at the poster of Rosa-Josepha, and smiles. "Why not think of her as Julia-Jules, like you could be a Gog-Magog? Or a Maire-Jules, or anyone. Even a Maire-Gog. I'd like to be Siamese twins with you, as long as we were divided, of course! But seriously, I don't know what clothes Jules wears. She keeps them locked up, though of course she borrows mine behind my back. As far as I'm concerned, I pay her and her sister to be Jules and Julia. If she's the same person she's getting a double wage for a double job, which is only fair. Poor dear Gog, you do *suffer* so. As if the truth mattered! Of course, it doesn't. Especially now, when the Nazis taught us how to burn the truth, liquidate it, rewrite all the past, brainwash a whole nation. What was that remark I liked? The one you always used to quote and hate? By Aaron Burr, I think you said. Truth is what is plausibly stated and boldly maintained. Well, I tell the truth then, don't I?"

Gog feels Maire's reasoning whirl his brains round like a tee-to-tum; but he concentrates at looking up at the blank ceiling, willing its still whiteness to clear his mind.

"The truth," Gog says, "is what happened. And I can check on that. With old friends. With people I trust. If you weren't a liar, you'd be able to confirm with me all I did with you since we met."

"Nonsense," Maire says. "Two people can lie just as well as one. Look at all the arguments that break out when you try and say, Didn't we do that? No, I say, we did this. And so on. We don't remember the past the same. We all remember it differently. We all remember it for our own purposes. We drag it up, if we want to make a good case for ourselves in the present. Otherwise, it's no use, is it? We live now. The past's gone.

There's no truth, Gog, except what you see before you this moment."

"So that's the truth," Gog says. "All this way through my mind, all this journey through the past, just to find out it's not worth a damn, this is all there is." He allows his eyes to travel slowly round the room, taking them off the square white safety of the ceiling. "This is the truth, is it? Just what I see now, your face and your body, Maire. That's the truth, the chair you sit on and the wall behind you and the poster of Jane Avril and Rosa-Josepha, that's the truth just for the moment I see them. And the truth's just what you say, the moment you say the words. And all else is the false past of hazard and chance and illusion, at the mercy of memory or post mortem or seeking for grubby motives."

"Yes, that's right," Maire says. "I knew you'd soon come round to my way of thinking. Perhaps it's a good thing you've lost your memory. Soon you'll think just like I do and we'll agree for once."

"So that's the truth," Gog continues, speaking for himself. "That's what I've journeyed all this way to find. I see a face and a background. I hear words. I smell and I touch and I taste. That is the fact for the moment and only for the moment. All else is slipping and going, going, gone before I can grasp it and set it down. And if there's really a truth which lasts, only God knows it and we can't know God. And if there's no God and yet there's still a true world, it can only exist in the treachery of our minds and the lie of our reasons and the innuendo of our motives and the bunk of our written history. Maire, Maire, why can't we have a true past? Why we can't we plan the future? Why shouldn't we make sense out of the nonsensical present? I don't believe you. I can't. Logic isn't pure idiocy. Experience does repeat itself."

"Speak for your own sex," Maire says grandly. "I've never understood philosophy. It's all rot, the sort of thing men waste their time on because they don't have children. Women are different. They know the truth and they know what's happened. It's biological. They're mothers. They have to pass on the wisdom of the race and all that. The truth all women know is," here Maire makes a pregnant pause and then gives birth to a delighted smile and the statement, "the truth all women know is that all women know the truth. And men had better believe what women say, or it'll be the worse for them."

Gog turns his face against the pillow and groans. "Maire, Maire. You impossible woman. Maire." He lies there, stupid and supine, and he feels Maire pull up the sheets and get into bed beside him and lie her silk-skinned body along his flank.

"There," Maire says, "there. That's better. I can't stay. I must go out with Jules. But I'll cuddle you for a moment, and you'll soon feel better. Don't worry yourself so. It'll soon be all right. Just do as I tell you, and it'll soon be all right."

Gog stays prone on his stomach and speaks out of the corner of his mouth pressed against the pillow.

"Tell me, I met Miniver with you before . . ."

"You were dreaming of Cambridge in 'thirty-seven."

"And the Bagman. Do you know who I mean by the Bagman?"

"Of course I do. That weird man you met on your walks before we met in Paris. You were full of him. You used to bore me all the time about him. You claimed he was a real prophet of the people, calling down fire and flood on London unless they gave him the B.B.C. I used to laugh at him, but during the blitz I wasn't so sure."

"Ah, you do know them, then. I didn't meet them just now for the first time."

"Gog, even if you tell me of someone you met who I haven't heard of, perhaps he's someone you've never told me of. A whore you'd rather forget."

"My son?" Gog says.

"Your son?" Maire says, starting up. "*We* have no children."

"My son," Gog says. "I had him by a fat girl in a Fairground. He's a Colleger at Eton. Arthur George Griffin Junior. My mother Merry brought him up, so the fat girl just told me."

"You've got a son?" Maire cries in fury. "And you never told me." She begins to beat at Gog's back with her fists. "A daughter. That I could forgive. I'd make her mine. But a son, another filthy *man*."

Gog laughs under Maire's blows, glad to have shaken her composure. "Perhaps I'm dreaming it," he says. "Like I dreamed the journey."

"Perhaps," Maire says, dropping her fists. "Perhaps. I'm not sure. Perhaps you're remembering the truth."

"Ah now," Gog says. He turns over to look at the sitting body of his wife, rounded yet firm as that of a Greek youth. "You do believe some of what I invent on my dream journey."

"I can check on that. I'll ring up Eton this very minute. I will." Maire rises and prepares to walk out of the room, but Gog holds her back by the wrist.

"Check on a statement of mine about the past?" he says. "Why should you be able to check and not I? I thought what's past was past. What has it to do with the endless present?"

"A boy's a boy. Let me go. And if he's yours, I'll see about that."

"But he was a slip-up in the past. I didn't mean him to be. It was before I met you. What earthly relevance has he to us, if he exists at all?"

"I won't have anyone else having your child," Maire says. "Will you let me go?" She yanks her wrist free from Gog's grasp and sits on the bed, rubbing the circulation back into her hand. "You've got a child. You're like a rabbit."

"We don't know I've got a child. And even if there is an Arthur Griffin Junior at Eton now, we won't know he's my son. He's a wise child who knows his own father. And even if the fat girl says he's my son, we've only got her word about something which happened fourteen years ago. And we can't put much trust in that."

"But the boy's *there*," Maire says, nearly weeping. "And if he looks like you . . ."

"It isn't proof," Gog says, swelling with joy at this first demonstration of his power to torture Maire in her turn. "A physical likeness may be mere coincidence. How do I know the fat girl wasn't sleeping with my half-brother Magnus?"

"If Arthur's at Eton now," Maire says, "Magnum had him when *he* was at Eton."

" It's biologically possible," Gog says with a grin. " And you said all truth was biology."

" That's why a child's the truth," Maire says. " You can't lie about a child who looks like you. He's a living proof of what a dirty, lying, fornicating bastard I've married. Well, I'll show you. I've always stood out against having any. Now you'll have a whole brood of kids running round the house. And if any of them are yours, it'll be my mistake."

" It'll be your mistake in more than one way," Gog says. " I won't recognize them. And I'd divorce you."

" You'll recognize them all right," Maire says, " when they look up at you and lisp, Daddy. And I'm a Catholic like you are. Just because we're lapsed, it doesn't mean to say I'll allow you to divorce me. You'll never prove a thing against me, you clod. So there. I may have been good as gold till now, but just you wait. You didn't deserve it. I'm ringing Eton."

Gog catches Maire again as she rises and pulls her back on the bed.

" I'm glad to see you're not always in control," he says. " I'm glad to see you're jealous. I'm glad to see you mind about anyone else having some sort of claim on me. At least you want me all for your own, even if you only want to torture me."

" Want you?" Maire screams. " I don't want to have anything to do with you. Why couldn't you stay in that old bugger of an army with all those stinking *men*. I'm sure it was made for you."

She begins to cry in real earnest, puckering up her mask of a face into creases and wrinkles that age her twenty years more than the ten years below her true age which her mask makes her appear. And Gog suddenly sees a human face by his, a face that is suffering and ugly and pitiable, and he puts his arm round Maire and he begins to kiss the swollen lids of her eyes and to lick away her tears with his tongue, tasting the salt of his sudden recognition of her equality with his condition.

" There," he says, " there. If I do have a son, it won't be the end of the world. You can have as many as you like. But have them by me, it really would be better. I loved you, you know. I'll learn to love you again. We've been separated too long. We don't know each other any more."

"Beast," Maire sobs. "*Man.*"

After a time she quietens and she lays her head in Gog's lap and puts her thumb in her mouth and is silent. And Gog looks out of the window over the garden, where a pile of ash smokes after a bonfire, he looks over Hampstead Heath to the city puffing out its breaths of soot and smoke against the bright morning. And he knows that he has sat here many times with Maire's head in his lap and her thumb in her mouth, knowing that he will sit here many times more.

"Here we are again," Gog says. "Round and round. It might be 'thirty-nine now, mightn't it? There might never have been a war, though it's still going on in Japan."

"It'll soon be over," Maire says from Gog's lap. "The Yanks dropped a single bomb on some Jap city ending with -ama or something like all Jap cities do. One bomb and it burned the whole city. It's in the morning papers. The Japs'll have to surrender now."

"The Bagman's prophecy," Gog says. "He told me the Lord would destroy two cities in the Far East like Sodom and Gomorrah as an Awful Warning to London. Two cities. Perhaps he's wrong, there won't be a second. He said God would do it though. Not the Americans."

"They act like God, if you ask me," Maire says. "A whole city with one bomb. I saw a photo of it. A dirty great white cloud like a mushroom or a fist."

"I'm writing to the B.B.C. to give the Bagman the airwaves," Gog says. "He's better than Nostradamus."

There's a knock on the door and Jules's voice saying, "Madam, the car's been waiting for half an hour and you're late for your appointment." And Maire rises, saying, "Blast, I've simply got to go. Extra ration cards don't grow on gooseberry bushes. And now you're back, I'll have to have some or we'll starve."

"Do you think we ought?" Gog says. "If everybody . . ."

"Everybody has nothing to do with me," Maire says, looking in a mirror and dabbing powder over the streaks of her tears. "And ought has nothing to do with anything at all. You don't know how bad it is back here. You're so used to living off the fat of the land in those occupied countries of yours, you've forgotten how the civvies starve at home. We've never been occupied, that's the trouble. So we've never been able to organize a decent black market, where you can get what you ought to."

She finishes her hasty job of powdering and strides towards the door. "You've only got a kimono on," Gog says. "It'll come in useful," Maire says, "if I want to get those ration cards." She reaches the door, turns back, and gives Gog a smile that is both sweet and menacing. "Anyway," she says, "I can tell you, if I meet a truck-driver, I'm coming back pregnant." She strides out, slamming the door behind her.

Gog sits at the window, hearing the car drive away from the front of the house, watching the still day set its polished lid over the great city. He wonders idly about his journey and decides that it doesn't matter how he took it. On his feet or in his mind, wasn't the journey the same? Think of the man who travels round the world and returns only to say, The view's better at home, compared with the man who sits at his window without moving and sees in his mind's eye the bowels of the earth or the rings of Saturn. To gallop without sight is worse than to squat with insight. If Gog has dreamed all from the ragbag of his recollections, yet he has travelled. Perhaps he has only travelled back down the roads he tramped as a youth and a man, back down the labyrinths of his research, back into the hidden places of his family and his blood and his island and his doings that he could never have understood without retracing his steps. He has travelled and he has travelled in hope that he will arrive. And he has arrived at his home and his wife in Ithaca, Hampstead. And it is all the same, the view over the heath towards London, the sight of nature's denial of man's brick sprawl.

Yet if Gog is satisfied that a journey by mind is as valid as a journey by foot, if he knows that the mysterious windings and caches of the mind hold all of the truth that any man can know, yet some curious hankering after proof makes him start as the acrid whiff of charred cloth floats into his nostrils from the embers of the bonfire. He walks out of the room and down the stairs and into the garden to see what remains on the ashes. A rake is lying by the twisted flakes of charcoal and Gog harrows the burned stuff, pulling out with the steel teeth what he can find. Here is surely the hobnail of a boot, but perhaps it is a tack from an old piece of wood. And there, the twisted shape of a button from a coat, yet perhaps again, it is nothing but a molten bottle-top. The fire has destroyed the evidence, has burned up the corduroys and the boots and the pack, as if they never were, and perhaps they never were. They rest only in the winding ways of the mind, which does not sort the false from the true, the fantasy from the fact, but retains both with the dreadful impartiality of memory.

And as Gog in his red silk Chinese robe looks down at the ashes of the fire and across the heath to London, he feels dizzy and sits on the grass with his back against the trunk of an old walnut-tree. And the sun beats in his eyes until flames seem to be flickering again out of the ashes and the blood thunders in his ears as dully as distant bombs and his sense of time sloughs off him as his limbs weaken and his strength dissolves and he remembers when the city of London burned in the blitz and the trees of the heath seem to topple towards him like a wall, like a wall falling, falling, falling . . .

The block of offices begins to fall forwards as though there is no back to it, a tall block with seven storeys, its front tilting into the street in a straight edge like a lid falling shut until it bangs on the block opposite. Then the dust and the explosion and the waft of hot air so that Gog bends forwards to lean upright against the battering ram of wind, and afterwards straightens, surprised to find that his clothes are still on his legs. And he looks up at the grating of the cross-section of the block, the flames skittering free in each room, yet the walls and floors making black bars longways and sideways that try to put grids of sense into the fire's riot. And Gog waits helplessly for the engines to be called, the red engines that work round the clock now to contain the springing flames. There aren't enough engines, there never are now, while London's burning thrice nightly, fire, fire, pour on water, pour on water, but don't bother to call the engines, they're all called away, and we're soon to follow, called away for ever.

An old man with a red bucket marked FIRE in his hand walks delicately over the rubble and considers the burning block and picks his spot and puts his free hand to the bottom of the bucket and swings it forwards, but he is too old and the fire is too hot for him to approach, so that the water falls on the broken bricks only a little in front of his feet, yet the old man nods and walks off to fill his red bucket marked FIRE, because he's doing his bit.

Gog begins to weep in the streets of the City as the fire falls down the bright-dark sky and the searchlights' meeting makes triangles in the night and the anti-aircraft guns pop paper-bags all along the Thames and streets are whiter with burning in the black-out than on a summer's noon and an aeroplane is Halley's comet until it hisses into the river and the shop windows are starred with sticking paper and white paint on the black walls says KEEP SMILING and pill-boxes squat in concrete lumps behind stickers that don't make them news-stands and the labyrinth of London loses its thread with the street names painted out and only the taxi-drivers know where they're going sometimes and the roads are a waste of brick except where St. Paul's rears its high round hat as a pointer and a tribe of natives wanders in the waste keeping to queues for comfort and the men wear plain colours under tin bald heads and the women are men in stripy trousers over stacked heels and the children are solemn from the secret knowing that London's burning here and now and it's not just a nursery rhyme and perhaps their little piping has made it all come true and they'll get a spanking for this super wizard of a bonfire if they don't get evacuated all ticketed like a parcel.

A fire-engine does come tolling in and the firemen roll out the hoses and the main is somehow working and the lone jet of water is gulped up in the maw of the burning building, no more useful than a stream of piss into an oven, and the firemen abandon the block to the flames and begin breaking and entering, thieves in a good cause, into the neighbouring houses, hacking with hatchets the windows into flotsam and the doors into jetsam, and watering with their hose the bricks as if these would flower in sudden geraniums. And they bring up the sandbags to barricade the inferno, poor little blue devils in shining helmets, part-time trainees for the fiery furnace, amateurs of the hot spot, but now war-made into Lucifers of the day and night shift.

The fireman with the red moustache like a hairy coal collapses near Gog and drops the brass nozzle of the second hose that he has rolled out so that its water spatters the rubble uselessly. And Gog picks up the nozzle, feeling the force of the screwing jet, and he waters the great dogrose of fire with its pistils of flame leaning forwards out of the white petals of the glow. And the fire feeds on water, opening out as under rain, until the skin on Gog's eyeballs puckers and his cheekbones feel hot flesh stretch upon them and his knuckles peel open so that he must flick water from the jet with his free hand to douse himself till the heat surrounds him in steam and he cannot see for the thorns in his eyes and his lungs suck and retch and he falls by the hose. And a shiny helmet bows down over him and takes the nozzle from him and speaks from the cloud of steam, " Thanks, mate, but you shouldn't really, you're not in the union."

Hands come from the hot heaven and reach under Gog's arm-pits and support him away from the glozing heat and he turns to one side to see the black round hat of St. Paul's come to the rescue, but it is a red-cheeked man with a bowler over his thin, long jowls. And on the other side, the original fat lady, her bun falling down from her hairnet in a draggle-tail.

" All right, lofty?" says the fat lady, speaking so warm and nasal that hot treacle might be flowing out of her nostrils.

" Take it easy, old man," says the bowler, clipped and mumbl-ing from white teeth too tight to let the breath through.

Gog nods, gulping down cool air in deep elastic gasps, and then says, " Thank " and must suck in and out again to say " you."

" Not a bit of it," says the bowler. " Just lending a hand. Like you."

" It's like Guy Fawkes," says the fat lady. " An' think what they did to 'im." She laughs her gurgling whine, then mutters darkly, " But the pussies don't like the bangs, not the pussy-cats." Then triumphantly accusing, " They didn't think of that, did they? Not when they started this lot."

" Never liked that block myself," the bowler says. " Had to deal with a real sod on the fifth floor. Now he'll have to camp in the basement."

" Ain't every day 'Itler do you a favour," says the fat lady and laughs with the bowler. Then she turns to Gog, " Chin up, lofty." And she goes back over the rubble towards the firemen, chatting to the tall bowler beside her with both hands pushing up her hair inside her bun. And when she stumbles, he catches her arm to steady her.

Gog sits until his ribs have settled back in a tight cage round his frantic heart. Then he stands on his feet and begins picking his way through the débris, back to Maire tucked away in Hampstead. Oh, they won't bomb Hampstead, Maire knows best, there's a gentleman's agreement, if we don't bomb Heidelberg, they won't bomb Hampstead, it's a fair swap of centres of culture, it's a tip straight from the War Office, an Official Secret, which Maire knows because Maire knows everyone and everything that matters.

Gog comes to a crater in the middle of the street between tall buildings without windows. Out of the crater protrudes the back of a double-decker bus, as though the red tin mastodon had suddenly become homesick for the womb of a motherly iron mine. Deep in the pit, the bonnet of the bus lies in a pool of bloody water, reflecting the glare from the sky. Severed pipes and wires, the sinews that hold together the body of the city, twist and prick upwards. The mud flat, upon which London rests like a hippopotamus upon its wallow, already seeps through the bus windows over the slanted front seats.

Ahead, a low masked light.

A chain of people passing bricks from hand to hand.

A tea-trolley, the signal of long labour.

The sound of iron on brick.

No voices.

Fatigue must have choked off the speech of the rescuers, for Gog has noticed that blitz brings the gift of tongues. Suddenly the English all talk to one another, as if the Holy Ghost has come down from heaven with the fire-bellied bombs from the Junkers and has touched the tongues of the Londoners with coals so that they can speak freely to one another in any accent.

A warden stops Gog as he is passing. Under his helmet, only two red spots show, the points of his chin and his nose, the rest of his face is darkness.

"Give us a hand, chum," the warden says. "There's three of them down in there." Gog turns and looks ahead at a break in a row of terrace houses, a ragged hollow with edges of wrenched brick that makes the symmetry of the houses on either side an affront to this city of destruction. "We've been digging thirteen hours," the warden says, "and we've had it. A big chap like you . . ."

Gog says nothing and walks forward along the chain of people passing bricks from hand to hand, the great chain of the living leading to the dying and the dead, the chain of old men and young girls, of women and weak men, but not of strong men who are conscripted away from this civilian chain of being and ending. For shelter is turned to slaughter; the bricks which housed men now bury men; tiles are bolts from heaven, and the rain cuts with window-glass, and the hail is chips of mortar, and the snow is a powder of plaster, and the sleet is slaying shrapnel, and the bomb blast pierces more than the North wind, and the streets are deeper than dug-outs with hollow walls that fall in to weigh down worse than sandbags. If the telephone wires set over the every man's land of the city are not barbed, yet the calls for help along them whine useless as spent bullets. The silver barrage balloons float over the parks on cables and the ack-ack guns are sunk within their bunkers and tanks rattle in the streets and the metal of war has forged the chain of the living and dying from Aldgate to Burma, from Aldermanbury to Libya, all Britons equal under the death-dropping clouds in the trenches of city or desert, all Britons the same in front of the total war that hammers their differences into one whole iron of resistance.

At the end of the chain of people passing bricks, two wardens and a sailor pull and dig and swing at the rubble; the sailor's hands are bleeding from tugging loose the bricks, and his face seems covered with stitched bandages until Gog sees that the bandages are his unhealed web of plastic surgery. Gog takes a pick from one warden and begins clunking at the broken bricks, enlarging a hole above a beam, an oak timber that has fallen across another oak timber at right-angles to make a chance roof over a hollow in the pile of masonry. Gog makes a rhythm of the swinging of the pick, hup now, ho down, stick, claw, loose and hup now, ho down, stick, claw, loose and hup now . . . till the hole's large as a shoulder's width and the warden shines his masked torch down into the hollow and under the end of the upper oak beam, two white parted woman's legs stretch down from the timber lying across her belly and between her two legs the black hair points down the apex of its triangle towards the entrance to her womb, open towards Gog with the black blood welling out.

The warden tries to enter the gap between the bricks, but Gog pushes him aside, weeping, and he blunders inside the hollow, scraping the cloth off his shoulders against the broken brick, and he crawls over to the upper beam where there is space between it and the rubble beneath and he hunches himself beneath the timber as tight as a foetus and he settles his lower back against the wood above him and he stretches mightily and the beam moves slightly and the woman beneath the timber gives a long moan and the sailor comes climbing into the hollow beside the legs of the woman and says, "Again, for Christ's sake. Again." And Gog crouches on all fours with bent legs and arms, kneeling on the rubble with the fangs of brick cutting into his shins and the teeth of the mortar biting his downturned knuckles, and he straightens his arms and his thighs, bearing the weight of the upper beam along his spine-tree of bone. And the sweat pricks his eyes out and the pain on the backs of his fists and the surfaces of his knees pierces him and his breast splits with the panting of his lungs. And he hears the sailor's voice say, "Okay" and he sags back on his haunches, the beam slipping and crushing him a little. And he squints sideways through stinging eyes to see the sailor with one arm round the back of the woman he has pulled forward by the legs. The beam has runnelled a furrow deep in her belly and, as she sits upright supported by the sailor's arms, her breasts fall forward beneath her rucked dress in bloody bags. And Gog squirms and scrabbles from under the beam with splinters of wood tearing at his back, and his spine crackles and a stabbing shiver runs up his vertebrae as if the marrow were full of needles. But he rises again beyond the beam on all fours and squints in the torchlight to see the woman's eyes widen in front of the sailor's face with its skin-like bandages as if he were not human. She stares, then a corner of her mouth twitches in a tic or a smile, and she says, "Itma," and she sags on the sailor's arm. And faintness or death rolls her eyes up into their sockets. And the sailor lays her back on the rubble, weeping and whispering, "It's that man again," then fiercely insistent, "Did you hear her? She said, *man again*."

Gog crawls out of the hole and the wardens pull him groaning upright. His spine is a burning spear from nape to rump and he walks away, weeping slowly and softly, cursing at God for having no mercy, so that the crushed woman has to call on Tommy Handley to ease her into limbo.

The sirens keen, wailing to the street wanderers to scurry into the cellars, as Gog walks on through the burning night City of London. And a lone church bell tolls for no reason on this last December Sunday of the year of Armageddon; it tolls the old monk's rhyme time and again on four notes through Gog's scalding skull:

"Men's death I tell
By doleful knell.
Lightning, thunder
I break asunder.
On Sabbath all
To church I call ..."

But the lightning and the thunder fall and the Sunday churches are mass vaults now, empty and shuttered, even the crypts made sepulchres for men's death by direct hit. God's in his wrath and all's wrong with the world.

"The winds so fierce
I do disperse.
Men's cruel rage
I do assuage."

The bell falls silent beneath the anger of the bombs that are not turned aside. Four crumps of explosions as regular as bell notes, approaching. A warden takes Gog by his unresisting arm and leads him into the square tomb of the entrance to an underground station. " Can't stay out in that, can we now?" he says, with no more concern than if he's offering to share his umbrella with Gog during a shower.

Gog lurches stiffly down the stalled escalators, the people lying in long sprawls down the unmoving stairways. He picks his way carefully down the slatted steps, avoiding heads and arms that lie slack with exhaustion or else twitch at his passing. And he reaches the long burrow of the platform, where the bodies under the blankets are laid out in rows with the regularity usually reserved only for military graveyards. An intermittent snoring and the whimper of sleeping children is all that disturbs the stale air. The overhead lights shine down; some of the sleepers have blindfolded themselves with scarves against the electric bulbs. One pale girl sits up, her back against an advertisement for Cherry Blossom Boot Polish; she is reading *Horizon* defiantly to separate herself from the war and the slumbering herd packed about her. But as she looks up at the looming Gog and knows that she has to be friendly because the time requires its own idiom, she says, " Penny for the diver," in the funny voice of the radio diver and Gog has to smile and say, " Can I do you now, miss?" in the funny voice of Mrs. Mop and she has to smile because the catchphrases of the Cheekie Chappie or Big-Hearted Arthur or Stinker or Funf Speaking link the people, who must laugh or there'd be no release in the explosion of the inner ribs from the fear of the explosions of the outer sky.

Gog sits cautiously on the edge of the platform and strokes with the tips of his fingers the base of his burning spine, but he must escape from the weary overused air and back to Maire and her unalterable arrangements of luxury that allow for no intrusion by war or circumstance. So he lowers himself inch by inch onto the cinders by the track and walks along by the skewers of light on the rails into the tunnel, where far ahead he can see the little glow of the next station. And it is cool and reverberate in the long cavern, with his soles scuffing the clinker, and a smell of soot and buried places, and the relief of solitariness and of moving towards something, anything, just moving away from the people gone underground, the Londoners fled to their caves as all primitive folk do when the thundergod hurls his bolts and burns with his lightning.

Gog issues forth out of the tunnel long as the burrow of a worm and pulls himself up onto the platform of the next station, which is unfashionable and nearly empty, and he climbs up the stopped escalator and goes out of the square entrance of the catacombs, past its sleeping warden slouched on a chair in his blue overcoat. And the All Clear is sounding in sweet monotony as Gog comes into the smouldering street, and he looks about at the mazy burning of the City with the flames revelling in the alleys in a rout of red and yellow and kicking behind the office windows in a cakewalk of catastrophe, with only the spires of God sticking up indifferent, black and sentry-still among the mighty bonfire.

A great cloud of jet, darker than the mirrored night, rolls upwards and hangs over the endless arson of London; a ragged canopy of sooty smoke blots out the searchlights and the moon. And Gog sees that the Guildhall is burning, the home of Mayors and maces and worshipful companies, of guilds and grocers and mercers and masons, of pomp and power in gilt and leather aprons, of petty ceremony and almighty consequence. And as Gog staggers down towards the Guildhall with the hot rod searing his back, an edge of the cloud of jet swoops down as the wing of a raven and through his skull sounds the doom of that first Jerusalem, that golden city which William Blake knew was builded in Albion, by Thames sweet river before machines and moneybags, before Moloch and Mammon:

> They groan'd aloud on London Stone,
> They groan'd aloud on Tyburn's Brook,
> Albion gave his deadly groan,
> And all the Atlantic mountains shook.
>
> Albion's Spectre from his Loins
> Tore forth in all the pomp of War:

Satan his name: in flames of fire
He stretch'd his Druid Pillars far.

Jerusalem fell from Lambeth's Vale
Down thro' Poplar and Old Bow,
Thro' Malden and across the Sea,
In War and howling, death and woe...

The wall at the west end of the Guildhall has fallen and the blue firemen are soaking the spluttering rubble so that they can pull their hoses forwards through the steam and douse the burning Council Chamber, where jealous aldermen always scheme for their privileges against King and all comers and win incidental liberty even for lesser people because the legal phrase Englishmen includes more than merchants.

The Rhine was red with human blood,
The Danube roll'd a purple tide,
On the Euphrates Satan stood,
And over Asia stretch'd his pride.

He wither'd up sweet Zion's Hill
From every Nation of the Earth;
He wither'd up Jerusalem's Gates,
And in a dark Land gave her birth.

He wither'd up the Human Form
By laws of sacrifice for sin,
Till it became a Mortal Worm,
But O! translucent all within...

Rearing out the smoke and steam before the Council Chamber, two brown giants stand in the fiery furnace. On the right, a Roman centurion with spear and shield, his hair bearing a wreath of laurel. His face is lean in the brown wood, arrogant and sneering from his fifteen foot height. The flames blister his wood with black boils so that dark wax runs down bubbling, but the fire seems to recoil from the authority of his beaky nose and will clamber no further than his chin. Yet, as Gog watches, the centurion splits open and peels apart in black charcoal bending and topples forward in a great hiss onto the paving, where he throws out a scattering of sparks and becomes thirty separate pieces of black wood, gently burning. So perishes Magog, one of the two guards set above the west door of the Guildhall of the City of London. Two and three-quarters of a century before, in the Great Fire of Pudding Lane, Magog was also burned; he was reconstructed to rule from the beginning of an Empire until its last gasp, then to burn again. For as long as men rule other men, Magog will stand above their door, and as long as men rule other men, great fires will be raised to burn Magog down.

Gog turns to the giant on the left hand, the wooden Gog that gives the living Gog his nickname. The flames run about the giant's leggy stand and eat his boots and lick up at his bare knees and at his short trousers under his kilt of wooden armour. A sudden gout of flame runs up the hollow funnel within the wooden Gog's ribs and sprays out in sparks and smoke from the laurel wreath also upon his shaggy hair so that embers fall over his cheeks and his long face, downcast and bent and brooding over the intolerable burden which the people must always bear because they are the people. His quiver of arrows slung on his back becomes a pile of blazing faggots, his quilted shirt leaps into a shroud of flame until only his right fist holding his spear still stretches forward from the pillar of fire about his body. And as the living Gog starts forward towards the giant, yellow wraiths run over the giant's hand and up the long spear to its tip, where a spiked ball hangs, the morningstar of the ancient Britons which they used to let the sky into the brainpans of their enemies.

The flame engulfs the wooden Gog in a great roar and rending and the giant totters and bends and crumbles away as his spear becomes a fiery rod blazing more fiercely than the living Gog's smouldering spine. Then, in thunder, the giant disintegrates into charcoal and the blazing morningstar falls with the rest of the spear-shaft to the stone floor and breaks free and spins towards the living Gog, who stops it with his foot and rolls it under the sole of one shoe against the ground to put out the flame, then he stoops to pick it up, forgetting about his spine's pain, which stabs him until he shrieks, so that he has to kneel before the pyres of the giants and scoop up the morningstar as gingerly as a hot potato, changing it from hand to hand so as not to burn his palms. And the morningstar has lost all its spikes and is nothing but a blackened globe.

The firemen now run by Gog with their hoses towards the flaming Council Chamber, their leader at the brass nozzle uniformed and helmeted exactly as his string of mates behind him, who hold up the coils of the jerking white canvas snake spouting out its clear venom at the furnace. And another fireman taps Gog on the shoulder and says, not unkindly, "Out of here, cock. Ta for the help, but you'll only get in the way." So Gog rises and walks out of the fallen west wall, bearing the last remnant of the wooden Gog, the weapon from the end of the giant's spear now charred to a round orb no more dangerous than the planet Earth itself, when it once spun through the universe with its crust cooling into soil and the first living things crawled out of the slimy sea to inhabit the land and form the first link of the chain of the living and the dead, until the fire and the hammer should come from heaven and destroy them utterly and the chain should be forged all over again. And Magog is dead, ground into cinders by the boots of the advancing firemen. And Gog is dead. And only the scorched globe and all that therein survives is left, and the survivors are equal under the fire and the hammer that fall to chasten them and purge them and temper their eyes into seeing that men are men and no more than men, not set over each other, but condemned with each other to trial by survival in their inescapable flesh.

Gog bears the burned morningstar of the dead giant in his cupped hands all the way up the hill to Hampstead, an offering and a pledge that, as New Troy once rose on London marsh when Gog and Magog were first chained to the gate at Aldermanbury, so now Jerusalem shall rise for a second time on the clinker of London, and Albion shall lie on the waters in green harmony as the ark of his people, whole and one and indivisible in peace as in war.

The fields from Islington to Marybone

To Primrose Hill and St. John's Wood,
Were builded over with pillars of gold
And there Jerusalem's pillars stood . . .

Gog wakes from the doze of memory to find himself on the grass under the apple-tree with the shadow of Maire upon his eyes. The small breeze plays at the black flaps of her kimono, baring the sockets of her thighs as far as the edge of her belly. In her hand, she holds several coloured and divided squares of paper.

"I just rang up Eton," Maire says. "There is an Arthur George Griffin Junior there. But the records say he's adopted by you. His father died in the pit and his mother of t.b. It's not a likely story, but it may be true. Just like it's not a likely story I didn't have to sleep with anyone to get these ration cards, and it may be true I'm not pregnant."

"Don't sound so tough," Gog says, "even if you are. We'll have to work something out. I'm sure we will. We've a lot of sins to forget we did during the war, but it's nearly over. If we didn't forget the sins of the war, there'd never be any peace. We'd always be fighting."

Gog rises and goes back towards the house with Maire, yawning in the backwash of the fatigue that will not ebb from him.

"We'll try," Maire says. "We got on all right before the war, when you loved me. I was pretty comfortable with you. I admit, I wouldn't like to go. Though I could, mind you. There's many who'd take me in. And they've got enough coupons to feed a regiment."

"I believe you," Gog says, laughing. "But you'd get fat if you ate enough to feed a whole regiment. Besides, we're all out of our minds, not only me. As if coupons really mattered. Clipping out our life by coupons."

"We do," Maire says, "we do. It's no use sneering. Oh God, was there ever a time when we didn't have to live by cutting out coloured squares of paper like children who never grow up?"

As Gog comes into the house, he sees in a small glass case hung on the wall a charred wooden orb that can only be the morningstar of the giant Gog which he carried home the night the City burned. And the black globe is so split and calcined that even a child would laugh, if it were called a world in play.

XXXV

The three days of summer after the destruction of Hiroshima and before the destruction of Nagasaki by brimstone and fire from a bomber, Gog spends trying to orientate himself in the new found land of his old self. All is familiar and yet strange, all is known and yet alien.

With the return of much of his memory, Gog finds that he has also recovered his powers of analysis. Until now, he has allowed everything to happen to him, whether dream or action. He has been merely a man in a landscape of fantasy or fact, part of the whole scene and its events, undifferentiated. He has had to choose nothing, for he has thought of no experience on which to base a choice. He has had to initiate nothing, except when driven by instinctive needs for food and drink and warmth and sometimes sex. He has merely reacted to the events and people which he has met, reacted unconsciously and blamelessly as a savage or a child. But now that some of the knowledge and some of the drives in him are explicable, now that he begins to understand his family and his researches and his old way of doing and living, Gog can judge his present feelings and actions on the basis of some past ones. His spontaneity has gone, his knowledge of causes and consequences come. He is no longer an Adam innocent and wild in the garden of Albion. He has eaten of the fruit of the tree of good and evil and he is George Griffin Esquire in London.

This power of analysis over himself and his surroundings leads to Gog's alienation from his world. On his journey, he did not even have to accept. He merely was. He had one simple purpose, to get to London. Now he has got there, he is like the millions of soldiers thrown out of the set rules of the army into an aimless civilian society where they must make their own rules and put down roots again, if they can. And Gog cannot. Hampstead seems to him no more than another temporary resting-place on his journey. For long as he has travelled, he still knows too little of himself or his life or his country. He has just set foot on the road, and already he seems to have arrived.

In the place which he apparently owns by deed and purchase, he is both a native and a visitor. He recognizes only to feel apart. Mishkin, the porcupine cat, lies in wait on the tops of doors or on the branches of trees, in order to leap on Gog's back with all twenty claws extended, yowling with simultaneous welcome and enmity. When Gog pulls Mishkin off his back and strokes its fur, the cat first purrs in ecstasy at its friend's love, then bites him for being a stranger. When the coast is clear of cats, Gog walks down a path through a rose garden, sure without looking that the tenth trellis will be set a little out of line with the rest; yet the white and red and orange and pink roses spreading out their shavings of lips stir him as if he had never before seen a rose. Before he turns the corner of the road outside the front gate, he is certain that he will see the Dick Turpin set back, black-beamed and white-plastered in its pub yard with the highwayman astride his black horse riding the painted sign on its gibbet and chain; yet he creeps into the dark public bar as if he were a foreigner and had never set eyes before on the curious and loved segregations of the English class system, public bar and private bar and ladies' bar and saloon bar, divided off from each other by leaded glass and wooden partitions, linked together by the vast mahogany horseshoe of the counter itself. He skulks by the walls of streets with names he can rattle off without reading the name-plate. He shies from the greetings of neighbours, avoids their houses as though these were enemy strongpoints, ducks welcomes like grenades, and feels solitary in a gathering of locals. When they ask him as they all do, "Glad to be home?" he shrugs as if the question had no mark.

Even in his own property, Gog cannot believe that anything is his. The overgrown lawn, the gardens for vegetables and flowers, the apple orchard, the tennis court, the greenhouse built like a miniature Crystal Palace, surely nature is taking them back from him, pushing up her long grasses and weeds to bind and garrotte these hopeless efforts of gardeners to contain her, gardeners all gone away to war, some to die and be buried and rejoin nature herself. The house, rambling in red brick and green with ivy, has too many rooms for one man. How Maire has managed to keep such a barracks from being requisitioned and packed with refugees, Gog does not know. But empty the whole place is, except for the suite that Jules-Julia occupies to the west, and Gog cannot even recognize the furniture in the empty rooms because of the dust-covers that cocoon them like six-pounders shrouded against the rain.

Maire has to be discovered again. Gog finds her contradictory and unpredictable, sometimes a termagant and sometimes a child, full of guile but given to sudden asides of trust, menacing only to provoke declarations of love, determined on her own way except when she feels like clinging, able to do anything as long as her concentration lasts, needing society and smart friends yet sacrificing them all to silence with Gog, ready to start for Timbuctoo now as long as she can turn back tomorrow, lying all the time except when the truth is funnier, teasing continually yet butter-soft if there is retaliation, sensual to the point of folly but disengaged from the consequences of any passing act. In bed with Maire, Gog becomes her sexual slave again, his fingers itching for the nap of her skin, his belly crawling at the touch of her breasts. Yet outside the bedroom, Gog can treat her in an amused and tolerant way, making her angry by his patronage and detachment. "You were never like this before the war," she storms, and Gog can believe her. Five years of worrying about little more than his own survival have given him an absorption with himself that does not allow for the total concentration upon another, which passes under the name of passion.

The new Gog's almost excessive awareness of his every thought and every action leads to a form of paralysis of will, in which he is so passive that his acceptance of the plans of others seems almost a form of unselfishness. Yet it is an indifference, an unwillingness to engage himself in anything that he has chosen. If this is really his home, if the old roots no longer hold him so that he blows hither and thither on others' whims like a dandelion puff on the winds, then there is no reason why he should stay in Hampstead rather than go elsewhere. He notices Maire artfully talking to him about projects for the future, about moving the rose garden to where the shrubbery is and the shrubbery to the rose garden, about selling some of his investments to buy others; she is trying to make him a servant to his own property in order that the management of what he owns can give him enough of a purpose to get through the days and stay where he is; but as he feels that he can barely hang onto his own body and consciousness, he cannot feel for mere things outside his own skin, which his wife and his society label artificially as *his*.

He supposes that he must work; but Maire tells him that he is too rich to have to do so. And what is he qualified to do? He was a teacher once, but he has forgotten nearly all he knew. The great research project, the History of Gog and Magog from the Beginning of Albion to the End of England, why, there is no trace of that. His study is more like a cell, bare of books, its shelves empty as the gums of old men. When he asks Maire about what happened to his library and his papers, she says, " Surely you remember? Your last leave, you burned them all. I tried to stop you, but you wouldn't listen. You said, What's the use of all this crap about the past? What we need to do when this bloody mess is over is to build a better future. And you burned them. In the bonfire. It took you days. Burning your books, just like the Nazis." Only now that the shelves are bare and the bloody mess of the war is over for Gog, he can only sit in a listless present and cannot imagine a future. The Labour Government, the government of the people, must be planning for that. And what room is there in the bright new England for a middle-aged rich man, who has burned his books so that he cannot even teach, who has forgotten nearly all he knows and is too old to learn new tricks, and who is too tired and disengaged to care about a future that is nothing to him but the repetitions of the aimless moments? When the Army sent Gog home from

Hamburg, it seems to have demobilized his senses along with his body, to have taken his identity away with the disc round his neck, to have removed his personality so thoroughly that he can concentrate on himself twenty-four hours a day and find no one very much.

So Gog sits, pulling out the empty drawers of his desk, so suspiciously empty that Gog is pretty certain Maire has assisted in the incineration of his past and his papers, jealous of the time and the passion which Gog once spent away from her on his obsessive grubbings after the ancient and the forgotten and the lost. Yet two reminders survive. Gog finds slipped down the back of the top drawer a chapter of his research, and a curious coloured print of a man riding a sea-monster, entitled *Gog's Map* or *A Caricature of Albion*. Gog sees that the print is actually a map of England and Wales. The north of England is the head of a countryman under a blue bonnet, the midlands are his brown belly, Wales is his blue cloak blowing behind him. But the southland, the greedy southland, is a green scaly fish with a huge mouth and fangs that are the Thames estuary, swallowing all into the red maw of London. Red also is the bobble on rural Albion's boot astride the fish, red the folds of his cloak in South Wales, red his arm holding a beermug with shoulder on Mersey and hand on Humber, and red the tassel on his bonnet by Tyne. Red London has set Portsmouth and Cardiff and Liverpool and Manchester and Birmingham and Sheffield and Newcastle to work in the red factories for the red money that is swallowed up again by the red mouth of the Thames. And all the brain of the north and the guts of the midlands and the freedom of Wales must be carried willy-nilly on the stickleback of the greedy fish that devours the sea and all that therein is.

Gog amuses himself by tracing the route of his journey in the Caricature of Albion; by foot from the tassel tip at Edinburgh to the bonnet's rim at Durham; by car down the edge of Albion's face to the corner of his mouth; by foot again over the moors of his beard into the mug at York; then by ambulance all the way down to the monster fish's arse-hole at Totnes; and then the final trudge along the body of the fish from Glastonbury to Brighton by way of Albion's ankle, until Gog also is swallowed up in the red gullet of London.

The second reminder of Gog's pre-war work is the last surviving fragment of his research. He would not know that he had composed the sentences, but that the written corrections on the typescript appear to come from his hand. He reads the piece as if it were by some strange author picked up in a second-hand store, a collection of paragraphs that hazard has brought to the reader and that can hardly be relevant to him in any way.

The typescript is headed, *Translation from a Local Chronicle, Which Tells of the Old Use of Hampstead Heath.*

It reads as follows:

For two days and two nights, the Romans link their shields between the columns of the temple to the false god-emperor, Claudius, those massy columns of stone that British slaves have hauled from the holds of ships in the harbour, and we come on them out of the town in flames, for the Druid Myrddin has made Boudicca swear the oath by the oak to burn all. At the end of the second night, the Romans have cast all their javelins with the soft iron shanks that drag down our shields and leave us at the mercy of their short swords. They are croaking with thirst, when I lead the last charge of my brothers of the British tribes. I smite them with my bronze ball big as man's head, studded with spikes on the end of an oaken pole, and I break through the wall of shields between the columns and crush their helmets as if they are clay pots and flail my way within the temple and the Britons pour after me and we put them all, each man and each woman and each child and each beast, yea, even to the mouse at the bottom of the jar of corn, we put them all to the slaughter and spread them with pitch, except those three score captives whom Myrddin reserves for the sacrifice. And we topple those pillars that still stand after the temple is burned, so that there shall be no mark that the Romans ever were, once the grass shall grow again over the ashes.

Outside the ruins, Myrddin orders the building of the Wicker Man. And he is built of osiers fifty feet tall; the pointed branches are plaited and stretch out from his wrists in long fingers of wood. And the captives are herded inside the Wicker Man, standing upon one another and moaning pitifully. And for his head, Boudicca, the widowed Queen, orders that a likeness of my own face shall be painted in blue woad upon the hides of calves; she calls me Gog, the Slayer of the Romans, and bids me mount her chariot at her left hand.

Myrddin has faggots piled about the Wicker Man bearing my image on his face and holding the captives within his body, and Myrddin faces the place where the sun will rise and lights a torch of pine and chants the due prayers with the host drawn up in a circle about him and, as the first edge of the sun shows on the rim of the world, Myrddin puts the torch into the faggots and the flames leap up the osiers and the captives, crying pitifully, are burned in the fire, falling out of the fiery Wicker Man onto the faggots. And when the last cry is mute and the hides that bear my image are consumed, the sun rises in a bronze ball big as a man's fist, studded with the spikes that are its rays. And Myrddin eats of the flesh of the captives, as do the few of the tribe of the Silures who are with us. But I stand beside Boudicca and will not eat of the flesh of men.

Boudicca prepares to climb upon her chariot to address the host of her warriors. First, she praises the gods for the victory, particularly Andrasta, Goddess of death and birth, sacred to women. Then Myrddin whispers in her ear and gives her a moving pouch, which she hides between her breasts beneath her cloak, clasped by the great cairngorm of the royal house of the Iceni. When she mounts the chariot, her two daughters sit on the shaft at her feet, their heads bowed beneath their red hair, as their mother points with her spear at them and tells of the Roman tax-gatherers who beat the Queen with rods and outraged her daughters so that the tribes have chosen her to lead them and avenge their wrongs. And she brings up Myrddin beside her to speak, Myrddin who also calls for rebellion because Suetonius is gone with the legions to destroy the holy island of

Mona and to slay the Druids and burn the sacred groves. And Myrddin counsels that now is the time to march on London and burn the cursed city, from where the Roman roads stretch out like bands to tether the earth of England and split tribe from tribe so that the Romans may enslave them one by one.

Then I speak, although Boudicca does not call upon me, for I am the mightiest of the Britons in battle. And I counsel that we should march day and night to the west country and meet with the rest of the Silures beyond the Severn river and catch Suetonius as he comes out of the passes of the western mountains. For it is hard to defeat the Romans by pitched battle against their armoured legions; but by stealth and by stratagem, we will destroy them. The British are many and if they fight, they will pick off the invaders one by one; it is the act of a fool to strike the trunk of a tree with his fist, when he may strip off the twigs one by one and break off the roots one by one until the tree withers of its own.

But Myrddin gives a sign to Boudicca and she reaches into the bag between her breasts and looses a hare, sacred to the moon; it twists in fear as it runs through the host of warriors. And Myrddin says that the twistings of the hare are a sign of the Gods that we should march on London; I think the old Druids practised divination for truth, but the new ones for advantage. I do not think that Myrddin means to give Boudicca good counsel in defeating the Romans; he means to draw Suetonius east by massing outside the Roman centre of London, thus saving Mona and the power of the Druids in their sacred groves.

So we march upon London, which Wayland, the smith of the Gods, first built by Thames side; in oak he built it, but the Romans have added stone. And we march to destroy our own city and our own kind; but we are beleaguered by bad omens. The estuary of the Thames turns blood-red and corpses are seen on the shore where no corpses are. Nine ravens fly on the left of us and a single magpie sits on a dead oak tree. We pitch camp, waiting for the omens to favour us. The days pass, with Myrddin forbidding Boudicca to advance. And messengers come, saying that Suetonius has already harried the Druids and the holy island of Mona and its sacred groves with fire and sword, so that they are destroyed utterly, and Suetonius is riding alone with his horsemen to London with all speed. And I counsel that we advance to destroy him as he is cut off from his legions; but Myrddin has cast a spell over Boudicca and she will not move. And I see that Myrddin did not wish to save Mona, but to destroy it, so that he may become the Arch-Druid. He does not wish to meet Suetonius yet in battle, but to sack London, so that he may bind the tribes to him by blood and booty before they meet the Roman army.

Suetonius abandons London, leaving it to the old men and the women and the girls and the children. He takes away its veterans and its garrison to prepare for the final battle. He leaves London to the slaughter so that he may build up the strength of his legions in the north. And I counsel pursuit before he can group his forces, but Boudicca will not heed me. For Myrddin guts the belly of a living goat and in its spilled entrails he sees that through London lies our victory. So we march towards the city on the clay and the marsh, where the Roman roads meet that bind us down and divide our island.

It is not for victory we go to London, but for vengeance. Boudicca cannot forget the rods on her bleeding back and her fouled children, Myrddin cannot forget the burning groves of Mona and the murdered priests. And we scatter the old men at the north gate of London and scale its walls and pass along the straight paved avenues flanked by columns as many as the trees of the forest and there are houses without number which have water beneath their stone floors and marvels beyond counting brought from beyond the sea. And we slay every living thing within the walls, each man and each woman and each child and each beast, yea, even to the worm in the ripening apple, except for the thousand girls and women that Myrddin keeps for sacrifice in the sacred grove of Andrasta on the hill called Hampstead outside the city, that same sacred grove where the sons of Albion were rooted after spawning the first race of the giants that fought with Gogmagog. And when London is empty but for the dead and when blood flows beneath the stone floors of the houses instead of water, we take up the booty and pile it outside the walls before Boudicca and Myrddin, copper and bronze and tin and iron and silver and gold, hide and cloth and silk and amber, beakers curiously forged and harness fit for the chariot of the sun, so cunningly is it worked, and corn and wine beyond measure. And Myrddin orders the city to be burned in vengeance for Mona, and we fire London. As the smoke rises in a great cloud of jet, we leave the city. And Boudicca shares out the booty among the tribes, with Myrddin advising her and blessing it so that the Gods shall not curse it for being denied to them. But it is borrowed booty; we never deny the Gods but for an hour.

At sunset Myrddin leads us up to the sacred grove for the sacrifice of the thousand captives, and from the hill called Hampstead I see the city below us glowing here and there in the night, as black and fiery as Annwfn beneath the world, where the flames burn on the great nothingness of molten pitch, where noon is as dark as midnight, and where we begin and where we end. And London's fires die and all is darkness and the red Thames grows cold and my heart is heavy to see this work of folly and destruction, when Suetonius and his army are still to the north.

Pine torches blaze from the branches of the trees, as the tribes drink and feast. And within the sacred grove itself Myrddin and his myrmidons sacrifice the women and the girls to Andrasta. The screaming of the victims is like swine flogged to death to make their flesh soft; but many of these victims are Britons, even if they lived with the Romans, slaves who had no will of their own. And Boudicca stands at my side and pleads with me, 'Gog, the Slayer of the Romans, be not angry. We do as we must do, we follow the laws of the Gods and the Druids. So did our fathers and our fathers' fathers, when they drove away Caesar. The Gods have given us two victories and they ask for their sacrifice, especially Andrasta, Goddess of death and birth, sacred to women.'

Boudicca bids me walk with her through the sacred grove, where the women would groan from the oaken stakes which impale them between their legs, but that Myrddin has had their breasts sliced off and sewn in their mouths. And I say, 'Boudicca, these are woman as you are. Did the Roman tax-gatherers do this to you and your daughters? Are not rods and rape better than the stake and the sword? Are we worse than the axe of the Romans?' And Boudicca says, 'What is is. As the Gods will.' And she is pale beneath her red hair and she vomits behind a bush.

So we come upon Myrddin, prophesying from the entrails of a living girl, slit open and tethered. And some women are hanged from the oak branches by the legs and some are cut by the spear and some are scorched by the ember and their screaming makes me grind my fists in my ears. And Myrddin has changed the commandments and has given some of the young girls to the warriors; they lie moaning with men about them as bees. And I reproach Myrddin, 'Will Andrasta never be satisfied?' And he turns to me, the blood falling down the long nails on his fingers as the gutted girl moans at his feet, 'Not until every Roman and friend of the Romans is dead on this island. The entrails say that we should sack Verulam.' And I say, 'More fire, more slaughter, while Suetonius gathers his army? You want vengeance, Myrddin, vengeance without victory.' And Myrddin looks at the entrails of the girl and says, 'This is the way to victory, Gog, the Slayer of the Romans. Shall any Briton who has been here ever be forgiven? What we do to the Romans will be done to us, if we lose. So we shall win and shall be ruled under the laws of the Gods and their servants, the Druids.' And I say, 'But these are not Romans, these are Britons.'

I look down at the gutted girl and I know her; the Romans

took her six years before as a slave when they came to get their taxes. And she moans, dying, and I take my sword and I slay her. And Myrddin threatens me, saying, 'You defy the Gods?' And I say, 'No, you defy the Gods. Your rule is murder and by murder you shall die.' And I raise my sword to slay him, but Boudicca holds my arm. 'Gog, shall you be an outlaw, with all men's hands turned against you? When you slay a Druid, there is no forgiveness, only wandering in torment until the beasts kill you.' And I lower my sword and I say, 'Boudicca, he is a false Druid and against the people.' And Myrddin smiles and commands the great horn with the boar's mouth to be blown and the warriors assembled. And he greets the leaders of the tribes and asks them and their hosts whether they are content with the rule of Boudicca and himself, and they are drunk on wine and rape and blood and booty, and they clatter their spears on their shields. And Myrddin puts a laurel wreath on my hair, mocking me and calling me Gog, the Champion of the Romans.

So we leave the sacred grove on the hill called Hampstead, we leave it a graveyard of women for the fanged Andrasta. Behind us is the black city of London in its acres of ashes with the Thames winding through. And we march on Verulam and we burn and we slaughter there. And we delay for another sacrifice and I know that the Gods are angry against us. For they have allowed Mona to perish and a false priest to make us butchers, to bind us by blood to the vengeance which must come.

Suetonius gathers his army in the north and we come upon him at last. He is a brave leader and he stands his men with their backs to the forest so that they cannot flee; a plain lies before them sloping down to our host. And we draw up our carts behind us, for our women to watch the victory. And we are as the sea in numbers and the Romans as mere rocks; we are as the clouds and the Romans as mere mountains; we are as the sands and the Romans as mere cliffs. And we charge up the slope in our hundreds of thousands against the line of the legions. But the javelins come down upon us as death from the heavens and drag our shields to the ground and the legions drive forwards and break us as an iron ram and we are cut in two and caught between the Romans and the carts and we are slaughtered in our thousands and our tens of thousands, until our piles of corpses even outnumber those we slew in the three cities. And the Romans spare no man and no woman and no living thing, yea, down to the little dog that runs at Boudicca's feet. And Boudicca flees, with the poison ready in the hollow of her cairngorm broach. And Myrddin flees, for what priest will stand in the battle-line if he can fall down to Annwfn from his bed? And I fight with my back to a cart, swinging my bronze ball big as a man's fist, studded with spikes, until the Roman dead are about me in a wall high enough to defend me. But the Romans throw in their darts until I bleed in thirty places and I sink to my knees, dying, as the standard of the XIV Legion bears down upon me, borne up by a centurion holding a painted shield, bearing the device of a red eagle in flight and from each wingtip hangs down a flail . . .

When Gog has finished reading the typed pages, he does not know whether he has been looking at the translation of a chronicle or part of a historical novel or a mixture of the two. There is nothing to show the source of the piece, whether it came direct from the inspiration of the pre-war Gog or whether it was a free rendering of some ancient manuscript, still surviving or destroyed by bombing. If he has invented it himself years ago, Gog is startled by his old preoccupations with slaughter and torture and war. Perhaps only in peace could he allow himself to depict the horrors which the human species reserves for its quarrels. Yet if the account is true ancient history, Gog can only feel that all wars are the same. An eye-witness has told him of the liberation of Belsen and the permanent enslavement of the liberators to the nightmares of their memory. Belsen will have its chroniclers, but Gog knows now that he is too weak to be one of them. How could he ever have chosen to translate such brutality from any source?

The piece is about a hero called Gog. True. But then, if it is so aptly about Gog, surely it is spurious. Granted, there is enough circumstantial historical detail, presumably correct, to convince the unwary that it is indeed a translation. *Ergo*, it is only a translation to the printed page of the ragbag of Gog's pre-war mind, his fascination with the people and his knowledge of the bloodiness of the mob, his hatred of the cruelty of power and his vainglory that he could use his own powers for the people without corruption. So Gog's new processes of logic speak, but they give him no answers, merely new questions. Why did he once spend years hunting down these stories of the people's revolts against London, unless he himself was in revolt, a leader without a following, a searcher in the butcher's shop of history and of the imagination for the dreams of glory that he would never dare to make fact?

Of all the evidences of the past that Gog has met in his journey, only the story of Boudicca in Hampstead's Grove remains in his hand. The rest, oh the rest, that is at the mercy of memory and memory must err. Gog sits at his empty desk by his empty shelves, looking out over the few safe trees that make Hampstead Heath now into a park for the people, he sits and looks out over a great city that is soon to be at peace and to rebuild for the third time its ruins and its errors and its power over Britain. He is no longer angry at the prospect, even if he does not welcome it. He is merely indifferent. For he knows that the city will rebuild itself despite him and without him. He can neither cause its destruction nor its flowering. If he spent all his money, he might be able to restore or knock down a whole street. But what is a whole street in a warren of avenues and roads and closes and squares and crescents and mews and dead ends?

So Gog looks at the nine pages of typescript in his hand that he cannot remember having written. He wonders whether this is ballast enough to keep him steady through his future voyage. Can he recreate on the evidence of these nine pages the obsessions that allowed him to live unaware through the overcast years of the rise of Mussolini and Hitler and Stalin and Franco? Were not these obsessions with the mythical *people* a denial of living persons? Was not this concentration on proving himself a populist hero on the page an excuse not to have to prove himself a mere man dying perhaps a coward's death for the Republic in Spain? They also serve who only stay home and write. Perhaps. But they serve best who work or fight as men among men.

So Gog walks out with his nine pages to the bonfire in the garden. He puts a match to each page in turn, holding it until the flames lick at his fingers, then he drops it onto the ashes until all but the corners of the pages, a few nondescript words, have been consumed. Gog remembers too little of his old self to return to his preoccupations. Even if he remembers just enough of the past to know that he may never escape it, yet he does not remember enough to know how to relive it. For all his concentration on himself, he may not know what sort of a man he is. Only future and repeated actions can prove his characteristics to himself. He cannot go back, he is too listless to go forward. So he condemns himself to the extended present. He waits for an elastic time of waiting.

Two events put an end to this drift in Gog's life at Hampstead, this dragging of the sea-anchor that touches no bottom. The Americans drop a second atom bomb on Nagasaki, thus fulfilling the prophecy of the Bagman and making the fourth and final burning of London imminent, unless the B.B.C. is made over to Wayland Merlin Blake Smith. And Gog's half-brother, Magnus, invites Gog to lunch in the City five days after the dropping of the bomb and the last warning before the end of the world.

XXXVI

The chophouse in the City has seen better days. Old wood adds dark splendour with time and labour; but where the cuffs and elbows of the customers have not rubbed the tables into a deep gloss, scars and roughness in the wooden surfaces show the absence of polish and servants. The wine-coloured leather of the cushions on the seats of the benches in the alcoves is worn through to brown underlining and even to coils of horsehair. The brass of the old carriage-lamps is green with decay, their glass is often cracked. The prints of coaching scenes on the walls collect more dust on their frames than the passengers of the Brighton Flyer ever did from the summer road. The long horn hanging on the putty-coloured walls, once creamy-bright, is almost black with the breath of disuse. There is one old boxing-print, too, that stirs Gog's memories back to the reading of his boyhood and the remembering on his road; Tom Cribb stands left arm forward and shoulders steady to meet the onrush of the mighty blackamoor Molineaux, while the Fancy and the dandies gamble about the Ring. An advertising model of a Regency buck striding along for the sake of elegance and Johnny Walker has lost his stick and both hands, war-wounded under his wrists of white china. Even the cutlery on the table is weary of jabbing too long into tough game; the prongs of the forks are bent and the edges of the knives are barely sharp enough to cut water. The one starched napkin in front of Gog, whiter than the dreams of nuns and folded carefully into the shape of a swan's body, only serves to accentuate the shabby-genteel squalor of the remainder of the room, where Gog sits waiting for his half-brother Magnus.

There is no one in the room, except for Gog and the waiter, who replies to every request for a different form of drink or food with the remarks, " We're out of stock, sir . . . Before the war, sir . . . What with rationing, sir . . . Sir? Sir? *Sir*! !" He is both deferential and condescending, with all the lordly humility of the wise underling, who, but for the grace and hierarchy of God, would be sitting in the place of Gog with enough inside knowledge to get exactly what he wanted. But Gog does not know what is hidden under the counter or in the cellar, so all he can do is to order nearly the whole length of the immense wine list in front of him and end with a weak beer, home-brewed and fit only for home consumption.

When Magnus comes in through the door, he is so much what

Gog expects that Gog can hardly believe such a parody of memory to be flesh and blood. All the shortage of clothing and cosmetics in London has not stopped Magnus from wearing a bowler hat as furry as the rump of a badger, a suit matte with newness, a white stiff collar with points sharp and untrimmed, a silk tie aslant with bars of garish and distinguished old school colours, and black shoes patent-fresh and fit to squeak, if their leather had not been stripped off the more aristocratic and infant of beasts. Under the bowler's rim the face of Magnus is another version of Gog's own, refined to the point of absurdity by the crucible of genes. Both have long chins and large noses; but the chin and nose of Magnus have been pinched in, not squashed broad. Gog's full mouth is compressed in him into a rosebud pout with two thorns at the edges. The heaviness of Gog's brows and forehead becomes a narrow protuberance of skull, which distends the skin so much that the pallor of the bone is visible. The eyebrows and lids of Magnus seem to be lifted in permanent surprise, as though both of his cheeks are caught in an invisible vice which squeezes the eyes back into their sockets and the features forward and upward in points of extension. Only Magnus's metallic helmet of greased yellow hair fails to remind Gog of a pinched version of himself, become a lank weed that nature forces to grow artificially high in its search for the light.

Magnus gives his hat and umbrella to the waiter, who bows to see such a patron. "My dear George," Magnus says, coming forwards. "What an age!" Gog does not know whether Magnus is referring to the long time since they have met or the bad time which they both endure. So he parrots, "What an age," as his half-brother sits opposite him.

"There's no need to drink that bog water," Magnus says, looking with distaste at Gog's glass of beer. "Surely I can arrange something better. Waiter, two doubles from the Black and White you keep for me. And rare steak and *haricots verts*. Green beans." The waiter notes the order, too overawed to say no, as though Magnus alone had the power to call forth good food from dearth and rationing. "You'll have the same, George, I hope?" Gog nods.

"There's not much choice, but at least, they know me here,

and I've always had a *faiblesse* for English cooking at its simplest and least execrable. And *sauce moutarde*, mustard sauce. I shouldn't have to translate, I know, but no one seems able to speak French any more, even the waiters. The war may have encouraged the biggest foreign invasion since the Normans, but paradoxically, it seems to have made us more irredeemably and rightly insular than ever."

Gog looks at the ageless face of his young half-brother, assured and prattling in his decisive tone. There are no wrinkles on Magnus's pointed face except for three lines on his forehead, the one place where significant furrows give the illusion of thought.

"*Merci, m'sieu,*" the waiter says in the voice of an aggrieved Parisian and stalks away, while Magnus gives a delighted chuckle at his back. "Why, those are the only two words he knows, and he simply had to show them off. Adorable!"

Gog cringes inside, as he always does when a diner dares to insult a waiter because he knows that he has bought the privilege to do so and can redeem a meal of insults with one coin too many in the tip. "What sort of war did you have, Magnus?" Gog asks. "Adorable, too?"

"Slightly more useful than yours, I imagine," Magnus says with some asperity, answering Gog's tone of irony. "Without organization, this country would have collapsed in 'forty. Sometimes we had to work night and day, night and day. You couldn't imagine the strain. Ah, the whiskies."

As the waiter puts down the drinks, Gog feels his nerves leap like fishes at the arrogance of Magnus's voice, at his assumption that the soldiers have done damn all except sun-bathe on the turrets of their tanks. But Gog controls himself, takes the whisky, downs it in one gulp, and says, "Another, please. Prove you're the Great Organizer."

"Another," Magnus says to the waiter, and as the waiter opens his mouth to protest, Magnus strikes him dumb by adding, "My friends in the Ministry suggest that the black market may even extend to places *we* patronize. Impossible, I say. There can be no investigation while *I* still patronize a restaurant."

The waiter goes off, and as he goes, Gog says, "Bring the bottle, while you're about it, *m'sieu*. We have to celebrate, my *brother* and I."

Magnus looks furious and puts a thin finger to his lips. "Must you?" he hisses. "In *public*. You know I hate any reference . . ."

"Why worry if you're a bastard," Gog says, "if you are?"

"Will you be quiet?" Magnus commands in a whisper. "Quiet, I said. Or I shall leave. At once."

"What does it matter, Magnus? I mean, only one thing matters now. The war's over and you're alive. Lots of people aren't."

"There are such things as decency," Magnus says. "Of course, my origins don't matter. This is a classless age, under our *present* government. In fact, I shall probably reveal my origins at the right time, if my antecedents seem to be a little too elegant for some of the hobbledehoy Ministers we find nowadays. I believe both Keir Hardie and Ramsay Macdonald were illegitimate; it's quite a tradition for leaders of the Labour Party. But I will not have you maliciously spreading it around to all and sundry. There are truths which all should know and truths which only some should know and truths which should never be known by more than one."

"Yourself, presumably," Gog says, as the waiter puts down the bottle of whisky on the table and leaves, sniffing. Gog pours Magnus another whisky just as Magnus covers his glass with his hand, so that the alcohol soaks Magnus's kempt nails. "Sorry," Gog says and pours himself half a glass of spirits and takes an explosive gulp, enough to begin the thaw of the cold reason of his mind and the melting of the logical wrath of his present state.

"You seem to have become quite an old soak," Magnus says. "They say that war improves no one. I had hoped you would prove the honourable exception."

"I'm never the exception," Gog says. "I'm the rule. Or at least, I try to be. And you're the ruler." He grins at his little joke. "I saw Mother, you know. She trod on me with a horse."

"Will you be quiet?" Magnus insists. "Walls have ears."

"Poor things. What they must hear."

"It is a figure of speech," Magnus says. "As you well know. A slogan I may take the credit for inventing, although I allowed my superior to take the official credit. More *diplomatique*, you know. I did not ask you here to get nostalgic and drunk about someone who was no real mother to me, but a mere conduit pipe into existence."

"Why did you ask me to lunch, then?"

"Didn't you know?" Magnus says, exaggerating even his air of accentuated surprise. "Maire asked me to see you. To straighten you out, she said. Knowing my influence over you, your envy of me and my career . . ."

Gog opens his mouth, ready to loose a bellow of anger or laughter, but in the end he only gulps. "Envy? You? I couldn't."

"But you always have, my dear George. Ever since the very beginning. Come, you must learn to admit the truth to yourself. You always wanted to get to the top, we all do. You wanted to be known for your intellectual powers. You wanted your place in society. Oh, I know, you liked to think of yourself as a rebel. But we all know what a rebel is, merely a man who wants to join those he rebels against on better terms. The moment you got your inheritance from that unlikely great-aunt of ours, who unfairly left me *nothing* as though I could have chosen the circumstances of my birth . . . the moment, I say, you got the money, you immediately began to behave exactly as I always knew you would. A large house, servants, respectability, a wife."

Gog laughs. "You could hardly call marrying Maire becoming respectable."

Magnus looks at Gog with astonishment and contempt. "What a caddish remark! How could a man speak of his own wife like that? Poor Maire. She really doesn't deserve her fate. She told me you weren't quite yourself, but I hadn't imagined such a vicious lie. Maire's often told me about her mother's family in France, very well-connected in the Bordeaux area . . ."

Here Gog does bellow with laughter. "Not the wine-barons of Bordeaux?" he roars. "Chateau Maire, bottled on the estate? They were really fishmongers."

"Will you stop it, George? I know Maire almost as well as I know you. We really became quite good friends while you were away. And if I had to rely on someone for an objective view of things, I know I couldn't do better than Maire. You were damned lucky a good woman like that agreed to marry you out of pity, to try to save you from your follies. She's often told me how she nearly gave you up when you insisted on keeping your inheritance, because people might think she was marrying you for your money. But she'd given you her word, and she felt she had to keep her promise. You don't meet many like that in these sad times."

"You believe her?" Gog asks, incredulous. "You really believe her, when she's playing the innocent slave of duty?"

"Maire has no motive," Magnus says, "to wish you anything but well. What she tells me of you coincides exactly with what I think of you."

"Doesn't that make you suspicious?" Gog says. "That's when you have to worry about your opinion of somebody, when you find another person agreeing with you too closely. Maire's taking you, Magnus. She's taking you like she's taken me all these years."

"Taken me?" Magnus says, smiling. "Perhaps she has."

The waiter comes back with a wooden trolley. From it he dispenses plates and steaks and meat juice and green beans and a silver sauceboat full of white thick liquid. "And a bottle of Mouton Rothschild," Magnus says. "I know you've only got one bottle left, I've kept account. But this is as good a day to drink it on as any." The waiter goes off, grumbling darkly. "I hope you notice how much I am celebrating your safe return, George. I'm doing you so well you wouldn't know there was a war on."

"There isn't," Gog says. "It's nearly over."

"Oh, yes. I'd forgotten. It's just about finished. Those marvellous bombs. Think of the millions of Allied lives they saved."

"Just like the two little white flowers of St. Francis," Gog says. "Just like two little white flowers blooming up there among the clouds. I wonder if anyone got out. Even Lot got out of Sodom and Gomorrah."

"Well, that's the end of the Yellow Peril," Magnus says. "Occasionally, one was worried. Singapore, you know. A damned bad show."

"I know a man," Gog says, "who swears that London's suddenly going to spring up in a little white flower just like that if you don't build Jerusalem here. And give him the B.B.C. Magnus, you know about all these plans and things. What's the future of London look like? Are you going to let St. Pancras and Kentish Town repose among golden pillars high?"

Magnus looks at Gog with infinite patronage. "My dear George, I did hope that the war would at least cure your exquisite romanticism. Golden pillars high? Highways more likely, skyscrapers, blocks of flats. Of course, we have proposals. And frankly, we can only blame one person for not getting the London we want. Adolph Hitler! If only he'd kept on with his Junkers and V-2's a bit longer, they'd have cleared a lot more land for us. But the trouble with the blitz was, it was so damned inefficient. We wanted open spaces for autobahns, and all we got was a few craters for children's playgrounds. If only they'd knocked us flat like Rotterdam! Mark my words, that'll be the great port of tomorrow, while the Thames docks will carry on slower and slower until they become the mudbank they once were. There's only one way to build for the future, that's on nothing. The Americans always knew that. They own the future because they never had a past to destroy. Let your friend bring about the entire destruction of London, I only wish he would. Then we could get on with doing a proper job of reconstruction, not a patchwork."

The waiter comes back with a webbed bottle of wine and the ritual of serving it is duly performed, the drawing of the cork, the wiping of the neck of the bottle, the laying of a tot in the bottom of the glass, the savoury sip, the nod of the head, the pouring of two glasses full, the cradling of the bottle on its bed of basketwork, the retiring of the waiter.

"If London reverted to the marsh it used to be," Gog says, "what would you build on it? Why start again? Ashes to ashes, marsh to marsh . . ."

"And where else would we run Britain from? And the Empire? You're a sentimentalist, George. You forget half the world is used to looking to these little buildings round these three small bends of a narrow English river. Habit makes them look here. And even if it were only a marsh again, habit would still make them look and expect orders from the marsh. Why do people still look to Rome? Not because of the ruins and the church there. Because of what was there. The strongest power in the world is the newest city on the most ancient site."

While Gog eats his meal and drinks the rest of the bottle of whisky and most of the bottle of wine, Magnus expounds on the London of the future. His voice is so assured that the new city seems almost to exist already, its elevated roads, its sunken garages, its columns of flats, its symbolic green spaces and belts, its shopping centres, its hub of offices and wheel of factories with the railway lines spoking out between them and the radial airports catapulting the aeroplanes round the surface of the globe. Precise as a proposition of Euclid, Magnus rehearses the *Quod Est Demonstrandum* of the New London, the New Troy, the New Jerusalem, a city of vertical and horizontal lines broken only by the arcs of great curves, a metropolis of men communicating without rest or stay, an urban geometry dedicated to movement without end and change without growth.

"Hell," Gog suddenly interrupts. "Hell, hell, hell, hell." The alcohol has dissolved his new and precarious foothold on the ice-floes of logic and analysis. He feels himself washed back, back into the unthinking sea of emotion and unconscious action, from which he first surfaced some weeks before. An ebb sucks at the healed wound on his right temple. The chophouse takes on a seaey motion, with the prints on its walls swirling and the tables bobbing and the napkins choppy as spume. The mouthing face of Magnus becomes as significant and unintelligible as the tolling bell of a strange metal buoy, warning of wreckage ahead but unmentioned on the charts.

"What do you mean hell?" Magnus says. "We won't get Utopia this way, but it'll be damn near it. And it'll be manageable. Run as smooth as a dynamo. We'll have everything. Productivity, efficiency, hygiene."

"Hell," Gog says. "You're making a hell, Magog. That's who you are. Magog."

"Will you stop calling me that? I won't stand for nicknames, even if you will. Magog, indeed! You're the only person who calls me that."

"Well, you are, aren't you? Magog. Whitehall. Running us

all. Shoving us around. Planners. You're right. Adolph didn't do a good job in the blitz. He didn't hit the Ministry of Town and Country Planning."

"An envious heart procures mickle smart, as the peasants say on their Scotch reservations. You and your obsession with Gog and Magog, which I see even the war hasn't cured. *Mon vieux*, don't you realize why you got the obsession in the thirties? The moment you met me first, you saw how much more attractive and intelligent I was than you, the *legitimate* Griffin. So you made yourself out to be some sort of popular hero, which you weren't. And you projected onto me all you secretly desired and hated in yourself, the Faustian drives to power and knowledge, the ability to organize and control. You ransacked and forged history to gild yourself and blacken me, because you couldn't be me. I am the man you want to be, George, young and successful. In me, there is yourself realized. I am the Man of your Gog, your Magog. I am the worst thing that ever happened to you, the person you might have been, had heredity been on your side. What is a successful brother but a walking reminder of your own failure?"

Gog looks at the thin face of his half-brother, the compressed version of his own that seems sharper in mind and tongue and face. And he feels his fists clench under the table in his urge to smash in the mocking caricature of himself that sits opposite him, his reflection in a fairground mirror of warped glass and iron rim.

"Did you ever, Magnus," he says at a tangent, "sleep with a Siamese twin called Rosa?"

"I'm not you," Magnus sneers. "I don't want to figure in your baroque imagination."

"I'm not you, either," Gog says, beginning to rap his knuckles softly on the underside of the table. "If I'd have been you, I'd be dead by now. Suicide. Your success I'd call failure. Power. Power corrupts. You know that. Look at yourself in a mirror. See yourself as I'm seeing you. Top civil servant. You look like the top of a barrel of new beer. The scum rises, you know, to the top."

Magnus puts up one finger in the air. "Waiter," he calls,

" the bill!" He considers Gog, dropping his finger. " I'll tell Maire it's useless trying to straighten you out. I might as well be talking to an ox. You'll find Maire leaving you and then what will you do? You're not really fit for society now, are you? Why don't you go away for a bit, George? To the country you like so much. Take a rest. I'll arrange it. Remember," here Magnus leans forward and lays a consoling hand on Gog's bicep, " everything I do for you is for your own good."

Gog stiffens his forearms under the table and rises suddenly, upsetting the table onto Magnus's lap. The plates slide their greasy juices onto the subtle stripes of Magnus's jacket, the cloth shrouds his hands. " I'm *so* sorry," Gog says, smiling.

A flush makes a sudden rash across Magnus's face, as he starts up, shoving the table to one side with a strength that seems strange, given the habitual languor of his movements. " Moron," he snaps. " You meant that."

" Oh, yes," Gog says. " I did. That's why you envy *me*, don't you, Magog? Because I *do* what you'd love to do. And you daren't. I do it, you daren't." Gog laughs. " I don't care about what people think. So I can do anything I like. Don't you wish you could, Magog?"

The waiter rushes forwards with a napkin and begins rubbing the mess on Magnus's suit, merely scouring the grease more irremediably into the cloth, while Magnus speaks with the clipped and stabbing anger of the English gentleman, who prefers a sword-stick to a club.

" You drunken oaf! I'll have you committed for this. Maire says you're mad, as it is. I'll have you examined by a specialist. Two specialists. And Maire and I, we know you're insane. We'll sign the certificate. A few months in an institution. I think that'll take care of your anti-social behaviour."

" Like this?" Gog says. And he swings his right fist into the rosebud of Magog's mouth. For it is Magog standing there before him, Magog of the nose like the iron blade of a scythe so sharp that his eyes lie far back in their sockets out of fear, Magog of the face both glib and bony, Magog the lord of Mammon and Moloch and Machine, with his servant kneeling in front of him and wiping away the mess from his feast. And Gog sees Magog's lips split on his knuckles and the blood spurt out from Magog's mouth and the body of Magog stagger back and fall against a table. And Gog looks down at his own fist in wonder, and lo, Magog's teeth have scored the back of his hand so that Magog's blood and his mingle and join on his fist, the blood of brothers.

As Magog comes forward, his left duke stuck out in the old boxing stance, as classy as Molineaux versus Cribb in the print on the wall, the waiter rushes at Gog, swatting him with his napkin as if he were a fly. Gog is unsighted, and Magog hits him four times, one-two to the belly, one-two to the face, before Gog can push the waiter back, white tie over tails under a table. And Magog weaves in again, one-two to Gog's left brow, a left and a right that strike and smart and make the lids swell up over the eye into a sudden patch of flesh. But as Magog dances back, his hip catches on the edge of a bench and he is checked, just as Gog swings his right fist into his enemy's body. Magog grunts and bends, but recovers; his flesh is hard with muscle under his dandy airs.

For every time that Gog strikes Magog unsatisfactorily on shoulder or side of the head, Magog dabs through a dozen blows to Gog's vital parts, raising up lumps and bruises, reducing Gog's sight to an oozy blur as if he were squinting through a slit in a tank turret in the rain. Yet Gog's huge advantage in weight and his own good condition from walking or war training makes him wear Magog down. Magog slips and falls once when he strikes Gog, because Gog is rushing at him so fast that the force of his own blow is turned against him. Gog drops his fists and begins to grapple with Magog, to wrestle with him and bend him and twist him and wrench him and knead him and pulp him and rack him, ignoring the blows which Magog rains on his sides and neck. At last, Magog is bent backwards over a table, with one of Gog's hands at his throat and the other confining his wrists in a single manacle. Gog leans forward with his weight to choke Magog; but his enemy does not fight. Magog goes limp, until Gog loosens his grip. Then he smiles and sits up on the table, dusting off his jacket with his hands.

" You can't kill me," Magog says. " You know that. Or you'd swing for it. As it is, you're going in the dock for assault and battery. The first policeman I see will put you in custody."

The alcohol explodes in Gog's boiling blood and he sees Magog's head in front of him become blue as a copper's helmet with a bright crown of hairy metal and he raises both of his clenched fists on high and he brings them down on his enemy, who slips sideways so that Gog dashes his fists onto the table. Then Magog is off and running through the door of the chophouse out into London, where the newsmen are crying, "Victory over Japan, Victory over Japan! End of the War! Read all about it!"

So Gog is off after Magog down the sunny streets, with the drunken people all about him, cheering and waving, off after the dapper dishevelment of his pin-striped quarry, whose lank height puts him head and shoulders above his fellow men. And Gog blunders on implacably in pursuit, cannoning off anyone in his way without so much as a sorry. He sees Magog go to ground in a crowd round a speaker on a box on Tower Hill, disappear by stooping and ducking among the heap of listening human heads.

Short of breath, drunk and dazy in the heat, Gog lumbers into the crowd. The Tower skitters and reels before him, its careful blocks jigging and slipping, its battlements askew. The voice of the speaker, who, who? It's proof, proof at last, the voice of the Pardoner. And there he is, head high and sharp as a splinter under his cockle-shell hat, addressing the people where Magog's gone to ground.

"Pardon, we must ask pardon, ask pardon from the Almighty, what have we done? We have destroyed cities as if we were the Almighty, without so much as a pardon. And we eat and we drink and we're merry, not to say tipsy, because we've won the war. But we haven't asked pardon. Oh yes, killing a Jap's not the same as killing a kraut which is not the same as killing a good fellow Britisher. But all the same, you've got to have pardon. Only three and six, pardons, done up in legal seals, worth it for the sealing wax alone, take you straight to heaven or wherever else you want to go eventually. Buy my pardons, three for ten bob, bargain family offer, don't leave a loved one behind. They're dipped in the holy water of Jordan itself, I went there special by submarine. I'd give 'em away for free, but I'm collecting for our poor blind toiling brothers, the pit ponies, who help to keep us warm o' nights. Pardon me, if you want to celebrate with a clean conscience, you'd better get a pardon for all what you did in the last war. Only another two and six and I'll give you another pardon you can date yourself. Keep it handy, and you'll be absolved from what you do in the next war too . . ."

As the Pardoner patters, Gog searches round among the crowd, ducking into any gap between the pressed bodies, looking for a squatting Magog but finding usually a child and once a dwarf. Then as Gog turns to the Pardoner to ask him if he has seen Magog, there is a heaving on the far side of the mob and Magog bursts out, doubled up and running down into the ruined City towards St. Paul's. And Gog fights his way out of the press, shouting, " Let me be, people, my people. There he goes, Magog. Catch him, catch him." But the crowd looks at him curiously and parts before him and lets him run off, none following.

Then Magog's sprinting down Tower Hill, so off at his heels, heart hammering, lungs gulping, the booze making a blitz on the walls still standing, so they reel and totter and fall thundering down the road. And it's slip on the cobbles, skid, recover. Turn down Thames Street past the pier, with Tower Bridge spearing up its spires, gothic-fantastical. Jog past the Customs House, taxes on the goods of the ages, duties on tobacco and pepper and ambergris, percentages on cinnamon and stinkwood and ladies' brollies, a cut on beaver pelts and whalebone and brass trays from Benares. Pay, pay, ye holds disgorging, pay to the man in blue uniform, pay out your imposts, the left wing of each Muscovy duck, a barrel and a half of sperm oil from Antarctica, half a hogshead from Oporto, the spare ribs of every carcass from Argentina, the stoppers from all the flasks of myrrh from Damascus, corkage on bottled Beaujolais and poundage on Copenhagen butter and tonnage on coals from Newcastle, strip off your sacking, your wrappers, your bindings, expose the entrails of bales and clots of wool and jute veins and hawsers intestinal, watch him pick out the auguries and note the sums to pay in his little blue book, see him peek out the crannies of the packets of poppy dust, the sweet cooked weeds of the orient that waft their takers on cloud and drift to nirvana, c/o Lavender

Wharf, London.

Pant on, blood pounding, feet pumping past Billingsgate, shuttered and reeking, afternoon sleeping. Salt stink of mackerel and cod and herring, who'll come and buy me, eel and flounder and whitebait, a pint for thruppence, shrimps and cockles and whelks big as soft tennis-balls, hangars of boxed catches inside those empty halls, who knows, in half a hundred crates the sections of the Loch Ness monster, only fourpence a fillet, gamey but tasty, maybe a whole mermaid on ice, serve her up with hollandaise and sea-shells on her nipples and an oyster in her navel, more likely find a manatee or a dugong or a dolphin, netted unwary but eaten by necessity, sad sea-flesh in slices from sources unknown, all sending out odours from Davy Jones's Larder big as the Seventh Sea, stinking of brine and the clinging odour of fish blood. Ho, ho, porters and boxers, now afternoon dozing, come and catch Magog, gut him like a herring and tan him like a kipper, gaff him in his belly-button and smoke him like a salmon, pack him in olive oil and can him sardinewise, slice off his blubber and render him for glycerine.

Stop to get breath under the viaduct of the new London Bridge, not fallen down, not fallen down, my fair lady. Magog stops ahead, panting and looking back, ready to run off if Gog moves, ready to gulp air as long as Gog does. All about among the bombsites, warehouses still stand, treasure cliffs, merchandise in its myriads, mountains, Matterhorns. Behind the walls high as China, citadels of goodies, counties of fleeces fit to wrap the ice caps in and melt the floes, making a flood lower than the deluge of molasses and treacle swilling out the brick caverns on either Thames' side. See, Magog's off again. Push feet, shove will, on, on.

What's in these canyons of cornucopia? Why, there's matches enough to blaze a bonfire to fry the moon, carpets in intricate patterns to maze the whole metropolis, strings of onions to peel and swamp the universe with God's blubbering, Andes of fat for soap heaving with maggots like Pacific swells, dried bananas in black sticks as if all the world's forests were burned for charcoal, metal Appenines of canned spam, Saharas of dried eggs, Kalaharis of powdered milk, vats of cod liver oil for Britain's bonny babies that would calm a North Sea of troubled waters, distillate of orange from all the groves in Florida, tea-leaves like plagues of ants in every nook and crack, sponges to dry up the Pool of London and not even be moist, argosies of turkish delight, cargoes of prunes, merchantmen of candied peel, convoys of marzipan . . . all to be consumed, consumed, consumed utterly and turned to sewage to wash away down the river that floated the fleets of Eldorados into its wharves.

But pound, pound down the pavements, under the railway bridge, trains hammering and roaring overhead, skull reverberate with their iron fuss, blood jangling with booze, bells clanging with peace come, sweet peace, now run sweet peace in peals of iron clappers, on after Magog, how can we have peace if Magog still rules, Magog high as the Monument, high as the high bowler of St. Paul's rising above the ruins just as Magog's yellow-metal skull rises above his dirty dandy suiting?

Turn up Bread Street Hill after the quarry. Breaths sharp as lances in the lungs. Stop and puff. Watch Magog duck his head between his knees to net air. There'll be no bread for you, my people, no bread except in coupons, in rations, in toil and sweat and labour, unless Magog's got his skull stove in on the gutters of the hill, unless we're blitzing in that round crown of power that sits on the cathedral of the shoulders of authority. So jog onwards up the hill, catch him bending before you, boot his arse forwards, strike at his shoulder-blades going away, so he turns in a fury, lashes back and stops you, then darts off up Bread Street Hill, as though he didn't always eat cake.

So Gog pursues Magog through the City in a running fight, coming up on him to hit him, briefly ding-dong ding-dong at each other like the church bells pealing victory, but all is ruin now, rubble and wrack of spire and office, boarded windows and tarpaulins over the doors, slug Magog with a haymaker, then gasp as his one-two thuds in your short ribs and he's off again, run, run, never catch him, no breath left, stitch in the side, stop and pant, see him halt ten yards ahead, watch each other, move and he moves, so we go through the shattered City with the bells pealing victory, so we go on to St. Paul's clanging out peacetime, so we go with Magog parted from his avenging shadow by ten yards, so we play tag through the streets never further never closer, ten yards between us, Magog dogged by Gog through the victorious people and the victorious ruins, only the great bowler of St. Paul's looming above the wasteland of fallen brick and fallen stone.

And it's down Ludgate Hill past the boozers and the singers and the yellers and the cheerers, crying peace on earth and good-will for all men, but Magog's still in front, power rampant and elusive, power to ground you down and blow you up, power to sweat you and beat you, power to thread your muscles into wet strings and scoop out your brains like egg-yolks. Kill that power, kill him, kill Magog, as he's under the railway bridge, looking, looking for a bobby, blue helmet and big boots. But anarchy's ablaze today, city on riot, roisterers and revellers, even the coppers dead drunk in the pubs, and there's no one to save Ma-gog as Gog clumps along after him, past the beery glass doors of the King Ludd, oh, you rebuilt the first Ludd's Town that's now corrupt to London, you girdled it round with towers innumer-able, making the citizens build stone houses full of silks and satins, that no other city should have fairer palaces within. Good King Ludd, old King Ludd, step down from your pub sign and clock Magog with your mace, bash in his slick hair till the blood runs out of his ear-drums. He wants to pull down your alleys and terraces and byways, he wants to gridiron your crazy quilt of a city and make it into barren arteries of commerce. Clobber him, good King Ludd, drop your board on his brainpan. Sweet King, hear your faithful Gog, always your liege servant for the past and preservation.

But Magog's across Ludgate Circus up Fleet Street, with the presses and the afternoon editions pounding out their lies and vans about him, pulping out their propaganda about peace for ever, no more war now, *Britain Wins War*, *Cock of the Walk and the World*, *Who'll Dare Tweak The Lion's Tail Now*, *Empire for Ever*. No, no, can't you see, it's either peace or power. Which will you have, Britannia? Throw in your trident, give up the seven seas for your puddle? Then you'll have the shield of security, who'd want such an isolated little island? So throw your type out at Magog, feed him into the flatbeds, stamp him with letters, use his blood as ink and bring out a new edition, *Magog Is Dead, Loud Sing Halleluia, Peace On Earth, Empire Ended, Each To His Own Back Garden, To Hell With Whitehall, To Heaven With Us All.*

But the newsvendors and the passers-by let Magog through, they don't lynch him, and Gog must pound on, till, sudden as a flicker, Magog whisks through a narrow entrance off the Strand just short of the Aldwych, nicks into a slit between offices that holds only a black door and a red light. And as Gog pursues him, the door opens and Magog's in and Gog just gets his foot in the jamb and shoves against the door closing, shoves and strains and heaves, till the door opens suddenly and Gog falls into a hallway on hands and knees.

Darkness with spots of fire. Slow stealth of seeing. Light creeping like a beggar into eyes. Gold blur. Gold shape becoming twin giant standing bombcases, joined at the side, fit for a squadron of Halifaxes to drop and disintegrate the moon. The interiors of each shell-case are scraped out. On two large wireless sets winking with red and white and green valves sit a girl, painted all over with silver except for her breasts, and a boy, painted all over with gold except for his genitals. As Gog rises to his feet before them, the girl says, " Which way, cock?" and Gog says, " Magog, which way did he go?" And the boy says disgustedly, " Bints again." And the girl points to a curtained alcove to the right and presses a button beside her, which causes a small mine to explode under Gog's feet and sends him scampering for cover through the alcove into the den of the Fat Girl.

Her room is fitted out like the cockpit of a vast bomber. Past the plexiglass windows, clouds elevating nude girl angels served by terrible priapic red imps float by in front of a duck-egg sky. Through the glass floor, an aerial view of London, from which tiny flames and puffs of smoke erupt and cut-out model buildings collapse and spring up again in an endless whirligig of destruction and reconstruction. Stuck onto various houses are pins holding up coloured flags to mark the peculiarities of the occupants. Here in Belgravia, MR QLP – WHIPS/PINPOINT HEELS; in Chelsea, MRS RFL – SAILORS/SPADES WITH GOATEES; in Soho, MR AAS – RAPE/THIN WITH DUMB

SCREAMS; in Pimlico, MISS HUP – SCHOOLGIRLS/SLIPS & CANES. The vices of London are each pin-pointed and docketed for blasting with brimstone and fire from the heavenly brothel, so that a glance serves to locate the target of a client's tastes and deviations for instant annihilation. Sitting before a gigantic dashboard of dials and wheels and levers, the Fat Girl billows out of a tight black leather flying-suit that cuddles each ounce of her overflow as lovingly as the hide covers a plump hippopotamus. And as Gog watches, she shouts, " 'Old on tight, me 'earties, loop t' loop, double jelly roll." And she pulls and wiggles a giant metal phallus labelled *Joystick*.

Immediately, the metal walls shake and shiver and shudder, some making revolutions like huge tin drums for blasting pop-corn. The air is howling and screeching and shrieking with pain and ecstasy. Thunderous detonations go *crrrp, crrrt, crrrk* over the loudspeakers. Gelignite by the ton blasts beneath Gog's lobes. In front of the cockpit, a film begins whirring like a propeller, a film taken from the nose of a diving Stuka. The earth hurtles towards Gog horrendously and horizontally, then at the last moment before crash it is stripped off as if peeled aside in débris and black fume. Gog feels his stomach lurch and heave and, dammit, yes, a foul itching of nervous desire begins to pluck at his groin. The cockpit steadies as the Fat Girl pulls the *Joystick* back to the level and the crescendo of bombardment and sexual appetite whimpers down to a distant bang or grunt. A girl enters, clad in spotless white dungarees cut away at each breast and at the crotch. The Fat Girl looks at her watch. " 'Alf after three, Laureen," she says, " time ter goo in Noomber Seven. 'E like boonk service. An' doant leave yer 'orsetail." The girl switches a hairy whip and goes off to one of the nine tin doors set into the walls; this one is marked *Fuselage 7*. As she yanks open the door and walks in without warning, Gog reads on the back of her white dungarees *Air Crew 3*.

" Well, well," says the Fat Girl turning to Gog, her loamy vowels already sharpened by a cockney whine, " if it ain't ole Goggie. 'Ow's yer keepin', luv? Oop in smoke fer long? Got all kinky after blitz, too? Theer's lots that way noo. They've got ter 'ave it sceery, like. Ain't t' same, reely, 'avin' a scroo noo without block-buster or V-2 breathin' fire doon yer arse. So Crookie an' Rosy 'ave blitz service ten time a night. 'Ave our aerothrills an' yer spills it, or yer mooney back. T 'appy direct 'it. Yer can be 'igh as kite an' yer doant leave t' ground. No vertigo in our gogo. But I'll treat yer special, luv. Thousan' bomber raid *an'* rockets. If that doant shift yer, yer better shoot oop shop an' min' t' pigs." She looks at Gog appraisingly, her small eyes glancing and her squashed lips wet as a trodden plum. "Still like 'em ploomp, ducks? 'Ere, I'll see if Crookie can tek a breather. 'E's workin' overtime these days. Those bloody atom-bombs 'ave got all t' fairies an' nymphos fair crawlin' oop wall, cruisin' fer bruisin' from ole Crookie. 'E used ter say 'e was like Channel, never dry oop. But noo, yer coold chuff off from Dover ter Calaay an' yer woant get yer boots wet."

At that moment, the naked Crook walks out of one of the fuselage doors, slamming it behind him. He is a bent and shaking man, barely recognizable, weary unto death, his yellow hair stuck to his body with sweat, even his rearing cock a limp cod. "Enough, enough," he croaks, "yer ruddy whoar, yer ladyship." He drags himself over to the empty pilot's seat, assisted by the Fat Girl. "Easy do it," she says. "Yer're all in, Crookie. 'Ave a joyride all on yer ownsome noo. Give 'em Bomb-plan Foor. In thirty secs, bomb-doors open an' drop stick of 'undred pounders. In three mins, sirens, searchlights in t' cabins an' ack-ack on theer arses with 'oses. Then give 'em a mo ter say theer prayers, then direct 'it, pull out all stops. An' if that doant mek 'em coom, they're mules. I've got ole choom 'ere 'oo wants reight spot of kip an' blitz. Fer ole times' sake, like. Doan't worry, Goggie, even if 'ouse blows oop, yer'll lan' soft on Rosie. I'm joost simple coontry maiden what all world takes in. 'Appen so, an' then again, 'appen not."

As the Fat Girl pulls Gog towards *Fuselage 6*, Gog sees the exhausted Crook slump against the dashboard and begin pulling at levers and pressing buttons aimlessly and blindly, muttering, "Cows, sods, bitches, queers, they turn me up. They do fair. I'm 'eadin' fer a nunnery, I am. Peace, quiet, an' none of that no more. Get shit of 'em. Apes . . ." The iron door of *Fuselage 6* slams on Crook jerking moodily at the controls, and Gog is left in a small metal cubicle with the Fat Girl unzipping herself from her black flying-suit and saying, " 'Urry, ducks. Oot with it afore bomb drops. Me arse is bigger'n better'n it ever weer before it weer scrimmed off unner that damn gippo caravan. So give 'er a try, Goggie. Chocks away! Okey-pokey, penny a loomp. More yer 'ave, more yer boomp."

But just as the Fat Girl's vast udders appear pulpy as twin pillows stuffed with curds and swing their sludgy and inescapable one-two at Gog to lay him flat on the narrow bunk bolted to the floor behind him, the inferno blasts off. Incendiaries flare from pits in the floor, the metal walls roll and rattle and bump and grind, hidden nozzles squirt out jets of scented water sharp as tracer bullets, a deafening din cataracts to a clattering caterwaul. Gog is flung pell-mell into the pneumatic Fat Girl, then bounces back askew-agley, thumping round the metal walls and ceiling that's now a floor, cannoning into the Fat Girl's tons of wet flesh slopping against him then skidding away, as the whole fuselage rolls over and over in a tail spin without end, then begins to corkscrew and gyrate, while thundering detonations begin splitting the metal sides and make bolts pop out and fly through the air in iron hail. " Christ, 'e can't stoppit. 'E's squetched an' skywannocked us. 'E's pulled t'ole works. 'E's pulled secret switch ter croosh t'lot inter sardine tins, if t'coppers coom in."

It's an abomination of disintegration, a desolation of dislocation, fragments and shrapnel, shards of steel and paint, shreds of flesh and sense ... whores flying by wearing only W.A.A.F. hats and blue murder in their mouths ... clients with paunches flapping, rumps slack with fright, shrieking and moaning ... Her Ladyship in gold garters embossed with coronets, yelling, " My carriage," as she straddles a tail-fin ... Crook spinning round the broken *Joystick* like a teetotum ... smell of sulphur and excrement, fire and ammonia, fume and sweat ... electric wires snaking out red and black nooses to twine around aged nudity and spark it into rigadoons and sarabands and schottisches and polkas of pain ... a dashboard dial smashes through a plexiglass pane and rivets itself into the eyesocket of a putrescent dandy, who glares aghast through his calibrated monocle ... But Magog, where's Magog, gone to ground in *Fuselage X*?

Gog hurtles from door to door with the tin and iron rending about him in squadron wreck and armageddon of armour ... There's rumps and thighs of fat whores, spreadeagled and saddled, red and golden and purple-haired where they shouldn't be ... bishops without gaiters, soldiers without boots, grocers without aprons, even civil servants caught with their striped trews down ... but Magog's got canned and sealed off so completely, he's as invisible as a slice of tuna in a tin without an opener ... Yet only one Fuselage door hasn't been busted and shattered, blown to smithereens and glory by Crook's pulling the switch for the annihilation of evidence which the police can use against him ... *Fuselage 3* still has its door clamped tight as a welded plate ... Then Crook's flailing leg kicks in the last red button and it's Etna and Vesuvius over the whole earth, Dresden and Hiroshima global, Day of Judgement and Night of Inferno ... Welling heat, molten metal, pea-soup gas, burning blindness ...

And Gog feels the Fat Girl yank him by the arm, pull him down through a trap into the cool bowels of *terra firma*, whispering hoarsely, " We'll get shit of it ... T' last kick, when yer cock's conked oot, a good shit ... T'toobe, floosh yer toobe daily ... Get yer toobe reight an' yer'll walk on air oop top." Gog is made to crawl on hands and knees through a dark dripping passage, stinking with acrid damp and reeking with soft droppings, until suddenly he's jerked upright and squashed against a mass of bodies, he's packed closer and closer, the blubbery give of the Fat Girl squeezed up behind him as she's pressed thin by the other clients and whores shoving in behind her, tighter and tighter into the squashed morass of people, yelling, " No more, no more, no more room," but still more and more latecomers pack in, until they're crushed like dates in a sticky-sweet goo in the depths of a hole blacker than Calcutta, darker than the terminus of the journey to the end of the night. Then suddenly the whole glob of humanity begins to shimmy as the floor beneath their feet hums and slithers and lights flicker by at the windows and the Fat Girl whispers, " T' toobe, t' toobe, t' commootin' toobe, direct link from t' aerothrill 'oar'ouse ter B.B.C. Bush 'Ouse, zero line, not on map, unschedooled, t' underground pipe what keeps us regular an' goin' on an' on an' on. All aboord fer radio city, three pips 'ooray, all aboord!"

The mass jammed into the Tube heave and paw and finger each other. By the sporadic lights passing by, Gog can see an old man picking at the nipples of a small nymph, dressed only in a stenographer's pad chained round her neck, try as she will to pull away, she's stuck where she is crammed without mercy, while a jowly brute behind her bites at the nape of her neck and palms her buttocks. "Help," she cries, "help!" but who can move to aid her, while the grinding wheels shriek louder than her thin wails for succour, and the lecherous press melds and mingles in the connubial crush of commutation, fresh food of flesh sucked in every morning to feed the city, evacuated nightly in filth and muck-sweat towards the suburban villas tidy as toilets. Glutton city, orgy porgy offices, fat-farting factories, gulping down humankind for breakfast like eggs and bacon, passing them out in the evening through the *anus mirabilis*, the underground intestines called the Tube, while the winding sewer river Thames buoys up the cargoes of the discharging boats that sail up its flow before ebbing with the excrement of the commuters to the salt-cleansing sea.

As a red light bobs by, Gog sees Magog's skull under its yellow helmet of hair protruding out of the cluttered mob. And with a mighty effort, he jerks up both of his hands out of the rubbing vice that shuts them in between the Fat Girl's belly and a plump dowager's back. And Gog grabs at the high knobs for standers on each side of the tube, and with a ho ho heave ho, he hauls himself up and sprawling out of the sucking quicksand of his species, until he's sprawling beneath the low metal roof of the rushing Tube on a knobbled pool of heads, screaming and cursing and jabbing up at his ribs with thumbs and brollies. But Gog winches himself forward by pulling at the knobs, he swims on the heads of the stewing and sardined people towards Magog, frogging forwards to that hated slick hair and loathly nape of neck, till he gets his hands round Magog's vertebrae and throat, and it's full throttle, grip the ridged muscles of the wind-pipe, as Magog's Adam's apple bobbles and gulps like a ball on a fairground jet, and all shout, "Murder, murder," yet none can free their hands to get at Gog spreadeagled on the heads of the helpless people crammed into the Tube. So Gog begins to choke Magog to death in the great intestinal passage set up between the Strand whorehouse of aerodynamics and the B.B.C. Overseas Service.

Just as Gog is squeezing the last of Magog's breath out of his gullet so that his enemy's tongue stands out like a blue candle between his teeth, the Tube stops with a jolt and a screech and the doors slide open and yellow light streams in and the mob spews sideways, carrying Gog briefly upon its heads, then dropping him as it spreads out. Magog wriggles free of Gog's grip and Gog stumbles to his knees and his hands drop to the underground platform and the commuters surge by rushing on their errands, trampling him indifferently with their millipede boots and shoes, the ten-thousand-toed-tramp of the Tube people getting on time to the City from the private fantasies of orgy they have each in his dark linen brothel at home, tucked up tight when the lights go out. So Gog rises among the bashing legs, he dives after Magog through the throng, he lunges again after Magog ahead, who looks back unseeing, then darts through a recess and a door, marked *Private – Do Not Enter*. But Gog is at his heels, and though the door slams in his face, he bursts it open again and enters.

He finds himself in a corridor leading to corridors leading to corridors in a vast communications centre. Iron pipes carry cables along the ceilings and red lights warn away from studio doors and technicians scurry about, self-important and armed with scratch-pads and screwdrivers. And Gog peers in through the thick soundproof panes set in the doors, peers in after the vanished Magog, lost without trace in the labyrinth of spoken words beamed out night and day as the Voice of England, calling Europe and Africa and Asia and America, contradictory yet self-congratulatory, state-controlled yet independent, oh people paradoxical, how do you manage it? But Magog's gone to earth with the green wire in a control room. So Gog prowls about aimlessly, until he sees through a square pane two familiar faces sitting opposite each other at a table, a microphone between them and the air-waves trembling to carry their syllables to the waiting millions of ears. One face is withered and glossy like a polished pippin, the other sprouts a millrace of white hair about its hook nose. And Gog could cry anger to see Miniver-Cluckitt coldly considering his notebook and he could cry halleluiah to see the Bagman, sitting transfigured with ecstasy by the microphone that rises holy as a chalice, rarer than radium, ready to bellow the Bagman's message to all the wondering flocks of Albion, ready to tell them to build Jerusalem now on the rubble and the warehouses by Thames' side.

And as Gog inches open the soundproofed door to eavesdrop on the interview between the voice of logic and the voice of inspiration, he hears the following words through the crack:

Q. "Your interviewer tonight is Professor Miniver, Professor Emeritus of Dialect at the University of Durham. And sitting with him in the studio is Mr. Wayland Merlin Blake Smith, a most interesting type of vagabond rarely met on the English highways and byways in these days of national emergency. You wouldn't call yourself a tramp, would you, Mr. Smith?"

A. "By their words shall ye know them. You wouldn't call yourself a squit, would you, Professor Miniver?"

Q. (HURRIEDLY) "Yes, yes, yes. Mr. Smith, this is a live recording and perhaps we should stick to the points in hand. As we all know, those that tramp the roads have the reputation of being philosophers, full of wise saws. In my researches, I've met many a fine phrase. (IN DIALECT VOICE) if ifs an' buts weer apples an' nuts, wooldna I fill me guts."

A. "I know a saying, too. There's no getting white meal out of a coal sack. Who's being interviewed, Professor? You or I? O, ye of little wisdom and much education, better that a millstone were tied about your necks and ye were drowned in the depths of the sea than that ye ignore the words of the Almighty spoken through the tongue of His servant, Smith, the prophet of the Lord."

Q. "What was the origin of your religious fixation, Mr. Smith? Psychologically, you appear quite an interesting case."

A. "The Lord came to me on Mona's Ancient Druid Sacred Isle, and He bade me say,

And I am come again in my fourth coming; Smith, the leader

of the Israelites, come to build again Zion.

And Magog is burned down in the accursed city, and Gog, his brother; the wrath of the Lord passeth, as the winter into the summer.

And the Lord saith, how shall I give thee up, Albion? How shall I deliver thee, Israel?

I am come to restore Zion and the temples of Jerusalem; this is my servant Smith, in him I place my trust.

I shall be as the dew unto Israel, if she will hearken unto him;

If she will deliver to him the waves of the air I have given her; if she will deliver to him the transmitters, or be cast into utter darkness . . ."

Q. "Your plagiarism of the Bible is really quite accurate. An inspired . . . *pastiche*! Well, Mr. Smith, you have been given the transmitters for a quarter of an hour in Strange Encounter, our Weekly Rendezvous with Odd Bods and Queer Coves. It's usual now to ask for one of your favourite bits of music to be played for our eager audience. Your choice is the *Messiah*, I presume?"

A. "The trumpet of Gabriel. The brazen voice of the Day of Judgement. Play that, Professor Miniver. And we shall have Jerusalem here at once."

Q. "What recording would you like, Mr. Smith? We have a very nice trumpet voluntary by Purcell. While our records department hunts it up, shall we resume? Time is short . . ."

A. "For us all, Professor. I do not intend to leave the transmitters while I still have breath to repeat the message of the Lord. He has destroyed in the Far East the two cities that I foretold would be an Awful Warning to the abomination and desolation of London, the accursed city. Repent ye, repent ye, in sackcloth and ashes, and give me the airwaves, or ye shall surely be the third city caught up to the flaming heavens by the fiery fist of the Almighty."

Q. "I'm sure the Royal Air Force will take care of *that* problem, Mr. Smith. Anyway, the United States of America is our ally, and no other nation will have the know-how to make atom bombs for decades. We're perfectly safe, Mr. Smith, except in your nightmares. Have you a following at all, people who believe as you do?"

A. " Woe unto them that do not believe the word of the Lord, for they shall perish utterly. Woe ..."
Q. " Yes, yes, but don't you think preaching is best left for the ordained ...?"
A. " Repent ye, London, for Gog is abroad in the land fighting against Magog his brother, and they are the signs and forerunners of the end of the world ..."

Here Gog sees Miniver clutch the microphone towards him and begin talking hurriedly into the metal ear of the machine.

" We cut our programme short here to hear Handel's *Water Music*, played by the Royal Philharmonic ..."

The light of battle transfigures the Bagman's face under the electric bulbs so that his white bush of hair glows with the same yellow light that sparks in his eyes, and he rises from the table, and he wrenches the microphone from Miniver's grasp with one hand, and with the other he slams Miniver's balding crown so that Miniver's face is squashed unconscious against the table. Then the thunderings of the prophet's denunciations are called down from the skies.

" Woe unto you, England, that drove the true religion from these sacred shores, woe unto you, London, that has swallowed up the fatness and the increase and the forests and the meadows of Albion, woe unto you, Magog, who has consumed the men and women and the children of Israel in the grinding mills of your machines, woe unto you, Gog, who has left the ways of the Lord and the people for your own selfish pride and your own selfish wrath, woe unto you, ye nations of the earth, for ye shall be torn asunder ..."

The Bagman suddenly howls with fury and drops the microphone and rushes across the room like a wild ram at a nanny-goat. Gog leans forwards from his eavesdropping to see the Bagman hurl himself through the door leading to the control-room of the studio, which has cut him off the air. Behind the plate-glass window of the control-room, Gog watches the fight between the Bagman and the male technician and the female technician, as if he were watching an underwater film of Tarzan the Elder taking on two Martians somewhere beneath the great grey green greasy Limpopo River all set about with wireless aerials. The

Bagman rips off metal ears that look like headphones, he tears off veins that look like wires, he flays skin that looks like white overalls, he shatters eyes that look like horn-rimmed glasses. When the two Martians are drowning at his feet, he begins pulling switches and turning dials and shouting, yelling, screaming behind the soundless window. The Martians swim off one after the other through the door and scamper away to seek help, while the Bagman barricades himself with a great metal cabinet inside the control-room and plunges into a dementia of manipulation. He yanks out leads and connects them to his armpits, he wreathes microphones round his head like laurel wreaths, he screws valves into his ears and plugs in his lobes, he strips his feet and shoves his toes into cable-sockets, he gathers wires like grasses to festoon about his body and mesh him in tendrils of communications. Then, with his whole flesh connected to the airwaves that will bear his prophecies to the four corners of earth, to all Albion and to all that hear the voice of Albion, the Bagman pulls the master-switch in the control-room. So the regiment of technicians and policemen who rush into the studio at Bush House are just in time to see with Gog the metamorphosis and translation of Wayland Merlin Blake Smith from his fourth incarnation back into the essence of becoming again that is eternal living. From every wire and socket, the blue teeth of electric particles flare and spurt and bite the body of the Bagman into a mad jig of death, a jerking and a blackening and a splaying and a charring and a kicking and a coaling in a frenzy of cremation. Before Gog's eyes, the Bagman is turned by the fiery waves of the air from a body howling dumbly in the ears of all mankind, he is turned to the effigy in ashes that will be the doom of all mankind. As the corpse of the Bagman withers and shrivels into charcoal among the myriad copper teeth of the radio wires that are his electrocution and his consummation, the metal jaws of the particles lock in one blinding forge of fire, one deafening hammer and anvil of detonation, and Gog is lifted up by the hands of the explosion, he is borne from the underground chambers of London where the machines feed on men in the name of linking them to one another, he is carried upwards through a fissure opening under the pavements of the Strand, he is handed up by the boiling black air and left sprawling in a daze on the front porch of Somerset House, alive and hardly kicking but certainly not calling inside to get a copy of his birth certificate or to hand in his official chips.

Blast and booze are Highland flings in Gog's skull, they are Irish reels and maypole dances. He rises, weaving and hobbling and lurching along the gutter. The walls are joining hands about him and tripping in a ring, the people are running past huzzaing halleluiahs, and Magog, goddam Magog, he's sauntering along unawares down the Strand, down the Strand with no lily in his hand, but clutching a new black brolly thin as a pencil, too smart to flower even in the rain. So wobble up behind him and clobber him with fists doubled into one, but they miss his head as he moves and they strike him on the back, so that he turns and sees his enemy and flees into the thickening crowd. So press on past Charing Cross in the wake of Magog into the mob, press on, Gog, fee fi fo fum, do I smell the blood of an Englishman?

See-saw, sacradown,
Which is the way to London town?
One foot up and the other foot down,
That is the way to London town.

The people are massed on the pavements of Whitehall, they're yelling and hallooing and hurrahing and waving, they're screaming themselves hoarse with victory and loyalty, as the golden coach is wheeling by, yes, the golden coach of His Royal Highness King George the Sixth, Emperor of India and Infinite Lesser Places and the Very Least Breed, yes, the golden coach is clopping by behind the black horses, postillion rampant and coachman resplendent and equerry mountant and footman flamboyant, the King's face tanned brown with make-up under the weighty crown that bends down his starveling neck, while the Queen's got her chin up, her skin rose-white and glossy, her hair spattered with tiara drops, we love you ma'am, yes ma'am, surely, the great British people throwing up their lungs loyally in bellows of devotion, many a bum show's been saved by twin Highnesses wearing the red and purple and ermine for the edification of their devoted subjects the people, they're just like me and you really only they aren't because they're royalty, even a king sits on his own arse says Montaigne, so hooray for Good King George and Good Queen Mary, hip ray and cap over the steeple, as they ride back in state after the Speech from the Throne in Parliament on this glorious day of victory, the Fifteenth of August in the Year of Our Lord, Nineteen Hundred and Forty-Five.

The crowds are swilling and brewing, fermenting liquor of people, the sun makes the very air beery and intoxicating, Gog's drowning like the Duke of Clarence fallen in the vast butt of malmsey which is the boozy lees of the people washing down Whitehall, as Gog struggles against the tide towards Magog making for the seats of power, Whitehall and Downing Street and the Houses of Parliament, where Magog after Magog after Magog Etcetera are sitting to rule all Albion and twist it to the use of England and London.

But Magog flits ahead, improbable and impalpable, his yellow hair flying off like a hawk to scratch at Gog's rolling eyes, his head bouncing high as a moon before settling back on his shoulders, his body a teasing tall lure always just ahead of Gog, who thinks he's pushing Magog invisibly just beyond his grasp a few inches ahead of his crooked and murderous fingers. Now they're level with the Cenotaph, where the dead are uncommemorated on this day of rejoicing, now they're past Downing Street, where the policemen are always ready to imprison the Prime Minister from his grateful electors, now they're into Parliament Square, with Big Ben glaring down a Cyclops eye to north south east west and the Abbey ahead jouncing and clanging with bells. And Magog's off past the front of the Houses of Parliament, past Oliver Cromwell glaring from his plinth so bronze and cruel, past the lobby entrance and the policemen guarding it into the recesses of the lawgivers of the red fifth of the globe. Gog does not stay for an invitation, he's through the bobbies faster than a blast of wind, up the stairs into St. Stephen's Hall, where the Commons are assembled to thank His Gracious Majesty.

Beneath the high ribbed roof falling in stone tracers; under the mosaic of King Stephen and Edward the Confessor kneeling before Saint Stephen backed by a tree cascading in green faith; below the eight scenes of picture-postcard past, King Alfred's first British fleet knocking off the Danes with beaky longboats, Richard the Lionheart setting off mailed like an armadillo for Cross and Acre, King John looking hag-ridden by barons at Magna Carta time, Protestants protesting by reading Wyclif's Bible in rural Utopia, Sir Thomas More telling off turkeycock Cardinal Wolsey in the halls of parliament, Queen Elizabeth the Faerie Queen of her Knights and Venturers handing a certificate of legal piracy to Sir Walter Raleigh, Sir Thomas Roe conning the Moghul Emperor into giving the British a toehold in India so that they could stamp it flat with their boots later, the signing of the Act of Union by which the Scots knuckled under to the English in order to rule them ever after; overtopped by the twelve great parliamentarian apostles mouthing silently in stone, Grattan for Ireland and Burke the House of Commons dinner-gong, he'll still be spouting after we've had eight courses, fat Fox for liberty with raised fist to get it, Mansfield and Somers and battle-doomed Falkland, trimmer Clarendon and ship-money Hampden, Selden and corpulent Walpole the everlasting premier, Chatham and Pitt the boy wonder, forever stone-set in youth, never grow up as old as your father; set in rows of temporary benches in this converted chapel, the new Commons men and women sit, displaced from their proper chamber by incendiary bomb-blast and from their leasehold on the Lords' Chamber by the King's Speech from the Throne that day. No one asks Gog about his business because no one knows who's present, there are so many new Members of Parliament after the election, three hundred and fifty fresh faces, most of them for Labour and the people.

The leader of the people is up by the Front Bench and by the geegaw Mace lying on the table to declare parliament's open. He's a crabapple of a man, his voice dry as an accountant's as he tabulates his call for revolutionary action. "We have had a General Election which has brought great alterations in the composition of this House. We have had a change of Government; but in the midst of change there are things which remain unaltered. Among those are the loyalty and devotion of the House of Commons to His Majesty. It is the glory of our democratic Constitution that the will of the people operates and that changes which, in other countries, are often effected through civil strife and bloodshed, here in this island proceed by the peaceful method of the ballot box . . ."

Does the will of the people operate through you, tally-man of royal blessings? Listen, O listen, ye people, are ye not betrayed?

". . . In rendering our congratulations and thanks to His Majesty we pay tribute to something more than the institution of kingship. His Majesty the King and his gracious Consort the Queen have shared our anxieties, our tribulations and our sufferings during the war, and the shadow of bereavement has fallen on them as it has fallen on the homes of their people. The King and Queen have throughout set us an example of courage and devotion which will not be forgotten. By this, and by their sympathy, they have strengthened the bond uniting them to their people . . ."

Why are ye dumb, ye massed backbenchers for Labour? Did they send you to Westminster to bow and scrape your gratitude for patronage and privilege? When you spoke down there in the election to the people, you were one of them, you swore to help them, there'd be no pulling the ermine over your eyes, you'd show the ritzy boys up there in London. But one step into Westminster and you're dumb as stones, while the old ritualists play the old games in front of you and speak in the name of the people, the forgotten people, the unremembered folk who put crosses on their ballots in faith that their hopes for equality and liberty will not be betrayed by their representatives, as they always are and always will be, Magog without end, amen.

Now the old leader's up from the Opposition Front Bench, corpulent and out-of-date as a magnum of aged brandy, a man to raise your hackles and warm your cockles, a damned aristocrat more dangerous than a rat in a tight corner and more courageous than a bulldog when you're in that tight corner with him. The sonorous phrases roll out like sugarplums off his gobby tongue, the phrases of glory and grandeur slowly sinking shrouded in the imperial banner to the purple deeps of the Seventh Sea.

" The good cause for which His Majesty has contended, commanded the ardent fidelity of all his subjects, spread over one-fifth of the surface of the habitable globe. That cause has now been carried to complete success. Total war has ended in absolute victory. Once again, the British Commonwealth and Empire emerges safe, undiminished and united from a mortal struggle. Monstrous tyrannies which menaced our life have been beaten to the ground in ruin, and a brighter radiance illumines the Imperial Crown than any which our annals record . . ."

Forgive the ancient warrior talking of time past in the bitterness of personal defeat and the last gasp of Empire, upon which the sun which never sets is already setting, and India is lost and all with it. Forgive the old warhorse, put him out to pasture, let him dream of Marlborough and Boer War and Gallipoli, he has saved his island and mortgaged its inheritance, he has sold away the estate to save the birthright, lead him slowly to the grave in glory, that is what is wanted and that is his due and that is what is dead and done.

The loyal thanks to His Majesty mumble humbly on, until there's a shiver of anticipation as the lone rebel rises at the back of the hall, rises in tweed and thick ripe Scots vowels to cast the sole voice of dissent.

" On such an occasion as this I would like to associate myself with the remarks that have been made. Whatever the future may hold – and with the coming of atomic energy some of us who hitherto considered ourselves quite dynamic figures may find ourselves well in the background – everyone must recognize the fact that as a constitutional Monarch, the King has, at all times, sought to serve the best interests of the country . . ."

So even you, workers' candidate, sole Communist and revolutionary, even you bow before the throne and the past and the pomp and the circumstance. Even you join in the thanks of the loyal House of Commons to His Majesty, Question put, and agreed to *nemine contradicente*, Address to be presented by the whole House, Privy Councillors humbly to know His Majesty's pleasure when He will be attended.

Then to round off the business, the Lord President of the Council's orating about matters really important on this conclusion of the great day of the first opening of the parliament of the people, prating its formulae to might and majesty.

"I beg to move, That during the remainder of the present Session, until the House otherwise order: (1) Standing Orders Nos. 1, 6, 7, 8 and 14 shall have effect as if, for any reference to a time mentioned in the first column of the following table there were substituted a reference to the time respectively mentioned in the second column of that table ..."

Call clarion to action, government of the people, call them to the barricades against poverty and class and war, call them not by lickspittle lackeydom before the palace, call them not by numbers and rote and Standing Orders and due attention to the iotas of proper business. Call the people thus, O representatives, and you will call to vain air, they will not hear you. They listen for the voices of fire and lightning, of blood and bolts from heaven, or else they listen to the voices of warmth and chuckling, of heart and home. How shall the people hear their chosen men speak in the chatter of typewriter keys, the time-tables of meetings, the agenda of business, the rapping of gavels, the intrigues of tea-rooms, the tolerance of precedence? Come in, Oliver, step down from your plinth, stride in again to St. Stephen's Hall, put your hand on your sword hilt, command them to take away this bauble, this gilt-and-silver Mace as trumpery as a Christmas-tree angel, bid them pack off their rumps home and let the business of government be, leave power alone to the nakedly powerful, ruling by sword and blood, without pretence of parliament in the name of Cromwell and Magog, set over Gog and the people.

As Gog looks round the packed benches of St. Stephen's Hall, Westminster, where the new Commons are assembled on this day of total victory and formal opening, he looks for the face of Magog his foe and kinsman so that he may crush in the skull of power, he looks from the face of the right hon. Member for Wakefield to the face of the right hon. Member for Jarrow, he looks from the face of the right hon. Member for Torquay to the face of the right hon. Member for the University of Oxford, he looks from the face of the right hon. Member for Montgomery to the face of the right hon. Member for West Fife, he looks from face to face to face through the several hundred faces of the Members of Parliament sitting in the Palace of Westminster, he looks for his archenemy and bloodbrother Magog. But the faces before him swim and blur and confuse like milk, then separate into clots piled on clots of faces, all alike, all the same, all the face of Magog, yea, each face the face of Magog, each face the face of power, even the face of the right hon. Member for Ebbw Vale and the hope of the people, every mouth the mouth of Magog, every eye the eye of Magog, every head the head of Magog, every voice the voice of power without end as long as many men shall suffer to be ruled by few men.

As Gog opens his mouth to howl havoc before charging forwards to pick up the Mace and stove in as many of the crowns of hydra-headed Magog as possible before the bluecoats of authority drag him off to the dock and the drop, he hears the screeching of the witches behind his left ear and a stinking moribund pussycat flies through the air to land squashy and reeking on the Government Benches. " Lower than vermin yourselves," shrieks Merry's voice, and Gog turns to see his mother dressed in scarlet coat and jodhpurs, in black bowler and riding-boots, pulling rotten carcasses of rabbits and dogs and grouse and woodcock out of a game-bag, she's hurling them high and away among the sitting Members on the Speaker's right side, coveys of carrion descending from the air, rains of maggots dropping from the flying clouds of stinking meat, gobbets of fur and feathers fluttering down in a stench of dark snow. " I'll give you vermin," Merry screams, " I'll give you vermin, you stinking rabble." She volleys the government majority with the refuse and offal of the chase and the chasers, until she's pulled out of the door by four enormous police officers, dragged out cutting at them with her whip and yelling to the high roofs, " Vermin, you're vermin, we're ermine, you vermin, vermin, vermin, vermin!"

Gog pushes towards his mother to help her against the blue fuzz dragging her away, but suddenly the House rises and bullocks out of the door towards the entrance, shoves out in a mob towards dinner-time at five thirty-five on the dot. House adjourned. Gog is swept on with the human mass of parliamentarians down the steps and he is thrown off sideways into old Westminster Hall dreamed upright from bomb blast with medieval monarchs nodding down kindly from their high embrasures. Treason, Gog, treason, you're thinking of treason, and here they try traitors, here they judged William Wallace, Perkin Warbeck, Thomas More, Protector Somerset, Edmund Campion, the Earl of Essex, and the greatest of them all, Guy Fawkes, remember, remember the Fifth of November, and gunpowder, reason and blow up the lot! Then black cap for Strafford, then his master Charles Stuart Himself, oh, even a King's head can topple from the block and roll like a bloody apple across the boards. Only the Regicides get topped, too, then Titus Oates perjurer extraordinary, then the Jacobite Lords, and there's even an acquittal, Warren Hastings, ruler of India and looter within limits of jurisprudence. But they won't acquit you, Gog, not if they know the plots of arson and riot and annihilation that flame inside your drunken noggin, waiting to burst out in a mayhem of London.

Look, there go the Beefeaters, all togged up in scarlet and yellow, in white ruffs and black lids, swords and halberds at the unready, having a last check-up of the vaults before shutting up shop for the night. And isn't that Magog, the last of the Beefeaters, tagging along disguised as an old man in ribbons and breeches? Yes, that tall old man at the end is surely Magog, trying to sneak off from the just wrath of Gog and the people. So creep down the steps behind them to the crypt of St. Mary's Undercroft, creep down itching to wrench up a fancy railing and let sense into the bloody ambitions of the masters of force and trickery.

As Gog reaches the curving ribs of the buried chapel, there's a scuffle ahead, a flailing and yammering of old men playing at apprehending Guy Fawkes again, a scattering of dignity and medals in all directions, a barrage of oaths and a hopscotch of black shoes trying to stamp out a fuse that hisses and splutters towards the sticks of gelignite piled under the chapel seats. And there's crookback Evans the Latin sending the Beefeaters arse over tip to the four points of the compass, there's a fluttering of bright uniforms and a rending of surcoats and a cracking of withered bodies as dry and bent as his own, as he yells his independence: "Freedom, freedom, you wouldn't give the Celts freedom, would you? I'll blow you to blazes, bloody London, indeed. For Wales and Arthur and the Celtic Union! There's shame on you, limeys, there's shame on you Nazi limeys. Give the Celts freedom, then worry about India. *Cymru ambeath*, Gog bach! For Wales and St. David!"

Yet just as the fuse is about to blow the Houses of Parliament to hell and perdition, a Beefeater is knocked over by Evans the Latin and sits on the spurting fire and rises, yelling with fury. But his rump has extinguished the vengeance of the Celts and Evans the Latin is carted off to the Tower by the uniformed pack. As Gog plunges in to the rescue, he sees Magog in his lobster military disguise edging away through the vaults, trying to vanish once more. So Gog shouts, "I'll be back, Evans the Latin, when I've put paid to Magog," and he's off in pursuit through the dark passages under the Palace of Westminster.

Through the narrowing vaults oozing slimy, stone petering out in gravel and packed clay, the passage thinning to a crack then to a burrow, Magog wriggling ahead and upwards like a slug or a worm. Follow him in the slippery blackness entombed in the gut of Westminster, after him into dank oblivion and claustrophobia, struggle upwards under his heels, work elbows and knees up the moist flue from the vaults, then suddenly a lid opens and lights pour down in a square and Magog's out and squirming away. And it's out, out for Gog blinking at the Gothic glory about him. He rests with his elbows on the golden throne, its seat pushed up like a lid behind him. He looks down from the red gold dais over the plushy woolsacks past the red seats of the departed Lords guarded by their wooden griffins and sphinxes and lions, he looks down to the bar of metal fleurs-de-lys that hems back the Commons from entering further, he sees the tall Magog pause by the bar like a black rod who happens to be a gentleman usher, only to thunder, "You will be hanged, drawn and quartered, George Griffin, for the crime of *lèse majesté*. Get off that throne!"

So Gog hoicks himself out of the entrails of the seat of all the power in Britain and the Empire, he clambers onto the red and gold dais in his dirty and dripping suit under the elaborate gilt canopy more bitty-brilliant than a falling fountain, he lumbers forwards down the aisle of the Lords' Chamber towards his enemy, tall and ready to strike him down for his traitorous sacrilege. And as Gog staggers towards the avenging figure of Magog, an old woman hobbles through the door behind Magog into the House of Lords. She raises both her blackthorn sticks on high and begins hammering at the head of Magog, screaming imprecations at him, " Where have they gone? The Bishops, where have you hidden them? They must open the box now! Joanna's box! Or we are all doomed! The Bishops, the Box, the Box, the Bishops, box the Bishops, pish and pox, or London burns!" As Magog tries to fend off the flailing sticks, so Gog comes up behind him and boots him down, saying, " Well met, Granny Maria." But she merely turns her sticks on him, bim bam, clonk clunk, till he's fleeing for his life out of the Lords' Chamber with Magog at his side, fleeing from the wrath now, never mind the wrath to come, fleeing Granny Maria as she screams.

" A pox on the Bishes and Gog and Magoggle,
If you don't open Joanna, fire burn and cauldron bubble."

So Gog and Magog flee beneath the high arches of the Peers' Lobby across the tiled pavement with its sixteen-starred centre, down the Peers' Corridor where painted Charles Stuart is still trying desperately to arrest the five Members for treasonable words spoken in the House. But Charles didn't catch them then and no one will catch Gog now, as he's out of the breach of privilege into the Central Lobby. There he skids to a stop before the bomb-ruins of the old Commons ahead, his lips agape under the pointed windows and the mosaics of the four Saints of Albion, while Magog slips aside into the nearest telephone booth. For ahead, wearing the robe of red and the breeks of white, the order of the Star and Garter and Bedchamber and Extravaganza, the Cross of St. Stanislas and the Faggot of King Wenceslas, the Emblem of the Knights Hospitaller and the Green Candle of King Ubu, stands Maurice, dolled up to the nines plus and sporting a long wig over his glib chops. While Gog watches, a whiskered old gentleman presses the bulb of a gigantic antique camera on a tripod, all bellows and rosewood, and Maurice drops his snooty pecker and waves a lordly arm in Gog's direction.

"Born to the people for to die of drink," Maurice declaims, "Now I'm in the purple and in the pink. 'Ow's tricks, Gog me old? What did I tell you, a grateful nation knowin' a good thin' when they see one 'ave elevated me to the 'ighest 'onours. Lord Morrie of Bethnal Green. If that ain't a triumph for the people, what is? For singular services rendered in the line of duty, gettin' the goods what people want to the people what wants 'em ... at a fair price, of course." Maurice bends over and whispers in Gog's ear. "'Ere, chance of a lifetime, I'm givin' 'em away, I'll lend you the 'ole gear, purple tosh and the lot, for only twenty nicker. Put 'em on be'ind the pillar, an' you too can 'ave your genuine photo took all togged up in the Lords. 'Oo's for equality? You can be a peer, too, for only twenty nicker, and the photo lasts more than a lifetime. 'And it on to future generations, Dad in 'is Sunday coronet, the kids'll lap it up. Free for all comers, anyone can join 'em, gents and ladies and kiddies, only twenty nicker. Seventeen an' a cow an' calf for you, special price for old pals what believes in the people like Lord Morrie of Bethnal Green. I tell you, I've even 'ad *real* peers took inside this gear, the moths 'ad all their togs and they didn't 'ave the coupons. 'Ow about it, Goggie, or don't you want to join the nobs?"

Just as Gog is about to reply, he sees a look of fright fly like the shadow of a sparrow across Maurice's face. The Lord of Bethnal Green puts two fingers in his mouth, lets out a splitting whistle, and he's hupped his robes round his waist and he's scarpering off with the old cameraman, who shows a nimble pair of young shins for all his false whiskers. Gog turns to see Maire bearing down on him, wearing a black widow's suit and attached to the right arm of Magog and flanked by six mighty policemen in a phalanx of authority.

"Officers, officers, there he is, my poor husband," Maire says. "He'll come quietly, I know he will. His brother, dear Magnus, won't bring a charge against him, though he's been dreadfully assaulted without rhyme or reason. Dear Magnus," Maire continues, squeezing Magog's arm and giving him a look of adoration. "I don't know where I'd be without you. Or where Gog'd be, for that matter. Officers, take him away till he's slept off the liquor, take him away. God knows what mad dreams of riot aren't troubling his poor skull right now. I shouldn't wonder if he doesn't imagine he's going to blow up the Houses of Parliament, or pop out of the Throne like a jack-in-the-box!"

The policemen surround Gog and begin to march him off between them, while Magog puts in a few paternal words, "Treat him gently, officers. He's been in the war, you know. We'll straighten him out eventually. Till then, time and patience. It's a pity *some* of them came back at all from the war in the state they're in. But still, we must learn to put up with them."

So the policemen march Gog inexorably off between them down the lobby towards the main entrance to Parliament. Maire and Magog follow after, chatting fondly and in control of the situation. Gog strains his ears to hear their talk, but all he can half-hear above the boots and the hubbub (or is it his mind whispering?), all he can hear is Maire's voice saying, "Yes, Magnus, tonight, if we can get him committed so soon. You and I'll get power of attorney over the property, naturally. You know, my dearest, I only married Gog to get at his *brother*."

As they reach the door of the street outside the Commons, Gog sees the wheeled box of the Black Maria waiting. But packed round the mobile prison is a dense mass of Londoners, West Enders and East Enders and up and down the towners, cockneys and costers and hawkers and buskers, skivvies and floozies and chippies and chars, soldiers and sailors and airmen of all the nations, tinkers and tailors and beggars and thieves, barrow boys and spivs and crooks and mudlarks, the people out on the spree round Big Ben because the pubs are open and the Japs are up the spout and it's a bit of all right, till the thick head in the morning. While Gog watches, twenty hefty marines pick up the Black Maria and dump it on its back, useless as a tin turtle. Before the policemen can hurry Gog back into the safety of Parliament, the crowd's seized them and scattered them like chaff before their fists. Gog's hoisted up on the mob's shoulders and passed from hand to hand, black bottles are thrust down his gullet so he chokes on liquid fire, they're singing and roaring *Tipperary* and *We'll Hang Out Our Washing On The Siegfried Line*, and he finds himself stuck up on the plinth of Richard Coeur de Lion, high under the bronze belly of the Lion-heart's nag. And the mob's roaring for Lofty, Give it 'em, Lofty, and Gog's yelling, Kill, kill, burn and kill, Pull it down, brick by brick, Bastille of the Thames. Tear 'em, rend 'em, slay and slaughter. Remember Boudicca. And the mob roars with laughter and shoves more bottles down his throat, bathes him with alcohol, breaks his back with slapping, while he shouts, Kill 'em, my people, Kill 'em, among the cheers and the roister and the aimless spill of men.

On the morass and eddies of the human marsh about him, Gog sees Maire carried off by a wave of sailors, carried like the drowned corpse of a black queen borne down the current, carried off to God knows what orgies in the hammocks and stokeholds of the docks, shanghaied perhaps for months for the pleasure of the crew, but sure to rise among them to be mistress of the boat, turning it pirate and sailing under the skull and crossbones, cruising back into London docks with damask sails on the black-backed freighter, Maire the Magnificent in white breeches and black shirt, a cutlass between her teeth and a pistol in her belt, always on top of God and the Devil and mere men.

There's Magog, too, tossed from hand to hand like an elongated bedding roll, slugged upwards like an aerial punch-bag, ripped and gouged by thousands of talons on the myriad up-reaching hands, his clothes in flayed cloth about his wrists and waist and ankles, his fluffy hair matted with blood, his scythe nose broken, his lank joints wrenched loose in their sockets, his plump purse of a mouth scattering screams like largesse in the claws of the mob. So Gog watches the drunken people rip Magog to pieces, scratch him and scour him and slice him and skewer him with their nails and callouses, until a gigantic stoker lifts him high on hairy forearms twined with strands of muscle thicker than a hawser, lifts him and throws him with crunch of snapped bone against the bronze flanks of the Lionheart's nag, so that Magog slides down dead to the world and half-way to heaven in the arms of his blood-brother.

As the mob roars about Gog for the kill, as the rabble chants for the sacrificial victim whom Gog has hunted from the Tower through the bowels of the earth to Parliament Square, as the people bellow for the blood sacrifice of the dandy ruler to bury below the cornerstone of a lasting peace on earth, Gog looks down at the face of Magog bloody in his arms.

The drink goes sour in his veins and his eyes become sharp as pickled onions and he sees that the face of Magog is the face of his half-brother Magnus, a man wounded and bloody and half-alive in his arms. The sickness of bad liquor, or else a pity for all things broken and blood spilt and life ebbing, makes Gog's guts heave. He cradles Magnus on his lap and he spits into his hands and he rubs them together and he wipes away the dark black goo that oozes from the cuts in Magnus's face. When the hands of the mob reach up pitiless to drag Magnus down and drown him in a crushing sea of boots below the statue, Gog fights them off and swings Magnus over his shoulders and climbs up the bronze tail of the horse, he scales the nag's rump to the back of the bronze Crusader in his mail and stillness, he drapes the body of Magog over the pommel of power and majesty, he reaches up the King's right arm as high as the tip of his half-broken sword, he wrenches the stabbing point free and squats down, jabbing at the rabble that comes climbing at him like breakers from the human storm below.

The whistles shrill for rescue and the horses of the mounted policemen come in inexorable as dredgers and the mob parts on either side of the ramming hooves and the line of booted blue-coats on their high nags reaches the plinth and Gog chucks down the body of Magnus onto the helmet of a riding copper, then he's jumped down the far side of the statue and scarpered off with the ebb of the mob that's sucking back down Victoria Street and Whitehall and the Embankment.

Once again Gog begins the slow trudge back to Hampstead and towards the North. But while the drunken people of London pad and roar like a great beast about Gog, he knows himself a man at last. While the revellers chanting peace and victory smash their fists in each other's faces, Gog feels his hands hang slack by his side. While the very lamplights waver boozily, Gog feels his head spark and logic hone his mind enough to know that the lamps haven't had too many beers, there's a power cut. Unbidden tears begin to streak his cheeks, his heart swells up and bursts inside him, he curses the heavens for making him too much of a coward to fight for his faith. He knows that the Gog before the war is forever dead and gone. For he loves the people no longer, they are the mob and the rabble. He loves persons, perhaps, if he can find persons to love. Even his arch-enemy, Magnus and Magog, why, he's a man, he bleeds like any other, he must be saved like each victim.

A man is a man is a man. He has only his body to inhabit. He fights for himself, not the people. He struggles for his own. He has no other. He is his champion. He battles for his cause. He does not want Liberty, but to be free. He does not want Equality, but to say sir to no one. He does not want Fraternity, but to have some brothers. A man's ribs are his own castle. There he dwells until he dies. As he can love his own person, so may he love each person and all persons.

In these words, Gog finds out a new conscience on the way to Hampstead. It speaks clearly enough to make choice and action possible for him for the first time, as he approaches the fork at Camden Town. Take the left fork and it's the Great North Road of learning self by feet and circumstance, the road that is just beginning to make a new man of Gog. Take the right fork to Hampstead, and it's the old life with the past and Maire to remind him of what he was and may be still. And Maire will be surely sitting there in judgement and welcome, saying, "Gog, Gog Griffin, you've been home drunk since lunchtime, Magnus brought you back straight in the taxi, Jules-Julia will swear to it and Mishkin will say miaow, too." And Magnus will turn up, suave and smiling and unmarked and saying, "Old man, you really should see a doctor and get those disorderly thoughts of yours into some sort of shape. I know a good mind-bender, he'll knock some sense into you." And they'll prove to him in Hampstead that all his journeys and his rebellions are fantasies of the mind, when it doesn't matter, it really doesn't matter if he lives half in cloud and half on earth, as long as there are no witnesses and liars to accuse him of falsehood and madness. Memory is all, memory is all, a man is his memory and it tells not the false from the true.

So Gog approaches the fork in the road at Camden Town. The left fork leads to the Great North Road and the journey that is only just beginning in search of Gog after Gog after Gog since the green sides of Albion first rose out of the North Sea. The right fork leads to Maire and Magnus and Magog and the power of London, stretching out its iron and brick fingers to pinch in all Britain. As Gog comes to the fork, sober yet unsteady on this August night of victory and peace on earth, he does not know which way . . .

ANTHONY POWELL

THE FISHER KING

Anthony Powell's first full-length novel since the completion of A DANCE TO THE MUSIC OF TIME

An ancient myth refashioned with contemporary characters in a modern setting produces an acknowledged masterpiece.

'His version of The Fisher King becomes an ironic romance, handled with the elegance of a master. And one can only be grateful to hear again the tone of that sharp, exacting Powell voice'

Malcolm Bradbury

'A thoroughly entertaining story . . . cleverly linking the myths of our common past to the humdrum present and casting rich light on both . . . This when you least expect it, is really what makes a great novelist'

David Hughes in The Mail on Sunday

'THE FISHER KING is a rare work of art for a number of reasons . . . Powell is above all funny, and makes humour out of both the gravity and perceptiveness to which narrative aspires . . . I could read whatever Powell writes from here to eternity'

John Bayley in The London Review of Books

'What Powell understands better than any other living British novelist is the importance of selection and emphasis in the telling of a story'

A. S. Byatt in Books and Bookmen

sceptre

NIKOLAI TOLSTOY

THE QUEST FOR MERLIN

Did Merlin really exist or is he just a figure of legend?

Where does myth end and history begin?

Do Merlin's prophecies mean anything and how are they related to other ancient cults?

The wizard Merlin – trickster, prophet and enchanter – has long exerted a strange fascination over academic and layman alike, and is a recurrent figure in European literature from Malory to Tolkien.

In this absorbing account of his lifelong 'Quest for Merlin', Nikolai Tolstoy plunges into the fields of history, anthropology, geography and psychology to elaborate his controversial but persuasive theory that Merlin actually did exist.

'THE QUEST FOR MERLIN will probably rank as the year's unlikeliest book, yet in the hands of Count Tolstoy we are persuaded not only that Merlin existed, but where he existed, and how he earned his place in English literature . . . Certainly he has written a book which fairly crackles with excitement as he produces his clinching pieces of evidence'

Yorkshire Post

sceptre

ALLAN MASSIE

AUGUSTUS

AUGUSTUS reconstructs the lost memoirs of Augustus, true founder of the Roman Empire, son of Julius Caesar, friend and later foe of Mark Antony, patron of Horace and Virgil. Massie has breathed conviction and realism into one of the greatest periods of the past, creating an unforgettable array of characters and incidents.

'All the drama of Graves's *I, Claudius* with an added mordant humour'

Harriet Waugh in The Spectator

'He makes Augustus credible as a man: wily, ruthless, shrewd, generous, admirable'

Andrew Sinclair in The Times

'A private and public history that never loses its pace or grip. Massie summons up a Roman scene that frankly exists as much in the late twentieth century as in the first century B.C.'

Boyd Tonkin in The Listener

'A great achievement by any standard'

The Scotsman

'A marvellous historical novel, written with style and verve . . . ranks with Robert Graves's classics *I, Claudius* and *Claudius The God*. All the colour, cruelty and splendour of a great pagan civilisation are given their due by a novelist at the height of his powers'

Dublin Sunday Press

MAURICE SHADBOLT

SEASON OF THE JEW

A novel about an astonishing historical event.

More than a century ago, the Maoris of New Zealand staged a ruthless battle for land ownership against the British settlers. Under a charismatic leader and prophet they fought with particular ferocity, for they had cast themselves as the Jews of ancient Israel, struggling against their imperial masters to reclaim their lost lands.

'An excellent historical novel. The story is absorbing and full of surprises. Shadbolt writes admirably with a tautness and an astringent humour rare in the genre'

Conor Cruise O'Brien in The New York Times Book Review

'A figure to be spoken of in the same breath as Patrick White of Australia'

The Times Literary Supplement

'Shadbolt writing at his very best'

Auckland Star

'An ironic and powerful novel . . . it is not just about the rape of a country; it is also an understated and unsentimental love story'

Time Out

sceptre

RONALD FRAME

A LONG WEEKEND WITH MARCEL PROUST

Seven stories and a novel
from the author of SANDMOUTH PEOPLE

'His style is achieved and elegant . . . On this form, he is one of the most interesting writers around, capable of narrative radiance, and of articulating the virtually unspeakable depths of his characters'
Douglas Dunn in the Glasgow Herald

'Aims straight for the intellect. Frame is a writer who relies on care, logic and distance, creating unsettling patterns with aplomb'
New Statesman

'Frame creates images of clarity, while at the same time suggesting layers of meaning, teasing the reader to return to them, as if to a painting for a more careful second look'
Rose Tremain in The Sunday Times

'Varied and talented . . . All exhibit a superb technique backed by clever twists in their plots'
Martin Goff in the Daily Telegraph

sceptre